THE
SHADOW
SAINT

As she walks towards the train station, she examines Sinter's gift. It's a fragment of burned metal. The hilt of a broken sword, she realises, blasted by fire, pitted by sorcery, stained by the ichor of a million dead worms. A piece, a relic, of Saint Aleena of the Sacred Flame. She remembers Aleena saving her from Jermas Thay's clutches, remembers the blessed fire. Imagines, for a moment, Aleena's rough hand holding the sword hilt. Eladora only knew Aleena briefly, but cherishes the memory of her stalwart presence, her unnerving, unyielding determination. Her knack for stabbing evil things with a fiery sword.

She tries to think why Sinter would give her such a valuable relic, but her head just spins in circles. A message? A gift? A threat, reminding her of the power of the Kept Gods? A clue about his intentions?

"Fucking fuckers are trying fuck us," whispers Eladora, recalling Aleena's most heartfelt prayer.

BY GARETH HANRAHAN

The Gutter Prayer
The Shadow Saint

THE
SHADOW
SAINT

GARETH HANRAHAN

www.orbitbooks.net

ORBIT

First published in Great Britain in 2020 by Orbit

1 3 5 7 9 10 8 6 4 2

Map by Paul Bourne, Handiwork Games

Excerpt from "Midnight" by Hugh MacDiarmid from
Complete Poems Vol II, Carcanet Press, 1996

A CIP catalogue record for this book is available from the British Library.

ISBN 978-0-356-51153-5

Typeset in Garamond by M Rules
Printed and bound in Great Britain by Clays Ltd, Elcograf S.p.A.

Papers used by Orbit are from well-managed forests
and other responsible sources.

Orbit
An imprint of
Little, Brown Book Group
Carmelite House
50 Victoria Embankment
London EC4Y 0DZ

An Hachette UK Company
www.hachette.co.uk

www.orbitbooks.net

To Edel

For a life with trees

HORDINGER TERRITORIES

HAITH

GRENA

GUERDON

● GUERDON TERRITORY
● ISHMERE TERRITORY
○ HAITH TERRITORY

LOST ASERIA

KHENTH

ULBISHE

MATTAUR

JASHAN

SEVERAST

N

SUNSET LANDS

To Edel

For a life with trees

GUERDON TERRITORY
ISHMERE TERRITORY
HAITH TERRITORY

HORDINGER TERRITORIES

HAITH

GRENA

GUERDON

LOST ASERIA

KHENTH

ULBISHE

JASHAN

MATTAUR

SEVER'AST

N

S

SUNSET LANDS

PROLOGUE

The spy climbs a stair of fire to get to heaven. The foot of the stair is in a battlefield, where the honoured dead lie mingled with the bodies of their foes. Below, tiny black dots move across the field. Bone-picker priests sort the corpses, matching disembodied limbs and heads to torsos before sending them for the funerary rites. The bodies of the enemy dead will be divided among the pantheon of the victorious – these days, all gods are carrion eaters. Old taboos no longer hold, not when every fragment of soul-stuff is needed for the war effort.

According to the tradition of the Sacred Realm of Ishmere, the souls of the honoured dead must struggle up this stair to get to heaven. Each step burns away some sin, some weakness, until they are pure enough to enter the sanctum of the goddess. This rule, too, no longer holds currency – the stair whirls across the battlefield, greedily sucking up every soul offered to the goddess.

Idly, the spy touches one step. The fires are cool as stone, and do not burn him.

Here, suspended in the sky, the spy can survey the whole battle-field. Over *there* is where the forces of Ishmere landed, bringing the sea with them, a fleet of mighty warships landing ten miles inland. And directly below is where the hosts of Mattaur made their stand, on the slopes of a sacred hill.

The hill offered a threefold advantage. It was a spiritual strong-hold of the gods of Mattaur, where the eyeless priestesses gathered to venerate their Stygian deity. It was a high ground, safe from the miraclous floodwaters brought by the pantheon of Ishmere. And most important of all – the spy can make out the wreckage of an artillery emplacement. Alchemical cannons, bought at great expense from the foundries of Guerdon. During the battle, those guns nearly – well, turned the tide is the wrong metaphor to use in a battle where one side long ago conquered the sea, but the alchemical weapons inflicted terrible casualties on the armies of Ishmere. Saints dying in agony, their bones transmuted to lead, their lungs seared by poisonous gas. Phlogiston fires that cannot be quenched still burn on the battlefield.

The cannons might have won the battle, were it not for divine intervention. From this vantage, too, the spy sees three huge parallel rents in the hillside, furrows each half a mile long and fifty feet deep, devastation in the heart of Mattaur. That is where the lion-headed goddess reached down and slashed her enemies with her claws.

The spy reaches the top of the stairs, and steps into heaven.

Mortals and gods mingle here. The navy has set up a command post and pitched tents in the middle of the Courtyard of Heroes. Young, smartly uniformed officers rush to and fro, ignoring the fabled champions in their midst. Two armoured demigods – one with the head of a serpent, the other a bird – block the spy's path. These are Sammeth and Cruel Urid, the guardians who watch the gates of heaven. Sammeth's blade drips with poison so potent one drop can kill a hundred men; Urid's spear can pierce a dozen elephants in one throw.

A young officer with a clipboard spots the spy and shoos the two demigods away. Confused, they wander back to a nearby tent and slump down.

"I've an appointment to see General Tala," says the spy.

"General Tala is dead," replies the young officer. "You'll be meeting with Captain Isigi of the intelligence corps." There's an undertone of anger in the young man's voice, a note of jealousy. The spy notes it, files it away.

"Follow me," says the officer. "Stay close." He leads the spy across the Courtyard of Heroes. They've painted lines on the ground, different coloured trails leading off in different directions. The officer keeps his eyes fixed on the paint, so he doesn't get distracted by the glories around him. They follow a black line across the shining stones of heaven's shore.

Glancing back, the spy sees Sammeth polishing his spear, even though the blade is already more brilliant than the sun. Cruel Urid sulks in his tent, trying to get his beak around the mouth of a scavenged hip flask.

The spy is brought to another, larger tent. The darkness inside is welcome, easier on the eye than the radiance outside. There, sitting behind a trestle table, is another young officer, a woman. In front of her is a file folder, and a wooden bowl piled high with human hearts, stacked like red apples.

"It's General Tala's eleven o'clock, ma'am," announces the male officer.

"Thank you, lieutenant," Isigi replies. Her face might once have been beautiful, but now it's covered in fresh scars that zigzag across her skin. "I'll be handling this briefing in the General's place." She starts to unbutton her shirt. "You may go, lieutenant."

The spy notes the way the lieutenant's hand clenches the fabric of the tent. There was definitely something between these two officers. So young to have attained such rank, too – the Godswar has made soldiers of children. The flap closes. The tent is almost completely dark, but the spy can still see Captain Isigi as she folds her shirt and lays it with the rest of her uniform on a stool. Then, shaking slightly with anticipation, she takes a heart from the bowl and bites into it.

And then they are no longer alone in the tent.

There is a timeless moment, when the spy isn't conscious of anything other than the goddess's overwhelming *presence*. He is with her on every battlefield, from the charnel field below to every other war across the world, and from the present all the way back to the first time someone picked up a rock and used it to bash an enemy's brains out. He is with her across the world, wherever the fleets of Ishmere sail. He is with her across the heavens, as she gathers the honoured dead to her banner and consumes their power so she can work further miracles, win further victories. Conquest without end, every victory adding to her power and her hunger.

But it's blind hunger, undirected power. The goddess knows nothing except endless destruction, conflict eternal. It takes a human element to lend purpose and structure to that holy wrath. In the tent, Captain Isigi is like a seed crystal, a framework around which the goddess can accrete.

Golden fur suddenly covers Isigi's brown skin, fur that blazes with its own divine radiance. A jewelled breastplate appears on her chest; a skirt of leather straps manifests around her waist, a skull threaded through each strap. Her own skull cracks and reshapes. Huge fangs sprout from her jaws as her head becomes that of a lioness.

The goddess Pesh, Lion Queen, war-goddess of the Ishmeric pantheon — or rather her avatar, made from Captain Isigi — purrs in satisfaction and settles back onto her seat. The spy notes without alarm that the simple wooden chair is now a throne of skulls, that the trestle table has become a blood-soaked altar. The hearts begin to beat again, squirting jets of crimson across the floor.

The file folder, though, is still a file folder. Isigi — or is the overlapping entity in front of him more Pesh than Isigi now? — picks it up, extends a claw and slices through the metal seal holding it shut. The spy shudders at the grace of the movement, knowing that those selfsame claws recently tore a half-mile rent in the hillside below. Isigi removes the papers, reviews them in silence. The tent reverberates with her divine breath, which smells of meat and sandalwood.

Everything comes down to this.

To avoid thinking about what's going to happen, the spy wonders how many times Isigi has channelled the goddess already. Not many, he guesses — the scars are too fresh. Gods are hard on their war-saints. One day, there won't be enough of Isigi left to return to her mortal form. He feels almost sorry for the young officer who bought him here. The boy has lost his lover to the embrace of a goddess, and from that union there is no easy path back.

"X84?" says the saint. It's his newly assigned code number in the files of the intelligence corps. It's the first name that's really his, and he finds himself unexpectedly fond of it. He nods.

"Sanhada Baradhin," reads Isigi. *That's* the name the Ishmere Intelligence Corps knows him by. "Of Severast. Profession: merchant." She glances at him with glowing yellow eyes. "'Merchant'," she echoes, sarcastically.

"I bought and I sold," offers X84. "What I bought wasn't always legal and what I sold wasn't always mine to sell."

"A criminal," she growls. The spy can tell that some balance has been tipped, that the gestalt entity he's talking to is now a little more Lion Queen than Isigi.

"Tell you what," says the spy to the goddess, "I'll count up everyone I hurt in Severast, and you count up everyone you killed there, and we'll see how the scales balance."

"War is holy," replies the goddess automatically. And here, in this heaven for warriors, that's true.

He shrugs. "You knew who I was before you called me."

"No surviving family is listed here," says the goddess, tapping a line in the file. "Do you have friends in the camps? Lovers?" All of Severast is an internment camp now, the survivors of the Ishmeric conquest held until they convert or are sacrificed to the victorious pantheon. Mattaur was the last of Severast's neighbours to hold out.

"No."

"Why, then, do you wish to serve the Sacred Realm of Ishmere?" asks the goddess.

"You're winning," says the spy, "and you'll pay."

Imperceptibly, the balance falls back, and it's Isigi who turns a page in the folder. "You imported weapons from Guerdon's alchemists."

"Yes."

"Do you still have contacts there?"

"I honestly don't know. I did. I can make more. I know the city."

"The city has changed," warns the captain, "and may change again, very quickly. Do not think of it as a safe refuge from the war."

"I was in Severast when your armies conquered it, captain. I know what safe means, these days."

Isigi ignores him, and flips through the rest of the folder in silence. The only noises in the tent are the shuffling of paper, the bellows-breath of the goddess and the soft clinking of the skulls in her skirt as when she moves in her chair. X84 idly toys with one of the beating hearts in the bowl.

"Leave that alone," growls the goddess.

"Sorry."

She reviews the last page, then – faster than the eye can follow – grabs his hand and slashes it with her claw. Blood wells up from the wound. She inclines her lioness-head towards the spy's palm to lap up the blood, but he snatches his hand back and cradles it in the crook of his other arm. "What the hell?"

Pesh growls. "We have no reason to trust you, Baradhin. So I will taste your blood and know you. If you serve us well, you will be rewarded. If you betray us, I will personally hunt you down and punish you. Give me your blood."

The spy nods, then extends a shaking, blood-stained finger. She gives it a perfunctory lick, then signs the last page of the folder, seals it with a divine word of command, closes it. As she does so, she recites: "You will make the arrangements for passage to Guerdon. You will accompany another of our agents on the voyage, and ensure he is delivered safely."

"Who's this agent?"

"My brother's saint. Chosen of the Fate Spider."

He feigns irritation. Blusters professionally. "God-touched? It'll be a hell of a lot harder to smuggle your spy into the city if he's got eight legs or whatever."

"The child is . . ." Does the goddess pause there, almost imperceptibly? As if she's tasted something bitter? " . . . still human. After that, we may have further tasks for you."

"Wait!" says the spy, "What about my payment?"

"Gold coins, one per—"

"Not gold. The price of gold has plummeted since your Blessed

Bol started turning his enemies into big golden statues. No, I want to be paid in Guerdon silver." The spy doesn't give a damn about the money, but it keeps the goddess's mind off the taste of the blood.

"You will be paid in gold," she says. "Unless you prove especially useful to us."

"What do you need?"

The goddess withdraws, and her final answer is strangely doubled.

"You'll be contacted when you arrive," says Isigi, and in the same moment, with the same mouth:

"War," says the goddess. "War is holy."

And with that, Pesh departs, and only Isigi is left. The captain staggers as her body shrinks back to mortal proportions, as her face shatters and retakes human form. She reaches blindly for a blood-stained towel she keeps behind the desk and presses it to the open wounds on her face. "Get out of here, Baradhin," she orders without looking at him. "The lieutenant will see you back down the stair."

The tent flap opens, and the lieutenant sidles in. He gasps as he sees the wounds on Isigi's face, the sweat and blood on her bare skin. He hurries to her side.

"It's all right," mutters the spy, "I'll see myself out."

Before either Ishmeric officer can argue, he slips out and hurries along the line of black paint, head bowed, dismissed from the camp of the conquerors. The line leads him back to the edge of heaven, and he descends the stair of fire that leads back to the mortal world.

Halfway down he takes the stolen heart he palmed from the bowl out from his shirt and drops it into the ocean, far below. He wipes his bloody hand clean, then uses a strip of his shirt as an impromptu bandage.

The goddess wounded him, but she did not taste his blood.

She doesn't know him.

CHAPTER I

I f Sanhada Baradhin had a son, then the boy's bones lay probably somewhere in the ruins of Severast. Perhaps he was turned to screaming gold by the weaponised wealth-curse of Blessed Bol, or speared on a shaft of moonlight. Even if he lived through the invasion, he was likely killed in the orgiastic rampage of sacrifice, when gangs of war-priests culled the city streets, murdering entire districts in accordance with the funeral rites of their respective gods. The spy saw priests pushing ornamented saltwater tanks, blood and water slopping out of the overflowing basins as they drowned worshippers to the Kraken. Mass graves marked with coins for Blessed Bol. Cannibal rites of the Lion Queen. Even the Fate Spider's slow embalmment could be hastened; mummification takes too long, but alchemical preservatives imported from Guerdon can do in minutes what used to take long years in the Paper Tombs.

If Sanhada Baradhin had a son, the boy is dead.

But while the spy is not Sanhada Baradhin, and the boy in the cabin with him is not his son, for the duration of this voyage from the southlands to Guerdon he is Baradhin and the boy is Emlin. Eleven or twelve years old, maybe, but sometimes something far older looks out from his eyes.

The boy didn't have a name when he was presented to the spy. They took his name away in the Paper Tombs.

Sanhada named him Emlin. It means *'pilgrim'* in the tongue of Severast.

Taking on the roles of refugees from the Godswar was easy for both of them. Walk like you're hollow. Keep your voice low, as though speaking too loud might attract the attention of some mad deity. Shudder when the weather changes, when light breaks through the clouds, when certain noises are too loud, too charged with significance. Flinch at portents. The man whose name is not Sanhada Baradhin and the boy who didn't have a name arrived on board the steamer a week ago with bowed heads, shuffling up the gangplank with a crowd of other survivors. Sanhada's contacts and god-wrought gold earned the pair a private cabin.

Taking on the roles of father and son is harder. Sanhada has no official standing in the Ishmere Intelligence Corps; nor is he a priest of Fate Spider. Nor, for that matter, was the spy ever a father before.

"I am chosen of the Fate Spider," said Emlin on the first night at sea, when they were alone in the cabin. "Your fate has been woven for you. X84. The thread of your life is in my hands, and you shall obey me." His adolescent voice broke as he recited the words they taught him in the temples. The boy's small for his age. Dark hair, dark eyes, the pallor of years spent in the lightless Paper Tombs. He stood straight, with the pride of one who knew he'd been chosen by a god.

Sanhada had bowed his head solemnly, and said, "My life in your hands, little master — but outside this cabin, I am Sanhada Baradhin, and you're my son. And I'll thrash you if you speak out of turn."

The boy frowned, his face flushed with anger, but before he could speak the spy added, "Live your cover, little master. It is pleasing to Fate Spider to keep secret that which is shadowed. No one outside this cabin shall know the truth, save you and I."

And after that the spy saw secret pride in the boy's face when he pretended to be Sanhada's son.

Emlin, the spy hears, grew up in a monastery in Ishmere, although he's not Ishmerian by birth. His family were killed in the Godswar; like many other war orphans, he was taken in by the church. In the morning, he tells the spy things he could not possibly know himself; the Fate Spider has been whispering in his ear as he slept, carrying intelligence reports from far away. No doubt there is another boy, or a blind old woman, or a young blade, or some other soul unlucky enough to be congruent with the deity, crouched in a prayer cell in the Paper Tombs, communing intelligence across the aether.

These reports are about the progress of the war, about advances and defeats. The Ishmeric armada has turned north.

Towards the land of Haith, Ishmere's great rival, perhaps its last true danger. Towards Lyrix, the dragon-isle.

Guerdon, too, is in the north. Although Emlin never speaks of it directly, the spy infers that the gods of Ishmere are wary of challenging Guerdon directly. They fear the weapons that Guerdon birthed in the alchemists' foundries, and worry that such god-killing tools might be wielded by other enemies, too.

In the privacy of their cramped cabin, the spy and the boy endlessly rehash their plans for reaching the city undetected, and what they will do when they get there. Neither of them has any knowledge of the intelligence corps' plans for them once they arrive in the city, beyond making contact with the Ishmeric agents already in place. Emlin guesses that his role will be to relay information back to the fleet. For now, the spy is just a courier, tasked only with getting Emlin past Guerdon's religious inspections. Foreign saints are forbidden in the city.

Sometime they eavesdrop on the conversations that filter down from the deck above. The spy paid extra to ensure he and Emlin have a private cabin, paid even more to ensure they'd be asked no questions. The pair remain mostly overlooked and forgotten.

Over breakfast on the fourth day out of Mattaur, Emlin asks him about Severast.

"Did you ever visit the temple of the Fate Spider there?" he says around a mouthful of fruit. He is always ravenous on waking.

The spy knows that Sanhada Baradhin visited that temple many times. The man was a smuggler, and the Spider is patron deity of thieves and liars as well as spies. Baradhin would visit the gaudy temple of the Many-Handed Goddess, the Severastian goddess of trade, and then stroll across the plaza and through the maze of alleyways in the medina, brushing past dancing girls, fire-eaters, smoke-seers, street vendors selling all manner of delights. The

Spider's temple in Severast was underground, hidden from view, connected to the surface by dozens of narrow winding staircases. Only one of these stairways was open at a time; to reach the temple, Sanhada Baradhin had to know which little shop in the medina was a front for the Fate Spider on a particular day. He bribed beggars to learn the secret of the streets.

"Once or twice," admits the spy.

"It must have been glorious," says Emlin, "before it became a den of thieves."

"Thieves were always holy to the Spider in Severast."

"Not in Ishmere," declares Emlin emphatically. Reciting what he's been taught.

No, thinks the spy. Not in Ishmere. The Fate Spider was worshipped in both lands, but in different ways. In Severast, he was a deity of the underworld, worshipped by the lost and the poor, the desperate and the disenfranchised. In Ishmere, in mad, cruel Ishmere, the Fate Spider was part of their militant pantheon, put into harness for the war effort. There, the Spider is a god of secrets, of prophecy and stratagems. God of endings, Fate-eater, poisoner of hope.

"The temple was beautiful," admits the spy. "It was all veiled in shadow, each altar and shrine revealing itself only by touch. I—"

"I don't see shadows," interrupts Emlin. "All darkness is light to me." His eyes gleam, and the spy realises he has never seen the boy stumble in the dim cabin. The fanatics of Fate Spider have robbed him of the beautiful gradations of shadow, of the softness of the dark, of the capacity for doubt.

That night, while the boy sleeps, the spy stays awake and remembers the fires of Severast. How the burning medina crashed and collapsed into the temple caverns below, the pale seers howling as the sunlight caught them. How all the delicious ambiguity of the temple was laid bare by the certainty of destruction. That night, while the boy sleeps, the spy watches him in the darkness and dreams of revenge.

*

Sanhada Baradhin is too long a name for the hasty Guerdonese, so the crew call him San. The ship's name is *Dolphin*, and the spy can think of few names less fitting. *Angry Metal Hippo* or *Ugly Floating Tub* would be more appropriate. Driven by her roaring, stinking alchemical engines, she wallows with great enthusiasm through the waves, smashing her way across the ocean.

X84 is not the only passenger on the *Dolphin*; two dozen other people huddle on the deck, and there are more in the holds below. Most come from Severast; some from Mattaur or the Caliphates, or more distant lands. Some mutter prayers to defeated gods. Others are silent, hollow-eyed, looking to the empty horizon for meaning.

Ostensibly, *Dolphin*'s a freighter, not a passenger liner; when she left the docks of Guerdon, her hold was full of alchemical weapons. The ship is double-hulled with reinforced steel, warding runes half occluded by rust and barnacles, to ensure that her cargo of death was safe until it arrived. The spy wonders if that's wholly necessary. The way the Godswar is going, the whole world will be consumed sooner or later, every living soul devoured in the hungers of the mad deities. If that's the case, then what does it matter where the bombs go off? The only difference between a battlefield in Mattaur and some marketplace in Guerdon is a matter of time.

Time and money. The master of the ship makes great profit by selling bombs that explode on the battlefield, and would be greatly irritated if a bomb went off in a marketplace in Guerdon. It strikes the spy that the master is uniquely suited to his ship – both are singularly ugly, both approach the world as something to be smashed through, and both are wrapped in iron hulls to keep something toxic locked away. The master is named Dredger; at all times he wears a protective suit, a thing of valves and filters and tubes, so that not an inch of skin is exposed. His hands are heavy stubby-fingered gauntlets; his face is a mask of lenses, ports and wheezing bellows. The story among the crew is that Dredger has been exposed to so many alchemical weapons over the years that his flesh is thoroughly permeated by toxins, that he'd explode into a cloud of poisonous gas if he ever removed his containment suit.

Having observed Dredger for the last few days on the journey north to Guerdon, the spy has another theory – that there's nothing wrong with Dredger at all, that the armour is a marketing gimmick. Certainly, it's helped Dredger protect his niche of alchemical salvage, reusing the unthinkable weapons brewed up by the guilds of Guerdon. Who would want to get into a business when the cost is writ in the tormented flesh of the market leader?

Sanhada Baradhin did plenty of business with Dredger over the years, but the two never met. They corresponded by letter and courier, and the spy's agents intercepted and read all those letters over the years. He feels as though he knows Dredger as well as Sanhada Baradhin did, that he has just as much claim to the man's friendship. In Dredger's eyes – lens-masked and hidden – the spy is Sanhada Baradhin, and that assumption is reality enough.

Dredger leans on the railing next to the spy. Some valve on his back hisses and spits steam as his pose relaxes a little.

"San," he says, "have you given any thought to what you're going to do when you get to Guerdon? I could probably find something for you, if you want."

"What sort of work?"

"Nothing in the yards. Got Stone Men for that shit. No, I'm thinking maybe . . . sales? You must have contacts down south that ain't dead, and if they ain't dead, they're buying, right?"

The spy considers the offer, weighing it, testing its balance like a fencer tests a sword. On the one hand, it's a plausible next move for Sanhada Baradhin, and would provide him with a base of operations. On the other hand, he wants to get a feel for the city, and tying himself down to the first offer that comes his way is the wrong move. Racing straight towards his goal means sprinting into a minefield. He must approach obliquely.

"I've got some, ah, outstanding business to take care of first, my friend. And I was able to bring a little money out of Severast, so I'll be all right for a few weeks. But thank you, and I might well take you up on it if the offer's still open in a while."

"Not like the war's ending anytime soon."

"Will there be a problem bringing money into the city?"

"Depends on whether or not you catch the eye of the customs inspectors. You're not a man of faith, are you?"

"Not especially."

Dredger points to another refugee, a middle-aged woman who has carried a number of small clay idols out of the sacked city. Bracing herself against the churning motion of the boat, she prays to them. Dancer and Kraken, Blessed Bol and Fate Spider. "They watch for foreign saints. They don't much care in Guerdon which gods you pray to, so long as those gods don't answer back," says Dredger. "'Specially not the gods of Ishmere."

"The gods of Ishmere were the gods of Severast," says the spy. "There were temples in Severast to the Lion Queen, too, and they did the rites just as faithfully there."

A lens in Dredger's helmet clicks and swivels, refocusing on the spy. "So what happened? Why'd the gods turn on Severast?"

"I'm not sure they did. There were saints of the Lion Queen on both sides, for a while. Those who say the gods are mad are right, I think, and mad people sometimes argue with themselves." There's a cloud in the distance that catches the spy's attention. It's moving against the wind. "And you can't blame everything on the gods. If a runaway chariot runs over a child in the street, do you blame the charioteer or the horses?"

"I blame the parents," mutters Dredger.

"Speaking of which," says the spy, "the boy's ... a little god-touched. Your city watch — can they be bribed?"

There's a gurgling sound from inside Dredger's helmet, like he's contemplatively suckling on the end of some tube. "Tricky, these days. Tricky." He shakes his head. "And in my position, San, I can't afford to piss off the watch by sneaking you into the city."

He's interrupted by one of the crew. "Master, there's another ship off to the west. It's a Haithi warship." The sailor hands Dredger a telescope, and he inspects the distant ship.

"Keep on. We've no quarrel with them. And nothing worth confiscating on the return trip, eh?"

"See anything in that cloud?" asks the spy. Dredger swings the telescope around, peers at the dark smudge on the horizon.

"Not a thing. Why?"

"Just a feeling."

The sound of praying voices grows louder. Several of the other refugees on deck gather around the woman with the clay icons. One of the icons is moving now, clay transmuting into scaly flesh. The tentacles of the Kraken break free of their earthy prison and thrash about on the deck. A collateral miracle.

"Dredger!"

"I see it! Turn! Turn!"

They're too late. The cloud's racing towards the Haithi warship now, and they're caught right between the two belligerents. The *Dolphin*'s engines roar and belch smoke as they're thrown to full power, but the blades can't find purchase in the suddenly glassy water. A miracle has seized the waves, stealing them and claiming them for a hostile god. The water becomes unnaturally calm and clear for a mile in every direction, an icy track running from the stormcloud to the Haithi warship. Looking through the impossibly clear water, the spy can see all the way to the seabed a thousand fathoms below.

Tremendous tentacles writhe there, like the ones on the little clay icon but ten thousand times bigger.

"TURN!" roars Dredger. In a fury he snatches up the woman's icons and hurls them overboard. They land on the surface of the sea and do not sink.

Emlin emerges onto the deck. "Go back down!" shouts the spy. "Stay below!" The boy retreats, half closing the door. Staring out at the transformed sea in wonder.

The Haithi warship is aware of the danger. She's an older ship, a sailing frigate refitted as best they could for the perils of the Godswar. Rune-scored armour, proof against lesser miracles. Phlogiston shells loaded in her cannon. No doubt key crew members are Vigilant, their souls bound to their bodies, so they can fight on despite death and dismemberment. She turns to bring her guns broadside-on to the threat.

The storm crashes over and past the *Dolphin*. The glassy water is whipped into razor waves that scour the deck, shredding anyone caught in their path to red ribbons. The old woman was at the railing, reaching for her lost idols. She falls back, keening, her hands ruined and bloody. The wind laughs in his ears, and he glimpses a shape flitting through the sky overhead.

Of course. Somewhere up there is an Ishmeric saint, a locus of divine attention. Kraken and Cloud Mother are vast as the sea and the sky; the gods choose mortals as channels for their energies in the mortal realm. Dredger staggers across the deck, shouting at the helmsman. The storm's passed them by, so if they can limp out of the afflicted patch of ocean, maybe they can get away intact. The *Dolphin*'s engines scream as the ship struggles in the water that is no longer water. A miracle of the Kraken. Still, they're making a little progress—

—And then the Haithi ship is right on top of them, less than a spear's throw away. The storm twists back on itself, pushing the *Dolphin* even closer to the warship. Cannons bark, and the spy throws himself to the deck as gunshots ring out over his head. To the credit of the Haithi gunners, not a single shot hits the *Dolphin*. Phlogiston shells burst in the storm clouds overhead, trailing blazing streamers as the alchemical substance burns mist and seawater and empty air alike.

The kraken rises, but there isn't space for it to surface between the *Dolphin* and the Haithi warship. By closing the gap between the two vessels, the Haithi sailors have constrained their gigantic enemy, closing off one line of attack. They're using Dredger's ship as cover.

Gigantic tentacles rise out of the glass-smooth ocean on the far side of the Haithi ship, and the cannons on the other side answer in unison.

The Kraken-saint screams. One blazing tentacle sweeps across the Haithi deck, knocking sailors and cannons and anything else it can scrape off into the ocean. It leaves a slimy trail of burning phlogiston behind it. Haithi sailors rush to dump buckets of fire-quelling foam on the greenish flames, fighting alchemy with alchemy. Then the storm engulfs the two ships again, plunging them both into a laughing lightning-riven darkness and the spy can't see the Haithi ship any more. There's the occasional flicker of fire, but he can't tell if that's the ship catching fire or the muzzle flash of cannon.

The spy whispers into the wind: "I'm an Ishmeric spy. I'm on your side, you idiot. Back off!"

There's no answer. He didn't think there would be. His conscience, he decides, is clear.

Another tentacle explodes out of the ocean and swipes blindly for the Haithi warship. It finds the *Dolphin* instead and paws at the side of the ship, tearing a yard-wide hole just above the waterline. A cannon blast sprays burning liquid into the air. The spy's lungs start to burn, and he coughs at the acrid smoke.

He stumbles across the deck in the direction that Dredger went. Climbs over the bodies of the other refugees – he can't tell if they're dead, clinging to the hull to avoid being thrown overboard, or just prostrate with divine terror. A short ladder leads up to a higher deck. He hears Dredger shouting orders, but there's no time to explain himself. He sees a rifle in a rack and grabs it. Chambers a round, a little ampoule of alchemical blasting-power and lead.

Somewhere up there is the saint. The spy points his gun towards the heavens, looking for the heart of the storm.

There.

His shot strikes true. A human figure, held suspended by the clouds like an elemental trapeze, suddenly visible, suddenly twisted in agony. The figure tumbles, clutching at its side. The spy reloads, fires again, misses, reloads.

Mists thicken around the figure, slowing its descent, cradling it. The cloud reddens like a giant's bandage as blood seeps into it, and as the cloud seeps into the saint's body. A miracle of transmutation – the man will become more and more cloud, just as Captain Isigi is becoming more and more Lion Queen. That injury would be lethal to a mortal man, but a saint is more than mortal. It takes more than that to kill the earthly avatar of a god.

It takes, for example, a whole platoon of Haithi marksmen.

Remorselessly accurate rifle fire targets the now exposed saint, shot after shot striking home. The Haithi gunners are Vigilant. Fear is only a memory to them. Undead limbs don't tremble, and undead eye sockets don't blink.

And then the saint falls. The storm breaks, unravelling with impossible speed as the natural order reasserts itself. The sea, too, is suddenly itself again as the Kraken-saint sinks away, releasing the waters from the grasp of its miracle. The *Dolphin* lurches forward, going from supernaturally becalmed to full acceleration in an instant. Even if they wanted to, it would be hard to circle back to the damaged Haithi warship, to the wounded but still dangerous kraken.

The *Dolphin*, after all, flies the flag of Guerdon, and Guerdon is neutral in this war.

Emlin cheers. The spy breathes again. He hands the weapon back to Dredger.

The armoured man takes the gun, methodically unchambers the last round, checks the barrel, weighs the odds. Then says:

"I'll get your boy across safe, San. And then we're square."

CHAPTER 2

"Just think of it," says Dr Ramegos, "as building a bridge. Opening a door."

Eladora Duttin nods, bites her lip to keep from stammering, then chants the spell Ramegos taught her. *It's not like opening a door*, she thinks, *it's like pulling an anvil down on your head.*

Eladora's unprepared for this lesson in sorcery, but that's true of this entire impromptu apprenticeship. She cannot quite recall when she first met Ramegos — sometime in the painful, chaotic haze after the Crisis. The days after that horror are lost in fog — Eladora vaguely remembers stumbling down from the Thay family tomb on Gravehill, body and soul wounded by her dead grandfather's blasphemous sorceries. After that, there were weeks spent in a hospital bed, the metallic taste of the painkillers, and a succession of half-remembered grey figures who questioned her, over and over. Men from the city watch, from the church, the alchemists' guild, from the emergency committee, all trying to piece together the events that had remade Guerdon. To take the broken, reeling city and give it an account of itself that made sense.

One of those figures never left Eladora's side, and, over the weeks, resolved itself into a bright-eyed woman, too energetic to be as old as her wrinkled dark skin suggested. The endless interrogations and debriefings slowly became conversations and one-sided confessionals, and along the way Ramegos declared that she was going to teach Eladora sorcery.

Eladora extends her hand, feels the power flow along her arm.

Feels the pain, anyway, and she assumes that means she's channelling *something*. She clenches her fist, slowly, imagining the spell paralysing a target, holding them in unseen chains of sorcery – but then she loses control, the magic slipping through her fingers. For a moment, her hand feels like she's thrust it into an open fire, the unseen chains suddenly turned to molten metal, her skin blistering. A spell gone awry can discharge unpredictably – if she swallows the power she's drawn down, she can ground it inside her body, risking internal damage. If she lets it go, she might ignite something, and this cramped backroom in the IndLib's parliamentary office is crammed with papers and books.

She holds her hand in the fire, trapped in indecision, until Ramegos leans forward and brushes away the errant spell as if it's a cobweb clinging to her skin. The older woman's casual use of power is impressive.

"That was a good attempt," says Ramegos, "but sloppy. You've been neglecting your practice."

"I-It's been hard to find time. Mr Kelkin—"

"Kelkin will work us both to death if we let him." Ramegos tosses a damp cloth at Eladora, who wraps it around her hand. "Not everything has to happen according to his schedule."

It's not his schedule, Eladora wants to protest, *I'm working to fix Guerdon, and you're … doing whatever a Special Thaumaturge does.* But she doesn't want to have that argument again. Ramegos may know, intellectually, what happened to this city, but she's not from Guerdon. She doesn't feel the same fierce urgency to save it that Eladora does.

She picks another conversational tack. "Whereas you intend to kill me at your leisure."

"Sorcery," says Ramegos, "is a perfectly healthy mental exercise, with only a small chance of self-immolation. If all you want out of life is wealth, power and sanity, go be an alchemist." In the last century, Guerdon's alchemical revolution has transformed the city – and the trade in alchemical weapons brought vast wealth in from overseas, as the Godswar consumes half the world.

I don't want to be an alchemist. Or a politician's adviser. Or . . .

"Now, again. But try not blowing yourself up this time."

Eladora groans and tries to clear her mind, or at least brush aside a few of her more urgent worries. She lifts her hand again, envisages the twisting, impossible shapes—

And there's a hammering at the door. Perik's annoying voice shouting. "The chairman's on his way! He's called—"

He's cut off abruptly. Eladora opens the door to reveal Perik's stand there, frozen by the spell in the act of knocking. Ramegos snorts in amusement, dispels the paralysis with a wave of her hand. Perik's standing there in confusion, caught in the action of knocking.

"—the committee," finishes Perik. He glares at Eladora and would glare at Ramegos if he dared. The sorceress ignores him, picks up her heavy grimoire and hurries off, floating through the uproar of the outer office.

"Remember to practise your Khebeshi," she instructs Eladora as she leaves. "You won't get far as a sorcerer if your Khebeshi is poor." Ramegos would say that – she's from the distant city of Khebesh – and mastering the obscure and difficult tongue is very, very far down Eladora's list of priorities.

Perik waits until Ramegos is gone before speaking. "Chairman Kelkin sent an aethergraph message an hour ago," says Perik venomously, "he wants your report. I didn't want to interrupt your time with the Special Thaumaturge."

Eladora curses under her breath. She squeezes past Perik and hurries over to her desk in the outer office. A dozen other assistants to the emergency committee glance up at her, then return to their work, every one of them scribbling frantically like it's the last minute of a final exam. The distant chatter of an aethergraph in another room; the hubbub of voices in the corridor, like a gathering wave. Kelkin's nearly here.

She piles papers into her worn satchel, praying to no gods they're in the right order. In her mind's eye she can see Kelkin – her boss, everybody's boss, chair of the emergency committee and de facto ruler of Guerdon – stomping up from Venture Square like a little puffing steam engine, dragging behind him a huge crowd of supplicants and clerks, beggars and bodyguards, lunatics and journalists, and heaven knows what else. When Kelkin appears in public these days, it's always one breath away from a riot. Normally, Eladora's nervous that something will happen when Effro Kelkin's out and about in the city he temporarily rules. Today, she almost wants something to happen.

Anything to slow him down.

She's not ready.

Eladora briefly wishes she'd been practising something more painful than a paralysis formula. Instead, all she can think to do is ask Perik for a favour. "Can you, ah, stall him? I just need five minutes."

In truth, she needs five months.

Maybe five years.

The gigantic report on her desk is an inquiry into the origins, demographics, structure and status of the New City. Ten months ago, at the height of what some call the Crisis and others the Gutter Miracle, a new city exploded into being within Guerdon. A warren of streets and tunnels, palaces and tower blocks, all made from pearly white stone, erupted from the corpse of a criminal named Spar and engulfed the south-east quadrant of Guerdon, inflicting untold damage on the Alchemists' Quarter and the docks. Since then the New City has been colonised at speed. Refugees, mostly, but anyone brave enough could go down there and stake a claim to one of the empty palaces the gleaming, silent arcades.

Guerdon was already reeling from a series of attacks; the city watch overstretched. There was no way to take control of the New City when it formed. The newspapers ran riot with lurid tales of depravity and crime. Anything's possible there; even reality isn't quite nailed down in the New City – her report is crammed with accounts of miracles and magic that she cannot attribute to any known god. There are cries and editorials demanding the New City be tamed, be purged, be quarantined or demolished or dispelled, but no one can agree on what should be done or how to do it.

Eladora's impossible task was to understand the New City, to map it and take stock of it. Others on the Industrial Liberal staff were to build on her work, as part of the great security bill that Kelkin demanded. He was once the great reformer, but his reputation of the last twenty years was built on law and order, and he was determined to bring order to the New City.

Eladora glances at one page, which is entirely blank apart from the heading "Proposed Solutions".

She's really not ready.

"Can I *stall* him?" echoes Perik incredulously. "He's already sent word to assemble the emergency committee. No, I can't *stall* him. If you won't take it, I will!"

Perik used to work for Mr Droupe of the alchemist-backed Hawkers, the main rivals to Kelkin's Industrial Liberals. The Hawkers are, officially, the City Forward party, but everyone still quotes a joke Kelkin made twenty years ago about how their only policy was selling weapons in the market, hence Hawkers.

Technically, Perik still works for Droupe, just like Droupe is still technically the head of parliament. But that parliament hasn't sat in ten months, and won't ever assemble again in its old form. During the Crisis Kelkin took control of the old Committee for Public Safety, declared a city-wide emergency and assumed special powers. Eladora has read enough history to know how fragile order can be, how easily the order of the world can be broken. Kelkin held law and order together through sheer determination and force of personality in those dark days, and for that she's profoundly grateful.

And as if to ensure that Droupe was forever routed and ruined, a scandal came to light three months after the Crisis. A forgettable affair involving bribery and corruption, but it was enough to make sure that he couldn't return to Guerdon and claim the chair of the emergency committee. Eladora is quite sure that it was Kelkin who leaked the scandal to the press, and wonders how long the old man has been holding that in reserve. Effro Kelkin is sometimes an idealist and sometimes a vicious opportunist; his biographers are already digging in for trench warfare.

"It's my work," snaps Eladora, pushing past Perik. His face reddens with anger, but she ignores him and calls for her assistant. Rhiado extrictates himself from a knot of aides and hurries over to her. He folds his lanky frame in an approximation of a bow – Rhiado's only a year or two younger than Eladora, but he treats her like some elder stateswoman, when she's only an assistant, too. He's assistant to an assistant – an awkward title, but everything about the emergency committee is improvised. The city was gutted last year by the Crisis, and they're holding its civic organs together like a pustulent bandage.

"I'm heading down to meet the chairman. What's on my schedule afterwards?"

"You've got the reception at the Haithi embassy this evening. That's it."

"Thank you," says Eladora. She steps around Perik and weaves through the maze of desks in the outer office.

"Oh," calls Rhiado, "your mother wants to see you. She's in the city."

Eladora walks straight into a desk. She stumbles, skinning her knee on the sharp edge. She loses her grip on the satchel, and papers spill across the floor. She can feel her cheeks burning as she bends down to pick them up, can hear Perik's exasperated mutterings.

"It's fine, it's fine," she insists and brushes Rhiado aside when he tries to help. It's not his fault – he doesn't know Silva Duttin.

Eladora has not spoken to her mother in more than three years. There are moon-shaped scars on her forearms that bear testament to that last encounter – she remembers sitting in the restaurant, digging her fingernails into her skin to stop herself screaming insults at the woman. In the Crisis, Eladora saw monsters and gods, but the thought of meeting her mother is still a knife in her stomach.

No time for that now. She forces herself to stand, brushes herself off. Perik's still glaring at her, but she has to ignore it. Kelkin needs her.

Eladora hurries out of the door. Parliament is a labyrinth of tunnels, halls, offices and archives, but she's learned to navigate it without thinking. It's mostly empty, anyway. With the great parliamentary chamber upstairs vacant for nine months, the place can run with a much smaller staff. She ducks down a spiral staircase and cuts across an assembly room to get to the main corridor.

She's just in time to fall in alongside Effro Kelkin as he marches towards the council chamber at the head of his entourage. He puffs as he walks and she can see sweat on his balding pate.

"Have section five to hand," he orders her. Eladora nods and hopes that section five wasn't left scattered across the office floor upstairs. Her heart's pounding, and it's not just the threat of her mother. She's worked for Kelkin since the Crisis, but this is only the third time she's accompanied him into the council chamber.

Briefly, during the Crisis, Eladora channelled the power of the nightmarish Black Iron Gods. Proximity to political power is a pale shadow of *that* divine glory, but it's closer than anything else.

Admiral Vermeil holds the door to the council chamber open for her. She ducks around the bulk of the older man. Vermeil has his own, much slimmer report in hand, in a red folder. Eladora dreads what might be hidden inside.

The admiral is Kelkin's security adviser. The contents of that red folder contain Vermeil's possible solution to the problem of the lawless New City. Ten months ago, at the height of the Crisis, the government bombarded parts of the city with rockets. Nothing's unthinkable any more, nothing's off the table.

The admiral bows his head and mutters a greeting as Eladora passes by, as if he's holding the door for her at a dinner party.

She takes one of the stools crammed around the walls of the little chamber. The emergency council consists of eight members and a few clerks, so the room gets uncomfortable at a dozen people. Today, it's more like thirty, and there are more crowding in the door. Eladora's stomach sinks at the thought of presenting her draft report to such an audience. Ramegos is on the other side of the room, deep in conversation with one of Vermeil's staff, and can offer no reassurance. Eladora catches sight of Perik's pinched face, scowling at being shut out of the council room again, but then Kelkin raps the gavel, the door closes, and they're on.

"I call the, ah, what's the count?"

"Ninety-four," whispers Eladora.

"Ninety-fourth meeting of the emergency committee to order. We'll dispense with a reading of the minutes. Jarrit, let's start with you."

Jarrit — an elegant, grey-haired woman from Maredon, largest of the outlying towns — rises and launches into roughly the same speech that's been made at the last seventy committee meetings. She eloquently argues that the immediate crisis has passed, and that it is time to call a new parliament and give rule of the city back to the citizens.

By which she means the alchemists' guild and their wealthy allies. Jarrit's a Hawker through and through. Without mentioning him by name, Jarrit insinuates that Kelkin has subverted democracy and six hundred years of parliamentary tradition. (Eladora, still a history student in her battered soul, can't help adding mental footnotes: the rotten parliaments when the institution was a room full of hostages to the king; the fifty-year gap when Guerdon was dominated by the monstrous Black Iron Gods; the blessed parliaments where the Church of the Keepers filled nine-tenths of the seats.)

No sooner has Jarrit sat down than another speaker springs up. Another Hawker, castigating the emergency committee for its lackadaisical and half-hearted response to the security problem facing Guerdon. No one knows what to do about the city that appeared at the end of the Crisis. It's flooded with criminals and cultists, the city watch lack the courage to patrol all the alien streets and the committee has refused to authorise the creation of new Tallowmen.

At that, Eladora smiles inwardly. The Tallowmen are monsters made by the alchemists' guild. At the height of the Crisis, the alchemists were given leave to grab suspected criminals off the streets and render them down in the tallow vats, to make an army of horrors to usurp the city watch. If Kelkin did nothing else, he'd still hold Eladora's loyalty for keeping those leering candle-man horrors in check. And she wouldn't be the only one who feels that way; if there's one thing Guerdon agrees on, it's that the Tallowmen are monsters.

It's just that half the city thinks they were necessary monsters, to keep the other half under control.

The chairman listens to the speech without expression. Midway through, he leans back and snaps his fingers at Eladora. She rifles through her satchel, and hands him as much as she can find of section five. He leafs through it, makes a few notes, then he takes Vermeil's red folder and lays it beside section five on the green baize of the conference table. She wonders if the admiral chose that red deliberately. It looks like a pool of fresh blood that Kelkin's about to dip his hands into. As he flips through it Eladora tries to read over his shoulder. Catches sight of words like *Tallowmen*. Like *prison ships*. *Forcible decontamination. Heavy gas.*

"Is there anything else before we move on to new business?" asks Kelkin when Abver's done. He lays his right hand on the red folder. "No?"

A hush descends over the conference room. Heads incline forward. Ramegos is unreadable, unmoving. Vermeil holds his breath. The Hawkers lick their lips. The Keeper priests fan themselves, their scratchy robes uncomfortable in this summer's dead heat.

"I have no new business," says Effro Kelkin.

Uproar. Every other member of the committee, and their aides and advisers, all shouting at one. Eladora looks to Vermeil in confusion, wondering what Kelkin's doing. Is he just taunting his rivals on the committee by dangling Admiral Vermeil and his proposal in front of them, then denying them a vote on it? Did he plan on calling a vote, then decide against it at the last moment, perhaps reading some subtle change in the room? Or – Eladora worries – is this a sign of Kelkin's ill health? The chairman is more than seventy years old, and was badly wounded during the Crisis. The city won't survive without a firm hand to guide it.

Now he's banging the gavel, demanding order.

"Old business," says Kelkin. "Jarrit's motion to recall parliament and hold a general election. I believe I postponed a vote on that motion at the last meeting."

He's definitely mocking them. That motion was made five months ago; he's postponed it more than fifty times since then.

"I second the motion," says Kelkin. "Let us vote on the proposal to hold a general election in the cities and hinterlands to choose a new parliament."

Dead silence. Jarrit, hesitantly, raises her hand. She has little choice. "Aye." They go around the table.

Two more ayes, then Abver. He looks at his allies on the council, whispers urgently with an aide, then speaks haltingly. "It's . . . this council's very purpose – is to, ah, deal with . . . After all, recalling parliament and holding an election will take weeks. You can't – I mean, would the chair not agree that it would be exceedingly remiss of this committee to leave the city in such a state, to aggravate the situation by calling a contentious election?"

"The city's survived for ten months since the Crisis. I think we can muddle through another six weeks. How do you vote, sir?"

Abver stares at Kelkin, incredulously. Kelkin's entire platform is built on law and order, on stability. Now he's not only poured phlogistonic oil over that whole platform, he's handed the Hawkers a match. "I vote aye. If the chair refuses to lead this emergency council in actually tackling the emergency, let's go back to parliament as soon as we are able. Let the people have their say."

Next to vote is Ogilvy, Kelkin's second in the Industrial Liberal party. Ogilvy's equally staggered by Kelkin's call for a vote. He looks as though he's about to vomit up a live fish as he raises his hand. "Aye," he says weakly.

The last is the young Patros, the head of the church of the Keepers. His features are perfectly composed, his eyes downcast in reverent prayer, but from her seat Eladora can see him nervously tugging at a gold prayer ring on one finger. The church of the Keepers used to be Guerdon's state religion. For nearly three centuries, the Keepers kept both gods and laws, commanding a huge majority in parliament. Their power has dwindled since then. Kelkin dealt them a crippling blow early in his career when he passed the Free City act, allowing foreign faiths to open temples in the city.

But ever since the alchemists and their Hawkers rose to power, there has been an uncertain alliance of the defeated between the Keepers and the IndLibs. Ten minutes ago, Eladora would have called Ashur one of Kelkin's closest allies on the committee, but now everything's uncertain. Finally, he lifts his head. Eladora's struck by how nervous he looks.

"This is a mistake, Mr Chairman, and the city will rue your decision. We looked to you for stability, and you've betrayed us. In the name of the most holy church of the Keepers, I vote nay."

Kelkin ignores his erstwhile ally. "The chair votes aye. The motion is carried. All other business is suspended until the calling of the one hundredth and fifty-third parliament. This committee shall only meet again if warranted by special circumstance. Until then, the chair thanks you all for your service."

He slams the gavel down.

There's a stunned silence for a moment, then it's like Kelkin just kicked over a beehive, as an incredible deafening buzz of urgent conversation fills the room. The door's unbarred, and the uproar spreads into the corridor. Eladora catches a brief glimpse of Perik, who'd already huddled in conversation with Abver; apparently his defection from the Hawkers to the IndLibs is already forgotten. Rats are quick to leave a sinking ship, of course.

And there's Kelkin, the captain who just steered the ship headlong onto the rocks. He turns first to Vermeil and hands back the red folder. "Bury it," he orders, "and burn any copies."

He gives Eladora back section five of her report. He's scrawled some numbers across a mostly blank page. Her estimated population of the New City, divided by the number of citizens per representative in parliament. Everyone else in Guerdon's ruling elite sees the New City as a threat to public safety, a monstrous aberration that must be excised. Kelkin's seen it for what it is – enough new votes to topple the balance of power in parliament.

He hasn't crashed his ship on the rocks. He's beached it on a virgin shore.

CHAPTER 3

Guerdon's a neutral city, a city of weaponsmiths, sailors and mercenaries, of rich men and poor – and of spies. Observers to watch the harbour, to spot where ships carrying cargoes of death are going. Eavesdroppers to listen to whispered diplomatic overtures, to hear the bargains and betrayals in the coffee shops along Venture Square. Pickpockets and codebreakers to intercept and decipher messages carried by couriers. Hedge-sorcerers to read the runes and interpret omens. All the pantheons have their agents here. The alleyways of Guerdon are a front in the war, where – for now – battles are fought by mortals, not gods.

That is why a man whose official title is Third Secretary to the Ambassador of Haith leaves the embassy by a concealed door. The embassy of Old Haith is perhaps the grandest of the mansions along Embassy Row, reflecting the long and close relationship between the two nations. The building is sombre, dark leaden windows and grey stone, no decoration other than the sigils of the various Houses whose scions serves as ambassadors to Guerdon over the decades. Many of the sigils are crowned with a bar of iron, which signifies that one ambassador or another inherited the family phylactery on returning to Haith.

The Third Secretary will never see his family crest mounted on the walls of the embassy. He's not a member of a great House. He's a Bureau man. He serves the Crown of Haith another way.

He walks past the embassy of Haith's rival, the conquering Sacred Realm of Ishmere. Statues of the Ishmeric gods watch him as he passes by, and he can feel their hatred like heat from an open furnace. Snarling Lion Queen, the war-goddess of Ishmere. Writhing Kraken, who steals the seas. The mocking face of Blessed Bol, whose touch brings prosperity. Smoke Painter, hidden behind a veil.

There's no sign of Fate Spider, which worries him. Fate Spider is the Ishmeric god of destiny and secrets. There's a belief – something between a running joke and an article of faith – among the intelligence staff at the Haithi embassy that Fate Spider's statue comes to life to eat unwary spies. The Ishmeric pantheon is always in flux, always changing as the gods of one island rise in prominence, or one god metamorphoses through sheer madness into some new aspect. There are staff back at the Office of Foreign Divinities whose job it is to interpret tiny changes in the rituals and decoration of Ishmeric temples, in an attempt to divine shifts in the balance of divine power.

The absence of Fate Spider might indicate that the secretive deity has fallen from favour. Or it might be a feint, to fool the watching spies. The line between madness and divine purpose has long since been erased in Ishmere.

There are still a few lights burning in offices on the upper floor of the Ishmeric embassy. The Third Secretary looks up at them, idly wondering about his counterparts there. They also creep out at night, no doubt, sending vibrations through all the threads and webs of the shadow world. They have spies watching the harbour, and the alchemical warehouses and the mercenary hiring halls. They also have agents and informants; they have cover identities just like him, bland bureaucratic titles that cloak their true purpose, just like his heavy coat conceals the gun he wears.

He wonders if they also call Guerdon home, as he does. He comes from Haith, but he hasn't returned to that land in decades. His career has been spent in the various outlying colonies and conquered territories. You could trace the long retreat by mapping his assignments. As the years pass, and the borders contract, his postings are closer and closer to Haith.

He has not taken leave in years, because if he took leave he would be expected to return to Old Haith, and he is no longer comfortable there. Haith hasn't changed, but he has. Of course, he's not wholly part of this city either; he may appreciate Guerdon's fierce energy, its animal passion, its sordid ways of survival, but he's still Haithi. His bones belong to the old Empire.

Glancing back down Embassy Row, he sees a pair of watchmen, patrolling. There was a killing on this very street only a few weeks ago, a rival spy shot dead. A little splash of violence, like the first tentative raindrop before a storm.

His business tonight is on the far side of Castle Hill. He ducks down a narrow flight of steps, slick with the afternoon's rain, then goes through another archway that leads to another staircase, and that brings him down to a subway station. He remembers being amazed by the subway when he first came here. Haith has a few train lines running between cities and the estates of the great Houses, but the trains of Guerdon are a modern marvel. The tunnels they run in predate the city in places. Old abandoned ghoul runs. There's more below the city than there is above, runs the old saying, although that's no longer true. The addition of the New City tipped the balance to the surface.

Assuming, of course, that there aren't new labyrinths and catacombs beneath the eerie marble streets and dream-palaces of the New City. He hasn't dared visit that part of Guerdon; there are dangerous powers in those streets, so he only interacts with the New City at one remove, through agents and hirelings. Watching from a distance, through the grimy window of the safe house on Gethis Row.

As the subway train rattles through the darkness, the secretary amuses himself by imagining impossible pleasure domes and subterranean mushroom gardens in the depths of the New City, lurking out there in the black void beyond the tunnel. Every so often, a spark from the train's wheels blazes, a flare that gives a flashing vision of the tunnels. It's always graffiti-covered greenish rock, but the secretary cannot help but feel that if the spark happened a moment earlier or a second later, he might behold marvellous vistas.

The train slows as it approaches the next station. Three other passengers get on. Two are young and drunk, in the grey robes of students. Laughing, they fall into a pair of seats near the door, kissing and pawing at each other. The boy's eager fingers dislodge the flowers braided through the girl's hair.

The other passenger is an older woman carrying a handful of leaflets. Silver charms and amulets jangle as she picks her way down the carriage towards him. The Third Secretary recognises the symbols: the old woman is an acolyte of the Keepers. These days, the church of the Keepers is forced to compete for worshippers like all the rest of the faiths in Guerdon. The Third Secretary feels sorry for the old woman, who must peddle her beliefs to a cynical city. When she was young, the Keepers practically ran Guerdon, and a life in service to the church was considered glorious and rewarding. Kelkin's reforms changed all that. The woman reminds him of an old crab on a dry beach, left behind by a wave that's never going to come back in, scuttling this way and that in search of some tide pool.

All his sympathy vanishes when, out of all the seats in this half of the carriage, she sits down next to him. The faint scent of incense clinging to her clothes does nothing to mask the yeasty old-woman stink. She proffers a leaflet. "The gods watch over you," she says. "Holy Beggar, Saint Storm, Mother of Flowers — there's a god set over each of us. They will not turn their faces from us. Only we turn our faces from them."

He takes the flyer to avoid argument. "I'll read it," he promises.

Mollified, the old woman points to the entangled students. "Disgraceful," she says loud enough for them to hear. "Like animals. Like whores."

He ignores her and pretends to bury himself in the flyer. One section is a cut-out-and-keep card, and the flyer exhorts him to carry such a card on him at all times. It's for those too poor to carry a symbol of the Keepers, or too faithless to be recognised as members of the Church. The idea is to carry the card until you die, so when the time comes to dispose of your body, you get buried with the proper rites.

The card doesn't describe those rites, but the Third Secretary knows what they are. These days, the dead of the Keepers are given to the carrion-eating ghouls, the remains lowered down deep corpse shafts into the depths of the city. It's a practical solution on multiple levels – not only does it reduce the need for graveyards in an overcrowded city, but the ghouls extract the *residuum*, the potent soul-dregs, from the corpse and consume it themselves. The Kept Gods take only the thin gruel of prayer, a starvation diet of faith that ensures that Guerdon's gods are weak and manageable, compared to the crazed titans of other lands.

The Third Secretary smiles inwardly. Death is a problem for other people, not a Vigilant-caste man of Haith. His soul isn't going anywhere.

The train emerges from its tunnel and rattles across a viaduct. Below is the tangle of streets and alleyways called the Wash, the most notorious old slum in Guerdon. The New City has engulfed half the Wash. Shimmering white towers and ethereal spires rise above the tenements and stagnant canals. This close, the Third Secretary can see that the New City is not as heavenly as it appears from afar. Washing lines have been strung between those spires; banners flutter in the night breeze. Graffiti scrawled across marble façades. Temples proclaiming themselves to be gambling halls, whorehouses, fighting pits.

"Disgraceful," echoes the old woman. "Filthy city. A canker, I tell you. A canker."

"This is my stop," says the Third Secretary, and forces himself to sound apologetic.

He rises, and she clutches at him, her hand grabbing his coat. He pulls free of her grasp, hurries away from her, down the carriage.

"Read it!" she calls after him. "Your soul can still be saved!"

He leaves the train and hurries down the platform. Behind him, the two drunken students peel themselves apart and stumble out, too. He crumples the flyer up and is about to throw it away when he spots something unusual. *The fires of Safid shall carry the soul . . .*

He uncrumples it, skims it, then folds it carefully and slips it into a pocket. As far as he can tell, the flyer's from some minority sect, the Safidists, who don't normally proselytise in the city. He'll send it home to the Office of Foreign Divinities, for their archives. The mainstream Keeper Church is faltering, overtaken by its radical fringe. He's seen too much of the Godswar to pay much attention to the divinities of Guerdon. Compared to the fighting gods of Ishmere, Guerdon's deities are somnolent, barely aware of their worshippers or their peril. But divinity isn't his department.

He strolls out of the station. Finds his focus as he mounts the stairs one step at a time, managing to make himself trudge like a tired labourer on his way home despite the adrenaline flooding his veins. The Wash is emptier these days than it was when he first came here, when he first built his web of contacts in Guerdon's underworld. Now, that underworld has shifted south and east, vanished into the unknowable white labyrinth of the New City. One day soon, he'll have to brave the new terrain of his adopted home, but tonight he has more urgent matters.

His destination is a house on Gethis Row, where he is to meet his contact: a dealer in alchemical weapons. Haith buys such weapons in great quantities direct from Guerdon through legal channels. But there are some weapons that cannot be bought for any amount of coin, and this meeting is part of a long and delicate negotiation to settle on a price that cannot be spoken.

The light above the door is dark. That's not right. His contact should be there, waiting for him, and why would she be waiting in the dark? The street is too quiet, too empty. The secretary sniffs the air, wondering if there's a hint of blood on the breeze. He doesn't break stride or show any reaction – just walks on by.

It isn't enough. The first attacker darts out of an alleyway, the second from the shadows of a doorway across the street. The secretary goes for his gun, but someone else in an upstairs room already has him in their sights.

He feels the impact before he hears the roar of the gun, and then he feels the pain three heartbeats after that.

He tumbles into the gutter, and one of the attackers is now on top of him. It's the girl from the train, the student who had her tongue down the boy's throat. She cuts his throat, with a single slash of a little knife. She doesn't twist his head to the side, though, so she's rewarded with a gush of blood over her hands and knees. She shrieks.

Amateurs.

The Third Secretary no longer has breath to sigh with, but he still has enough control to roll his eyes. Daerinth is going to kill him for dying. Sloppy. Sloppy. It's not just the black mark on his career, it's all the little bits of living he'll miss. Not just pretty girls, but good food and wine. Damn it, now he's going to miss the reception tonight, too. He was looking forward to that.

Approaching footsteps, accompanied by a stronger smell. A young man's voice, nervous and excited. The knife-wielding girl is joined by her lover from the train. "I hit him! The gods guided my hand!" he says. "Did you see that! What a shot! What a . . . ugh!" And then the sound and smell of vomit.

Definitely amateurs.

They lift his corpse by the feet and shoulders and carry him into the alleyway. He considers his options. His training urges him to continue to play dead — play a corpse, to be precise, because he's genuinely dead. He waits for his opportunity.

As he waits, he ponders: is his death connected to his contact's apparent absence?

He's pretty sure it is — it's not likely to be a coincidence that he'd get murdered right outside the house where he was supposed to conduct a major illegal arms deal. Still, stranger things have happened, and it's remotely possibly that the two supposed students from the train just happened to rob and murder him here. If they go for his coin purse, that might be a clue.

They dump him in a pile of garbage. The stench is overwhelming in his dead nose. He can feel some of his senses sharpening, others diminishing. The sensation of concrete pavement and rotten fruit against his face is very far away, and seems just as unimportant to him as the blood draining from his throat wound or the gaping bullet hole in his right side. His sense of smell has improved, and beyond the sickly sweet rot he can smell his blood on the woman's hands, her floral perfume, her partner's oniony breath. The distant, fainter tang of alchemical discharge from the gun that ended him. It's a temporary condition – he's read that when the necromancers flense him down to polished bone, he'll lose his sense of smell. Enjoy it for the moment, he reflects.

The girl turns the Third Secretary's body over and starts rifling through his pockets. His dead eyes stare at her face. It's hard to tell, but he can't find a trace of remorse on her features, which irritates him.

"Go and tell her we got him!" orders the girl.

Definitely not a coincidence. Definitely a conspiracy.

He's waited long enough.

They trained him for this moment, over and over again, so when it comes it's forgettable. All the practise runs blurring into the only real one. With an effort of will, the dead secretary relinks body and soul. There's a flash of heat as the iron periapts implanted beneath his skin fuse with his bones. Necromantic energy suffuses his dead body, and he feels strength flood into his stiffening limbs.

The woman shrieks and slashes him with her knife, but he's too fast for her now, too strong. He catches her wrist, crushing it with his undead fingers, and then slams his other hand into her sternum. She crumples and falls off him, gasping for breath.

The young man looks on in terror, frozen to the spot as the man he shot springs to his feet, blood-drenched, still gushing from two mortal wounds. The gun's still in the boy's hands, but it might as well be a thousand miles away.

Run, says the Third Secretary in his new voice. It sounds ever so terrifying and sepulchral, and it works – the boy drops the gun and sprints down the alleyway. After all, he's seen a ghost.

Maybe, reflects the Third Assistant Secretary, being Vigilant won't be that bad. He spins around and delivers a brutal kick to the woman's forehead, knocking her out. He can have her questioned. Find out how she knew about the deal, discover who she's working for.

First, though, he needs to find out how much of this vital

operation can be salvaged, find out what his life was worth. He picks up her knife, runs one finger along its sharp blade, finds it pleasing. He pads down the alleyway, testing the balance of his reanimated body. He finds that pleasing, too; in his new state, he's faster and stronger than before. The soul realigned with the flesh. Or, well, with the bone anyway. The flesh is dead weight now.

A light burns brightly within the safehouse. The Third Secretary grins with lips that are already stiffening, then throws himself through the door with blinding speed. The dead move fast.

The old woman in the safe house moves faster.

In her hands, a flaming sword.

The Third Secretary's last thought is that he really, really needs to tell the Office of Foreign Divinity what's happening, because this changes everything. But then the fire catches his bound soul, and he burns, and there's nothing left.

CHAPTER 4

The *Dolphin* enters the great harbour of Guerdon. The city proper is another hour's travel; Guerdon straddles what was once the mouth of a river where it spilled into the bay. The river is now mostly buried, dissected and diverted into a hundred canals and underground waterways.

The bay is flecked with islands. From the deck, Emlin and the spy watch them pass by. Dredger plays tour guide, offering running commentary. He's glad to be back in his city.

Some islands are crowded with guns and fortifications, naval bases ready to protect the city from invaders. Guerdon remains unaligned in the Godswar because of commerce, not idealism. They do not trust to the mere fact of their neutrality to protect them from invasion, and the war is closer every day.

In the distance, they spot the Bell Rock, a reef so low in the water that it is visible only at ebb tide, and invisible and lethal when the seas rise. Dredger points out the ruins of a lighthouse on the rock, and the teetering steel frame of the temporary replacement light. The legs of the frame are stained a sinister bright yellow, just like the rocks around them, and Dredger explains there was an accident there a few months ago. A freighter carrying alchemical weapons broke its moorings and ran aground, spilling a cargo of bombs and poison gas on the Bell Rock. He points to another boat, similar in design to the *Dolphin*, moored off the island. The tide is low; men in breathing masks and rubber waders clamber amid the tainted rocks. Dredger explains they're some of his employees, collecting strands of a seaweed his alchemists bred. The seaweed soaks up the poison, concentrating it. Later, they'll dry out the seaweed, grind it up, and resell the dust to some merchant of death like Sanhada Baradhin.

Beyond the Bell Rock, closer to Guerdon, is a long flat island or sandbar. More than half of it is artificial, created by dumping barge loads of poisoned earth into the bay. That's Shrike Island, Dredger's little kingdom. Even at this distance, the spy can see chimneys and refineries on the stable part of the island; the yards where Dredger turns the leavings of the alchemists into weapons for resale. His own alchemy, turning used poison into gold. Never a death wasted.

Between the *Dolphin* and the Bell Rock is another island. It's crowded with ships of all sizes, berthed wherever they can find space along the long piers that splay out into the bay. There's a low building, and beyond that an encampment. Tents, fences, guard towers. Hark Island, where Guerdon filters those fleeing the Godswar from those who bring the mad gods with them. An internment camp for the divine. Rogue saints, blessed monsters and true believers get detained; the faithless and the fearful get to go on.

Dredger grunts and points at the western side of Hark. There's an old prison there, a crumbling fortress of greyish stone, its walls partially overgrown with ivy. Rising over the walls of the fort, the spy can see signs of construction – skeletal frameworks topped with metal tanks, alchemical engines.

"Been building that all year," says Dredger, glancing at Emlin. "Prison for saints."

From his perch on the railing, Emlin stares at the rugged isle like it's a slumbering monster.

South of Hark, two hundred yards or so from the shore, there's a jagged tooth of rock poking from the water. The spy can see more figures moving around that little island. Collecting more tainted seaweed, maybe, although there's no yellowish stain on that tiny outcrop.

Naval patrols – fast little gunboats – circle around Hark Isle. No doubt the *Dolphin* has already been seen, and if Dredger does not dock there so that his passengers from Severast can be poked and probed by the city's inquisitors, there will be trouble.

They cruise past the Isle of Statues, a quarantined land for sufferers of the ghastly stone plague. A low, grassy island about a mile across. Grey shapes stand sentinel, unmoving, and the spy cannot tell if they are natural rocks or the stony husks of the dead. The sound of a church bell comes mournfully over the water. It's time for Sanhada and Emlin Baradhin to drown tragically.

The spy slips over the rail of the *Dolphin* and drops into the waters of the bay. The summer sun is warm, but the water's still chilly. He signals for Emlin to follow. The boy throws a waterproof bag to the spy, then jumps into the water, before eagerly striking out for the nearby shore. The spy collects the bag and sees Dredger at the rail. The big man says nothing, but one armoured hand gives an almost imperceptible salute, and then the ship is gone, heading for Hark Island.

It's only a short swim to the shore but the water smells off, tainted by some chemical runoff from the alchemists, and it's a relief to scramble up onto the rocky beach of the Isle of Statues. The shore is littered with stones. Some are jagged, like broken shards of pottery. Others are rounded and shiny, and then he realises what he's walking on. The gleaming stones are bullets, washed clean by the tide. The jagged pieces ... he picks one up, turns it around. Runs his fingers over the shape of an eye, a nose, half a brow. The beach is all broken Stone Men. Probably from the early days of the quarantine, when they tried to rush the boats in their stumbling, awkward fashion.

Emlin sees the stone face, opens his mouth to ask a question, then thinks better of it. Good. He's learning.

The spy strips off his wet clothes, and uses the stone face and other body parts to weigh them down when he throws them into the sea. Emlin does the same. The boy's back is marked with ancient scars and bite marks. Ritual exposure to the venomous spiders of the Paper Tombs.

From the bag Dredger gave him the spy removes a pair of hooded robes. He puts one on, pulling the scratchy garment over his head. A disassembled rifle and a few other treasures remain in the bag as he seals it up and hefts it over his shoulder. As the spy walks across the beach, he adopts the hunch-shouldered, downcast demeanour of a Keeper priest. *Live your cover*, he thinks.

"This way," says the old priest to the young acolyte who follows behind him.

A narrow path leads off the stony shore in the direction of the church bell. From the top of the path, they can see the church spire in the distance. The island is all scraggly green grass and grey stone, a jagged outcrop in the midst of the bay. A few half-wild goats watch them from the crags. Other than the church, there is no sign of habitation; other than the goats and the gulls wheeling overhead, there is no sign of life. The priest wonders at the absence of the island's cursed population. Are all the Stone Men in the little church?

Then he sees a pair of eyes, watching him from what he mistook for a standing stone, and he realises that the Stone Men are all around them. He does not know if they let him pass willingly, or if these particular specimens are so far gone that they cannot move or speak. Some of them are certainly paralysed. These ones have little wooden bowls next to them to catch rainwater; their more mobile fellows and visiting priests or family members do them the questionable kindness of feeding the locked-in Stone Men, of pouring little sips of icy cold rainwater past frozen lips, of spooning mouthfuls of mush into their mouths.

Their route across the island brings them past one such Stone Man — a weathered dolmen, a living gravestone. One eye peers at the spy from beneath a mossy brow; the other eye is encrusted with thick flakes of granite. The Stone Man's arms have fused to his torso; the legs have sunk into the soil. The creature's mouth cracks open, but no words come out, just a rattling, like pebbles tapping on stone. *Tuk-tuk-tuk.*

"Come on, let's go," says Emlin, repelled by the diseased creatures.

The spy is not, by nature, a merciful man. He is ordinarily unmoved by suffering. But he is about to set foot in a new city, and he needs all the luck he can muster.

"We can afford a little kindness." The spy stops and picks up the Stone Man's water bowl. Raising it to the Stone Man's lips, he lets the liquid dribble into the grey-streaked mouth. The creature's teeth have become stalactites and stalagmites. A half-stone tongue, like a grotesque cancerous hybrid of snake and tortoise, rolls around behind the stony teeth, licking at the edge of the bowl.

"Remember us in your prayers, friend," whispers the spy. He returns the bowl to its niche.

From all around him comes scraping and shuffling. Mouths crack open, eyes stare pleadingly. Semi-mobile Stone Men crawl closer; others just click and grunt, for they can no longer make human words. Emlin backs away from the wretched creatures, tugging at the spy's robe.

They can't stay to help them all. They have an appointment. The spy leads Emlin along the path. The church bell has ceased to ring, and now the only sound is the wind and the waves and the gulls.

The church doors are closed when they arrive, but another, more distinct path runs down from the church to the little harbour. Following that, they soon come upon the other priests. A knot of a dozen men, dressed like the spy and Emlin – loose grey robes, thick rubbery gloves to protect against infection. Some come from the little island chapel, others from their ministrations along the shoreline. They hurry to join them, just two straggler priests who lingered a moment to tend to another poor soul. The boy stretches himself, stands as tall as he can, tries to pass for a grown man. At the harbour, the fourteen priests climb into a long rowing boat, and, if any of them notice their new brothers, they say nothing. Dredger's used this route before to smuggle people into the city. Or maybe smuggle Stone Men off the island, to bolster his workforce at the yards.

Once clear of the Isle of Statues, one of the priests passes around a heavy glass jar the size of a milk pail. Removing their gloves, the priests scoop out handfuls of clear jelly and rub it on their skin. The spy does likewise; the slime is gritty and stings his skin. Alkahest, in case any trace of the Stone Plague contagion made it past their gloves.

With slow, hard-won strokes, the rowing boat crosses the waters between the Isle of Statues and the city of Guerdon. As it approaches the city, their little boat must jostle for space with much larger vessels. Huge freighters and merchant ships – older ones with sails or oars, and newer ones, iron-hulled and driven by alchemical engines. Hulking refugee ships, scarred by passage through the Godswar. The spy sees kraken-size tooth marks on some of the floating wrecks. Fast-moving customs cutters, racing past, trailing foul streamers of chemical smoke. Bright sunlight makes the water glisten with a sheen of oil. Floating debris bumps against their hull.

The priests are bound for the Church of Saint Storm, an ancient temple venerated by the sailors and fishermen of Guerdon for centuries. The church stands near the docks at the seaward end of the district called the Wash, notoriously the poorest and most dangerous part of the city. The tenements of the Wash visible from the boat appear to be empty; a row of vacant towers, empty windows like the eye sockets of piled skulls at Severast. That part of the city is eerily quiet.

The rowing boat heaves around the stern of a freighter anchored in the middle of the harbour, and for the first time the spy can clearly see the New City. Instantly, he is reminded of the heavenly camp above the battlefield of Mattaur. Impossible towers, airy-light and stacked like dreams. Palaces piled on palaces, stairwells rising and splitting into a dozen branching walkways in the sky. Minarets and unlikely plazas jostling in the wild growth; a jungle of marble. The unnatural stone of the New City is pearl-white and gleaming, and now the light of the setting sun sets the marvellous sight afire with unearthly beauty.

It might be a heaven.

Emlin nudges him and points at a flurry of movement in the distance. A woman appears at one of the balconies of the New City overlooking the bay. If the spy were closer, he's sure he could hear her screaming. She throws one leg over the balcony, hesitates an instant as she looks down at the grimy waters hundreds of feet below. That moment is enough – two men emerge onto the balcony, grab her and then drag her back into the shadows. The other priests pay no attention to the distant spasm of violence, which tells the spy that such things are not uncommon in the New City.

It might be a heaven, but it's full of sinners.

What the spy looks for, though, is the towering fortress of Queen's Point on the other side of the bay. Guerdon's stalwart defender, a granite mountain bristling with cannons. There are other emplacements, too, watching over other approaches to the city, ready to spit the worst horrors of the alchemists at any invader.

The rowing boat enters the inner harbour, picks its way through the canals and arched channels of the old river, down scummy waters to a jetty at the side of Saint Storm. The spy notices open sewer entrances, tunnel mouths and narrow wynds that slope up from the water's edge – a hundred possible exits. He nudges Emlin, nods towards one alley almost at random.

The two help the priests unload their boat. They have brought next to nothing back from the Isle of Statues, other than a great box full of empty syringes with steel needles. Alkahest in a more concentrated form, for the treatment of the plagued. Hoisting his own bag, the spy follows the priests up the slick steps to the door of the church, but turns at the last moment and hurries down the side alley that runs behind a dockside tavern. Emlin follows his lead perfectly – the boy has met his first challenge, and performed well. They vanish in an instant.

In the backyard of the tavern, hidden by barrels of empty oyster shells, the spy removes his priestly disguise and helps Emlin struggle free of the damp robes. Their brief vocations abandoned, he takes two final sets of clothes from his bag and stashes the robes in their place. The nameless priest joins Sanhada Baradhin as an identity shucked by the spy. They're folk of the Wash now, the dregs of the city.

The spy leads the boy along the street, looking for an inn or dosshouse where they can stay for a few days. The city leers at them, bubbling up a cavalcade of strange voices and faces. Limbless veterans beg in the gutters; barkers and con men look for marks. Initially, the spy's pleased at how well he and Emlin fit into the flow of the crowd, how quickly they seem native.

Soon, though, he sees the same face twice. They're being watched. The thought perversely amuses him; they've been in Guerdon less than five minutes, and already their cover might be blown. It's unlikely to be the city watch – they wouldn't observe him, they'd just grab him and beat him with truncheons, another illegal trying to steal into the city without passing through Hark.

He considers the possibility that it's one of the other agents from Ishmere. He's not supposed to make contact with them for another week, but if he were running things here he'd pick the new asset up early, keep surveilling until they were sure he wasn't a security risk. But he's reluctant to give the new guard in the intelligence corps that much credit.

So. Someone else, then.

"Son," he whispers to Emlin. "Keep your head down." The boy's looking around, overwhelmed by the crowds and the hubbub of the city.

The spy lets Emlin walk a few paces ahead of him. He watches for people watching the boy. There. A grey-haired woman, in a habit. Very similar to the priestly robe he just discarded. A Keeper priestess? She hurries to catch up with Emlin. Catches the boy's arm.

"Wait," she says, "don't run."

"Run?" Emlin echoes, playing dumb. The spy approves.

"I saw you come off the rowing boat. You came in from the Isle of Statues."

"What if I did?" The boy bristles, clenches his fist.

The spy steps in. "What concern is it of yours, old mother?"

"You didn't want to go through the checks at Hark. You were marked in the war, weren't you? Let me look at you." She reaches up to turn Emlin's face to hers, and the spy sees that her left hand is scaly, clawed, disproportionate to her arm. A magical transformation gone awry perhaps, or a battle scar of the Godswar. "I can't see any marks," she says, "but you were in the wars, weren't you?"

"At Severast," says the spy. It's true, after all. There and many other places, but it was Severast that changed him.

"I am Jaleh," says the priestess, "I have a place where you can both stay for a while. The Holy Beggar looks after his own. Tell me, what's your name?"

Sanhada Baradhin has drowned. X84's dormant for now. And the spy believes in his own luck.

He plucks a common name from the air, a Guerdon name. "I'm Alic."

CHAPTER 5

Eladora arrives late to the reception at the Haithi embassy. She's surprised she's come at all, having spent the last four hours at the Industrial Liberal party headquarters. Her fingers are ink-stained, her throat raw from talking in interminable meetings. She went home and changed into an evening dress for the reception, but it took all her willpower to walk out of the door instead of collapsing onto her bed and hiding from the world.

After the council meeting, Kelkin made a brief, hoarse speech to the faithful, declaring that the time had come to strike, that the New City would be their salvation as it had sheltered so many others. When he praised Eladora's work in surveying and investigating the New City, she'd shrunk back into herself. Gambling parliament on an unfinished report unsettled her, but what could she say? Kelkin had thrown the dice; they're all committed now.

She's senior enough in Kelkin's staff that it would be impolite if she didn't attend this reception – the Haithi are very sensitive to matters of protocol and etiquette – but she can leave as soon as she's made one circuit of the ballroom. First, though, she must pass through the entrance hall. A queue of guests snakes through the room, all waiting to be greeted by the ambassador. Eladora joins the line to meet him, grateful that he's standing in front of a huge open fireplace. The Haithi embassy is uncomfortably cold in contrast to the warm night outside. The old building is draughty, but that's not enough to explain the icy air. She wonders if there's some sorcery that replicates the chillier climes of

Haith. Or maybe the undead guards somehow sap the warmth from the air.

The ambassador – Olthic Erevesic, she recalls – looks like he should be dressed in furs and waving a battle axe, not sipping champagne from a little glass that's lost in the massive paw he calls a hand. A warrior prince from Haith's distant barbaric past. He's young for his post, only a few years older than Eladora, but he's already won a slew of victories in battle. Medals and campaign ribbons adorn his barrel chest, recounting his proud military career, and a ring of iron on his upper arm indicates his noble destiny.

As the line inches closer, she can make out the family crest of a sword, and the chains they've added to the armband so it can fit Olthic's huge bicep. The armband signifies that he's one of the Enshrined, the highest death-caste in Haith's stratified society. The scion of one of their great houses, heir to a family phylactery.

Just as her turn comes to speak to the ambassador, an aide slips through the crowd and whispers a message to Olthic. The ambassador has to incline his massive head to hear the aide, and Eladora catches the words "Third Secretary". She doesn't mind the delay; basking in the warmth of the fire she takes a deeper drink of her champagne. Maybe, by some miracle, she can avoid talking politics all evening. They're less than four hours into campaigning, and already she feels battered.

"Miss Duttin," rumbles the ambassador. "Forgive me. I have something to sign, apparently, even though I know the First Secretary can forge my signature perfectly."

"Of course, my lord." *See*, thinks Eladora, *that's one conversation avoided already. Just do that until you can leave politely.* The ambassador grasps her hands in one of his. "I want to have a word with you about my proposal to parliament. You know Mr Kelkin's mind, and I would appreciate your advice. Please, do not leave until we have a chance to speak."

"Certainly, my lord." She even manages to smile, not that he notices. He's already striding off through the crowd towards the private section of the embassy. Eladora lingers by the fire's warmth for a moment, then ascends the marble staircase to the main ballroom.

Heavy gold chandeliers hung with crystals reflect the light of a thousand candles. Apparently, no one at the embassy has heard of aetheric lamps or gaslights. The room's already crowded, even though the line behind Eladora stretches to the front door. She immediately spots several members of parliament, each one accompanied by a gang of aides and assistants. Like a mother duck surrounded by a troupe of ducklings, she thinks at first. On consideration, she should probably revise that to "warships surrounded by flotillas of tenders and gunboats", but the thought of fuzzy little ducklings quacking in parliament amuses her, and, also, she's finished her first glass already.

She skirts around the edges of the crowd, one eye fixed on the buffet table at the far wall. One more glass, one complete circuit of the room, and she can go home.

She makes it six steps before she's intercepted.

"Eladora! Come and join us!" It's Perik. Face flushed, brimming with false charm. He's surrounded with Hawkers. She spots several men and women in expensive clothes all wearing the golden eye-and-flask of the alchemists' guild – the Hawkers' chief patron. No friendly faces here. Before she can slip away into the crowd, Perik grabs her elbow and manoeuvres her into the middle of the circle. She's trapped.

"Now, Eladora here is the veritable *architect* of Kelkin's grand plan," crows Perik. "She's an expert on the New City. Apparently, it's just crawling with eager voters. We've all seen them, haven't we, arriving in god-blasted coffin ships, thin as skeletons, mad as saints, all waving ballot papers and shouting—"

She tries to interrupt. "I helped write it, I wouldn't take responsibility—"

"Shouting 'we have crossed the world to vote for Kelkin! A vote for Kelkin is a vote for' – what, exactly? What does the man stand for, these days?" Perik shrugs theatrically. "He spent the last fifteen years deriding us as pedlars and grubby merchants who were selling the honour of the city, and accused us of putting Guerdon in peril – when we're the ones who built up the navy! We're the ones who brought prosperity to all!"

"I-I-I—" stammers Eladora. She's never been good at confrontation or quick thinking. She casts her eyes around the room for someone to rescue her, looking for a way out, wishing she could sink through the floor.

Perik continues "Kelkin castigates us for endangering the city and neglecting law and order, but he voted against the Tallowmen! He voted—"

"Emergency measures," hisses one of the other Hawkers, sotto voce. The Hawkers are so closely associated with the alchemists' guild that the two are virtually one entity, and the monstrous Tallowmen were created by the alchemists' guild. The Tallowmen were intended to augment the undermanned city watch, and for a brief few days during the Crisis they replaced the watch entirely. But it turned out that people didn't like been "protected" by a collection of ghastly psychotic waxworks who had the troubling tendency to punish even minor infractions with frenzied stabbings. The vats were destroyed in the Crisis, buried beneath the New City.

"He voted against our emergency measures to stem the Crisis. And when he seized control of the emergency committee, he showed us what neglecting law and order really meant! Now half the city has gone feral. No order but the whims of crime lords, no law but the law of the knife! That is the work of Effro Kelkin that the people will remember when they go to the ballot box!"

Eladora bites her tongue. She is one of the few people in the city who knows what really happened in the Crisis, and she is sworn to secrecy. Instead, she fumbles for words, finds only platitudes. "Mr Kelkin believes this is still a welcoming city, and that the people of the New City will make Guerdon stronger in the long run. We will campaign on a platform of, of—"

"Of bleeding hearts and foreign gods. And if the franchise is extended to the New City – a proposal that should be very, very carefully considered from a legal standpoint – then I say the IndLibs are welcome to every seat they can win there! Because for every New

City seat they win, they'll lose two in the old! The people turned to Effro Kelkin to guide them out of the Crisis, and he did nothing! He let the city slip into anarchy, and now he cuts even the emergency committee loose! We are adrift!"

"Perik," interrupts an older woman. "Miss Duttin's glass is empty. Go and fetch her a full one."

Her rescuer slides a wrinkled hand through the crook of Eladora's elbow and guides her away from the circle of Hawkers.

"You have to excuse Perik. Actually, no, you don't. He's an ass."

Eladora recognises the woman as Mhari Voller, an elder states-women of Guerdon. The Vollers are one of the oldest families in the city, largely because they've always been politically astute and sided with the victors in every conflict. Mhari was an Industrial Liberal when she was first elected to parliament, but crossed over to the nascent Hawkers before Kelkin's government fell. Her father, Eladora recalls, was a theocrat; presumably, a few generations before that, they were sworn servants of the long-vanished kings of Guerdon – or maybe even the Black Iron Gods.

Voller swipes two champagne flutes from a passing waiter. "He's not wrong, though. I've known Effro for a long, long time, and I can tell when he's made a mistake. Thirty years ago, his mistake was being too harsh, and it cost him his government. Now, he had a second chance, and he's squandered it by being too soft."

Eladora frowns. "You're talking about the Stone Plague?" Thirty years ago, the city was wracked by a plague that turned flesh to stone. Kelkin controlled parliament back then, and he'd ordered an infamously brutal plan for forced quarantines, containment – even, according to long-standing rumours, cleansing plague-ridden neigh-bourhoods by having his agents start fires. Anyone with the slightest symptoms was forced into the camps at gunpoint. Hundreds died in riots. Then the alchemists' guild found a treatment, and overnight Kelkin went from city's saviour to monster.

"I told Effro he was losing perspective, that his cure was worse than the disease. I told him that the alchemists were the answer. But it was too late. Tell him something before he makes a decision, and he'll listen. But get him to change his mind once he's made it up? Never." Voller sighs wistfully. "I'll say one thing for Effro, though – he has an eye for talent. Come and work for me."

Eladora chokes on her champagne. "I'm sorry?"

"You're a Thay through and through. This city is in your bones," says Voller. "Come and work for me. I can use you."

Confused, Eladora flounders. "Ah, I owe Mr Kelkin a great deal and I'm determined to see this election through at least."

Voller sucks her teeth. "The captain goes down with the ship, not the navigator. If you wait until then, you'll be tainted with Kelkin's defeat. Stay with him, and you're a loyal fool. Jump now, and you'll be the aide who warned him he was steering his party into disaster, and left when no one listened to your wise warnings."

"Did you commend Perik when he switched parties?"

"No, I told him he was an idiot, and that he should wait out the term of the emergency committee." Voller takes a sip of her wine. "And he's being an idiot again if he's running back to the Hawkers. They needed Kelkin to stay in power for another year or so, let people forget that the Crisis was mostly their fault. Jumping from the IndLibs to the Hawkers is jumping from the frying pan and swearing allegiance to the arsonist."

Eladora's head spins. "But you're a Hawker. How can you say that?"

Voller smiles. "Things change. Other powers rise. Consider my offer, young lady, and we'll talk no more of politics tonight. There'll be enough of it to choke us all over the next few weeks." She takes a generous mouthful of wine.

"If you'll forgive me, Lady Voller, the Haithi ambassador asked to speak with me, so I should go and see if he's free."

"Of course. Please, do think about what I said."

Eladora had mentioned the Haithi ambassador as an excuse, but now that she thinks of it, it strikes her as a good idea. She can have a brief word with Ambassador Olthic and then leave the party. If she hurries, she can be home before midnight, and she knows that will count as an early night in the weeks to come. What does Mhari Voller know, anyway?

It's too many people and too much politics on too much free wine for Eladora.

She cuts across the main floor of the ballroom, smiling and nodding at every smiling face. She dodges a journalist from the *Guerdon Observer* who tries to ask her about the fall of Severast; slips past a trio of her fellow Industrial Liberals who are haranguing some unfortunate Haithi merchant about trade treaties; avoids a drunk, lecherous Keeper priest. Then pauses to exchange a few brief words with Admiral Vermeil, who's deep in conversation with the ambassador from Lyrix. Eladora's out of her depth there. She knows little about the land of Lyrix, other than tales of dragon-run criminal syndicates who quarrel with mad gods amid fabulous jungles. The ambassador from this land of wonder salutes her with a champagne glass and grumbles about seasickness.

"Two weeks to cross, all because your navy demands we go in convoy. The delays are entirely on your side, Admiral."

Vermeil shrugs. "We are short of escort gunboats, and, with the war so close at hand, delays are inevitable."

The ambassador raises his glass. "The gods send dragons to scourge the sinner and honest man alike." It's an old Lyrixian saying that used to mean *don't blame me, look to the gods instead*, but these days refers to the Ghierdana crime families that increasingly control Lyrix's trade.

Vermeil introduces her to the ambassador, and the man's eyes gleam at the mention of Eladora's name in a way that disturbs her: avaricious and reptilian. "Miss Duttin. Your name has reached the ears of my great-uncle. You are a historian? Come to the isles of the Ghierdana with me, and I will introduce you to one who remembers a thousand years!"

"It's, ah, very interesting, but, ah—"

Vermeil steps in. "Miss Duttin has responsibilities here that preclude her leaving the city for the foreseeable future." He whispers in her ear, "They want to question you about the Crisis. Tell them nothing."

She moves on, hastily.

There's still no sign of Ambassador Olthic in the entrance hall. His place has been taken by the First Secretary of the embassy, a withered figure so pale and fragile that at first glance Eladora isn't sure he's alive. Daerinth something? Or something Daerinth, some honorific that she can't recall on three glasses of wine.

Glancing back into the ballroom, she spots Perik holding court and decides that returning to the party isn't an option either. She's visited the ambassador before, in the company of Kelkin or other members of the emergency committee. His office is just down that corridor, behind the oak door. She remembers a quiet bench outside it. Perhaps she can wait there until the ambassador passes by.

The noise of the party fades as she walks down the corridor, replaced by the mausoleum silence of the empty administrative wing of the embassy. Brass plaques on each door note the absurdly overcomplex titles beloved by the Haithi, and runes note the death-caste of each official. The Under-Secretary for Trade, Supplicant. The Assistant Supervisor of Customs, Vigilant. She finds the door she recalls leads to the corridor outside Ambassador Olthic's office, and it's ajar.

She goes through it, finds the bench and sits, hands folded, demure. She closes her eyes and rests for a moment. The party's exhausted her more than the last week's work on the New City report. She lets her mind wander.

Worm-fingers at her neck, her dead grandfather's voice hissing from behind a golden mask. The chill of the embassy becomes the deeper cold of the family tomb where he imprisoned her during the Crisis.

Eladora gasps, sits bolt upright. There's no one around to witness her momentary lapse of composure, for which she's grateful. She takes the memory, folds it neatly like a sheet of paper, and pushes it down as deep as she can, mentally stacking heavy cloth-bound history textbooks on top of it. She struggles to calm her racing heart. Her grandfather is dead; he died twenty years ago, and again ten months ago, but either way he's definitely, incontestably, gone.

There's a map on the wall. It's old and hopelessly out of date, which, as a student of history, makes it all the more fascinating to her. It's centred on the city of Old Haith, a hundred miles north of Guerdon. The Empire of Haith – a necrotic purple – spreads out inland north and west. It arcs north-east, along the foothills of the icy mountains, into Varinth. South, the map is speckled and blotched with purple. Speckles, for trading stations and outposts. Blotches for lands conquered by Haith in centuries past, when the undead legions and magic blades of the Empire were invincible.

There are gaps in the purple. Guerdon, for one, a little spot of farmland on Haith's southern doorstep, a vassal city state. The island of Lyrix to the east, and off its coast the smaller islands of the Ghierdana, full of dragons and thieves. And to the south, Ishmere, Mattaur, Severast, the trader cities of old. If this map were accurate, all three would be stained red, not purple, bloodied by the soldiers of Haith who died and died again on those shores in a dozen wars.

It shows Haith at nearly its greatest extent, covering almost half the map. These days, Haith's just a smear: the heartland, Varinth, a few outposts. Still a great power, but no longer unassailable.

If the map were accurate, it would show Guerdon in brilliant silver, with silver trade routes spiralling out to all four corners and off the map to the Archipelago, carrying wonders of the alchemical renaissance. The dead of Haith might stand vigilant in their endless ranks until the end of time, but the living folk of Guerdon don't have time to wait. There's always another deal to be made.

And if the map were accurate, she reflects, it would be on fire and screaming.

She hears footsteps approaching. It's one of the embassy's Vigilant guards. She's seen the walking dead before, but never unmasked. The creatures aren't allowed out onto the streets of Guerdon without prior permission from the watch, and they aren't allowed to go out without masks. Apparently, the watch once thought that the common folk of Guerdon would be terrified at the sight of ambulatory skeletons. An old law, as out of date as the map – there are far more unsettling things in the city these days.

Still, she suppresses a shudder as the skeleton approaches her. His jaw drops open. **Forgive me, but you cannot be in here. Go**

back to the reception, he says in a voice from the grave. Firmly but respectfully, he places a dead hand on her arm and lifts her off the bench, escorting her to the door.

"What's going on?" she asks.

The skull doesn't look at her. **There's been an incident. Return to the reception, you'll be safe there.**

Down the corridor, one of the guards shouts in alarm, she hears more uproar and running feet, Olthic's booming voice, but the dead man closes the door in her face, and she's left alone in that mausoleum.

The next morning, Kelkin's office is bedlam. Eladora wonders where all these people came from, this fevered host summoned by the magic word 'election'. After being ignored for a few minutes, she tackles one running clerk and learns that Kelkin is breakfasting in the Vulcan. The coffee shop was Kelkin's regular haunt and de facto office when he was just a lonely voice in opposition in a parliament dominated by the Hawkers. After he took over the city through the emergency committee, he needed an actual office with luxuries like doors. Going to the Vulcan now is, Eladora suspects, more about showing his face in the city than getting any actual work done.

She has work to do, but she needs to talk to Kelkin first.

When she arrives at the Vulcan, Eladora finds that Kelkin's retinue has taken over the entire coffee shop and spilled into the street outside. Junior clerks and attachés juggle papers as drovers herd pigs past them, up to the market in Venture Square. A line of supplicants snakes around the block. There's a watchman at the door, turning regular customers away, but another of Kelkin's senior aides spots Eladora at the entrance and waves her in.

"He's in the back," she's told. "Go on. Ten minutes."

She passes Dr Ramegos on her way in. Eladora nods at her and pushes past, but Ramegos calls her back.

"Did you finish those exercises I assigned you?"

"I had to go to the Haithi reception."

Ramegos snorts. "A true adept has perfect focus, and commits wholly to the act. There is no distinction between spell and sorcerer – the two become one entity, one single timeless monad 'tween earth and sky. Is there room for any extraneous thought?"

"Uh, no."

"Well, then." The older woman smiles, wrinkling her dark skin. "Get to work."

Inside, Kelkin's at the same table he's reserved in the coffee shop for half a century. As usual, it's covered in papers, used plates and stained coffee mugs. The papers at the bottom of the largest piles haven't been referred to for decades, and Eladora shudders to think about the oldest coffee mugs. She slides into the seat opposite the old man.

Kelkin has no time for pleasantries. "The new parliament will have two hundred and eighty-two seats, or thereabouts, up forty-eight from the last election – and all those new seats bar two are in the New City and the lower town. We need to win every bloody one of them, *and* hold most of our vote in the city proper, and that's just to get enough to go into coalition."

"You'd work with the Keepers over the alchemists?" she asks in amazement. Kelkin spent half his life breaking the power of the Keeper's church in the city.

"I'd go into coalition with the Crawling Ones if I get to set the agenda. The church has no damn business being in politics, not any more. Their support is rotten as old timber, but people still vote for them out of—" He waves a hand, as if unwilling to contemplate why anyone would do such a thing. "No, the church is done as a political entity in this city, but it'll last one more election, especially with the alchemists on the run."

"At the embassy party last night," begins Eladora, then she catches herself. She decides that she doesn't want to mention Voller's offer, not until she knows enough to have a considered opinion of it.

"What about the embassy?" snaps Kelkin, irritated by the delay.

"Th-th-the Hawkers crowed that you'd made a mistake by calling a snap election. They said that you'd be punished for not tackling the city's problems while you had the emergency committee's powers at your c-command." She chooses her words and tone carefully – her place in Kelkin's organisation is an unusual one. She's young and inexperienced but she's one of the few people who knows most of what went on during the Crisis, and that makes her valuable.

"Punished for not cleaning up their mess, more like." Kelkin shrugs. "They're right. If we have another horror show like the Crisis, it'll all be on me, and we'll lose. But the election's only six weeks away. We make it through six weeks without the city burning down around our ears, and we win." He snaps his fingers at her. "Enough. I want you to work with Absalom Spyke. He's run things down in the Wash for us before, and he'll be making sure we win the New City."

"Working with?" she echoes. "Doing what?"

"Identifying the bastards in the New City who can reliably deliver voters to the polls, and finding out how much we have to pay for 'em. Campaigning, girl. Honest graft."

"I thought I'd be preparing a brief on the Free City case." The Free City Act, passed by Kelkin nearly forty years ago, ensured near-universal suffrage within the city of Guerdon. It's the cornerstone of any plan to win new voters in the New City, so the other parties are likely to make a legal challenge and argue that the New City is not actually part of Guerdon. The case is almost certain to fail, but if the challenge were to be upheld, then Kelkin and the Industrial Liberals would be utterly routed. Eladora doesn't want to risk that, and it's a rare opportunity for her to use her academic knowledge in the service of politics.

Kelkin snorts. "We'll give it to Perik. Wait, no, he's fucked off, and good riddance to that walking snot. Give it to" – he waves his hand vaguely – "the carrot-headed one with the bad beard. Give it to him, then go and find Spyke."

She nods.

"By the by, the Derling chair in History in the university is to be filled by the start of the college year."

She freezes. That was Professor Ongent's chair, vacant since his death. "That's to be expected," she says, carefully.

"Don't be coy. If you want your arse in that chair instead of this one" – he shoves the battered coffee-shop chair she's sitting on with his good leg – "then it can be arranged. Get me those ivory towers, and you can have yours."

As she leaves, a half-dozen people push past her, trying to get Kelkin's attention. The square outside the Vulcan is crowded with criers, hawkers and protestors. Overnight, the streets have blossomed like a meadow in spring: every wall and lamp-post has sprouted posters. People shout at her; someone presses a flyer into her hand, and then another and another.

Feverish, pugnacious, the city is alive in a way she hasn't seen since before the Crisis.

She can almost forget that, less than a year ago, this square was besieged by monsters.

When the gutters ran with blood, and the sky filled with vengeful gods.

CHAPTER 6

Terevant Erevesic – Lieutenant Erevesic of the Ninth Rifles of Haith – stares at the page. He can't think of a good rhyme for "slaughterhouse".

Obviously, "mouse", "louse" and "grouse" can work, and, while they all neatly describe different facets of himself right now, he wants to write about that day on the shores of Eskalind. About the soldiers who died – and rose and died again – under his command.

Terevant writes down the word "spouse", stares at it for a moment, then crosses it out heavily. He flips the page over and tries to apply himself to what he should be doing. Another letter from the Office of Supply, addressed to his father; more demands for the war effort. Beef and grain and timber and hide, all from the sprawling Erevesic estates. And more soldiers, ditto. More peasant levies.

Terevant volunteered, once, but that was half the world away. And before Eskalind.

He scratches his wrist, takes another sip of wine and tries to read the letter again. The archaic script – written by some long-Vigilant clerk – is hard to parse. "The eternal Crown, in the person of the 117th Laird, does command and require—"

A bell rings, signalling the arrival of a visitor. Grateful for the interruption, Terevant hurries out of his father's office, striding down the marbled corridors of the mansion, down to the entrance hall. Expecting some corpse up from Old Haith, some Bureau factotum from one Office or another.

Two living people wait for him at the foot of the stairs. One of them Terevant doesn't know – a little man, blinking at the grandeur of the hall, with unruly hair and a face that looks like it stretched to fit his huge pointy nose. Civilian clothing. The other, though, Terevant knows instantly.

Lyssada.

The stranger, the servants, the mansion, the sunlit lawns and the great estates beyond them, the sky and the sea and the land all shrink away. In his eyes, Lyssada is the only real, meaningful thing in the universe. Terevant finds himself suddenly at her side, and he's not entirely sure if he ran down the stairs or fell down them, and it doesn't matter. Her hair is tightly bound; she wears a heavy military greatcoat that looks to be several sizes too big for her, although they probably don't make them for her small frame. Borrowed from Olthic, he guesses; his brother, her husband. One hand's buried in the pocket of her coat; the other swings free, carrying an envelope. His stomach sinks at the sight of that even as his heart leaps at the sight of her. He worries he might rupture something, tear open some old war wound.

"Lys, I—" *Lady Erevesic*, he should say.

"Let's walk outside," she says quickly, gesturing to the still-open door, to the sunlit grounds.

"Aren't you tired? It's a long ride from the capital."

"I want to see the old place again. Come on, Ter."

Terevant falls in beside her, stepping back a dozen years as he does so. In his memory, summer sunshine again fills the lawn, and she runs ahead of him, barefoot on the grass, her light dress billowing as she races for the safety of the trees. He often thinks of that moment. On the battlefield, it was one of his talismans, something to remind him of what he fought for, just as the lower-caste soldiers held little cardboard tokens of the Crown. They had their vision of heaven; Terevant's vision is still, despite everything, that sun-drenched lawn. Now, just like then, they're not alone. Back then, it was his brother Olthic, striding ahead; now, it's the strange little man who pauses at the threshold, a bemused expression on his face.

"I'll only be a few moments," says Lyssada. The man nods, and

Lyssada leads Terevant across the lawn, into the grove of trees where they once played.

Out of earshot, he realises, of the servants.

The little man watches them from the shadow of the doorway. "Who's he?" asks Terevant. Something about the man marks him as a foreigner. Not Haithi, at least not from Old Haith. Maybe one of the Empire's few remaining territories.

"My assistant," replies Lyssada absently. She glances around the grove. "This place hasn't changed at all."

"Father keeps it that way." Lys had been fostered for a few years here in the mansion, after Terevant's mother and sisters drowned in a shipwreck off Mattaur. The day Lys arrived was the day his grief started to lift; those few years were happy years, carrying him away from sorrow.

"How is the Erevesic?"

Terevant shrugs. "Still hanging on. Still hoping for Enshrinement." The highest of death-castes. His mother's death was sudden; by contrast, Terevant's been preparing for his father's death for many years. It's an inevitable fact of his mental landscape, as solid and familiar as the grey mansion beyond the trees.

Other feelings are less certain. He pushes at his emotions, scratches the scabs over his heart. "I presume Olthic is here?"

"No, he's still in Guerdon. I'm heading back there tomorrow night." She rubs her thumb over the seal of the cream envelope, as if suddenly hesitant to give it to him. "And so are you." She holds out the letter to him. "I came here to fetch Lieutenant Terevant of House Erevesic, formerly of the Ninth Rifles."

A scion of an Enshrined House like the Erevesics wouldn't normally be assigned to a regiment like the Ninth, but they were his comrades, and the "formerly" hurts.

"How come you're the one bringing this?" he asks in excitement. In surprise. In apprehension. Shame that she knows what he did. A little flash of anger at Olthic for not being here. In a roil of emotion he can't name. The letter's from the military. Lys is part of the Bureau, the civil service. There's supposed to be a strict division between them. She could get into trouble for handling a letter like this.

She shrugs. "I knew it was in the offing. I was in Old Haith anyway. I thought you'd appreciate seeing a friendly face."

Three half-truths, maybe, none of which add up to honesty, but he can't worry about that now. He breaks the seal and reads the letter inside. Skims the description of the battle on Eskalind, of the fighting with Ishmere forces. How Cloud Mother manifested on the battlefield, snatching up soldiers and hurling them into the sky, ripping them apart so that blood came down like rain. The seas draining away, replaced like something like liquid glass that cut and burned you at the same time.

They ordered him to take the guns on the shore. He'd done that, pushed ahead to the temple, charged right into the maw of the gods. Reading the cold description on the page, it's like they're describing the actions of someone else, someone long dead and far away. He cannot recall giving those orders, can't recall that mad rush for the temple.

Did he squander the lives of his troops on a foolish quest for glory? Did he draw the wrath of enemy gods, and lead the survivors out of the maelstrom? Terevant doesn't know, and if *he* doesn't know, how the hell can a bunch of dead generals in Haith decide?

Two hundred Haithi soldiers landed on that beach at Eskalind. Only seventy-two sailed away. And only a dozen of those still live.

"You fought bravely," says Lyssada quietly.

"Opinions differ." There's nothing exonerating here. No mercy from the review board. No reason for them to spare him, but he reads to the end. His jaw drops.

"I'm to keep my commission, then?"

She says nothing, just smiles knowingly.

He quotes from his new orders. "'You are hereby temporarily attached to the diplomatic security corps, and are to review the guards assigned to the embassy at Guerdon.' Olthic stepped in, didn't he? He told the committee to exonerate me. Is this his way of making sure his little brother doesn't embarrass him again? He wants me down in Guerdon where he can keep an eye on me. Hells, Lys, I'm not a child. I can stand on my own." He puts as much conviction into his voice as he can muster, but he suspects he comes off sounding petulant. Everyone knows the truth: where Terevant struggles to stand still, Olthic strides ahead. But he can't help but be excited and relieved, too, by the news of his exoneration. He might prefer to have prevailed on his own merits, instead of Olthic's intervention, but it's still another chance to prove himself.

"The Crown commands, not your brother," says Lys.

"Did he step in?" he demands again. *This time, it's going to be different.*

"I don't know."

"I thought you were omniscient down at the Bureau," he mutters, sullenly.

"Oh, we are." She laughs, and he can't help but be lifted by her amusement. "I read your poetry, you know. I pulled a few strings with the Sedition office."

"Death," he curses. Years before, he'd applied to and been rejected by the Bureau. He followed Lys there, throwing away his place as the second son of House Erevesic to chase her into the onyx labyrinth of the Bureau – only to have the very first door slammed shut in his face. He couldn't go home after that ignominy; he'd fled overseas to one of the Empire's far-flung outposts in Paravos. Spent a few months living in a dissident commune, drinking with other poets, actors and revolutionaries, publishing awful poetry under a pseudonym – it was fun for a few months. At least no one there ever compared him to Olthic and found him wanting.

Then the Sacred Realm of Ishmere conquered the outpost, and he was forced to flee. When he reached Haith he got blind drunk, and signed up with the army.

"It was really bad poetry," says Lys. "Atrocious."

"Some of it was about you."

She mockingly presses a hand to her forehead, as if about to faint. "Oh, if only I had seen through your cunning literary devices. Oh, wait, I did, and it was still bad." A flash of a smile, to soften the blow. "Now, are you ready to serve the Crown?"

"By watching some soldiers strut around a yard in Guerdon? I think I can manage that." He's Haithi; he'll do his duty. Struggling against what they expect of him has brought him only sorrow; why not try to do what's right for once? Live up to his family name.

"Things are more complicated than that. I'll brief you on it later." She hands him another envelope. Train tickets. "We're leaving tomorrow evening on the sleeper." She pauses for a moment, reaches out and grips his forearm. "There's something else, which is why it has to be you for this."

"What?"

"Olthic needs the sword."

The bedroom is stiflingly warm. It's still early afternoon, and the sun must still be shining beyond those thick curtains, but there's a huge fire blazing in the grate. The scent of burning pine can't quite hide the smell. Terevant's father – *the* Erevesic – sits by the fire, the family sword naked across his lap. His fingers run over the spell-forged steel of the blade, tracing the runes, the family crest. Communing with the weapon.

Also on his lap is a folded letter; the same paper, the same seal as the one brought to Terevant. The Crown commands, the Crown requires.

A young necromancer sits in the corner. The heat of the room has forced him to open his heavy robes; his face has a sheen of sweat.

"I want to go," croaks the Erevesic. "I want to go. I did enough, didn't I? Accomplished enough. But they won't let me in." The old man's wrists are marked with hundreds of scabs and thin white scars. "I want to go."

"I know you do. But ... Olthic needs the family sword, Father, and you know how proud you are of Olthic. You told me so yourself. You tell me very, *very* often."

"He should come himself, then. He could tell them to let me in. I'm still the Erevesic, am I not? They should listen to me!"

"Forget about the sword, Father." After months of nursemaiding the old man, Terevant has little patience left. "I've got my orders. Look, I'm still an officer."

"Still an officer. Still an officer. Idiot. The Bureau doesn't have officers."

"I didn't join the Bureau. That was years ago. I joined the army, like you wanted." *Five years late. From disgrace to disgrace.* "They're sending me down to Guerdon. I'm leaving tomorrow night."

"Fine. Go, all of you. Leave me alone. Just leave me with the sword."

Terevant straightens up. "If you were going to be Enshrined, they'd have taken you already. There's no shame in Supplication."

Everyone says that. No one believes it. The lowest, commonest death-caste is for low, common people. The ambitious strive to become valuable enough to Haith that they warrant preservation as Vigilant; only members of a few noble families, like the Erevesics, can even hope to be Enshrined in a family phylactery.

"I am the Erevesic!" shouts the old man. He tries to grab the sword and rise from his chair, but the weight of it is too much for him, and he topples. Terevant catches him, letting the ancestral blade crash to the ground, ringing. "I am the Erevesic!" insists his father, sobbing. Gently, Terevant lowers him back into the chair. Careful not to touch the blade, he wraps his hand in a blanket and replaces the weapon on his father's lap, then steps back.

His father clutches the blade, knuckles white, blood oozing from cuts on his thin hands. The blood is absorbed by the metal of the sword. "Mother, uncle, grandfather, all of you. I'm here," whispers the old man to the sword, "I'm here. I am the Erevesic, too. Let me in."

The necromancer whispers from the corner. "It will not be long now. The phylactery has closed itself to him – if that channel were still open, he would have passed on quite naturally by now. He must choose quickly which of the other castes to die in. And I fear he has lingered too long to achieve Vigilance. I shall do what I can for him."

They wait there in silence, the necromancer and the soldier, until the old man's breathing becomes rhythmic, until his hands stop their spidery tracing of the runes. *It wasn't supposed to be like this,* thinks Terevant. Olthic should be here, and all the Erevesic officers, the Vigilant warriors who've served the family for generations. Old Rabendath, Iorial, all the rest. If they were here, then maybe his father would have the strength to achieve Vigilance. Or maybe they know he doesn't, and that's why they stay away.

Death and duty are inextricably entwined in Haith. Dying well is a duty. The skeletal Vigilants and the iron vessels of the Enshrined watch their living kin not with jealousy, but with cold expectation. *I did not flinch*, they say silently, *will you be the one to fail? To break the chain? To let down our great lineage?* Haith is full of monuments to past conquests, past glories. Die well, and you're part of something greater.

Instead, he'll die with only Terevant and an anonymous necromancer for company.

Terevant remembers his father being angry when news of his mother's death came. Being angry, again, when Terevant followed Lys to the Bureau. Both times, the chain was tested nearly to breaking point.

I came back, didn't I? I'm trying again, thinks Terevant, hoping that his father understands. But the Erevesic's head droops forwards, and he begins to snore.

Terevant fetches a pair of heavy riding gloves from his father's dresser. The gloves fit him, he thinks, but would be comically undersized on his giant brother. He puts one glove on before taking the sword. When he lifts it, he hears a distant roaring, like the echo of his blood in a seashell. He transfers the sword to his old kitbag and closes the drawstring.

"Go," counsels the necromancer. "Attend to your duty, and I shall attend to mine."

"No," says Terevant, sitting down by the bed. "I'll wait."

CHAPTER 7

In Jaleh's house, Alic and his son share a room with a man who wakes up screaming every night, and another who has roots and branches growing from his flesh. There are other prodigies in other rooms; a dying man whose innards are turning to gold, a woman whose skin blisters when she speaks the name of any god but the one who's claimed her, a child who laughs and dances on the ceiling. It's a refuge for those damaged by the war. A gentling-house, they call such places, where those too close to mad gods are carefully cleansed of their spiritual entanglement. Half of Jaleh's residents would otherwise be interned on Hark Island as dangerous miracle workers, and she reminds everyone that the only prayers permitted under her roof are ones to the safe, weak gods of Guerdon. The prayers are deliberately dull and droning, meant to numb the soul, not stir it. To replace divine rapture with deadened, uninspired, half-hearted belief. Taking a saint away from a god is like trying to take a ball away from a toddler. Reach for the soul directly, and they'll snatch it away, or throw a tantrum. Ignore it, show no interest, make it boring, and they'll abandon it.

Alic watches Emlin as he prays. The boy eagerly took part in the rites for the first few days they spent in the house, overly fervent as he tried to convince Jaleh or any other observers that he'd abandoned his devotion to Fate Spider. After that, he started to avoid the evening prayers, looking for excuses — work to be done, stomach cramps, or just vanishing into the warren of alleyways around the Wash. Jaleh warns Alic that unless the boy submits to gentling, the gods of Ishmere will never let him go. Alic nods, says humbly that he'll talk to the boy, make him join the rites.

He needs to maintain the boy's sainthood, but to refuse would be suspicious. So, he compromises. Some days he brings Emlin along, and on others he lets the boy slip away. The gods can make of the boy's soul an unseen battlefield, tugging it this way and that, but as long as Emlin keeps his silence no one will be suspicious. The boy is young. He can endure, live his cover.

The spy mouths the prayers with the rest of them. There will be no effect. No god has any claim on him.

Not everyone can be saved. Some of the people in the House of Jaleh are too deeply changed for the curses ever to be undone; others cling to their curse, finding strength in it. Others simply don't understand what Jaleh offers. The screaming man, Haberas, for example: his wife Oona was touched by the Kraken-god of Ishmere, and transformed into a sea creature. Every morning, Haberas stumbles downstairs and prays for her curse to be lifted, then he spends the afternoon down by the dock. He watches Oona swim through the murky waters, her mermaid tail kicking up mud. Oona breathes through gills now, and, no matter how fervently he prays, Haberas can do nothing for her. The god's touch remade her physical body, not her soul. All the prayers in the House of Jaleh won't change her back.

Those who can, work. There's plenty to do. The old house was abandoned before Jaleh claimed it, so roofs need endless patching. She has arrangements with a few grocers, so every day boxes of the market dregs must be collected and boiled down into huge cauldrons of vegetable stew. Some beg on the streets by day; others find casual work down at the docks. And some of the residents have their own needs; Michen, for example, must be pruned every night, so the spy cuts bleeding branches from the cursed man's back. They keep the branches for firewood, even though it crackles and smells like pork when burned.

The spy watches for a week, biding his time. He sees the half-gold man die when his bowels transmute. The spy cleans the blankets off the stinking deathbed and washes the gold-streaked chamber pot, while outside family members squabble over ownership of the half-gold body. They were happy enough to leave him with Jaleh for the slow decline, but now he's dead and no longer shitting everywhere, they want his precious corpse back. They'll be disappointed; gold is cheap these days.

He watches other comings and goings. Some of Jaleh's former residents have moved on; once their magic has faded, or they learn to hide their divine gifts or curses, they can be treated like any other refugee and seek their fortune in Guerdon. They come back sometimes with donations of coin or food, or just to help out. Jaleh blesses all of them with her claw-hand and prays to the Holy Beggar; cautions them not to make trouble, to avoid the attention of the authorities. Guerdon is open to the coin of the faithful, not their gods. Temples are permitted, but no miracles on the streets. Another balancing act, like the city's tenuous hold on neutrality in the war.

One of the regular visitors is a ghoul woman. Unlike the other miracle-blighted prodigies of Jaleh's house, ghouls are a common sight on the streets of Guerdon, so this one named Silkpurse isn't a former resident. Unlike the other rag-clad ghouls who skulk in the sewers and catacombs under the city, Silkpurse puts on a scavenged approximation of human clothing and walks in the sun wearing wide-brimmed hats. She carries a bag stuffed with election leaflets, and talks about Effro Kelkin and the Industrial Liberals with a zeal that could conjure miracles if a god were listening. Many years ago, Kelkin passed the Free City Act that gave the ghouls free run of the surface, and for that he has won her undying loyalty.

Twice in that first week, Silkpurse arrives with new residents for Jaleh's, folk she plucked off the streets of the New City before anyone else saw their divine curses. A young girl with a scarred face, just like Captain Isigi — some animal-headed god once used her as its earthly vessel. An older woman who's recently been beaten — the spy recognises her as the woman from Dredger's ship, the refugee with the clay icons. She made it through processing at Hark Island, but the others fleeing Mattaur still suspected her of being an Ishmeric spy and drove her away, her clay idols broken along with her fingers.

Jaleh binds her fingers and sets her to work in the laundry, while the the actual Ishmeric spy in Jaleh's house fixes the roof and watches.

They watch him, too, wondering who he is. Still, as long as he works, he's welcome to remain for a while longer.

Days go by. His orders from Ishmere were to wait a week, then show up in the common room of a tavern, the King's Nose. Someone will meet him there, some other spy from Ishmere. He wonders how they know he's coming. Do all newly arrived spies from Ishmere go to that tavern? That sounds like a death trap: for all the spy knows, Guerdon's counter-intelligence has the place staked out already. Did some other courier bring word of his arrival? Or do the spies in the city have some magical method of communicating with their masters in the south – and, if so, why did they need him to bring Emlin?

One evening, the spy is pruning Michen in their shared room while the screaming man – Hebaras – sleeps fitfully. Each night, it gets harder to trim the branches from Michen's skin without gouging out huge chunks of flesh. Emlin watches from the top bunk, not daring to blink, barely breathing.

"Did you fuck a dryad, man?" mutters the spy.

Michen laughs, then winces in pain as two twigs tangle. "I was a mercenary for Haith. We ran into a god. He was thirty feet tall and covered in these vines that ate people, so he wasn't my type."

"Was that up in the Grena Valley?"

"Nah, further off. Varinth. The Haithi broke the old gods there, but the bastards are still up on their sacred mountains, and come shambling down whenever anyone breathes a prayer. We thought it'd be an easy tour – easier than going to the Caliphates, anyway. But no . . . half my troop just turned into trees when He came down, and I was right on the edge of the miracle."

"Hold still, this is a deep one." Michen braces himself as the spy tries to wrench a branch out. It's right above the small of Michen's back. "What about him?" asks the spy, nodding towards the sleeping form of Haberas. "Was he in Varinth, too?"

Michen shakes his head. "Him? Last ship out of Severast. He stayed until he found a captain that would tow Oona along."

"Ah." Alic wasn't there, but Sanhada Baradhin was at the fall of Severast, too.

And so was the spy.

There's a knock at the door, and Jaleh comes in. "Alic, could you and Emlin go and fetch some clean blankets, please?" She wants to talk to Michen alone, because the gold man downstairs has died and now the room next to the infirmary is available. The room for the dying. In a few days, there'll be a half-wooden corpse there instead of a half-gold one. Alic, the spy has decided, is kind and tractable; Alic's always happy to help. "Come on, son," he says. Emlin slips down from the bunk, landing like a cat.

The spy makes a circuit of the upper floor of Jaleh's house after fetching the blankets, checking every window. When he comes back, Jaleh and Michen are gone, and Michen's bed has been stripped down to the mattress. Haberas moans and mutters in his bed.

The spy sits down on his own bed, thinking again about his appointment. His thoughts turn to Emlin and he wonders what happened to their previous saint. Were they killed? Captured? Or did they succumb to the terrible pressure of the divine, warped like Haberas' wife into something inhuman? The touch of the gods makes no allowances for mundane anatomy, for the base necessities of the flesh. The saints of Smoke Painter have no faces, just a caul of skin like the veil that covers the god's face. As long as they remain in the god's favour, they have no need to eat or drink, no need for eyes to see. But if the god rejects them, the sorry creatures are doomed.

"What will become of her?" groans Haberas. The spy looks up, sees the man staggering towards him, caught in a waking dream. "Give me an oracle!"

He's mistaken the spy for one of the priests of the Fate Spider. In Severast, the priests once predicted the future, traced the strands of fate for the faithful. Another mask the spy once wore that he's had to cast aside. Still, there are lingering obligations. He can't refuse the old man's plea out of hand.

"Hey," the spy whispers, "remember the temples at Severast before they burned? Remember the dark alleyways of the market? There was a candle-seller's place, right in the shadow of High Umur's tower – remember?"

"I . . . remember."

"Remember the secret door at the back of the chandlers. How cool the shadows were there. How restful. Like still water after the hubbub of the market."

Haberas never went there in his waking life, never knew about that secret door, but the spy knew it so well, his whispers conjure it in Haberas' mind.

"Walk through it. It's dark in there, so you can't see, but there's a staircase winding down. Feel the steps with your feet," insists the spy, "they won't find you there."

The shadows in the bedroom in Jaleh's house grow darker, grow legs, scuttle around the room. Haberas isn't a saint, but he's spiritually dislodged, polarised by his experiences in Severast. It takes only a little push to align him with one deity or another.

Fate Spider, god of thieves and secrets – and spies – is shared by the pantheons of Severast and Ishmere. Down in that hidden temple were little cells where saints lay, whispering to one another across the world, sharing holy secrets through vibrations on a magical web. All-knowing omniscience takes a lot of legwork, and Fate Spider has many legs.

The temple of Fate Spider in Severast is gone now, but it still exists in thought, and in thought Haberas enters it. Without quite knowing why, he curls up on a stone shelf in the blessed darkness of his dream, and curls up on his bed in the House of Jaleh.

"She will live," whispers the spy, and Haberas echoes him, "and through all the storms she'll find her way back, and her hands will run with silver for the alchemists' cure." A liar's prophecy, and without any power behind it, but it's comforting for Haberas.

The man slips back into a deep sleep.

After a few minutes, Emlin comes back, clutching a bundle. He looks at Haberas in surprise, amazed at the silence in the room, the lack of weeping or screaming. The spy just shrugs.

Emlin crosses to sit next to the spy and shows him the bundle. Inside is an alley cat, fur filthy and matted, half starved. The creature's alive but stunned, breathing shallowly. "I caught it," whispers Emlin, "I need a knife."

"Why?"

"I need to be ready." The boy's quivering with excitement, too, his heart racing. "For when we meet the others. They'll need me to walk the web. I should make an offering."

The spy takes the kitten from the boy. "Is that what they taught you in Ishmere? That Fate Spider would be pleased by such cruelty?"

"How can I please Him, then?"

"Go and find six ways to enter and leave this house without being seen."

CHAPTER 8

The morning after his father's death, Terevant takes a carriage to the city of Old Haith.

Old Haith, greatest of the cities of the north where the grey towers rise from the mists to vanish into the sky. Old Haith, whose dictates shape the world. Old Haith, where death is bound by law.

Old Haith, the disconcertingly empty. As Terevant's carriage clatters through the streets, he doesn't see more than a handful of living souls. Oh, the dead are here in great numbers – soldiers walking the newly fortified walls, engineers entrenching cannons and defensive spell-wards, Bureau clerks and functionaries working tirelessly to manage the sprawling Empire – but there are fewer living than even the last time he was here. Only a fraction of the living in each generation attain the higher castes and become undying, but the balance between living and undead tipped in the days of Terevant's great-grandfather. In a few generations, he imagines, there'll only be a single living soul in this vast grey city, the mortal bearer of the eternal Crown.

His first destination offers a premonition of that fate. The vast estates of the Erevesics lie to the west, but in the heart of the city each of the great Houses maintains a fortress. The Houses farm the land and feed the armies; the Bureau manages and monitors, and the Crown commands. His carriage draws to a stop outside the tower of the Erevesics.

The Vigilant guards salute him as he passes, but do not speak. He walks down long silent corridors, passing by silent monuments. The memorials speak of ancient victories; he doesn't know if they stopped adding new plaques and monuments because the armies stopped winning, or because memorials don't matter when the survivors are still extant to bear witness, even centuries later. In Haith, you're nobody until you're dead.

He's unsure which of the family's lieutenants are here today. He recalls visiting the tower when he was a young boy, when his father wore the sword, a memory of Lys laughing as her father swept her up in a bear hug. Then, there were almost as many living lieutenants as undead ones – but times have changed and the war has taken its toll. If Terevant's brother Olthic were not ambassador to Guerdon, then he'd be here, at the head of the long table. Ordering the dead, commanding the disposition of the family's forces, and all the lieutenants would whisper to one another, asking if they could recall another general so fine in all their long service. Voices like the rustling of dead leaves.

He enters the council chamber. A dozen skulls turn to look at him. Commander Rabendath. Iorial, his fractured skull laced with veins of gold. Kreyia, still blackened by Lyrixian dragon fire. Lyssada's father Bryal, his bones with the sheen of relative youth.

They can all sense the sword he carries. Terevant's tempted to take it out – as a member of the bloodline, he could draw on the blade's magic, bolster his strength and courage and presence, but he dismisses the idea. These dead are veterans of the House; they've fought alongside the bearer of the sword for centuries, they know it better than he does. It would be absurd. He'll just have to be himself.

"My father died last night," he tells them.

A message arrived ahead of you, my lord, says Rabendath. **Will he be joining us?**

"He died Supplicant," says Terevant, trying to keep any quaver from his voice. Rejected by the sword, his father could not die Enshrined as he wanted. Instead, Terevant watched through the night as the dying man fought to hold onto his soul, struggled to bind his spirit to his old bones. Dying Vigilant, though, is hard for the old. It takes concentration and discipline to lash the soul to the body, and his father kept mumbling about Olthic, about old battles, about the shipwreck. He never mentioned Terevant as he died, at least not that Terevant heard, but there was a long time between when the old man's mumbling became inaudible and when the necromancer gently teased his father's soul out of the body and into a jar.

Terevant feels like a jar, thinking about it. Hollow, empty, a little fragile. In other lands, dying in bed, old and rich, with one of your children holding your hand would be a fine way to go. In Haith, though . . .

There is no shame in that. The sepulchral voices of the Vigilant seem to come from deep underground, and Terevant can't detect pity or sincerity or anything else in that grinding groan.

Will Ambassador Olthic return to Haith immediately? asks Kreyia, a little too eagerly.

"I don't know," admits Terevant. "I've been asked to bring the family sword to him." The dead shift, uncomfortable in their iron chairs. They read the reports from Eskalind, too. Any of them could probably carry the sword to Guerdon. Any of them, instead of the unreliable second son.

He dislikes feeling hollow. He wants to be on his way already, to fill himself with purpose. He resents being second-guessed by the dead, no matter how loyal or courageous they've proved themelves.

It would be more fitting, says Bryal, **for the Commander to carry the blade, at the head of an honour guard.**

"The Crown commands me to go to Guerdon," says Terevant, "quietly."

The Crown, says Kreyia, **does not command the Sword Erevesic.** She's right – the Crown is the greatest of the phylacteries, but its power is not absolute. The Crown, they say, rests atop one head, but also three pillars – the functionaries of the Bureau and the Houses of the Enshrined.

"My brother is now the Erevesic. The sword is his."

His place is here, with us, says Iorial. **Or ours with him. I pray you, lord, remind him of this.**

He will understand, says Rabendath, **when he claims the sword.** His dead voice makes him sound like a judge handing down a sentence to a condemned prisoner.

As Terevant leaves, Bryal follows him out. **Please**, he says, **give my regards to my daughter. It's been too long since she returned home.**

It's only when he's back in the carriage, on the way to the train station, that Terevant considers how odd it is that Lys should travel all the way back to Old Haith and not call on her father.

The sentry at the train station salutes Terevant as he passes. He returns the gesture awkwardly. After months out of uniform, he grew used to the subtle, scornful looks the soldiers gave to civilians of military age. He even welcomed the censure, after the retreat from Eskalind. Unconsciously, his hand brushes against the shiny new insignia on his collar, marking him as part of the embassy staff.

A cloud of sooty smoke floods the station platform as the engine gets up its head of steam. It's an old steam train, pressed back into service on passenger routes. The new trains use more powerful alchemical engines imported from Guerdon, but they need those trains to bring bodies and souls down from the hinterlands to the western front and the sea ports. This route – south to Guerdon – has been secured following a rare victory in the Godswar, and Terevant spots only a handful of uniformed troops among the passengers. There's no lightless mort-carriages for the Vigilant, no train-mounted artillery pieces. Why, it could almost be a sight from a generation ago, a train full of tourists and merchants, if it were not for the snipers atop the guard's car and the heavy barricades welded over the windows that block out most of the light, leaving only a narrow firing slit of illumination. He clambers on board, wrestling his kitbag through the narrow entrance. A few alchemical lanterns dangling from the roof of the corridor shed pools of flickering, sickly light, enough for Terevant to find his way to their compartment.

The sword hidden in his bag catches on every corner, as if unwilling to leave Old Haith. Terevant considers reaching into the bag and touching the hilt; maybe his ancestors really are having second thoughts about the trip south. Instead, he hastily shoves the kitbag into the luggage netting above his seat and tries to ignore the rustling whisper of the voices in the steel.

He settles into his seat and looks for something to read. Lyssada sent him a report on the garrison at the embassy, but it's a long ride south and he'll save that joy for later in the trip. Instead he fetches a battered copy of the season's fashionable book – *The Bone Shield*, something wonderfully patriotic about a Vigilant soldier and the necromancers who love her – and tries to find his place in that, but his attention keeps sliding off the page. He stares at the empty seat across from him, imagining his brother's outsize presence crammed into it. Olthic would have to fold up that armrest, and his knees would be jammed uncomfortably up against Terevant's. His booming voice, commanding, echoing through the train. People would recognise Olthic without seeing him, whisper to one another about how lucky they were to share a train with such a celebrated hero. Soldier, diplomat, victor – Olthic was not larger than life. No, his life swelled up to match his frame.

Especially after Eskalind. While Terevant was getting his men killed in a futile charge on the temple of the Lion Queen, Olthic was capturing the Ishmeric flagship in the harbour. While Terevant was testifying to the committee of inquiry, Olthic was being made the new ambassador to Guerdon. Just some of those little ironies that makes life worth throwing under a train.

They'll write novels about Olthic one day. Maybe they already have. A suitably inspiring topic for propaganda, with the respectability and devotion to duty that the Crown likes. *The Bone Shield* is a little too intimate to be ideal, a little too hot-blooded. These days, Haith prefers its heroes to be made from marble and polished bone. That doesn't quite fit Olthic, but he could play the part with conviction, of that Terevant has no doubt. Some judicious editing, some ghost-written humility.

Just as the train is about to depart, the door to the compartment opens. Terevant looks up, hoping for Lyssada's face, but it's Berrick, the assistant who accompanied her to the Erevesic estate. A pair of men flank him, in plainclothes but Terevant can tell they're Bureau secret police. He wonders who Berrick is, to warrant such protection.

"May I?" Berrick gestures towards the seat facing Terevant, and sits down without waiting for a nod.

One of the secret policemen — the living one — hands Terevant a leather folder, sealed with a spell-ward. "Lady Erevesic has gone ahead. She will meet you later on the journey. Deliver this folder to the embassy, and don't let it, or him" — he glances at Berrick, who shrugs gamely — "out of your sight."

"With my life and death," answers Terevant, suppressing a smile. It seems absurd, like children play-acting at being soldiers and taking it all deathly seriously. Guerdon's as far from the front lines as you can get. He can guess already that the embassy guards he's being sent to command will be mostly fuck-ups, or rich idiots who've bribed someone to be sent far from danger. Maybe, if he's lucky, there'll be a few competent ones who do all the work.

He hopes he falls into the third category, but he could make an argument for either of the first two.

The two policemen vanish, and moments later there's a whistle and the train departs. Grey light shines through the viewing slit as they pass out of the station's canopy, flashing staccato shadows as they pass by towers and buildings along the railway. Berrick stands so that he can look out of the little slit as they pull out of Old Haith.

"I've never seen the city!" he marvels.

Old Haith is certainly one of the world's great metropolises — or, rather, in its case, necropolises. Still, Terevant's surprised at Berrick's wonderment. He takes the measure of his travelling companion, trying to fit the pieces of Berrick together. His hands aren't callused, suggesting he's not a labourer or a soldier. His accent is hard to place. No caste marks on his clothing, no periapt scars. He's in Lyssada's service, officially, and Lyssada works for the Bureau. Is he a spy? A defector? What's Berrick's purpose in all this?

The sealed folder on the seat next to Terevant mocks him. He snatches it up and stuffs it into his luggage overhead, next to the Erevisic sword. He can let his ancestors worry about it.

"What's *that*?" gasps Berrick, pointing to a huge window-less pyramid.

"The Bureau." *He must be a foreigner if he doesn't even know that.*

Terevant knows that building. Remembers sitting outside it, weeping. Lyssada had surprised them all by quitting the service of House Erevesic and taking the Bureau exams. His father had been furious. Olthic silent, working his anger out with sword and shield. And Terevant – he'd run after Lys, followed her to Haith. Taken the entrance exams for the Bureau, too. A scandalous act, for a scion of a House to try to join the anonymous ranks of spies and bureaucrats.

It was even more scandalous for him to fail. The Bureau rejected him. And he'd fled rather than return home, taken ship and sailed to the most distant province of the Empire he could afford.

The city vanishes, swallowed by the darkness of a tunnel.

"I have," says Berrick, conspiratorially, "a bottle of rather good wine in my luggage. More than one, in fact."

"I think I'm technically your bodyguard," says Terevant, "at least until Lys shows up. I just got my commission back, and I'd rather like to keep it a little longer. So, no drinking on duty."

"Oh, we're not meeting her until the border, and I am a man who needs to get through the very last of his wine cellar before this train gets to the border. So, let us toast the Erevesic!"

Father or Olthic? wonders Terevant, but he drinks deep either way.

Eight hours later, Terevant is the only one still awake in the compartment. Across from him, Berrick snores, his head lolling against the shoulder of one of the Guerdon girls they'd met while leading the charge into the second-class carriages. Outside, in the corridor, he hears a drunken soldier belting out a familiar marching song. A spilled bottle of wine soaks into the floorboards of the carriage. Disgraceful behaviour, reflects Terevant. Unbecoming of an officer. He imagines the eyeless glare of Commander Rabendath, or Bryal, grumbling about him in the voices of the dead.

And with all his ancestors watching, too. He reaches up and makes sure that the Erevesic sword is still safe in his kitbag. Even through the thick canvas he can feel the energy of the blade, the magic coursing around it, looking for nerves and veins and bones to infuse.

The girl on the seat next to him mutters something when he moves his arm, then falls back to sleep, lulled by the rocking of the train as it rattles south through the night. It's cold. Terevant reaches up to pull down a jacket from his bag and drapes it over . . . Shara? Shana? What was her name? They'd found her and her friend a few carriages down. Wealthy sisters from Guerdon, on a trip with their chaperone, taking advantage of the recent reopening of the rail line between the two nations. It had been easy to spirit them away with the promise of wine and merriment. Their chaperone, a bearded, middle-aged man, had fallen asleep with his nose in a newspaper, the paper trailing in the remains of the dinner on the table, news-print soaking up brown sauce. Allowing Shara? – Shana? (was one sister Shana and the other Shara, daughters of a family sorely lacking in imagination?) – to sneak out and run laughing up the corridor with Terevant.

Her mouth, when he'd kissed her, tasted of summer.

He tugs part of the long jacket over himself. Curling his arm around Shana – definitely Shana, he'd compared her eyes to those of a lioness roaming the savannah – she turns and nuzzles into his neck. He imagines for an instant that it's Lys instead, as he begins to drift off. Distantly, he knows that he should give some thought to getting the girls back before their chaperone notices his charges have been out cavorting with strange men (very strange men, he thinks dreamily, still wondering who Berrick is), but he's drunk and warm and, he realises, happier now that he's been a very long time. He'll be with Lys and Olthic again. After death, just like before.

Ten years have gone by, ten strange and hard years, but, despite that, they're still the same people. Or so he tells himself.

Outside, dull grey light as the night begins to give away to morning.

The sword above his head nudges at his mind; some atavistic family bond makes him dream of ancestors whose names he cannot, offhand, recall.

Better than his usual dreams, of Eskalind and the war.

CHAPTER 9

Seven days after X84 arrived in Guerdon, the spy who calls himself Alic walks out of Jaleh's house and makes his way through the winding streets of the Wash.

He leaves Emlin behind. Tells the boy to act normally, live his cover. If Alic doesn't return, he's not to panic; instead, he should go to Dredger and ask for shelter there. Dredger owes Sanhada Baradhin a favour, after all. The boy's eyes are full of defiance — he wants to come with the spy, to be part of the shadow world — but he obeys. He doesn't use any of the hidden ways to leave the house unseen that he's discovered — the attic window, the back door by the kitchen, the old coal chute in the cellar that opens onto the alleyway at the back of the house. Ways he brought to the spy shyly, as offerings.

Alic ambles down the street, whistling. A smile for everyone. Alic's a friendly sort.

He stops in a clothes' merchant, buys a coat and a hat, cleans his face when he passes a drinking trough. Alic the poor labourer who lives in Jaleh's halfway house vanishes, replaced by a man who might be Sanhada Baradhin the merchant. The new coat and hat draw the eye away from Alic's stained trousers; his gait changes, fatigue dropping away. He hurries; time is money, business is business. San's always hustling.

Ahead is the looming loaf-shaped mound of Castle Hill, the great rock on which Guerdon was founded. Atop that massive lump of stone, he can see the towers of the parliament building. Stairs zigzag down the cliff, and a brightly lit road runs from the foot of the steps down to Venture Square and the edge of the New City. Looking over his right shoulder, the spy can see two of the other great power centres of the city – the glimmering cathedrals up on Holyhill, seat of the blessed Patros, head of the Church of the Keepers; and the thicket of cranes and scaffolds and smokestacks that marks what remains of the Alchemists' Quarter, destroyed during the Crisis. Glancing behind him to check that no one is following, he catches sight of the New City rising impossibly from the harbour.

As he pushes on through the crowds, the spy is struck by the notion that the city's buildings and monuments are far more permanent and real than the people who live there. Everyone else around him is fleeting; a rush of water or a tongue of flame or a breath of air, but the stone remains. The city is immortal as gods are immortal; the city needs its citizens like gods need worshippers, to feed on their prayers and the stuff of their souls.

He climbs up narrow streets, shadowed by Castle Hill, and comes to the tavern that glories in the unlikely name of the King's Nose. The sign outside shows a man's head in profile, eponymous namesake prominent. The tavern's busy enough that another customer goes unnoticed, quiet enough that he can find a table on his own. He orders a drink – a local speciality, some alarmingly brightly coloured synthetic sugar water shot through with alcohol – and waits. Someone's left a newspaper tucked into the corner of the chair; he smoothes it out and pretends to read it while he listens.

Snatches of conversation about politics. Most people here voted for the Hawkers last time; most people here work, indirectly, for the alchemists. But as survivors share their stories of the Crisis, it's clear that the mood's against the old order. Too many people were hurt, or killed, or menaced by nightmarish slime monsters and Tallowmen, or blown up by rockets fired on the city. The events of the Crisis are still opaque to most people, but the one thing that can be agreed on is that something has to be done.

But what that thing is, no one can agree.

There, thinks X84. Those two. A couple, the woman middle-aged, hard-faced, a shopkeeper or a schoolteacher or something else forgettable. The man's a little younger, weather-beaten, callused. A sailor? No, a mercenary. The spy intuits a cover story for them; the widow, and the returning veteran she took up with after her husband's death.

X84 waits for them to approach him. He wonders which it'll be. The "widow", maybe asking the "merchant" about business?

No, it's the man. He saunters across, draining his pint and putting the tin mug down on the bar as he passes. "Borrow that paper when you're done?" he asks the spy.

"I'm finished." He hands the paper over. The man runs through various job advertisements, circling promising ones with a pencil.

"Why do they call it the King's Nose anyway?" asks the spy, idly, nodding at the pub sign outside.

"There was a king in Guerdon, once, and I guess he had a big nose. Maybe they all did. Royals fucked off three hundred years ago when the Black Iron Gods took over. People say the good days'll come back again when the king returns. Or a queen," replies the mercenary, grinning widely at some private joke. He rips out the page, hands the remains of the newspaper back. "Thank'ee for that. Have a good night."

He vanishes back into the crowd. When the spy looks up, the pair are gone. He opens the newspaper. Written in the margin of one page is a message. An address in Newtown. *Tomorrow night. Bring the boy.*

The spy takes a last swig of his drink, then carefully slops the dregs of the chemical brew over the message, erasing it forever.

A day later, they arrive at the Newtown house. Alic and Emlin are ushered into a small dwelling that smells of cabbage. The pair from the King's Nose attend to Emlin first, and dress him in priestly robes which are much too large for the boy, but his solemn mien robs the sight of any potential humour. His sainthood is no laughing matter. Emlin pushes the overlong sleeves back, and picks up a bundle of papers.

"I'm ready," he says squaring his shoulders.

The woman whispers a word into his ear, anoints him with oil from a lion-headed vial. The boy descends into the cellar. There are no lights, but his feet find the uneven steps unerringly.

They show the spy into a little parlour where he sits down on a worn couch.

"I'm Annah," says the woman, lighting a cigarette. She offers him one, too. "That's Tander." The mercenary grins and reaches over to shake the spy's hand. As he does so, Tander runs his thumb over the spy's palm, checking for the scar left there by Captain Isigi back in Mattaur.

From downstairs, the spy can hear Emlin chanting a prayer to Fate Spider. Soon, he'll be in a trance, his whispers heard across the seas. He'll chant those notes all the way back to Ishmere.

"Call me San," says the spy.

"You didn't come in under that name, though." Annah takes a sip from the mug of coffee by her chair. "Dredger smuggled you in."

She's testing him, checking his account. "Via the Isle of Statues," he replies.

Tander reaches over to a cabinet and pulls out a small jar of alkahest, smears the slime over his hands. "You're safe," says the spy.

"Suppose it's better than going through Dredger's yards," says Tander to Annah. "Remember that one last year? Came out of the crate stiff as a board and all yellow?" He's grinning, his tone light, but there's a current of manic anger running beneath the surface. An easily tapped potential for violence.

Annah ignores him. "What's your code number?"

"X84."

"What have you done since you arrived?"

"We've kept quiet. Staying in a flophouse in the Wash. I told Dredger I might look him up in a few days, but haven't talked to him since I arrived."

"A flophouse?" Annah's face is unreadable, but Tander's isn't.

"Jaleh's gentling-house, you mean! What the fuck are you doing there?" His grin vanishes, face contorting with sudden anger. *Volatile*, thinks the spy. "Amateurs, that's what they send us."

"The boy knows who to pray to," says the spy. There's a note of pride in his voice that surprises him. "He'll do his job."

"That's what Rhyna said, and that went well, didn't it? Fucking marvellous, that was." Tander jumps up. The man has too much uncontained energy for the spy's liking.

"Who's Rhyna?"

Annah glares at Tander, but the mercenary keeps talking. "Our former whisperer. Stupid cow couldn't work a miracle on her own, despite all her prayers, so we had to smuggle her up to the Ishmeric embassy in Bryn Avane. There's a shrine there."

The spiritual potency of a saint is magnified in a holy place. It's easier to work miracles at a shrine, easier for a saint of Fate Spider to whisper secrets across the ocean. "You were intercepted?"

"That's enough," snaps Annah. "We'll take the boy from here."

"What?" *That would be a mistake*, he thinks instantly, but it takes a moment for him to decide *why* it's a mistake. It'll damage his cover. That's why.

Nothing more.

The boy is a tool. An asset, to be used. A weapon, made by the gods.

Nothing more.

"You'll get your money now," says Tander, "if that's what you're worried about."

"Your job was to bring the saint to us," says Annah. "Nothing more." The spy looks up, startled as she echoes his thoughts.

"Thought you'd want to be rid of the brat," laughs Tander.

"Emlin's my son. I've told people he's my son," says the spy. "It'll draw attention if I just hand him over to strangers."

"We may need to use him at short notice." Annah studies X84. "You shouldn't have claimed him as your kin. It complicates matters."

She leans back, her expression unreadable. There's an awkward silence, broken only by whispering from the cellar room.

The spy isn't sure if Tander and Annah can hear it, but he can. Emlin's voice, overlaid with the chittering of the god.

"I want to help. To serve. I was on the wrong side in Severast."
Live your cover. "How can I please the Sacred Realm?"

The silence lasts another heartbeat. Two, three, four.

And then Tander laughs loudly. "Oh, we can use you, all right."

Annah lights another cigarette. Her fingers are mottled, the brown stains mixed with bleached spots from alchemical work. "We need information. The trade in illegal weapons has stepped up – and Haith and Lyrix are doing most of the buying. We need to know what they're buying. How much, what sort of stuff. Whether it's salvage, or new material."

"I'll see if any of my old business contacts are still active."

Of course, the spy isn't Sanhada Baradhin, and, while certain aspects of the dead man's life are known to him, others are not. The spy knows, for example, that he visited the temple of the Fate Spider many times. The man was a smuggler after all.

"I'll see what I can do," says the spy. "And I'll take my payment. A man's got to eat, after all."

Annah produces a purse and hands it to him.

"I was promised silver. Not miracle-cheap gold."

"I know what the gods said," says Annah. "But this is my operation, and I'll run it how I choose."

He pockets the money.

"Leave a message for Tander at the King's Nose if you need to talk to us in an emergency. Otherwise, we'll use chalk signals."

She recites a list of public places in the city they can use to leave messages disguised as graffiti or random scrapes. A mark on the steps of Saint Storm's church means he's under surveillance; a mark in the lavatory at Phaeton Street station means he's got useful information and so forth. A mark near the door of a dockside tavern near Jaleh's means he's to bring Emlin back to this house that night.

"Anything else I should know?" asks the spy. Thinking of invasion fleets surging north, about the gathering wrath of the gods. About the god bombs.

"Tander will find you if circumstances change. Otherwise, we'll review the situation in a few weeks," says Annah. She finishes her coffee, stands and walks downstairs to the cellar room.

The whispering doesn't stop. It's more insistent now, as though Emlin's words have sprouted legs and are crawling up the walls. The whole house is thick with stolen secrets, a parade of encrypted messages scuttling up the chimneys, to take flight on the warm summer winds that blow south.

Tander senses it too, shudders. He takes out a metal hip flask and tops up his coffee. He waves the flask at the spy. "Welcome to Guerdon, friend."

"It's safer than Severast, anyway," says the spy, and Tander laughs. He pours a generous measure into the spy's cup, too.

"Aye, well, you weren't here for those bastard Tallowmen," says Tander. "Thank the gods they stopped making those things."

"Was it the Tallowmen who caught your previous saint?"

"Nah. City watch. It was only a few months ago. After the Crisis."

"Rhyna, was it?"

"Aye. They grabbed her coming out of the embassy, and tried to drag her into a carriage. But I had a loaded gun in me pocket, praise be to the gods. Shot her from forty yards away."

"How'd you escape?"

"Same way I survived the Godswar. Ran like fuck." Tander grins. "Give me the watch over gods any day. At least Rhyna died *like* an honest woman. Much worse ways to die than a bullet in the head. I tell you, better to see out the war here than anywhere else. Never does anyone any good to get too close to the gods."

Is this genuine cynicism, or a trap to test X84's devotion to the Sacred Realm?

"The gods bless us all," he replies.

Tander seems about to reply, but then the whispering stops and he too falls silent. After a few minutes, Annah returns, with Emlin. The boy's dressed in his street clothes again. He's shivering, leaning on Annah for support, but there's a look of immense pride on his face, a grin that he can't hide.

"Come on, I'll walk ye back down to the Wash," says Tander,

slapping the boy on the back. As they leave the house, the spy glances back and sees Annah watching them from the upstairs window. There are few lamps on the road and the night is dark, but he feels her gaze on him all the way down the hill to the watch post and the stairs leading down to the Wash. He can hear invisible spiders of divine attention scuttling over the walls around him, stalking him down the street.

That night, Emlin is restless in his bunk. The spy lies awake, listening to the boy thrash and turn in the bed above him. Muttering prayers under his breath. Across the room, Haberas sleeps soundly.

"What's wrong?" asks the spy.

"Nothing."

He waits.

"I just . . . I wish the gods were closer. They're very far away."

"You said the message got through. You did well."

"I don't want to go to Jaleh's prayers tomorrow."

"You have to." The boy stinks of divinity after the miracle. If the city watch caught him, with their thaumaturgic lenses and their saint-hunters, it would all be over.

"I guess, but . . . " Emlin turns over heavily. "You wouldn't understand."

Emlin's tasted sainthood. In the cellar of that house in Newtown, he channelled the power of a distant god. No wonder he can't sleep. No wonder he's praying in secret, trying to reach the god again.

He thinks the spy wouldn't understand the divine beauty of the gods. How it feels to *know* them, to look beyond the portents and manifestations in the mortal world, and see the gods in all their glory on the other side. The unutterable radiance, complexity beyond measure, that divine certainty and oneness of purpose. The euphoria of knowing all the world's secrets, seeing all the connections in Fate Spider's web. The power to shape destiny, to navigate the threads of the future.

The terror of being separated from the gods. The nauseating fall back to the flesh. The sensation that you've left parts of your soul behind as you struggle to return to mortal existence, the long unwelcome journey back from divinity.

Alic wouldn't understand that. Neither would X84.

The spy understands.

He should stay silent, but Alic feels compelled to give some words of comfort. "It'll get easier. The gods are closer than you know."

"But they're going to make war on Lyrix, I think." The boy whispers, careful not to wake any of the other sleepers in the shared room. "They're not coming here," he adds bitterly.

"You need to sleep," says the spy. "And stay hidden. Fate Spider is patient, isn't he? You've got to be patient, too."

"I guess," says Emlin again, unconvinced. "What do you think of Annah and Tander?" he asks quietly.

What does he think of them? Tander is, in the spy's estimation, an idiot. Probably a useful one – the man seems physically competent – but sloppy, undisciplined, unreliable. He's an attack dog. They must have leverage on him, some sure way of controlling him. A leash, pulling him to heel.

Annah, now – Annah's a rarity in Guerdon, but something the spy has seen elsewhere. She's a true believer. She understands that the gods dictate the laws of reality, that the mortal world is just a shadow cast by the unseen powers. That sort of person is always on the watch for omens, for traces of divine intention made manifest in material events. The spy wonders what she makes of Guerdon, where the local gods are weak and docile. When the gods fall silent, anything goes. Annah, thinks the spy, warrants careful handling. She'll take nothing on faith from mortals. She needs the right sign.

He admits none of this to the boy. Instead, Alic shrugs. "I don't know. I hope they don't push you too hard."

After a moment he says, "Tander said I should stay with them. He said I could stay in the cellar and make it a shrine, and work in Annah's shop by day. He said they're rich."

"A son belongs with his father," says Alic.

"But you're not my father. We're just pretending."

The spy gets out of bed and stands so that he can look Emlin in the face. He doesn't bother to light a candle – the boy can see in the dark.

"Listen. The first rule is to live your cover. Every day, every heartbeat. You've got to *be* my son. Think it and know it, so that when the city watch stop you or some sorcerer comes sniffing, you don't hesitate. And you've got to step lightly. Give the world no reason to notice you. Understand?"

The boy nods.

"Does Emlin know Annah and Tander? Does Alic?"

"No."

"That's right. X84 knows them, not you or I."

"What about the shrine?"

The spy considers the question for a split second. Sanhada Baradhin knows little about gods and saints. The merchant made his devotions at the temples, but never stepped beyond the first mystery. *Live your cover* is the first rule, but not the only one.

"A shrine?" scoffs the spy. "A shrine would *help*, but it's not the important thing. Living your cover is all about the face you show to the world, right?"

"I guess so."

"Well, there's more than one world, isn't there? There's the world most folk see, where everything's solid and it's all real things. And there's the world people like you see. The god's world. The aetheric plane, the alchemists call it. To be chosen by the gods, your soul – your face there – has to be pleasing to them, aye?"

"Yes."

"So, what do you think would please Fate Spider more – you sitting in some cellar, or out in the world, listening and learning secrets?"

"In the monastery," says the boy, "I sat in a cell and listened to the whispers in the shrine."

"Aye, well, that was in Ishmere. The air's filled with gods there, and they'll lay claim to anyone who breathes a prayer. They've nothing to fear there. Things are more *delicate* here. Fate Spider isn't the only god walking the night here. You've got to meet him in secret, and make yourself known to him by the right signs and watchwords.

"Now get to sleep, son. We've got work to do in the morning."

The boy studies his face for a long minute in the darkness, then turns over, apparently satisfied.

"Sleep," insists the spy.

He waits until the boy's breathing becomes regular. Waits as the hours of the night wheel by.

He whispers into Emlin's ear a prayer of his own.

And when the boy wakes, sobbing, from a nightmare, the spy is there to comfort him. To chase away his fears, and dismiss his terrors as nothing but a dream. "There were these masked men there, and they were dragging me away to a carriage. And – and Tander was there, and he had a gun, and ..." the boy whispers, clutching his head as if he expects it to burst.

The spy cradles Emlin, whispers his fears away. Just a dream, he says, but the lesson has been taught.

The boy doesn't pray again that night.

CHAPTER 10

Terevant's woken by screaming. Shana, lying on the floor, eyes open, staring blindly. Her sister, bending over her, in shock.

Berrick stirs in confusion. "What . . . huh?"

Someone hammers on the door of the compartment. "What's going on in there? Open up!"

"Shit." Terevant drops to his knees, examines Shana. She's not bleeding, and she's still breathing. He grabs the sister's arm. "What happened?"

"I . . . the train braked, and she fell. Hit her head." He glances at Shana's face, pale in the shaft of morning light that now streams into the compartment. No sign of a mark in the slightest. He turns her head so she's facing into the sunlight; her pupils don't react. She touched the sword, he realises. The Erevesic sword, like all family phylacteries, is only for members of the bloodline. It rejects other bearers. Shana's lucky to be alive; she'll be luckier if she's still sane.

Why did the damn fool open his bag?

"Open up I say!" shouts someone from the corridor. The train guard. Terevant wrestles Shana back up onto the seat. She convulses as he pulls her off the floor, and for a terrifying moment he fears she's going to have a fit of some sort, but then she takes a gasp of air and vomits across her sister's lap.

Terevant flicks the door clasp open and sees the beefy face of a train guard, eyes bulging with fury. "Uh, a young lady in here is unwell. Everything's fine."

"That's them!" An older man with a great bushy beard behind

the guard extends an accusing finger. "They took my girls!" It's the chaperone. Terevant struggles for words. Behind him, Shana and her sister are both in hysterics, and Berrick's crammed himself into a corner as if he's trying to hide. The train's brakes squeal; they're coming into a station.

"Everything's fine," repeats Terevant. "One of your, uh, ladies slipped and fell, but she's unhurt. And nothing untoward happened. We were just, ah, discussing current events." He could try pulling rank by producing the Erevesic sword, but he imagines Olthic's reaction to seeing the news in a Guerdon gossip-rag. A titanic sigh not of disappointment, but of confirmation. "Look, let's give the young ladies a moment to collect their belongings, and nothing more need be said."

"They're robbers, I'll wager! Got my silly girls drunk and had their foul way with them, then stole from them. I want them arrested! Search their bags!" shouts the chaperone. He points accusingly at Terevant's kitbag.

"On my honour as an officer, nothing untoward has happened here," says Terevant hastily. The guard pauses for an instant – he doesn't have the authority to arrest anyone, but he's clearly on the chaperone's side.

"Search their bags! Fetch the watch! What if they're demons?" The man's drawing quite a crowd with his theatrics.

"Step out of the compartment, sir," orders the guard, making a decision.

The bearded man crows. "Arrest them!"

Terevant reaches up to his bag, and then the door to the corridor opens again and he hears Lyssada's voice. More clipped and commanding than he recalls. Whatever she says to the guard works: he backs off as though banished by a spell. The bearded chaperone quails and vanishes back into the crowd, abandoning the unconscious girl and the sobbing one.

Lyssada takes in the sorry contents of the cabin at a glance, wrinkling her nose in disgust at the state of it. "Change of plan. You're both getting out here. Come on."

She moves like an efficient whirlwind in the cramped compartment, stepping over Shana's twitching form, sweeping up Berrick and his belongings and hustling him out the door. Terevant follows in her wake, grabbing his kitbag off the shelf. The weight of the Erevesic sword almost throws him off balance. He tries to bid farewell to Shana, but Lyssada grabs him by the arm, pulls him out onto the platform and slams the door behind him, over the protests of the guard. The train takes off again.

The three of them trot along the deserted platform in silence. They are the only passengers to alight here, and the train moves off before they reach the station's concourse.

Lyssada marches in coldly furious silence. Terevant follows, knowing he should be ashamed, but the situation is so farcical that he wants to laugh. Lys can tell; he knows by the way she bristles, by the set of her shoulders, and that makes it all the funnier.

The rest of the station is equally deserted, and looks like it hasn't been used in decades. Vines hang down from the broken glass roof, the paint peels like dead skin and there are deep cracks in the walls. Terevant spots crates of military supplies stacked in the concourse, but otherwise the place looks completely dead. This clearly isn't a regular stop on the train line between Old Haith and Guerdon.

"Lys, where the hell are we?"

She doesn't answer him but points at an archway and says to Berrick: "Go on. The carriage is waiting for you down there. I'll meet you there in half an hour." She clicks her tongue in irritation. "We'll talk about this on the way."

Berrick catches Terevant's eye and shrugs, as if to say "such is life". He ambles off into the darkness, whistling. It's clear that he, at least, was expecting to disembark in this ruin. Terevant's head spins.

"This way," says Lys, guiding Terevant towards another archway. A tunnel, with passageways and chambers branching it off it. Terevant guesses it's deeply buried beneath a hillside; storerooms and corridors for moving troops, maybe, safe from artillery fire or miraculous bombardment. The walls are pocked with bullet holes, spell-scars. In places, the walls are scorched; in others, stained with a glistening mud. Lys warns him not to step in it, but he's already giving it a wide berth. He's seen such things before in the Godswar.

"This is Grena, right?" he asks her, and she nods. It makes sense – the little valley of Grena lies on the route between Haith and Guerdon. The rail's only open again because the valley was recaptured by Haith six months ago.

"That's good," she mutters, "you're not a complete idiot. I expected it of Berrick, but I thought you'd have a bit more sense."

"He and I got a little drunk on the way to Guerdon. You and I' – *and Olthic*, he mentally appends – "have got more than a little drunk on the way to Guerdon." Then, though, they went by sea. He remembers Olthic standing at the prow, wind in his hair, staring out to sea like he was already plotting his conquests. And, in retrospect, Terevant got drunk because he had nightmares about shipwrecks.

"That was a long time ago. Now you're an officer, and I'm an ambassador's wife. We're not children any more."

"What, are you afraid my behaviour's going to reflect badly on the family? Like anyone on that train cares if the second son of a Haithi house got drunk with some city girl. I can cart the sword drunk or sober, you know."

"I take it back," spits Lys, "you are an idiot." She's genuinely angry with him. His amusement turns sour. *There's* the shame, oozing into his stomach, like he's distilling the darkness of the ruined station into something cold and sickening. Terevant stops in the middle of the tunnel, spreads his arms wide as if inviting a dagger to the heart. "Enlighten me."

Lys turns around, looks up and down, peering into the shadows. She leads him into one of the little side chambers and speaks in a low, urgent voice.

"This train station and the town around it was taken by the Free Grenan Devotees twenty years ago. Their fertility goddess sent war-naiads up the river and swarmed our defences. She slaughtered our troops twice over. The loss of this route cut our primary rail link to Guerdon, so obviously we had to get it back."

None of this is unknown or surprising to Terevant. He's heard war stories of similar campaigns overseas all his life. Local deities, caught up in the Godswar and infected by the same divine madness as the forces of Ishmere. Gods cannot be killed, only crippled, and doing that is exceedingly difficult. Destroy the god's avatars, and you only blunt the god's attention and focus in the material world, forcing it to choose another saint. Victory means a slow and bloody grind: kill every worshipper, tear down every temple, break every relic, dispel every miracle – and do it all again, over and over, until the god's a forgotten shadow, shrieking in the void.

The cynics say humanity will be extinct long before the Godswar ends.

"Sounds lovely. Nice little local war," he mutters.

"We threw everything we could spare at Grena. Vigilants. Bone hulks. Armoured trains. Tried landward assaults, tried landing at the shore and moving up along the river. Nothing worked – their goddess had deep, deep roots in this valley. Divinity's best projections guessed it would be fifteen years before we retook the rail line, and thirty before the valley was desecrated."

Now this is interesting. The only quick victories in the Godswar come when the gods themselves clash, and that's not an option for Haith. Their spiritual strength is primarily in near-divine relics like the sword, and in the Vigilant. The death-god of Haith will not rise until the world's ending. "What happened?"

"Swear on the sword that you shall not speak of this." Lys's eyes gleam in the darkness. "Not to anyone. Not even Olthic."

Terevant pulls the Erevesic sword from his bag. The weapon's magic aura whirls around him, surging with power. His fatigue melts away. The darkness recedes as his eyes sharpen. He can smell Lys's scent, perfume mixed with the smoke from the train on her skin.

He hesitates for an instant before grasping the blade by its cross guard. Suddenly, the little storeroom is crowded with invisible ghosts, his ancestors there to witness his oath. Some seem to crowd close to him, as if eager to hear whatever secrets Lys is about to reveal. "May the ancestors reject me if I speak of this."

He places the sword on the ground between them. Releases his grip, and the ghosts vanish.

"There was a rocket launch. Not us – a Guerdonese naval vessel. One shot, and the goddess was dead. No physical damage to the valley, but a complete annihilation of the deity."

"Death's face," he swears. A weapon like that changes the war. He imagines fighting the battle of Eskalind again, when the gods of Ishmere attacked the Haithi invasion force. He remembers Kraken rising from the ocean, and Blessed Bol dancing on the surf, golden statues in the shape of dying men tumbling around him. To be able to snuff out those terrors with a single shot . . . "Why aren't we using those?"

"The alchemists' guild won't even admit they exist. Neither will Guerdon's emergency council. The city's still in chaos. Bureau and Crown are both agreed, Ter – we need to secure those weapons. It's our only hope of stopping Ishmere when they come for Haith."

His heart's pounding in the silence of the little tunnel. "What do you need me to do?"

"Edoric Vanth – the Third Secretary at the embassy. He's gone missing. There are rumours he's been killed. He's prepared for Vigilance, so if he was killed . . . "

Terevant flexes his wrist, feels the iron periapt implant pull against the skin. The mortal body is fragile – one stray shot, one cut, and that's it. The Vigilant of Haith, though, are another breed. Much harder to kill. If Vanth simply went down the wrong alleyway and got his throat cut by some footpad, he'd already have reported back to the embassy.

"Either he's dead, or he's being held. Either way, it's spooked the Bureau. They're worried that the Guerdon embassy is compromised, that we're already under attack." Lys's intense gaze transfixes him. Every atom of her being is focused on him, on this mission. There's no one around, but Lys still lowers her voice. "Ter, I don't trust half the embassy staff. Previous ambassadors have run Guerdon as their own private fiefdom, and I don't know if they're reliable. And Olthic and I . . . things are fraught."

"Fraught?"

"Very fraught."

Terevant rubs his wrist. His hangover is back with a vengeance. "We've got to find out what happened to Edoric Vanth."

"You do. I'm not coming back to Guerdon with you. Not yet."

"Where are you going?"

"I can't say." Terevant envies her ability to neatly section off aspects of herself — how she can tell him one set of secrets while keeping another, how she can be a spy one day and a socialite the next, how she can be his friend and his brother's wife at the same time. He envies her control. She knows who she is, what she's supposed to do, and so can slip on one mask or another. "But it's important, too. Go into the valley, you'll see how important."

Lys nods towards the waiting carriage. "I need you to find out what happened to Vanth, Ter. You're in charge of the embassy garrison — you can take control of the investigation. If Vanth was betrayed by someone in the embassy, then they might be able to conceal their involvement by bringing in one of their own creatures to handle the inquest. It has to be someone I can trust." She takes a breath. "Can I trust you?"

Once, he'd have died for her with a song on his lips. Maybe that's who he's supposed to be. "Of course."

She shifts from foot to foot. A nervous tic he remembers from when they were young. She lays a hand on his arm to steady herself.

"You'll have to leave the sword with me, now," she says, eyes bright.

"It's the Erevesic blade. I must guard it." It's unthinkable for him to leave the sword. Even Lys, who's part of the family by marriage, cannot safely touch the blade.

"Ter, listen — that incident on the train means there'll be city watch waiting for you at the border. Our treaty with Guerdon bans us from having phylacteries in the city, same as they don't allow saints in the other embassies. They will impound it as a divine weapon. I need you to go onto the city, to find Vanth, but you can't bring the sword."

"So, what, I'm going to leave the blade of my ancestors in the bloody lost-and-found office of a bombed-out train station?" He already failed his ancestors by not securing it in the train.

"I've got a plan. Trust me, Ter. Quell the blade as much as you can, and we'll stow it in my coach – there's a concealed and warded compartment to hold it. In a few weeks, you or Ol or a Vigilant can come and fetch it. It's not ideal – but it's more important to get you into position in the embassy."

He lifts the Erevesic sword and feels the flow of power through the rough leather of the binding. He wonders what would happen if he drew on that magic. What wonders could he perform? How would Lyssada look at him then?

"Quell the sword," she prompts him.

The souls swirling in the blade sense his presence; his hand tingles as their magic pushes against him, seeking to use him as their vessel. He can feel the nerves in his hands, feel the flow of blood through individual veins and arteries, feel the interplay of bone and muscle, becoming aware of them as he has never known them before. His flesh transmuting into fire; his nerves to flashing light, his bones to unbreakable adamant.

"Quell it."

He pushes back. Whispers that now is not the time, that they must sleep. The light from the sword fades, and it becomes suddenly heavy in his grasp.

"Here," says Lyssada, passing him an embroidered cloth, enchanted to dampen the blade's magic, and he carefully binds up the sword. "Come on."

They walk back through the dark tunnel to the deserted station, and he follows her through another archway into a small courtyard. A carriage waits there – an old one, battered. There's no suspension, and the one concession to modernity is the raptequine in the harness instead of a horse. The alchemist-grown monsters are stronger and faster than anything natural-born.

Berrick is snoozing inside; Lys shoves him out of the way so she can show Terevant where to conceal the Erevesic sword in the hidden compartment. Even quelled, the sword is dangerous. It can unravel spells, cut through strands of fate. Old stories tell of the horrible accidents that befall those who betray the Houses of Haith.

"We're late," she says to Terevant. "One of my agents, Lemuel, he'll meet you at Guerdon. I'll see you as soon as I can." She squeezes his hand, and then she's gone – the carriage rattles off down the overgrown road south, running parallel to the rail line, leaving Terevant alone in the deserted station.

He feels as if some part of him has gone with Lyssada, and tells himself that it's just some lingering connection to the sword.

He returns to the platform, finds a bedroll in his kitbag and lights a little fire to heat a tin of soup. The new service to Guerdon only passes through once a day, so he has nearly twenty-four hours of boredom ahead of him, and he's nearly finished *The Bone Shield*.

Tomorrow morning, he decides, he'll go out into the valley and see what the grave of a goddess looks like.

Dawn does not improve the prospects seen from the train station.

Terevant watches the sun climb into the sky, but the light is muted, hesitant, as if some pall hangs over the Grena Valley. Everything has an artificial quality to it, as if it's paper-thin. The valley is a landscape painting. He's worried to step too heavily on the path, in case he puts a foot through the fragile canvas and falls out of the world.

It'll be midsummer in a few weeks, but there's no heat in the air. No chill either. His skin feels numb.

He walks down from the station along an overgrown path, but the plants don't slow him down. The blades of grass crack and crumble when he pushes through them; the thorns snap off instead of catching on his uniform. Everything's weak and hollow, going through the motions of growing. Signs along the path warn of dangers – unexploded ordnance, unbestowed curses.

There are unlikely orchards on one side of the path. Conjured by some vanished miracle he guesses, as the trees sprout from ground broken and blighted by artillery bombardments. They are almost bare. Only a few of them have fruit, and he has no desire to taste any of it, even though he breakfasted on meagre military rations and the last of Berrick's wine. The fruit doesn't look rotten or poisonous or tainted, just . . . flat. Hollow, again. There should be a great buzz of bees around all those blossoms, but the valley's deathly silent.

He leaves the shadow of the trees, trudges over a blasted land. The valley was a battlefield in the Godswar. He steps around glistening alchemical fallout, steps over fragments of bone and twisted metal. The wind whistles through the rubble of this scarred land.

The path leads down towards the ruined city of Grena. There's a Haithi flag fluttering in the breeze from a newly constructed fort. That flag is almost the only motion in the leaden valley.

Almost. There are a few people listlessly working in the fields. They look confused, as if unsure how they got here. Swinging the scythes awkwardly, as though they've never used them before, even the horny-handed old farmers whose weathered skin speaks of a lifetime outdoors. They bow their heads, flinching away from Terevant when they see his uniform.

The Empire of Haith once occupied the land of Varinth, across the ocean. There, they banned worship of the local gods. Killed the priests and saints, tore down the temples. They provoked the gods until they manifested in some form, then blasted those manifestations of the gods with cannon fire until they fell. Gods of winter and justice, sun and moon, harvest and poetry – their titanic corpses all lying in the surf by the shore, ichor mixing with the foam of the waves. The occupying forces declared that anyone who prayed to the old gods would be punished. They were part of the Empire of Haith now; their only loyalty should be to the distant Crown. New rules: no prayers. No rites. No saints. The dead get handed over to state necromancers for processing.

Still, they'd creep away in the night to worship. They'd hide shrines in their homes, or sneak off into the forests. Smuggle the dead out to be buried according to the old rites, so the residuum of their souls would feed the gods.

And the gods came back. Rolling down from the mountains and the forests and the wild places to besiege the forts of the occupiers. The Empire of Haith maintained such occupations only at great cost – and great cruelty. And those are minor deities, local gods like the goddess of Grena, unlike the expansionist gods of Ishmere.

Terevant wrote poems decrying the Crown's actions, then carefully burned them when he joined the army. No doubt some clerk in the Office of Sedition has copies.

He avoids entering the shattered town, circling around it, following the river down towards the sea. Lumps of mud on the riverbank vaguely suggest humanoid forms, piled in great numbers on either side. Naiads, maybe, servitors of the goddess, annihilated with her. A mass killing.

Along the estuary, he walks amid rushes. Some seabirds wheel overhead, calling to one another. Other birds of the same species stand stock still in the middle of the path, paying no attention to his approach. Like the people of the valley, they're wounded. Thrust into a strange world of surfaces with nothing beyond. Weeds grow along the shore in profusion, and that eerie stillness of the upper valley is gone. The estuary is being reclaimed, the emptiness left by the goddess filled by something else, an anonymous, blind natural order.

There's a different quality to the plants that grow by the shore. They grow in fierce profusion, sprouting like a conquering army.

Out there in the bay, according to Lys, was where the god bomb went off. A war ended in a flash. And there are other such bombs somewhere in Guerdon. Half the spies in the worlds must be crowding into the city.

How frustrating it must be for the gods, to have to work through mortal agents.

A sudden shiver runs through him, like he's being watched. In other lands, he's heard people compare the feeling to someone stepping on one's grave. The phrase makes no sense in Haith, where only the disgraced casteless have graves. In Haith, they call it the eye of history, and say that it portends great deeds in one's future.

He turns and hikes back up the valley.

After a few hours, the train to Guerdon arrives, shattering the silence of the station with the roar of engines. He climbs on board, eager to be on his way.

He's seen the grave; now he's going to the city that murdered a god.

CHAPTER 11

Absalom Spyke, Eladora decides, is a monster grown in some alchemical vat, with legs of steel and stomach of stone. On Kelkin's orders, the pair of them have walked every street and alleyway in the Wash, visited every ale house and watering hole in the lower city. Politics for Spyke, it seems, has nothing to do with the policy papers and grand debates of parliament. It's backslapping and drinking with old friends, all of whom are quietly influential in their districts. Some of these friends bring Spyke problems to be solved – a troublesome gang, a leaking sewer, a tale of unexploded ordnance from the Crisis – and Spyke promises to take care of it. Others come with a list of names, their own name usually at the top of it, and Spyke ceremonially folds these and slips them into a pocket. They'll be remembered, he says, after the election.

When all else fails, when the friend brings nothing to Spyke except crossed arms and a smile that's a little too wide, that's when Spyke reaches into another pocket, and brings out a roll of notes – as much cash as Eladora has ever seen in one place, and her grandfather was the wealthiest man in the city. She bites her lip.

From time to time, Spyke remembers that she exists, and introduces her to his old friends and ward-captains as "one of Kelkin's". One of Kelkin's what, she wonders. Mostly, though, she's invisible, trotting after Spyke like a stray dog.

After the Wash, they climb into the New City. Spyke walks more slowly here, his route is more uncertain. The dance is the same, but the tempo is slower and his partners are different. Refugees fleeing the Godswar occupy many streets in this conjured city, and Spyke meets with their leaders. Hesitantly, he makes his overtures to them, but he doesn't understand their problems or can't solve them, and they're not interested in the kickbacks and sinecures he can offer. They complain about new powers that have arisen to take advantage of the fall of the old Brotherhood, like Ghierdana criminal gangs and the Saint of Knives.

Spyke is less sure of himself here and turns to her for counsel, asking her questions about the New City and its denizens. She can quote figures at him, tell him the numbers she got from Hark Island or compare the histories of Severast and Ishmere, but they're effectively speaking different languages. After a swelteringly hot afternoon made frustrating by spending long hours trying to get to a seemingly inaccessible tower block, clambering up and down the stairs and alleyways that wind like intestines around and through the buildings, Spyke announces a retreat. They fall back to the Wash, to a tavern not far from Lambs Square.

Spyke's carrying a king's ransom in his pocket, but sends her to buy the drinks.

When she returns, he's in conversation with yet another rogue. Spyke's grin lights up the room, his cackle is like jingling gold, and his backslaps echo like thunder. He's a fountain of enthusiasm.

The other man leaves, and Spyke slumps down in his seat. Takes his drink from Eladora with a grunt of acknowledgement, and stares into the brown liquid inside the mug.

Eladora sips her drink – it's better than what she had to stomach earlier, but still rancid. The city hasn't had good wine since the fall of Severast. "Isn't it rather inefficient to approach these people one at a time? Shouldn't we rather hold a public meeting where we could describe policies, talk about how to reform the New City?"

"Too early for speeches an' rallies. And half those fuckers would knife the other half, I'll wager. Nah, t'would be a riot. Maybe when we know who our friends are, in the New, but not yet."

"Still, you've hardly mentioned policies. How will people know what we stand for if we don't tell them?"

"Standing is shit," declares Absalom Spyke. "These people stand all day – at work, in the factories or the boats, or in queues. They don't care, girl. They don't care who rules the city as long as it ain't the Tallows. By nature they won't vote at all, except where there's graft to be made. We bribe 'em, church bribes 'em, and a few old fools vote for the monarchists or some other loons."

"Bribery," says Eladora, "is illegal."

"Paying for votes ain't legal. Paying folk to get voters to the polls is legal, and old as the hills." Spyke leans over the table, so close that she can smell his foul breath. "Let me guess, girl – you're Bryn Avane born and Glimmerside bred, and you think you know how this city works. You think everyone else is stupid or crooked, and that it's up to you to fix everything so's the common folk can curtsey and thank'ee. You don't know nothing."

He slumps back in his chair, drains the last of his beer. He digs into his pocket, pulls out the roll of notes. Waves one at Eladora. "Get me another, there's a good girl."

She stands. "I have a previous engagement, Mr Spyke. I'll bring your concerns to Mr Kelkin when I meet with him. And since those are party funds you're spending, I trust you'll be responsible with them. Good night."

The air in the street outside the inn is warm and sticky. For the last few months, the skies above the city have been unusually clear, as the majority of the alchemists' factories were shut down by the Crisis, but the weather tonight makes for choking smog that hangs low over Guerdon. The streets are awash with a yellowish, gritty fog, making the city look like it's been submerged below a polluted sea. Wrapping her scarf around her mouth for protection, Eladora hurries away from the tavern, heading for the small apartment that Kelkin arranged for her.

It's not far to walk. Still, these streets aren't safe, so she hurries and keeps one hand on the little pistol concealed in her pocket. She's never fired the little thing in anger, only practised with it.

Miren showed her how to use guns.

She takes that memory, folds it neatly and pushes it into a mental folder that's crammed to bursting with similar little notes. She then returns the folder to a heavy iron safe, wrapped in chains, and submerged in the deepest, coldest part of the ocean. She does *not* think about Miren Ongentson any more.

Instead, she runs through the sorcerous incantations Dr Ramegos taught her. At Eladora's degree of sorcerous talent, trying to use a spell to defend herself is unlikely to be a very effective weapon, but it'd certainly be unexpected – and reciting the chant in her mind reassures her.

Eladora reaches the apartment building without incident. The walls of the stairwell are covered with election posters. She counts the number of IndLibs compared to Hawkers. They're outnumbered two to one, and this is supposed to be a part of the city that supports Kelkin. Another bad omen.

When Eladora comes to her door, she turns the lock, then the second, heavier lock she had installed. Then she stops, takes a deep breath and presses her fingers to the centre of the handle. Runes flare red for an instant, then vanish in a puff of sulphurous smoke. Her stomach lurches. Eladora picked up the basics of thaumaturgical theory at university, but she never dared cast a spell until after the Crisis. The warding spell that guards her door marks the limit of her abilities so far, and the spell takes such a toll on her that she's unsure if she wants to go further. Humans aren't meant to wield such powers directly, so most thaumaturges die young, their bodies ruptured or minds corroded by arcane energies. Heavy-duty sorcery is the domain of inhuman entities like Crawling Ones. Alchemy is a much safer way of handling such fundamental forces.

She hesitates before entering. For an instant, she imagines that her grandfather is waiting for her beyond the door, his gold mask reflecting otherworldly lights, his worm-fingers glistening with unholy magic. Or Miren, with a knife.

A deep breath. No. Jermas Thay is dead and gone. Miren's gone. She takes that memory and locks it away in the same prison as the memories of Miren, and Ongent, and the rest of the Crisis.

She lingers for a moment, though, on one element of that

catastrophe. Her cousin Carillon Thay was at the very centre of the Crisis. Eladora is one of very few people in the city who know the truth about her – that she was created by their grandfather as a conduit to capture the power of the imprisoned Black Iron Gods. An unwitting, unwilling saint. Spyke's insults earlier still sting. Eladora's determined to make the most of this second professional life of hers, to be a better political operative than she was a scholar at the university. She failed to connect her cousin's supernatural curse with the ancient history of the city and the Black Iron Gods until after Carillon had fled Desiderata Street on that awful night. If she'd better smarter, braver, then so much suffering might have been averted. Every widow in black, every missing child, every wound and scar is a potential accusation, a victim of her failing. That truth is unerasable; when they finally write the histories of this time, her guilt, and the guilt of her family, will be plain for all to see.

She can't undo the Crisis, but she can ensure that the new Guerdon that rises from the ashes is a better, fairer place than the city of Tallowmen and worms and chained gods it used to be. Mentally, she retraces her steps through the New City. Recalls every fruitless conversation between Absalom Spyke and the various leaders and chieftains and power blocs he met there. What's needed is information, a divine perspective on the New City. To know their desires before they do.

Church bells echo across the city from the triple cathedrals on Holyhill. Eight o'clock. She shakes herself from her reveries, curses, and hurries over to her wardrobe, stripping off her street-stained clothes as she does so. Fretting, for a moment, at her appearance in the mirror. She finds a dress that's clean and moderately flattering – and, as a bonus, modern enough to annoy her mother. She pulls it on hastily, then sits to apply some makeup. Her mother's dinner invitation is for nine o'clock, so she has to hurry.

The creak of a floorboard makes her jump, spilling powder across her dresser. She carefully wipes it away, listening intently as she does so. The floorboard was on the floor above, wasn't it? Not in the room outside? Her door is locked. No one can get in. *But Miren could*, she thinks, and wipes that thought away, too.

It's been a week since the first invitation arrived, the day after the reception in the Haithi embassy. Eladora parried that initial summons with a note saying that she was regrettably busy with election-related matters, and suggesting a lunch meeting the next day. Her mother riposted with another letter, pointing out that the next day was a holy day for the Keepers – the feast of Saint Storm – and so it was of course impossible for any of the devout to contemplate a lunch engagement. They sparred back and forth by messenger, and Eladora had even dared hope that things would end like they had on the previous three occasions when Silva Duttin came to the city – that they'd go through this dance of conflicting obligations and clashing appointments until Silva had to go home, and the two could avoid having to spend any time together. Avoid acknowledging that mother and daughter had taken opposing positions on church, state and everything else.

But no – Eladora's last thrust resulted in an invitation to dinner at a terrifyingly expensive restaurant, and she can't tell if this is a victory or a hideous mistake. Arrayed for battle as best she can, Eladora hurries down the stairs – first checking the spell-wards that guard her front door – and then down again, into the city's subway.

Waiting for the train, she stares into the dark mouth of the tunnel, and remembers her grandfather's worm-fingers draping a black amulet across her chest.

She wonders, not for the first time, what Silva Duttin had known of her father's heretical, monstrous work.

The restaurant her mother chose is in Serran, one of the wealthiest districts in Guerdon, although its star has faded in recent decades. The king's pleasure palace is at its heart, although it's been abandoned for more than three hundred years, after the royal family fled to escape the Black Iron cult. The same cult Eladora's grandfather revived.

On arrival, Eladora confuses the maître'd by inadvertently asking for the Thay table, not the one booked under the name of Duttin. The Thay family is best remembered these days for being mysteriously murdered one night fifteen years ago, so the waiter's confusion is understandable. Eladora corrects herself, and follows him, cheeks burning, through a maze of wood-panelled corridors decorated with paintings and relics from the old Barbed Palace.

"Mrs Duttin is in the Rose Room," announces the servant. "Wine has been served already, although if there is anything you would like, pray name it and it will be provided." As he opens the door, Eladora hears the sound of what she can only describe as cackling from within.

Her mother's sitting there, along with – to Eladora's surprise – Mhari Voller. Both women have nigh-empty glasses in hand; Silva's wiping away tears of merriment.

"Eladora! Join us, my dear!" says Voller, pouring the few drops from the bottom of a bottle into a third glass. She waves the empty bottle at the waiter, who takes it and vanishes like a ghost.

Eladora watches her mother warily as she sits down. She's become old in the five years since Eladora last saw her. Her hair has gone grey, her eyes are too bright, feverish. There's a croak in her voice now. Mhari Voller must be thirty years older than Silva Duttin, but she looks younger.

"I-I-I didn't know Lady Voller would be joining us," says Eladora. For that matter, there's a fourth place set at the table, implying another unknown guest.

"Forgive me," says Voller, "I've been trying to catch up with dear Silvy for *days* now, and this might be my last chance for a while. We're all busy people, after all, especially with all the fuss." Her fork describes a little circle in the air, which Eladora takes to encompass parliament and the city and the election and the state of the wider world.

"And it might be best to have a referee. Or a witness." Silva spears a piece of grapefruit and raises it, dripping, to her mouth.

"It's just . . . there are a few, ah, private matters that I'd like to d-d-discuss." Eladora bites her lip; her stammer is always worse when she's nervous or feeling childish, and she can feel herself slipping backwards in time as she sits down opposite her mother. All her cultivated masks – senior adviser to Effro Kelkin, postgraduate scholar at the university, radical anarcanist who believes the gods are nothing more than magical phenomena gone rotten, without any moral authority – fall away, and she's the nervous, sniffling little girl crying because neither the gods or her mother love her.

"Mhari's an old family friend. She's known you since you were a baby. And she knows all our secrets." Silva sighs. "Ask your questions."

The first question that arises is *why are you doing this?* Eladora expected an awkward dinner where she and Silva went through the motions of being mother and daughter, as she promised to write more and fended off her mother's suggestions that she marry some suitably devout landowner from Wheldacre. Where any questions about Jermas Thay or Carillon or related matters would be met with accusations that Eladora was a godless whore who had turned her back on the path of moral righteousness. This is something else entirely.

The waiter ghosts in. Eladora has him fill her glass to the brim, and drains half in one gulp, to Silva's disapproval. Voller, though, reaches across the table and clinks her glass against Eladora's. "We've ordered for you, dear," she says. "We couldn't wait. Hope you don't mind."

Food is the last of Eladora's priorities. Her thoughts go back to the interrogation rooms down in Queen's Point fortress, when they questioned her for weeks after the Crisis. The same questions, over and over, asked by different people. Now it's her turn to be the interrogator.

"Did you know Jermas Thay was still alive, all those years?"

"My father died fifteen years ago," says Silva. "The thing that ate him and . . . imprinted his personality was not him."

"Did you know the Crawling One was out there?"

Silva shrugs. "No. I knew that Jermas had . . . intentions towards survival after death, but I thought they were just the ravings of a dying man. He wasn't always coherent."

"Did you know about his experiments? About his worship of the Black Iron Gods? About Carillon?"

"Yes. The whole family knew, to some degree. I even . . . " Silva trails off, then pulls back the sleeve of her dress, revealing an arm pockmarked with hundreds of old burn marks and scars. "He led us all astray with his obsessions, and when I recognised the evil in my father, I escaped. I atoned – and I saved you from it. Oh, he would have loved you, child, if he'd had the chance to mould you. All that arrogance – he'd have damned your soul and mated you to devils from the pit! Why do you think I left? Married your father, moved out to that horrid little farm in Wheldacre? To get away from him!"

"But you went back. You brought me back." They'd visited the Thay mansion several times when Eladora was a child, before the Keeper's saints attacked it and killed the family in the dead of night. "And it was Kelkin who reported him to the church, not you!" Eladora tries to keep her voice under control, but she can't keep her last words from becoming an accusation.

"I was weak," admits Silva, haltingly. "Your father had no head for business, and we needed money . . . and I didn't understand entirely what was going on, either. It wasn't always bad, at the start. And . . . " Silva falls silent, and Mhari Voller steps in.

"Everyone knew that Jermas was, ah, eccentric, Eladora. He always associated with radical alchemists and sorcerers, and helped Effro Kelkin bring foreign religions into Guerdon. Everyone knew he was strange – we just didn't know how far he'd gone. The real rot was only in the last years – after Silva left, after you were born. After little Carillon . . . why, Silvy, I dare say you were a brake on his worst excesses. Things only got abominable after you left."

Eladora ignores Voller and fixes her gaze on Silva. "What about Carillon? Did you know what she was?"

"My brother's bastard? A child who I thought I could rescue from a house of sin? A wound in my heart?" Silva hisses. "What?"

"Bred to be a Black Iron Saint."

"I knew she was tainted. We all are – you and me, too. I tried to save you for years! I thought I'd failed when you came to this city of corruption, but it's not too late! The fires of Safid will purify our wounded souls, if only we have faith!" Spittle spatters over the crystal and china plates. Mhari Voller gently takes hold of Silva's hand.

"It's all right, dear. Jermas is gone."

"Is she?" hisses Silva, and her hand clenches. "The monster child?"

Voller hastily pushes Silva's hand out of view under the table. Eladora frowns – something just happened there, but she can't tell what. Did her mother draw blood, cutting her own palm with her fingernails? Or break something? There's a faint smell of burning, too.

"The past is done with." Voller takes a breath. "We must think about the future. Eladora, child, you were instrumental in stopping the Crisis that Jermas precipitated. You – and Saint Aleena – destroyed what remained of Jermas, and stopped the alchemists from taking control of the city. Jermas wasn't the only lunatic trying to steal the gods – equal blame should fall on the alchemists, on the late Guildmistress Rosha above all. But also on myself, and the rest of the City Forward party. We were so drunk on power and wealth that we lost sight of what was right.

"All of us have sinned, child. And it's time to make amends."

Is this all a Safidist suicide pact? wonders Eladora suddenly. The Safidists believe that burning reunites the soul with the Kept Gods. She envisions a phlogiston bomb under the tablecloth, her mad mother hitting the plunger while Voller finishes the last of the wine. The thought is so absurd that she bursts out laughing.

Silva frowns at her.

Voller continues. "We can build a stable future for the city. You're Effro's assistant. He listens to you. You can bring him our proposal."

"Who's we?" asks Eladora.

"The church," croaks Silva, "the blessed church of the Faith-Keepers. The true faith of Guerdon."

"So you want, what, an electoral pact? A proposal for a coalition against the Hawkers?"

"We want Kelkin to come back to the faith," says Voller. "Did you know he was in training to become a priest, once? We want Kelkin to return to the fold. The city needs a government of unity to see it through the Godswar, unity both spiritual and temporal. We want worship of belligerent gods banned from the city. Your grandfather was right about one thing – this city needs strong gods to guard it against attack. We don't have much time."

Eladora's left speechless. Voller has just casually discarded forty years of her own beliefs and policies. What could possibly force her into such a total reversal? "And what else? No more neutrality? Repeal of the Free City Act? Are you both utterly insane?"

Silva's face goes red, and her eyes blaze with anger. Eladora sees a flash of divine light in them, and when her mother speaks it's like thunder bursting in the little dining room. Crystal goblets shatter, staining the tablecloth red as blood. "This is our chance at redemption, child! DO NOT SCORN IT!" Silva springs to her feet, a tower of wrath. Her withered hands clutch at the table, and her fingers break the solid hardwood. She's suddenly clad in shining armour, haloed in fire.

Eladora topples backwards out of her seat and cringes in the face of her mother's borrowed divinity. The horror of sainthood.

"Silva, please, please sit down," says Voller. She's scared, too, but not shocked. The blazing holy light fades, and Silva crumples back down into her seat. The armour vanishes. She hunches over and starts to weep, and Eladora can't tell if they're tears of sorrow or religious ecstasy.

"Come on, Silvy. No more displays like that. Let's get you cleaned up." Voller gently leads Silva towards the powder room. "Eladora, please wait a moment. This is . . . there's nothing more important."

The two older women leave. Eladora, shaking, sits back down at the ruins of the table. Her mother's brief, terrible blast of sainthood broke all the crystals. An antique mirror on one wall has a crack running down its face like a frozen lightning bolt. There are faint brown marks on the tablecloth that Eladora suspects are letters, the Litany of the Keepers burned onto the cloth in a miraculous transcription.

She hears the door behind her open. "M-my m-m-m-mother broke a glass," says Eladora, assuming the waiter has returned.

"Looks like I missed a party."

A bald man, middle-aged, grinning with broken teeth. Sinter. A priest of sorts, the spymaster of the Church of the Keepers. She met him briefly during the Crisis, shortly after he'd tried to execute her cousin to stop her using her powers. Sinter sheltered Eladora for a night, until one of his men betrayed her and sold her to Jermas Thay's agents.

Eladora suspects that Sinter was one of the people who questioned her in the days just after the Crisis, but it's hard for her to recall that week. Other parts of her past – like Miren, like Ongent – Eladora deliberately doesn't think about, but the time just after the Crisis she cannot recall, other than blurry faces and the taste of bitter medicine.

"Miss Duttin," says Sinter, sitting down in her mother's chair. He puts his three-fingered hand into the dents left by Silva. "Gods above," he mutters, "mysterious are the ways of the Kept Gods, for they reserve their most potent blessings for the most bloody awkward of women. I take it you and your mum are getting on like a house under artillery fire."

"Mhari Voller made a proposal. I rejected it. My mother was displeased. And, apparently, is chosen of the gods."

"We have a sudden surfeit of saints."

"I thought Aleena was the last." During the Crisis, the Church of the Keepers had only been able to muster a single war-saint, and while Saint Aleena of the Sacred Flame had worked miracles, it still marked a precipitous decline of the church's power.

"She was. Things have changed." Sinter shrugs. "The Crisis stirred up our friends upstairs. There've been miracles out in the hinterlands. Old village priests and strapping young farmboys getting blessed with sainthood. A good *harvest* this last year. Best I've known."

She imagines the gods fleeing Guerdon during the Crisis, bolting like animals attacked in their own stables. Running for the hills, looking for shelter. Looking for weapons. The gods blindly grabbing the most convenient mortal tool – and finding her mother. It's what Silva always wanted. "'To offer up the soul entire to the will of the divine'," quotes Eladora, "although I don't know how much choice anyone had in the matter."

"That," says the priest, grinning, "is fucking heresy. To imply that the gods are not all-wise and all-knowing. To suggest that saint-hood's a matter of bad luck and circumstance, like getting caught out on the moor by a sudden storm and getting hit by lightning – it's shameful. Didn't your mother teach you anything?" His greasy bon-homie is unpleasant, but it's less terrifying than her mother's wrath.

"Saint Aleena compared the Kept Gods to cows. She said they were like beautiful, dumb animals."

"Aye, well, she should have known, right. Although . . . " he swills his wine around, stares into the glass, "it's not that fucking *simple*, is it? They don't fucking know that. Everything's off balance."

"With the Kept Gods?" She wonders who *they* are.

"With everything." He picks up a fork and devours the remains of Mhari Voller's starter as he talks. "Here's how I see it. This city's like a big machine, right, an engine rattling along the tracks. If you keep it fuelled and oiled, bread and money and shit, and don't fuck with the levers too much, it'll run along nicely as long as the tracks stay safe. Sometimes, someone would step out of line – like your grandfather – and have to be put back in their place to make sure things kept running smoothly."

He snarls. "But people stepped out of line, and we weren't strong enough to knock 'em back– I mean mainly Rosha, but she wasn't the only fucker. Now everything's spinning out of control and we're all just hoping it doesn't fucking explode." He points a fork at Eladora. "Your man Kelkin knows. Everyone knows it. Look at them. No one wants to be stuck driving the engine when it's like this. You think the Crisis is over? This is the Crisis, still. Rosha pulled the big red lever, and no one knows how to stop it."

Eladora decides that she's tired of cynical old men telling her how the world works. "Tell me, Mr Sinter – are you here as a represent-ative of the Patros?" If Sinter's still working for the main church, and the Patros shares his views about the city careering towards disaster . . .

"I'm just hanging on, child. A humble servant, I." He picks up a napkin and goes to dab his face, picks some broken shards of mirror from the cloth instead. "Gods below."

Mhari Voller and Eladora's mother come back in, along with a swarm of waiters, who change the tablecloth so quickly one might suspect the use of sorcery. Broken crystal is cleared away, spilled food swept up, fresh cutlery conjured. One of the waiters scoops up a knife from the ground near Silva's chair; the handle's crushed, four dents matching Silva's fingers as they clenched it, and the blade's scorched as if held in a flame. Without breaking stride or changing expression, the waiter whisks it away with the rest of the mess. In a trice, the only signs of the divine intervention left are the damaged table and the unnoticed crack in the mirror.

"Your holiness! So glad you could extract yourself from affairs of state," says Voller to Sinter. She helps Silva lower herself into a chair. Silva's head lolls, her eyes unfocused. She's muttering to herself. Eladora wonders if her mother has had a stroke, and discovers that she has absolutely no desire to get any closer or provide any aid or comfort whatsoever. "We'll have no more exuberance," Voller proclaims gaily, patting Silva's hand.

Waiters whirl around again, bringing in the entrées. Sinter digs into his steak; Eladora shoves her fish around the plate. It's exquisite, but she can't stomach it.

"How much have you told her?" asks Sinter around a mouthful. He's nearly done already.

Eladora answers before the other two. "You want the impossible from my employer, and want me to convey your absurd r-request to him."

"In some respects," says Voller, "there is room for negotiation. If Kelkin wants to save face, for example, we can frame it as a coalition pact. But the gods cannot be denied."

"Fire shall destroy the blasphemers," adds Silva, "storms shall wash them away, and from the ashes, flowers shall grow." She hasn't even touched her food. She's staring at the floor, and Eladora has the horrible impression that her mother doesn't even know that she spoke. Eladora has seen creatures like elder ghouls use human mouthpieces before.

"And campaigns change." Sinter wipes his lips with his sleeve. "I like Kelkin, really I do. Honestly, he runs the city better than whatever pious yokel our lot would put in charge. But he needs to come back to us, not fight us. He hasn't seen half of what the church will bring to the field, if we have to."

Eladora's had enough of this ambush. She pushes back her chair and rises. "Rest assured I shall give a full accounting of this meal to Mr Kelkin — threats and all."

Mhari Voller slumps back as if defeated and takes a large gulp of her wine. Silva Duttin doesn't move or react as her daughter leaves.

"Good night, Mother, Lady Voller. Thank you for the . . ." Eladora waves vaguely at three largely untouched plates, "wine."

Sinter hurries out after her. "I'll see you to the station."

"This is Serran, not the Wash. It's not necessary."

"You never know," mutters Sinter.

"The last time you offered me protection, I ended up kidnapped and lying on a sacrificial altar before the night was through." Eladora plucks her coat off a hook, ignoring the horrified expression of the footman who was about to fetch it for her. She knows she shouldn't speak about the events of the Crisis openly, but if her mother — her sainted mother — is throwing around minor miracles over dinner, then apparently the seals of secrecy have been broken.

"Fair enough," says Sinter, "but let me offer it again. Like I said, you don't know what's coming. When all seems lost, look to the gods for aid."

He presses an object into her hand and vanishes back into the private dining room.

As she walks towards the train station, she examines Sinter's gift. It's a fragment of burned metal. The hilt of a broken sword, she realises, blasted by fire, pitted by sorcery, stained by the ichor of a million dead worms. A piece, a relic, of Saint Aleena of the Sacred Flame. She remembers Aleena saving her from Jermas Thay's clutches, remembers the blessed fire. Imagines, for a moment,

Aleena's rough hand holding the sword hilt. Eladora only knew Aleena briefly, but cherishes the memory of her stalwart presence, her unnerving, unyielding determination. Her knack for thumping evil things with a fiery sword.

She tries to think why Sinter would give her such a valuable relic, but her head just spins in circles. A message? A gift? A threat, reminding her of the power of the Kept Gods? A clue about his intentions?

"Fucking fuckers are trying to fuck us," whispers Eladora, recalling Aleena's most heartfelt prayer.

CHAPTER 12

When the train reaches the border, Guerdon city watch sweep through the carriage, inspecting papers and souls. One of them, her face hidden behind a mask of whirring lenses, stands over Terevant as he digs out the travel documents Lys gave him. The woman flips through the papers, then calls over her supervisor. The second guard examines the papers again, cross-referencing them against their own lists.

"You were supposed to be on yesterday's train."

"We stopped at Grena, and I went to stretch my legs. The train left without me, so I caught this one."

"You're travelling alone?"

"Just me."

They search his baggage anyway. Terevant sits there, trying to keep his knee from jiggling. In a few hours, he'll be walking the fabled streets of Guerdon again; the arcades off Mercy Street, the great fortress at Queen's Point, the Barbed Palace, Holyhill . . .

It is strange, this combination of apprehension and excitement. He thinks back to the landing on Eskalind. Then, he'd trained for the task, rehearsed it over and over. Led his troops off the boat and up beaches along Shipbreak Strand a hundred times, so the landing on Eskalind was ultimately an anticlimax, the same dull routine again. Until the gods struck. Guerdon promises a different form of action, and he's eager for it. He's spent too long knocking about the Erevesic mansion, sitting at his father's interminable deathbed, or writing endless reports about Eskalind. Six months of preparation before, six months of dissection afterwards, for sixty minutes of action.

The guards move on, and he exhales. He's tired of waiting. He has a mission again, a way to serve the Crown. A place in Haith. No longer a poet, no longer quite a soldier. Another life before death.

Slowly at first, the train moves on, too, gathering speed as it rushes down the rails towards Guerdon. A tunnel swallows them. Terevant packs up his bags in the dancing lamplight. He wonders what the inspectors would have done if he'd had the Erevesic sword. They must some sort of supernatural backup, he guesses, a sorcerer or something at least. The Guerdon/Haithi border is possibly the last frontier in the world where divine wrath is a likely prospect, but surely they don't leave this flank unguarded? Out through the little viewing port, he saw new fortifications, towers and tunnels and spiked walls facing north. At the station, he passes through a maze of little offices, a clerk hiding in each one. Like birds in a crumbling wall, he thinks, nests feathered with papers. There were sea-cliffs off Eskalind, where tens of thousands of seabirds nested. When Cloud Mother descended, the birds had risen up as one, wheeling round until the whole flock took on the shape of a woman, a giant made of wings. Hands made of a hundred ripping beaks. The clerks snatch his papers, check the details, but they don't bite. They hand back his documents, point him towards the exit.

He walks away from the clerks, and for the first time in months he doesn't hunch his shoulders against the shrieking of the gulls. He walks across the marble floor of the concourse with military discipline, heels clicking against the stone.

And so he enters into Guerdon.

Night has fallen over the city, and alchemical lanterns blaze in rows along the streets, while a radiance like frozen moonlight shines from the great bulk of the New City down by the harbour. The streets are crowded even after dark, and everyone in the crowd is alive, full of heat and noise. Overwhelming, compared to the cool quiet of Old Haith. The crowd feels like it's a heartbeat away from becoming a mob – or a street party. He smiles despite himself.

They're like children at play, blessed in their innocence. None of them, he guesses, have ever seen the Godswar. They press leaflets into Terevant's hands, offering him anything from the pleasures of the flesh to a cheap hotel to eternal joy in the Dancer's embrace to something about a vote for Kelkin being a vote for stability.

Across the square comes a figure in a Haithi uniform, the mole-skin hat cutting through the crowd like a shark's fin. To his surprise, the soldier's wearing a mask and heavy gloves. He must be Vigilant, one of few in the city. Most of the embassy staff in Guerdon are living. There are long-standing restrictions on the numbers and movements of the Vigilant in the city – a legacy of old rivalries and old suspicions. Haith has meddled in the affairs of Guerdon many times before. City watch guards glare at the Vigilant as he crosses to greet Terevant.

Welcome to Guerdon, sir.

"I'm – uh, yes. Thank you." Terevant salutes awkwardly around his kitbag.

You don't recognise me, do you, sir?

This strikes Terevant as an odd question as the Vigilant's face is hidden, and wouldn't tell him much anyway – one skull is much like another. Terevant tries to make out the family sigil on the soldier's chest, but it's too dark.

Yoras, sir. I was with the Ninth Rifles at Eskalind.

He remembers Yoras as a new recruit, as green as the seawater he puked into at Shipbreak Strand. By the time they set out for Eskalind, though, he'd been as well trained and ready as any soldier in that invasion force.

He remembers Yoras dying, too. A scaly thing that crawled out of the sea – a god-birthed monster, a far-gone saint, who knows? It had claws, though, and rifle shots bounced off its hide like rain-drops. He remembers Yoras stabbing it through the mouth even as it disembowelled him. Terevant hadn't looked back – the temple was within sight, and he'd urged his troops onwards.

"Of course, Yoras."

I didn't get a chance to thank you, sir. You saved my life.

Terevant coughs to hide his involuntary laugh.

In the retreat, sir. We were surrounded by enemy troops, and your company came at them from the flank. Cut us a way out, sir. They had holy relics, sir, that we could not abide in undeath.

That, he can't remember. The retreat is a blur in his memory "Have you been assigned down here long?"

Best part of five months, sir. Half the embassy guards got killed in the Crisis, so they needed replacements. An honour to guard so distinguished a hero as your brother, of course. I didn't know you came of such a family, sir.

Yoras leads him to a waiting carriage.

We'll be a few moments getting out of here, sir. There was a big Hawker meeting in the hotel across the square tonight, so there's a lot of traffic. I don't hold with it myself. The election, that. Seems unreliable, like building on sand. Haith has had the same ruler for more than a thousand years. The Crown, forged of steel and magic, is eternal. The wearer of the Crown changes – when one dies, a successor is chosen by the necromancers – but the collective intellect in the Crown, the braided souls of all previous rulers of Haith, continues to rule, now and forever.

"It seems exciting, though."

Secretary Vanth thought so too, sir. Yoras opens the door for him.

Waiting inside the carriage is another man. Sprawled against the seats, longish dirty-blond hair, high cheekbones, thin and bloodless, like he's been bleached of colour. He wears a battered army jacket without insignia. Three fresh scratches on one cheek, parallel lines like he's been raked. The man doesn't rise to help Terevant on board, he just waves a hand in a vague greeting.

Terevant involuntarily checks the man's wrists for implant marks – nothing. Supplicant-caste? Or undercover – deliberately risking dying out-caste in order to hide anything that might tie him to Haith. Lys took the same risk, earlier in her career. Or perhaps he's not even Haithi at all. "And who are you?"

"Lemuel," says the man, and adds nothing more. His accent is all Guerdon. His own gaze travels languidly over Terevant, sizing him up. Then he smirks, and there's something knowing about it, like he's making Terevant the butt of some unspoken joke.

Terevant settles in the seat opposite. "Where's my brother?"

"His Excellency is at the embassy. Things are a little . . . fraught, what with the election and all."

"Fraught" was how Lys had described the situation in Guerdon. And while his Excellency is technically the proper honorific for an ambassador, it's also a mocking nickname that Terevant and Lys sometimes used for Olthic. An old joke based on a school report, when Olthic was rated "excellent" by every tutor. Terevant finds he resents this stranger being part of their private joke. Unless . . . he has to think like a spy now, look for hidden messages. Maybe Lys is sending him a signal, telling him that this Lemuel is part of their circle, that he can be trusted despite appearances.

"Fraught," he echoes. "Who are you at the embassy?"

"Oh, I help out where I'm needed," says Lemuel airily.

"Which Office?"

"None of them," says Lemuel, and smirks again.

Terevant nods at the man's cheek. "What happened?"

"Trouble with a girl." Terevant imagines long nails clawing at the man's face. Lemuel rubs his scratched cheek gingerly. "They gave you a folder in Haith, right?"

Terevant digs the folder out of his kitbag. Lemuel reaches up and pinches his cheek, squeezes the deepest scratch until a little droplet of blood wells up, then smears the blood on the wax seal of the folder, disarming the magical ward. He starts reading through the documents in silence, using the streetlamps they pass for light. Alternating bands of light and darkness cast Lemuel in different shades, catching the bones of his lean, wolfish face. Lemuel's lips curl in amusement as he reads some tidbit or aside in the Bureau folder, but he doesn't share his insight with Terevant.

Terevant decides he doesn't like the man very much, in any light.

*

The gates of the embassy swing wide to receive them. Somehow, Terevant can tell he's back on Haithi soil. It's colder, quieter. The servants in the yard – all living, he notes – hurry over to take charge of the snarling raptequine, but they don't run, don't raise their voices.

Lemuel vanishes so quietly that Terevant only notices his absence. He has taken the folder with him.

This way, sir. Yoras escorts Terevant through a doorway. As soon as he's across the threshold, Yoras removes his mask and strips off his gloves. There are runes burned into the bones of his wrists, the patterns matching the periapt implants beneath Terevant's own skin. Spiritual anchors to keep soul and bodily remains together.

The embassy is silent apart from the shuffling of papers.

I'll show you to the ambassador.

They stop outside a pair of ornate double doors, marked with the family crest of the Erevesics. The ambassador's study. Terevant can't help but note the freshly painted bar above the crest, signifying that the presence of *the* Erevesic, the head of the family and bearer of the phylactery.

Yoras takes Terevant's kitbag. **I'll stow this in your room, sir.** He pads silently down the corridor, leaving Terevant alone on the threshold. He raises his hand to knock, then thinks better of it and just pushes the door open.

Olthic rises from a stuffed armchair beside the fire, drops the book he was reading, and strides across the room. "Ter!" he booms.

Terevant salutes. "Lieutenant Terevant Erevesic, transferred from the Ninth Rifles, reporting."

"Welcome to the comfortable side of the war!" Olthic returns the salute, shuts and locks the heavy door, and gestures to the other chair by the fire. He rings a bell by the desk and slaps his belly as he sits down. "Come in. Sit down. Eat. The food's good here. You'll like it better than the front lines." Olthic's still in fighting trim – of course. Too disciplined to let himself indulge, despite this diplomatic post. "I've missed you, Ter. What news from home? How was your journey?"

"Lys said—"

"You'll have to remember to call her Lady Erevesic in public. She's the ambassador's wife, and we can't be informal."

"Lys told me—"

"But first." Olthic looks around eagerly. "Where is it? The sword?"

"It's with Lys. She's smuggling it across the border, hidden in her carriage."

Olthic doesn't reply for several long moments. His breathing is so loud that Terevant swears the flames in the grate dance back and forth in time to his inhalations.

"You left the Erevesic sword – the enshrined souls of our ancestors, the foundation of our house, seventeenth of the treasures of Haith – behind?" He doesn't shout, but Terevant can tell he's furious.

"What else was I supposed to do?" Annoyed, Terevant flings himself into the chair opposite his brother. "The Lady Erevesic said it was dangerous to bring it in to the city. I assumed you'd discussed the care of the family sword – the enshrined souls of our ancestors, the foundation of our house, seventeenth of the treasures – with your wife."

There's a knock at the locked door, the smell of food. "Go away," shouts Olthic, and he hurls his book at the door for good measure.

"Don't blame the servants."

"Oh, I don't. I blame you. And her. That is my sword. I am the Erevesic." Olthic paces.

"She said it would be noticed, but that she'd smuggle it in later, or one of us would go and fetch it in a few weeks—"

Olthic snarls, springs across the room, tries to yank open the door. It's locked, but he pulls it with such strength that the heavy door nearly cracks. "Get out. Get out," he snaps, turning the key. "Get out before I do something unwise. Weeks. Bloody weeks."

This reunion is going marvellously. "My orders are to review the guards."

"So you can lead them into an ambush? I read the reports from Eskalind. I saved you from a court martial." He flings the door open. "Get out."

Terevant steps into the corridor. "Always a pleasure, your Excellency."

"Daerinth!" roars Olthic. Another door across the corridor opens instantly – this Daerinth must have been waiting for the call. He's old enough to be Terevant's grandfather, but he shuffles across to Olthic's office with remarkable speed. Instinctively, Terevant's gaze flickers over the old man's robes. A house sigil he doesn't recognise, with some obscure curlicues whose meaning he can't recall. Lys was always the best of them at studying the books of heraldry, at recalling the honoured dead.

The door slams in Terevant's face. Muffled conversation from the far side.

Yoras steps out of the shadows, holding a tray of food. His skeletal face is, of course, unreadable.

Your room is this way, sir. He gestures down the corridor with his free hand. Terevant and Yoras instinctively fall into lockstep, the cadence of their march drilled into both of them at Shipbreak Strand.

Symbols of past diplomats and their great deeds loom down from the walls, reminding Terevant of his failure to find a place in the great order of Haith. Every step takes him away from his brother, away from what remains of his family – away from the wreckage of his career. Where next? He could refuse the assignment to the embassy. He might be able to accept a demotion and get back to the lines, give his life and death to the Empire on some distant battlefield. End up like Yoras, here, a skeleton endlessly patrolling some outpost of the faltering Empire.

For a moment, he imagines Haith's fall. Imagines the palace of the Crown and the Bureau in ruins, the temples of death fallen. All empty, no sound except the click of skeletal heels on marble, as the last Vigilant patrol the tombs forever. *There's no shame in being Supplicant*, he'd told his father. The usual platitudes one says to the dying, without believing them yourself for an instant.

Behind him, the door to Olthic's study opens again.

"Terevant! Come here!" shouts Olthic.

Yoras stops, inclines his skull quizzically. Terevant waits a fraction of a second, a little personal rebellion, before turning on his heel and marching back. Olthic waits at the door.

"Terevant Erevesic," says Olthic, formally, "by will of the Crown, you are appointed captain of the embassy garrison at Guerdon, with all the responsibilities and duties of that role. Do you accept?"

"I—" A thousand objections. He's not a diplomat, or a spy. He's not even vaguely qualified. He doesn't want to stay in Guerdon, with Olthic raging at him. Being around Lys and Olthic will be like putting his emotions into the teeth of some grinding engine. A thousand reasons to say no.

"Do you accept, damn you?"

Only one reason to say yes. It's his duty to obey, and he's done with running from duty.

"Yes."

Olthic gestures into the study. The old man's at the desk, hastily filling out some forms. "Sign there." Olthic sighs. "Your job is to command the embassy guards and protect the embassy grounds and staff. March them up and down, keep the living out of the worst of the whorehouses, don't get obviously drunk on duty. That's it."

"And Edoric Vanth? Lys said—" Terevant stops, corrects himself. "The Lady Erevesic said I should look into it."

Olthic scowls. "Lemuel's handling it."

"Your grace, it would be better to have Lieutenant Erevesic, ah, oversee the inquiry. More proper to have an officer of a great House involved. Lemuel can assist, if it proves necessary." Daerinth's voice is like the rustling of paper; as if the effort of speaking exhausts him. Still, he manages to smile weakly at Terevant.

Olthic bristles for a moment, then stalks away across the room, picks up the book he flung, smoothes out the pages and slams it back onto the shelf. "Fine."

Daerinth takes the signed letter, folds it neatly, slips it into Olthic's desk drawer. "That will be all, lieutenant," whispers the old diplomat. "It will be good to have you here at the embassy."

Yoras is waiting outside. It's impossible for a skeleton to raise its

eyebrows in surprise, but something about the inclination of Yoras'
skull suggests exactly that.

Your quarters are this way, sir.

"And my office?" He's tired after the journey, but eager to get
started. His task is important, vitally important, to the security of
Haith. Lys is depending on him.

Yoras pauses. **I'm afraid I haven't been told where to
put you, sir.**

"Well, Vanth's office is free, isn't it?"

Quite so, sir. This way. Yoras leads him down another corridor.
The Vigilant sorts through a bundle of keys as he walks, looking for
the right one for the office of the Third Secretary. **It's been locked
since he left, sir.** He finds the key, unclips it from the ring, and
hands it to Terevant. **Your bedroom's right above this office, sir,
two levels up. Do you want me to wait and show you up when
you're finished, or ...**

"No, you can go. We'll discuss the embassy guard in the morning."

All the same to me, sir. I don't sleep any more.

They come to a stop outside the office. A band of light shines from
under the door. Terevant tests the handle. It's unlocked.

Sir? Yoras lays a bony hand on the hilt of his sword.

Terevant pushes the door open. Lemuel looks up at him from
behind a messy desk, strewn with papers. "That was a quick reunion," he mutters. "Figured you'd have more to say to his Excellency."

You should not be in here, vagabond.

"What are you doing in here, Lemuel?" asks Terevant.

"Just looking for some papers. They're not here." Lemuel springs
up. "You're welcome to it." He hurries to the door, tries to push
past Terevant.

Terevant grabs the wiry man by the arm. "You're supposed to
assist me. Where are you going?"

"Out." Lemuel twists free. "I've got contacts to meet. Got to
go alone."

"All right." Terevant gestures to Vanth's files. "Where should I
start, then?"

"Bureau training, ten fucking years ago," mutters Lemuel. "I don't know. Vanth never talked to me. I wasn't one of his little club." A clock in the office behind him chimes, and Lemuel winces. "I'm late." He hurries off down the corridor.

Yoras makes a sound that might approximate a throat-clearing cough, if he had a throat to clear.

"Something to say, Yoras?"

Lemuel is a disagreeable and base creature, by all accounts. I would not rely on him, sir.

Terevant enters the office. Pages of scribbled notes, maps, diagrams litter the desk. Thick folders of typed documents, too. A wine glass and the remains of a plate of food left balanced atop one pile.

"What did he mean about Vanth's club?"

The Third Secretary and many of the permanent staff have worked under the First Secretary for several years. They are all Haithi. Lemuel may work for Haith, but he . . . Yoras inclines his head. **He's very mortal, sir. I don't know what use the Lady Erevesic finds in him.**

"I see," says Terevant. He picks up the plate of food, the wine glass, puts them on a side table. "Well, you may go."

I'll stay on watch, sir. Just in case.

Yoras closes the door, leaving Terevant alone in the office.

The chaos of the room – and the wine glass – remind Terevant of his own rooms in Paravos, and the thought cheers him.

Olthic, he thinks, will be easier to deal with in the morning. In a few days' time, they'll fetch the sword back from Lys, and all will be well again.

He works for a while, sifting through documents, looking for any mention of the god bombs or a clue to where Vanth might be, but something distracts him. The noise from the city outside, maybe. Old Haith's quiet as a tomb, and, before that, he was used to the silence of the Erevesic mansion, the stillness of the night broken only by his father's coughing in the next room and the hooting of the owls in the east tower. Guerdon never sleeps. Trains rumble by underground; there's shouting and singing from distant taverns, the clatter of carriage wheels on cobblestones.

He crosses to the little window, stares out across the nighted city. From here, he can look down. In the distance, beyond the dark outline of Castle Hill, he can see the weird shape of the New City, glowing with its own light. An alien cityscape, like some baroque moon had crashed into Guerdon. Half of Vanth's notes are reports about the New City – mapping it, establishing networks of informants on its streets, ferreting out its secrets. The New City's said to be dangerous – maybe Vanth went there, disappeared there. There are reports in his archives about the streets shifting, archways snapping shut like monstrous jaws.

But, no, it's not the distant city. It's something closer at hand. His gaze is drawn across the street, to the shapes on the roof of the Ishmeric embassy. Statues of gods, shapes out of his nightmares. Blessed Bol and Cloud Mother. High Umur, his bull horns glimmering in the moonlight.

And, there, hunched as if about to pounce, the savage Lion Queen. The bringer of war. If she brings the Godswar to Old Haith . . . the long, long lines of the ancient Houses, the eternal Bureau, the divine Crown have all endured for centuries, and now they might all be destroyed before the end of the war. The last stand of the Empire of Haith, brought down by fire and storm and savage divinity.

Sometimes, he imagines that it's him and Olthic and Lys, standing side by side against the gods.

And sometimes, in his private dreams, it's just him and Lys, and he has the sword.

CHAPTER 13

E ven before her cousin's miracle, Eladora knew the city was alive.
Guerdon shambles on from age to age, incorporating its scars
and eating its scabs, surviving as best it can. Eladora waits with
the rest of the crowd gathered outside the House of Law, with the
reporters and doomsayers, and the runners who'll sprint down to
the speculators in Venture Square when the verdict's announced.
The mob presses in on her, adding to the uncomfortable heat of the
morning. Someone jostles her, sending a shock of pain through her
side – the wounds she suffered during the Crisis have never fully
healed. She lets the crowd push her away from the House of Law,
finds a doorway where she can wait in peace. The lintel over her
refuge is soot-stained; a legacy of the Tallowmen that once stood
guard here, before everything changed.

A gutter-press reporter stalks through the throng, notebook
in hand, looking for vulnerable aides like herself. Eladora presses
herself into the doorway to avoid being seen. She doesn't have the
verbal agility needed to fend off questions; she's cursed with academic honesty. If they ask her about this court case, she'll answer
honestly. By law, anyone who can claim a 'hearthstone or gravestone'
in Guerdon has a vote. This universal suffrage was one of Kelkin's
triumphs; under the previous rules, the franchise was determined
by attendance at the churches of the Keepers. But the law was not
written to account for miraculous eruptions of architecture, and it's
possible that, legally, the New City doesn't count as part of Guerdon.
If the judges rule against Kelkin, the Industrial Liberals will lose

the election. Someone more adept at handling the press, like Abver, might be able to bluster and spin, but not Eladora.

Fortunately, the reporter spots Perik in the crowd, and Perik's only too happy to give a quote. He flushes red as he shouts to be heard over the noise of the mob, and she catches fragments of his response. He's talking about security, about the need to elect more Hawkers in order to protect Guerdon. He gestures up at the remains of the House of Law to underline his point. The House of Law was Guerdon's chief courthouse and city archive, until a bomb destroyed the bell tower and set fire to the archives.

Eladora knows that the bomb was planted by agents of the alchemists' guild, the Hawkers' own patrons. She knows that the bell tower of the House of Law was once the prison for a slumbering Black Iron God, and that the alchemists plotted to reforge the monstrous deity into a god bomb. She knows so much she dare not speak. Perik, unencumbered by secret knowledge – or any knowledge at all – produces a fluid, burbling stream of half truths and slogans.

Firefighters managed to save parts of the House of Law, and now the city has adapted. What remains of the archive now extends into the warren of lawyers' chambers and clerks' cubbyholes in neighbouring buildings, with salvaged court records stacked in precarious piles in every available corridor. The court itself was at the far end of the quadrangle from the explosion, so it survived, but the chambers of the Lords Justice and Mercy were destroyed. The judges have taken over a nearby inn as their sanctum, and Eladora suspects this "temporary" arrangement will persist for centuries. Neither is especially convenient to the functioning of the court, but they work, and so the city continues.

It reassures her. Whatever happens, Guerdon will muddle through. Kelkin will step in and find a way forward.

The doors of the court open. The crowd presses forward, then gets pushed back by city watchmen. In the crush, Perik's separated from his reporter. He shouts one last quote, waving his arms like a drowning man sinking into a sea of flesh.

The Lords Justice and Mercy, sweating beneath their ceremonial masks, troop across the grass of the quad in the direction of their inn. Behind them, the courtroom spills out lawyers, petitioners, scribes and gawkers in great profusion. The House of Law was full to bursting. Eladora can't see Kelkin, but he must be in the centre of that tide.

The crowd parts, and a massive monster pads towards her. Stinking of the grave, his horned head, with its face like a skinned horse, would be eight feet above Eladora's if he wasn't hunched over. The King of the Ghouls, the Great Rat of Guerdon. Hurrying along by his side is his spokesman and clerk, a young man carrying a bundle of papers.

The glowing yellow eyes spot Eladora. The ghoul's mind brushes against hers, and it's the feeling of someone walking on your grave. Rat stops, and the crowd pouring out of the courthouse flows around him as if he were a boulder in a river. The clerk massages his throat and looks as though he's about to faint for an instant, then speaks – elder ghouls find human speech unpleasant, but can force others to speak for them. She recalls the hideous sensation herself and wonders if the mental discipline Ramegos taught her would be enough to block Rat's commands, but the ghoul is polite enough to restrict himself to his designated spokesman.

"MISS DUTTIN. GOOD AFTERNOON."

She owes Rat her life; the ghoul carried her out of the tomb. The city owes the ghouls; there are rumours of a secret war fought beneath the streets between the ghouls and the Crawling Ones. Jermas Thay's true kin, thinks Eladora – sorcerous demon-worshipping worms, not her.

"Lord Rat." She bows her head, hoping he doesn't see her press her nose to a scented handkerchief, knowing he doesn't care. "I take it you triumphed in court."

"KELKIN DID. THE REFORM ACT HOLDS. THE NEW CITY CAN VOTE."

"And so can the undercity," she points out. Rat shrugs his shoulders, and flakes of mould cascade down his mountainous flanks.

"KELKIN SHALL HAVE MY SUPPORT IF HE LISTENS,

AND IF MY KIN ARE FED." He bares his teeth at that, sharp and yellow-brown, each tooth as long as one of Eladora's fingers.

Abruptly, he sniffs the air near her face, tasting her breath. Yellow eyes narrow, and again comes the psychic grave-tread, only this time it's more intense, the sensation of digging, of claws ripping at the surface of her mind. She steps back and draws on her rudimentary skills of sorcery to put up a mental barrier as Ramegos taught her. She senses the elder ghoul could push past it without effort, but it stops him. He tilts his monstrous head.

"YOU SMELL OF DIVINITY." The elder ghoul is a sort of necrotic demigod; during the Crisis, Rat was able to hunt down Carillon and tried to kill her because of her connection to the Black Iron Gods. At first, she panics – what can he smell on her? In the tomb, under Jermas' spells, she was a sort of proxy saint for Carillon, and she's had nightmares about the ghoul crawling in through her window, about those claws slashing her throat, those teeth ripping at her dead flesh. Then she realises that it must be smelling the lingering magic of her mother's presence.

The thought of her mother being eaten by a hulking monster from the underworld is not an unfamiliar one to Eladora, but it's unworthy of her. She pushes it away.

"I'm looking for Mr Kelkin. Where is he?"

The ghoul laughs, and the crowd parts again, abruptly, as everyone on one side of Eladora takes one step towards Castle Hill and everyone on the other takes one step in the opposite direction, down towards the New City. All psychically shoved by the elder ghoul, clearing a straight path between Eladora and Kelkin.

The crowd goes quiet for an instant, the silence broken only by the chuckling of the ghoul.

Cheeks burning, Eladora hurries down the path cleared for her. Kelkin watches with bemusement as she approaches, then sees the ghoul and scowls.

"Bloody idiot," he snaps, and she hopes Kelkin means Rat and not her. The old man's temper is legendary. He grabs her roughly by the forearm and leans on her. "The Vulcan," he barks, like she's a cabbie.

It's only a short walk down to Venture Square, but he's breathing heavily by the time they arrive at the coffee shop. In the junior ranks of the Industrial Liberal staff, Kelkin's health is the subject of endless speculation. Usually, his energy is boundless, but though he snaps orders at various passing aides as he and Eladora cross the square, she can feel him wince as he limps, and he sits down heavily in his armchair when they get to the backroom.

"Unanimous," he crows, "without so much as a half-penny bribe. That's good lawyering. What the devil do you want? What's the point of me ensuring that every beggar in the New City can vote if you're not up there telling 'em to vote for ME?"

"I'm ... well, that is, we ..." Eladora's thoughts swirl and her words trip over one another.

"Bah? Is it Spyke? He was complaining about you, too. If you can't work together, I'll pair you with someone else. Here." He grabs a sheet of paper from his overburdened desk, glances at it, hands it to her. A few names are underlined. "These ones are working the New City. Talk to them, see if they're more suitable. Just get it done."

"It's not about the New City. It's about my m—about the church."

"The Keepers. What?" She has Kelkin's full attention now.

"I, ah, met my mother for dinner. Mhari Voller was there, too." Kelkin's eye twitches at the mention of her name, but he doesn't interrupt. "And ... I don't know if you know him, but—"

"Sinter," he snaps. "Quickly now."

"Voller hinted ... more than hinted, really, that she was rejoining the Keeper party. They proposed a coalition, a p-pact. They even talked about you returning to the fold."

"And in return, a ban on foreign faiths."

"I think so. They want to meet with you."

Kelkin snorts. "Do they have the backing of the Patros?" he asks.

Eladora shrugs. "I don't know. I asked Sinter that, but—"

"Ach, it doesn't matter what Sinter says. I've never known a more faithless man. The bastard should have found his calling as a book-maker on the race-track, not a priest."

Now that Kelkin points it out, Eladora can see the resemblance.

Sinter, with a stable of hobbled gods and bridled saints. *He wanted to run me,* Aleena said of him once.

"On a related matter, what do you think of this?" Kelkin hands her another document. This one is fine parchment that glimmers with its own internal radiance, ornamented calligraphy and heavy with wax seals. From the hand of the Patros himself. Eladora skims it. It's a notification that the Keepers are shutting down the corpse shafts underneath their churches. For centuries, there's been a secret bargain between the Keepers and the carrion-eating ghouls of the city. The Keepers gave the ghouls most of the dead, and in exchange the ghouls kept watch over the subterranean prison holding the monstrous servitors of the Black Iron Gods.

During the Crisis, those servitors escaped and were destroyed by the Gutter Miracle. There's no need for the bargain now – but paying off the ghouls was only part of the arrangement.

"What . . . what will they do with the dead instead of giving them to the ghouls?" she asks.

Kelkin raps his stick on the table. "Exactly! The city's gods are weak because the church starves 'em of soul-stuff. If they go back to the old rites, if they give them the residuum of all the faithful dead, then soon the gods start getting *notions* about their divinity! How long before Guerdon turns into Ulbishe or Ishmere?"

"At the dinner last night, my mother demonstrated . . . spiritual gifts."

Kelkin lowers his voice, and there's a note of uncertainty in it that she's heard before only once. "All right. This needs looking into. I'll send for you when I need you. Right now, get back to work."

"What should I tell my m-m . . . ah, Lady Voller?"

"Nothing yet. If they contact you again, say you talked to me, that's all. I don't know if this is just Voller and a few Safidist lunatics, or if the Patros supports this play." He pokes the fire burning in the grate, even though it's a warm day outside, and stares into the flames.

Even though Eladora has to venture through dark and perilous streets alone, she does not miss Absalom Spyke's punishing pace or his abrasive company. She's able to walk as she pleases, making her way down by degrees into the Wash. The summer heat drives away the shadows, but conjures up an incredible stink; effluent and dung and alchemical runoff combining in a witches' brew. The streets are mostly deserted in the afternoon heat.

She looks at Kelkin's list of volunteers again. One name on it she's seen before, in a very different context. During the secret inquest after the Crisis, everyone who'd associated with Carillon and the other key figures was investigated by the city watch's saint-hunters. Eladora recalls an endless parade of names, some of which she knew, and others that meant nothing to her. Spar, Rat, Heinreil, Rosha, Aleena, Sinter, and other names she's locked away and doesn't think about.

One of Carillon's tangential associates was a ghoul named Silkpurse.

Elabora has an idea, but it's not one she's willing to acknowledge yet. It scuttles through the back of her mind, an unwelcome visitor. She tries to squash it, but it's tough. She tries to lock it away in the same place she keeps all those other things she doesn't like to think about, but it's got its hooks into her and won't be relegated to the category of things from her past life. It's a grubby, unwholesome, poisonous idea, and she doesn't like it at all, but it won't go away.

Eladora picks her path, following sea breezes and open spaces where the air is less foul, until she finds a door off Lambs Square with the symbol of the Industrial Liberals painted on it. The door is unlocked and inside the hall is dark and mercifully cool. She climbs a short stairway that leads to a large hall. There are painted sets stacked against one wall, and stained curtains hang down over a small stage. A bar, closed at this hour. A row of trestle tables, mostly empty, although there are a few stacks of election posters that should, ideally, be pasted on walls across the Wash. There should be a throng of volunteers here, too, but the place is deserted apart from a pair of old women.

"I'm Eladora Duttin," she introduces herself, "I'm looking for Silkpurse."

One of the women ignores her and ostentatiously neatens a stack of leaflets. The other points with a knitting needle towards a door at the side of the stage.

"Thank you."

The door leads to a row of dressing rooms. All open, apart from one. Eladora knocks.

"Please, come in," says a voice both sing-song and guttural, like a lost child calling from deep underground. Silkpurse is the strangest ghoul Eladora has seen; her face hidden by a veil, her claws carefully trimmed, her dress spotless instead of the rags and stolen burial shrouds most ghouls wear when they bother with clothes at all.

"I'm El——" begins Eladora, but Silkpurse interrupts her. "Eladora Duttin! Hello! I saw you talking to Lord Rat earlier. I was listening from under the courthouse. Such a blessed day. Of course, I didn't think they'd defy Mr Kelkin, but it's nice to have it all proper and legal-like – but where are my manners? Can I get you something to eat?"

"Um, no, thank you," says Eladora. Ghouls are known for eating carrion, preferably corpses rich in residuum, in lingering spiritual energy.

"It's surface food!" crows Silkpurse, producing a biscuit tin. Eladora refuses. Her stomach is still roiling from the smell outside – and from the overbearing perfume in Silkpurse's room. "What can I do for you, miss?" asks the ghoul.

"Mr Kelkin's asked me to work on the campaign in the New City. I was dealing with Absalom Spyke, but I'm not sure if he and I are quite the right fit. You were recommended by Mr Kelkin." In fact, Eladora has no idea who prepared that list of campaign volunteers working on the New City wards, but the praise makes Silkpurse preen and clap. "I'd like you to show me around the wards you've been canvassing."

"Oh, I'd be delighted." Silkpurse leads Eladora out of the hall and back onto the streets. "Come on, we've a few stops to make here in the Wash, and then it's up to the New City."

The ghoul's energy is irrepressible. As they walk, Silkpurse frequently lingers to stick up a poster or rip down a City Forward banner, then races to catch up with Eladora, or bounces ahead to proselytise at some passer-by, shouting that a vote for the IndLibs is a vote for Guerdon's future. Prosperity preserved, all ills put right.

Back at university, one of Eladora's friends – a wealthy girl named Lucil – had a puppy, and Silkpurse reminds her of that enthusiastic little animal. That puppy vanished a few weeks after Eladora moved into Professor Ongent's house on Desiderata Street.

Now that she thinks about it, Miren disliked the animal. It always snapped and growled at him. Now that she thinks about it, she can explain the animal's disappearance all too easily.

She forces herself to focus on Silkpurse's constant chattering. The ghoul's anecdotes roughly match Eladora's own studies of the New City's population – around half the residents come from Guerdon and the countryside, and the rest fled the Godswar, in search of the fabled neutral, godless city. Eladora's interested in the latter group. She needs to know how these newcomers will vote. When she explains this to Silkpurse, the ghoul nods enthusiastically.

"Oh! Oh, you should talk to Alic. He's new. He'll help. This way!"

Silkpurse leads her to a large, semi-derelict building in the lower Wash. The bells of Saint Storm ring from the nearby church. The notes are different from what they used to be; they've replaced the bells since the Crisis. Silkpurse scurries into a side door, leaving Eladora to wander around the small vegetable garden in the courtyard.

Faces look down at her from windows on the upper floors. She smiles up at them but when she looks closer the faces vanish.

A older woman emerges from a different door to the one Silkpurse used. A Keeper priestess, by her robes, but she isn't wearing the ceremonial keys. One of her hands is monstrously warped, like the claw of a dragon. "I am Jaleh," she says, "and this is my house. You don't look like you're in need of refuge." The woman stares at Eladora for a moment, muttering a soft prayer under her breath, and Eladora feels the inkling of spiritual force brush past her. An invocation of some sort. "I might be mistaken," says Jaleh. "You have been the instrument of the gods before, I think."

"I'm just waiting for Silkpurse," says Eladora, uncomfortable under Jaleh's scrutiny. It disturbs her that even a brief contact with her mother could leave such a clear mark on her that both Rat and this priestess sense it instantly.

The older woman makes a dismissive gesture with her claw. "The gods know those who have walked on the other side. Those who have gone there, even briefly, are never the same. It is . . . easier to return to that place if you've been before, even if you take a different road." Jaleh looks at Eladora, clucks her tongue. "Have you got a guide, child? Have you taken precautions? It's better to choose a path and walk it knowingly than to wander blindly."

"I d-don't know what you mean." It's not entirely true – some of what Jaleh's saying makes sense. The gods use saints as their instruments in the physical world; points of congruency, as Professor Ongent once put it. Once one deity has created or discovered a point of connection between the realms, then presumably another god could make use of it. Eladora realises that she might be proof of that – her grandfather tried to make her a channel for the Black Iron Gods in that botched ritual under Gravehill, and she was able to contact the Kept Gods. She resolves to do some research on the topic, to talk to Ramegos. To fill her brain with information and certainty, and leave no place for fears to nest.

Jaleh stares at Eladora for another long moment, and mutters a prayer. Then she sighs, shakes her head, and says, "I'll send Alic out as soon as I find him." She withdraws inside the rambling sanctuary, leaving Eladora alone and uncomfortable. When she was a child, Eladora caught a fever and nearly died; she remembers her mother sitting by her bed for days, watching over her without actually seeing her. A pitiless determination, as though Eladora was just the terrain on which her mother's will contended with the fever. Jaleh's gaze had something of the same steel in it.

Before long, Silkpurse comes bouncing back, with a forgettable man in tow. Average looking, middle-aged, carrying a pile of rolled-up posters and a bucket of paste. His tan suggests he spent time somewhere sunnier than Guerdon. His voice is soft and surprisingly pleasant, though, and there's a glint of humour that she finds charming. He's a welcome distraction from her unwelcome thoughts. He's easy to trust − or would be, if she had trust to give. As it is, she smiles thinly and extends a hand. He tucks the posters under his arm and returns the handshake.

"This is Alic," says Silkpurse. "He's eager to help out, and he only arrived from Severast a few weeks ago, so I thought he'd be ideal for what you wanted. Alic, Eladora Duttin is one of Mr Kelkin's chief advisers, and she's a scholar and a great lady and—"

"I'm just looking for perspective on the New City," insists Eladora.

He grins. "I haven't been here long. I'm still learning the streets. But maybe I can offer fresh eyes at least."

"Thank you."

"Wait a moment," he says to her, then raises his voice. "Emlin!" A pale boy, rake-thin, emerges from the shadows of the house. He reminds Eladora of Miren, somehow.

Alic puts a fatherly hand on the boy's shoulder. "I have work to do, all right, important work. Can you take care of yourself here?"

The boy nods.

"And Aunt Annah wants to see you this evening for dinner. If I'm not back, can you find the way there?"

"I can."

"Holy Beggar, light your way." Alic hands his son a few coins, sends him on his way. A foolish smile on his face as he watches the boy run off.

Eladora leads the trio out of Jaleh's courtyard and down along the docks towards the edge of the New City.

"Let's start with Sevenshell Street," she says to Silkpurse.

"That's a nasty part of the New City. Some of our lads got attacked up there, canvassing," warns the ghoul, but she doesn't quibble. Instead, her demeanour changes: she drops lower to the ground, sometimes scurrying on all fours. She removes her gloves and flexes her sharp-clawed paws. She darts from shadow to shadow, growling at anyone who pays too much attention to the pair of humans walking behind her.

For her part, Eladora checks her little pistol concealed in her handbag. It clinks against the chunk of broken sword that Sinter gave her. "You came from Severast as a refugee?" she asks Alic.

"Indirectly. I went to Mattaur first. I was lucky – I was a merchant, before, and I knew some people in Guerdon already. I was able to get passage out." He sighs. "Other people weren't so lucky. There were thousands left behind. Survivors of Severast, wading into the water after each ship, begging to be taken away from the Godswar."

"Silkpurse said you volunteered to help out. What drew you to the Industrial Liberals?"

Alic pauses for a moment, considering his words. "What do you know about the sundering?"

"It was the start of the war between Severast and Ishmere, right?" She's read reports on it, but it made little sense to her. Any news out of the Godswar reads like the ravings of a madman.

"Sort of. Both lands worshipped some of the same gods – Lion Queen, Cloud Mother, Blessed Bol. But in Ishmere they were deeply embroiled in the war, whereas we were on the fringes. Not neutral, but not as involved." They start climbing up one of the many winding staircases from the Wash into the New City. Six months ago, this was the alchemists' docks, and ships came from all over the world to trade for dreadful weapons. Now, the ruins of that docks are under fifty feet of conjured stone, and the alchemists have to transport their wares from the regular docks down in the crowded Wash. Alic stops every few minutes to paste up another election poster whenever he spots a free patch of wall. A dozen Effro Kelkins stare down at Eladora.

Alic talks as he works. "And then the gods went mad. Not all at once. You'd hear stories of miracles out of the east, of new saints and monsters. Old ways getting swept away – but it was hard to tell what was incipient madness and what was the normal churn of events. I think the gods – our gods, in Severast – saw it first. That the sundering was an act of self-preservation. They tried to break themselves in two rather than remain part of an infected whole. Some of them didn't manage it at all. Others did. There were two

Lion Queens, for a little while. But the one from Ishmere was stronger, and without mercy."

"Professor On— a professor of mine at university, he once compared the gods to a burning forest, and human souls to trees. So the sundering was like – digging a firebreak?" She's enjoying this conversation. Partly because she's never been outside Guerdon and has no direct experience of the Godswar, but mostly because it's deliciously heretical. Talking about gods as quasi-natural forces, or phenomena that can be manipulated meant imprisonment and death by burning even a century ago – and is still forbidden in many other, less liberated places than Guerdon. Even the greatest mysteries can be unravelled, catagorised, tamed ... and the conversation would really, really annoy Eladora's mother, which is an added bonus.

Alic nods. "Something like that. But it wasn't a clean break. There were still sparks in the air in Severast, so to speak. The fighting started in heaven, and spread to the mortal realm. And then the city burned." His hands are quick and precise. He smoothes out one poster, steps back to admire his work.

They pass a building that bears the symbol of the Keepers. There's a small crowd outside, and robed Keeper priests move through them, distributing alms and blessings. Distributing little paper rosettes, too – badges of support for the Church in the election.

There are guards there, too, wearing old-fashioned armour. They scowl at Silkpurse, who hisses and crosses to the other side of the street. Eladora starts to follow her, but Alic catches her arm and brings her closer to the crowd.

There's a fire burning in a brazier outside the church, and another priest throws a log onto the coals and declaims a Safidist prayer. He raises his arms and calls to the Kept Gods to reach down and grant him their blessing. His face is ecstatic, his eyes bright and bulging as he begs for transcendence. He holds his hands so close to the flames that his skin blisters, but nothing happens. The gods do not answer his prayer. They answered my mother, thinks Eladora. But Aleena Humber who was their greatest champion didn't ask for their blessing – they just picked her at random from some country farm, like a spark landed on her. *Our Kept Gods, they're fucking dumb. All instinct, all reflex, no forethought.*

Alic whispers, "The Keepers have a half-dozen other missions like this one; bread and soup for the converts. For some who fled the Godswar, that's what they want – to exchange the mad gods for kinder ones. But the gods of Severast were our friends and family; not everyone can deny 'em."

He gestures back down the hill, and from this vantage point they can see the whole bay of Guerdon, with its isles and fortresses, and the harbour crowded with so many ships it looks like the city spills a mile out into the water.

"If the firebreak wasn't enough to cleave the gods of Severast from the mad gods of Ishmere, then perhaps an ocean will work."

CHAPTER 14

There's a small courtyard in the heart of the Haithi embassy. In the middle stands an urn, marked with the sigils of the mort-god whose name is never spoken. It's for the Supplicant staff; if they die here on foreign soil, their spirits will be collected, stored in the urn, and eventually shipped back home for their final service. Terevant touches the urn, but it's just cold metal, empty – not like the swirling, flowing strength locked away within the Erevesic sword. The urn isn't a true phylactery – it can only keep the souls from decaying, from sinking into the material world and dispersing as ambient magic. One merely stores the souls, he reflects, the other channels them, unites them in a common purpose, exalts them. The difference between a mere vessel and a weapon . . .

Between an urn and a sword, obviously. Gods, he needs coffee.

The luncheon table is like a conjuring trick. One moment, the courtyard's empty, and then the servants come out with a table. One throws a white cloth over it, and suddenly it's laden with fruit and cold meats, and hot coffee. Another servant comes out with a pair of chairs.

"Good afternoon," booms Olthic as he emerges from the embassy. He dismisses the servants with a wave. He's no longer angry – his rages are like summer storms, quick to pass. "Sit down and eat, damn you. I'm trying to apologise."

"For what?"

Olthic covers a slab of sourdough bread with jam as if he's trying to bury it. "I was angry, last night. About the sword – and what I said about your role here. I want you by my side, Ter, like when we were young. I need people I can trust. It's not just to keep you out of trouble. There's trouble enough here."

"What exactly is going on?"

"I can't tell you yet. I'd like to, but ... " He sighs. "By the way, they called a Fifty last month, and I was among those named."

"Congratulations," says Terevant flatly. The Fifty is a list of the most worthy and promising Haithi from across all the castes. It's a worrying omen for Haith, as a Fifty list is assembled only if the necromancers expect a new host for the Crown will soon be warranted. Either the current Crownbearer is sick – or, more likely, they fear Haith will be attacked and want a young, vigorous Crownbearer. But still – it's the highest honour, the shortlist for godhood.

"So was Lys."

"Aaaah." Both Lys and Olthic rose by supporting one another, their alliance catapulting both of them to success in the army and the Bureau, but only one head can wear the Crown. Next to the Crown, the Erevesic sword is a lesser afterlife.

"Are ... are you sure you want the sword, then?" asks Terevant. The Crown demands loyalty. If Olthic believes he's a serious contender for the Crown, then he might choose to voluntarily give up his claim on the sword, which would raise his standing in the estimation of the necromancers. It would show his devotion to Haith, not just to a single House.

The Erevesic blade would go to Terevant instead. He'd have the weapon's power, be the family champion. A demigod, all his weaknesses burned away, bolstered by the strength of his ancestors.

"I need the sword, Ter," says Olthic, crushing that momentary fantasy. "This city isn't stable any more. Imagine what would happen if Guerdon entered the war? If they joined Ishmere? You weren't here last year, during the Crisis. We lost six of the guard to Ravellers. If I'd had the sword then ... you don't know how different things might have been." Olthic's eyes are bright – no doubt envisioning himself cleaving through the tide of demons, thwarting the cultists, saving Guerdon, and winning the undying loyalty of Guerdon's people for Haith.

"As soon as Lys sends word—" begins Terevant, but Olthic interrupts him.

"Her little pet has been in touch with her already. A week, and the city watch will no longer be quite so watchful. I'll get it then."

"Her pet?"

"Lemuel," says Olthic, removing a stuck fruitfly from the jam pot. "Once the sword is in my possession, it's done – as long as I do not draw on the most potent gifts of the blade, they will not dare offend Haith by challenging my right to carry it. All in all," he says, scraping the dead fly onto a napkin, "you were lucky."

Terevant nods slowly. If Lys hadn't been waiting at Grena to collect Berrick, then it might all have been far worse. Then again, if he hadn't gone drinking with Berrick, hadn't met up with the sisters, or if their bearded chaperone hadn't been so insistent, then it might all have gone smoothly. Tiny little nudges, each one almost insignificant, conspired to shape his fate. He wonders if that's true of everyone, if every soul is a little boat adrift in a sea of chaos – or if he's unusually rudderless.

In comparison, Olthic's like a steam-driven dreadnought, his constant course unaffected by little whims of fate. "I am the Erevesic now," says Olthic. "I need to look to the future of our House. Should I die without issue – or become otherwise unable to bear the sword – it would fall to you."

"What a calamity for House Erevesic," says Terevant, as lightly as he can, but both of them know it's not wholly a joke.

"This isn't about blame or the errors of the past. It's about ensuring that the family sword has an acceptable bearer." Olthic plunges his thumb into the skin of an orange, flays it. "Daerinth has arranged a meeting for me at the alchemists' guild in a while, Do you want to spar before I leave? We have to keep in fighting shape, set an example for the living."

Terevant finishes his coffee. "No. I want to take a walk. See some of the city, get the lay of the land." He leaves *I haven't beaten you in a fair sparring match in twenty years* unspoken.

Olthic leans forward again, the chair creaking under his weight.

"I'd prefer if you didn't leave the embassy compound except on official business."

"As his Excellency commands." Terevant rises, salutes, waits to be dismissed.

"Oh, don't stand on ceremony. Go on."

Terevant strides across the courtyard.

A withered hand attached to a withered frame topped by a withered face stops him at the door. "Lieutenant?"

Ter suppresses his first question, which is *why are you not dead yet?* "Yes, First Secretary?"

"Young Lemuel has news from the city. He awaits you in your office."

Terevant nods. "Ah, thank you."

"Don't let yourself be misled by him. The boy's a useful gutter-snipe, but he's not . . . not . . . " Daerinth trails off, as if he's forgotten what he intended to say, but he doesn't release his grip on Terevant's arm. "You don't look much like the ambassador, do you?" Daerinth's eyes are so whited with cataracts that Terevant can't tell if the old man is making an observation, or genuinely asking for information.

"My brother's always been a bigger man than I."

"You must not be angry with him," says Daerinth. "It is very hard."

"Why not? I mean, what is very hard?" Terevant begins to wonder if this man's mind is as frail as his body seems to be. The First Secretary is supposed to be the embassy's premier diplomat, the ambassador's right-hand man in negotiations with Guerdon. Why entrust such a vital role to so fragile a vessel? Why not a younger man, or at least a dead one? He glances at the old man's wrists, but they're clear of the magical scars that mark a Vigilant. His house sigil doesn't indicate they have a phylactery. When Daerinth dies — which might be before the end of this conversation, from the look of him — he'll just die a Supplicant and end up in the jar in the courtyard.

"To be one of the Fifty. I should know."

"Are — were you?"

"Not me." The old man smiles like a child. "My mother was. Long, long ago. She was a poet. She won a place in the Fifty, and suddenly she couldn't write like she used to. Everything became rimmed with knives, she said. Everything became a potential failing. I was only five, but if I couldn't recite my histories in school, then that was a mark against her as one of the Fifty."

"I'll keep that in mind. Now, if you'll excuse me."

The withered hand clutches tighter.

"She won, you know. This was before the war got bad, and the Crown cherished her voice. I grew up in the palace, and they called me the Laughing Prince."

"That was you!?"

Daerinth bows ironically, although he can only manage a barely perceptible bend at the waist.

"I feared that she would stop loving me, you know. How could she not, I thought? She was part of the Crown then, a thousandth part of a soul so glorious so how could she still love her mortal child when she was mother of the nation? But I was wrong. She loved me. She did, for a while. She wasn't my mother, but the Crown loved me." Daerinth inclines his head towards the man in the courtyard. "He will remember you, too. Even afterwards."

The spy looks down on Guerdon's crowded harbour, at the spires and bulwarks of Queen's Point across the bay. "Then perhaps an ocean will work."

He mentally steps back for a moment, to listen to his own words, to study their effect on Eladora Duttin. Apparently his Alic identity is partial to poetic notions. Alic likes feeling useful, too; he's enjoyed fixing Jaleh's roofs, and putting up posters for the Industrial Liberals. But Alic isn't the spy, even if the spy is currently Alic.

Duttin is hard to read. At first glance she reminded him of something delicate and nervous. A hare, maybe. A library mouse, burrowed into a cosy paper nest. Or a clever bird, a parrot that can recite speeches, but would be best kept in a comfortable cage. The more he talks with her, though, it becomes clear that there's a slow, deep strength in her. She's a glacier, moving forward irresistibly. A little cold and wet on the surface, but iron-hard and remorseless.

She senses his scrutiny, smiles awkwardly. Keeps talking about Kelkin. She's slow to react, prone to second-guessing herself. The spy can work with this.

The path to Sevenshell Street wends through the most confusing parts of the dream-like architecture of the New City. Wide boulevards suddenly contract into alleyways, unfinished towers stand forever on the brink of collapse. A mansion like a doll's house, missing its front wall.

They pass a profusion of temples and shrines. Icons watch them as they go by. Some are ancient relics, probably salvaged from a loser's temple in the Godswar. Others were made here, cut out of the shimmering stone of the New City, shaped from river clay, assembled out of junk. The spy recognises some of them – there's Lion Queen, and Cloud Mother, and Blessed Bol, his statue made of thousands of copper coins glued together into his fat grinning face. All those are gods from the south, but there are other deities, too – Mother of Flowers and Holy Beggar from Guerdon, Yellow King and Masked Prince, Ishrey the Dawnmaiden and Uruaah Mountainmaker from the Silver Coast.

"Look at this one!" exclaims Eladora. She's gone into one shrine that's lost in shadow. He follows her into the cool darkness. It's a shrine to Fate Spider. Eladora stands next to a huge statue, as tall as she is, depicting a monstrous spider. She reaches out and brushes her finger over the marble. "I wonder how they brought this here. It must weigh several tons."

The spy doesn't dare speculate. He moves cautiously, wary of disturbing whatever powers are connected to this place. The walls of the shrine are covered in messages and prayers, each one written in a private code. There are offerings, too, little burned scraps of paper with secrets scrawled on them. They rustle under Eladora's boots as she circles the statue, an echo of the Paper Tombs.

Silkpurse hisses from outside, and it breaks Eladora's enchantment with Fate Spider. As she hurries out, she brushes past him in the darkness. Quick as a ghoul, he dips his hand into her bag, holding the coin-purse tight so it doesn't jingle. Eladora doesn't notice.

Outside, in the sun, he asks her, "What's in Sevenshell Street, anyway?"

"My, ah, cousin. I've been there before, but it was a few months ago and I came at it from a different route."

"Fallen on hard times, has she?" The spy tries to square how Eladora — clearly well educated, moderately wealthy, and close to Effro Kelkin and the IndLib inner circle — could have a close family member who lives in one of the most dangerous rookeries in the New City.

"Jumped, more like," mutters Eladora.

Silkpurse leads them on down this street of foreign gods, and then through an archway into an unexpected market. Sellers shout at them in a dozen languages, gesturing at the wares spread out on brightly coloured blankets. The stalls here deal in alchemical goods – salvage from the warehouses, weapons, medicines in cracked glass jars. A Stone Man haggles for a syringe of alkahest; there's a butcher dealing corpse-meat for ghouls under the counter. Across the market, there's a woman giving a speech, and Eladora insists they go over and find out which party she's from, but it turns out she's a recruiter for a mercenary company.

The spy lingers for a few moments, talking to the alchemical vendors. He'll have something to report to Tander and Annah, something for Emlin to whisper to her fellow saints of Fate Spider. Enough to keep Captain Isigi satisfied. He wonders idly if the captain is still alive, down in Mattaur. Maybe her mortal form has broken under the strain of sainthood.

Silkpurse circles back to him. "How much further?" he asks her.

"Not far." Silkpurse looks at the bundle of Industrial Liberal posters and flyers that she's still carrying, and sighs. "Oh, Alic, she's not going to Sevenshell because of the election, is she?"

He shrugs. "Everything's political."

"Let's get it done, then," says Silkpurse. She scurries off to fetch Eladora out of the crowd, and finds her at a bookseller. The spy watches the interaction from a distance, as if it's a mummer's play: Eladora crowing as she finds some unexpected treasure of a book, the ghoul plucking at her sleeve urging her to go, the merchant quoting a price, Eladora reaching for her coin-purse and finding it missing. She looks around in alarm; Silkpurse's mix of pity and exasperation – what did Eladora expect, walking into the worst part of the New City?

The spy dodges out of sight, waits a few heartbeats, then pushes through the crowd to Eladora. He makes himself breathe heavily, as though he just won a footrace. "I caught the little thief. He got away, but . . . " He holds up the purse he stole from Eladora.

She thanks him profusely while cursing herself for not paying more attention. Her face flushes with embarrassment; she stammers as she tries to bargain with the merchant. The spy steps in and haggles for her in the cant of the Severastian markets, all hand gestures and throat noises. He buys the book for half the asking price, and hands it to Eladora.

"Thank you, sir," she says, still embarrassed. She pretends to flip through the book, but he catches her glancing at him with a new appreciation.

It's best not to appear too eager. In a day or two, he thinks, she'll come by Jaleh's, ask him to go walking with her in the New City again. Infiltration is part seduction, part patience. He has to wait now for her to contact him. She's got to be one to spot Alic's potential, the one to ask for his help, to take him into her confidence. She has to trust him – and then he'll be able to report to Annah and Tanner that he's infiltrated the Industrial Liberal party. From Eladora, it's only a single strand of the web to Effro Kelkin and the highest echelons of Guerdon's government.

And Emlin will whisper these secrets back to their superiors in Ishmere.

And the heavens will burn.

CHAPTER 15

Lemuel's snoozing, cat-like, in Edoric Vanth's chair when Terevant arrives. From the doorway, Yoras makes a bony click of disapproval.

"What news do you have for me?"

Lemuel slowly opens his eyes. "I've found Vanth, maybe. Up in the New City, I'm told by my contacts. Sevenshell Street. I thought you'd want to go up and take a look."

"Quick or dead?" Among the folk of Haith, "quick" covers both actually *living* and the long post-mortem Vigil allowed by the necromancers.

"Dead, I'm told," says Lemuel.

"How?"

"I'm not sure. The story is some saint got him." Lemuel stands, stretches. "Come and see."

"Aren't saints banned in Guerdon?" Terevant asks, remembering the watch thaumaturges on the train, Lys's insistence that he hide the Erevesic sword.

Lemuel rolls his eyes. "City watch tries to ban the foreign ones. Send those they catch out to the camp on Hark, but some slip through. And the New City's dangerous."

Terevant turns to Yoras.

"Yoras," he calls, "get your mask."

The Vigilant are not to leave the embassy without permission, sir.

"Can't I give you permission?"

Not as such, sir. Not unless it's an emergency.

"Dash it all." There are living soldiers in the garrison, too, but he doesn't know them yet, doesn't trust them. "All right. I'll be back in a few hours."

I look forward with bated breath, sir.

He double-takes at that, but Yoras is always grinning these days. Terevant grabs a weather-stained cloak to drape over his uniform, and follows Lemuel out of the sprawling building.

Lemuel moves with a long, loping stride, quickly covering the ground between the compound and the Bryn Avane train station. They pass the grotesque idols of Ishmere's embassy, the sullen high-walled darkness of Ulbishe, the shining minarets of the Twin Caliphates. Terevant remembers one of Vanth's reports, about some Ishmeric spy who was shot right here in the gutter, and the outline of a satirical poem rises up in his mind. The street is the Godswar in miniature, told from the perspective of the rats who dodge the titan footfalls of the incomprehensible giants who walk there. He tries to quash the idea – he's an officer again, with duties and a reputation to rebuild, and no time to write it anyway – but it distracts him enough that he walks past the entrance to the station, and Lemuel has to pull him back.

The walls of the stairwell are thick with election posters. Lemuel digs into a pocket and produces a pair of rosettes, hands one to Terevant. "Pull your cloak over your uniform," he advises, "and fasten it closed with that."

The rosette is made of crepe paper, with a cheap brass pin in the shape of a crown. "What is it?"

"Party supporter badge. Keeps the worst of 'em from annoying you, if they think your vote's spoken for."

Terevant does as Lemuel suggested. "Which party?" he asks.

"Monarchists. Bunch of lunatics who think the king's going to come back to save the city." He puts his own rosette on, replacing one with the sign of the Keepers.

"You said a saint killed Vanth – what saint? What god?" demands Terevant.

The train platform is almost deserted, but Lemuel still shushes him. "Not here. Too many ears."

They board the nearly empty train. Thunder down through the tunnels. They sit in silence, facing each other. Lemuel yawns, brushes down the buttons of his military jacket.

"Where did you serve?" asks Terevant, nodding at the jacket.

"Oh, I took this off a dead man." Again the insolent smile. "I'm told you were a poet."

"Ah, yes. Before the war."

"I always preferred the theatre," smirks Lemuel at some private joke.

"Do you know where Lys – where I might find the Lady Erevesic?"

"You might find her almost anywhere. She gets around, our Lys, doesn't she?" Lemuel picks another speck of lint from his sleeve. "She trained me, you know. I've been with her for years."

"Do you know where she is?"

"If she wanted you to know, she'd have told you."

Shame battles with irritation within Terevant. If he hadn't screwed up on the train to Grena, then maybe Lys would have revealed more of her secrets to him. And he had such grand plans to investigate Vanth's death, to prove himself that way – but instead, Lemuel's found the trail already. His face flushes with anger.

Lemuel laughs. "Gods below, you're easy to provoke." The words delivered not as an insult, but as an assessment, the way a mechanic might triage a damaged piece of artillery. "They'll eat you alive in this city. You've got to learn to act."

"Blend in, you mean?"

"You're not going to do that, not with that accent of yours – and everyone knows your glorious brother, anyway." Lemuel chuckles again. "See? There you go again. Compare you to his Excellency, and you twitch. You're an easy mark. You've got to give less away. Hide what you really care about. It's caring that'll get you killed."

He becomes more serious, leans forward. His voice drops. "I'll give you an example. Back before the Crisis, I had this girl bedding an alchemist from the guild. I'd known the girl – her name was

Jenni — since I was ten. She'd convinced lover boy to bring some documents out of the guild, alchemical secrets that the Bureau wanted, right? Only the Tallowmen got wind of it. They follow Jenni to where she was supposed to meet me."

Lemuel swallows. "I spot 'em. I work out what's going on. And I walk away. I walk right past Jenni without looking at her. And I don't look back when the Tallowmen grab her. I don't look back when she screams. I'm just a bystander, as far as they're concerned. Like she had nothing to do with me."

"You sound proud of being a bastard."

"I'm from the Wash. Can't afford *pride* where I grew up." Lemuel throws himself back in his seat, theatrically offended. "See, once they know you, who you really are, they can *use* you. You can't give 'em an opening. That alchemist — soon as I found out he wasn't happy, I put Jenni in his way, and I had him by the cock after that. Other people, it's something else. Money, fear, revenge, love. Doesn't matter. Once you're hooked, you're gone." He crooks his finger, mimicking a fisherman's hook tearing through soft flesh.

"You should get out before anyone gets their claws into you," adds Lemuel. And then he turns his gaze to the flickering lights beyond the window, his expression blank as if he and Terevant are strangers who just happen to be sharing a carriage for a moment.

Sordid, thinks Terevant. The vile man is projecting his own gutter sensibilities onto the whole. Surely the Bureau isn't all like that. In his youthful imaginings, in the books he read in Paravos, it was all daring intrigues, high-level diplomacy, cleverness and guile. Not some poor girl used as a lure, then gutted on the street like a fish by Tallowmen.

The city presents its many faces to them, station by station, like an impressionist. At Five Knives station it's a street tough, daring them to disembark. At Castle Hill, a doddery clerk, fussy and busy. At Venture Square, a rich speculator.

And down by the old docks, something stranger. They're on the edge of the miracle-spawned New City here. This station nearly collapsed in the Crisis, but was saved through divine intervention.

Ribs and spars of shimmering stone bear up the roof, having broken through from above like the roots of some petrified tree. The iron rails end halfway along the tunnel, replaced with matching rails of stone.

"Stick close," says Lemuel. "Vanth got ended here. It'd be awkward if you went, too."

Lemuel clearly knows the New City well. He leads Terevant through a maze of stairs, corridors, winding streets, unlikely turns. Moving faster now, hurrying through the strangeness. Terevant wants to linger, to take different turnings – he spots a market, a street of shrines, a tower decked in bright banners, things that might be buildings or sculptures or the graves of monsters – but he follows doggedly after Lemuel.

Until Lemuel stops. There's shouting in the distance, gunfire. Terevant's hand goes to his sword, but Lemuel stops him. "Shit," says Lemuel, his confidence visibly shaken, "wait here. Don't fucking move." He hurries through a door, closes it behind him.

Confused, Terevant cautiously advances down the alleyway. The brief spate of gunfire stops, and the city's abruptly silent, holding its breath. The walls around him *creak* suddenly, like the solid stone's transmuted to sailcloth caught in the sea breeze for a moment. Terevant draws his sword, ducking low. The air is full of *presences*, as if some god is close at hand. It reminds him of the landing at Eskalind, before the miracles rained down like artillery. His heart's pounding, his stomach turning to water. *Vanth was murdered by a saint*, Lemuel said.

Lemuel told him to wait. To hell with that. Terevant tries to find his way towards the fighting, but the streets are impossibly twisted, and every route seems to lead away from where he heard the gunfire. Doubling back, he tries to find a doorway that might let him follow Lemuel. The one Lemuel went through is locked, but Terevant finds another one down the alleyway.

It opens into the cool, unexpected darkness of a little chapel. The sigils of the Kept Gods above the altars. The chapel is brand new, born from the same miracle-conjured stone as the street outside, but there's an ancient golden casket on the altar. A holy reliquary,

Terevant guesses, older than the New City. Maybe older than the old city, too.

The church is deserted, except for a bald-headed priest who rises from the frontmost pew.

"Put your sword away, sir. No one will trouble you here."

"Don't you hear the gunfire?"

The ugly priest clasps his hands together. He's missing two fingers from one hand. "Perils and monsters abound here, but here we are safe in the hands of the Mother of Mercies." He smiles beatifically through broken teeth. "My name is Sinter."

"Here we are," says Silkpurse, "Sevenshell Street." A little snug row of townhouses, facing out over the open sea. Parts of the New City jut out over the ocean. Down below, mudlarks pick through the rocks for shellfish and flotsam. One part of the wall below is discoloured a sickly yellow-brown, and moisture drips from it. An old sewer entrance, maybe, accidentally walled up in the Miracle. Behind the houses, a curved wall like a frozen wave, like someone built a seawall two hundred feet above the shore and then decided to add a row of houses at its base. It makes as much sense as the rest of the New City.

The street's empty, but the spy glimpses fearful faces in windows. He can smell trouble.

Trouble and soot.

The last house in the row is burned out. The door's been smashed open, the windows are hollow-eyed and blackened. Soot streaks run down the walls. Wordlessly, Eladora runs ahead, steps over the threshold. Inside, the room's been blasted. It was no natural fire. Even if every scrap of wood and cloth in the place had been piled in a bonfire and set alight, it couldn't have produced this inferno. Magic, then. Or a miracle. Or alchemy.

"This . . . Carillon lived here."

The spy glances around the remains of the house. Two other rooms, similarly destroyed. No other exits.

Silkpurse sniffs around, pauses, sniffs again, then scrabbles at one pile of ash. There's a body in there, partially burned. "Oh, no.

Oh, gods," says Eladora, staring in horror. She turns away, steadying herself against the scorched wall.

The spy kneels, helps the ghoul uncover the remains. Some of the ribs have been shattered – a gunshot. And in the wrists . . . iron periapts.

He flinches, expecting the skeleton to leap up and attack them.

Silkpurse glances up at both of them with ghoulish amusement. "What, did you think it was Cari?" She chuckles, running her claw almost tenderly down the length of the scorched femur. "This is a man's corpse."

"A man of Haith," says the spy. "He's got periapt implants."

Silkpurse examines one of the little iron talismans grafted to the corpse's ankle. "Oh, is that what those things are?" she says with distaste. "Shouldn't he be prancing around, then, not lying dead here?"

Eladora, still deathly pale, joins them around the body. She doesn't dare touch it. "What . . . Can you tell what happened to him?"

"Shot. Cut. Burned," says the spy, pointing at the wounds in turn. The body's been burned, but not as much as the spy would have expected, given its surroundings. He's about to explain – when the windowsill behind him shatters in a shower of dust and debris. The whip-crack of an alchemical pistol, the acrid smell of phlogiston. Attackers on the street outside.

He flings himself to the side, out of the line of fire. Silkpurse scampers over to the doorway, daintily removes her hat and veil, and then roars an animalistic howl. Eladora's frozen in surprise. Blood runs down her cheek, but she's lucky, it's just a graze from flying shrapnel. The spy darts across and drags her into the cover of the wall, pushing her head down. Her blood sticky on his fingers. More shots from across the street, and the sound of someone scrambling on the roof. Who are they? It's a good question. But it's only the second most pressing one in the spy's mind, on the heels of *do I have any better weapons than this poster stick?*

"Take this!" Eladora presses a gun into his hand. It's a small alchemical pistol, single-shot, little more than a lethal toy. The spy hesitates for an instant, wondering if Alic should be a good shot, and then one of the attackers comes through the front door of the house and it turns out that Alic is a brilliant shot. The intruder crumples, clutching the ruin of his kneecap, blood gushing from between his fingers. Gods, he's only a few years older than Emlin, another child sent to war.

Eladora shrieks. Silkpurse grabs another enemy who came too close to the front door. Her claws, made for tearing dead flesh, sink into his living wrists, and blood spurts freely. She swings him around, like it's a grotesque waltz, leading him by the arteries, positioning his body between her and the gunmen across the street.

The spy dares to take a look out of the window. Four or five more foes across the street, emerging from doorways, climbing down from hiding places. They're good, whoever they are – they advance cautiously, darting from cover to cover. They were lying in wait, he guesses, ready to ambush – who? Eladora? Her mysterious cousin? Did they expect the dead Haithi to spring up?

Shouting. A man comes rushing up the street, frantically waving his arms, his long army jacket billowing behind him. "Not now! Not now!" he shouts. "Get rid of them, quick!"

One of the attackers unholsters a flash-ghost grenade. The aetheric discharge from that would kill everyone in the house. The spy snaps off a shot, forcing the bastard to duck before he can throw it. The shot goes wide, catches Army Jacket in the shoulder. The newcomer falls in the street, cursing. The spy fumbles for another cartridge, but reloading the tiny gun is like trying to pick a lock, and by the time he's reloaded Army Jacket's crawled out of sight.

"We've got to leave!" the spy shouts at Silkpurse. The ghoul nods, shifts her grip on her human shield. Stepping out of that door means stepping into a hail of gunfire.

"Miss Duttin," calls Silkpurse, "stay behind me. I'll guard you as much as I can."

"W-what about that door?" asks Eladora, pointing to the back of the house.

There's an opening in the wall that wasn't there a moment ago. An archway, leading to a narrow staircase. A way out. The edges of the stone archway are still fluid, the ghostly marble flowing like liquid moonlight.

It's a miracle.

A miracle they have no time to question.

"Go!" hisses Alic, and Eladora stumbles towards the archway, tripping over the Haithi corpse. Alic follows her; Silkpurse comes last, dragging her waltz partner as a shield.

Their foes pursue them as they scramble up the steep stairs. The ceiling is low and cramped, and the steps wet and treacherous. Gunshots behind them make Eladora flinch. Wet cracks as Silkpurse's waltz partner gets hit and goes limp. The ghoul discards the body, dropping it to block the narrow stairwell and force the enemy to clamber over the remains of their own. Glancing back down, Alic sees the fellow with the flash ghost at the archway at the base of the stairs.

"Look out!" he shouts. Silkpurse sees the danger, bounds down the stairs, but she won't get there in time to stop—

There's a flash of purple light and a sound like tearing, and the attacker's flung against the wall. Eladora's outstretched hand blazes with the same purple light for an instant, the bones limned in fire. Silkpurse reaches the man a split second later. She picks him up, smashes him against the wall again, and he's down. A roar of ghoulish pain as Silkpurse is wounded. The house below is full of foes.

Alic hustles Eladora up the stairs. She's wobbling after throwing that spell, so he has to half carry her until she finds her feet. Her fingernails are bleeding; almost absently, the spy filches a handkerchief from her purse and catches the blood. He pockets the cloth.

The tunnel ends in another archway, opening onto a deserted alleyway, a canyon between two towers like stony cliffs. He shoves Eladora out into the alleyway, then turns to help Silkpurse up the last few steps. The ghoul's limping, and blackish blood stains the fresh marble of the steps. "It's all right, it's all right," mutters the ghoul.

They emerge into the alleyway, and find it empty.

Eladora's vanished into thin air.

*

Another door in the chapel, and Lemeul tumbles in, breathless, his army jacket covered in dirt like he's been rolling in the gutters. Terevant feels like he's backstage at a theatre, watching the cast enter and exit through the wings and trapdoors, that there's some drama happening outside that he's missing. Lemuel double-takes at the sight of Terevant.

"What's happening out there?" asks Terevant.

Lemuel's bleeding from a gunshot wound to his arm. "Half-dozen armed bastards," he spits in frustration, "versus some bitch saint."

"I have spoken to Lemuel here of the threat posed by the hateful Saint of Knives," proclaims Sinter, "and I fear it was she who murdered your Edoric Vanth. This New City is an an abhorrence, and she is part of it. A demon child, a murderous footpad granted unholy powers. Once, she preyed only on criminals, but her bloodthirst grows. The city watch try to catch her, but – alas – to no avail!"

"The watch are on their way up now," adds Lemuel. "We have to go."

Sinter looks surprised for a split second, then nods. "Indeed, young Lemuel is right – it would be better if you left here now, before the watch find you. Old Haith has few friends in the city."

Terevant looks towards the door Lemuel came through. He takes a step towards it, sword in hand. "We should get Vanth's body, even if he's fully dead." Thinking of Lys on the station at Grena, of the oath he swore.

"Fucking come on," snarls Lemuel.

Sinter glides forward. "The city watch will bring any remains they find to the morgue at Queen's Point."

Terevant hesitates. He wants to charge out there, but . . . *You charged on at Eskalind*, a voice whispers at the back of his mind, *and see where that got you.*

"We'll go. I'll demand the remains from the city watch." He tries to sound commanding.

Sinter bows his head. "Mother of Sorrows, bless his passing. You have my condolences on your loss."

CHAPTER 16

Eladora stumbles, and a hand catches her and pulls her to the side. For an instant, she has the disconcerting impression that she was pulled through the wall, because the way back seems impassible. Her rescuer – kidnapper? – drags Eladora up a narrow staircase and along a gallery cut into the seawall. Narrow shafts of sunlight from the windows illuminate the room, and Eladora catches a glimpse of the other woman.

"Cari?"

It's been only a few months since she last saw her cousin, but the changes are marked. Cari looks like one of the miracle-shocked mercenaries that come back from the war, her face gaunt, her expression like flint. The hand that's locked around Eladora's wrist is covered in scabs and calluses. Her grip is stronger than Eladora remembered, but it's a strength born of training and street-fighting, not a divine gift.

"Silkpurse is back there – and Alic. And someone's attacking us."

"I fucking noticed. Same bastards burned down my house a month ago." Cari seems to listen to some unseen, unheard message for a moment, "They've split up. Silkpurse is clear. They won't catch her if she heads that way." Cari grins. "Can't catch a Guerdon ghoul."

"What about Alic?"

"Dunno." She concentrates for an instant. "Shit. Sorry. They got him." She abruptly changes course, dragging Eladora through another door. "They're after us instead."

They hurry through another tunnel. From behind, Eladora hears shouting, running feet.

The tunnel brings them to a twisted spiral staircase. "Climb," orders Cari, and Eladora obeys, but her cousin doesn't follow. Instead, she sees Cari unholster a pistol and aim it down the empty tunnel.

The shouts behind them grow louder, but Eladora can't tell how close their pursuers are.

Carillon can. She squeezes the trigger an instant before the first attacker enters the little tunnel. The shot strikes true, and the lead pursuer roars in shock as his gun explodes in his hand. Eladora shrieks and scrambles up the stairs on her hands and knees. The stairwell seems to wheel around her, as if it's spinning on its axis, trying to throw her back down into the carnage.

She glances back, sees Cari retreating up the stairs behind her, knife in hand. The man is behind her, snarling, slashing at her with a curved blade. He's clumsy, fighting with his off-hand. Cari moves like a dancer, perfectly anticipating her foe's every swing, dodging and jumping on the narrow, uneven steps as surefooted as if she was on level ground. The man swings again, her knife flashes, and his shirt is suddenly marked with blooming red stains.

There's a second attacker. She glimpses the pistol in his hand, looks right down its muzzle, *sees* the phlogiston flash – and then suddenly Cari jumps in front of her.

The bullet hits her cousin squarely in the chest– and all the walls in the stairwell crack simultaneously, like it's an earthquake in this room only. Huge wounds opening up in the stone, showering them all with dust and shards. Cari falls to her knees, winded, but she's alive and unhurt despite taking a bullet at point-blank range.

The city took the blow, some part of Eladora thinks, but at the same time she's stretching out her hand and reflexively reciting the incantation Ramegos taught her. The spell goes awry again. Every muscle in her arm, her side, her shoulder goes numb as the spell's backwash runs through her. She grabs something heavy from her bag – the sword hilt Sinter gave her – with her left hand and swings at the attacker. She gets lucky, catching him when he's off balance, and he falls backwards, striking his head against the wall. *Run*, she thinks or says or shouts, she can't tell. Pulling Cari upright, sending pain arcing through her right arm. Eladora feels lightheaded; as she stumbles up the stairs, she sees that her fingernails are all burned. Her hand was already bloodied and blistered from her incantation earlier; if she tries the spell again, she'll burn out the nerves or burst the veins in her hand.

Cari grabs her, hustles her onwards, leads her through another bewildering series of nonsensical rooms. Some are empty, some are littered with debris from parts of the city consumed in the Crisis. Eladora picks her way over pipes and tanks bearing the sigil of the alchemists' guild, over a pub sign from Glimmerside that she recalls passing in her university days. Over pews and statues from a Keeper chapel. The statues had vat-grown jewels for eyes, once, but now they watch Cari and Eladora through empty sockets. They pass through a room that might be furnished for a banquet, but all the tables and chairs are pushed up against one wall like driftwood.

Cari drags her towards one blank wall.

"In here."

The wall miraculously quivers and reshapes itself at her touch, the stone pulling apart like flesh. Sinews of mortar breaking and snapping. A cold wind blows in through the growing aperture, and Eladora gasps at the sight revealed. They're high above the New City, a dozen storeys or more. She can see the street with all the saints down there, and all the other glimmering towers and mansions and twisted coral carbuncles of the conjured city. Then, beyond that, stretching to the horizon, is old Guerdon. She can even see the green-stained roof of the nearest Victory Cathedral, so they must be up very high indeed.

"Come on."

There's a narrow bridge, a spit of stone, no more than two feet wide, arching between this building and another tower, leading to another blank wall. This tightrope of stone is at least a hundred feet from end to end, and looks slick with moisture. Cari steps onto it without hesitation.

Eladora has hesitation enough for both of them. "I can't. Oh, gods, I can't."

"We won't let you fall," says Cari, taking her by the arm again and pulling her out onto the narrow span. Eladora slips and clutches at Cari, but Cari seems rooted to the stone, able to bear Eladora's weight with ease. Her cousin strolls over the bridge with insolent grace, and at the far end the other wall convulses and opens, too, revealing a room in the building beyond.

Eladora glances back to see if the first opening is still there. Not only has that first impossible door closed, but the bridge behind her is melting away, the stone retreating like an icicle in spring.

"He's showing off," says Cari. They step through the wall into the second tower, and the wall shuts behind them, cutting off the winds whipping off the harbour. Eladora discovers she's been holding her breath for at least a minute, and sinks down to sit with her back against the suddenly solid wall. She shakes silently for a few moments, closing her eyes as she tries to recompose herself. She cradles her wounded hand.

She remembers endless interrogations and debriefings – in front of the emergency committee, or with Sinter, with Dr Ramegos, with Admiral Vermeil, with a dozen nameless, blank-faced men and women – where they asked her the same questions over and over: *where is your cousin? Where is Carillon Thay? Is she still a saint of the Black Iron Gods? Is she still a threat to the city?*

And afterwards, when the interrogations were over, they decided that Carillon wasn't a threat. They sent Eladora to confirm – her final test, completing her rapid ascent in the ranks of Effro Kelkin's assistants. Eladora's assessment was that Carillon would soon leave the city, running away to sea just like she did before. Eladora thought that her cousin was done with Guerdon, done with sainthood.

Clearly, she was wrong.

"Soup?"

Eladora looks up to find Cari awkwardly holding out a steaming bowl. Eladora takes it, stirs the greyish lumps around the greyish liquid, puts it to one side and looks around her. The room they're in is mostly bare apart from a small nest of blankets in one corner, a shelf crammed with knives and other tools, and a small cooking stove. A door in the far wall. No windows, just the glimmer of an alchemical lamp.

"Huh," says Cari, stripping off her shirt. There's a fist-size hole where the bullet struck. "I was wrong. The other guy you came with – Alic – he's alive. I could have sworn they caught him." She thumps the wall with a fist. "You're losing it, big man."

"Alic's quite resourceful," says Eladora, relieved. "I was at your house. There was . . . there was a body there."

"I didn't kill him. I don't even know who the fuck he was," Carillon says indignantly. "They dumped him in my old place an hour ago. I was trying to work out what the hell they were doing when you showed up. I mean, yeah, they were trying to frame me for *something*, but . . ." She falls silent for a moment, then rolls her eyes.

"He was a man of Haith," offers Eladora.

"Huh," says Carillon. "That's interesting."

"Your house was . . . ah, destroyed *before* the body was left there?" asks Eladora, cautiously. Questions make Carillon uncomfortable. Eladora thinks of her cousin as a feral alley cat: try to box her in, and she'll bolt. She has to be relaxed before she'll talk. Also, she'll eat anything and is probably diseased.

"Yeah. I pissed some people off."

"Who?"

Cari shrugs. "Lots of people. I kicked the Ghierdana syndicates out two months ago – they tried to take over Heinreil's old operations. They didn't see me coming, and they don't have their boss dragons over here. Might've been them. Or that glass-witch from Ulbishe. Or some of the fucking gunrunners. Or . . . "

She pauses. "Yeah, or the spies. We've had a lot of *them*, lately, haven't we? Poking around where they don't belong." Cari glances at Eladora. "I wonder if they mistook you for me."

"And tried to kill you on sight?"

"To be fair . . . " Cari reaches down, and removes a wickedly sharp knife from some hidden sheath. "I've been busy. Not much happens in the New City that I can't see, and if someone crosses the line—" Her hand twitches, and the knife embeds itself in the wall next to Eladora. "At least, El, that was the fucking plan. The Saint of Knives, that was me." She pauses again. "Us."

Eladora gingerly touches the wall behind her. "I take it that your friend Spar is still . . . " She searches for the word. Spar fell to his death in front of hundreds of witnesses, but the New City was conjured from his remains. "Extant?"

"He's extensively extant," says Cari, "in places." She sighs and leans back, staring at the ceiling. "It's getting harder to reach him, though. Up here's one of the few spots left where things are still, I dunno, fluid. He's close to himself, up here, and he can do stuff to the stone. Down at street level, though, he's more . . . " She pauses – no, listens. "Constrained. He can show me what's happening anywhere in the New, it's like the visions, only he doesn't shout at me to free a bunch of evil monster gods all the time. But he doesn't think like we do any more. His soul's sort of smeared – I don't know, you tell me – all right, his soul encompasses the whole New City, but he's still human, not a god. So, he's all cracked and bitty. There are streets where the only part of him is anger, or places where it's just his memories, and I can't talk to his, uh . . . "

"His conscious mind," suggests Eladora. The whole situation is fascinating and bizarre. The desperate final act of the Crisis – Carillon channelling the collective power of the trapped Black Iron Gods into her dying friend – has created something new. Not just a new city, but a new order of being. A living city, a *genius loci*, with Carillon as something like a saint. She really wants to talk to Dr Ramegos about this. "Would you come down to Queen's Point with me? There's someone I'd—"

"Fuck off."

"Like you to meet."

"El, no."

"Let me talk to Kelkin. We can—"

"No."

"All right."

Cari eats in silence for a few minutes.

Eladora stirs the soup, then puts it aside again.

"I see your vigilantism has ensured the New City is a place of safety and public order."

"I'm trying, all right?" Cari spits out a fishbone. "There was a bottle of wine around here, wasn't there?" she says, addressing the air. Talking to Spar. Whatever the response is, it's not to Cari's liking, and she wrinkles her nose in irritation.

"I can see you're trying." Eladora gestures with her spoon towards the small arsenal of blades and guns by the bed. "But surely it's folly to attempt this alone – well, physically alone."

"It is all going fine, mostly." Cari applies a whetstone to her knife blade with irritation. "I'd be doing a lot better if those fuckers weren't sending death squads after me."

"Well, that's an even better argument for being reasonable, isn't it?" says Eladora. "Carillon, if Mr Idgeson is amiable, you could work with the emergency council, use your talents with official sanction . . ."

"El," says Cari, "no. Gods below, you're maybe the one other person in Guerdon who should understand what it's like to have the gods of the city nesting in your skull. You know what the watch would do to me if they caught me. Best fucking case, I end up in a prison cell for the rest of my life."

"That's not going to happen."

"Send me to Hark as a dangerous saint. Dissect me in some alchemist's lab. Burn me at the stake."

"Well, those are more plausible." Crestfallen, Eladora watches her cousin sharpen the knife. She remembers the night Professor Ongent showed up at the door of the house on Desiderata Street with Cari in tow, stunned and scared by her mysterious visions, unaware then that they stemmed from the nightmarish Black Iron Gods. Cari looked so fragile and exhausted that Eladora had almost forgotten the mutual loathing of their childhood, and had reached out to help.

Carillon doesn't look fragile now. There's an angry strength in her, a confidence born of a willingness to act, to do violence. She scares Eladora now, in a way that she never did before. Cari always carried a knife, but somehow Eladora could tell that she'd never killed with it.

The knife in Cari's hand now seems well used.

An image flashes through Eladora's mind, a vision as clear as any divine foresight – Carillon lying dead on a rooftop, gunned down by some foe. Too much strength can be dangerous, if you forget when to stop and regroup.

But Eladora can't think of the words to make Carillon see that, and she certainly can't force her to listen. If she knew how to make Cari see sense, she'd have done it long ago. In the house on Desiderata Street. Or back on the farm where they grew up, out in Wheldacre.

"I ran into my mother."

"How is the hag?" asks Cari, still sharpening.

"She's a saint now."

"Fuck!" Cari's knife slips, cutting her knee. Blood spurts from a shallow wound. "A what? A Keeper saint? Are you fucking serious?" She laughs as she presses a rag to her bleeding leg. "Silva's a saint?"

"The Kept Gods have chosen her as their vessel. It's all very solemn and holy."

"Well, she must be happy. What was that thing she kept talking about? Saffy-something."

"Safidism. The belief that it is right and proper to seek sainthood, and that one achieves sainthood through humility and concordance with the divine, by suppressing one's own will in favour of sub-mission to the gods." A reddish liquid, thin and flecked with little chips of stone, oozes from the wall near Cari. Eladora stares at it, but doesn't say anything. Some sort of echo, she guesses, Carillon's wounds mirrored by Spar.

"Well, she must be happy."

"Actually," says Eladora, "she was quite . . . fervent in her attitude towards you. I think you should stay well away from her. Honestly, we all should. I think she's gone mad."

"'Gone', yeah." Cari closes her eyes, looking inwards. "Well, that's nice for Silva. May she get martyred really fucking memorably."

Eladora sniffs, unsure how she feels about Cari's casual wish for her mother to meet a grisly end. On balance, she decides, she's mostly fine with it.

"You're still working with Kelkin's lot?" asks Cari.

"By 'lot', you mean the emergency committee delegated power by parliament for the duration of the present crisis? Yes, I'm still one of Mr Kelkin's aides. For the moment."

"Have you ..." Cari pauses, then asks her question in the most casual tone she can muster. "Seen Rat lately?"

"This morning, actually. There's some friction between the ghouls and the Keepers, so he is consumed with politicking."

"Poor bastard," says Cari, with little sympathy in her voice. "You know there are corpse shafts under the New City? Miles of tunnels, too, just like the rest of the city. Spar was thinking of the ghouls when he built this place."

"I can pass a message on, if you'd like."

"Don't you fucking dare. The bastard tried to kill me. Rat's dead, and something else is wearing his name." She gingerly peels back some of the bloody rag. The bleeding's stopped.

Eladora doesn't argue.

"How about Miren?"

Eladora freezes. She hasn't seen Professor Ongent's son since the Crisis. She believed herself to be in love with the cold boy for a long time. It was only afterwards, in the months since his disappearance, that she's understood something of his true nature.

Miren's knives, too, were very well used.

"I haven't."

"I thought I spotted him, once or twice, poking around the New City, but he's a sneaky fuck. He vanished when I went after him."

"He can't have retained his teleportation, can he? It was a gift of the Black Iron Gods."

"Yeah, well, he got away somehow, the shit." Cari removes the rag, probes the wound with a grubby finger.

"Come here," orders Eladora. She finds a jug with some relatively clean water. She's dropped her handkerchief in the carnage, so she makes do with a strip of cloth cut from her own dress, and expertly cleans out the wound.

"You've been practising." Eladora nods – after the Crisis, she found it calming to study what to do in an emergency. She'd make a passable nurse now. "And thanks for that spell, too."

"I don't know if it was necessary. You seemed to be very—" *murderous* springs to mind, but Eladora manages to says "competent" instead. "The knife wounded you, but the bullet didn't?"

She shrugs. "Some saints can teleport, some get flaming swords. I've got a city with a martyr complex looking out for me. I can . . . sort of shunt injuries to him, but it takes concentration. We can do other stuff, too. Those fuckers got off easy. If we'd been a few floors higher, I could've closed the walls on them." She considers her words, then adds, "Maybe. It's getting harder all the time, or he's getting weaker." Carillon looks up at Eladora, suddenly subdued. "It's all the same, over and over, isn't it? Spar and the stone. And Silva and me, too – instead of her chasing me around the kitchen with a wooden spoon, she'll be chasing me around the city with a flaming sword."

"Some patterns break," offers Eladora. "You didn't run away. It was, ah, assumed that you had, but you stayed and you've tried – in your way – to help the New City."

Cari flexes her wounded hand. "Not entirely my idea. I have a friend who's civic-minded."

"Actually," says Eladora, almost shyly, "that's why I sought you out. As I said, I'm working with Mr Kelkin's Industrial Liberals in preparation for the upcoming elections."

"So?"

"Well, given your unique insight into the New City, I was hoping that you'd be able to assist in selecting promising candidates for election. We're looking to recruit leaders and champions from the newly arrived communities, groups that—"

"You came to me for *polling advice*?"

"I just thought that you might have an invaluable perspective."

"Fuck off," says Cari, bluntly.

And then, louder, incredulously, and clearly directed to the ceiling above her. "Fuck off. No. No."

She turns back to Eladora and says in hollow tones. "Oh, gods below. He's interested. He wants to help."

Eladora wishes that there was a shrine or a statue or a manifestation of some sort, instead of speaking to the empty air. "Ah, Mr Idgeson, I know that your father and Mr Kelkin had considerable disagreements once upon a time."

"Kelkin had his dad executed, but, sure, considerable disagreements," interjects Cari.

"However, circumstances have changed for all of us, and I'm sure we can find common ground and areas of mutual interest."

The building quivers slightly, as though a train passed beneath it, or the earth trembled. Cari clutches her head. "Ow. Gods, you've got him all riled up now. Like I said, he doesn't think like we do any more. I can't make sense of what he's saying – I'll need to move around the city, pick up different bits of the thought from different streets." She crosses the room, finds a battered coat in a pile of clothing. "Thanks a lot," she adds, sourly. "Like I had nothing better to do than wander around, dodging assassins, for fucking *this*."

"I am in your debt," says Eladora.

"Get some sleep. While I'm out, I'm also going to find out who the fuck that Haithi corpse was, and why they wanted someone to think I killed him."

Eladora stands. "Before you go . . . you said people were combing the New City for leftovers of the Crisis. What are they looking for?"

Cari scowls.

"You don't want to know, El."

"Of course I do. It's important. Tell me."

Her cousin's face darkens with anger. "But it wouldn't be telling you, would it? It'd be telling Kelkin, and Rat, and all the rest. Fuck. That. And stay here." The wall opens at her touch, swallowing her, resealing behind her.

Leaving Eladora trapped in this tower with no doors.

CHAPTER 17

The spy walks out of the New City, wearing the mask of Alic. He draws a worried frown on this mask as he descends, passing through the bizarre transition zone between the New City and the Old. The district of Glimmerside, where conjured shapes interweave through structures built with mortal hands. Stalactites of stone cling to the façades of taverns and bookshops like some angelic fungus.

A chattering gaggle of students outside a tavern, all sitting on a delicately beautiful spiral staircase that springs from the tavern yard and ascends to empty air. An entire apothecary's shop sits on a tongue of stone that lifted it into the air nine months ago, so the Gutter Miracle could conjure a dancing fountain where the shop once stood. A crowd laughs at a puppet show, where Kelkin beats the previous First Minister, Droupe, with a stick until he bursts in a shower of golden coins. Toy violence, only a few minutes' walk from where people died in the streets.

The crowds change like the sky as he moves through the streets.

Up in the New City, people were like autumn leaves, many colours all tossed on the wind, each one different, all fallen from dying trees across the sea.

In Glimmerside, close to the university, the shapeless grey robes of students are dark clouds scudding across the sky.

And here, down near Eladora's apartment, it's like a brilliant sunset. With the Festival of Flowers in a few weeks, the bohemian section of Glimmerside is alight with summer finery and laughter.

His own clothes – drab, forgettable – remind him oddly of a bird on the wing, a lonely flyer crossing many skies. He's never liked birds before.

Eladora's apartment is on the second floor of a townhouse near Venture Square. He's watched this building before. Watched her and several other senior aides in the Industrial Liberals come and go. Waiting for an opportunity. His fingers clench the opportunity in his pocket.

Even if he hadn't seen Eladora blast that attacker with a spell, he'd have suspected her home was magically warded. The party would have seen to that. These days, with sorcery taught in universities and mass-produced in weapons factories, it's a necessity to protect important people and information from supernatural attack. Picking a lock is trivial for the spy; bypassing magical wards without being detected is harder.

The stairwell outside the apartment is empty. There's another flat on the far side of the landing, but the spy can't hear anyone inside. He kneels down and blows softly on the lock of Eladora's door; traceries of magical sigils glow blue in response. Some wards blast trespassers; he doubts Eladora would employ such lethal counter-measures, but it would sound the alarm, maybe capture his image.

The bloody handkerchief is his key. With an effort of will, he can mimic the spiritual identity of the person behind the blood. Like making a duplicate key, pressing it into the shapeless darkness of his soul. He wraps the handkerchief around the fingers of one hand and presses on the sigils while picking the lock with the other.

It's almost anticlimactic, how easy it is.

The spy enters the apartment, closing the door silently behind him, unseen in the heart of Guerdon.

Lemuel insists Terevant keep silent until they're well clear of the New City, as if he expects this Saint of Knives to hear their whispered conversation, as if he expects the demon girl the priest described to suddenly appear in front of them, materialising in a puff of smoke to murder them both with burning blades. He waits in silence as the train carries them north, stained fingers pressed against his wounded arm. It's only when they're past Venture Square that Lemuel proves willing to speak.

"You should write up a report. Make it an elegy if you want." A warning about mad saints. He seems to think the matter is settled – Vanth was simply unlucky. No grand conspiracy.

In any other city, Terevant wouldn't think twice. He saw plenty of mad saints in Paravos, mortals lifted out of the everyday world by the touch of the gods and put back down askew. Mad saints at Eskalind, too, laughing as they killed.

But Guerdon's supposed to be different. And he's supposed to be different. The old Terevant might have taken the easy answer that Lemuel offers, to agree that Vanth's death was a cruel act of god and call it done, but he's going to do better this time. He wants to show Lys he can do better.

So, when they reach the embassy, he returns to Vanth's office. Sits down at the paper-strewn desk and starts to work again. He needs to make sure he's not missing anything, some clue that might unlock a deeper mystery.

This time, he starts with older files. Vanth kept dossiers on various key figures in Guerdon. It's confusing to Terevant's eyes. Back in Haith, the names don't change. The Crown is always the Crown, the Enshrined families are always the same, regardless of who currently bears the family phylactery. The masters of the Bureau are all long established on their Vigils. If one were to compile similar dossiers on the rulers of Haith, you could safely carve them in stone. The living are footnotes to the dead.

It's not like that in Guerdon. Names appear and vanish, factions form and dissolve. There's no order, only temporary arrangements. A few people are threaded through the folders – Effro Kelkin, for example, has had a hand in everything for decades. Prince Daerinth, too, has been a quiet player in Guerdon's politics for decades, ever since he was exiled here after his royal mother's passing. Other folders end abruptly – one day there are sheaves of newspaper cuttings, reams of notes in Vanth's copperplate handwriting, and then there's nothing but a clipped obituary or a brief note describing their fall.

Rosha, the genius guildmistress of the alchemists, vanishes during the Crisis. The former Patros dies. Edwin Droupe hastily exits. The power structure of the city washed away overnight.

Tucked at the back of Rosha's file, there's a single handwritten list. Terevant takes it out and stares at it. A list of Haithi family names, old ones. It takes him a minute to work out what they have in common — it's a list of noble families that have died out without heirs. Their phylacteries taken to some arsenal under the royal palace. He tries to think of what such a note has to do with Rosha, but it makes no sense. Misfiled, he guesses. It's not the only error he's found.

He reads through other files. One heavy folder describes secret arms deals with alchemists, conducted through intermediaries. Hints of new weapons, more potent than any that had come before — and from the timing, these must be the god bombs Lys talked about.

The price was the "accidental" destruction of a Keeper monastery on Beckanore. Even after reading the file, Terevant's unsure why the alchemists wanted the monastery burned, but there's a copy of Vanth's letter of commendation sent by the Crown itself, so it must have been a success.

But Rosha's gone, and the alchemists are in disarray. It appears that Vanth was still obtaining alchemical weapons after the Crisis, so who was his supplier?

An arms dealer? There are plenty of files on those, and going through all of them takes hours. By the end, Terevant knows far more than he ever wished about the arms trade in the city, and how lucrative it is — his head spins from reading endless columns of numbers.

Heavy footsteps from outside. He hastily closes the folders. Olthic strides into the room, not bothering to knock.

"Next week, you're going to come with me to parliament. You need to see diplomacy at work."

"What's going on?"

"Simply put, I'm going to propose an alliance, between Haith and Guerdon. A mutually beneficial pact — we get all the alchemical weapons they can make, we protect them and their shipping."

"This is going before their . . . emergency committee?"

Olthic shakes his head. "Their damn election makes everything more complex. We'll be meeting with the emergency committee, but nothing will be signed until after the election – and it means we'll need to convince all of the party heads, so we're assured of victory no matter who wins."

Terevant looks his brother in the eye and asks a question that's been troubling him since he arrived. Maybe longer. Maybe since the retreat from Eskalind.

"Olthic," he asks, "why are you here? You could have had your pick of assignments. I visited the family commanders before I left Haith – Rabendath and the rest are desperate for you to return and lead the House troops. Why take the posting as ambassador?"

His brother stands, paces. Doesn't look at him as he answers. "The Crown wants Guerdon, Ter. When I get the sword, I'll be able to stand toe to toe with a demigod. But we're up against gods, and we'll need all the weapons they make here.

"Once I get the sword," continues Olthic, speaking to himself. "Then I'll lead the defence of Haith. I'm not like the rest of the living, Ter. I never lose my nerve." He turns to leave, then stops and turns back. "I'm told you found Vanth's remains. That was quick work. Well done, brother."

"Who told you?" asks Terevant, but he can guess.

"Lemuel. A mad saint, he said. I'm not surprised – the Godswar's in the New City already, but the rest of Guerdon won't admit it. If they'd seen what you and I saw at Eskalind, eh . . . " Olthic shakes his head. "They need Haith as much as we need them. We have to band together against the storm."

"Practising your speech for parliament?"

"Something like that." Olthic taps the doorframe with his hand, like he's patting it on the back. "The Bureau keeps pestering me for news on Vanth. They've got a bee in their skulls about his case."

The god bombs, thinks Terevant. He takes a moment of secret pleasure in knowing a secret that Olthic does not.

"Muttering about assassins and conspiracies. They fear Ishmeric spies infiltrating Guerdon and targeting the weapons foundries. You know the Bureau – full of paranoids. Endless wheels within wheels, endless reports and schemes, and still they turn to the Houses to get anything *done*." Olthic rolls his eyes. "Write up a report on Vanth's death, then go and fetch the sword. I'll need it before parliament."

Olthic walks out, vanishing silently down the corridor. He can move like a panther when he wants to.

To die at the hands of a saint is to be struck down by the wrath of a god, and the gods are mad. So everyone says. Vanth's death, therefore, has no more meaning than a storm at sea sinking one ship and not another.

But if that's true, there's equally no reason why Terevant survived Eskalind and the other soldiers did not, and Terevant doesn't like that thought. There has to be some meaning to it. Some unseen poetry that makes destiny rhyme.

Terevant waits until Olthic's gone, then closes the files, locks the office door. In Haith, it is said, the dead speak honestly. And he's yet to hear from Vanth's body.

Eladora isn't sure how long she has to wait in that windowless, doorless and shamefully bookless room. She jumps at every noise in the building below her, imagining it's assassins creeping up the tower to murder her. Or Miren, returning for Carillon, and finding her instead.

It's dark outside when Cari returns for her, and her cousin stops to scrub blood from a knife before they depart. "I had to check something. The bastards who came after you are the same ones who dumped the body," says Cari. The knife blade's gleaming now, but she keeps scrubbing. "Spar couldn't *see* where they went. Someone knows how to hide from me. Some relic or a spell or shit. Don't like that."

Eladora thinks back to the night of the reception at the Haithi embassy. The uproar over some incident. "Could you learn anything about the dead man from Haith?"

Cari ignores her, asks a question of her own. "Gethis Row's down by Seamarket, isn't it?"

Both locations are in the Wash. Eladora knows them from canvassing and her walks with Absalom Spyke. She nods.

Carillon bites her lip, picks up a different knife, circles around the apartment. "What is it?" asks Eladora.

"You're pretty high up with Kelkin and his lot, right? You'd hear things, watch reports, that sort of stuff?"

"I-I'm one of Kelkin's aides. Yes, I'm sometimes privy to sensitive information and secrets. Especially given our, ah, shared involvement in the Crisis."

"Know some guy called Edoric Vanth?"

The name is vaguely familiar. "I think he's Third Secretary at the embassy of Old Haith, or some similar title."

"And Haith's the place with all the dead guys who worship magic crowns, right?"

"I thought you travelled the world," sniffs Eladora, recalling a long-ago conversation where Carillon was more than happy to show how parochial Eladora's life was in comparison to her own former wanderlust.

"Never went north."

"Ah. Well, Haith's ruled by a Crown that's said to hold the wisdom of all previous kings. The aristocratic families all have a phylactery of their own, like the Crown but of less stature. And there's an elite class of intelligent undead, the Vigilants."

"So, I was right."

"I wouldn't be so reductive."

"What can kill one of those Vigilants?"

Eladora's hardly an expert on such matters. "I don't know. I understand they're quite resilient – after all, they're already *dead*, so mere wounds wouldn't suffice. I suppose the most effective way would be some sort of counter-magic."

"Saint stuff?"

Eladora remembers Saint Aleena in the tomb, parrying the spells of the Crawling Ones. Her sword of fire, its blaze incinerating Jermas

Thay, the firelight driving away the darkness. "I suppose so." She touches the hilt of Aleena's sword for comfort.

"Huh," says Carillon. She flexes her hand, looks at a faded scar on her palm.

Eladora weighs how much she should trust her cousin. By rights, she should report this meeting to the watch. She may no longer be the saint of the monstrous Black Iron Gods, but her supernatural connection to the New City is a worrying development.

"I don't know. If I hear anything, I'll ... well, how can I find you if I do hear anything?"

"I'll find you. Don't come back here, El. Don't look for me."

Eladora nods.

"All right! All right!" snaps Cari in frustration. "I'll give it to her." She digs into a pocket, producing a handful of boiled sweets, a few coins and a list of names scrawled on a scrap of paper. She hands the list to Eladora. "There, happy?" she asks. "He's really fucking excited about this. Now come on."

The return journey is surreally quick. Descending the many floors of the tower is like a whistle-stop tour of the wider world. On every level, the residents have decorated the walls of the landing with symbols and tokens of their vanished homes. Those who fled Ul-Taen have drawn protective sigils, and left an eerily lifelike mannikin watching over the stairwell. Those who left Lyrix to seek safety in Guerdon are guarded by a painted dragon, with teeth made of cuttlefish bones.

Outside, Cari hustles Eladora through back alleyways and secret stairs that open into a subway station. At this hour of the night, the trains run only infrequently, but there's one waiting there at the platform.

Cari shoves Eladora on board and closes the door without a word of farewell. A moment later, with a hiss of smoke from its alchemical engine, the train departs. The last Eladora sees of her cousin is Cari hurrying down the platform, muttering to the walls.

Carillon, she thinks privately to herself, has never looked more like Silva. It's not just that they're both sainted — it's a family resemblance, something Thay-ish about them. The Thay family was once tightly bound to Guerdon's fortunes, and now that the link to the city's future has been severed, Cari and Silva are both adrift. Finding new ways to shape Guerdon's fate.

It's only a short ride before Eladora's back on familiar territory, and the train pulls into the Venture Square stop only a short walk from her apartment.

There's a pile of rags on her doorstep. As Eladora gets closer, the rags unfold and rush towards her. It's Silkpurse.

"Oh, thank goodness, thank goodness. We looked all through the New City, Alic and I, but we got separated for a while and I couldn't find you. He's probably still up there looking, I'll tell him you're safe." The ghoul's clawed fingers pluck at Eladora's wounded forehead, her torn clothes. "I can fix up that," says Silkpurse, poking at one rip. "I'm good with thread." The ghoul's own dress is blood-stained, and she's limping, but ghouls heal quickly.

"I just need to sleep," insists Eladora. Silkpurse fusses about her, but she's suddenly too tired to explain what happened, so she just stumbles upstairs, falling through the door into her flat. She shuts it behind her, feels the cool darkness on her skin.

Her heart races as a sudden fear washes over her; every time she comes home, she imagines she'll find Miren waiting there for her, with a knife. But no assassin emerges from the shadows. No monstrous boy, stepping between the cracks of the world. She takes a breath and pushes the fear away.

She scoops up a pile of letters from the mat, stumbles down the hallway without lighting the lamp, seeing by touch and memory. In her study, she finds a smaller reading light and conjures a harsh glow from the aetheric tube. Cobwebs brush against her face; she hasn't cleaned in weeks. At least, she reflects, it's not quite as bad as Carillon's place, and the cobwebs tell her that no one's been here.

The note Carillon gave her falls to the floor. She picks it up and peers at her cousin's atrocious handwriting. As promised, it's a list of names and addresses in the New City, the people Cari glimpsed in her visions who would make good candidates. They'll all need to be vetted, of course, but the few names Eladora recognises are promising indeed. She places Cari's list on her writing desk, next to a pristine sheet of white paper. In the morning, she'll transcribe the list into her own perfect handwriting. Almost as an afterthought, she adds one more name to the bottom of the list. Alic is at least worth consideration by the party.

She sinks into an armchair and tries to focus on the letters. Calling cards from various IndLibs in Kelvin's orbit, drafts of speeches and policy papers, committee circulars. A memo talking about the upcoming Festival of Flowers and how the Keepers will use it for electioneering; lists of ideas on how the IndLibs can garland themselves in the trappings of the faith without making any commitments to the Keeper's church.

Every time the building creaks, she flinches. The toes of her boots are splattered with blood. She removes them and hides them in a closet.

Next is a folder of sensitive documents, sealed away behind wards. Eladora's letter opener has a retractable needle in the hilt so she can prick her finger and bleed on the wax, certifying her identity and disarming the magical traps. If she'd cast the spell herself or had a key to it, she wouldn't need this little blood sacrifice, and her finger wouldn't have developed a semi-permanent scar over the last year.

Inside she finds notes on trade and diplomacy, news from abroad that might affect the election. There's a draft of a speech on the navy that Kelkin wants to give. Kelkin's draft is rambling, written in haste, talking about new defences for the city, more escorts to defend against pirates from Lyrix and raiding krakens. The first of a new class of fast interceptors, to be launched just before the election.

From the writing, she can tell Kelkin is rattled, and he always overreacts when he's defensive, giving up his grand designs and leaps of progress to protect against much smaller slights. She imagines him as a dragon – slow, lumbering, ancient and scaly, vicious and cruel on the ground, but able to soar to the heavens when it takes flight. Sleeping on his hoard of voting ballots, the backroom of the Vulcan as his lair.

The thought makes her laugh and drop the pen, which rolls under the chair. Getting up to fetch it is intolerable, and the chair's so comfortable. She sets the letter aside, slipping it back into the folder and resealing it. The wax heals itself, flowing and merging. Like the flesh of a Tallowman.

As sleep comes, she remembers something, but she can't catch the thought. It's like a little spider, scurrying through her mind, hiding under the furniture. She glimpses it, but it's too fast, and it vanishes down into the deep places she doesn't like to think about any more, the sealed files.

If it's important, it'll come back.

CHAPTER 18

Queen's Point is the city's clenched fist. It's a fortress that commands the bay; a naval base with a dozen gunboats tied up at the docks, and the grey shark-shapes of larger steel-hulled warships out to sea; it's a prison and a barracks and a headquarters for the city's watch. All spikes and barricades and gun barrels and fluttering flags and military discipline. All reassuringly familiar at first, but, as Terevant moves through the fort, it becomes jarring.

Everyone's alive here. The dead of Haith make everything slow and stately. When the dead can work through the night without light or rest, there's less need for haste.

By contrast, Guerdon teeters on the edge of anarchy. Everything gets done, but it's sloppy.

He finds a clerk who directs him to another clerk. Terevant fumbles through Edoric Vanth's papers, and finds the name he's looking for. "Ah, the office of criminal sorcery, please. I'm looking for Dr Ramegos." If the priest was right, and the watch is holding Vanth's remains, they'll be under the jurisdiction of this Ramegos.

The clerk leads him down a narrow but well-lit staircase into the bowels of the fortress. Not a dungeon – no prisoners down here. It's a maze of offices and storerooms. Walls four feet thick, fortified against cannon fire and miracles. The distant drone of air-purifying fans, proof against alchemical poison and dust bombs. A modern fortress, unlike the ancient castles that guard the approaches to Haith.

"In here." The clerk shows him into a small waiting room with a few chairs. There's a map of Guerdon on one wall, flanked by a yellowed notice about registering sorcerous talents; on the other, a framed portrait of Droupe where some artist quested valiantly to find the man's chin.

Terevant sits. The whirring of those fans and the flicking aetheric light makes it hard to concentrate on the papers he brought with him, so he pulls out his novel, *The Bone Shield*, and loses himself in that story until the door opens. He glances up; a woman, a few years younger than him, her face bruised beneath makeup, one hand bandaged. She sits down in one of the other chairs to wait, taking out her reading material. He glances at the page she's studying — weird glyphs crawl across the paper. Some sort of technical notation, alchemical or thaumaturgical maybe.

He finishes the last few pages of *The Bone Shield* and closes the cover with a flourish.

"Any good?"

"A few passages. Not the ending though — a dull, predictable moral lesson about the folly of esteeming love over duty." He grins and offers the book to her. "I'm done with it, if you want it."

"Oh, I couldn't."

"It's fine. I'm *fantastically* wealthy." Which isn't wholly a lie; the Erevesics are rich landowners, but the family fortune mostly goes on maintaining the House troops battling the Godswar. Debts owed to Guerdonese alchemists, Ulbishan money-lenders.

The woman doesn't appear impressed, but she still takes the book and examines it. "It's from Haith," he explains as she scans the frontispiece.

"I gathered that. Do you mind if I borrow it?"

"As I said, I'm done with it. But you can return it to me at the embassy, if you like."

"Th-thank you," she says after a moment. "I'm Eladora Duttin."

"Terevant Erevesic, of the Ninth. No, wait, I'm with the embassy now."

She stares at him for a moment. "You're the ambassador's brother?"

"You know Olthic?"

"I've met him a few times, at the embassy. He's a very impressive man."

Terevant decides to change the subject. He's lost count of the number of conversations that have turned into people praising Olthic at him. "What are you doing down here? Reporting something?" He points to her wounded hand.

"No, no. Another matter. I can't discuss it. And what about you?"

He's about to explain that he's here to demand the remains of Edoric Vanth, but he remembers he's supposed to be a spy, and bites his tongue. "I can't discuss it either."

"Ah."

A long awkward silence follows. Footsteps in the corridor rise and then fall into the distance, and the silence returns again. It's Eladora who cracks first.

"Do you know why they call this fortress Queen's Point? When the Black Iron cult took over the city, the royal family fled rather than serve the new gods. Legends claim that the first Black Iron God was an idol, drawn out of the ocean by a fisherman, although Pilgrin theorises that early experiments in, ah, Haith, may have permitted the local gods to m-manifest in material form. Anyway, a priest smuggled the royal family out of the palace at Serran via a secret passage, and they made their way down through the ghoul tunnels to here, where there was a little fortress."

Apparently, her idea of small talk is a historical lecture.

"The queen ordered her troops to raise the royal pennant so the enemy would know that she was here. The Ravellers hurled themselves against the walls, and eventually consumed her, but . . . " She pauses, apparently lost in thought. "Forgive me. Anyway, while the enemy was distracted, the young prince fled Guerdon in a ship and went to seek allies against the Black Iron G-Gods. After the war, the place was named Queen's Point in her honour."

"The prince never returned?"

"No. The c-common legend is that he'll return in the city's darkest hour, but records show that he toured the east seeking allies, spending years at various courts trying to scrape together an invasion force, before he ran out of money and vanished."

"No cousins? There must have been someone else who could stake a claim?" A momentary and unfamiliar sense of shame – there are no heirs to the Erevesic sword, except Olthic and him, no one else to carry on the line. The Guerdon kingship was meaningless in the grand scheme of things; their crown just a piece of jewellery, not the living sword of the Erevesics.

"The Keepers consolidated power after they overthrew the Black Iron Gods." Duttin continues, clearly more confident when reciting from a history book than speaking off the cuff.

The door opens, interrupting Duttin's lecture. Standing there is a grey-haired woman who must be Dr Ramegos. Her robes are decorated with brightly coloured bird motifs, a splash of brightness against the grey concrete, but she also wears an armband with the sigil of the Guerdon city watch. Behind her is a young aide, who carries a gigantic grimoire chained to his wrist.

Duttin obviously knows the older woman, and rises to greet her.

"Are you all right?" asks Ramegos, "I heard you were attacked." She grabs Eladora's right hand, examines the injury. "Ach, I remember how much this hurts."

"I'm ... It's nothing." Eladora gives the doctor's hand a squeeze. "I'd like to learn more about warding spells, though. Just in case I'm followed home."

"Yes, yes. I'll show you."

"And, ah, teleport wards. Are such things possible?"

Terevant hastily interjects himself into the conversation, before he's forgotten. "Dr Ramegos – I'm from the embassy of Old Haith and—"

"Yes, yes. I did notice the periapts. This way."

Ramegos leads them both down the corridor, whispering to Eladora as they go. According to Edoric Vanth's notes Ramegos is, among other things, the city's thaumaturgical coroner, called in to consult on deaths involving sorcery or miracles. He wonders if she's native to Guerdon – her accent and appearance are both foreign. In Haith, the Crown would never trust an outsider with such responsibilities.

There's an aetheric tension in the air as they walk down the corridor, and Terevant wonders if there's some huge sorcerous engine on the other side of those concrete walls. When he blinks, he sees runes and sigils bursting against his eyes.

They stop at Ramegos' office. Through the doorway, Terevant can see the office walls are lined with books and heavy binders. Chains of tiny divine icons hang from the ceiling, gods from many different pantheons. Fate Spider and Lion Queen jostle for space with the Keeper pantheon, the death-god of Haith, the Star and other gods he doesn't recognise. All the icons are made by the same hand and are of the same size; the world's gods classified and collected like butterflies under glass. Then Ramegos closes the door in his face, leaving him outside.

Eladora settles into the chair opposite Ramegos. The thaumaturgist takes her hand, clucks at the injury. "Well, at least you've been *trying*."

"It was, ah, a practical application of sorcery."

"Oh?" Ramegos sits back in her chair. She waves her hand, and a kettle begins to boil. "Do tell."

Eladora picks her words carefully – for now, at least, she wants to avoid mentioning Carillon's name. Her cousin's like an alley cat that will have to be lured down from the New City, and trained to put this second set of god-granted talents to proper use. Ramegos is kindly and generous once you get to know her, but she's also an extremely powerful sorceress, and doesn't appreciate insolence. No, best to leave that meeting for another day.

"An altercation in the New City. An attempted robbery, I think. No lasting damage."

"To you or them?"

"Uh, to me. My assailants were, ah . . . "

"You know," says Ramegos, pouring a cup of spiced tea, "if you run around throwing dangerous spells without a full licence, you'll

answer to the Special Thaumaturgist. Who will tell you to practise more."

"I actually came here with a question." Eladora sips her tea.
"About words to block teleportations, yes?"

Ramegos snorts. "Teleportation's almost impossible, you know.
I've only known a handful of human adepts who could manage it.
Of all the things to worry about—"

"What about saints? Saints who teleport."

Ramegos puts down her cup. "No one," she says gently, "has seen
Miren Ongent in the last four months. You don't need to worry
about him."

Eladora blushes and tries to hide behind her teacup, embarrassed
at her transparency. "I, I – in my rooms, I thought ... well, there
was nothing actually there, but I thought, for a moment ... "

"He's gone, Eladora. I give you my word. You'll have to *trust* me
on that." Is she hinting at some secret? Did the city watch catch
Miren, despite his talent? "Although," muses Ramegos, "his miracles might make it easier to use similar sorcery here in Guerdon.
Might be worth looking into, when I have a spare year. All that
aside, there are ways to block or deflect teleportation. Not especially
useful, but good practice for you. We'll start with our old friend, the
Transactional Analysis ... "

Eladora groans inwardly as Ramegos pulls a well-thumbed textbook
on sorcery out from a drawer. The *Transactional Analysis of the Khebesh
Grimoire* is the foundation of modern sorcery, but it's infamously
complex and dull. She's not sure how long they spend applying the
techniques of *Transactional Analysis* to the problem, but by the time
they're done, her head feels like it's full of the alchemists' fire-quenching
foam – heavy, sticky, her thoughts thoroughly extinguished.

"That'll do for now," mutters Ramegos. "I've got work to do." She
sounds reluctant to stop.

"Thank you." As Eladora rises, Ramegos picks up *The Bone Shield*
and flips through it. "What's this?"

"A Haithi novel. Speaking of Haith, I should—"

Ramegos interrupts Eladora. "If this is about the dead Haithi spy that the watch found in the New City, then don't say anything more. Best you keep clear of *that* mess."

Eladora holds her tongue. Ramegos turns another few pages, then looks up. "Did your grandfather ever go to Haith?"

"I-I, uh, I don't know. Many aspect of J-j-j, of his life are obscure, and family records were destroyed when the family was, ah, also destroyed. Why do you ask?"

Ramegos hands the book back. "No reason. Now, run along. And don't forget to practise your sorcery."

The young scribe smiles awkwardly at Terevant as they wait outside for Eladora to finish her meeting with Ramegos. "She won't be long," he says, and he's right – Eladora and Ramegos spent only a minute or so in conversation, but when Eladora emerges she looks exhausted, as if many hours have passed. She yawns as she bids farewell.

"Thank you for the book." Her voice is scratchy, as if she's been talking for a long time. "I'll return it to you in the embassy."

"I look forward to it."

Ramegos calls him in. Her desk was covered in papers an instant ago; now it's bare as bone. He blinks.

"Please, be seated."

"I'm here about a Haithi citizen, Third Secretary Vanth. I've been informed that you have his remains."

She wrinkles her brow. "Informed? By the First Secretary?"

"No, by other sources."

"Other sources." She snorts. "How decorous."

"Do you have the body?"

She reaches up to her chain of gods, taps the Haithi death-god so that it starts swinging. The vibrations of the oscillating deity run up and down the chain, setting all the other gods clattering and clinking into one another. "It would be better," she says quietly, "to let me handle this."

"I'm in charge of embassy security. The murder of one of our diplomats falls under my purview."

The icons stop moving. Some of them have become tangled, caught in the spindly legs of the Ishmeric Fate Spider. Frowning, Ramegos reaches up and disentangles the Haithi death-god from the rest.

"Well now," she mutters to herself, "*that*'s not good." Shaking her head, she stands. "Let's get this done."

She leads him through a maze of corridors and stairs. Despite her age, she sets a fast pace, impatiently ushering him on.

"Did you know Edoric Vanth?" She pauses at the door of the morgue.

"Not really." Terevant feels like he got to know the man a little, through reading his notes. Vanth loved Guerdon, its messy intrigues and its changing ways. He was observant; he had an eye for quirks of personality or biographical details that provided a key to understanding a case. He was close to Prince Daerinth – both men had been stationed here in Guerdon for years, one in exile, one in comfortable obscurity, while a string of ambassadors came and went. Some of Vanth's notes reminded Terevant of his own relationship with his father – keeping affairs in order while the older man slowly slips away.

Perhaps he's been too hard on Daerinth. Haithi decorum would never let the First Secretary admit it, but he must feel Vanth's death keenly.

Dr Ramegos unlocks the heavy door and invites him into the morgue. There, on a slab, lies a fire-blackened corpse. It's unsettling to see it in such a condition – Vigilants are customarily stripped of their dead flesh as soon as possible. Death isn't supposed to be so disorderly.

The worst of the damage is to the head and upper chest, which have been burned almost to the bone. Cracked leather fragments cling to the ruin of the man's face – it might be scorched skin, or the remains of Vanth's clothing. Terevant checks the wrists. There, beneath the roasted skin, he can feel the telltale lumps of the iron periapts.

Ramegos sighs. "Do you know what he was doing in the New City?"

"That's an internal matter."

The doctor stares at him, and for a moment Terevant feels a sudden weight in his hands, as if he was carrying an object, heavy and invisible — a sword. Sorcery's crawling through this room, in ways he doesn't have the talents or training to detect. Subtle forces moving beyond his perception.

Ramegos pauses. "You're Olthic's brother, aren't you?"

He suppresses a sigh. "Yes — what of it?"

"You don't look much like him, that's all." She sounds saddened for a moment, immensely weary as she gestures to the corpse. "I can tell you how he died." She points at the ghastly wounds. Terevant's seen much worse in the war, but it's different here. The stark silence of the morgue is oppressive; seeing a mangled and burned corpse should come with the sound of shouts and screaming, with distant artillery and miracles booming out of heaven. Not this silence, broken only by the ticking of a clock and Ramegos' low voice, pointing out the gunshot wound, the knife cut, the evidence of sword and fire.

Vigilants can be immensely resilient. Wounds that would kill a mortal are easily shrugged off — it doesn't matter if you've got a punctured lung if you don't need to breathe any more. Decay, dismemberment or widespread damage are harder to withstand. Still, the body's mostly intact despite everything.

"Miraculous." Ramegos touches the burned skin, which flakes away like ash.

"I've heard a name — the Saint of Knives."

Ramegos frowns. "Maybe." She draws out the word, lets doubt seep in.

"You have another theory?"

"Not yet. I don't know enough. I need more time." She brushes some ash off Vanth's sleeve. "We all need more time."

A thought pops into Terevant's mind. "Could it have been an Ishmerian?" *Ishmeric agents disrupting the supply of alchemical weapons from Guerdon, while their invasion fleet closes on Old Haith.* "The chosen of High Umur can hurl fire."

"If there was an Ishmeric war-saint in Guerdon, I'd know," replies Ramegos. She sounds tired.

Terevant bends over the corpse again, staring into Vanth's eye sockets. "You're still searching for the killer, I presume," he asks.

"Not personally, but rest assured that the watch is poking sticks into gutters and beating up witnesses as we speak."

"I'll take custody of the body now," says Terevant, sharply.

Ramegos goes to the corner, tugs a cord. Somewhere far away, a bell rings. "Someone will be down in a minute to bring you and the body back to the embassy." She sits down on a bench at the side of the room, suddenly showing her age. Her young scribe hurries in to tend to her, still carrying his huge book. Muttering to herself, Ramegos opens the tome and pages through to find the first blank page. She takes a pen and starts to write, the nib scratching across the heavy paper.

Terevant circles the table, examining the body closely. Laid out on a tray next to the body are Vanth's possessions. A steel knife, well used. A few silver coins. A ticket stub, too badly burned to make out any details. A scrap of paper, also burned. He peers at it. It's a leaflet, crumpled and scorched, but still legible in parts. *The fires of Safid will carry the soul*, he makes out.

"I want to show you something," announces Ramegos, startling him. Terevant spins around.

"What's that?" he asks.

"In Khebesh," answers Ramegos slowly, "it is the custom to record every act of sorcery. Every action, every spell or miracle, deforms reality. We write them down so that one day we can restore reality to what it should be." She finds the page she was looking for, and turns the book around so he can see.

There's a whole section of the book that's a wild scrawl, entries bursting out of the neat lines to cascade down, twist back on themselves, sigils burned into the paper. She flips back one page, then another and another. A litany of madness. One page is just a blotch of ink; another is stained with tears.

"I don't understand," says Terevant.

"That's when I passed through the Godswar," says Ramegos. "I know you've seen it, too. So you understand, I hope, how blessed we are here in Guerdon. How we must do everything we can to keep it that way."

Ramegos struggles to her feet, groaning. "Someone will be with you soon."

She walks out, leaving him alone with the dead.

CHAPTER 19

Today, the spy knows, will be a day of many faces.

His first face is the one he wakes with. X84, watching Emlin sleep. Three nights in a row, the boy was called by Annah and Tander, to whisper miraculous messages to distant gods. A litany of weapons sales and cargo shipments, whispered to heaven. The toll on the boy's health is obvious. It's not merely the effort of communing with the deity – it's essential for a covert saint like this one to disengage cleanly. There can be no collateral miracles, no physical manifestations, no secondary blessings. Nothing that could be detected and traced by the city watch. He must reach out for Fate Spider and hide from his *attention* at the same time. Cut away the portions of his soul that are wholly claimed by the god, while still being devoted to him.

It's a balancing act that's driven stronger men mad.

X84 makes the considered decision to leave the asset to rest, because he'll be needed tonight. But it's Alic who tugs the blanket over Emlin, who goes downstairs and fetches breakfast, then leaves it by the boy's side for when he wakes.

Over breakfast in Jaleh's, he is Alic. He's given away that he can read and write well, and now half the god-touched crowd round his table in the big common room every morning. Some want him to write letters to the city watch, pleading for the release of relatives from the internment camp on Hark Island; others want him to deal with the city's bureaucracy, and he's become very familiar with the rules for guild membership, council fees – and the electoral rolls.

There are letters home to Mattaur or Lyrix or Ulbishe (and, as he reads those, Alic lets the spy in him surface a little more, skimming them for sweetmeats of useful information). Letters to other addresses here in Guerdon, written by the god-touched whose stigmata are too visible to allow them to walk the streets beyond the Wash and New City.

It's become part of his morning routine, of late, to spend a little time with Haberas and his mer-wife Oona. Haberas has found work down in Dredger's yards; it's mostly Stone Men who do the dangerous labour down there, but some tasks call for nimble fingers. Haberas and Alic sit by the water's edge and talk of the old days in Severast, while Oona listens from the shallows. She has no lungs left, only gills, so she cannot speak. The spy idly wonders if the Kraken-god was being cruel when he transformed Oona, or if she was just caught in the wake of some greater miracle.

When the factory whistle echoes across the harbour, Haberas shuffles down to the docks, and Oona vanishes into the deeps to hunt.

It's Sanhada Baradhin – recalled from oblivion – who shows up at Dredger's offices down by the docks. Dredger greets his old friend warmly; sticky wine is poured into glasses; they gossip about war and doom and profit margins. Sanhada's evasive when Dredger asks him what he's been up to. Again, Dredger offers Sanhada work; again, it's the spy who refuses. He makes sure, though, that he's seen walking out with Dredger. The armour makes Dredger easy to spot. Everyone in the Wash knows him, and everyone will mark who he's talking to. They'll remember Sanhada's swagger, and his thick accent, and his hat, and not the face beneath.

Setting off at a fast walk, the spy casts off Sanhada Baradhin and becomes X84 again, the Agent of Ishmere. Anonymous, unremarkable. He takes precautions now, a twisting path through the alleys and wynds of the Wash. Passing through one temple and another, so the divine incense of many gods clings to his cloak. He ducks into a subway station, leaves again without getting on a train. At Phaeton Street he draws an X in chalk by a lavatory stall, and then it's Alic who returns to Jaleh's house.

To wait. To write, furtively, notes jotted down as he works in the attic room, patching holes in the roof.

Emlin skulks around the attic, avoiding the spy. Flinching at random moments, like he's hiding from thunder only he can hear. Staring at spider webs, and cracks in the glass. The boy's going hallow – slipping out of the mortal world, seeing too much of the divine. Alic watches with concern. X84 frets about the loss of a vital tool.

"Fate Spider's getting closer," whispers the boy, "but He won't talk to me."

"Patience," says Alic as he writes. "Our god must hide."

"Is He hiding from me?"

"From our enemies."

"Tander said I'm not trying hard enough." The boy's hand strays to his face, rubbing his grimy forehead. Probing, as though he can poke holes in his skull and let the god in.

"Tander's an idiot."

"But *he's* loyal."

The spy stops writing. He looks up at the boy, who's perched atop a bunk.

"What do you mean?" *He's* loyal. By omission, someone else isn't.

Emlin doesn't answer. He just hunches over, scratching at the bristly dark hairs that have started growing at the base of his neck.

Definitely going hallow, thinks the spy.

"Jaleh's holding an evening service in a while," says Emlin suddenly. Emlin's skipped most of the gentling rites; if the boy wants to attend one, then he, too, can tell that's something wrong. The bland, placid worship of the Keepers is a balm to the soul, compared to the fierce, frantic skittering of Fate Spider.

"I'm meeting Tander. Go if you want to."

"If you're meeting Tander," replies the boy, "then Annah will need me tonight." Shivering as he speaks, despite the summer heat.

You don't put more weight on a thread than it can bear.

"Here," says Alic, handing the boy a few coins, "run down to Lambs Square. Get out of this house for a while."

Emlin stares at him for a long moment, then snatches the coins. "Be back before dark," cautions Alic as the boy runs off.

Twilight, and the lamps light up across the city. Flickering gas flames or torches or just darkness in the Wash, eerie alchemical lamps with their sickly, steady radiance in richer districts. Miraculous light in the New City, welling up from the stones. The sound of doleful singing emanates from the little chapel attached to Jaleh's house. Evening prayers to the Kept Gods, hymns that never soar.

Outside, the spy sees Tander, standing under a lamppost. Shimmying up to light a cigarette from the gas flame.

In the course of leaving Jaleh's house, the spy becomes X84 again. Alic's smile falls from his face; Alic's height and strength from his shoulders. He walks past Tander, ignoring him for the benefit of anyone watching. He makes his way to the IndLib workers' club, open late tonight. He brushes past knots of men and women, overhears snatches of conversation about rumoured plots by the alchemists, tales of the Godswar abroad. The spy exchanges pleasantries with a few as he passes by, but goes alone to a corner table.

Tander shows up a few minutes later, sits down opposite him. Just two working men, nothing to see here.

"I like this." Tander holds up his pint, admires it in the light. "Watch won't dare follow us in here, not so close to an election. And the beer's better, too, even if you have to pay for it. At the Hawkers' places, you can get the alchemists' slop for free."

"You always have to pay for quality," says X84. Under the table, the deal is done; Tander passes across a bag of coin, and X84 hands over a tightly wrapped scroll of paper. To the spy's professional horror, Tander unrolls the pages and looks over them right then and there. He coos and laughs as he reads the documents – the spy's handwritten notes on Guerdon's naval readiness, on proposed alliances and trade deals, on new alchemical weapons. All copied and reworked from Eladora's letters.

"Where did you get this?" marvels Tander.

"Asking questions in dockside bars," lies X84. "Is it good stuff?" he asks. "Worth the money?"

X84 cares about the money. The spy doesn't.

The spy watches Tander read, praying the man sees it, sees the vital secret wrapped up in those pages.

He doesn't see it. He flips past the pages about Guerdon's navy without stopping.

It all depends on Annah now, thinks the spy. He takes a drink of his beer and smiles, choking down his frustration.

Patience, the spy tells himself. *Live your cover. Hide.*

"This might need to go out tonight. Bring the boy up to us later." Tander gulps his beer, stuffs the papers into his shirt. "Little bastard is losing his knack, though. You brought us a shit saint, mate. Can't commune properly at all. *Probably* not your fault." He grins, showing too many clenched teeth. "But, I mean, you're the one who thought a fucking *gentling-house* would be a good place to hide. And now it's me who she's got crawling around on my hands and knees in the cellar, looking for fucking spiders to feed to him. Offerings, too. Sacrifices." Tander pats the hidden bundle of papers, his excitement turned to sudden nausea. "We'll need another sacrifice tonight, to make sure this gets through. And it'll be more than a fucking stray cat. I should make you fetch it."

The spy takes a long sip of his own drink, avoiding eye contact.

"We'll be in touch," says Tander after a minute. He rises, drains his cup and stumbles off into the crowd.

The spy lingers, finishing his drink in a way that won't draw attention – anyone who knows him here knows him as Alic, and Alec doesn't have money. So, Alic wouldn't leave a drink unfinished, nor would he guzzle it like Tander just did. Alic is a slow, thoughtful, helpful fellow. Alic's a good sort. He relaxes into the Alic identity, drawing it around him like a comfortable overcoat. Alic doesn't have to worry.

So, Alic sits there, drinking his beer and listening to the songs. They're old songs, forty years old, from the heyday of the Reformist movement. Songs about the corruption of the Keeper's church, about how the gods don't answer prayers no more, but how the alchemists will change honest sweat into gold. He overhears snatches of gossip about the election; they're all for Kelkin, the big beast of Guerdon. Kelkin, all gristle and sharp elbows. A survivor, winning yet another election by sheer tenacity.

The spy listens, too, and watches the crowd. Who might be useful? That woman there, her clothes bleached in spots, and faint marks on her face suggesting she wears a mask – does she work in the alchemists' factories? That merry trio at the bar – sailors, he'd wager, but are they navy deckhands or the crew of some merchant? Those two in the corner, whispering to one another – what might they be up to? He smiles at the thought that they're spies, too, and it's not impossible – Guerdon's crawling with spies and informants. Are they conspiring, too, sending secret messages back to the dusty lords of Haith, the poisoners of Ulbishe, or the dragons of Lyrix?

A tall man stalks over to the table and sits down in the chair vacated by Tander. He's got another beer in his hand for Alic.

"Absalom Spyke," he says. It takes a moment for the spy to realise it's an introduction.

"Alic."

"Aye. Duttin was singing your praises. Says you're a man worth keeping an eye on."

"Is she all right? She got hurt when we were up canvassing in the New City."

Spyke rolls his eyes. "Maybe it'll knock some sense into her. I don't know what Kelkin was thinking, sending a soft girl like that up there."

Alic shrugs. "It was a rough patch. We all nearly got our brains knocked out, sense and all. They were heavily armed."

"So Silkpurse told me. She also thinks you're worth talking to, and she's good at sniffing out worthies."

"High praise indeed."

"Maybe," says Spyke, leaning back.

"Tell me about yourself, Alic."

The spy lets Alic talk. This identity is his own creation – not stolen, like Sanhada Baradin's name and history, or imposed on him like X84. He allows Alic to speak freely, to talk about how he wants to help, about how Guerdon welcomed him when he fled the Godswar. Spyke nods slowly, brings over a few other people who fled Mattaur. They share stories, and Alic's tales might be made up on the spot but there's enough truth in them to pass muster. More people crowd around them; tables get dragged over. Spyke buys a round of drinks for everyone, and there's cheering.

"All of ye," says Spyke, "can vote. Mr Kelkin's reforms saw to that. As long as you live in the city and can prove it – and that ain't hard, just need someone in good standing to vouch for you, and I'll do that. And when you vote, you'll vote for Mr Kelkin's man in this borough – whoever that is." His dark eyes stare at the spy as he says that.

"I have to go," says the spy abruptly, pushing back his chair.

Spyke grabs him by the arm. "We'll be in touch, all right?"

Alic leaves Emlin sleeping. The boy disobeyed his instructions, came back well after sundown, missing both the spy's curfew and Jaleh's evening prayers. Emlin thinks he crept into the house unseen through the cellar door, but Alic watched him from their window, and said nothing. The boy deserves a little taste of freedom.

The spy sneaks out of the house via the same route, makes his way through the dark streets of the Wash. Heads west, west and up, crossing the old canal they call Knightsgrave, and bribing the watchman to get through the gate into Newtown. It's only a short walk from there to the safe house.

Tander meets him at the door, and scowls. "Where's the boy?"

Alic steps over the threshold, and Tander suddenly grabs him, twisting his arm in an interestingly painful way, frog-marching him into the kitchen. Slamming him down into a chair, and suddenly there's a gun in his face.

"Where's the fucking *saint*?" demands Tander. The man's good at violence, if nothing else, notes the spy.

"In bed." Alic cranes his neck to look past blustering Tander, to

Annah who sits by the fire, smoking, the stolen papers on her lap. "Emlin needs to rest. You're working him too hard."

"That's not your judgement to make," says Annah. "Emlin belongs to the Sacred Realm. We all belong to the Sacred Realm, and if it pleases the gods to destroy any of us, we shall go to our death without hesitation." Tander shoves the barrel of the gun into the spy's nose for emphasis, and Annah makes a disgusted noise. "Oh, put the bloody gun down, Tander."

He obeys instantly, like a whipped dog. Stomps off to the hallway, but he's still listening. Stations himself by the door, gun in hand, as if he's expecting trouble. Emlin's not the only one under stress.

"I've read through these papers," says Annah. "There's something I want to discuss."

"What is it?" asks the spy. *He* knows the answer, but X84 doesn't, Sanhada Baradhin doesn't, Alic doesn't.

"This new warship they mention may be significant," says Annah.

"How? What's one new ship going to matter?"

Annah pauses. "Last year, just before the Crisis, the alchemists made a new weapon. A new warhead. They sent a gunboat up the coast to Grena and test-fired it."

The spy knows this. He's known it since before he climbed the stair of fire to Captain Isigi's holy office. Known it since before the fall of Severast. He knew it the instant the goddess was destroyed, irretrievably unmade by the divine hatred of the bomb. But he's a good liar, and when Annah describes the god bomb to him he injects just the right amount of surprise and dawning realisation into his reaction. A weapon that can kill gods, my word. But that would mean – gasp!

Everything, from his first careful approach in Mattaur to his new identities as Sanhada, as X84, as Alic, has been towards this moment. He holds his breath as Annah reinitiates him into the secret of secrets.

"We're not sure how many of the weapons survived the Crisis. The alchemists had at least one more working model, but they didn't get a chance to launch it before the gutter miracle. There may be more warheads. We've been looking for them, but," she puffs on the cigarette, "so has everyone else, and we don't have the resources of Haith."

"You think they've got one of those bombs on the new ship?" asks the spy.

"That's how I'd do it," Tander calls from the hallway. "A new ship, fast, heavily warded, but lightly armed? She's a god hunter."

"Maybe." Annah's unconvinced. "Certainly reads that way." She pokes the dying fire in the kitchen grate into life, puts a kettle of water on to boil. Points to a shelf, at mugs and a coffee jar. The spy takes them down. She stares out of the window, into the darkness of the night. The lights of Queen's Point fortress burning beyond the Newtown terraces. "It could be a bluff. For all we know, the weapons were all destroyed during the Crisis, along with the alchemists' foundries. I could see Effro Kelkin doing something that brazen – threatening every god in the world, when he's got nothing."

She hands him a coffee. The heat of the cup makes the scar on his palm hurt.

"Who would be fool enough," the spy asks, smiling, "to lie to the gods?"

CHAPTER 20

The blank page is like a wall of white stone; the words Terevant tries to write feel inadequate to the task. A dozen false starts. *Report to the Bureau concerning the death of Third Secretary Vanth*, he writes, then crumples that page up and takes another blank sheet from Vanth's desk.

A knock at the door. Lemuel. Eyes red-rimmed, just back from some nocturnal mission in the sleepless city outside the embassy walls. His bandage, too, is red-rimmed; the wound has opened again. "Are you done yet? The night train won't wait."

"Come in," orders Terevant.

Lemuel enters, curses when he sees the blank page. "What's the delay? I found Vanth's fucking body for you. The Saint of Knives did him." He picks at the edges of the bandage, wincing at the pain.

"I found this on Vanth's body," says Terevant, sliding the half-burned leaflet across the table. "A pamphlet from—"

"The Keepers, aye." Lemuel glances over the paper with disinterest. "What of it?"

"Maybe it means something."

"Maybe it means fuck-all. Gods below, it's election season – you can't walk five feet without some party hack pushing something into your hand."

"The Special Thaumaturgist, too," argues Terevant, "she suggested . . ."

"What?" snaps Lemuel, irritatably.

"That it wasn't the Saint of Knives. Maybe Ishmere had a hand in Vanth's death. We can't be certain that there are no enemy saints in this city."

"So which is it, then?" Lemuel raises his voice in anger. "Keepers, or Ishmere?"

Terevant taps the blank page. "This letter," he says, "will go out with my signature on it, and the seal of House Erevesic. I need to be sure of what happened." *Vanth's death is only the starting point. It can't have been a random killing by some mad saint. It must be connected to the god bombs.* "We need to investigate more."

"We? *We?*" echoes Lemuel, "*I* found Vanth's body. I know Guerdon. You have your fucking name and the seal of House Erevesic, and what else? I know all about you, you know. You're the *other* Erevesic, the one who failed. And failed. And failed. And now you presume to give me orders?"

Terevant's hand clenches in anger and shame, crumpling the blank sheet. Everything Lemuel said is true. He could have written that litany.

"Write the fucking letter," insists Lemuel.

"Not until I'm sure."

"When have you ever been certain of anything?" mutters Lemuel. Terevant tries to ignore the barb, but it troubles him. It's too well aimed to be a random shot – either there's another file somewhere in the building with Terevant's name on it, or Lyssada has told Lemuel all about him.

Lemuel scratches his chin. His skin's pockmarked and reddened by some irritant. He stalks across the room, looks at the ticking clock on the wall. "All right," he says after a dozen ticks, "let's go and talk to her."

He brings Terevant out of the embassy, through the streets of Bryn Avane to another building. Long and grey, with many dark windows. A hive of bureaucracy; rows of offices and clerks' cubbyholes, but at this time of night it's almost deserted. Lemuel, it seems, knows the night guard, knows he can be bribed. Inside, the building smells of floor polish; a maze of grey and beige. "Board of Trade," mutters Lemuel. "This way."

The building would be utterly mundane by day; by night, when it's empty, it's eerie, as though they're exploring a ruined city after some catastrophe. In Haith, of course, such a place would never be empty, even at night. The Vigilant work without cease.

They pass through a conference room, unlit lamps sitting on a mahogany table topped with green baize. A map on the wall shows Guerdon's exports of alchemical weapons, red lines like veins linking the city to the wider world, the Godswar beyond the seas. The thickest lines pump to Haith; other trade routes connect to Lyrix, to Ulbishe. The map must be out of date – it shows Severast and Mattaur, and they've been swallowed by the great rival.

"Here we are." Terevant's heart jumps with excitement – maybe Lyssada has crept into the city for some clandestine meeting, and she's waiting in the next room – but Lemuel opens the door to a small windowless chamber. There's nothing inside except a table, a single chair and a curious machine: a cross between a typewriter, an accordian and some sort of aetheric lamp.

"Clever thing, this. Alchemists make 'em. It's an aethergraph. Lets you talk to people far away," mutters Lemuel. He adjusts the machine, plugging in a thick silver cord, pressing a key that makes the central column of the machine glow with an eldritch werelight. "They've got them all over the city – city watch, parliament, guild-halls. Even some out in the hinterlands. The Bureau's got friends that let us borrow their set, when we need it. But we won't have much time." The machine clatters, the keys moving on their own. "Here we go," he says. "Put your fingers there." Terevant sits down at the machine and places his fingers over the keys. Lemuel presses another control, and suddenly there's the *sensation* of someone else in the room. A warmth in the air; the ghostly scent of Lys's perfume. Wind rustling in treetops, as if a vast forest has sprung up in the street outside.

The glowing aether-tube is like a temporary phylactery, bringing both their souls together in a brief sorcerous union.

His fingers move of their own accord, pulled irresistibly to tap out a message, a letter at a time. H-E-L-L-O. T-E-R.

It's weirdly intimate, as though he can feel her fingertips on the other side of the brass keys.

WE FOUND VANTH, he types.

The keys move again. Lys is typing. I KNOW. WELL DONE. Terevant finds an involuntary smile creeping across his face.

DO YOU TRUST ME? she asks. It feels like she's sitting at the table with him, staring into his eyes.

ALWAYS, he replies instantly.

THEN TRUST LEMUEL.

The light in the aethergraph flickers, and Terevant's suddenly aware of another phantasmal presence. He gets the impression it's another woman. Older, greyer. He distantly hears the sound of bells ringing, and he doesn't know if he's hearing with his own ears, or if it's coming over the psychic aethergraph link. His mouth fills with the taste of wine.

I HAVE TO GO, types Lys. I WILL SEE YOU AT THE FESTIVAL. KEEP—

And Lemuel reaches over Terevant's shoulder, pulls the cord from the aethergraph. The machine shuts down abruptly, leaving a sickening psychic absence in place of Lys. The sensation of standing on the edge of a great emptiness.

"Time's up," says Lemuel, "but you heard her: send the damn letter."

Back at the embassy, Terevant writes the letter. A few scant words, confirming that Third Secretary Vanth was killed by a criminal saint in the New City. Lemuel takes the letter, the wax seal of the Erevesics still warm and soft, and hurries off to the train station. There's still time to catch the night train to Haith. Terevant imagines the letter flitting north, vanishing into the great machine of the Bureau. Bone-white hands breaking the seal, the empty eye sockets of some Bureau mandarin reading his hasty note.

He's done what was asked of him. Swallowed his doubts. Done as Lys asked.

He wonders what he's set in motion. He can dimly apprehend the movement of invisible powers, intrigues unlocked by that letter. The Bureau was worried by Vanth's disappearance; they feared enemy action. Now, they've been reassured. Maybe it's all as simple as removing a possible blemish on Lys's record, so the necromancers don't hold it against her in consideration for the Crown. He curses Ramegos – if she hadn't planted these doubts in his mind, he'd never have thought twice about the flyer.

That's when I passed through the Godswar. I know you've seen it, too.

At Eskalind, the saints of High Umur hurled fire from the sky. The saints of the Lion Queen grew claws that could pierce any armour. He sits in Vanth's office and stares at the ranked folders and towers of notebooks, and remembers Eskalind.

What if we're wrong? What if Ishmere's already here? He remembers Ramegos' chains of divine icons, the Fate Spider entangled with death. And her book – why did she show him the book? To warn him that rivals in the Godswar were already in the city?

He thinks of Lys and Olthic, pulling him this way and that. Each one trying to command his loyalty and trust. Intrigues between the various Haithi Houses and the Bureau are never-ending, grudges and schemes perpetrated by the undying, and by the living desperate to earn a place among them.

What if they've missed something?

Vanth is dead. His vigil has ended. But there might be something left in him.

"Yoras," calls Terevant quietly.

The door to the office opens a crack, and Yoras pops his skull in. **Sir?**

"We're not done yet," says Terevant, surprising himself. "Go and wake the necromancer."

The dead don't sleep.

Terevant does. He snatches a few hours in the middle of the night. Wakes before dawn, hurries back down to the basement vault where Yoras stands guard. From inside, low chanting, a prayer to Death.

Vanth's remains lie on a cot bed before the empty altar.

"How goes?" he asks the embassy necromancer.

The necromancer — a young woman, auburn hair beneath her cowl, rings and necklaces of polished bone clinking as she moves — rolls her eyes. "There wasn't much left of body or soul here. We must be grateful for whatever we receive, no matter how meagre. But we are nearly done." She's dressed the former Third Secretary in a grey shift, and now she's taking a knife to the tattooed flesh on his wrists and ankles, his heart and neck and groin, gently exposing the periapts that made him Vigilant-caste. To reanimate him, she needs to remove him from the death-castes entirely.

It, thinks Terevant. The corpse on the floor isn't Vanth any more. Anything that was Vanth got burned away when he was destroyed with holy fire. And all they want from it is some lingering memory, a name or a clue engraved in scar tissue in the brain.

"This body has been tampered with," says the necromancer.

"Other than getting shot, stabbed and set on fire?"

"Yes." She peels back an incision to reveal Vanth's guts, sorts through them. "It's beyond my skill to read these signs."

"Can you still bring him back?"

She taps an exposed periapt with her knife. "Little life will cling to these bones, but I will try," she whispers. The temple seems to swallow all sound. Even the scraping of the serrated knife is muted.

Yoras comes in and watches the knife work in silence for a few minutes, then says **it itches, sir, when they flense you like that. Strangest thing, having itchy bones.** The skeleton shivers.

"Quiet," hisses the necromancer.

The silence that fills the cellar room becomes a prayer, a hymn to Death. There are words in that silence. The necromancer draws on the urn of souls in the courtyard above to fuel her sorcery — the books in the Office of Supply will have to be balanced later, but the Erevesic estates produce plenty of peasant souls to recompense the embassy account. An eerie bluish mist precipiates in the room. A ghostly miasma, chill to the touch. It adheres to periapts — both Terevant and Yoras end up with streamers of ghost-mist trailing from them, but the necromancer gathers the greater mass of soul-stuff and herds it towards Vanth's corpse. His periapts swallow it.

Terevant has seen the dead rise before, many times. Most often, it was the Vigilant soldiers of Haith rebinding their souls to mortally wounded bodies. There, the body moved like a marionette for the first few minutes, and you could see the glowing shadow of the spirit, anchored to the iron periapts. The Vigilant didn't really come back, because they never really left. They lashed themselves to their bones rather than cross over. Like a shipwrecked man clinging to a rock while the current tries to drag him out to sea.

He's seen enemy dead rise, too, resurrected by the mad gods. In their blind haste, the gods vomited up souls and crammed them into bodies called back into service or shaped by remorseless miracles. He's seen soldiers rise up on the battlefield, alive but horribly mangled. Seen them return in bodies assembled from the stuff of the gods, brought back with tree branches replacing arms, or scabs of solid gold to staunch arterial bleeding. The resurrected never come back clean.

This is different.

Edoric Vanth doesn't come back at all.

The thing they've made moves like an animal, snuffling and whining to itself. It crawls off the bier in the necromancer's shrine, shambles upright to walk in halting steps.

The Vanth-thing prowls around the cellar room, sniffing and pawing at everything. Terevant keeps one hand on his sword in case it turns violent.

Without looking over at the necromancer, he calls out, "How long will it last?"

"A few days." She takes a deep breath, "Unless I renew the spells again then. Not as hard, but . . . " She pauses. "Where are you going to keep it? You can't leave it down here."

A good question, and not one Terevant has an answer for yet. "I'm not going to keep it," he says, "and do not speak of this to anyone. It's a matter of state security."

Yoras escorts the thing into an anteroom and dresses it in a hooded cloak, in an attempt to hide the worst of the burns. On a dark night, in the rain, if you were blind drunk, you might not spot that the cowled figure you just passed was not alive – but if you're that unobservant you probably won't make it home alive yourself.

"Let's see what he remembers." Terevant steps forward, raises his voice. "Vanth?"

The undead thing flinches, turns its gory head to face him. There's something in there, some intelligence beyond the rote motions of a zombie, but it's not Vanth.

"Do you remember who killed you?"

The ruined jaw moves soundlessly. The thing paws at its throat in frustration.

Then nods its head.

CHAPTER 21

They leave the embassy through a side door. Yoras pauses at the threshold. **As Vigilant, I'm not allowed to leave the embassy grounds.**

"This counts as official businesses. Come on."

It really should be in writing, mutters Yoras, but the Vanth-thing is already shuffling down the street, so he follows, fastening his face mask into place as he runs.

Vanth leads them towards a subway station. Terevant suppresses a nervous laugh as the zombie-thing pats its rags, looking for a coin to buy a ticket. Terevant circles around the undead thing and buys three tickets from the clerk.

"Your friend all right?" asks the clerk, nodding towards the hooded figure.

"God-touched." The cruelties of the Godswar explains all sorts of weirdness. "We'll take care of him."

At this hour, the train is mostly empty, and they have a carriage to themselves.

Vanth's half-burned neck struggles to hold the weight of his skull. His head bobbles back and forth in time to the rocking of the train as it rattles through ghoul tunnels under the great city. The carriage fills up as they pass through Five Knives, through Glimmerside, through Castle Hill. A few look suspiciously at the hooded figure and the masked soldier, but Terevant just smiles and waves back, and they look away.

We're past the junction for the New City, observes Vanth, *next stop is the east Wash, and then the docks.*

Terevant shrugs. "Let's see what comes of it."

At a stop in the Wash, the Vanth-thing lurches up. Terevant hurries to make sure the cloak doesn't fall away. Guerdon has its share of horrors and monsters, but walking corpses aren't a usual part of the menagerie.

They follow Vanth back to the surface, follow it through the warren of little streets in this ancient part of Guerdon. The creature's moving easier now, as if taking up the habits of its life as it gets closer to where it died.

This part of the city is the shoreline between Old and New, the westernmost extremity of the Crisis and its spasm of impossible building. On their right, dark-windowed tenements and rookeries leer out, a warren of alleyways and thieves' hiding places in the spaces between ill-built walls. On the other side of the street, the same – but punctuated by the eerie angel-built intrusions of heaven. A footbridge arcs above their heads – three-quarters of the span is Crisis-built, an elegant arch of moonstone, but it fell short of the far side, so the locals closed the gap with a tangle of ropes and planks salvaged from a wrecked ship.

Unfriendly eyes watch them from the alleyways on either side.

It's dark; the only illumination comes from the stone lamps that glow on the left-hand side of the street. The moon's a thin sliver in the sky. They duck into alleyways to avoid the crowd spilling out of a tavern, circle around to bypass the fleshpots near the Seamarket by night. Hide from a passing city watch patrol.

The corpse leads them to an alleyway, pauses there for a moment. One hand strays to its throat, probing the wound. The jaw moves, but it still can't talk. The other hand flexes, paws at its waist as if looking for a weapon. An alarming thought strikes Terevant – what if it's looking for *revenge* on its killers? While Terevant wants to see them identified and brought to justice, he doubts the zombie retains the same appreciation for legal niceties – and it would be a hell of a diplomatic incident if the former Third Secretary of the Haithi embassy were found to be running around Guerdon murdering people, even those who arguably deserved it.

"Vanth," calls Terevant. "We need information. How did you die? What were you doing that night?"

The zombie turns to him. The jaw moves spasmodically – and then it's off again, heading back towards the street.

They pass a line of abandoned townhouses. He spots a street sign, naming it as Gethis Row.

Some of the houses have wreathes of fresh flowers laid at their doors. **Memorials**, mutters Yoras. **This street got cleared out in the Crisis. People got killed here, or brought up to the Seamarket.**

Vanth pauses outside one house, then turns to climb the stairs to the front door.

"Hold him there," orders Terevant. Yoras hurries forward, pulls the zombie back. The Vanth-thing doesn't resist, but again one hand goes to its throat, the other searching for a sword or knife at its belt.

Terevant brushes past the two and walks up to the front door. It's unlocked.

Inside, the house is deserted. He walks through the rooms, reconstructing the history of the place as best he can. There were families living here before the Crisis, crammed seven or eight to a room. Three rooms on the ground floor. All empty now, but there are signs of later occupation, squatters and thieves. The rooms have been stripped of anything valuable. His boots tread on shattered plates, on rags, on chunks of fallen plaster from the ceiling. A broken alchemical lamp smears greenish light across the walls of the backroom.

Up the stairs, though, things are different. There's a toppled wardrobe blocking the upper landing. Two large holes have been punched in it – gunshots, by the look of them. And there's a reddish stain on the far wall, amid cracked plaster, that lines up with one of the holes. There was some sort of squabble between rival gangs here. Weapons smugglers, he guesses.

Burn marks. Someone waving a torch around – or a flaming sword.

The rooms on the middle floor have been looted. It reminds him of a military encampment that's been overrun. That room was the barracks, four beds crammed in. That was the mess hall. Rats scavenging whatever scraps of food remain. And this room . . .

This one was definitely the armoury. Broken boxes stuffed with straw, bottles of watered-down phlogiston, grenades and other weapons lying scattered on the floor. A canister of withering dust kicked under a chair. The room stinks of something caustic, a smell like vomit mixed with ash. There are spots on the shelves untouched by dust or soot, suggesting weapons have been removed recently.

Terevant kneels down and examines a broken crate. There's a sigil on it, one he's seen thousands of times before. It's everywhere in the city, but he first saw it in the war. The brand of the alchemists' guild of Guerdon.

He tries to put it together. Someone with a flaming sword – Vanth's killer? The Saint of Knives? – comes in the front door, smashes their way up the stairs. The defenders try to stop this assault, but are overcome. The attacker ignores this trove of valuable weapons; someone else steals them a few days later, literally after the dust has settled.

The ceiling creaks.

Someone else is in the house, on the floor above.

Drawing his sword, Terevant creeps up the narrow stairs to the topmost floor. He passes a window, sees the street below, Yoras standing sentry outside the house. He waves, catches Yoras' attention, then signals silently for the guard to come up. Yoras nods and advances up the steps with the Vanth-thing.

The next floor's like the one below. A deep gouge in the banister – someone clumsily swung a blade and missed. A broken door, smashed into a hundred pieces. Old bloodstains on the floor. He moves cautiously, looking for his fellow intruder, but there's no sign of anyone.

He enters a bedroom. Next to the bed is a chest of drawers, and it's been shoved out into the room at an angle. In the gap behind it, Terevant spots a neat hole cut in the thin dividing wall, big enough to crawl through. A hidden room.

He kneels down and peers into the darkness. It looks like an attic room beyond; he can see a trestle table covered in rolled-up papers and maps. He waits for a long moment, listening. There could be someone waiting on the other side of that wall, ready to stab him when he sticks his head through.

For a moment, he debates retreating and grabbing that canister he saw earlier. Withering dust is a toxin that rots flesh; he could send a cloud of it wafting through the hole, clear out any ambushers. The dust is a horrible way to go, though, and dangerous to handle without the right protective gear.

The canister is still downstairs.

Of course, whoever's in the attic doesn't know that.

"Hey!" Terevant shouts. "I've got withering dust," he lies. "Come out peacefully, or I'll dust that attic."

A woman's voice replies. "Fuck you. You don't have it."

"Yes, I do. One swing of this thurible, and your lungs will turn to jelly. Horrible way to die."

"You don't have it." There's absolute certainty in her voice. "So fuck off."

From the sound of her voice, she's close. Just on the far side of the divide. He sidles up, pressing himself against the wall so he can't be seen through the hole, trying to judge where she—

—a knife punches through the wall, piercing the crumbling plaster, cutting into his cloak, his tunic, his skin. It's a shallow cut, but it hurts. The woman slithers out of the hole, rushing past him, driving her elbow sharply into his throat as she runs, winding him.

Terevant chases after her, gasping for breath. The woman's already down the stairs onto the first floor. Leaping down with divine grace. Saintly grace. The Saint of Knives. *Lemuel was right*, he thinks as he charges down the stairs onto the landing below.

She's waiting for him in the doorway of the armoury room. Small and lithe, dressed in a leather jerkin and dark clothes. Her gamine features are oddly familiar; her face is pockmarked with tiny scars. A pack at her side is stuffed with papers clearly stolen from the attic room. In her hands she's holding a metal canister.

"I've got withering dust," she says. "Fuck off peacefully, or I'll dust the landing." Her finger brushes against the release valve. Terevant suppresses a smile – she doesn't know how to use the weapon. There's a safety catch that needs to be pulled first before you press the valve.

"All right! Look, look." He puts down his sword. He feels his tunic sticking to his skin as he bends – he's bleeding from the knife wound. "I just want to talk." At least until Yoras and the zombie-Vanth get here. "My name is Terevant Erevesic. I'm from Haith."

"*Really* don't care. Leave."

"One of our men—"

"I didn't kill him."

"Then why did he lead us to you?" demands Terevant. Yoras should be here any second.

The woman glances to one side, as if she can look through the walls, and she seems to see the danger, too. "Get back!" she hisses, and presses the valve. Nothing happens.

Terevant lunges forward, but the woman's faster than he is. She ducks nimbly to the side, then dodges out of the door. Yoras comes rushing up the stairs from the ground floor, but she's already moving, running back up the stairs, always just out of reach.

"Fuck! Spar, how does this thing work?" No one answers, but she seems to listen for a second, then unerringly finds the safety catch. "Got it!"

"Back!" shouts Terevant. Yoras throws himself backwards as a greyish cloud of heavy dust hisses into the landing. The Vigilant doesn't need to worry about inhaling dust motes, but a concentrated burst could rot his bones and destroy him.

Edoric Vanth – what's left of him – doesn't stop. The zombie runs through the cloud of withering dust, stumbling as caustic grains pepper its skin. Dead flesh puckers and withers; one outstretched hand takes the brunt of the damage. The flesh sloughs away, the bone crumbles, leaving the zombie with a jagged stump. The dust canister must be an old one, though, as the zombie survives the cloud and crashes into the foot of the stairs. Still moving.

The woman flings the canister through the glass of the window, then follows it out, levering herself up onto the windowsill and climbing onto the roof of the house. The zombie follows, undead strength and single-mindedness compensating for its patchwork clumsiness, its dust-withered limbs. Two sets of running foot-steps — one soft and quick, one heavy and stumbling — thunder across the roof.

"Yoras! Stop Vanth!"

Yoras glances at the dust cloud — dangerous even to him — then runs back downstairs, out onto the street, in pursuit of Vanth.

Terevant finds a bathroom, a cloth that he can soak in water. Waits until the worst of the dust has settled. He presses it to his mouth and nose to protect his lungs, wraps his cloak tightly around himself, then sprints through the dust field. They used tons of with-ering dust at Eskalind, to cover the retreat. He hastily checks the hidden room upstairs. Most of the papers are gone, and those that remain are clearly the dregs — he finds old maps of the city, a plan of the subway system you can buy for a copper at any station, a battered library book, dog-eared and crammed with notes.

The title: *Sacred and Secular Architecture in the Ashen Period.*

He prowls around the room, looking for something, anything, that might explain why the Saint of Knives murdered Vanth. And why Vanth would come here, to this hideout. Maybe he was killed here.

There's a thunderous crash outside. He darts to the window in the stairwell, sees only a cloud of rising dust. Shouts of alarm.

Sir? calls Yoras from below.

"In here."

I fear I lost them, sir. And the city watch are coming — we must go before we're discovered.

Terevent gathers up the papers, stuffing them into the book to keep them bundled, then follows Yoras down the stairs onto the street outside.

The right-hand side of the street, the row of tenements, is as it was when they arrived.

The other side, the New City, has changed: the rooftops have sprouted spikes. The footbridge has vanished. That shimmering trade hall has lost all the windows on its topmost level.

She ran through there, sir. Before the windows, ah, disappeared.

"And Vanth?"

Yoras points to a faint line of brownish patches on the wall – marks left by a one-handed zombie-thing as it scrambled over the rooftops in desperate pursuit of the mysterious intruder.

He's gone, sir. We must go too.

"This," says Terevant, "could have gone a lot better."

Two days later, he listens to Olthic rage. Someone saw Vanth, or maybe Yoras – either way, Guerdon accuses Haith of letting undead Vigilants out onto the streets without permission, in breach of agreements between the two cities. Newspapers and rumour-mongers accuse Haith of plotting against Guerdon.

Lemuel warns that this will prompt the watch to tighten security again, that there's no way to smuggle the sword back into the city before the upcoming Festival of Flowers. Olthic will have to wait.

His brother threatens to send Terevant back to Haith. It's Daerinth who intervenes, Daerinth who calms Olthic down. He points out that it would reflect badly on House Erevesic, on Olthic's prospects in the Fifty.

"Patience," he whispers. "None of us know when we shall be called to serve, so we must stand ready as long as the Empire endures. Death is no release from duty."

In the yard outside, Terevant marches the embassy garrison back and forth, back and forth, until his throat is raw from shouting orders and he's so exhausted he can't remember which troops are dead and which ones are still alive.

CHAPTER 22

So, fuck, there's a zombie chasing her.

Cari runs across the footbridge, but the thing's right behind her. Not breathing, but there's the fast patter of dead feet as it closes. Bastard thing is Tallow-fast.

A miracle would be handy around now, she thinks. But she's down on the edge of the New City, where such things are hard to come by. It's difficult for Spar to manipulate the magical stone of the city down here. In fact, it's getting harder for him everywhere, but she can't think about that right now.

She flings herself through an open window on the far side of the street, landing in a dusty attic, and then *pushes*. Cari's learned that when Spar's miraculous strength fails, she can make up the difference, martyr herself. It costs her; it hurts her. It feels like she's birthing the miracle, like it's taking her blood and bone and transmuting it into spell and stone. She lets out a yelp of pain, and the attic abruptly goes dark as the windows clench and vanish. From outside, there's a crash as the other half of that jury-rigged footbridge collapses onto the street below. A heartbeat later, a thump as the fucking zombie slams into the wall that used to be a window. A scrabbling noise as it climbs onto the roof.

"Great," she whispers.

He's looking for a way in. Go through the door on your left.

She can see the undead creature, sort of. Down here, Spar's perceptions are fractured and imprecise. It's like trying to catch a reflection in a broken mirror – either she loses sight of it, or she sees it from multiple angles and needs to work out exactly where it is.

"How do I kill it?"

Her knife's useless against something that doesn't bleed and doesn't care if its organs are punctured. The withering dust didn't work, either. She could double back and try to get to the weapons left in the Gethis Row house, or maybe head onto the cache of weapons she already stole . . .

I think I should, suggests Spar, and he's right.

It's a simple tactic, one they've used several times before. Against Ghierdana cutthroats, against a Gullhead. Cari sets them up, and Spar drops the stone on them. Splat.

"Can you do it down here, though?" A quick miracle like that is costly for Spar. Too costly.

I think so. His voice in her head fades in and out. Memories that aren't hers come with it, carried like windblown leaves on the breath of his thought. His father's body, twisting in the noose. Looking out of the window at Hog Close at the city's skyline. Falling, always falling.

That memory means he's hurting. That he's pushing too hard.

Cari shakes her head, and whispers: "No. I'll lure him further up into the City. Then splat."

She stuffs the papers she stole from the hidden room into her shirt, then sneaks across the attic. *Loose floorboard. Sidestep right*, warns Spar. Her heart pounding as she walks as silently as she can. The zombie's still skulking on the roof, not ten feet away, but she's the best thief in the world these days. Well, in Guerdon anyway. The Saint of Knives, angel of the New City.

A bony hand smashes through a roof tile just overhead. Bony fingers claw at her face. She yelps and dodges forward, running blindly now. Crashing through a door as the revenant forces its way through the roof and into the attic behind her.

Left now. She turns, find herself in some little garret room with a single window. She forces it open, crawls out onto the rooftop again. Runs along the gutter. Behind her, the glass shatters as the zombie takes a more direct route.

She stumbles, catches herself. The night air is clearer than usual – fewer fires in summer, and the new factories are on the far side of Holyhill – but her lungs still burn as she runs. The heavy bag throwing her off balance.

Get back to the New City. Get back to where the streets love her, where the living stone enfolds her. Get back home.

Ahead, there's the domed mountain of the old Seamarket. To her left, the tonier parts of town, Venture Square and Mercy Street and the Tower of Law where her old life ended and her new one began.

The one where she's being chased by a fucking zombie, and her dead friend is making the rooftops sprout stone caltrops to slow the fucker down.

Faster, Cari.

Easy for him to say. She slides down a slanted roof, hops across a gap – a six-storey drop to some pissy alleyway – and clambers onto the next rooftop.

The skeleton leaps the gap and lands right in front of her, blocking her path.

Change of plan. She throws herself backwards off the rooftop.

Her connection to Spar manifests in three miracles.

Visions.

Stoneshaping.

And a third trick.

Spar can take the force of a blow, absorb most of the damage from an injury or impact. But it's not guaranteed. They both have to *will* it, at the same moment. He's got to *catch* her, like it's a trapeze act.

Be ready, she prays. *Also, we've never done this outside the New City so I pray to*

fuck

it

works

Impact.

Carillon lands heavily, six storeys down, smashing into the cobblestones. Alive, unbroken. In the distance, there's a noise like a crack of thunder as some part of the New City suffers in her stead.

She lies there an instant, winded. There's no sign of her pursuer.

"Spar, where is he?" she asks, as she tries to call up a vision. Nothing. No response.

"Spar?" Cari staggers to her feet, limps down the alleyway. The people on the street outside are all looking up at the New City, at the cloud of dust that's rising from a broken spire, glittering in the moonlight. They don't pay attention to the thief girl who emerges from the alley and pushes through the crowds.

Still. Here. Spar's thoughts are slow and laboured. Catching her cost him.

A moment later, a vision of the zombie drips into her mind. It's stopped chasing her. It's following the street north, heading inland. Heading in the rough direction of the Haithi embassy.

"Ow."

Tell me about it.

Carillon follows the streets as they rise towards the New City, as the grimy soot-stained greyness of old Guerdon gives way to miracle-spawned wonder. She feels better the closer she gets to home.

If that Haithi creature comes back, then *I'll splat it.* Spar sounds stronger, too, closer.

"Sure," she mutters. Drawing on Spar has to be a last resort, she tells herself. She worries that too many miracles will diminish him, snuff out the last remnant of his consciousness. *I can't let him go again*, she thinks, in a private part of her mind that she hopes he can't read.

Later, Cari finds a quiet rooftop and takes out the papers she stole from that hidden room. She mentally curses the other Haithi guy, the living one who disturbed her. Curses herself, too – she should have found that hidden attic earlier, searched it thoroughly instead of grabbing whatever was on top of the pile.

She looks through the papers. Her eyes water, and she blinks rapidly, washing out little specks of white stone grit. Spar's reading through her eyes.

Some sort of alchemical machinery, he guesses. She can't tell – there's a semicircle of boxes that might be a floorplan, and lots of weird runes, and some sort of structure on the edge of the design that reminds her horribly of Professor Ongent's sorcerous constructs. "No clue."

She opens another page. Stops in horror. "Fuck."

This one she can read clearly. This one she sees in her dreams.

It's a map of the city, New overlaid on Old. A map of Guerdon as it was before the Crisis, with the Alchemists' Quarter clearly visible, all their foundries and vats. The outline of the New City sketched atop it. And there, drawn in ink and pencil, a map of the tunnels and vaults below.

All the vaults. Even the ones where Spar locked away the worst of the alchemists' creations.

That zombie isn't the only undead thing out there.

Carillon imagines what might happen if this map got out. The alchemists would rip up the New City. They'd gut Spar, blast him open to reach those secret vaults. Anything to get what's buried there. This is what all the spies and treasure hunters seek.

"It's all right," she tells him, tells herself. "They're all dead." The Gethis Row house was *abandoned*, right? Whatever happened there, whatever killed them all, they didn't find this hidden map. Maybe this is the only copy. Maybe whoever assembled it is dead, too.

Maybe, for once, they'll get lucky.

She closes her eyes, searches the visions. Two streets over, there's a woman smoking a cigarette. A box of matches in her pocket.

Carillon brushes past the woman a minute later. Steals the matches. Climbs back up to the rooftop.

The papers burn quickly. A fiery blaze against the dim glow of the New City, and then it's gone, and so is Carillon.

INTERLUDE

Lyrix.

Rasce waits by the shore for his uncle's ship. The island's docks are a rough place – lots of mercenaries and pirates – but no one dares bother young Rasce as he sits and waits. The sun turns the stones of the harbour into an oven, so the sea breeze is welcome. A tavern keeper hurries out with an even more welcome goblet of iced wine. A gift, for a scion of the Ghierdana families.

It's good wine. Rasce takes out his dragons-tooth dagger and displays it openly on the table, signalling that this tavern has the blessing of the Ghierdana.

Uncle Artolo's ship arrives, and Artolo is first off the gangplank. Limping down, supported by two of his brute squad, he presses a hand to his side. "Don't touch me, boy," he says when he sees Rasce. "Bitch saint opened me up like a fish. Is there any more wine?"

Rasce finishes the last of the goblet. "No. Great-Uncle wants to see you right away." There's a carriage waiting, to take them up the steep spiralling path to the villa atop the cliffs, to their great-uncle's cave.

Artolo groans as he climbs on board. "He knows, doesn't he? About the Saint of Knives?"

Rasce hops up nimbly behind his uncle. "I'm sure he's read your letters."

"They told me Guerdon didn't have saints. The Tallowmen were gone, Heinreil arrested – they told me it would be piss-easy!" complains Artolo. "She was everywhere. Knew everything. And we couldn't kill her. Look at this!" He produces his own dragons-tooth knife from his pocket. "I cut her fucking throat with this."

Rasce takes the blade, runs his thumb over the edge. It's blunted, like someone tried to use it to cut stone. "Well, tell Great-Uncle that. I'm sure he'll understand."

"I'll go back. We need more men, sorcerers, too. Hire some Crawling Ones. Get the blessing of Culsan. The city's ripe for the plucking, don't get me wrong. I just need more time."

The carriage races around a steep bend. Now, they're on the south side of the island, looking out over the sparkling blue ocean. In the distance, there's a line of greenish steam rising from a lurid scar slashed across the waters. A fence of acid seeds, one of the defences against invasion by Ishmere.

"Now that," says Rasce, "is going to be more of a problem."

The carriage comes to a stop at the end of the road. Rasce leads his uncle past the guards, brings him right through the oldest part of the villa. Relatives watch the pair go by, but say nothing. Even Artolo's own children dare not approach him.

Rasce brings him down the stairs. The air is full of sulphurous smoke, dark and thick and hot.

Great-Uncle hears them approach.

Great-Uncle has famously keen hearing.

Artolo falls to his knees at the entrance to the lair. "I ask your forgiveness, Great-Uncle. I know that I've failed you, but I've served the family faithfully for many years. You know how hard the gods can be, and—"

The dragon interrupts him.

"Did you find the lost weapons, Artolo? The things of black iron?"

"No. I looked, I found traces, but—"

"Rasce?" calls the dragon.

"Yes, Great-Uncle?"

"Come in. Bring the knife."

CHAPTER 23

One month to election day.

One month before the mobs march or ride to the polling stations, the ballot boxes in every watch-house and square. A grand harvest of ballot papers will mark the end of this searing summer, as the city chooses a new parliament. *And then what?* thinks Eladora.

It's been ten days since her ill-fated visit to Carillon. Ten days spent mostly huddled in backrooms in the Industrial Liberal headquarters that hasn't changed since her grandfather's time, far from the changing streets of the New City. She passed Spar's list of names onto Absalom Spyke, who'd read it, snorted – and come back a day later with a wary newfound respect. Eight of them have already signed on to stand in the election; the others are considering the offer. Kelkin's pleased, apparently, although it's hard to tell.

But they need to hold on in the old city, too, and that's what today is about. Law and order, strength and stability. The outer office of the IndLib rooms in parliament is crowded, but she pushes her way through. Jealous glances as she walks into the inner rooms. Only senior party officials have dispensation to enter the sanctum without an escort or appointment. Eladora occupies – awkwardly, as always – a unique position. She's not a lawyer, unlike half the other junior staff, and she's not the scion of some political family that's been with the party for fifty years.

At least, not as far as they know. She's careful never to use the Thay name.

Jermas Thay's mask was made of gold, she remembers, and

behind it were the worms. Cold slimy fingers pressing against her, writhing lips reciting the spell to call monstrous gods . . .

She doesn't break stride as she crosses the room, but recites one of Ramegos' incantations in her mind to drive away the memories of the Thay family tomb.

The others can't know that her experiences in the Crisis are the reason why she's trusted above other, more experienced political operatives. She's *initiated* into that terrible constellation of secrets. She knows all their sins, and they know hers.

She smells Rat from outside the committee room – a distinctive stench of dirt and rotting flesh, and something sharper, a tang of sorcery. That means this isn't just a regular meeting; the lord of the ghouls wouldn't crawl up from his throne in the depths without good reason. The guard at the door lets her into the high-ceilinged room. It was a feast hall in the days of the old kings, she recalls, back when parliament was a toothless drinking club for courtiers. Now, oil paintings of stern-faced ministers and clerics stare down from where royal banners once hung.

All the chairs at the long table are already taken by various senior Industrial Liberals. At the far end of the table squats Rat, sitting cross-legged, too huge for any chair. His horns, like monstrous antlers, would scrape against the ceiling if he stood at his full height. The only person willing to sit next to him is Dr Ramegos. Neither Rat nor Ramegos are IndLibs or even politicians, but they're both loosely aligned with Kelkin's goals for the city. The fact they're here at this meeting suggests it's about the city's security and defence.

She takes a seat along the side of the room. Kelkin's reading some letters with another aide. He looks up, addresses the room. "We'll start at eleven. The Council's got a meeting with the Haithi ambassador at noon, so if you have anything to say when we start, talk bloody quickly."

That sets off a buzz of conversation; little knots and conspiracies form as they try to decide who'll talk, whose concerns are most pressing, what requests can be combined. She could save them time – the whole party's looking to Kelkin for reassurance, for the promise that he'll corral the votes they need by sheer force of will. They don't have anything to say, so much as a generalised fearful wail. She looks in her bag for a notebook, finds instead the Haithi novel that Erevesic loaned her. She flips through it, bewildered by the sheer weight of the genealogies and histories at the start of the tome. Half the book is prologue.

A shadow falls across the pages. She looks up into the face of a pale young man. His suit, expensive but slightly grubby; his lips pulled back from his teeth in a ghastly approximation of a smile. It takes her a moment to place him as Rat's lawyer and spokesman. "YOU WENT LOOKING FOR CARILLON," says the young man, but she can tell he's not the one speaking. There are little telltale twitches in the muscles of his face, flashes of pain in his eyes as Rat takes control of his mouth from across the room. Like the words are leaden ingots that fall from his lips. "DID YOU FIND HER?" Eladora looks across at the massive ghoul, meeting the gaze of his yellow eyes.

"What business it is of yours?"

"SHE IS HARD TO FIND. OTHERS GO LOOKING. EVEN THE GHOULS. FIND ONLY EMPTY ROOMS AND DOORS OF STONE. SHE IS CLEVER, OUR CARI." The yellow eyes flare. "WHAT BUSINESS OF IT IS *YOURS*?"

"She's my cousin," whispers Eladora, "the B-Black Iron Gods are gone. She's not a d-danger to anyone any more."

The young man snorts, as does Rat across the room. "THERE'S ALWAYS DANGER AROUND CARI. BEWARE."

"That's a strange way to talk about your friend."

"NONE OF US," says the boy, "ARE WHO WE ONCE WERE. WE MUST ... EAT OUR PASTS AND GROW STRONG, SO WE CAN SURVIVE WHAT IS TO COME. HE TRUSTS YOU," Rat extends a clawed finger towards Kelkin, "AND YOU MUST ... REMIND HIM OF WHAT MUST BE DONE."

"And what must be done?"

"THE GODS MUST BE KEPT FROM THE CITY. ALL OF THEM." Rat withdraws; the young man gasps for breath, gulping in lungfuls of air, then mutters an apology and stumbles back to his master's side. A few people, including Ramegos, look curiously over at her; she waves them away.

The ghoul puts one titanic arm around the boy's shoulders and smirks at Eladora – and then her own mouth moves, and words come crawling out of her throat in the monster's voice: "I SAVED YOUR LIFE IN GRAVEHILL. REMEMBER IT."

Kelkin rises, taps the table. The room falls silent.

"The committee's hearing the Haithi proposal today, so I don't have time for questions. Shut up and listen." He begins to speak, outlining his plans to secure the city against supernatural threats. A bargain with the ghouls, trading the city's dead for assistance in sniffing out saints and sorcerers, keeping order on the streets. "If a cult wants a temple in Guerdon, then they can have the worshippers in life, but no unsanctioned saints or miracles, and the city gets the dead." Kelkin coughs. "We'll make them all Kept Gods." Eladora spots a gleam of savage joy in Kelkin's eye; his battles against the Keepers are legendary, even though he was once an initiate of their priesthood.

No unsanctioned saints. That would include Carillon. She hasn't told anyone, not even Kelkin or Ramegos, about her meeting with her cousin. Another secret she'll have to keep. She finds herself wondering what Aleena would have made of all this. Sometimes, when Eladora's nervous, she recalls the saint's comforting presence, her righteous, profanity studded wrath – and the mercy she showed Cari.

Thinking of Aleena reminds her of her mother. Kelkin's plan to use the ghouls means he'll have to reject Mhari Voller's offer of coalition with the Keepers – unless he's already thinking several steps ahead, establishing an extreme position for some future negotiation with the Keepers.

She's lost track of the speech. Kelkin's moved onto the navy, to alchemical weapons. Louder murmurs of approval. He boasts about the new fast interceptors that will guard Guerdon's coast – and, glancing around the room, Eladora can guess who's initiated into the secret of the god bombs by who cheers and who bows their heads, cowed by the thought of deicide.

Kelkin finishes up. "All right. The next few days are going to be rough. Expect the alchemists and Keepers to make up ground on us. Expect bad press, hard slog, and dissent in the ranks. The Festival plays to our opponents' strengths, not ours. But once it's done, and everyone's back in the city, that's when we make our big push. Hear me? As soon as the last fucking flower is handed out, that's when you run like the Tallows!" He thumps the table. Ragged cheers.

"Now, let me go and entertain some bloody approaches."

Kelkin stomps out of the IndLib room and up the stairs towards the main body of parliament. Most of the other IndLibs head down towards the exit, hurrying to get back to the city and the campaign. Eladora's about to go with them, when Admiral Vermeil intercepts her. "You're wanted for the next meeting, too, I fear, Miss Duttin. In case some ancient skirmish or dispute between Old Haith and Guerdon comes up, and a historical perspective is warranted."

All of the major parties have suites of rooms on the lower level of parliament, and they are all sending delegations to this meeting with the Haithi ambassador. Flowing like tributaries into the main corridor, joining the churning crowd. She spots Perik trotting along-side the head of the Hawker group, giving some last-minute briefing. Ramegos, huddled in conversation with some Old Haithi diplomat.

And there's Sinter, as part of the Church group. It's strange to see him out in daylight, in some official capacity. He's a creature of backrooms and alleyways and private threats. A gargoyle perched on some cathedral gutter, eavesdropping on the city below. He slips away before they enter the committee room.

There are places at the conference table for the Haithi ambassador and his two aides, and for the committee. Everyone else has to crowd around the edges. There's a lot of awkward shuffling and whispering; this Haithi entreaty might shape the long-term future of Guerdon's fraught relationship with its northern neighbour, but, right now, it's a distraction from campaigning.

A clerk rings a silver bell, signalling the arrival of the Haithi delegation. First comes Ambassador Olthic, towering above the rest. He's smiling, but his eyes dart around the room, identifying potential allies and enemies. First Secretary Daerinth toddles after, leaning on the arm of Olthic's brother Terevant. Now that she sees them together, she sees how similar they are, and how different. Terevant's clean-shaven; Olthic bearded. Both keep their hair short, but Terevant's is unruly. Both dressed in Haithi military uniforms, but Olthic wears dozens of medals and campaign braids, whereas Terevant's is almost bare. Olthic strides, he roars, head held high; Terevant looks subdued, and takes the seat furthest away from his brother. It makes her think of Carillon; she and her cousin both have similar facial features – the Thay look – and were mistaken for sisters when they were children. Eladora did whatever she could to distinguish herself from her troublesome foster-sister; if Cari was covered in mud and scratches from playing in the woods, then Eladora kept herself pristine and stayed indoors, and told herself she didn't want to go playing anyway.

Casting his eyes around the room, Terevant spots Eladora – probably the only person he recognises in the crowd of suspicious faces – and smiles. Perik shoots her a suspicious glance, doubtless suspecting her of plotting with Haith.

Kelkin taps the table, and the room falls silent. "Ambassador, the floor is yours."

Olthic stands. One hand strays to his belt, and then he snatches it away and holds onto the back of his chair. "Thank you, Mr Chairman. Honoured friends, I bring the greetings and blessings of the Crown of Haith, undying and forever loyal."

Kelkin grunts and waves his hand, indicating that the ambassador should get on with it. It's extraordinarily disrespectful – either Kelkin's trying to undermine Olthic, or else he's letting his impatience get the better of him. Eladora shifts uncomfortably in her seat – Kelkin's got his back to her, so she can't read his face.

Olthic continues. "Haith and Guerdon share common ancestry. Our mutual forefathers crossed the sea from Varinth, and we were one people for many centuries. We share a common tongue, a common history."

"If I want a history lecture, ambassador, I have my aide for that," says Kelkin sourly. "Duttin bends my ear for hours about Reconstruction-era plumbing. Please, move on." A ripple of laughter runs around the room. Eladora forces a smile, not wanting to give Perik the satisfaction of seeing her discomfort. And Reconstruction-era plumbing is important, damn it, People take the works of the past for granted but the city would be awash with sewage if the Reconstruction hadn't been so thorough.

The only person more uncomfortable at the laughter than Eladora is Olthic himself. His knuckles whiten as they grip the chair. He takes a breath, and keeps speaking. His baritone voice remains mostly calm as he continues.

"As the chair wishes – but there is one more similarity which must be noted. You have your Kept Gods, who remain gentle despite the war that presses on your shores. In Haith, we have but one god, Death, but it too remains unsullied by the Godswar. Both nations recognise the folly of untrammelled divinity, and see that the madness of other lands can only lead to doom. Haith wants no part of the Godswar."

As a historian and a former teacher, Eladora gives the ambassador a failing grade for that summary. While he's correct in claiming that Haith hasn't succumbed to the same reality-churning divine madness that marks the other belligerents in the Godswar, it's wrong to claim that Haith's pursued the same studious neutrality as Guerdon. Haith has territories and satrapies all over the world that they defend; early in the Godswar, they took advantage of the chaos to hugely expand their overseas holdings. Now they're in retreat, pulling back to defend their homeland.

She turns her attention back to the speech.

"Haith is one of Guerdon's best customers. We purchase four in every ten weapons sold by the alchemists; we buy more ships, hire more mercenaries from you than any other nation. For that matter, half the food in Guerdon is imported from Haith; wood and furs, too. We are like siblings – we have quarrelled in the past, we have disagreed, but we are inextricably entangled.

"As you are all aware, there has been a material change in our mutual circumstances. For decades, since the early days of the Godswar, the valley of Grena has impeded overland traffic between our two nations. The mad goddess of that region attacked anyone who tried to pass through the valley. The railways, built at great expense, fell empty. Now, the railway is open once more – a renewed connection between us. The first of many."

Olthic's finding his rhythm now as he talks – the last line rolls across the room like thunder.

"That may be a premature assessment, ambassador," snaps Kelkin, peevishly. "We've not forgotten other people who had *connections* to Haith." He's referring to a scandal of a few years previously, when a ring of Haithi spies was discovered in the alchemists' guild. Fear and mistrust of Haith runs deep in Guerdon, and Eladora guesses Kelkin's theatrics are aimed at a domestic audience. Insulting the Haithi ambassador plays well with the groundlings in the election, but that comes at a cost in the long term – the dead of Haith remember grudges and slights as keenly as the living. There isn't an audience in the room, and no journalists, but she's sure every moment of the meeting will show up in the city's newspapers in the evening edition.

Olthic ignores Kelkin's interruption. He leans across the table, speaking directly to the assembled leaders in urgent tones. He talks about the bonds of trade and culture that tie Guerdon and Haith together, but Eladora's unimpressed with that part of the speech. She can't help mentally footnoting it, correcting it. Odd, she thinks, that someone from a land thronged with immortals should be so ignorant of history – though she's heard enough old men talk nonsense about the great deeds of their past, telling burnished myths instead of accurate histories. Nostalgia and regret poison memory, and why should the dead be immune to such failings?

Olthic's better when he talks about Haith's undead-bolstered strength, about battling in the Godswar. His prowess as a warrior is well known. But he doesn't mention Haith's long retreat, and that's what matters here. Haith's overmatched in the Godswar, and all Olthic's victories in battle don't change that.

"When I first came to Guerdon, I expected a cynical city, a city that honoured no traditions or gods, where nothing counted except coin. In my time here, I have come to see Guerdon as an honest city, ruled by practical people. The trading cities are falling, one by one. Severast and Mattaur are gone. Will you lock yourself up behind walls, like Khebesh, and hope the war ends before the hungry gods turn their eyes to you? Will you fight alone if the mad gods send their hosts against you? The alternative I offer, that the Crown offers, promises protection, a steady market for your goods, and undying friendship."

Olthic sits back down.

Kelkin's the first to speak. "I like to think we have a few morals left to us, here in Guerdon. Free trade and freedom of faith being two of them. Your proposal would turn us into a protectorate of Haith at best. You'd take eighty per cent of our trade, you say? And would we be free to sell the rest to, say, Ishmere?"

"There are other buyers for your weapons. Allies of the Crown will take all you wish to sell, I assure you. As for freedom of faith, you have already shaved that reed exceedingly thin. Worship freely in Guerdon, but not too fervently – that's the rule, isn't it? Honour whatever god you wish, but pray they don't answer your prayers?" Olthic shrugs "If you find virtue in clasping vipers to your bosom, I suppose it's better if you pull their teeth first. Haith has no objection to your policies, and we promise no interference in your domestic affairs."

"And our foreign ones?" asks Kelkin. "We would be tying our fate to that of Haith. And, well, Haith's losing. Most of your overseas colonies have already fallen, and you're trying to consolidate what's left. We're not a scrap to be swept up, or a bauble to decorate the magic crockery collection you call a government."

Eladora can see the result coming long before the committee members make their little speeches and cast their votes. It's as clear to her as if she was reading tomorrow's newspapers, or a textbook written a hundred years hence. Kelkin and the IndLibs will reject the proposal; Kelkin gets to show how he's standing up to Old Haith, how he's the only one to decide the city's course. The alchemist-backed Hawkers will be split, taking whatever positions will maximise the prospects of future arms sales. And the Church will vote in support – partly because of Olthic's words about foreign cults, partly to draw a clear contrast with Kelkin. The course of events is obvious to her, was obvious from the start of Olthic's speech.

She's unsurprised, bored even, when the votes come in exactly as she predicted.

Olthic, though – the great general is taken by surprise. He contains himself long enough to give the assembled politicians a curt nod, then strides out.

Olthic almost contains his fury until they reach the carriage. He draws his sword, to the alarm of the guards by the side door of parliament and smashes it against a stone wall, over and over. Terevant's sickened by the sight – he's rarely seen Olthic lose, and never with such bitterness.

"That was a disaster!" Olthic roars. "Kelkin was against me from the start!"

Daerinth tries to soothe him. "That's only to be expected, but we have assurances that he'll lose, and—"

"Assurances! From Lyssada! And where was she? Where . . . Is . . . The . . . Sword?" Punctuating each word with another sword blow against the wall, until the blade snaps.

He rounds on Terevant, shoving him against a wall. "You were supposed to bring me the Erevesic sword before that meeting! I should have walked in there augmented by all the strength and wit of our ancestors! I needed every edge to convince them, and I had nothing!" He raises his fist.

Terevant tries to push back, but he can't even budge Olthic. His own guilt is stronger than the iron bar of Olthic's arm, anyway. Terevant tells himself that he couldn't have known that the resurrected Vanth would escape, couldn't have known it'd block the return of the sword, but he doesn't believe it. "Is this how the Erevesic is supposed to behave?"

Olthic releases his brother. Picks up the remains of his sword, then flings them down again and climbs into the carriage. Terevant follows; Daerinth totters in, too, and closes the shutters.

"You went in there with a half-baked plan and then gave them a reason to tear it apart," snaps Terevant. "You know they don't trust us. Why didn't you wait until after the election?"

"There isn't time." Olthic clasps his hands, restraining himself. Then, in another sudden spasm of anger, he pulls a ring from his finger and hurls it to the floor of the carriage. His wedding ring. Olthic glares out of the window at the passing lights of Guerdon. Greenish lights flare in the smokestacks of the alchemists' factories beyond Cathedral Hill. Terevant can tell that his brother's fury is settling. Undiminished, but sinking deep into his bones. Like rainwater from a sudden storm, seeping into the earth to emerge later as an irresistible river.

Daerinth lays a withered hand on Olthic's arm. "Calm yourself. This is a setback, not a defeat. It's said that Ishmere's moving north. The closer they draw to the city, the more alluring our offer becomes. Fear shall be our ally. Soon, they'll be scrambling to embrace our aid. But for that to work, my lord, you need to show calm in the face of danger."

"Gods, give me actual bloody danger instead of this posturing. Give me something I can hit."

Daerinth shakes his head. "This can all be salvaged."

"Salvaged. Salvaged, he says. Like I'm some mudlark, grubbing for coppers in the sewers."

The jolting of the carriage sends the ring rolling against Terevant's foot. He bends over and picks it up. "What can I do to help?"

Olthic doesn't answer, so Daerinth steps in. "The ambassador will be occupied with matters of state for some time, and I must assist him. There are various administrative duties in the embassy that can be moved to your desk."

Sit there and do nothing, in other words. He rolls Olthic's over-large wedding ring around his palm. There's an inscription inside the band – *"Should heaven fall and earth crack asunder, still I will find thee".*

He looks up, finds Olthic staring at him.

"Do you want this back?" Terevant says, holding out the wedding ring.

Olthic frowns. He takes the ring, jams it back on his finger. "Trying to ensure there are no heirs ahead of you, Ter?"

"You and she seem to be doing that all by yourselves."

"You sound like Father," says Olthic. "He thought I should marry some dull girl from the Westfolds who'd give him a litter of grand-children. After you left, there was a parade of them through the house. All good Haithi women, impeccable lineages.

He sighs.

"But none of them were Lys."

"Lady Lyssada," says Daerinth, quietly, "is Bureau. Do not forget that."

Olthic fidgets with his wedding ring, turning the band over and over. Digging the metal into his flesh. "We'll see her," he says darkly, "at the Festival."

Daerinth leans close to Terevant, to whisper in his ear above the rattling of the carriage's wheels over the Bryn Avane cobblestones.

"The Bureau has proven untrustworthy, of late. I still have friends in the Crown's palace. They whisper that the Bureau is not as loyal to the Crown as it should be."

Terevant rolls his eyes. Daerinth's clearly fixated on the Bureau. Some paranoid delusion, maybe, that the Bureau sabotaged his career, and that they exiled him to Guerdon all these years. Terevant had similar thoughts, sometimes, in the dark of night. "Maybe the Bureau believes the war is lost already. Why, I've even heard tell that some there secretly worship foreign gods, to curry favour with our enemies. Conspiring against the Crown from within."

It's nonsense, Terevant tells himself. The Bureau uses

underhanded schemes, but only in the service of Haith. Bureau and Houses, all working together to preserve the eternal Empire and the eternal Crown.

That's how it's supposed to work.

So where is Lys? Where's the sword?

CHAPTER 24

Patience, thinks the spy, and as Alic he looks over his shoulder at Emlin. The boy's scrubbed up and in new clothes for once, courtesy of money from the Industrial Liberals. Determination on his small face – here to do a man's job, not play – but he keeps glancing over at the row of shops.

"Let's stop here." This shore of the New City, within view of old Guerdon and its harbour, is one of the more respectable parts. You can walk down the alleyways here and have a good chance of losing only your purse, not your life. The promenade's been colonised by entertainers and amusements. They stop outside a stall selling sugared jellyfish, just down from a new temple to the Dancer.

From here, they can see right across the bay. See right across to the artificial mountain of battlements and cannons and aetheric vanes that composes Queen's Point.

Alic takes a paper-wrapped bundle from his satchel and tears it open. Inside are hundreds of leaflets. Emlin takes one and stifles a laugh, looking at the stipple-print portrait of Alic's face under the logo of the Industrial Liberal party.

The Industrial Liberal candidate for the fourth district of the New City grins. "When opportunity arises, one has to seize it." He runs through his counter-arguments if Annah objects: that being a candidate lets him move around the New City and talk to anyone he wishes at any hour of night or day, making it excellent cover for spying. That this brings him closer to Eladora, and Eladora is close to Kelkin, and that he's only a few steps away from the highest offices and most closely guarded secrets of the city.

Alic hands his son a sheaf of flyers. "Go and talk to people. Tell them that a vote for me is a vote for Kelkin, and a vote for Kelkin is a vote for Guerdon's future."

Emlin takes the flyers. He's hesitant at first, shyness born of his time in the temple and his natural aversion to strangers. But he's a saint of the Fate Spider, and the blessings of that god are manifold. The spy watches the boy as he slips into a new role, a new identity – the loyal son, a determined believer in his father. His demeanour changes; he intuits the desires and secrets of those he speaks to, insinuating himself into their confidences. Using rumours and gossip, using snatches of conversation he overheard from his rooftop explorations in the Wash. Alic watches proudly as Emlin spins a web of connections across the promenade.

Alic joins his son, stopping passers-by with the same zeal as a proselytiser from one of the temples. Have you heard the preachings of Effro Kelkin? Give your soul to whatever god you want, but give your vote to the Industrial Liberals.

Across the glittering bay, frigates and destroyers and patrol boats sail in and out of the naval base, and Alic notes their comings and goings on the back of one of his election flyers.

The sun's setting beyond Queen's Point, turning the sky above the promontory to fire and filling the bay with liquid gold. Alic and Emlin have made their way all along the western perimeter of the New City and back again; he can't count how many voters he's talked to, how many hands he's shaken. Emlin sits on a bench, clutching a glass of some syrupy drink from the alchemists.

Two more people approach Alic. He turns, readying himself to go into his now-polished patter, then he recognises them.

"Alic!" says Eladora, her face beaming with a rare smile. Beside her, Silkpurse grins. "I heard wonderful things were happening down here."

"I've made a start, at any rate." He hands one of his leaflets to

Eladora. "Could I get a word with the man himself, I wonder? Five minutes with Kelkin could help a lot."

"I'll arrange it if I can," says Eladora. "It'll have to be after the Festival of Flowers. Are you attending the fair?"

Alic shakes his head. "I've asked around. The only people going to the Festival from here are Guerdon born and bred, and their attitudes are pretty much set. Most of the newcomers aren't going – they see it as a Keeper festival more than anything else. So, I should stay here and keep canvassing."

Emlin sidles up beside them. "Oh," he pouts, "everyone says it'll be fun."

He introduces the boy to Eladora and Silkpurse. "My son," he says, "Emlin. I brought him out of fire and the Godswar to knock on doors for me." Alic laughs.

Eladora nods awkwardly at the boy

"Getting late," mutters Silkpurse. "Want me to walk you back to Jaleh's?" She sniffs the air near Emlin, freezes, and then a smile spreads across her snaggle-toothed muzzle. He can guess what she's thinking – why would Alic choose to live in a gentling-house, a halfway house for saints and god-touched? Clearly, Emlin is the missing piece – he knew his son has unwanted divinity that he needed to shed. His choice of Jaleh's reinforces Silkpurse's rosy image of him; now he's also a good father, quietly delivering his child from the clutches of the mad gods.

The spy lets a matching smile spread across Alic's face. "No – we've got more ground to cover here. Enjoy the Festival." He bows in farewell.

Eladora is about to depart when a thought strikes. "Ah, if Emlin wants to attend the Festival, I could bring him along with the IndLib staff? It would involve a few hours of work, and a lot of standing around listening to pompous speeches, but he could slip away for while."

The smile freezes on Alic's face. It makes sense for Alic, doting father, to trust the woman who's his friend and political sponsor to chaperone his son for a few days. Eladora clearly intends it to be a kind offer, a note of appreciation for Alic's efforts on behalf of the IndLibs. But all that's a lie. Alic doesn't exist, and the boy isn't his son – he's the saint of a monstrous deity whose armies are closing on Guerdon.

And that's why he must go. A few days away from Jaleh's should maintain the boy's fragile sainthood long enough for the work to be done.

"That's very kind of you, Miss Duttin. With all he saw back home, it'd be good for him to walk in the sun and be around mortal folk."

"I'll call by Jaleh's house in the morning. There's a special train booked by the party, and I'll make sure he has a seat."

When he tells Emlin, the spy permits Alic to take a moment of joy in the boy's happiness.

They get back to find that Jaleh's moved them to another room in her house, a small attic room barely large enough for the two cot beds to fit. A small window sheds moonlight on the two beds, and on the battered copy of the *Testament of the Keepers* that Jaleh left lying on Emlin's bed.

As Emlin sleeps, the spy searches the little room, making sure no one can overhear them here. He probes knots in the floorboards for spy holes, presses his ear to all the walls to see if he can hear breathing in the adjoining rooms, gathers dust in his hand and lets it sift through his fingers into the shaft of moonlight – sometimes, the presence of scrying-spells will distort the air around them, making the dust dance in patterns of runes and spirals.

Nothing.

The spy settles himself onto his own bed, fully clothed. Idly, he picks up the *Testament* and leafs through it. It's a child's version, telling the stories of the Kept Gods with big illustrations and simple words. The Mother of Mercies, Mother of Flowers, protector of children. The Holy Beggar, the stranger who is a friend. Saint Storm, the perfect knight. Holy Smith, who labours with mind and hand. A child's book for a child's finger-painting of a religion. These gods of Guerdon are clumsy, slow, simple things compared to the gods of Ishmere.

The Godswar will be a massacre, if Saint Storm and Mother of Mercies are pitted against High Umur and Lion Queen. Sheep against lions.

The spy remembers the faithful in Severast crowding into the temple of Fate Spider. They cast lots for sacrifice, blindfolding themselves so the identity of the killer would remain a holy secret. They drank the venom of the temple spiders, dying in hideous contortions. The priests walked the web of fate, searching for a path out of darkness. With each step, the priests diminished as they spread themselves over a hundred possible futures, a thousand.

And all the while, the faithful of Severast knew that the faithful of Ishmere were a hundred times more fervent and godly than they, and that the gods would favour the invaders in the bay.

Across the city, a bell sounds the midnight hour. It's time for the spy to go.

He climbs out of the window, crosses the roof without a sound, shimmies down a drainpipe. He's learning how to move in Guerdon without being seen, and there are routes above and below the streets. Tonight, he doesn't have far to go.

Tander's down by the docks, talking with a group of mercenaries. They're just back from the Godswar, bearing the scars of that conflict. Haunted and hollow-eyed, those who still have eyes. X84 loiters nearby, in Tanner's line of sight, close enough to eavesdrop, and waits.

After a few minutes, Tander detaches himself from the crowd and walks away. The spy follows him, and around the corner falls in beside him. They walk along the maze of jetties and docks that's the shoreline of the Wash.

"My old company back there," says Tander. The former mercenary grins at X84, but there's panic in his voice. Old trauma or new woes, wonders the spy. "Good lads, good lads. One of them's ex-navy. Used to work at Queen's Point, knows the place well. She says the fortress is . . . well, it's a fortress, isn't it? It's locked up tight."

The spy nods. Queen's Point is impregnable.

"Annah wants me to go in. Take a look at that fucking ship you found out about. See if it's really got the weapon on board. Walk into the fortress, she tells me, like it's nothing. Like I . . . " He rubs his neck, scratching furiously. "Half the base is given over to the city watch, right, and the watch are shit. So, break in on the leeward side, find a way through — a connecting corridor or a waste pipe, maybe. I'd fucking crawl through the sewers if it weren't for the damned ghouls."

Tander stops by the waterside, lights a cigarette. The flare of the lighter's reflected for an instant in the dark waters beneath them, and matched by the smear of light across the bay, all the floodlights at Queen's Point.

"No miracles, she said. They'd be detected. No fucking miracles. But I need a miracle," mutters Tander, apparently to himself. The mercenary takes a few long drags on the cigarette. "Do I call you Sanhada or Alic these days, you sneaky fuck?"

X84 shrugs. "Whichever."

"Alic, then. Alic, my lad, my chum, my fucking bosom pal, did I ever tell you how I got into this game?"

"This sounds like a conversation to be had over a drink," says the spy, gesturing towards a dockside tavern.

Then suddenly he's on the ground, face pressing into the slimy wood of the jetty, Tander's knee crushing his spine.

The pain is interesting.

"We're having it now, all right?" hisses Tander in the spy's ear. The pressure vanishes, and the spy rolls over to see Tander pointing a gun at him.

"What is this?"

Tander ignores him. "The lads and I, we were good. Gods below, we were good. And stupid. We held our nerve when the god-husks came shambling. Divine things, gods that had been beaten down so many times there wasn't much left of them, just teeth and miracles. Saintless and witless. We made a fortune off the Haithi, putting down husks for them. Came back here, and Bena made sure we spent most of that fortune on new gear. Proper weapons out of the alchemists' best workshops."

The spy shifts, moving so that he's got a wooden post at his back. If he needs to, he can twist and slip into the water like an otter.

"Next time out, we go down south. Get hired by the Severasti, to hold the line against Ishmere. More money that we've ever seen, good wine, girls from the Dancer's temple, and everyone's telling us that the Godswar's not coming, that Ishmere won't attack Severast. Same gods, right? Allies as long as anyone can remember.

"We lasted a month."

Tanner's cigarette scatters ash over his shirt as his mouth trembles. The gun shakes, too, and he squeezes his hand to keep his grip on the weapon. His trigger finger quivers.

"They captured me. Cloud Mother just plucked me off the ground, threw me into the sky. I wake up in . . . in their fucking heaven. Annah was there, she's intelligence corps, but there was a g-g-god there, their spider. Fate Spider. He . . ."

Tander turns his head to the side and throws up into the waters of the bay. The spy darts forward, but Tander's faster, and he brings the gun up to point straight at the spy's face.

"Back!"

The spy retreats.

"It's a terrible thing to meet a god. The Spider . . . dissolved me. His venom burned me away. There wasn't anything left, except some little screaming thing. And they gave me a way out. Wove me a new fate, bound me to Annah. See, I have to do what she says, or she breaks the thread and I . . . I don't exist any more.

"She says jump, I jump. She says die, I die.

"So if she says get into Queen's Point and verify, I have to. You're a smart bastard – you're going to help me."

"I can't."

"I'll kill you."

The spy doesn't move. The threat doesn't hold much fear for him.

"I'll kill the boy. I'll burn down that fucking gentling-house. Burn them all. Think I won't? I fucking killed our last saint, I'll do this one, too. Happily. The bastard Spider won't find me if I put out all its eyes." Tander's finger tightens on the trigger.

"Don't!" Alic says. "I'll help. I'll help." The image of Emlin burning leaps into his mind and won't leave.

Tanner sobs in relief, great gusty choking tears wracking his body. The gun's still in his hand, shaking as he struggles to breathe.

The spy sits there, disgusted with himself. Disgusted with the man in front of him. But his mind is already moving, changing plans. He can turn this to his advantage.

"You don't know what it's like, being like this. It's no way for a man to live, dangling from a thread. To be used like this . . ." He wipes snot from his nose with his sleeve. Sheepish, he pockets his gun. "I owe you, understand? I won't forget this. We're mates. We're in this together to the end, whatever happens."

A terrible thing, indeed.

"San!" booms Dredger. "Come in, come in. Sit. Have a drink."

Dredger's office smells so strongly of fresh paint that Sanhada Baradhin considers borrowing a gas mask. He sits down on a new couch, pours himself a glass from the crystal decanter on the side table. "Business is good, I see."

"Oh, aye. With the alchemists still rebuilding, supply of new weapons has fallen, but demand has only increased. Ishmere is on the warpath again, it seems."

"Are they coming here?" asks the spy.

"Nah, not a prayer. They'll go for Lyrix, probably. Maybe Haith. They don't have the strength to take both at once, and they've got to be wary of pushing one into alliance with the other." Dredger rubs his gauntlets together. The metal digits clink. "Uncertainty leads to fear, fear leads to a desire to own weapons of terror and irresistible fury. For pity's sake, tell me you're here to work in sales."

"Actually, I've had something of a change of career." The spy hands Dredger one of Alic's election flyers.

Dredger hoots with amusement. "This is you? Alic? I've heard some of the lads in the yards talking about you. You might even win. Why 'Alic'?"

The spy shrugs. "A clean start."

"Well, what do you want? My vote? Or are you here to pick my pocket like the rest of your filthy political kinfolk?"

"Campaign contributions."

"Of course, of course." Dredger lumbers around to his desk, opens a drawer. "How much?"

The spy counts on his fingers. "A few underwater breathing masks and suits. The use of your launch. A brace of flash ghosts. Waterproof guns. Thaumic goggles. Oh, and forty thousand silvers."

Dredger turns around slowly. His face is hidden behind his own breathing mask, but the spy can guess at his expression. "That sounds like an . . . unconventional campaign. What the *fuck* are you playing at, San?"

"I can't say."

"San . . . Alic . . . whatever. Is this a scam? Are you trying to gull me?"

"No." The spy picks his lies carefully. "Like I said, it's a fresh start, which means I need to resolve some old business, old debts. I owe a bunch of pirates out of Lyrix. They've got a job in mind that needs specialised equipment."

"And the silver?"

"Some of it is for them. Some of it is for me – for the election."

"Just why," asks Dredger, "do you think would I give you all that? Ask me for a few hundred, San, not a bloody arsenal on top of a fortune on top of . . . the rest of the stuff."

"Because you're buying me. I'll be your man in parliament. I'll vote as you tell me, lobby as you tell me. Go against Kelkin if you ask me. Forty thousand is cheap for utter and complete loyalty. You have my word, Dredger."

"Cheap if you win. Bloody expensive if you lose. For both of us. I'd have to do unpleasant things to you, San, for the sake of my own reputation." Dredger closes the drawer, moves over to a painting of a burning ship. There's a safe behind it. He lays a gauntlet on the dial but doesn't turn it. "Why are you doing this, San? Really? If you've got debts, there are easier ways to clear them. If you've got ambition, why chain yourself to me?"

The spy takes a drink. "Right now, everything's uncertain. Kelkin's thrown the dice, and no one knows how they'll land. And, like you said, that scares people. And scared people do stupid things. I'm doing this because of what I saw in Severast, my friend. I'm doing this so the people with your weapons of terror and irresistible fury shoot them in the right direction."

"You're asking for a bribe on the grounds that you've found your principles?" Dredger puts a heavy bag of coins on the desk, then closes the safe. "It's a thin cord you're hanging by."

CHAPTER 25

Terevant doesn't know what is worse — the spine-shattering shocks that come when the old carriage runs over stones at speed, or the sweltering, airless heat of the cabin. It's made in the traditional Haithi style, as befits the ambassador's official vehicle, which means small windows and lots of furs against the cold of winter — a winter six months away and hundreds of miles north. On midsummer's day in Guerdon, it's an oven on wheels, slowly broiling them alive. Prince Daerinth withers in the heat, occasionally flapping a bone-white fan over his face. Olthic stews, his face purpling behind his beard. His massive hands flex as if gripping the hilt of an invisible sword, or strangling a thin neck.

Terevant tries to read. He pulls out the book he found in the abandoned house that Vanth led them to, *Sacred and Secular Architecture in the Ashen Period*. A bookplate proclaims it the property of the Guerdon University Library, but it's clearly a long time since this book was stored neatly on a shelf. It's tattered, smeared with dirt and blood, and crammed full of loose notes. The notes are in several different styles of handwriting, and seem to be mainly concerned with the tunnels under the city. There are maps of tunnels, too, and on several someone's drawn in the outline of the shape of the New City, overlaid on the older charts.

"What's that?" growls Olthic.

Terevant hastily closes the book. "Some old guidebook."

The Festival of Flowers is a huge affair. Half the city decants itself to the countryside for a day or two. Ostensibly, it's a religious celebration of the Keepers — a big ceremony where they invoke Mother of

Flowers for the upcoming harvest, a place where farmers could recruit seasonal labour from the city. In the last century, though, the Festival's grown and mutated, becoming a trade fair where Guerdon's guilds can show off their wares; a pleasure garden full of amusements and delights; a recruitment fair for mercenary bands and a military parade ground. A hundred smaller festivals and exhibitions all rolled into one.

The Festival's always associated with nature, with sunshine and flowers and bucolic countryside, but the brochure map shows a temporary city bigger than most permanent ones. Tens of thousands of people decamp from Guerdon and the hinterlands to this fantasy of plasterboard and canvas. They come by ferry and train, or by carriage, or walk along thronged roads singing half-remembered hymns and well-rehearsed drinking songs.

This year, no doubt, it'll also be a political battleground. Every candidate will be there, giving speeches. Those not of Guerdon have a presence here, too; the government of Haith has a tented pavilion, and so does Lyrix and a dozen other nations. Looking at the map, Terevant notices that even some nations that no longer exist in the real world have their place in this wonderland – exiles from Severast and Mattaur have erected tents celebrating their defiance of Ishmere.

It's slow going along the roads – the carriage has to force its way through the crowds. Finally they roll into a secure yard at the back of the Haithi pavilion. Guards – living ones – help Daerinth disembark. Olthic jumps to the ground and strides off into the pavilion, shouting orders. Terevant tags along after him. Inside, the pavilion is dark and cool and mostly empty. There's a display of marble sculptures, a paean to Haithi military triumphs. He touches one – they're plaster casts, taken from marble artworks back home in Old Haith. Ersatz monuments of crumbling plaster, to impress upon Guerdon the eternal endurance of Haith.

Terevant hears Olthic roaring at some subordinate, and decides to make himself scarce. He doesn't have any official duties here anyway, not until later. When Lys gets here, he'll complete the mission he began nearly a month earlier – he'll take the Sword Erevesic from its hiding place and deliver it to Olthic.

He slips out of the tent, back into the thronged field, past endless rows of food stalls and beer tents. The Festival crowds are somewhat different from the city folk. No Stone Men, for one. No ghouls that he's seen. Fewer foreigners – he'd stand out even if he wasn't dressed in a Haithi military uniform. A few people look warily at him, but there's remarkably little trouble. Sunlight and laughter and merriment; the city relaxed for the first time since the Crisis. Even the electioneering is muted.

He spots Eladora Duttin at the IndLib booth.

"Miss Duttin," he hails her. Eladora looks up from her papers. A dark-eyed boy slouches behind her; his eyes widen in alarm when he sees Terevant's uniform.

"Lieutenant Erevesic." Eladora gestures at her young companion. "This is Emlin, my charge for the day. How are you finding the Festival?"

"I just arrived. You've been here for a few days, I take it?"

"My tolerance for whimsy is quite exhausted, yes." She gives him a wan smile. "Emlin here may be a better judge."

Emlin doesn't speak, he just shakes his head. Shy, or scared?

Eladora continues. "I hope the ambassador did not take Mr Kelkin's responses to his proposal personally. Mr Kelkin can be a bit, ah, b-brusque."

"Calling the Crown a magic crockery collection?" Terevant smiles, to show that he at least was not insulted.

"Uh, that sort of thing."

"I'm sure he'll survive. How are you finding *The Bone Shield*?"

"Oh, I'm afraid I haven't had much time to read of late. I'm scarcely halfway through."

Impulsively, he takes out the book on architecture or archaeology and shows it to her. "You seem to know a bit about history. What can you tell me about this?"

"Gods below!" she swears. "Where . . . where did you get that?" She tries to snatch it off him, but he holds onto it tightly. "That's mine!" she says.

"It says 'property of the university library'," he points out.

Eladora looks around. Emlin and several bystanders are watching the altercation with interest. She lets go of the book. "Mr Erevesic, I'd like to discuss that book with you — at your convenience, of course." She digs around her purse, hands him a printed card with her address. "At your earliest c-convenience."

She's shaken, he thinks. The book means something — and whatever it is, she's unwilling to discuss it in public.

He bows, bids her farewell, and strolls off in triumph. The day is looking up — maybe the reanimation of Vanth wasn't completely futile. He's getting the hang of this intrigue business, while Olthic has shown that he's not infallible.

The thought buoys him up. He feels like he's one of the colourful kites that soar above the Festival ground. The heavy book in his pack seems suddenly light, as if it too might go whirling into the sky on the warm breeze that blows across the vast Festival field.

He buys a glass of beer at a stall, finds a table and takes a long drink. A week trapped in the embassy with Olthic has worn his nerves to the bone. The news doesn't help either — it's hard to reconcile the thought of apocalyptic war with the sunshine and merriment of the beer tent, but daily reports from the Bureau all confirm that Ishmere's invasion force is moving north towards Haith. Part of him wants to rush back home, fight in the defence of the city alongside the honoured Vigilants of House Erevesic — get away from Olthic's accusatory stare. But his duty is here, the Crown wants him here. Well, not *here* in this beer tent, exactly, but in Guerdon. And whatever else, it's safer here. He's rushed off to war before, and that ended at Eskalind.

Lys will be here soon, he thinks. He can talk to her, let her clever mind unpick the tangle of his thoughts, tell him what to do. He always listened to her, unlike Olthic. He laughs — here he sits, surrounded by tens of thousands of strangers, in a city far from home, and still making endless pilgrimages to the grave of thoughts he'd buried years ago.

Tens of thousands of strangers — and one familiar face. He looks twice to make sure, but there's no mistaking that unfortunate nose. There, in the corner of the beer tent, sits Berrick. No wonder

Terevant hadn't spotted him earlier – the little man is clothed similarly to most of the crowd in the tent. Country farmers in their holy-day best, all dressed up for the last day of the Festival. Shiny buttons, muddy boots, fresh bright feathers in their caps.

He pushes through the crowd over to him.

"Berrick!"

The little man looks up in alarm. "Let's not use names," he says quickly, tugging the hood of his cloak down to conceal his face, but he pushes a stool out for Terevant to sit down.

Oh, death, thinks Terevant. Perhaps the little man is undercover.

"It's nice to see you again," says Berrick. "And though the wine isn't as good, the company is, ah, welcome." His breath smells strongly of alcohol. He's several glasses ahead of Terevant.

Terevant follows Berrick's lead. He can't hide his Haithi military uniform, but he hunches over as best he can, shuffles his sword under the table, so that not every passer-by will take notice. He's not the only soldier in here – a few at the bar are Guerdon navy, probably attached to some demonstration of the city's defence forces.

"Half of Guerdon must be here," says Terevant, gesturing at the crowds.

"Only half? I've never seen such a mob." Berrick does seem overwhelmed. "Not even in my dreams. I dream of Guerdon often, lately."

"It's full of life," agrees Terevant. "Especially the New City."

"I've never been. To any part of it, that is. They don't let me go there."

"Who doesn't?"

"In the army, when they give you orders, did you ever question them?" asks Berrick.

"It depends on who's giving them, and why. In battle, you don't hesitate, because that gets people killed. Other times . . . well, there are ways of questioning an order without disobeying it. Spirit of the instruction versus the letter, that sort of thing."

"I suppose the virtue there is that one's orders are very clear. Go here, do this, shoot that thing." Berrick scratches his prominent nose.

"Dig a latrine, watch that wall. Oh, and wait. That's the big one. Waiting for something to happen."

Berrick swirls the wine around his glass. "But the intent is clear. You know what you're supposed to be doing, even if you don't always know why."

"I guess." Terevant shifts awkwardly on the stool.

"I don't think it matters if I question my orders. Things are going to happen whether I agree or not."

"Berrick, you can tell—" Terevant's interrupted by an alarmingly tall man in a long coat, who throws a pair of pamphlets onto the table. "Vote for Kelkin and the IndLibs!"

"Friend, you sow your seeds on stony soil here," replies Berrick, showing a Keeper rosette. The tall man sneers and shoves a pamphlet into Berrick's wine glass before stalking off.

Berrick fishes the paper out of his glass. "If I could, I'd have stayed a wine seller, I think. I like telling people about good wine. But we all have our commandments." He stands. "I shall see you again, when we have other commandments to obey."

"Is Lys here?"

"She'll be watching." Berrick stands, lingers a moment. "It was good to share a last drink." And then he turns and walks away, pulling his bright green cloak around his shoulders despite the heat, tramping down the hill to the main field. His heavy tread reminds Terevant of a condemned criminal going to the gallows.

Terevant has his own obligation. It's nearly time to bring the sword. He has another drink to calm the buzzing in his head. A fourth for the Ninth Rifles, in memory of the lads who fell and rose and fell again at Eskalind.

He's finishing the fifth when they call him back to the Haithi pavilion.

At four o'clock, they'll hold the Blessing of Flowers. Eladora checks the clock yet again. Just over an hour to go.

The blessing is the one fixed point of the Festival. Everything else is ad hoc, or pushed around, or competes with six other events.

Various IndLib events that Eladora carefully scheduled have been moved or cancelled. One rally ended up getting timetabled opposite a demonstration by the navy, so the IndLib tent was almost empty, Ogilvy speaking to twenty snoozing greybeards. He's hoarse now, from trying to shout over the sound of explosions and rifle fire from outside.

Her volunteers are phantasms. If she doesn't keep them under constant surveillance, they vanish off to the amusements or just stand around staring.

It's worse than herding undergraduates.

Alic's son Emlin has proved surprisingly diligent. When Eladora offered to take the boy along, it was out of charity. Emlin came out of the carnage of Severast – he deserves to see some wonders that aren't the work of monstrous mad gods. Gratifyingly, Emlin seems fascinated by everything, even mundanities. Whether it was helping out in the back tent, where Kelkin and a few other IndLib leaders worked the guild masters for donations, or walking the avenues handing out pamphlets, Emlin is always wide-eyed, drinking everything in.

She's tried, over the course of the day, to engage him in conversation about his life in Severast, or his father, or anything, but the boy is evasive. Through diligent excavation, Eladora manages to get a few details out of him – he went to some sort of religious boarding school, he stayed with an Aunt Annah and Uncle Tander while Alic was at sea. When he doesn't want to talk, he finds something to busy himself with. His elegant, long-fingered hands stacking flyers, tidying things away. And always alert, always listening.

Eladora remembers her own visits to the Festival, when she was younger. Her mother would always take her and Carillon. Invariably, Carillon would slip away and vanish for hours, and Silva would drag Eladora to the great open-air prayer field of the Kept Gods. Silva would pray angrily there until the watch found Cari. When they were young, Cari would normally be found asleep in some corner, or sitting under the counter in a sweet shop being fed treats by an indulgent stall keeper. In her later years, the watch would drag Cari

back by the ear, and accuse her of pickpocketing or fighting or trying
to climb the frame of some tower or aerial railway.

Eladora's own memories of the Festival are mostly of standing in
the full glare of the blazing summer sun, trying not to faint while
her mother and the rest of the congregation prayed. Hearing, distantly, the joys of the rest of the Festival. It got worse after Carillon
left; instead of coming here, to the main festival outside Guerdon,
Silva took to attending a much smaller Blessing of Flowers up in the
mountains run by a Safidist sect. No merriment, no big fairground
full of delights, just a raging bonfire and endless prayers, begging
Mother of Flowers to take her faithful as vessels for her power.
Bloody-footed pilgrimages over the mountain to the little village
where Saint Aleena of the Sacred Flame had gained her blessing.

It's nearly three o'clock. Kelkin's supposed to give a speech at three,
taking advantage of the crowds gathering for the Blessing of Flowers.
The IndLib pavilion's emptying out already, the party members leaving to push through the crowds down to the middle field. Eladora
and Emlin are the last in this part of the tent, tidying away papers
and dragging heavy tables over to the side – there'll be a reception
here later, after Kelkin's speech. Eladora's been to similar affairs
before, and is already plotting her escape routes from drunken, lecherous old goats who think that because she's part of Kelkin's circle
she has a liking for old men who used to be someone important.

Suddenly Emlin makes a quiet yelping noise in his throat and
ducks behind a trestle table.

"Don't be afraid, child." Silva's voice. Eladora turns, sees her
mother there, dressed in the brown robes of a lay helper of the
Keepers. The old woman leans heavily on a cane, but she seems
healthier than she did three weeks ago at the dinner. "Come out."

"L-leave him alone," snaps Eladora, positioning herself between
her mother and the table. "What do you want?"

"I thought I might find you here in this den of sin," says Silva.
"Drawn to false idols. Oh, the evil runs thick in our veins. Only
the fires of Safid can burn us clean." She puts down the cane, then

shuffles around to one end of the table. "Your grandfather would be so proud of you. Kelkin's handmaiden. His whore."

The long tables are so heavy that together Eladora and Emlin can only drag them across the floor. Silva shoves the table one-handed, flinging it over to the side of the tent. A few other IndLibs at the far end of the tent look around in confusion; Eladora waves them away.

"And what are you?" hisses Silva as she exposes Emlin. "There's a stench about you. Let me see." Silva raises her hand, which suddenly blazes with its own internal light, a fiery reddish-golden glow that burns deep within. The bones of the old woman's hand black against the flames. With her other hand, Silva rips down the ties of the tent flap and lets it fall down, blocking the sunlight from outside. Suddenly, the only light source in this part of the pavilion is that burning hand, and it throws huge dancing shadows against the canvas walls.

Silva's shadow is crowned with flowers of fire, cloaked in storm.

Emlin's shadow, as he crawls away across the floor in terror, seems to have eight thin spindly legs. Some divine contamination.

Silva grunts and grabs her cane from the table. The flames from her hand run down the stick like water, setting it alight. She advances towards Emlin.

"Mother, stop." Eladora grabs Silva's arm, but it's as futile as grabbing the door handle of a carriage to stop a whole steam train moving.

"Abjure the unclean one! Abjure the weaver of lies!" demands Silva as she advances on Emlin. The boy writhes on the floor like he's pinned there, his limbs flailing. "I shall know if you lie! Abjure him!"

Horrified, Eladora puts herself between Silva and the boy again. "Stop!" Silva scowls and brushes her out of the way. Her cane has become a blazing sword. Emlin curls into a ball, hiding his face from her wrath.

"ABJURE HIM!"

Silva thrusts the flaming sword towards Emlin, pressing the searing metal to his skin. He shrieks as the sword burns him, and shouts something in a language Eladora doesn't understand.

"Mother, stop!" Eladora slaps her mother in the face, as hard as she can. It's gratifyingly effective – the flames go out, the sword is a cane again, and Silva's sent staggering. The tent seems to spin around both of them; somewhere, in the distance, Eladora hears thunder smashing across the sky. Saint Storm's voice, the Keepers call it.

Emlin crawls away across the floor, whimpering, cradling his burned hand. Then, absently, as if she's wiping away a speck of dirt, Silva leans down and brushes her hand over Emlin's blistered flesh. Another miracle – his wounds are healed in an instant, leaving only a patch of reddened skin.

"He ... he is ... " Silva's leaning heavily on her cane again, swaying back and forth as if about to faint. The cane smokes. "And you – you too. You ... " She's drooling a little now, her face slack. "Carillon. You've seen her." Silva's voice is strange, and again Eladora has the sickening impression of something speaking through her mother.

"Yes – in the New City. She saved my life."

"Treacherous false friends. But the path to the true gods is a thorny one."

Silva totters forward and takes Eladora's hand with shocking gentleness. "Oh, do you remember going up into the mountains, dear, and over the hills to Saint Aleena's shrine? The sunlight like bright knives, flaying the skin from the world and showing you what matters. Salvation for our family. Salvation for our city. Oh, my child, we're so close." Silva embraces Eladora, liver-spotted arms with bones of steel closing around her like a cage. Eladora freezes.

The tent flap opens again to reveal Mhari Voller. She hurries over, strokes Silva's arm, whispers to her. "Silva Duttin, dear Silvy, you mustn't go running away from me. You see the gods so clearly, you'll fall over your feet. Come along now, you need to get ready. Remember, it's the Blessing of Flowers today, and you're needed to serve." She ushers Silva out of the tent, glancing back with worried eyes at Emlin. There's a russet torrent of people outside – other lay Keepers in robes identical to Silva's marching by, chanting and singing hymns as they proceed down to the Festival field. Voller gives

Silva a gentle push, and Silva totters into the crowd, joining the procession. Instantly, she adds her voice to the chorus, and it's beautiful, like the music of a great church organ rising up in harmony.

Eladora hurries over to tend to Emlin. The boy's shaking, and he pushes her away when she kneels down next to him. "I'm all right," he mutters. His wounds have vanished so quickly that Eladora's unsure of what she saw.

"Let me see," she insists, but he jerks away from her and bounces to his feet like he's being pulled up by invisible strings.

"I'm fine," he insists. He wipes his face on the shoulder of his shirt, spits, and then suddenly he's smiling again.

Her occasional assistant Rhiado sticks his jug-eared head into the tent. "Kelkin's speech. It's time."

The damn speech. She has to go, much as she'd like to stay and watch over Emlin. Eladora beckons Rhiado in. She hands him a few coins, and asks him to take Emlin away and take care of him. Buy him whatever she wants. Get a healing salve. The boy's recovery is suspiciously swift, thinks Eladora, and she makes a note to talk to Alic about his son. If he has a lingering spiritual taint from the Godswar he could be a danger to everyone around him. He'll be sent to Hark if the watch catch him.

She finds Voller waiting at the door of the tent.

"Lady Voller, if you're going to appoint yourself my mother's keeper, then please keep her from assaulting my assistant." *Starve her*, Eladora's tempted to say, *lock her away in a gilded cage. Keep her docile, because who knows what she'll do with that terrible strength. Do to her what the Keepers are supposed to do to their gods.*

"She wanted to see you. She worries about you – I hear that Effro has you clambering around the New City, endangering yourself."

"Her concern is touching."

"It's genuine. She doesn't ... You're seeing her at her worst, Eladora. You upset her, and she loses control. It's because she sees you so rarely. If you saw one another more, she wouldn't be as highly strung."

"I must walk down for Kelkin's speech." Eladora picks up her own bag. The leather's scorched – Silva's flaming cane must have brushed against it. Nothing inside seems to be damaged – a few folders of IndLib documents, her notebook, her coin-purse, the broken hilt of Aleena's sword that Sinter gave her, that terrible *Bone Shield* novel.

"Is something wrong?" Voller hovers over her, peering over her shoulder. Eladora snaps the bag shut.

"No, it's all fine."

The Bone Shield reminds her of her brief meeting with Terevant Erevesic earlier. He had a copy of *Sacred and Secular Architecture* – and not just any copy, but *her* copy. During the Crisis, she'd fetched that book from the university library and ended up carrying it around the city. The book illustrated the reconstruction of Guerdon after the war with the Black Iron Gods three hundred years ago. Showing how the reconstruction had built over the scars, burying temples and sealing off dungeons sacred to the monstrous deities of the past. The last time she'd seen the book had been in a safe house run by Sinter. She recalls reading it, losing herself in study, to avoid thinking about her predicament. Hiding in the bedroom, while outside assassins slaughtered everyone else in the house.

How had the book followed her out of that nightmare? Hunting her, like it had grown legs and crawled out of the past, pages smeared with blood.

Everything goes dim and distant. The sun in the sky seems to press down on her, like it's inside her skull, scorching her brain. Eladora's distantly aware that she's doubled over, retching. The festival ground spins around her. Voller's there, clucking, holding back her hair as Eladora vomits. Some passers-by jeer, laughing at the woman.

"It's all right, dear." Voller produces a handkerchief, wipes her mouth. "I always get nervous before a big speech, too, even if I don't have to say a word. You wrote some of Kelkin's, I know." She produces a small silver flask and hands it to Eladora. "Wash your mouth out with this. It's a medicinal tonic, wonderful stuff."

Eladora takes a mouthful from the flask, half chokes on it, then takes a second gulp.

"Also, gin," admits Voller.

Voller thinks her nervousness is due to Kelkin's speech But the election is her balm. It's wonderfully petty and grounded. Hearthfires and gravestones, streets and wards, nitpicking legal arguments. Everything's about the here and now, not about gods and monsters. This is something else.

"I must go to the speech," says Eladora again, and stumbles down towards the Festival ground. She's so dizzy she has to lean on Voller's arm as they go.

CHAPTER 26

O ne of the Haithi guards finds Terevant in the beer tent, and tells him his presence is required at the pavilion. The Lady Lyssada has arrived. Terevant follows the guard out. He can hear the murmur of the vast crowd in the distance, and the droning of the Keeper priests. The laneways between the tents are much less crowded than they were an hour ago. Everyone's gone down to the centrepiece of the Festival of Flowers.

Almost everyone. Daerinth's waiting for him outside the tent, along with a few clerks from the embassy. The former prince dismisses the clerks and shuffles alongside Terevant as they walk to the pavilion. It's cruelly hot. Daerinth is a withered weed, scorched by the sun.

"This is unseemly." Daerinth fusses at Terevant's uniform, scowls at the alcohol on his breath. "Mercifully, there are few witnesses, but word will get back through those treacherous dogs at the Bureau. Spies are worse than fishwives for scandal. Idiot."

Terevant's drunk enough to find the old man's anger amusing rather than insulting. "I think Lys will understand."

"I had a cousin once," whispers Daerinth as he fixes the clasp on Terevant's cloak, "who brought shame on the family. Rhaen, her name was. We shipped her off overseas, but she came back. Sent her to the academy, and she was expelled."

"A woman after my own heart."

"After my mother won the Crown, Rhaen fell down the backstairs at the palace. She'd been drinking. Such a tragedy." Daerinth pulls

the cloak noose-tight and fastens the clasp again. "She wasn't prepared for Vigilance, and the necromancers didn't get to her in time
for her to be Supplicant. She died dishonoured, casteless and *quietly*."

"A cautionary tale to all second sons."

Daerinth stops by Lyssada's carriage. Lowers his voice so the
guards standing nearby don't hear him. "Don't hand it over. Take
the sword yourself."

"What?" Terevant stares in confusion at Daerinth. Has he gone
mad from sunstroke? Why, in the name of the nameless god, is
Daerinth telling him to *steal* the Sword Erevesic? Daerinth, his
brother's closest adviser, First Secretary, a damned *prince of the
Empire*, is urging him to commit an unthinkable betrayal. *Or maybe
I've gone mad.*

Daerinth hisses at him. "Take the sword and go. Your brother's
attention is divided. He is trying to save both the Empire of Haith
and the House Erevesic. He cannot attend to both tasks at once."

"You're a lunatic!" splutters Terevant, but Daerinth continues.
This isn't some whim of the old man's — he's clearly rehearsed
this speech.

"He desires the Crown, but is held back by his duty to the sword.
Better to remove it from reach. You will benefit from this, too, oh,
oh." Daerinth paws at Terevant's jacket. "Oh, you shall be outlaw
for a while, for stealing the sword — but when your brother wins
the Crown you can be pardoned and take your place as the Erevesic.
Until then, you can forge a new reputation for yourself. There are
two straight paths to glory in Haith, the army and the Bureau, and
you stumbled and fell on both of them. Take the sword and cut your
own path through the thickets!" Daerinth reaches into the carriage,
presses some hidden catch beneath the seats. A panel slides open.
The sword's in there. Terevant can hear the blade whispering.

"Olthic — he'd never forgive me."

"I shall make him understand. Do this, and he will be crowned.
He shall make a fine ruler. And the Crown sees farther than the
living or the dead. He will still love you. Take the blade." Daerinth
steps back. "I said none of this," he croaks. His hands are shaking.

The old man turns his back and shuffles away towards the pavilion, gnawing on his knuckles, leaving Terevant standing by the sword.

Kelkin's march down to the Festival field becomes a procession, then an ambulatory rally. Musicians and performers dance ahead of the crowd; others hold banners high, or chant and cheer. Kelkin ignores them all. Eladora tries to push through the crowd to get to him, but the mob's too tightly packed around him for her to break through — and down at the field, a hundred times as many people wait.

It's well after three before Kelkin reaches the podium, and there are interminable speeches by lesser party figures before he'll be allowed speak. Eladora doesn't need to hear the speech — she's written parts of it, other parts Kelkin's been preaching for half a century, word for word. Any new material will be about his proposal to hire the city's ghouls as part of the watch to guard against hostile saints; he'll take what they said in the meeting and through some alchemy of charisma make people eager to have the ghouls watching over them.

Chants of "KELKIN! KELKIN!" fill the field, swell up and fill the sky.

Kelkin raises his hands, and the crowd falls silent.

His speech is hectoring, impatient, full of numbers — everything that should be uninspiring, but Kelkin's confidence and always bubbling anger give his oratory a fire that elevates it. He manages to be simultaneously the wily old trickster who knows how to pull every lever and work every cheat in the system, and the firebrand who's going to burn it all down and build something better. He promises to chart a course between the heartless buccaneering of the guilds and the stifling hand of the church; to bring reform and wealth to the city while obscurely hinting that he'll deal with any threats. A better tomorrow, if only you'll believe in him — and yourself. No guilds, no gods — just honest hard work, charity and integrity.

"He's always been so good at this," says Voller.

Eladora's feeling better now that she's out in the air, away from the tent and her mother. "Tempted to rejoin the Industrial Liberals?"

"No," she replies. "Look at this crowd. They're here for the Blessing of Flowers, not him. Oh, some will vote for him, but it's not his city, and never was. He knows love for the Keepers runs deep. The city for the church, and the church for the city."

"Love?" scoffs Eladora. "That's l-l-like saying marrying someone is the same as locking them in your cellar. The Keepers monopolised the souls of Guerdon for centuries! The people had no choice but to worship the Kept Gods."

"They're the gods of our city, child. Our gods, not the monsters of other lands. They love us – why should we not love them in return?" Voller leans in close, whispering in Eladora's ear so she can be heard over the roar of the crowd. "You should know better than anyone how they delivered us from the Black Iron Gods, and shielded us from the Godswar. Imagine where we'd be without their blessings! Do you really think a few alchemical guns can stop Ishmere from conquering us?"

"And going all S-S-Safidist is your solution? We have to defend ourselves from mad gods, so let's feed the worst impulses of our tame ones, goad them until they go mad, too, and turn some of us into m-mothers – into monsters!"

Voller steps back. "Eladora, child, please. Stop and think – I know you've a good brain. The Keepers are not your enemies. Gods below, they're not even *his* enemies." She points at Kelkin, who's boasting about trade with the Archipelago. "We all want what's best for Guerdon. We all want peace – and to put an end to the Crisis. And I'd be the first to admit that the Keepers have made mistakes in the past, but the gods have never stopped loving us. The city needs its gods."

"That," says Eladora coldly, "is exactly what my grandfather said."

"Oh, you poor broken thing," sighs Voller. "It's unconscionable that Effro has you running around the New City, when you still haven't healed from the Crisis. You should have a chance to rest. To go home and—"

"Home to Wheldacre? To my mother? How would that be rest-ful?" A memory runs through Eladora's mind, an image from many years ago when she was a child. Carillon – always Carillon – stole a jar of honey from the pantry, ran off into the barn to eat it. Ants came, drawn by the sweetness. Cari saw that the ants were eating the droplets of spilled honey, so she upended the jar for them on the ground. Eladora remembers the ants drowning in the honey, caught in its sticky kindness, dying of what they most most desired. The terrible kindness of a god.

Voller continues to plead. "Eladora, please, you could help. Effro could help. Just—"

Her words are drowned out in the roar of the crowd.

"The answer is no," says Eladora. "There'll be no pact between us." She expects Voller to be angry, or to plead with her to reconsider, or say – correctly – that Eladora's only one possible conduit between the Keepers and the Industrial Liberals, and that she can't speak for Kelkin, let alone the whole party. She expects that false façade to crack, for the feigned honey-sweet concern to turn to something cruel and icy.

Instead, Voller takes her hand, and says, "Please, keep him from doing anything foolish when he loses." She speaks with a terrible finality, as if Kelkin's defeat is absolutely certain. But how can Voller be so sure? The election is still weeks away, the church has scarely budged in the polls, and here, here in the heart of the Keepers' Festival, the crowd is chanting Kelkin's name.

Her mother threw a bucket of water over the dying ants and washed them all away.

Terevant stands under the sun, feeling the world rotate beneath his feet, trying to make sense of Daerinth's bizarre outburst. In the distance, across the fairground, twenty thousand people cheer.

He climbs into the carriage, pulls the sword from its hiding place. The ornamental hilt, the family crest drawn in gold, and the ancient dark metal of the blade, damascened with lighter ripples that in some lights look like faces or humanoid shapes.

The sword's a better size for him than it would be for Olthic. Ter has just the right proportions to wield the blade; Olthic's massive physique is better suited for some two-handed monster weapon. When Terevant lifts it, it recognises him. The strength of his ancestors surging through his hands, his arms, flowing into his heart, suffusing him. Memory-flashes of other days, of grand battles.

The sword wouldn't be his by rights – Olthic's the heir. The ancestor-souls living in the blade might reject him. He'd never be allowed to join them when he died, and his soul would be left to rot. But oh, before then – he lets himself dream, for a moment in the dark, of being some fabled roguish wandering hero, a dashing renegade flashing like a lightning bolt across the world. The sword would give him strength and speed, a blade that could cut gods and monsters. A mercenary, maybe. Wading through blood and gold, with the burghers of a dozen cities begging him to fight for their cause. Or a hero who fights against cruel and corrupt gods, kicking over the altars of monstrous deities and putting their saints and priests to the sword. Angry gods raging in the heavens, spitting poison and thunder at him, while he flourishes his blade and laughs at the sky . . .

It'd make a good poem, but it's not his life.

No, his last throw of the dice was at Eskalind, and look how that turned out. The words of the necromancer who attended his father: *He must choose quickly, now, which of the other castes to die in.* Advice for life.

He wraps the blade up again, then climbs out of the carriage. There's another distant roar from the crowd in the main field, as if they're cheering him on. He salutes the guards as he enters the Haithi pavilion. He glances around, wondering if Berrick's here, too, doggedly following after Lys, but there's no sign of the little man.

There, at the far end of the tent, stand Olthic and Lys. Daerinth's there as well, waiting like some monstrous clergyman. His eyes flash with fury when he sees Terevant carrying the sword, but he says nothing.

Olthic's impatient, Lys with her enigmatic half-smile that he loved to see break into a laugh. She's wearing a dress for the celebrations tonight, after the conclusion of the festival. She's heart-breakingly beautiful.

He walks towards Lys. He walks away from her, too.

After the speech, Eladora watches Kelkin and his immediate coterie depart, followed by various guild masters and politicians. She should be with them, but the press of the crowd around her is too great. She's trapped in the throng. At the far end of the field, the sound of a choir swells, and the hymn is taken up by everyone around her. The crowd reorients, shuffling around to face the altar to the south, and Eladora's forced to move with them, too. The hymn's one she's heard many time before, a song of praise to the Mother. Her four sacred aspects, corresponding to the cardinal points of the year. Mother of Hopes, of Flowers, of Sorrows, of Mercies.

The faithful raise wooden standards, each bearing the name of the village they come from. The standards are made to resemble barren trees, empty branches like skeletal hands.

Soon, when the priests bless them, they'll be garlanded with flowers, symbolising the rising life force, the bounty of the harvest and the gifts of the goddess. Children get to climb up on the standards to hang the flowers. Carillon always insisted on climbing to the very top of the Wheldacre standard, when they were young, balancing atop the swaying pole and hurling flowers heedlessly.

The hymn grows, and Eladora finds herself singing, too, in unison with the crowd. Eladora's voice soars – she's never been comfortable singing, she usually stumbles over the words, but today they come like a fountain of honey. Part of her recoils. There's something sickeningly warm and comforting about this, a soporific heat that makes it hard to think. The sun wheels overhead, as if the whole field is spinning. The sky is brilliant, brilliant blue, marked only by a few puffy white clouds. For a moment, the clouds seem to draw themselves into vaguely humanoid shapes, reaching down from that heaven.

It would be so easy to give in, to let the crowd carry her. Let her feet shuffle forward with the rest of the faithful. Let her soul flow into the sunlight, or the sunlight flow into her soul. She remembers

Saint Aleena carrying her out of danger, fighting for her. Watching over her as she slept. The sword bright in her hand, as bright as the sun.

She pushes back, tries to fight against the crowd, and suddenly the sun is a lance stabbing at her eyes, blinding her. Her voice breaks, and she can't remember the words of the hymn any more. She staggers. Someone elbows her in the side, hard, and she stumbles into the path of a large man, who treads on her foot painfully. Eladora struggles through the crowd, going against the flow, and fights her way to the side of the field.

Here, she can catch her breath. She's shaded from the sun by one of the tents, and the pain in her head diminishes. Twice today she's had that strange disorientation — once in the crowd, and earlier, in the tent, when her mother manifested her saintly gift.

To calm herself, she runs through some of the magical exercises that Dr Ramegos taught her, draws in her sorcerous energies and lets them run out again. Her limbs tingle as the power discharges, but her head is clear again. The clouds are just clouds.

From here, she can see the line of red-robed helpers, handing out smaller garlands of flowers to the faithful while the priests chant the Blessing of Flowers. People in the city say it brings good luck.

She recognises one of the helpers, even at this distance. It's her mother. Silva's one of a hundred helpers, passing out garlands. The daughter of the Thay family, once part of the wealthiest elite in Guerdon, handing out little bunches of wildflowers to the crowd. A long queue of people pass by the helpers, each one taking a garland. Soon, they'll hang them on the standards, and the patrol will say a prayer, and it'll all be over.

The downward stretch now, she tells herself. There's nothing between now and the election. None of the other parties have a leader who can challenge Kelkin. The Industrial Liberals will win, and Kelkin will credit her in his victory speech. Appoint her to some position on the university board, and she can go back to her studies. Return that copy of *Sacred and Secular Architecture* to the library, and apologise for its lateness.

Eladora stares across the crowd at her mother, as if trying to catch her eye. *You enjoy the sainthood you sought, Mother. It's probably easier for the gods to fill you, since you're missing a soul.*

And then the hymn rises in her again, the words of prayer becoming irresistible, and she's pulled back out into the sunshine. The crowd surges forward, carrying her towards the altar. She stumbles, and when she looks up into the sky she sees them.

Gods above.

There, raising his lamp of truth, is the cowled form of the Holy Beggar. A giant, taller than the sky. His cloak is the night sky; his eyes hold all the wisdom that can be found through suffering. Beside him, standing in the midst of the industrial pavilion like a colossus, is the Holy Smith. He shambles forward, lifting his hammer.

Does anyone else see them? she thinks. Maybe a few do – Safidist fanatics, god-touched mystics, sensitive children. The rest of the crowd are almost insensible to the proximity of their gods. The presence is seen only in aggregate – the hem of the Holy Beggar's robe brushes over the crowd, and a line of people abruptly shiver despite the heat.

Eladora's seen the Kept Gods before. She glimpsed them in the Crisis, when Saint Aleena perished. Then, they were frail phantasms, confused and frightened. Now, they're much stronger.

Saint Storm strides in from the east. His armour is encrusted with salt and barnacles, but his sword of fire burns bright across the sky. He looks down at Eladora – she cannot see the god's eyes behind the helmet's visor, but his *recognition* blasts through her like a thunderbolt, leaves her twitching on the ground. Hands in the crowd pick her up and carry her, another pilgrim overcome by religious ecstasy. Someone puts a garland of flowers on her neck, but it comes loose and falls to the ground to be trampled by the mob.

Eladora tries to fight back. Tries to recite a defensive incantation, but she can't find the words. All that comes to mind is a lecture from Professor Ongent, snidely dismissing the Kept Gods. *A typical example of a minor rustic pantheon ... patterns drawn from the cycle of life and death, from divisions between us and not-us ...*

unsophisticated, unremarkable ... no more intent or wit than a round-worm or a tick ...

The Mother rises from the fields around her. On her brow, a blazing crown of flowers. This is the bright time, the joyous time, before the toils of autumn and the bitter winter. Joy like honey, too-sweet. Eladora retches.

But this changes nothing, she tells herself desperately. *It's just an aetheric spasm, a spiritual fluctuation. The Keepers lost their grip on parliament a generation ago, when the gods were just as strong. Kelkin still won then.*

The gods look down at her, judge her – and move on.

They begin to fade from her sight. The Crown of Flowers on the Mother's brow shrinks. It's an implosion, an artillery bombardment in reverse. Concentrating, compressing down to a ring of fire ...

Terevant proffers the sword to Olthic.

His brother, absurdly, glances back to Daerinth for an instant. Daerinth shakes his head, briefly, but Olthic still reaches for the sword.

He raises it, and souls run down the blade. Pulses of energy flow through him. He's magnified by it. Already strong, he becomes invincible. Already handsome, he becomes glorious. Already commanding, now divine.

The three others – the three mortals – in the room are affected differently. Daerinth kneels, groaning as his old joints bend. Terevant can hear wild cheering, exultation, and for a moment he can't tell if it's from the Festival outside or from inside his own head.

Lys hears the shouts from the Festival. She laughs, kisses his brother on the cheek, and whispers just loud enough for Terevant to hear. "I win."

Silva hands a garland of flowers to one little man in a bright green cloak, and there's a crash of thunder, a flash of sunlight so intense it sears a ring of fire onto Eladora's vision. Everyone's vision – the whole crowd staggers, thousands of people struck half blind by that moment of divine glory. Eladora blinks furiously, but the ring's still there, a miraculous circle of golden light that recedes, contracts, until it's a crown. A crown of fire. The garland of flowers has become a blazing crown. Silva's still holding it, as is the man in the green cloak.

The Patros runs down from the high altar, shoving bishops and prelates out of the way. He pushes through them to Silva's side. She's still holding the crown, frozen like a figure in a painting. The whole scene is like a scene from a religious painting brought to life – the red-robed saint, the holy beggar, the Patros in his shimmering cloak.

Then the man kneels before the Patros. The Patros takes the crown and places it on the little man's head, in full view of the whole crowd.

"The king! The king has returned!"

CHAPTER 27

The waters of Guerdon's harbour are dark and murky this evening. The seabed's choked with mud and runoff from the factories, so every step throws up clouds of silt. Even if the spy were to light the lamp attached to his diving suit, he wouldn't be able to see more than a few inches. He can only trust in the tugging of the rope that's wound around his waist. It tugs him forward, and he walks forward into the utter darkness.

Tander's somewhere behind him, tied to the same rope. Ahead of the spy, the rope runs to the mer-woman, Oona. She's also holding the end of a second rope, the bridle for two of Tander's mercenary friends, Fierdy and the Relief. The Relief answers to no other name, and the spy doesn't begrudge him that. The four of them are all wearing diving suits that Dredger swears are watertight, but the growing chill in the spy's right boot suggests otherwise.

On their backs are breathing cages. Take gills cultured from some aquatic species, keep them alive in a vitalising gel. Clamp the gill inside a mesh, have it squirt liquid air into the back of the user's helmet. As long as the gill-creature thrives, you can breathe underwater.

The spy can feel the creature in the cage gurgling against his spine as he walks, leaden-footed, across the floor of the sea.

Somewhere, far above and far behind, is Dredger's launch, where Haberas and Annah wait. When the job is done, Oona will lead the four divers back to that launch; they'll shuck their weighted belts and boots, and she'll carry them up to the surface, one by one.

They're supposed to be down here for an hour at most, pushing the breathers to their limit. The spy doesn't know how long it's been so far – without sight, without hearing, without anything but the sensation of cold and the taste of copper. He's never been so aware of the blood in his body, the motion of his lungs. He can hear his heart.

Oona flashes by, a moment of light in the porthole of his helmet. Underwater, parts of her scaly body are luminescent, the holy litany of the Kraken written in her flesh. The sigils are brighter now, the gills on her flanks more visible. The longer she spends down here, the more she succumbs to her change. The spy's promised her and her husband a considerable payment for this job, but no amount of money can reverse her transformation. She belongs to the god now, and the sea.

A tug, and they move forward. A march into darkness. Someone stumbles – the spy can tell by the rope going slack, and then the water rushing past him as Oona swims over to lift the fallen diver. They're moving too slowly, the spy guesses, but they have no way to communicate.

After an endless, timeless march, the seabed begins to slope upwards. There are lights, far above, and the distant rumble of engines. Something passes overhead, an ironclad warship, huge and terribly present as a god. They're getting closer to the secure harbour at Queen's Point. The plan is to stroll past the fortress's walls and guards, past all its defences, by taking the decidedly unscenic route along the seabed.

It's an easier route, but it's not undefended. Oona leads them around underwater obstacles. Spiked chunks of metal.

At his belt hangs a heavy pistol. It's waterproofed – phlogiston can burn in water just as easily as in air – but he doubts he could hit anything with it while wearing this clumsy suit. Instead, he unclips the flash ghost and holds the weapon in his gloved hand. Press the clasp, and the little grenade discharges a howling storm of aetheric energy. Raw sorcery, gone sour.

Flash ghosts are hard to detect at a distance. An observer just sees a whirling flash of light, a phosphorescent catfight that blazes for an instant. Better yet, they're good at dealing with magical defences, they can overwhelm wards and other spells with sheer chaotic force. There's little a flash ghost won't fuck up on some level. The downside is that that they're largely indiscriminate, attacking the most vulnerable targets first, taking the path of least psychic resistance to oblivion. If the spy lets off a flash ghost here, the discharge will arc to Oona or one of the mercenaries. Still, he keeps the ghost ready.

The lights from the surface are getting brighter as they climb. Huge aetheric lamps mounted along the cliffs, banishing the gloom of twilight from the cove. Queen's Point was a cove once, a steep-sided gash in the headland. The fortress has consumed the headland, wrapped the sea cliffs in concrete. They've expanded the cove, blasted and dredged it, making it into a secure, sheltered harbour, narrow and high-walled.

Another ship moves overhead, eclipsing the blazing lamps. The spy can see the smaller shadow of the tug dragging the ship, as Oona's dragging them. As above, so below.

As part of their preparation Tander and the spy worked their contacts. Talked to Dredger, to ex-military, mercenaries, alchemists, sailors, anyone who'd been inside Queen's Point. The cove's entrance points almost due east, and their accounts all agreed that the main moorings are on the northern side of the cove. There's a small rocky ledge that starts halfway along the south side, and runs to the western end, close to the *Grand Retort*'s berth. That's their target. They can climb up there and spy on the docked ship up close. Confirm, somehow, that there's a god bomb there, ready for use on any invading deity.

On the sketch map Tander drew in the tavern, it all looked so easy. They'd crowed about how there'd be fewer guards on watch, with so many people away at the Festival. Talked about how they'd be in and out in a few minutes, how easy it would be. But the air in his helmet already tastes stale, and there's still a long walk back to the launch even after they finish the job. The other three divers worry about making it back alive.

The spy has other concerns.

Suddenly, there's a bloom of mud, a muffled, rumbling explosion of movement. A blur of brown and blue as Oona flees, the dropped ropes coiling like sea serpents in her wake. Movement – it's Tander's mercenary pals. One's fumbling with his pistol, the other's somewhere in the cloud of mud ahead. The spy catches a glimpse of something with teeth and tentacles, a polyp grown gigantic and carnivorous. The product of some alchemical vat.

He throws the product of another alchemical vat at it, the flash-ghost grenade tumbling slowly through the water. It explodes, too, silently, vomiting out a whirling cloud of pale phantasms that quickly vanish into the mud. Underwater, the shrieking of the weapon cannot be heard.

The thrashing stops, and it's all still.

Silt begins to settle, the water begins to clear. He sees the cut end of the mercenary's rope, a few shredded pieces of rubber diving suit, and a mud-covered carcass torn apart by long rasping tongues. The surviving mercenary – he can't tell which one it is – drags himself upright. The flash ghost got whatever monster guarded the approach to the cove.

Got one of the monsters, anyway. But who knows how many more creatures lurk in the mud and rocks ahead?

The spy turns. Behind him, the dark shape of Tander, still tied to him by the rope. Tander walks up to him, presses his helmet against the spy's glass faceplate. He can see Tander's mouth move, hear distinct vibrations transmitted through the metal, but he can't make out words. Instead, the spy unhooks his lamp and flashes it – once at the other mercenary, and once in the direction Oona went.

The other mercenary stumbles over to them, holding the cut end of his rope like a lost child. The spy takes that end and loops it around his own waist. All three divers are now tethered together again. They wait there in the murk for a long silent minute until Oona swims back into view. Compared to her aquatic grace, they are clod-footed and slow. Through gestures, she makes it clear that she's not going any farther. She'll wait at the mouth of the cove, and lead them back to the launch when they return.

She points in the direction of the rocky ledge that's supposed to be out there in the murk, somewhere along the southern edge of the harbour. She then swims off in the opposite direction, leaving the three alone. They can't talk to one another, and their own gloves are too bulky to make anything but the simplest gestures.

It's the democracy of the rope – they all have to follow the course set by the majority, come what may.

Lights stab down from above. A small boat, probably checking out whatever made the disturbance in the water. Guerdon's harbour is mostly empty of fish, but some must survive in the tainted waters. The guardian monsters must snap at the occasional flounder or dog-fish. Not every disturbance means an intruder. Still, the three divers hurry to get clear of the light.

Tander's in the lead. If he's picked the wrong direction, they're doomed. If he doesn't hit that rocky ledge, they'll march past it, off down the length of the secure harbour. There's nowhere to climb out unseen there. They might make it back to Oona before they run out of air, but there are no guarantees of that.

It's getting harder to breathe.

Far away, Emlin flinches away from the unrelenting fire of the Kept Gods, in the hands of Silva Duttin.

Farther away, the fleets of Ishmere sail north – to Lyrix or Haith, it doesn't matter. Cloud Mother's breath fills their sails; Kraken swims ahead, seizing the seas. Lion Queen stands on the prow, roaring a challenge. High Umur on his throne of stars. Fate Spider sees it all from the shadows.

The spy's light-headed. He can't remember a time when he wasn't walking through these murky waters.

And then the rope drags him up a slope. Tander's found the ledge.

They haul themselves out of the water, hunching down behind rocks and discarded fuel drums to hide from any sentries. Shucking off the diving suits, helping each other out of the heavy brass helmets, the clomping weighted boots, the alchemical cages. The gills in the cages are exhausted, their bluish scales now flushed pink. Little trickles of blood oozing from the feathery membranes. Tander's mercenary friend – the surviving one, Fierdy – has used these sorts of breathing tanks before. He pales and mutters an oath under his breath, tells them that he'll need to stay here to wash out the tanks before they can be used again. The spy unties Fierdy's rope from his waist. He stays tethered to Tander.

And then there were two.

Tander and the spy creep along the narrow ledge that runs along the edge of the cove. They're at the mercy of the tide here – the high-water mark is two feet above the spy's head as he clambers along, his feet sliding on seaweed and shells. They're halfway along the canyon of the sheltered cove, with Queen's Point opposite them across the deep, dark water. The southern cliff wall soars behind him. If there are sentries up there, they'd have to be right at the brink of the cliff to spot them.

There are sentries on the other side of the cove, of course – thousands of them. The massive fortress of Queen's Point stands there, cannons pointing out to sea, watchtowers gazing at the horizon. The fortress is piled upon itself, new bulwarks and towers engulfing older ones. Grown like a coral, a concrete cancer. The spy cowers at the sight of the fortress's hundreds of windows. Older ones are arrow-slits and gun-loops; the ones in the flank of the new-built sections are glassy portholes, gleaming like red eyes as they reflect the setting sun.

The long barrels of guns look like fingers against the orange-red clouds above the cove. The larger gun emplacements can fire clear across Guerdon's island-strewn harbour. They could smash the dying on the Isle of Statues, wipe Dredger's yards on Shrike clear in a flash. Smaller gun emplacements command the approaches to the city, watch over the entrance to this cove.

They crawl on, closer to the warship that's docked at the end of the cove. The *Grand Retort*. Built to take advantage of the latest alchemical engines.

Maybe a god bomb, too.

The spy fishes out out a spyglass and scans the *Retort*. The crew on deck lumber around in protective suits. Most have their helmets off—there's no danger here, just standard procedures. No danger *yet*, that is—the weapons they handle are a thousand times deadlier than any bullet or sword. How much of that canister of acid seeds would it take to kill every crewman on the deck, to melt their flesh and turn their bones into a sticky, chalky mess? A hundredth of the barrel? Less?

The spy isn't Sanhada Baradhin, but these ironclads look other-worldly to him, impossibilities conjured by alchemy and ingenuity.

"We have to get closer," Tander insists.

They shuffle faster. Fierdy's out of sight now, lost behind the rocks. They can see the deck of the *Grand Retort* more clearly now. There, mounted dead centre on the main deck, is the frame of a rocket launcher. Heavily reinforced, wound around with protective sorcery-runes and blast shields.

If the weapon were on board the *Grand Retort* right now, it would be there.

It's empty.

"It's not here, Tander."

"We've got to be sure," says Tander. "Annah *said*."

There, beyond the *Retort*, is a metal door set into the stone wall of the cove. Some natural sea cave that's been expanded, reinforced, locked away behind steel. A narrow-gauge railway runs from the door to the docks. It's an armoury.

The spy can't stop himself looking at it. It draws his eye. He feels he has to watch that door, in the same way he'd keep watch on a poisonous serpent sunning itself in the middle of the road. He doesn't like that door.

Tander spots it, too. To get to the door, they'll have to climb across from the one side of the cove to the other, crossing the western end. The rocks are jagged and scarred; it might be possible to clamber above the stew of garbage that's collected at the water's edge and make the crossing.

Tander goes first, and the rope tugs the spy along. He follows Tander along the rocks, using the same perilous handholds and toeholds. Digging his fingers into the slimy cracks.

As they get closer, the spy feels a growing weakness. It's a sickening sensation, as if invisible particles are penetrating him and encrusting his bones. His blood thickens, curdles, rots inside his veins. His fingers go numb, then his limbs. He's a sack of flesh, limp and heavy. Laboriously swinging one leg, then another, placing his arms on handholds like a sailor tying ropes, knotting his fingers around the rocks.

It's not enough.

He slips, plunges down towards the jagged rocks below, suddenly boneless.

The rope catches him. Tander holds on, clinging to the rocks, his fingers bone-white as he carries his own weight and the spy's.

"Climb," Tander orders, eyes wild. The Fate Spider's poison gives him strength born from desperation; for Tander, there's no fate worse than failure, than being unmade at Annah's command.

The spy can't do it. He's suddenly exhausted beyond all experience. He can only cling here, exposed. If a sentry glances towards this end of the cove, he'll be spotted instantly.

"Climb," hisses Tander, again. He shifts his grip on the stone – Tander's frightfully strong – so he can get to his knife and cut the rope if he has must.

He'll leave the spy to die here. Drown here. And then he'll go after Emlin.

The spy flails his limbs. Can't remember which ones are arms and which are legs, or what the difference between them is supposed to be. It's Alic who saves him, Alic who takes over. Alic who clambers across the cliff. Alic, now, who's helping Tander cross the last few feet of cliff before they reach the north side of the cove.

They're in Queen's Point now. Ahead, by the door, stand two sentries. They're watching the causeway that runs along from the docks to the armoury door, not the cliffs. They haven't yet seen the two bedraggled figures, huddled behind a barrel.

"What was that shit?" whispers Tander. "You had a fit or something?"

"It's nothing," says Alic. "Let's get this done."

Tander has his gun out. It's a gun made for fucking underwater use, it's not supposed to be accurate at any range, let alone shooting at targets a hundred feet away in near-darkness, but desperation does funny things to a man's nerve.

The crack-crack of two gunshots rolls out across the water, and two bodies fall, vanishing into the darkness. Tander breaks into a run, racing towards the armoury door. Frantic, furious, one last effort. The spy has to follow, running up onto the causeway. Along the railway, following the two bright lines of polished iron. They race up to that terrible door.

Behind them, the spy hears distant shouts, movement in Queen's Point. No siren yet, but it's only a matter of time. The fortress-god has felt a sting, heard the buzzing of a sandfly. Soon Queen's Point will stir itself to swat this intruder.

Tander gets to the door first. Spins the wheel to open it.

On the other side, a stone corridor. Racks, vaults of weapons.

They both see it only for an instant, before alarms sound in the depths, but that instant's enough. The god bomb's stored just inside the armoury door, ready to be loaded onto the *Retort* at a moment's notice.

A thing of ugly black iron, plates of twisted scrap metal welded together. Misshapen, mangled, a scab of divine ichor. So appalled at its own existence that it screams for annihilation. A shaped charge of blasphemy. Undeniable in its awful power, loathsome in its totality.

The spy shrieks inside his head – in triumph, in terror, he doesn't know.

Alic – he's more Alic than he's ever been, at this moment – grabs Tander by the shoulder. "We've got to go!" His heart pounding in his chest, he tenses for the pain of incoming gunfire. He wants, desperately, to live. To hear his name toasted in the IndLib meeting hall. To make it back to the gentling-house and hug Emlin. To stay Alic.

"Run!" Sirens howl. Searchlights flare. They dive into the water, swim for their lives. A short, filthy swim through the garbage, praying that the light doesn't find them. They reach the southern ledge again. Alic hauls on the rope, pulling Tander back up. Side by side, they crawl back towards the landing site. Towards the third mercenary, towards those breathing cages and the open harbour and Oona and the boat and safety and not dying on this fucking ledge . . .

The searchlight finds them.

"Move!" shouts Tander. Gunfire explodes around them. Shards of rock shower down into the water below. Tander's hit, bleeding from at least three wounds, but none fatal. It's a miracle, a bloody miracle granted by no known god that they're not killed, either of them.

Fierdy sees them coming. He half stands to usher them into cover where they can put on their diving gear, then his head explodes as a bullet catches him. Brains and skull splatter the waiting helmets in their neat row.

Tander grabs one helmet and jams it onto Alic's shoulders. Seals it roughly, slams the breathing tube home with such force that it startles the gill-creature in the tank.

"Do me!" shouts Tander.

It's the spy who reaches down, the spy who lifts another helmet, nearly drops it — it's slick with Fierdy's blood — and places it on Tander's head. "Quick, quick!" Tander turns around, gestures at the hook-up for the breathing cage. "We've got to go, got to tell Annah it's real, that it's here."

Tell the war fleet of the Sacred Realm of Ishmere that Guerdon is defended. Tell them that the first god to trespass here — proud Lion Queen, resplendent Cloud Mother, sullen Kraken — will be struck down, annihilated so utterly that they will know death as mortals do. Tell them of their peril. Tell them to stay away from Guerdon, to keep to their present course.

The spy takes a knife and makes a quick cut, stabbing through the protective mesh over the gill-creature in Tander's pack. The thing barely has enough of a nervous system to feel pain, but it still quivers as the steel slices through its fragile tissues. Then he clips the breathing tube home.

There'll be boats on the way soon. They don't have time to check their suit's seals, don't have time to do anything but clamp on the weighted boots and slither down into the water. Every step away from the god bomb is a blessed relief; the darkness of the water is cool and silent, like the shadows of the temple in Severast.

Tied together, they march into the lightless depths. The spy throws the last few flash ghosts ahead of them, clearing a path in case there are any more of those guardian polyps. He catches glimpses of Tander in the light from the flashes, but then it's dark again, and he can only walk straight ahead, following the taut rope.

The rope slackens.

Goes limp.

He finds Tander, swaying back and forth in the tide. Rooted by his weighted boots, planted in the seabed like some strange anemone. Silenced forever.

The spy drops the last flash ghost and walks away.

Oona appears out of the darkness like a psychopomp, here to carry his soul to some forgotten sea god. The mer-woman frowns when she finds him alone. He holds up the tattered end of the rope. She makes a face to express her sympathy, then dives down and unbuckles his weighted boots. Freed, he floats up into her arms. Her tail beats the water, and they rush upwards.

Behind them, watch patrol cutters spread out, searching for the intruder. Soon, they'll find the bodies. One, dead on the rocks. Another who tried to escape via the seabed, and never noticed that a stray shot had damaged his breathing apparatus. The poor bastard, marching to his death, not knowing he was running out of air. His remains shredded by the flash ghost, ensuring he could never be identified.

Oona speeds him out into the harbour. There's the little boat, Dredger's launch, idling in the water. Oona pushes him up, breaching the surface. Annah and Haberas help him in.

Annah's face is expressionless, unreadable, even when Oona gestures that there's no one else coming, that the spy is the only survivor.

Now is the most dangerous moment of all.

When Annah lifts the helmet off, he whispers to her, urgently. Like the words are fire, a burning torch he's carried out of the dark waters, passed from hand to hand in a relay. Tander and the others died to bring you these words.

"They don't have the god bomb," he lies, "they're bluffing. The city's wide open."

Annah takes a long, long, draw on her cigarette.

She cups the cigarette in her hand, shielding it so the little flare of light doesn't give her position away.

She exhales.

Drops the butt overboard.

"That changes things."

She turns, shoots Haberas neatly in the chest, dead centre. Fires again, into the water, hitting Oona. The mer-woman thrashes and flails in pain, her webbed hands splashing through the moon-silvered water, but then she sinks and vanishes. Annah fires at the water, twice, then sits down at the tiller and starts the engine.

The spy lies there, in the bottom of the boat, as they race south, away from Guerdon, following the coast. Passing the islands, past Hark and Shrike, past the Isle of Statues. Past the Bell Rock.

Exhausted, untroubled, the spy falls asleep next to the cooling corpse.

He's woken by the sound of Haberas' body slipping into the water, weighed down by the spy's leaded belt and weapons.

It's still night, but the eastern sky is brightening. It'll be dawn soon. In the half-light, the spy makes out the shape of coastline to the west. They must be a few miles south of Guerdon. There's a distant smear of light inland that the spy guesses is the Festival field.

Annah lifts the spy's breathing cage to throw it overboard, then pauses. She peers into the tank, holding it up to the dawn light. "You were lucky," she says, "the gill-fish died." She opens the little grille, pulls out the remains of the little alchemical monster. A burn mark on its gelatinous flesh – a flash ghost must have caught it. A spark of arcane energy, arcing from Tander's death to the spy's tank.

"It was hard to breathe," admits the spy.

"Surprised you weren't dead," mutters Annah. "Thank the gods." She squeezes, hard, and the little creature bursts in a shower of goo. She rinses her hand off in the water.

They sail on in silence, the only sound the rumble of the boat's engine. After a while, she turns the tiller, bringing them close to the shore, to land at a sheltered beach in the middle of nowhere. The spy hops into the surf and helps drag the launch onto the sand.

"Just leave it," she tells him. "Ory will take care of it."

She leads him up a narrow path to a little cottage atop the cliffs and knocks on the door. After a few minutes, a large man opens it. He yawns at them, but doesn't betray any surprise as he hustles them both inside.

This is Ory, guesses the spy.

Wiping sleep from his watery-green eyes, Ory manoeuvres his bulk around the cottage like a man carrying a sack of fish. At first glance, the spy thought him old, but Ory's voice is young. His skin glistens unhealthily, and when he brings over a plate of breakfast the spy sees how boneless and long his fingers are.

The fleet's still far away. This saint can't manifest the Kraken yet. But soon.

The spy is told to eat quickly. Ory finds him clean clothes – a fisherman's clothes, ill fitting, and not really suited to Alic or Sanhada Baradhin or any of the spy's other identities, but he can tie and tuck the excess fabric to not stand out overmuch. While he dresses, Annah and Ory talk in low tones. From some hidden coffer they produce three separate sums of cash – X84's payment, recompense for Dredger – it seems the launch is to be buried, to conceal it – and a small amount of travelling expenses, enough to get the spy back to Guerdon.

All paid in Guerdon silver.

Ory tells him it'll be easy. Just walk to the nearest village, and then he can catch a train up the coast. There'll be crowds coming back from the Festival. Easy to blend in. Easy to be forgotten.

Annah goes out to watch the dawn. Once the spy has his gear

packed away – the money and the weapons hidden beneath the absurd clothes – he joins her outside the strange high house. She's staring out to sea, methodically chain-smoking through all her remaining cigarettes.

"I'm not coming back with you. I have my own channels," she says. "Send the word. Then go silent. Maybe get out of the city altogether. We'll contact you through the boy if needed."

"I'll need your blessing to send a message to the gods."

"Aye." She digs into her pocket, finds the little vial of oil and hands it to him. The Lion Queen's face on the stopper is the same face he saw in the tent at Mattaur, half the world away.

He slips the vial into a pocket. "How will it happen? If it does, that is?"

Annah shrugs. "You were at Severast. It'll be like that."

Kraken's seas, rushing into the city like a flood of molten glass. God-spawned monsters, riding the mists of Cloud Mother. Miracles like fire. Ships landing in the streets, disgorging priests and fanatics to tear down the altars of local gods and reconsecrate them to the invaders with sacrifices. War-saints striding into battle, a hundred feet tall. Beautiful and terrible at once, the hosts of heaven making war upon the mortal plane.

"Will She be there?"

"She is on every battlefield. Of course She'll be there. But it'll be Fate Spider first. He'll weave our victory, and then She shall claim it." Annah finishes her last cigarette, and throws it over the cliff.

The rising sun makes it look like she's just set fire to the sky.

CHAPTER 28

The tail end of the king's procession streams past Terevant, the same words on everyone's lips. The king has returned! The whole fair's electrified by the news. Guerdon's suspicion of miracles doesn't apply here – this is their king, blessed by the old gods of the city. The Festival may be ending, but the celebration is only just beginning. They'll sing all the way back to Guerdon.

Terevant caught a glimpse of the king as he passed. Only from a distance – the new king, anointed by the gods, rode in a palanquin alongside the Patros of Guerdon, but still, close enough to recognise him. Close enough to see that distinctive nose, close enough for the king to catch Terevant's eye and give him a private little shrug. As if being chosen by the gods and acclaimed king of Guerdon was just another indignity of fate to be endured by Berrick.

The procession passes on.

Terevant, still stunned, ducks back into the Haithi pavilion. There's a private tent, off to one side, for the ambassador. Olthic and Lys went off there earlier. He brushes past Daerinth and his clerks as they tear down the main pavilion. He finds Olthic sitting on a cot half dressed, buttoning a shirt.

"Where's Lys?"

"Already gone back to the city. To the Palace of the Patros. Or the palace of the king, I suppose. King Berrick the First." He laughs ruefully. "I have to go to some official reception. Give me a hand, would you?"

Olthic's jacket is heavy with medals as Terevant lifts it from its stand. "What happens now?" asks Terevant, cautiously. The defeat at parliament was losing a battle — now, it seems, he's lost the war.

Olthic pulls on the jacket and sits back down, the cot creaking beneath him. "Lys has won. The new king — he's the Bureau's man. The Keepers will win the election, and they'll give us the alliance Haith needs. What I couldn't win by . . . " he shakes his head, as if amazed at his own folly, "by diplomacy, the Bureau wins by stealth." He shakes his head again. "I owe you an apology, I think. She played us both."

"Keeping the sword from you?"

"Indeed." Olthic lifts the blade, testing its perfect balance. "Once it fell into her grasp, she held onto it long enough for her to work her scheme. If I have to lose, then at least it's to her." He shrugs. "Daerinth was less philosophical."

"He suggested I take the sword," says Terevant, "instead of bringing it to you. It was . . . bizarre."

"Take the sword? Keep me in Guerdon?" Olthic laughs. "That's desperate, even for him," echoes Olthic. "I wonder if he thinks the new ambassador will finally get rid of him. Oh, I'm quitting," he says in response to Terevant's confused look. Olthic grins. "I'm going to go back home, and be the Erevesic. Lead our House army, like I should have done months ago. There is a war on, you know."

Olthic springs up, and it's like he's left some huge weight behind him. He claps Terevant on the shoulder. "Done with politicking, done with diplomacy, done with Daerinth whispering in my ear, telling me what to say and which arse to lick. Done with this fucking city of Guerdon, and to hell with it." He takes a deep breath. "All right. One last reception — have to stay on the good side of the alchemists' guild. Each glass of sherry's worth a thousand rounds of ammunition, or somesuch. Go and find a tavern, and I'll join you when I'm done."

The Erevesic walks out, humming.

Terevant stares in disbelief for a moment. When the Bureau rejected him, when his own future fell apart, he ran off and hid in the colonies for a year. When his brother has the Crown – the *Crown!* – snatched away from him, Olthic laughs about it.

Maybe Olthic's right. To hell with Guerdon. He'll drink to that.

Outside, the fair is ending. Hawkers and merchants whisk away their merchandise; dray-carts and wagons suddenly fill the laneways that earlier were crowded with people, here to haul the remaining goods and the collapsed stalls back to the city, to wait in some warehouse until next year. The clerks from the Haithi embassy lug heavy boxes back to waiting wagons; they watch Terevant keenly as he passes, no doubt jealous that he's off to relax while they've still got back-breaking work to do. Ahead, the grand exhibition hall of the alchemists has already been partially stripped down to its steel framework, like the corpse of some titan, its flesh partially melted to reveal the skeleton beneath. The disassembling fairground has an air of apocalypse about it: it's all frantic looting amid the ruins, or the melancholy emptiness of abandoned delights.

Terevant kicks himself. It's just the last evening of a country fair, not a harbinger of doom. Not everything needs to be drenched in poetic significance. His instructors at the military academy used to despair of him. They'd show him a painting of a landscape, and he'd notice the hillside pines outlined against the sky, their branches like serried ranks of spearmen. He'd see the cottage in the foreground, a little island of light and laughter in a dark landscape. He'd notice the name of the artist, and vaguely recall which school she belonged to.

He would, however, completely miss what they wanted him to see – the strategically important bridge, the ridge nearby where a competent commander would put his alchemical cannons and rockets, the thicket where one should station one's living troops, the bottleneck there where the Vigilant should stand, unyielding and undying. He can leave all that to Olthic again. Terevant wonders idly about his own future. There are still unanswered questions here in Guerdon, about Vanth's death, and the god bombs, but right now they take second place to another, more pressing question.

Somewhere, amid the wasteland of abandoned delights, is there still an open tavern?

He finds the beer tent he'd visited earlier, but it's closed. He walks around the back of the place, wondering if there's a way in, if there are still a few staff finishing the last of the kegs. Nothing.

In the distance he hears music, and follows that instead. There's a bonfire blazing up ahead, a circle of men and women around it. Mercenaries, he guesses; some are armoured, some are scarred, all of them drinking with determination, trying to cram as much life as they can into this summer's evening.

A woman approaches him, a pair of drinks in hand. She's partly dressed in elaborate, old-fashioned armour: bracers and greaves and a heavy steel collar. There's no way she'd wear anything like that outfit into battle. She must be a mercenary recruiter, in full regalia to impress the customers.

"If the Crown of Haith's looking to hire us, you're too late, friend," she says, passing him a drink anyway.

"No, I'm just looking for some company."

"You have found *the* company." She gestures with her goblet, "The Company of Eight."

There are at least two dozen warriors behind her. Some of them cheer and echo her toast to the Company of Eight.

"Join us," she says. "We've just signed on with Lyrix, so we're celebrating."

He does as she suggests, finding a space in the circle. The Company of Eight, he learns, actually did have eight people once upon a time. Five are dead, one's immensely rich and living up in Serran; the fate of the other two is obscure, as that part of the story is told to Terevant by an old mumbling mercenary who starts snoring in the middle of the tale. They're off to Lyrix, hired to bolster the defence of the island. One fellow desperately tries to persuade Terevant to buy a dragon-scale breastplate from him – he picked up the piece at the fair, and only later realised that going to Lyrix wearing the hide of a dead dragon might be deemed impolite.

The mercenary recruiter sits down next to Terevant. She's

exchanged her armour for a shirt and a long skirt that glitters in the firelight. She crosses her legs, and the skirt rides up, revealing a muscular calf. She leans in a little closer than she needs to, introduces herself as Naola.

It turns out she's the new captain of the Company, the previous captain having died of plague down in Mattaur. She came home to Guerdon – the daughter of factory workers – to learn that her parents and her younger brother had been killed during the Crisis. She raises a drink to them, laughing. They worried that she'd perish on some distant battlefield, but the Godswar found them in the safest city in the world. So much for certainty.

Terevant matches her with a toast to his own father, who would probably have preferred if he *had* perished at least once on a distant battlefield.

After a few toasts, someone mentions Paravos, Terevant unwisely admits he was a poet there and suddenly he's reciting for the company. One of them produces a set of pipes, and manages to compose a melody that fits with the rhythm of the words. He recites one about a warrior woman that he wrote about Lyssada, but Naola smiles as if he composed it for her on the spot.

As the fire dies down and the stars spread across the sky, it grows chill. She pulls him close and whispers that the Company's not leaving for Lyrix for another few days, another few nights. The warmth of her banishes any worries about the future. He kisses her neck; across the fire, one of the mercenaries hollers and jeers.

A hand taps him on the shoulder. It's Lemuel, of all people, but his customary mask of languid disinterest is gone, replaced by fury. "It's urgent. Come with me."

Reluctantly, Terevant disentangles himself from Naola. "I'll be back."

Naola stretches. "Don't be too long."

Lemuel hustles him away from the company, drags him into the maze of half-collapsed tents. He scans the field behind him, looking over his shoulder as if he expects trouble. "What's wrong?" asks Terevant.

"Nothing. Have to get you out of here," Lemuel insists.

"What is it?"

"You were seen meeting—" Lemuel stops talking for a moment as they pass a knot of labourers. Sweaty browed, tools in hand. "Seen meeting with Berrick Ultgard, here at the fair."

"So?"

"You were *seen*," repeats Lemuel. "We install our own fucking king, and you nearly blow it all by going drinking with him in full uniform."

"I didn't know who Berrick was at the time."

"What difference does that make?"

"I'm going back to Naola," declares Terevant suddenly. He'll leave the city with Olthic – hell, maybe he'll leave it with Naola – but, either way, he doesn't have to listen to Lemuel any more. He turns around. Strides back towards the fire. He can hear the singing of the mercenaries ahead; behind, Lemuel mutters some obscenity.

He quickens his pace, pushing through the last of the crowds.

Something strikes him from behind, and everything falls away and goes dark.

Hands bear him up. Strong arms carry him, bundle him in. The creak of wagon wheels; the hiss of a raptequine.

His throat is burning. Has he been drinking? Dreaming? Olthic's voice, indistinct, like it's coming from deep underwater. The embassy's built on quicksand. There are tunnels under the city, he remembers, and the world's falling into them.

He dreams, briefly, of the courtyard in the embassy.

A rotting skeleton stands there, not one of the armoured, polished-bone Vigilant. Its skull-face gleaming in the pale light.

Then oblivion swallows him like a wave.

CHAPTER 29

The IndLib special train back to Guerdon is overcrowded, with every seat full and the corridors packed, but when Kelkin snarls the carriage still clears. Only his inner circle remain. Eladora takes the vacated seat nearest the door, unsure if she should stay – she wants to go back and check on Emlin. She feels guilty at dragging an innocent boy into all this. Her assistant Rhiado will take good care of him, Eladora tells herself. The carriage is filled with familiar faces: Ramegos, worried and clacking her chain of god-tokens like she's praying. Absalom Spyke, red-faced, angry. Ogilvy, the old party functionary, looks shaken.

Kelkin passes around a shimmering Keeper-scribed scroll, and a few hastily typed copies. The letter is lengthy, but stripped of pomp and formality the actual message is quite short.

"'The Keepers recognise and acclaim the heir to the throne of Guerdon, and welcome him to the Palace of the Patros, until the king comes into his own,'" mutters one of the party elite. "'The Patros calls upon parliament to restore the throne to its appropriate station as swiftly as can be accomplished . . .' Effro, what the hell is this?"

Kelkin starts to answer, then coughs, turning purple. To cover, Ogilvy turns to Eladora. "Miss, er, ah, Miss Duttin. This goes back three or four hundred years, so a little context, please."

Everyone in the carriage turns to look back at Eladora. Heads craning around seats, bodies hidden, giving the disconcerting impression that some enemy has hunted down the entire party and mounted their heads like trophies. So many eyes on her make her nervous. She stands unsteadily – both from the motion of the train, and her earlier experiences at the Festival – and clears her throat. But this topic, at least, holds no uncertainty for her.

"For much of our history, Guerdon was ruled by a king, who was advised by lords and priests – and parliament, eventually. The first dynasties date back to Varinth, but the kingship passed from one family to another. There were pirate kings, conquerors, rival branches ... the full history is quite complex, but the kingship came to an end when the B-B-Black Iron Gods took control of the city. They held the royal family hostage for weeks, until the Keepers smuggled the king and his family out of the city."

Kelkin beckons her up and points her to one of the seats near him. She advances down the carriage, steadying herself on the leather loops hanging from the ceiling as the train sways. "The last king took a ship and sailed away, hoping to find allies to retake the city. We know he circled around the Firesea, visited the Caliphates, the exiles at Lyrix, Severast – all to no avail. History does not record the eventual fate of the king of Guerdon, though it's likely his ship foundered in a storm off Jashan."

Kelkin's recovered from his coughing fit. "Not quite." He gestures impatiently for Eladora to sit. She sinks down into the seat next to Ramegos. "The last king ended up in Haith. I know that because a few years after the Keepers defeated the Black Iron Gods and took over, the Crown of Haith asked if they wanted the king back. The Keepers decided that they didn't want to share power again, and told the Crown to keep the king." Eladora desperately wants to know more about *that* hitherto secret episode in Guerdon's history, that balance of power between kings and priests, but now's not the time. Kelkin coughs again, and continues. "It seems they kept the king for another three hundred years. I'm guessing this is some descendant of the line, not the actual fucking original. But ... necromancers, so who knows?"

"Even if he's the original," argues Ogilvy, "he has no claim to rule the city. The church can recognise him as the king, but parliament runs the city. We run the city."

"Aye, and the church clearly isn't demanding he be reinstated.

'Appropriate station' could mean anything, a figurehead or some such. The new Patros has only just settled his arse on the holy seat, he's not going to move aside to let some bumpkin from Haith move in." Kelkin snorts. "A show of hands – does anyone think that this is a genuine miracle, that it's pure coincidence that the secret heir to the throne shows up in the middle of the election?"

A few hesitant hands, quickly withdrawn.

"Who thinks this is a setup?"

The whole carriage, except Ramegos. The sorceress hasn't moved. Kelkin looks satisfied for a moment, then frowns. "Ramegos?"

"The two aren't exclusive propositions. The gods shape fate. What looks like coincidence can be divine intervention."

Kelkin groans. "All right," he continues, ignoring the theological detour. "This fellow is not the king. Do not fucking call him king. He's got no title unless parliament gives him one, and we're all here to ensure that doesn't happen. Call him citizen . . . do we even know what his name is?"

"Berrick Ultgard!" shouts someone from the back of the carriage. Spyke nods and adds, "Sure I saw the bastard drinking with a Haithi before the ceremony."

"The Keepers can rally their faithful around this new champion, and draw off those who might have switched to us as a last resort. Makes winning the New City more important than ever. Don't call him a king, call him a tyro. Ask folk if they want a steady hand on the tiller, or some farmer who'll be a puppet of Haith and the Keepers." Kelkin raps his cane on the wooden frame of a seat. "You've got a day to prepare, while the mob rolls home from the Festival. Day after tomorrow, I want to see every one of you out there with a strategy and an army of ward-beaters."

He circulates through the carriage, gathering small groups for various tasks. Eladora sits, fretting about what task he'll assign to her. She wants to be useful, to wash away this sickening, irrational feeling of shame that's been hanging over her since her encounter with her mother, or maybe since her brief vision of the gods, when they judged her and found her somehow wanting.

Out of the corner of her eye, she catches Ramegos studying her. The sorceress mutters under her breath, runs that chain of god-talismans through her fingers. Before Eladora can ask what she is doing, Kelkin sits down heavily in the seat opposite them, followed by Ogilvy.

"Gods below," curses Kelkin as his joints creak. His voice is hoarse, his left hand shaking. He pokes some young assistant with his cane. "Get me a drink." He closes his eyes.

Ogilvy lowers his voice. "You know that if you took Mhari Voller's offer, you'd win in a landslide. It might be worth it. Take the Keeper's support, win, and then fight them in parliament instead of the streets?"

"I'm not going back," insists Kelkin. "Not after all this."

"All right," says Ramegos. "Let's talk about something else. Kings and queens, for example."

"Didn't you hear me? Don't call the wretch a king." Kelkin's eyes snap open. He's angry.

Ramegos is unmoved. "It doesn't matter what I call him. It's what he's perceived as – and not by us. By the gods." She lays half a dozen tokens down on her lap. The gods of the Keepers: Saint Storm, Mother of Flowers, Holy Beggar, all the rest. The symbol of the Mother of Flowers seems bigger, more weighty. Eladora inhales, catches the distant scent of wildflowers. "How best to put this?" wonders Ramegos. "Effro, the gods follow paths laid down over many mortal lifetimes. The energy of worship, the portion of the soul given over to the gods, flows down those paths, lets them shape magic, make miracles. Now, if you reinforce those patterns, it makes it easier for that power to flow. Like clearing debris from a canal."

Kelkin sits forward, suddenly awake again. "What will having a king in Guerdon do?"

"The Kept Gods were worshipped under the aegis of a king for a long time. It's familiar to them, fits with their patterns. They'll become stronger. The more our world conforms to what their patterns think it should, the easier it is for them to reach down and intervene. That's why the Keepers refused to accept the return of the king when it was first offered – they were trying to keep their gods reined in. They starved them of residuum from corpses, changed the litanies – refusing the king was part of it."

"The Safidists are in ascendance," says Kelkin. Eladora can almost hear the clack of cogs and abacus beads in Kelkin's head as he strips influence from one branch of the church and reallocates it to the fringes. Sinter falls, Silva Duttin rises. Mhari Voller, always drawn to power, is a weathervane, a bead of mercury that flows downhill. He coughs, hawks up a glob of mucus that he spits into a handkerchief. Eladora has the impression that his decision came with the spittle, like the ringing of a cash register when a transaction's completed.

"We hold firm. Show stability. Show fucking backbone," declares Kelkin. "I'll hold the old city." He jabs a finger at Eladora. "Make sure we win the New."

The train approaches Guerdon, coming from the south-west, and the city accretes around the tracks. Buildings heave out of the night, and the sky ahead turns from inky black to a soiled yellow-grey, the city's lights reflected off the smog clouds that hang above it. The city hides from the night sky, raises ugly industrial towers in defiance of it, as if that smog is a shield, a blanket drawn over the heads of the multitude. They pass church spires that remind her of vertical bridges, of narrow stairs, that strain to pierce the clouds and invite the gods to climb down from heaven. She can feel the presence of unwelcome forces all around her.

Once, Eladora might have welcomed this. When her mother first embraced Safidism, first sought sainthood and tried to drag her daughter along, too, Eladora would have given anything to sense the presence of the gods, probing at her soul, brushing against her mind with revelations and holy inspiration. As she grew and her relationship with her mother soured, the thought of the gods embracing her felt like a violation, a psychic intrusion. Going to university, exchanging the blind, groping faith of the Safidists for the cool reason and formality of study was a relief. Guerdon was a relief. The chatter of the streets, the ceaseless noise of the factories, the churning harbour left no unattended quiet where the gods might sneak in.

This is how Carillon must have felt, she reflects. Cari fled Wheldacre, fled her mother's house, because she felt the presence of unseen gods more strongly than anyone else.

Thinking of Carillon reminds her of a loose thread. She gently rouses Ramegos, who's snoozing in her seat.

"Whuh?"

Eladora hesitates. She promised Carillon she'd stay quiet, but she has to know. "You said I shouldn't ask . . . but the Haithi diplomat who got murdered. Did you ever find out what happened to him?"

Still half asleep, Ramegos mutters, "A . . . witness came forward." She wipes sleep from her eyes, then peers at Eladora like she's a specimen. "But I can't talk about it," she says. "Why do you ask?"

Eladora stammers. "A-a Haithi official dies just before all this happens. It seems s-significant."

There's a long pause. "Practise your spells if you have nothing else to occupy your mind." Ramegos falls back asleep.

Or pretends to do so. Eladora can sense the sorceress watching her, eyes glittering beneath heavy lids. Unseen forces swirl around them as the train rushes into the twilight.

CHAPTER 30

It's well after midnight by the time they disembark. Eladora searches the train until she finds a sleepy Emlin, sitting with Rhiado and a couple of clerks. Emlin and Eladora walk through the dim labyrinth of the station, descending to the lower levels to Guerdon's subways.

The carriage is crowded at first, buzzing with conversation about the appearance of the king out of legend, but most of the passengers empty out at Venture Square. A passing watchman peers at them as they wait for the train to depart, his expression questioning. The lower Wash is dangerous at night; Eladora mentally recites her sorcerous invocation, just in case they do get into trouble.

Dr Ramegos was right; the ritual is calming.

The train jerks, drags itself forward and rattles into the darkness. They're alone in the carriage now.

"Emlin? I wanted to apologise for what happened at the Festival. That woman was my mother. She was looking for me, not you. She's . . . "

"I don't want to talk about it," he says. The poor boy's scared of Eladora, too. He presses himself back against his seat like he's pinned there. Eyes wide with fear, and Eladora remembers how for a moment she glimpsed eight points of light, eight eyes reflecting the fire of her mother's divine wrath. *There's a stench about you. Let me see.*

It would be the simplest thing to report him as an illegal saint. She could even do it through unofficial channels, have Ramegos look into it. Spare Alic the scandal. Kelkin would probably insist that Alic step down quietly; she can already imagine how he'd do it. Absalom Spyke looming on Alic's doorstep, his deep voice explaining how it's for the good of the party.

Hypocrite! part of her shouts. Eladora's own brush with sainthood was covered up, along with the sins of everyone else involved in the Crisis. The Keepers, the alchemists, the Thay family, Kelkin – everyone's soiled by it all.

"I'll bring you straight home," she offers.

"Don't tell my father!" says the boy, suddenly.

There are guards everywhere when they arrive at the train station in the Wash. Emlin flinches as they pass by. Eladora looks at the soldiers curiously – they're naval troops, not the usual city watch. There was some sort of incident at the harbour last night, she's told. A break-in; no damage done, and the thieves killed, but some may have escaped. They're waved by without question.

With so many armed guards around, the streets of the Wash are empty of civilians, but every window is watchful – except at Jaleh's house. There, every window is shuttered and the whole house is asleep. Eladora has to hammer on the door for several minutes before it's opened.

The old priestess, Jaleh, beckons them inside with her clawed hand. "Your father's still out," she tells Emlin. "Go to bed. Ask the Holy Beggar to light his lamp for you ten times before you sleep."

Emlin rushes upstairs without a backward glance.

"Where's Alic?" asks Eladora.

"Out," snaps Jaleh.

"When will he return?"

"I don't know. Hasn't been here since last night." She peers at Eladora. "You've been here before," says Jaleh. "With Silkpurse. From parliament. What do you want at this hour?"

Eladora waits until she hears a door close somewhere off in the depths of the house. "Actually, I'd like to ask a few questions, about Emlin and your house."

Jaleh grunts, gestures for Eladora to sit. "Already talked to the watch."

"About Emlin?"

"About my house, and about those who come to me for gentling."

"Tell me how it works," asks Eladora.

"Seems to me you'd already know all about it," mutters Jaleh. She pulls the sleeve of her robe down over her scaly arm, tucks her clawed hand away. "Have to be close to a god to receive their blessing, in whatever form it takes. Close in body or spirit, or close to a place of power. Shrines and temple and holy places – dangerous. Some get so close the god acts through 'em. Takes hold of 'em and won't let go. Like getting caught in a thorn bush."

Even though it's a warm night, Jaleh piles some logs in the grate, pokes the dying fire until it burns again. "Here, I help them who want to get free. Best not to suddenly tear free by denying the god who holds you – it rips the soul open. Better to slowly work the thorns out, one by one. Dull prayers help, smoothes the mind. Some gods hold you through your actions, others through your feelings."

"It's like a reverse of Safidism," says Eladora, "praying to one god to ensure another doesn't notice you, so your soul isn't in alignment. Does it always work? Can you always free someone from sainthood?"

Jaleh shrugs. "None of us are wholly free. There's always a chance, even here, that some god will reach down and claim any of us. But if someone wants to be gentled, wants their burdens lifted, I can help."

"Are you helping Emlin?"

"I help everyone who takes shelter under my roof."

"Is everyone here a former saint?"

Jaleh laughs. "Not since your lot opened Hark Island and started arresting people. No, most of them are just lost souls from the Godswar. A lot of god-touched, changed in body. They don't let true saints through any more. Just them who are a little blessed. One thorn in the soul." She chuckles and pokes the fire again, making it blaze up.

"Can you tell when someone's a saint?"

Jaleh's eyes glitter in the fire. "Sometimes I get a feeling. A sense of it."

"What happened to your arm?"

"What gives you the right to come here asking so many questions?"

Eladora pauses, then speaks quietly. "You know, parliament intends to employ the ghouls to assist the city watch, to sniff out saints and dangers to the city. Silkpurse speaks highly of you, but she's a generous soul. Others might be more intrusive. Or so Lord Rat suggested, when I last spoke to him."

"And will the ghouls be sniffing around you, too? I got a sense of it when you were here before – you were sainted, weren't you? You tried to tear free, and it broke you. Who was it? You sound like you've never been out of Guerdon. Did the Kept Gods stir and try to claim you? The holy fire of Safid? Or something else?"

"My mother," admits Eladora, "is a Keeper saint. She, ah, implied that Emlin might also be gifted. I want to know if you've seen any signs of spiritual gifts in him."

"And what then? Will you call the watch? Whistle up them ghouls? Send him to Hark?"

"Is that warranted?"

Jaleh reaches into the fire, takes out a hot coal, holding it on the bare scales of her warped hand. "I lived in Lyrix, a long time ago. I worked for the Ghierdana, the old dragon families. I stained my soul with all sorts of sins. Culsan, god of murderers, recognised himself in me, claimed me for his own, but I didn't know that for a long long time. Maybe if I'd seen that, I'd have come home before . . ." She clenches the coal, crushing it to black dust. "Some gods work in secret, child. And just because someone's a saint don't mean they owe anything to the god who claimed 'em."

She looks up at Eladora. "The gods cursed me after I strangled a priest of Culsan. That's what warped my arm. Divine punishment." She brushes the dust back into the fire, making it flare up. "I didn't even know I had been a saint of murderers until Culsan tore his blessings away and cursed me instead." A shower of sparks.

Is she hinting that Emlin is unaware of his sainthood? Or that she thinks the boy isn't a threat, that whatever vestiges of power he retains are too weak to be dangerous?

"I'll leave a note for Alic. Please see that he gets it." Eladora fishes in her bag for pen and paper. "Also, if you would ensure that Emlin is diligent in his gentling, I would consider it a personal favour."

Part of Eladora is uncomfortable at any sort of prayers to the Kept Gods, now that they're so much more active. What's needed is some secular gentling process, not beholden to any deity. Something like the sorcerous exercises that Ramegos insists she—

Oh. Eladora nearly breaks the pen.

Ramegos was part of the inquiry into the Crisis. Knows everything about Eladora's experiences. Took an *interest* in Eladora, tutored her in sorcery. *Like Professor Ongent did.* What gods does Ramegos suspect still have a claim on Eladora's soul? The Black Iron Gods are dead, they told her. Were they lying?

Jaleh, outlined against the fire, watches her. A vision of the future of the city, maybe, a scarred survivor that has made her own accommodation to the unseen powers. Unable to hide from them fully, unable to deny them, but able to balance one against the other. Blessed and cursed, faithful and faithless all at once. Eladora finds herself suddenly envious of the older woman. Jaleh has found her place here in this house. Eladora thought her place was in the university, amid the books. Where history is set and the rules of the world don't change according to the mad desires of unknown gods. Now she's not so sure.

The door rattles, breaking the moment. Jaleh undoes the heavy locks, opens it awkwardly with her human hand, keeping the clawed dragon-hand raised like a knife until she's sure it's safe.

It is safe. It's Alic. He enters, grinning, dressed in an absurd outfit of overlarge clothes.

"Miss Duttin," Alic says, and bows. "Is all well?" he asks. "Is Emlin all right?"

"He's upstairs. What in the world are you wearing?"

He looks down at his oversized clothes. "Oh, I was out with friends, and fell in a canal. Had to borrow these. What's this I hear about a king?"

"Apparently, the heir to the throne of Guerdon has returned."

"Really?"

The spy listens as Eladora hastily describes the events of the Festival. He dismisses the miraculous appearance of some long-lost king as irrelevant. The people of Guerdon are unsophisticated when it comes to divine intervention – they live in a land of Kept Gods and the dregs of the Godswar. A magic crown appearing to some distant heir? That's mere sleight-of-hand compared to the real wonders the gods can perform. If the kings of old clawed their way out of the tombs, or if every member of parliament suddenly fused together into a fleshy giant that bestrode the city, carrying Castle Hill as a shield and waving the three cathedrals as a trident, then the spy might be impressed. No, the return of the king isn't worrisome. It doesn't matter who's in charge when the Ishmeric fleet arrives.

Tomorrow. Tomorrow night Emlin will send the message.

Eladora continues. "They've sent Absalom Spyke to investigate this new king. I'll be taking over the New City campaign until polling day."

"You'd better take this, then." A bag of coin, so heavy that Eladora has to use two hands to hold it. "Campaign donations. From the merchants of the harbour in general, and Dredger in particular." He considers the matter. "I'll walk up to Lambs Square and fetch you a carriage. Better not to walk through the Wash carrying that."

"You did."

He grins again. "Sometimes the gods smile on fools."

The silence of the train station in Grena is the silence of a tomb.

A century ago, when the station was built, it was busy as a feast-day market. Primitive trains roared down the tracks, carrying the bounty of the goddess – a dozen harvests a year – north and south. South to Guerdon, as that city swelled with traders and sailors. North to Haith, eternal icon of stability and order. Some trains would rattle through the station on the express line, not stopping at Grena, going straight from one city to another.

Then came the war.

Then came the madness of the goddess.

Then the bomb.

Then silence.

Now, that silence is broken by a military train from the north. It races through the station, moving at full speed, its aetheric lights flooding the platforms with a false dawn. Row after row of skulls can be briefly glimpsed through the windows, mort-carriages full of dead men. There are living soldiers, too, next to the new weapon-carriages. The train's equipped with Guerdon-forged artillery. For now, these massive guns slumber under tarpaulins. The train doesn't stop. It passes through, and the silence of the tomb returns.

Then another train.

Then another.

Then another.

Then silence.

CHAPTER 31

Terevant wakes to find Yoras shaking him. Opens his eyes to look into the eye sockets of a skull.

The ambassador is dead.

It takes him a moment to connect the title to the man who holds it. A moment in which he's walking without noticing the ground has fallen away.

The ambassador is dead. Olthic's the ambassador.

Terevant's in the embassy. Back in Guerdon, somehow. A vague memory, last night, of being bundled into a coach. Rattling down country roads at speed. His stomach's awash with acid. His legs are shaking, and he has to lean on Yoras for support. His head feels like an overripe fruit, and every movement brings pain.

Come down, quick.

Terevant staggers down the stairs, grabbing his sword by instinct, buckling it on as he runs. He's still in his clothes from last night. Yoras follows close behind him. From ahead, shouts, running feet. The stillness of the early morning broken. Two Vigilant guards stand outside the door of Olthic's study. More inside, living and undead.

And one dead.

In a heartbeat, Terevant sees it all.

His brother's body lies on the floor by the fireplace. Half dressed – parts of the uniform he wore at the Festival on the floor, but he's wearing his old swordbelt, his spit-polished marching boots.

He's been stabbed. The blade was driven through his stomach, emerging from his back, then torn free. There are other wounds, too, smaller cuts. Blood, great red floods of it, over the ground, soaking into carpets and running in little regular rivers along gaps in the tiles. Furniture hurled about, as if caught up in a hurricane. The window's been smashed in. There's glass everywhere.

A look of confusion on Olthic's face that mirrors the one on Terevant's own.

There's no sign of the Erevesic sword.

Terevant stumbles towards the body, but, before he can cross the threshold into the study, Daerinth bars his way.

"Where is the sword? What did you do?"

Confused memories. Did he talk to Olthic last night? The last thing he recalls clearly is sitting with the mercenary woman, Naola, by the fireside. A dream of talking to Olthic. Jumbled memories of fleeing with Lemuel. A blow from behind.

Daerinth doesn't hesitate. He snaps orders at the Vigilants. "Detain the lieutenant!"

Terevant backs away as the skeletal troops advance. Bony hands reach for him. "Only you could have done this!" croaks Daerinth. "Surrender, Erevesic, and face the judgement of the Crown."

Instinct takes over. He draws his own sword, and the Vigilants draw theirs. The dead are faster than he is, stronger, but they're not trying to kill him and he doesn't need to worry about killing them. His blows hammer at them, wildly. Bones splinter as he hews at the Vigilant troops. Everything's a red haze. Olthic's dead, and the world's broken, and all he can do is fight. Blindly, through the tears. There's more than two Vigilants now, it's four or five, six, the whole garrison turning out, living and dead. The living hang back, confused – do they follow the orders of the First Secretary to arrest their commander?

The dead don't hesitate. Daerinth shouts an order, and the Vigilant redouble their attacks. His sword's ripped from his hand; another slash opens up his forearm, spraying blood across the marble wall. They're trying to kill him now. It's not murder if he can self-resurrect, turn Vigilant.

A sword thrusts at him, aimed at his heart. One of the Vigilant deliberately falls in the path of the blade, blocking its compatriots. It's Yoras.

Run, sir, he whispers.

Terevant runs. Shouting behind him, half the embassy in hot pursuit. He races up the stairs, vaults out of a window onto a low roof. Slipping down the tiles towards the courtyard. He catches himself on a gutter – his bloodied arm explodes with pain as it takes his weight and he nearly blacks out, but he stumbles across the yard to the gate. The dead are at his heels, but he's over the threshold just ahead of them, crossing the line from Haithi territory to Guerdon.

Eight Vigilant skeletons stop dead on the threshold, unwilling to pursue. Their hesitation won't last – either they'll fetch masks and gloves so they can move among the living, or Daerinth will send them out anyway. Or the living troops of the embassy will give chase. Terevant doesn't stop, keeps running.

Falling into the city.

In the morning, the spy's woken by a scratching at his window. He crosses the small room he shares with Emlin, stepping around his bed. Emlin's hidden somewhere under a pile of blankets despite the summer heat. A garland of flowers lies discarded on the floor. The spy kicks it away under the bed; Emlin has one more miracle to perform tonight, then Jaleh can gentle the boy all she likes.

Outside, Silkpurse perches on the windowsill, three storeys off the ground. She's got the sure hooves of a mountain goat. "Don't have time to knock downstairs, dear," she explains as she hands him a bundle. "Lord Rat's called us down, so I must be off."

"'Us', meaning?"

"All the ghouls of the city. Haven't had a gathering like that in a few months, not since we cleared out the Crawling Ones." She sucks at her sharp teeth, as if remembering a particular satisfying meal. "That's from Miss Duttin. Says it's urgent. Well, the food's from me. I was going to the market anyway, before going below." She pats a satchel at her side that bulges with fresh-baked bread and cold meats. Alic looks confused; behind the mask, the spy is knowingly amused. She's going into the deep places of the city, the old kingdoms of the ghouls, so she carries surface food to eat instead of corpse-meat. Her own version of gentling, a way to fend off the unwanted transformation into the next stage of ghoul-dom. Silkpurse's bread and Emlin's garland are both symbols that align them with forces other than the ones that lay claim to them.

The ghoul slips away. He opens the bundle, removes the matching loaf and paper-wrapped meats she left for him. The rest of the bundle is papers from Eladora. A letter, repeating what she told him last night, that she's now in charge of the campaign in the New City. A bag of coin (a third of what he gave her, he notes), a list of engagements, a list of ward-beaters and other party officials. A letter of writ, authorising him to act in her name – and her name means Kelkin's name. Plenty of work for Alic to do.

And why not? He's almost Alic entire, now. The spy's job is nearly done.

Emlin's awake. Watches him from the shadows of the blanket.

Alic holds out a hunk of bread. "Let's eat this here before going down to the common room for breakfast."

"Not hungry." Something's wrong, Alic can tell. The boy won't meet his eyes.

"You'll need your strength." He lowers his voice. "Aunt Annah wants you to *work* tonight."

Emlin draws back into the nest of blankets, shaking his head. "I can't."

The spy sits down on the bed, gently excavates the nest so he can see Emlin's face. "What happened?"

"There was ... there was another saint. Miss Duttin's mother, I think. She knew what I was."

"What happened?"

Silence.

"Emlin, what happened?"

The boy sits up in bed, his face streaked with tears. "She burned me, she made me ... she said I had to ab-ab—"

"Abjure," says the spy, bitterly. The word is ash in his mouth. The Keeper bitch has burned Emlin, spiritually. Forced him to deny the Fate Spider, to blaspheme. And the boy's sainthood was already tenuous. He's useless now! Broken!

"I can't hear the whispering any more."

"She hurt you?" Alic asks, suddenly furious. He grabs Emlin by the shoulders, turns him this way and that, looking for wounds.

"She healed me, too," says Emlin, his voice thick with shame. He was even denied martyrdom.

"A mad saint," whispers Alic. "She'd have killed you. It wasn't your fault. There's nothing you could have done to stop her. And I'm glad she healed you. It's better—"

And then a cold chill crawls through Alic. The spy speaks through his mouth, whispering into the boy's ear. "I know how to fix this. We'll go tonight."

The spy spends the day waiting. *Patience*, he screams. *Patience*, as he wants to gnaw his legs off.

Alic has plenty of work to do. Alic is everywhere in the Wash and the New City, tirelessly campaigning. Rallying the dispirited voters, laughing at the idea that Guerdon should have a king again. Reminding them that Kelkin saw them through the Crisis and has kept the city safe. It's easier to convince the inhabitants of the New City to dismiss news of this new king – those who fled the Godswar know better than to trust divine intervention, not in a city that's supposed to be blessedly godless. In the Wash, though, reverence for the lost king runs deep. It's in the shape of the streets, in the names of the old families. Shot through the city like sinews through meat.

He keeps Emlin close. Keeps the boy from dwelling on the events of the Festival. They talk about what they'll do after the election.

The summer day stretches endlessly. Alic fills the hours, but the spy watches the horizon. He wishes he could poison the sun, or drag it from the sky. Anything to hasten twilight.

When Emlin tires, he sends the boy home. Alic stays working. He eats in the IndLib hall. Laughing and joking with friends and allies. Dredger's money sliding down their throats, filling their bellies. It takes him half an hour to leave when he's finished his meal. Everyone wants one last word with him, to shake his hand and slap him on the back. Emlin waits for him back at Jaleh's.

The boy has abjured the Fate Spider. Denied the god. Broken their connection.

Blasphemed.

There are ways to re-establish the bond, though. Things best done under the cover of night. Atonement is not easy, nor will it be cheap.

Alic lingers as long as he can, delaying his return to the House of Jaleh.

Delaying the inevitable.

Guerdon stirs around Terevant. The city rising with the dawn. Ships leaving the harbour with the morning tide. Factories whistling the day shift. Markets and stalls unfolding around him like flowers. A fresh crop of election posters like dew on the walls.

He criss-crosses the city, train to street to alleyway to rooftop and back again. Moving at random. He wants to go to Lys, to talk to her, but he can't. Olthic said she was at the Palace of the Patros, but he can't show up at the gates and ask for her. *Excuse me, I'd like to talk to my sister-in-law. You can't miss her, she just manoeuvred her pawn onto your throne to seal her own coronation. Can she come out and play?*

And where is the sword, anyway? Still in the embassy? Only a member of the House Erevesic could carry it without harm – a blood member, so that excludes Lys. Terevant's the last of the line. An unknown cousin? Some bastard child of Olthic's? Of his? Or – a Vigilant could carry the blade. Maybe a human with sufficient magical protections, a saint or sorcerer, but only for a short time, before the blade's magic unknotted any spells of containment. But all the Vigilants in Guerdon are back there in the embassy, and how could a saint or sorcerer powerful enough get in without being detected? Absently, he walks down a winding staircase to another train station. The platform is crowded with workers heading to the alchemists' factories. He doesn't get on the train – he walks the length of the platform and leaves by another stairwell. Hide and seek.

He's not sure if he's hiding from Daerinth or Lys or himself. The looming fact of Olthic's death stalks him, like a giant crashing through the streets. As long as he keeps moving, he can stay ahead of that giant, hide behind buildings and towers. He knows if it catches him, it'll break him, crush him. That if he gives into his grief, then whoever did kill Olthic will get away with it.

Words of a poem echo around the hollow spaces of his skull.

> Haith is dust
> And Grena a grave
> But Guerdon's a mad god's dream

Five Knives to Glimmerside to the New City, then looping back along Holyhill, over the viaduct to Castle Hill. Morning rolling into midday, midday becoming a dull grey afternoon, the city subdued and hungover after the Festival of Flowers.

He walks until he can't feel his feet, exhausting himself. He can keep walking until he dies, then enter the Vigil and keep walking without breaking stride. Walk off the edge of the world into the sea.

> But Guerdon's a mad god's dream
> Fitful and dark
> Till stonily
> From soaring battlements
> The city eyes eternity

It's a moonless night. The stars are bright, but the streets below are dark enough. The city's quiet, a collective hangover after the excesses of the Festival. The gutters are choked with discarded garlands and poesies of flowers. Alic leads Emlin through the Wash's alleyways, and into the New City.

They pass under a makeshift gallows – from a window far above hangs a body, turning on a noose. Emlin flinches and moves closer to Alic, but it's just a grisly monument. The body is wax, not flesh. One of the city's defunct Tallowmen, now held aloft to be pelted with stones and rotten fruit.

They walk down the Street of Shrines without stopping. Out of the corner of his eye, the spy spots a city watch sentry. The shrines are under surveillance. The figure is masked, their eyes hidden behind lenses and thaumic probes. The mask's machine-gaze focuses on Emlin, holds for a moment, then the sentry waves him on. This part of the New City is no place to bring a child.

"Wait five minutes," the spy tells Emlin, "then get to the Spider's shrine, over there. I'll distract the watch." He forces himself to smile. "Ask the Spider for forgiveness, then send the message."

The shrine is a place of power for the Fate Spider. It will bolster the boy's connection to the deity, force Emlin's soul back to proper alignment. But it'll hurt. Mortals are such fragile, changeable things, but gods are constant. Remorseless. Their love and hate equally terrible, equally heedless.

The spy takes out the lion-headed vial and anoints the boy. Giving him Annah's mark, her seal, so the Ishmeric fleet will know this message comes with her blessing.

Emlin squares his shoulders and looks towards the darkness of the shrine. "I'll do it," he says to Alic, but it's the spy who answers.

"Good boy. Tell them the city's ripe for plucking."

In the shrine, Emlin kneels before the statue of the Spider and prays.

The shape of the statue is the same shape that's in him. His soul is *unfolded* by it, cracked open and pulled apart, losing its human aspect, extending eight legs to skitter across the web of whispers. Sprouting eyes that see beyond the material world. He digests the words that Alic spoke to him, wraps them in psychic silk, carries them onto the web.

It's hard. It's much harder than before. The shrine gives him the strength to try, like the statue's taking the weight of the burden.

Emlin fears that the god will be angry with him, that when he meets Fate Spider he'll be judged. Punished.

It would be fair. It would be just. He's sinned. He deserves whatever he gets.

And Alic wouldn't send him into danger.

Emlin rips free of his mortal body – unsure, in divine ambiguity, if his body is the eight-legged statue or the two-legged boy – and moves across the web. There are others like him, he can feel their movement in subtle vibrations. Spies in other cities, other lands. The web covers the world.

The strand he's crawling along is one of the northernmost. Most of the web is in the south, centred on Ishmere. There are thousands of saints there, thousands of his counterparts, soul-siblings. The web's so thick in places that it smothers the material plane beneath it; in those holy temples, fate is malleable.

He resists the temptation to take certain paths. The web is timeless, and some paths lead into the past or future. As an initiate, when he first came into his power, he succumbed to weakness, and crawled back into the past to look at his own family. Watched his own childhood, and saw his mother's face again. The priests chastised him for that, his first failing – and then Fate Spider forgave him. The Spider is his family now, his only parent, his greater self. He pushes away the thought of Alic's face that flickers through his mind. The future-paths are more perilous still, especially now that the web is wounded.

He crawls around the fringes of the damaged region, the aftermath of the sundering, and tastes sorrow and ash. The temples of Severast burned, and their priests vanished into the future. The web was torn. So much was lost. He does not envy the work of the spirits who toil there, reweaving fate to bring certainty to the ruins.

But Severast isn't his destination. He stops, senses the vibrations. He thought he'd continue south, to the heart of the web, to Ishmere.

But the god isn't there. For an instant, he's confused, wondering if he somehow got turned around, because it seems like Fate Spider is right on top of him. Then, he finds the right path. No wonder it was hard to read the vibrations – Fate Spider is not at the centre of the web today. The locus of the god is off in the fragile, unsteady regions where the web crosses the sea. He crawls along quivering strands until he approaches the divinity.

He asks for forgiveness.

The god considers him. Tastes him. Dissolves him, injecting venom into his brain so it can read all his thoughts. He is still pleasing to the Spider; his offence was grave, but there's still a place for him in Fate Spider's plans.

Moving out of time, now. He is Fate Spider, and the web is Fate Spider, and all things are Fate Spider. The message is delivered, always was delivered, for all things are known to Fate Spider. With eight eyes, he beholds the cosmos. He knows all secrets now. He sees the web of causality and chaos that births the future.

His mandibles, dripping with the Poison Undeniable, speak the secrets he brought out of Guerdon.

The weapon is a lie, whispers Fate Spider, *Guerdon has no weapon that can slay us!*

Emlin – his name is Emlin, he reminds himself – struggles to reassert his selfhood as other gods move around him. The pantheon of Ishmere gathers. Mercifully, Cloud Mother cloaks them in mist, so Emlin is not annihilated by the radiance of their divine majesty. He senses rather than sees them – the Kraken slithering beneath the surface of the world, vast and timeless. Blessed Bol, drawn back from his dreams of the dragon-hoards of Lyrix, hands running with coins. Smoke Painter, sliding past him, trailing perfumed vapours. High Umur, infinitely remote, attends this divine council by sending an emissary of holy fire, and Emlin recoils from the heat.

He's too close to the gods, too much of him has been sublimated into Fate Spider.

And prowling, stalking around him, something huge and predatory. Hot breath as the beast snuffles at him. The mists cannot wholly conceal the regal divinity that examines him. The Lion Queen's claws tear the web as She moves. Circling around the Fate Spider. Eight glittering eyes watching two of gold, brighter than the sun.

The Spider cringes. Emlin cringes, his heart racing, his eight legs coiling beneath him protectively. Shuffling back into some dark corner of heaven. The glory of union with the god goes sour; there are other powers in the pantheon, divinities stronger and fiercer than Fate Spider, and they are ascendant. Lion Queen considers the message.

"War," she says. "War is holy."

Lion Queen roars, and heaven breaks. Emlin falls, plummeting out of the realm of gods, falling back towards the realm of mortals. He's lost the protection of the god's favour – where once Fate Spider might have eased this transition, handled the fragile mortal vessel gently, now the god discards him like something soiled.

His offence was only partially forgiven. He must still suffer.

Emlin tries to become human again, but it's not easy. His skull cracks, again and again. Pain shoots through his head. Weeping wounds rip open along his side as four of his spiritual legs are severed as he drops to the physical realm.

He falls to the hard floor of the shrine, his face burning in agony from half a dozen wounds. Screaming in pain. His eyes screwed tightly closed, hiding from the Lion Queen's terrible radiance.

Alic appears next to him, helps him up, wipes his face.

Blood flows from six wounds on Emlin's forehead, stigmata of the Fate Spider. In time, those wounds may ripen into eyes.

"It's done," says Alic thickly, hugging the boy close.

And they are left alone in the shrine, all gods gone for now.

The customs post at Guerdon's northern border could, perhaps, have coped with a single train. There are a few watchmen there, a few guns pointing towards Haith. The border commander is woken in the middle of the night by the arrival of the first train. While he inspects the train's travel paper, he sends his watchmen down to inspect it. They peer in through the windows with their alchemical masks, scanning for concealed miracles and hidden saints. It's absurd, and they know it – Haith has no saints save the Enshrined, and what miracle could be more obvious than the hundreds of Vigilant soldiers who sit there patiently.

An examination of the travel papers reveals a hitherto unfortunate discrepancy between Guerdon and Haithi law on the topic of death. The regulations covering the train link between the two cities strictly limit the number of Haithi *soldiers* who can pass through Guerdon's territory, but have a much more generous allowance for the number of civilians.

The commander of the forces on the train smiles at the border guard. (Skulls always smile.) Why, all these Vigilant soldiers are on leave, and aren't currently soldiers by the letter of the law. They're off duty, unarmed and out of uniform.

The border guard points out that the city has an even stricter limit on the number of undead permitted in Guerdon.

Ah, says the train commander, the undead soldiers on leave aren't going to the city. They won't enter Guerdon itself. They're going to holiday in the countryside. And the restriction on the number of Haithi civilians makes no mention of whether those civilians are living or dead.

It's patently absurd.

The border commander could order the guns to fire on the train. He could blow up the tracks, protect the city from this potential threat. But there are more lights coming down the track, more trains approaching. His watch post would be overrun. He and all his border watch would be slaughtered.

He's also uncomfortably aware that tomorrow is supposed to be a busy day. Haith has stepped up its purchases of alchemical weapons in the last few weeks, and more of those weapons are being transported by train instead of ship, to avoid Ishmeric krakens or sky pirates from Lyrix. A fortune in trade. What will the alchemists' guild do to him if he closes the border unnecessarily?

The commander huffs and puffs, his nervous breathing in time with the wheezing of the idling train engine outside the window. He rereads the regulations again, consults his timetables, all under the unblinking scrutiny of the train commander's eyeless gaze. He digs out old railway maps.

A compromise – a blessed way out. There is, the border commander crows, a disused siding yard just north of Guerdon city.

Big enough to take all four of the "holiday trains". He can send a message ahead, have the city watch rush troops to monitor the yard, ensure that the Haithi "civilians" behave. The train commander grins and agrees.

The watch confiscate firing pins from the train's artillery pieces, promising to return them when the Haithi leave Guerdon soil. The Haithi do not object. Indeed, they cooperate, helpfully disassembling the cannon mechanisms. It's the living troops who operate the artillery, not the dead. The dead are slow to learn new tricks. Slow, but steady.

One by one, the trains pass through the border post.

As ordered, one by one, they stop at that siding, arriving in the dead of night. Guerdon is a looming shadow to the south-east, fitful and dark, sleepless on this sweltering summer night.

CHAPTER 32

Terevant spends the first night at a flophouse in the Wash. He doesn't sleep – or, if he does, he doesn't recall it. Sleep would bring nightmares, and nightmares are indistinguishable from the waking world.

His second day he spends wandering again, hiding, thinking. He feels like a hollow vessel, a soul-urn without a soul, filled instead with questions that rattle around his skull.

Olthic is dead. That fact feels too huge to fit in Terevant's tattered mind. He has to focus on fragments of the fact to keep his thoughts from straying. He's a man making his way across a narrow bridge, a dark gulf on either side.

Olthic is dead. What caste did he die in? Not Vigilant, clearly. Did he make it to the Erevesic sword in time, did the ancestors accept him? Or, did he die casteless and ashamed? A Supplicant, his soul trapped in the husk of his body until it's extracted by the necromancers and put to use in the temples of the nameless?

If he stops thinking, stops moving, he'll never move again.

Olthic is dead. How was he killed? He had the Sword Erevesic in his possession, able to draw on the stored strength and skill of a hundred generations of Erevesics. He must have been taken by surprise. Ambushed in a moment of weakness.

Killed by someone he trusted.

She played us both.

Haith is built on two pillars, the Houses and the Bureau, two arms of the state, directed by the immortal Crown. Every schoolchild knows that. The Crown desired Guerdon, so Houses and Bureau both went to work. The Houses sent Olthic – a war hero, a living legend – to dazzle parliament and convince them to ally with Haith. The Bureau sent Lys, to manoeuvre their pawn into place.

To ensure Olthic failed, Lys kept the sword from him. She took advantage of Vanth's botched resurrection – did she also take advantage of the incident on the train at Grena, or did she *engineer* it? Terevant's stomach sinks with realisation: *Lys asked me to bring the sword instead of having a Vigilant honour guard carry it because she knew she could manipulate me.*

Terevant's aware he's mumbling to himself. People on the street give him sidelong glances. He takes to the alleyways, sinking deeper into the Wash.

Lys manipulated him. Outmaneovred Olthic. Betrayed their trust. But . . . that doesn't mean she killed Olthic, does it? Even if she saw Olthic as a rival for the Crown, and was willing to commit murder to win the highest prize in Haith, then Olthic was a *defeated* rival.

"They'll eat you alive in this city. You've got to learn to act." Lemuel told him that. But Lemuel is Lys's creature. It was Lemuel who followed him at the Festival, drew him away from the warmth and safety of Naola's fire. Terevant touches the tender lump on the back of his head. He can almost feel the churning of his thoughts beneath his bruised skull.

And what to make of Daerinth? Did the old man suspect something? Is that why he tried to get Terevant to flee? No, that can't be – Daerinth was quick to accuse Terevant of Olthic's murder. Daerinth's no ally.

Terevant doesn't have a single living soul in the city he can trust. Guerdon's full of unfriendly eyes. City watch everywhere. Every time a watchman passes, Terevant flinches. Newspaper barkers all over the city shout about the Haithi troops encamped on the edge of the city, about the murder of the Haithi ambassador. It's only a matter of time before someone recognises him. He's still wearing a Haithi uniform beneath his cloak, for death's sake. He turns back the narrow alleys and teetering buildings of the Wash, full of places he can wait, where people are more interested in the contents of his purse than his face or uniform.

Olthic is dead. Olthic is dead, and he's not coming back.

Terevant is the last Erevesic.

He's light-headed from lack of food. He finds a street stall, buys a meal of mushy vegetables and fried fish from a one-legged vendor. When Terevant digs in his pocket for a coin, he finds a small hard rectangle of cardboard.

ELADORA DUTTIN, it reads, ASSISTANT TO THE EMERGENCY COMMITTEE, and, below it, an address.

Duttin. He could go to Duttin. But that book on architecture is back in his rooms in the Haithi embassy, and he can't go back there. He could go to her empty-handed, throw himself on her mercy, but that's a last resort.

Another tavern welcomes him in. It's crowded and raucous, full of sea shanties, toasts to the returned king, drunken prayers to Saint Storm and all the other sea gods. Sailors are the most ecumenical of souls, offering prayers to all the deities that share custody of the open ocean. He buy a drink, nurses it while he waits for the right moment. Tries to hold himself together. The crowd in the bar swirls around him, a sea of people that threatens to drown him. Olthic is dead, and so is their mother, their sisters, drowned long ago. Olthic is dead, and so is their father, and what would he say to see Terevant in another tavern?

Terevant clings to the calling card in his hand, turning it over and over, an emotional periapt.

And then a familiar face swims suddenly into focus, up out of the churning mob. There, a few tables away is the girl from the train. Shana. She's in conversation with two men – well, one man, and one hulking *thing* in a baroque suit of armour, the creature's body entirely concealed beneath hissing rubber pipes and metal plating.

He can't tell what they're talking about, but he does hear her mention a name.

Edoric Vanth.

*

Across the city, the spy waits.

Too many days have gone by since that visit to the shrine. Hot summer days, sticky and bright, the nights so fleeting they seem to slip from dusk to dawn without any true darkness. And by day, the spy is Alic, candidate for the Industrial Liberals, so he canvasses and campaigns and meets with people across the New City. Listens to them, reassures them of their bright, hopeful future in Guerdon, promises them that they will prosper. Allays their fears of war, while every night the spy creeps out onto the roof of Jaleh's house and looks out to sea.

Before the attack on Severast, the sky boiled, and there were terrible divine shapes in those angry clouds. Before the attack on Severast, the sea turned to glass. Before the attack on Severast, there were many signs and portents. Statues walked or wept. God-touched lunatics roamed the streets, shrieking about the wrath of the gods. Gold coins became sharp as knives when touched, and the alleys of the market ran with blood. There were sainted assassins on the streets, too, sent by the Fate Spider of Ishmere. They murdered the Kraken-saints of Severast, so they could not take on their war-forms and wrestle for control of the sea. Murdered the Spider-priests in the temples, calling them schismatics and heretics, until the shadows ate them. There were many omens before the gods came.

In Guerdon, the sky is cloudless. The sea that laps the Wash's shores is polluted, garbage-bobbed, but it's seawater.

There are signs and portents, but none are the ones he looks for. The city becomes restless, feverish in the summer heat. More saints of the Kept Gods appear. Crowds gather on Holyhill, looking for a glimpse of their new king, praying to the old gods of the city, and they are rewarded with minor, spasmodic miracles. Astounding, to the folk of Guerdon who have not seen significant divine intervention in two hundred years. The ambassador from Haith has been murdered, and the two governments trade angry letters. Haithi troops cross the border, encamp just outside the city, but there's no fighting, just posturing and flag-waving.

Days have passed, and there is no sign of the invasion. The *Grand Retort*, with its fearsome weapon, slumbers in its dock.

Alic laughs, slaps people on the back, hosts meetings in the IndLib hall, smiles. Alic, the bastard, is happy. He spends IndLib money on healing-salve for Emlin's wounds. Meets with Eladora, with Ogilvy, with other new friends.

The spy cannot find the patience that has defined him for so long.

Days have passed, and the wounds on Emlin's face reopen every night.

Terevant waits in the tavern, out of Shana's line of sight.

It's clear that she's not who she claimed to be on the train from Grena, that she's not the sheltered daughter of some prosperous merchant. If there ever was any truth to that tale, then the father must have gone bankrupt long ago and his daughter learned to survive on the streets. She haggles with the two men, pleads with them, but whatever she's selling the armoured man isn't buying it. After a few minutes, he rises – a puff of steam jetting from his suit – and stomps off. Despite his bulk, the crowd makes space for him.

Whoever the armoured figure is, he's respected in the Wash. The other man follows; so does a brutish Gullhead bodyguard stationed at the entrance of the tavern. Terevant wonders what Shana has that could interest such a creature.

Shana tries to slip off through a side door. Terevant hastily drops a few coins on the bar and follows her. She hurries through the streets, head down, jumpy as an alley cat.

He steps up behind her.

"Shana?"

She tries to bolt, but he shouts, "I just want to talk," and a spasm runs through her, driving her to her knees. Her face contorts. For a moment, it takes on an expression that reminds him eerily of his own mother. *She touched the sword*, he remembers. All the souls of the Enshrined Erevesics, briefly intermingling with hers before rejecting her as an unsuitable host.

She rises, and stands there waiting for him, like she's rooted to the ground.

*

Shana takes him back to her bedsit. The room's tiny, with only a single chair next to the bed. She sinks into it and draws her shawl around herself. She won't look directly at Terevant; she addresses her account to a spot on the floor.

He stands rather than sit on the bed. He draws the ragged curtain, just in case anyone might spot him from the street.

She speaks like she's exhausted from a long argument, too tired to fight or lie. "Lem hired us. He brought us on the train. He said to cause a scene when we got to Grena."

Terevant blinks. "Lemuel was on the train?"

"He was wearing a false beard. Pretending to be my dad or something."

The chaperone. The one who'd called the guards, tried to get Terevant arrested.

"Why?"

Shana shrugs. "He didn't tell us. Just said that we were to cause a fuss. He hired us for other stuff, too. Spying on people."

"That's why you tried to take the sword?"

"I didn't know! I swear. I was going through your bag, I'll admit that, but . . . ." She looks up at him, and it's not *her* behind those blue eyes. She speaks in a different tone, a different accent. "Claim thy sword, Erevesic. War is coming, and too long has it been since we have gone into battle." She trails off, then whimpers and scrapes at her face with her nails. "They're still there! Your ancestors, haunting me. I thought they'd gone, but you – you bring them back."

She looks at him. "Please," she asks quietly, "go away."

"What else did Lemuel tell you?"

"Nothing."

"What happened to the other girl? Shara?" Terevant can barely remember her name, and can't recall her face at all. He curses himself for not paying more attention.

"She – we were at the Festival. And she saw the king, and recognised him. Oh, we thought it was so funny, that she'd dallied with the godsent king before he was crowned. We were laughing about it, and then Lemuel found us.

"He took her away," she says. "He'll be back for me. I've got to get out of the city." She's trembling. Eyes like a trapped animal's.

Terevant rests his head against the wall. Lemuel's cleaning up, erasing anything that might connect Berrick to the Bureau.

"Please," says Shana again, not looking at him, "go away. You're Erevesic. You being here makes it worse."

He has to press her a little more.

"What were you doing in the tavern? What does it have to do with Edoric Vanth?"

"You weren't the only man Lemuel had us spy on. The Third Secretary . . . he'd stay here, some nights. And when he was asleep, I'd go through his bag. Take letters, papers, give them to Lem." She touches her cheek; in the half-light, Terevant can't be sure, but it looks bruised. "Sometimes, I'd give them to Lem. I kept some, hid them from him. I thought I could sell them to Dredger, buy passage out of the city." A little half-smile crosses her lips. "Maybe see Old Haith again, before the end. But Dredger wouldn't buy it. He said it was incomplete."

Pity wells up in Terevant. Shana was used just like he was – another of Lys's pawns to be moved and discarded once they'd served some cryptic purpose. Unseen schemes have murdered his brother, taken the family sword, brought him to ruin. Everything's turned to mist, all the fixed points of his universe have come unmoored. He doesn't know who he is, or what he should do – but he can save Shana at least.

"Here," says Terevant, emptying his purse on the bedside table. "Take this. Go. Not to Haith, the war's going there – run to the Archipelago or somewhere. Don't tell anyone where you've gone." She snatches the money from the table and bolts for the door – and then stops, frozen by some last echo of the Erevesic sword. She points to a drawer then vanishes, her feet pounding on the wooden stairs as she runs. Terevant waits until he hears the front door slam downstairs, then opens the drawer. Inside are papers. Some are diagrams of machinery, of alchemical engineering, and he feels dizzy with excitement – *Vanth was looking for the god bombs*. Other pages are covered in some thaumaturgical notation that reminds him of marginal notes in Duttin's book.

He can't decipher them.

But he's sure Eladora Duttin can.

CHAPTER 33

P *oor Alic looks exhausted*, thinks Eladora. Or maybe thinner – like he's fading away. The confident smile and boundless energy he demonstrated at the start of the campaign has diminished. He stares out of the carriage window at the city lights, too tired to read the documents on his lap.

Eladora suppresses her own yawn, then gives in to it. A most unladylike gesture, but Alic doesn't even notice. The raptequine pulling the cab hisses and yowls in answer.

She thought she was tired before the Festival, but the last few days have shown her what war must be like. Taking over managing the New City campaign from Spyke was enough to fill her days to overflowing, a dozen candidates to meet and another two score clamouring for attention. Most of them off the list she provided – or rather Cari and Spar provided – and full of passion and concerns and ideas, and hungry for party cash. The money that Alic provided got added to another pile from Kelkin, but the safe at the party head-quarters is almost bare again.

The cab slows as it approaches her building. She knocks on the ceiling so the driver can hear her. "Just here, please." To Alic, she says, "I'll see you in the morning. Don't walk home – take the cab. You need the rest, and the party will pay your fare."

"All right," he says. "Goodnight, Miss Duttin."

She alights, grabs her satchel, and turns towards the archway leading to the stairwell—

Yelps in alarm as she sees something moving in there. *Miren*, she thinks, imagining a pale face in the shadows. Her heart's pounding, but there's nothing there. Nothing that she can see. There are two flights of dark stairs up to the door of her flat, and the street's deserted apart from the departing carriage.

The carriage stops again, and Alic hops down. He slaps the back of the cab, and the cabbie drives off towards the busier environs of Venture Square.

"Heard you shout," says Alic. "What's wrong?"

"It's nothing." She discovers she's holding the broken hilt that Sinter gave her. She stares at it in confusion, then shoves it back in her bag.

Alic peers into the dark archway. "Can't be too careful, these days. Could be all sorts of thieves and spies lurking." He shrugs. "I'll walk you up."

"Thank you."

They climb the stairs together. Halfway up, Alic tenses. Pushes her back down a step, takes the lead. Walks soundlessly ahead of her.

There, sitting on her doorstep, head in hands, is an unfamiliar figure. A beggar? Street-stained cloak – and a Haithi uniform.

"Lieutenant Erevesic?" she says in confusion.

"I can't go back to the embassy," Terevant insists, over and over when they get him into Eladora's flat. "I don't know what to do. Olthic . . . " Terevant can't sit still. He moves from couch to chair, to pacing up and down, to the window, back to the couch. Alic busies himself in the kitchen, brewing coffee and getting food. She's grateful for his discretion – Alic has clearly decided that this is none of his business, so he's just making himself useful, bless him.

Eladora watches Terevant warily. By rights, she should go to the watch. Go to Ramegos – or Kelkin. Sheltering a fugitive criminal from Haith could blow up into a huge scandal, and she can't forget the impending election. She has no doubt that Kelkin has agents like Absalom Spyke who can make problems disappear.

But she remembers sitting in a cold alleyway off Desiderata Street, after ancient horrors suddenly exploded out of the history books and destroyed her old life. She remembers wandering the city, alone and penniless, and how Kelkin and Jere Taphson took pity on her.

"Tell me what happened."

Terevant's account of his time in Guerdon is that of a man picking his way across a causeway of slippery stones over dark water. He hesitates, he backtracks, he lingers at one place or another because the way ahead is dangerous and he must gingerly test each possible foothold. She guesses that much of his hesitation is connected to Haith's mysterious Bureau of spies. Figures rise out of the narrative and fall back into the shadows, their significance obscured. He talks about his walk in the Grena Valley, about the grave of the goddess there, about intrigue in the embassy, about Haithi internal politics between Crown and House and Bureau.

He talks about Eskalind, which has little to do with recent events, but he still returns there. Eladora's not familiar with the particular battle that Terevant fought in, but she's heard of Eskalind. The peninsula is strategically valuable, so it's been the site of innumerable clashes in the Godswar, changing hands over and over. The sands soaked in blood. The foundations of the world there torn up by miracles, leaving the place hellishly unstable.

He doesn't talk about his brother at all. He circles around the topic. Eladora recognises the habit – she and her mother never ever talked about how the rest of the Thay family were exterminated by Keeper saints. Some things are so vast and terrible they go unspoken, because afterwards, really, every conversation you have is about them to some degree.

Start with what you know, Eladora tells herself. "The book, *Sacred and Secular Architecture in the Ashen Period* – where did you find it?"

"A house on Gethis Row. Vanth led us there."

"After you resurrected him?"

"It wasn't him. He wasn't on Vigil. Just a sort of echo of him. I don't know how the necromancer did it."

Eladora makes a mental note to ask Ramegos about necromancy. "And Vanth was looking for, ah." She hesitates herself. She's sworn not to discuss the secret events of the Crisis. The bombs, though, are an open secret. Terevant passed through Grena. He saw what they can do – and something tells her she can trust Alic. "The god bombs."

Terevant nods.

"Did you read the book?" she asks.

"I glanced at it. Most of it didn't seem relevant. Discussion of old buildings. Demons in the depths. Maps of the city. Lots of hand-written notes in the margins."

"Some of those notes," Eladora admits, "were written by me. Last year, in the middle of the Crisis. I was looking for the hiding places of the Black Iron Gods – the raw materials the alchemists used to make those bombs. But I lost the book. It got left behind in a safe house belonging to Sinter." She tries to think of how it might have ended up at Gethis Row. Sinter's safe house was, she vaguely recalls, searched by the city watch in the weeks after the Crisis, while Sinter was missing. Did Sinter spirit the book away before they found it, or did it end up in some watch evidence locker at Queen's Point?

"And there's this," says Terevant, producing a few loose sheets covered in notation. The glyphs are similar to those in other sorcery texts she'd studied. There's a commentary in Khebeshi – Ramegos taught her that the best sorcery texts are written in the tongue of Khebesh. And diagrams, wiring charts, schematics.

"Where'd you obtain this from?"

"Someone who knew Edoric Vanth," answers Terevant. "I can't read it."

Alic settles on the couch next to her and reads over her shoulder. He points at one diagram. "Doesn't look like any bomb I've ever seen."

"The god bombs are much simpler," says Eladora. "Brutal even. This seems to be precision work."

"An aetheric engine. Some sort of industrial ward generator?"

"Not a ward," mutters Eladora, puzzling over the glyphs. "More . . . the inverse. A summoning circle. A very powerful one." Parts of a great machine. She turns one page, finds an illustration of a glass tower unlike any she's seen in Guerdon. Turns another, and is confronted with densely written Khebeshi text.

"What does the Khebeshi say?" asks Alic.

"I'm trying to work it out." She translates it haltingly. "'To ensure complete annihilation of the aetheric weave, it is necessary to achieve a local maxima of divine presence. A lesser concentration of teleological elements would result in only a partial erasure of the weave.'"

"What in the heavens does that mean?" asks Terevant.

Eladora recalls her own experiences, during the Crisis, when she was trapped in her grandfather's tomb and her soul was exposed to the horrific attention of the gods. The Black Iron Gods, reaching for her from their iron prisons, dark tendrils stretching out across the city. The Kept Gods, though – they were inchoate. Everywhere and nowhere. A million little flickering candle flames, all across the land.

"Targeting. It's a targeting problem. How to strike a god."

Terevant laughs hollowly. "I saw gods at Eskalind. They were . . . really big. Not hard to miss."

"No," says Alic thoughtfully. "It would be a problem. If Fate Spider is all secrets, he's here in this room. If Lion Queen is war, then she's on every battlefield. You encountered manifestations of the gods. Saints or avatars, pieces of the divine, not the whole of the god."

"Grena must have been an ideal test case," says Eladora. "The goddess they killed was the goddess of the valley – a localised deity – and she was manifesting through a saint at a time of impact. Her whole essence was concentrated to a single point."

"So the bombs on their own aren't enough?" asks Terevant. "Haith would need something else to kill an Ishmeric god?"

"Possibly. It would depend on circumstances. Without a-a 'local maxima of divine presence' – maybe a temple full of saints and fervent worshippers, where the god's close at hand. Or you'd need to wait for the god to manifest fully, which would be . . . "

"Terrible." Alic sounds broken. "It's terrible to face a god." He stands. "I should go."

"Now?"

"I need to get back to Emlin," he says quietly. He doesn't sound like Alic at all for a moment, and then he's back. "And anyway, Miss Duttin, all this sounds like something I'd be better off not knowing about."

She walks Alic to the door. He whispers to her, out of earshot of Terevant. "If you want my advice, miss, you'll bring him to Mr Kelkin right away. It sounds like he's found out some secrets about the city's defences, and you don't want that falling into the hands of your enemies. He's Haithi — and for all we know, he did kill his brother."

She nods. "Thank you. Please, don't mention this evening to anyone."

"I can keep a secret," Alic says. And then he's gone, hurrying down the stairs. Shoulders bowed like he's carrying the secret and it's a heavy load to bear.

Eladora closes the door.

"Is there anything about the actual bombs in here?" asks Terevant, leafing through the Khebeshi papers. She can almost hear Kelkin snap *it's a matter of state security* in her head.

"No. But there's no order to these papers. Lots of missing sheets."

"There's something else," says Terevant. "The house Vanth led us to — there was a woman there. About your age. She had powers of some sort — it was like she knew what was coming, or could see things."

"Knives? Little scars on her face, like freckles? Immensely frustrating to deal with?"

"You know her?" Terevant's eyes widen.

"She's my cousin. Carillon Thay."

"She stole more of the papers," says Terevant. He pauses a heartbeat, then adds, "I think she killed Vanth."

"Ah. That I can shed some light on." She has to think for a moment to work out how long it's been. It feels like months. "Just over three weeks ago, I met Carillon in the New City, and she warned me that unknown persons had, er, planted a body in her house. The ruffians attacked me, too."

"Did you see them plant Vanth's body?" Terevant asks morosely. He picks up his coffee cup and looks into it, as if checking the dregs for poison or doubting its existence. His capacity for trust has taken a pounding.

"No. Carillon has certain . . . spiritual gifts. She was, ah, integral to the Crisis last year, and it left her . . . changed." Eladora pauses, mentally reviews what she was told. The inquest determined that Carillon was broken, her sainthood lost. That her amulet was magically inert, and that Spar was gone completely. That the Black Iron Gods were all destroyed. But who made that determination? Did they make a mistake, or did they lie to Eladora?

"I think," says Eladora, "that we should talk to Cari."

"She tried to stab me."

"Yes, that does sound like her."

The streets around Venture Square are crowded – a backwash of revellers from the Festival of Flowers, mummers who've hastily written or exhumed street-plays about the kings, hawkers and Hawkers. Children and drunkards climb on monuments to forgotten saints or great victories. Eladora steers them around the side of the square, avoiding the crowd near the Vulcan coffee shop. Even at this hour, it'll be full of IndLibs, and she doesn't want anyone she knows asking questions about Terevant.

The crowds thin out as they head towards the sea and the New City. Ahead is the half-demolished, half-erupted bulk of the Seamarket, where the Gutter Miracle began. Somewhere in that twisted mess of masonry and magic are the remains of Spar – and Professor Ongent, too.

People who associate with Carillon Thay end up changed. Or dead. Or both.

"I'm not quite sure how to find her. I roughly know how to get to where I last saw her, but she may have moved on."

Terevant gives her a sidelong glance from the hood of his own cloak. It covers his uniform, barely, but it's too small for his frame. There's something strange in the sky, black pillars of smoke rising from Holyhill, from the Wash, behind Castle Hill. Eladora stares at the smoke, wondering if there's been an attack – and then the wind shifts, and the smell hits her. They're cleaning out the corpse shafts. Beneath the churches of the Keepers is a network of deep wells that lead down to the ghoul tunnels. For hundreds of years, the church has given the dead of Guerdon to the corpse-eaters. Eladora remembers the funeral of a neighbour; once the ceremony was done and the mourners departed, a black-trimmed cart left the village church in Wheldacre and rattled down the road to Guerdon. No one thought it strange. After death, the body becomes property of the church. It was Eladora's family who were seen as eccentric, with their Safidist insistence on burning the dead.

Now, wafts of greasy smoke billow from the corpse shafts. The Safidists are in the ascendance, and the holy fires will carry what remains of the soul's spiritual energy, the residuum, up to the Kept Gods. The smell turns Eladora's stomach.

Somewhere, in heaven, a dam is close to bursting.

She quickens her pace, and Terevant follows her down the warren of confused streets south of the former Seamarket, on the edge of the New City.

"We're being followed," he says after a few minutes. He takes her by the arm, leads her down an alleyway. Rats scurry away from them as they wade through drifts of trash, a humus of torn-down election posters and broken boxes. Shapes bound along the gutters overhead.

"Two of them," says Terevant. "In grey robes. They've been following us since we left your place."

"Students." She recognises the grey robes. University students, a common sight on Guerdon's streets. A common disguise for anyone who wants to walk unseen.

"Are they the ones who attacked you at Carillon's house?"

Eladora tries to remember. It's all a mess of gunfire and stabbings and botched spells, but she recalls her attackers then as burly, hard-faced. "I don't think so."

Terevant pulls her into another side street, picks up a rock from the mud. It's pearly stone, a broken shard of the New City. Eladora dips into her pocket for her own pistol before remembering that she gave it to Alic. She finds the broken hilt of Aleena's sword and hefts it. It'll do in a pinch.

"Ready?" whispers Terevant.

Eladora stammers, then just nods.

"Now."

He charges out of the alleyway, unhesitating, into the teeth of danger – then skids to a stop.

"What the hell?"

The street they just left has been transformed into a garden of flowers. It's too dark to see the colours, but the perfume from the blooms is overwhelming, sweetness mixed with the roast-meat stink from the corpse shafts that drifts over the city. Every surface sprouts flowers, growing from the mud, from cracks in the walls, from trash, from window frames, even from the metal flanks of a half-barrel. Terevant turns slowly around, holding his rock.

There's one patch of floral growth, in the heart of this sudden garden, where the flowers grow thickest, and beneath it is a ragged piece of grey cloth. A student's robe.

A miracle.

This time, she's the one who pulls Terevant away. Behind them, she hears the rustling of the flowers.

A prayer comes unbidden to her lips. Mother of Mercies, Mother of Saints.

Mother of Flowers.

Whatever it is, whatever this miracle, they can't fight it with a rock.

Running now, through dangerous streets. Through what used to be part of the Alchemists' Quarter, but is now the heart of the New City. Eladora looks for the tower where she met Carillon last time, but she can't see it. She doesn't know if she's simply lost, or if the city's geography shifts.

She glances behind. She can't see any grey robes in the grey gloom, but there's something there. She can feel it. A gathering presence, like a wave.

Terevant's pulling her along, dragging her by the arm, but he doesn't have a clue where he's going. He plunges blindly through the city, into regions where the Gutter Miracle faltered. Where Spar's vision of orderly streets and civic pride became blurred, mixed with his own thoughts and fears. Distorted buildings, shapes in stone that might be faces. A row of stone fingers rise from the street like bollards, carved so intricately Eladora can see the whorls of the fingerprints in the moonlight. Eladora stops to lean against one, to catch her breath. Sweat runs down and pools at the base of her back; the city presses close around her, hot and airless.

A house on one side of the street is slurred, the left-hand side perfectly shaped, the right-hand half an unformed mess of flowing stone, like the sculptor had lost interest in the piece.

And standing in that half-door is Carillon Thay.

"I know you." Carillon's eyes gleam in the darkness. "You're the fucker who sent that zombie-thing after me."

"Lieutenant Terevant, of the House Erevesic." Terevant half bows, but he doesn't take his eyes off her.

"Fuck it. Come in." Cari turns her back on him and opens the working half of the door, inviting them into the half-house. Empty bottles clink underfoot as she closes the door after Eladora.

"I didn't see you on your way up," remarks Carillon.

"We were followed – a Keeper saint, I think."

Cari concentrates. "No one nearby now. Guess you lost 'em. Or they're hiding from me."

"Carillon," says Eladora, "do you know anything about the death of the Haithi ambassador? Or the theft of his sword?" It feels like asking an oracle for divinations, but in her mother's stories prophets lived in caves or forests, and didn't have so many knives close to hand.

"Who?"

"What do you know about Edoric Vanth? What were you doing on Gethis Row?" demands Terevant.

"Who's asking, Eladora? You, or the bloody city watch and parliament and the Patros and Effro Kelkin and all?"

"Right now, just me."

Cari rolls her eyes. She leads them into a kitchen, finds a bottle on a shelf. She takes a swallow, then offers it to Eladora. Eladora refuses; Terevant holds his rock in a vaguely threatening manner while still reaching over to take a drink.

Cari twitches her nose, and the rock leaps from Terevant's hand, flying of its own accord across the room to merge with the stone wall. She keeps talking like the minor miracle didn't happen. "Right. Edoric Vanth." She takes a drink. "After the Crisis, every fucker was running around the New City trying to find the god bombs. The alchemists captured four of the Black Iron bells before . . . before it all went to shit. Beckanore Bell got used for the test run." There isn't any furniture in the unfinished room, so Eladora shuffles about, uncomfortably. Carillon leans against the wall; it reshapes itself subtly, the stone growing a lip for her to sit on.

"At Grena," says Terevant. "I visited there. It was . . . strange."

"Yeah, well, it was fucking apocalyptic here. The Ravellers were everywhere. Anyway, they got three other bells in the confusion. The Tower of Law, the Bell Rock out in the harbour, and the Holy Beggar. They got all of them back to the forges in the Alchemists' Quarter and started the conversion process before—" She shrugs.

"Before the Miracle." Eladora takes over. "The other Black Iron Gods, the ones still trapped in bell form, were destroyed when you transferred their power to Mr Idgeson. The three bells that were in the process of being converted to weapons – well, I know at least one survived and is usable as a god bomb." *The other two might have survived, too. Their stored power gone, but not their malice.*

"That's the Tower of Law bell," says Cari. "They converted that as quick as they fucking could, because they knew they might have to use it on the city. Kill the Black Iron Gods and the Kept Gods, too."

"The city watch recovered that bell from the rubble. What about the other two?" asks Eladora. Mentally, she tries to reconstruct the scene, to map the Alchemists' Quarter to the New City. Damn it all, this is *archaeology* – why wasn't she involved in this?

Cari swirls the liquor in the bottle. "Spar buried them deep. It's hard for him to *see* them. From a divine perspective, they're fucking awful to perceive. Like looking straight into the sun, if the sun were a black void of poison and death and screaming hatred." She pauses for a moment, listening to a voice only she can hear. Shakes her head.

"So, like I was saying, afterwards every fucker was looking for the remaining potential bombs. City watch, obviously. Alchemists. That shit Dredger from down the Wash. Adventurers. And spies. Lots of spies."

"Edoric Vanth," says Eladora.

"Among others, yeah." Cari takes a drink. "None of those fucks could be trusted. There's too much shit down there. After his body got dumped in my old place, I backtraced him to that house on Gethis Row."

Terevant spots something tucked in a corner of the room. A wooden crate, and a leather satchel on top of it, brimming with canisters and guns. "You're the one who stole the weapons from that house."

"A girl's got to eat." Cari gets up, moves to stand between Terevant and the crate, daring him to cross her. He doesn't move, and she continues.

"There were maps upstairs, too, documents and stuff – I don't know who made 'em, but they were good. Someone worked out *where* Spar put the bombs."

"Where are they?" demands Terevant.

Cari glares at him. "Aren't you listening? Fuck off, Haith's not going to dig up all that alchemical shit again." She waggles the empty bottle. "Look, El, I'm being responsible."

Terevant probes the half-formed stone frame where there should be a window. "What happened to Vanth, zombie-Vanth I mean? I saw him chasing you."

Cari shrugs. "He didn't follow me into the New City. If he

had . . . " She grinds the base of the bottle against the wall, like she's crushing a bug.

"He's still intact?"

"Was last time I saw him."

Terevant drums his fingers on the stone. "I was told that you killed him. I think they wanted me to find his body, to make me believe you did it. To hide . . . " He trails off, his face ghastly pale. He pushes at the stone frame again, pressing at the cracks. "You're a seer. Give me an oracle. Tell me, what happened to my brother?"

"The embassy," says Eladora, "is too far from the New City, I fear."

"Yeah," says Cari. "Anything north of Castle Hill, I don't have eyes on."

"The Sword Erevesic – it was gone from the embassy." Terevant's shivering despite the summer heat. "Did you see who took it? Did they pass through your domain? Where is the sword now?"

"What's it worth?"

"Money," he says. "The Erevesic estates can pay."

"You don't have two coppers," laughs Cari. "You're not even worth robbing."

"My money is in Haith."

"And we're not."

"Can you find the sword, Carillon?" asks Eladora, quietly.

Cari shrugs. "Maybe. If it's in the New City, or close enough."

"I know what you can give us," says Eladora to Terevant. "The election. Expose the new king as a Haithi plant. We all know that's what he is. Give us proof."

Terevant rubs his wrists, his fingers probing at something beneath the skin. He stands up, shakes his head. "I can't. I'm sorry, but I can't. I took an oath to the Crown. I made a promise."

"Well, then, fuck off." Cari marches into the half-made hallway and flings open the front door. "Go on, I'm not—"

A gunshot. A crack in the night, a different sort of gunshot to any Eladora's heard before. She freezes. Shards of stone and dust tumble through the air above her head. In that moment, she's not sure if she's been hit.

Terevant throws himself on top of her, tackling her to the ground. Another crack, and Terevant's hit, his body suddenly crumpled, limp. Eladora feels the shock run through him, hears him grunt and gurgle in shock. Blood spurting over her, everywhere, a red flood. Running through her fingers.

"Sniper!" shouts Cari. "Fuck, I'm sorry, I'm sorry. He's up there, four streets away. Shit." Another shot rings out, but Cari's ready for it. It hits her in the back, and the walls shake as they take the impact instead of her. Eladora hauls Terevant away from the door, blood trailing behind him. Cari slams the door.

She tries to remember what she learned about treating gunshot wounds. *He can reanimate*, Eladora tells herself as she tries to staunch the bleeding. Everything's very distant, suddenly, like she's watching it all from far away and far above.

"Spar," prays Cari. The unmade half of the house *shimmers*, like it's carved from ice that's beginning to thaw.

From outside comes a voice that makes them both freeze.

"COME OUT, CHILD. IT'S TIME." A voice of thunder and music and, divine glory, a sound that should come from no human throat, but one they both know so very well.

Silva Duttin.

CHAPTER 34

"Shitshitshit." Cari concentrates on the wall, and the stone flows sluggishly. Long tendrils slither out, interlacing like fingers to barricade the entrance.

"Come out!" Silva's fist smashes into the door, making the whole building shudder. The barrier cracks.

"At least six or seven of them." Cari speaks breathlessly. "Silva, sniper, more coming up. I think one of them's a saint. Fuck." She nearly slips in Terevant's blood as she backs away from the door.

"A girl of flowers," says Eladora, unsure how she knows. "A young saint." Young, drunk on power, newly transfigured by the flood of divine grace set loose by the belief in a king.

"Leave him," says Cari. "Maybe we can get out the back."

Eladora shakes her head. "I'll stall Mother here. You go."

Carillon doesn't hesitate. She darts upstairs and vanishes.

Saints are blessed with healing powers. There's nothing else that she can think of to do. Eladora stands, staggers to the door. "Mother! It's Eladora. Cari's gone." She feels dizzy, like it's a horrible dream. The air's thick with the smell of wildflowers; somehow, even though it's night outside, and the windows are stone, sunlight seems to be streaming into the room.

"ELADORA, MY CHILD. I SHALL CARRY YOU OUT AND BRING YOU INTO THE LIGHT OF SAFID! BURN AWAY YOUR SINS. DON'T YOU REALISE, CHILD? WE'RE MARCHING TO FREE THE CITY FROM THE TYRANNY OF MONSTROUS GODS! WE SHALL CAST DOWN THEIR

TEMPLES AND RESTORE THE THRONE ON HIGH." Again, the door quakes. More fingers of stone break. "HOLY FIRE SHALL BRING DOWN THE WORKS OF BLACK IRON!"

She's talking like it's three hundred years ago, when the forces of the Kept Gods – before they were Kept at all – freed the city from the Black Iron pantheon. The war of saints.

"Mother, listen to me. The world's changed. The gods don't understand that, they can't change, so you have to do it for them. The Black Iron Gods are gone! Cari's not their saint any more. Things are different!"

"FIRE SHALL DESTROY THEM. STORMS WILL WASH THEM AWAY. FROM THE ASHES, FLOWERS SHALL GROW."

A sword of holy fire cleaves the door in two. Eladora scrambles back, staring in horror. The figure outside is unrecognisable. Clad in ancient armour, wielding a sword of cascading flames. A cloak of storms, armour forged by the Holy Smith. A crown of flowers transmuted to steel.

For an instant, Eladora's perspective flickers, and somehow she's looking at herself through her mother's eyes. Her beloved daughter, steeped in lies and sin. The same horrible taint that runs through Silva's own veins, the sins of the Thay family who strayed so far from the path. The fires in Silva's blood burn away the taint; she accepts the agony as penance. Eladora must be made to understand the same. The city must be cleansed, too – the fires will burn away the taint. The towers will burn, and be washed away by summer storms, and from the ashes, temples will grow like flowers, and they will worship the true gods of Guerdon, now and forever and forever—

A flash of explosion.

Carillon flings herself out of the upstairs window of the half-made house, dropping the flash-ghost grenade as she does so. Trusting to Spar's guidance that the blast won't hit Eladora or whatshisname.

The sniper across the city snaps a shot while she's in mid-air, and it hits. Spar's miracle protects her, transfers the wound from her fragile mortal flesh to the stone of the streets. Most of it, anyway – it still fucking hurts when a bullet hits you in the face. She hits the ground, rolls, and grabs another weapon from her bag of tricks, spoils of that house on Gethis Row.

A can of withering dust. She twists the handle and throws it down the street, towards the girl-of-flowers. The canister skitters across the ground, hissing and spitting a cloud of lethal dust-grains. The girl falls apart, her body dissolving to thousands of glowing seeds that float on the breeze and drift until they find a place to land and take root. Most of them alight on poisoned earth, too close to the grains of withering dust to survive.

Behind you. Spar's voice. She dodges to the side as Silva charges, flaming sword in hand. The grenade doesn't seem to have sapped her at all. Fuck. Still, for all her god-given strength and speed, she's just an old woman, flailing with a sword she doesn't know how to use.

Back in the farm in Wheldacre, as a child Cari used to infuriate Silva by refusing to submit to punishment. She remembers dodging and climbing and hiding around the farmyard, while Silva stalked her with a wooden spoon.

Now it's knives. And a fuck-off sword.

Cari slashes at her aunt. Her blow skitters off Silva's armour, but she can tell it's not real. It's a miraculous protection. All Cari needs to do is keep dodging, break Silva's concentration, and her aunt won't be able to maintain her connection to the gods. Cari knows as well as anyone how hard it can be to maintain saintly gifts, to find that point where you're lifted out of the mortal realm enough to channel miracles, but stay grounded enough that it's you in control and not the gods.

Incoming. She flings herself to the side as the sniper shoots again. She sees the bullet from a dozen angles. All the windows are her eyes.

He's gone. Strong, callused hands grab the sniper from behind. Someone got him. She was wrong – there are two groups out there. Silva, the flower-saint, the sniper – and a second group.

She doesn't know who her unseen allies are, and the sniper's right on the edge of Spar's perception, but right now that's less important—

—than the big fiery death sword that's coming right for her face.

Carillon rolls to the side. Silva may be a little old lady, but it's like fighting the Fever Knight. Blundering and clumsy, but also fast and terribly strong. She needs to get off this wide street. *Left* is covered in a carpet of withering dust and flowers.

Right is a maze of alleyways.

Left has her bag of alchemical weapons. There's a big pistol in there, the sort they use to put down Gullheads.

Right urges Spar, but she hesitates for an instant, and the sword catches her.

She's not hit. It was a graceless, stumbling swipe, one she can easily avoid, and the blade whistles by her harmlessly. It's the flames surrounding the sword that catch her. Holy fire scorches her, and instinctively, she draws on Spar's miracle, transferring the injury to the New City.

Fire lights the night sky. The skyline is suddenly outlined in flame. Towers become burning torches as the stone bursts into flame.

Spar's voice in her head becomes a bellow of pain.

Shit. It's holy fire. It burns the soul.

Burns the soul. This whole city is Spar's soul, made tangible.

Silva swings again, wildly. Cari ducks again, scoops up the pistol from the top of the bag, but again she's brushed with flame. Again, more buildings become candles. She can't hear the screaming of the people in those towers, but Spar can.

She runs to the right. Silva leaps after her, jumping thirty feet in a single bound. The sword comes down a finger's breadth clear of Cari's head, and again the flames scorch her. This time, she cuts Spar off, rejects that grace.

Takes the fire.

Blinded, her face blistered and scorched, Cari slams headlong into a wall. The wall reshapes as she collides with it, becomes a staircase she dances up blindly, climbing out of Silva's reach. Leaving the street behind, reaching for the rain-gutters. Silva jumps again, scrabbling at the walls like a mad dog, but she can't find purchase.

Cari reaches the rooftop. More flowers are sprouting up here, growing impossibly quickly, their closed heads unnaturally large. She pays them no heed, doesn't have time for their weird shit when there's Silva with a flaming sword down there. She loads the pistol, and the bullet's a year's worth of anger. The pain so bad she can hardly stand, she sways back and forth on the precipice, choking on the smell of her own scorched flesh and burning hair, but she's not missing this shot.

You knew and you could have warned me, she thinks. Silva's a Thay. She knew what her family was doing, knew what they made Carillon for. And when Cari first started hearing the Black Iron Gods in the night, Silva should have known what that meant, too. Cari ran from Guerdon, and should never have come back. Coming back led to the Crisis. *You knew and you deserve this.*

Cari doesn't even need to aim. Even with one eye burned, the side of her face blistered, Cari can see everything down there. Spar shows her what she needs. She sees Silva, sword upraised in challenge. Eladora stumbling out of the shattered doorway.

She fires. Silva staggers under the impact, her miraculous armour flaring with light, then vanishing. Her aura of divinity vanishes. An old woman, stick-thin, in a tattered dress, stands unsteadily on the street below. She drops her sword, unable to bear the weight of it. Blood gushes from her mouth, her nose. She topples to the ground.

For a moment, Carillon senses an immense movement, a dislodgement of forces. Like a mainstay has come loose and is now whipping around the deck. The divine power that Silva channelled is loose. The grace of her sainthood broken. Nothing more than human.

Cari loads the gun again.

Suddenly, one of the flowers swells impossibly, convulses obscenely, birthing a human form. The young girl-saint slithers out of the flower, body slick with nectar or amniotic fluids or some other gunk. She slides out with enough speed to come flying at Cari, punching her in the side. Grabbing for the gun. The girl's nowhere near as strong as Silva, but she's in the first flush of her power. A new-minted saint, drunk on miracles.

Cari lets their combined momentum carry them both off the roof.

They land in a tangle of limbs and bodies – but only one of them has Spar's gift. The impact of falling four storeys is safely shunted to the stone around her, throwing up dust in a circle around the spot where she lands, cracking the pavement.

The flower girl isn't blessed in the same way. Flowers sprout where her blood pools on the sidewalk.

Still, Cari has the wind knocked out of her. She lies there, gasping for air. Without looking, she knows that her knife has fallen from her belt. She reaches out, finds the handle.

A booted foot steps on her hand. The pavement's crushed instead of her fingers, but her hand's trapped.

Silva, clad in armour once more, her sainthood recovered.

The sword catches fire again.

Eladora hides by the door, frozen in fear. She clasps her hand over her mouth as the wind catches the withering dust, but the doorway's sheltered. She watches in horror as her mother's sword burns Cari, and the city catches fire in response.

A touch of holy fire against Cari's skin, and those towers burst into flames. What will happen if Cari's killed by a saint's blade? Will the whole New City burn? She visited half those towers while campaigning, knows how crowded they are. Tens of thousands will die.

Run, she urges Cari, and it's as if her cousin hears her above the carnage. She watches as Cari springs up the side of a building, steps forming and vanishing just in time for her feet to catch them. Cari's out of reach of Silva, who's left raging on the street below. Her mother hacks at the wall in a fury.

If Cari keeps running, then maybe Eladora can talk Silva down. Eladora stands and walks, shaking, towards the avatar of divine wrath that's supposed to be her mother. Overhead, storm clouds have gathered, and Eladora can see shapes in the sky. Mother of Flowers, Saint Storm, Holy Beggar. The gods of Guerdon are abroad tonight.

"Mother—" she begins.

And then Cari pops back into sight, gun in hand. Aiming right at her.

The shot rings out. Eladora dives to the ground, convinced that the bullet is about to strike her. A sudden burst of pain in her chest, but there's no blood. The clouds wheel overhead.

It's like being back in the tomb under Gravehill. The same wrench in her soul, the same terrifying feeling of being exposed to terrible and vast *attentions*.

Saint Storm reaches down. His armoured gauntlet, lightning-clad, bigger than the city. Steel-clad fingers the size of towers. The pain vanishes as the god offers her a sword. Reminds her she already has a sword.

And then she's back on the street. Her mother crumpled on the ground ahead of her. She watches as Silva's fingers scrabble at the ground, as she wipes blood from her mouth, drags herself upright using a walking stick as leverage – and then rises, stronger than the storm. The stick becomes a sword. Her bloodied clothes become shining armour. Her eyes, fire.

Carillon's down, too. Eladora watches in horror as Silva stalks towards her cousin, sword held high. Cari goes for her dropped knife, and Silva steps on her hand. The sword bursts into flame.

Eladora reaches into her own bag. Takes out the hilt that Sinter gave her, the broken remains of Saint Aleena's sword. Aleena saved her in that tomb. Called down the Kept Gods and defeated all the monsters.

She holds the sword and prays.

Her sword, too, becomes fire. She, too, rises. Armour – translucent, frail, hesitant – appears around her. Strength flows in her like waves, dizzying her. One moment, she feels like she could shatter the city with one blow; next, she feels as fragile as glass.

The shapes in the clouds lose their symmetry. They clash and swirl.

She raises her sword. It blazes, and the flames on Silva's sword gutter and die.

Thunder booms overhead. The storm god roars in confusion, unable to tell which vessel is his saint.

"Wicked child," screeches Silva. She tries to stab Carillon, but she lacks the strength to hold her sword, and the blade falls harmlessly to the ground. Cari wrestles her hand free, and it comes up holding the knife.

"NO!" shouts Eladora, and Cari's sent tumbling away across the ground by the force of her cousin's command.

"Ungodly child! Thief!" Silva's weeping now. "Faithless as father!" She shuffles forward, hands outstretched. Eladora recoils, but her mother's not trying to embrace her.

Instead, Silva embraces the flaming sword Eladora holds. "The fires of Safid! Carry my soul!" The crackle of burning flesh. Eladora drops the sword in horror. The flames go out, leaving Silva clutching the cold blade with hands so scorched Eladora can see bone.

Eladora's armour flickers, reappearing around Silva. Her borrowed sainthood returning to the true vessel. The gods vacillating between two choices.

But in that instant of transfer, that brief gap, another shot rings out from across the city. The sniper rifle, again.

Silva sprawls on the ground. Eladora can't tell if her mother's dead or mortally wounded, but her divinity's gone.

Cari struggles to rise, and a second shot catches her in the forehead. The wall behind her cracks asunder, saving her life, but she's knocked unconscious. One side of her face burned, the other now marked by a hideous purple welt that runs from her hairline to the middle of her cheek.

Overhead, the clouds weep; hot summer rain falls across the city.

After leaving Eladora's flat, the spy walks and thinks. The city's afire with rumour – that the new king has brought an army with him, the new king is actually the old king returned from sea, the king was grown in an alchemical tank and it's all a plot by the guilds to regain power. Alic hears snatches of stories about troops from Haith, but he dares not show too much of an interest.

The evening passes into night. The streets grow quiet, and he's left alone with his furious thoughts. Outwardly, he looks calm, but behind the mask of Alic a frustrated storm rages. The stolen documents, the Khebeshi notes – they point to a terrible flaw in his plan.

There is a solution. A cruel one.

Everyone, he realises, has thought of the god bombs in the wrong way. They think of them as bombs – as products of the alchemists' foundries. Machines made for a task. A blind chemical reaction.

But they're gods, and gods demand faith. They demand a sacrifice, proof of devotion. Even the mangled, truncated, ruined Black Iron Gods demand their divine due. He should have seen that long ago.

The spy walks in a great circle, encompassing the Wash, only to end up back at Jaleh's. The house is sleeping now. Emlin's sleeping, his pillow sticky with blood. The boy stirs in his dream, muttering the names of ships at sea. Something he recited for Annah, maybe, or an echo of some other spy's report.

Alic strokes the boy's hair, and Emlin rolls over, reassured.

The boy's so fragile, so defenceless as he sleeps there.

The spy makes Alic reach under the bed for his bag. Underneath the rifle is a priest's robe, still stinking faintly of seaweed and alkahest. He bundles it up.

Alic is conscientious, a hard worker. No one pays any attention as he moves through the house, doing odd jobs. Securing the attic window. Nailing down a loose roof tile. Checking to make sure the back door is locked. But when he's done with that, he keeps working. Cleaning out rooms, scrubbing the kitchen. Stalling.

Live your cover, Alic tells himself.

Emlin comes downstairs, tousle-haired, still half asleep. "I'm thirsty," he says. One of his six wounds has opened again. Alic fetches the boy a cup of water, makes him sit on a stool while Alic smears some of the alchemists' balm on the cut.

"Is there any word from Annah?" asks the boy.

Alic's about to answer honestly, but instead he nods, and whispers: "Yes. She's told us that it's time to leave." It's only half a lie – they should have fled Guerdon immediately after sending the message. Got clear of the cataclysm, instead of waiting here for the coming of the gods. Waiting for the blast. *You can come back*, Alic tells the spy, *let me get Emlin clear, and you can come back.*

"We'll go on one of Dredger's ships again. Maybe go west, to the Archipelago." As far from the Godswar as possible.

"What about your election?" Emlin frowns. Touches the wound on his face, suddenly worried. "Is this because of me? I didn't mean . . . "

"No, no. It's not that. It's – it's orders from Annah. Can't disobey the intelligence corps, right? But she told us to hide, to go quietly. Can you do that?"

Emlin nods. "I'll go and pack."

"Good lad." Emlin hops off the stool and runs upstairs. Moving silently, even on the creaky wooden stairs. Good lad.

We'll leave tonight, he thinks.

But the spy's older than Alic. Colder and cleverer. Alic's just a name, a smile, a stance. A few lines of background, a handful of lies. His whole identity is as fragile as a spider's web – and it's anchored here in Guerdon. Everyone who knows Alic is here. He's a creature of the city.

And without those anchors he's so weak that the the spy can brush him away. Discard a disguise that's no longer needed. He slips out of the kitchen door, locking it behind him. Every step he takes away from Jaleh's makes the spy feel more like himself. It's liberating – but he still needs a mask to wear. It's not yet time for the spy to move openly.

Alic's last job is to move a barrel in the alleyway, rolling the heavy container along until it blocks the old coal chute. No more secret ways out.

Alic is a liability, the spy decides. *Live your cover* is good advice for mortal spies, but he's gone too far. Created a false life, a false name that's become too real. He has to end it.

Walk away. Kill your cover.

Alic can join X84 and Sanhada Baradhin. Dead men without a grave.

So he becomes the priest again, slipping the rough cloth robe over his head, becoming old and tired. No – the priest's bones are old, but they're warmed by the aftermath of the Festival. The king has returned! The Kept Gods are waking from their long slumber! The priest would feel the change. He hurries along the alleyway, breathing heavily.

The priest mutters to himself. Castigates faithless beggars and godless pickpockets as he climbs the twisted stairs of the New City. Wild-eyed, utterly fervent, utterly sure of his righteousness – *live your cover* – he finds a city watch sentry on the Street of Shrines.

I will tell you such a tale, says the priest.

Eladora stands in the rain, the fiery sword in her hands smokes with her mother's blood. Heaven-forged steel armours her; her heart feels like it's a blazing sun, flooding her with infinite light.

Men, armed men, appear out of the gloom. Eladora recognises some of them, faces out of nightmare. They're the ones who attacked her before, on Sevenshell Street. They say nothing, but they surround her, weapons ready, but not daring to come too close to a saint. To her.

Another one approaches, dressed in clerical robes. This priest drags a prisoner with him, a young man, of an age with the flower girl. His other hand holds a long-barrelled rifle. The sniper, Eladora guesses, the one who shot Terevant. The priest drops the boy to the ground, and rests the heavy weapon on his shoulder. Eladora recognises him too, and he knows her.

"Eladora Duttin!" shouts Sinter, and it works like a spell. She feels the gods withdraw from her mind – not completely, but it's enough to ground her. The broken sword hilt is a broken sword hilt. Her clothes stay her long-suffering, travel-stained dress and cloak, not shining armour.

Sinter grins at her, showing broken teeth. "Well, that was a bit fucking touch and go there. Thanks be to the gods that the gamble paid off, though. And what a prize!"

He glances down at Silva's body. "This isn't on me, understand.

This is on them. They fucking brought this on us. The gods. Still, I warned your mother not to cross me. Bloody awkward woman." He shrugs. "Heal her."

"W-w—"

"Heal. Her." One of the other men points a gun at Eladora. "I've seen bloody Aleena do it. If she can, you can. Lingering grace, am I right?"

"I can't."

"She's your fucking mother," says Sinter. "Try. Blessed Mother of Mercies, heal those who come to thee for solace, aye?"

Eladora bends down, next to her mother's body. There's a strange heat in her fingers – and the words of a prayer to the Mother of Mercies come to mind instantly. She recites them, and grace flows through her, honey-sweet and warm. Silva's wound closes.

"Not too much, now." Sinter tries to push Eladora's hand away, but she's too strong for him to do it easily. He has to use both hands to move her arm. "Don't want her waking up and causing a fucking fuss, do we? None of us want that. Look, I'm sorry I had to do this, but what choice did I have?"

"Y-y-you used me." Eladora was already spiritually *wounded*, open to the gods. She'd channelled the Kept Gods before. Sinter took advantage of the connection, used her to confuse the gods. Giving her Saint Aleena's own sword, bringing her close to her mother – and Eladora looking more like Silva every day. Enough to fool the Kept Gods. *They're so fucking beautiful, it breaks my heart*, Aleena told her once, *and so fucking stupid, I want to smash them.*

Unable to distinguish between Eladora and Silva, the gods split their gift of sainthood between the two – weakening Silva enough for Sinter to bring her down.

"Aye. Can't have a rabid dog on the streets. Can't have a mad-woman riling up the gods. But I swear to you she'll be spared," says Sinter. He raises his voice. "How are the others?"

Sinter's men have spread out across the street. One by Cari. "Still alive."

One by the flower-saint. "Here, too. Barely."

"All right, do her, too," orders Sinter. They bring the broken form of the flower-saint over, lie her down next to Silva's unconscious body. It's harder for Eladora to summon the power this time, but she manages it. The flower girl gasps for aid, then turns over and vomits a mix of bile, blood and petals. She stares in terror at the unfamiliar faces surrounding her.

Sinter drags the boy over, dumps him next to the girl. She reaches for him, but Sinter's boot blocks her.

"Fucking Safidist idiots. First whiff of sainthood and they think they're the fucking chosen ones." He slaps the boy away. "Right, you little Safidist idiot. You work for me, now? Not her!" He gestures at Silva's unconscious body. "For me! For the true Church. Understand?"

The boy shakes his head. Mouths the words "false priest" through bloodied lips.

Sinter gestures. One of Sinter's men draws a dagger across the boy's throat. Blood, again, in a terrible red gush. Eladora reaches forward, her fingers burning with healing magic, but the killer has a gun in his hand and clucks his tongue. She recognises him from Sevenshell Street. Sinter's men planted Vanth's body, she thinks. She wants to tell Terevant, but he's bleeding to death a few feet away in the house behind her.

Sinter kneels down next to the girl, grabs her head with his hands, forces her to look as the boy dies. "Now, child, you work for me, now, see? You're *their* saint, but you work for *me*. Fucking swear it, by the Mother."

She nods, helplessly. Eladora wonders if she's about to be forced to make the same oath.

"I swear by the Mother," says the flower-saint, and Sinter grins with his broken teeth.

"Sweet child," he says, kissing her on the forehead. "Pray for me. Pray for him, too."

Eladora stares sullenly at the priest. "I should heal Carillon, too." She can feel the connection to the Kept Gods slipping away. She could fight to keep it and the power it brings, but she remembers her mother's madness. That's what lies at the end of that path.

"Heal Carillon?" echoes Sinter. "Fuck no."

"Kill her?" suggests the gunman.

Sinter stands, looks at the towers burning in the distance. "Last time I tried that, it cost me two fingers, and that was before she was proper sainted. No, let's keep her alive until we know how to safely dispose of her." He raises his voice, addressing his men. "All right. This one—" nudging Cari with his foot, "to Hark. Have her put in the deep cells, mind you. With the special prisoners." He nods at the flower-saint. "Bring our new little sister to the House of Saints, and keep her there. Proper rites and offerings. Dump that dead one in the sea, weight 'im with stones. And Mrs Duttin goes back in her box, aright?" He takes out a little vial of what looks like smelling salts, uncorks it, and tucks it into the bloodied remains of Silva's clothing. Silva stirs but doesn't wake. He does the same with Carillon.

"A friend of mine's been shot. He's inside," says Eladora. "May I go to him, please?"

Sinter rises, circles around. He glances inside the half-house and laughs. "My! We've found the runaway, too!"

Two more of Sinter's men hurry over, pick Terevant up.

"What do we do with him, boss? Bring him back to the embassy?"

Sinter considers. "Nah. Fuck that turd Lemuel. Bring him to the palace, let Lyssada Erevesic have him. Call him a consolation prize."

"The Erevesic sword isn't here," observes one of them.

"I have had enough of swords," says Sinter, kicking away what remains of Silva's weapon. "They always leave a fucking mess."

They carry Terevant past Eladora. He's alive, but very pale and shivering. Blood drips on the ground. "Heal him, too," orders Sinter.

She complies. What else can she do? She could try to call down armour from heaven, to beg a blessing from Saint Storm, but one mistake would end her, and she feels hollow. Defeated. She pushes her fingers into the bloody well of the wound, feels the hard shape of the bullet, and concentrates. The power flows more slowly this time, reluctantly, but it still works. Heat rushes from her, and his flesh spasms, pushing back against her. Forcing her fingers back out, the bullet and all its little shards with it. The wound closes, leaving an ugly red scar like a brand.

She takes the handkerchief that Sinter offers her, wipes an ocean of blood from her hand. She feels faint, and shivery.

They carry Terevant away into the night. The armed men vanish in twos and threes. Silva's taken away. The flower-saint is wrapped in a robe of samite cloth and carried reverently down the street by men who look like mercenaries, but sing like choristers. Cari, in chains, is brought down a different road to the sea.

Until it's just Eladora, and Sinter, and the man with the gun.

She wants to be as brave as Cari. To find that strength she felt earlier. But that gun doesn't waver.

Sinter picks up Cari's knife, tests its balance. "And what are we to do with you, Ms Duttin? That boy was unreasonable, and I had to end him. Your mother wouldn't listen, and I had to use you to counter her, divert the gods' blessing into a more . . . reasonable vessel. I take no pleasure in this work. I'm just trying to do the best for my city. Same as you, I think." He sighs. "Are you going to be awkward, too?"

"I-I—"

"If you stammer I will end you."

Eladora swallows. "You still need Kelkin. You need Kelkin more than ever – if the church wins the election, who's going to run the city? You? A puppet from Haith?"

"Need is a dangerous word, but . . . aye, a steady hand and familiar face would make what's to come *easier*," says Sinter. "Can you get him?"

She looks him in the eye and lies. "Yes."

"Good girl. Give me the sword."

He takes Aleena's hilt back from her. Wipes it off, kisses it, puts it away inside his robe. "Back to the House of Saints with this, too." Sinter appraises Eladora. "I don't think you'll end up there. Not if you're sensible."

Sinter stoops and plucks a few flowers that sprout, miraculously, from a pool of blood. Their stems have intertwined, making them grow in a ring. A crown.

"The blessings of the Festival on you, child. Rejoice. It's going to be a good harvest."

And then he's gone, leaving her alone in the rain as the towers blaze in the distance.

Chapter 35

That night, as the spy walks back along the docks to the House of Jaleh, the sky's on fire. The New City's burning.

Are they here at last? thinks the spy. Crowds gather, looking up at the blazing towers, but the spy alone rushes to the railing, looks out across the dark water. No – Queen's Point is unchanged. There's no corresponding flurry of activity there, no rush to battle stations. The city's not under attack – at least, not by some external invader. His sacrifice isn't too late.

Alic would go up there. Alic would want to help. And it's better that the priest vanish again, he's given the watch all they need to know. He removes the priest's robe, throws it into the sea.

He puts on the Alic identity like a mask, but it now feels stretched and ill fitting. His movements awkward, the cadence of his speech is off. Still, at night, no one will notice.

As Alic, the spy hurries up to the fires, running along the same streets that the priest limped along. Becomes part of a stream of citizens who rush towards the flames. Alchemical wagons push through the crowd, carrying tanks of fire-quenching foam. The spy clambers aboard one of the tanks, helps direct operations. Rallying the people. He plunges into one burning building after another, pulling victims from the fire. Vanishing into the smoke again and again. He's heedless of the danger to his own life, onlookers whisper admiringly.

He works through the night. Later, they'll say that it was Alic's leadership that saved hundreds of people, that without him the disaster would have been much worse. That he fought to save the New City.

Towards dawn, it seems to snow. He stops, wondering if this is a miracle.

Then he touches one of the flakes, and it crumbles rather than melts. It's ash, falling from a thousand burning election posters.

Silkpurse finds the spy among the soot-streaked crowds. She comes rushing up to meet him, bounding on all fours. Breathless with alarm.

"Alic! The watch!" she yowls, gasping for air amid the lingering smoke. "Someone talked. Jaleh. Harbouring dangerous saints."

Alic wouldn't hesitate. Alic doesn't know what's happening, but he trusts his friend, so he would break into a run. He'd sprint downhill, through the narrow streets, towards the House of Jaleh. So, the spy does likewise, even though acting as Alic doesn't come as naturally as it did before. He can't bring himself to run headlong – it would spoil everything if he actually *rescued* the boy in time. No, he runs just slowly enough to miss the nick of time.

The House of Jaleh crawls with ghouls. Like a stone turned over, revealing the worms beneath. The ghouls scurry out of doors and windows, sniff the ground, jabber to one another. As the sun rises over the city, they whimper and cower, retreating to the shadows. They stink of the underworld. They're not young surface ghouls like Silkpurse; they're middle-ghouls, they haven't seen daylight in decades. But they're here now. City watch, too, soldiers with guns, lending a legal imprimatur to the whole affair.

Jaleh's in the courtyard, arguing with a huge horned ghoul. An elder, much larger, much older, much stronger than its kin. The spy guesses that's Lord Rat. It's a one-sided argument. Not only does the ghoul reply by speaking through Jaleh, but his responses are monosyllabic. Whatever her concerns are, it dismisses them with a shrug.

Even from a distance, he can sense the terrible power of the creature. It has senses far beyond those of any mortal. Those yellow eyes see things that should be invisible.

"Alic, you've got to talk to him! I can't make him listen!" urges Silkpurse.

The elder ghoul stirs. Heaves its massive bulk past Jaleh, extending its long hoofed legs. Stepping out of the little garden in front of the house in a single stride, turning down the street away from them.

"WHO IS THIS ONE?" says Silkpurse, but it's not her voice coming out of her mouth. Her eyes narrow. She studies the spy for a long moment.

Deflect, he thinks. "I'm a candidate for the Industrial Liberals in this ward," he declares. Finds a soot-stained leaflet in his pocket, shoves it in Silkpurse's face, so whatever's looking through her eyes can see the stippled picture. "I demand to know what you're doing to my constituents."

—and then that terrible attention withdraws, and Silkpurse is herself again.

The elder ghoul laughs. It leaps onto a rooftop and vanishes into a thicket of chimneys.

"Alic, you have to go to Mr Kelkin! You're Industrial Liberal now, they'll listen to you." Silkpurse flaps her hands in panic, her claws ripping through her lace gloves.

Jaleh staggers up, pale and shaken. Her dragon-scaled hand is bleeding from a wound. "They took half the house. Arrested all my flock. The ghouls and city watch. All my sainted ones."

"Emlin?"

"He . . . they could smell him. They broke into your room. He tried to run, to get out through the cellars, but they caught him. They took him."

"Where?"

"The docks. They're taking them to Hark Island."

The detention camp for saints. The spy rejoices – the sacrifice has been accepted! The machine is in motion! The web of fate is inescapable now.

The spy's triumph is certain.

But in that moment of triumph, he's distracted.

It's Alic who speaks. Alic whose stomach lurches, whose heart is frozen with panic and fear. Alic who thinks quicker, acts quicker than the spy.

Alic who grabs Silkpurse by the shoulders. "Arrest me!"

"What?"

"I've made a mistake! Tell them you smell sainthood! Tell them anything! Get me on that boat, quick! Arrest me!"

The boat of saints casts off from the docks, under the eyes of ghouls and the guns of the city watch. It is not the only boat to make the crossing to Hark Island this morning. The white wakes of a dozen more criss-cross the waters of the harbour.

Alic's seated by the rail, watched over by more ghouls. The saints huddle in the middle of the deck. Some pray to gods too far away to listen. Others pray to gods that do not care. Alic can see the hunched shape of Emlin a few feet away, but they've put a cowl over his head, and restrained his hands with bonds of some rubbery alchemical slime. Alic raises his voice when demanding that one of the guards give him a blanket against the early morning chill, so the boy knows he's there.

The spy has retreated. He's fled far inside Alic, hiding in some dark crack in his mind. For now, he watches and waits. For now, the spy's cover is alive, the mask moving of its own accord.

Driven by its hissing alchemical engine, the boat races across the harbour, threading its way past sandbars, past huge freighters, past barques and schooners, their sails furled as they wait for a tug. Off there is the Isle of Statues; on their left hand is the poisonous wasteland of Shrike.

Ahead, lonely amid open water, is Hark Island.

The boat has to circle the island to get to the landing jetty. Sheer cliffs of some grey stone, atop them the white walls of the old fortress. The spy can see other structures there, too, newer ones. Thin metal pillars – floodlights, maybe, or watchtowers. The roofs of new buildings within the walls. Small pillboxes, warded against hostile magic, and their guns pointing *inland*, towards the prison.

And *there* is the little tooth of stone the spy saw months ago, from the deck of Dredger's ship. A rocky pillar, rising from the sea, four hundred yards or so offshore. There's some sort of machinery there now, connected to the main island by thick pipes and weed-draped cables. Parts of it look brand new; technicians in the robes of the alchemists' guild scramble amid the rocks like crabs. They don't look up from their work as the boat passes.

The boat of saints lands at a little jetty, and its unwilling passengers disembark. Alic tries to stick close to Emlin, but the guards separate them, arranging the prisoners into a double file, like they're children on a school tour. Emlin's shivering, but he doesn't struggle or stumble as they march him blindly up the jetty. He and the spy discussed, over and over, what do to in the event the city watch came for them. Escape, if you can. Endure, if you must. The boy's getting ready to endure.

The ghouls stay on the boat, eyes gleaming hungrily as they huddle in the shade. There's a cart waiting on the jetty, and two of the guards stay to unload it, throwing its contents to the ghouls. Whatever it is lands on the deck with a wet thump, and the ghouls scrabble for it hungrily, taking their grisly payment in the meat of saints.

The spy may have condemned Emlin to the same fate. As they march up the jetty, along the narrow switchback path to the fortress gates, Alic swears a silent oath to himself, and to the boy. *I'll get you out of this.*

As they pass through the gates, the guards unholster gas masks and strap them on, but do not afford the same courtesy to the prisoners. They enter into what was once a wide internal courtyard, but is now the strangest prison Alic's has ever seen. A three-quarters circle of cells, fronted with prison bars.

Less than half the cells are occupied, and the prisoners are arranged seemingly at random. The northern end of the arc is almost completely unoccupied, while the southern portion is triple-occupancy in some cells. A circular guard tower with many mirrored windows stands at the centre of the yard, watching the open-faced cells. It flashes with blinding light as the sun rises over the lip of the fort.

Spindly metal structures with bulbous heads, like skeletal watch-towers, dot the yard. They pass near one, and Alic suddenly realises why the guards wear masks. There's some sort of mist-sprayer up there, hissing a thin stream of vapour into the yard. The spy's thoughts suddenly feel leaden. A sedative drug, he guesses, something to block the concentration needed to wield miracles or sorcery. Fatigue settles on him more thickly than the soot from last night's fires.

The guards bring them past that mirrored tower to a cluster of low-roofed temporary structures. Processing. A clerk – his mous-tache poking around the edges of his gas mask – examines each newly arrived saint, fills out some forms and assigns them a cell number. Some prisoners don't seem to fit whatever classification system the clerk's using, so they're sent to a holding area. False pos-itives perhaps. The ghouls don't always catch the right scent.

There's no sign of the elder ghoul. No ghouls at all. No, this place seems entirely clinical, born out of the designs of alchemists and architects. Alic relaxes, very slightly. They'll follow a protocol, obey a bureaucratic checklist. They'll be predictable cogs in a great machine. The spy's good at manipulating machines. That ghoul scared him, but these are just mortals.

Emlin is ahead of him in the queue. He's assigned a cell next to another prisoner from Jaleh's house – the old woman with the clay icons of Kraken. The clerk orders the guards to take especial care of Emlin, and they escort him out of the room like an honour guard.

It's Alic's turn now.

"What god?"

"None."

There's some confusion and delay – they don't have entry papers for him. On the far side of the island, there's a inspection station where immigrants to Guerdon are processed, but he avoided going through it when he first arrived. He's far from alone in that. And when he points out that he's an Industrial Liberal candidate, it adds further confusion to the whole affair. The little of the moustache he can see droops nervously.

"I need to talk to my son," he insists.

"Not now."

After a while, they take him away through a different door, and lead him back across the courtyard, giving him another look at the strange arrangement of the new part of the prison. He watches them lock Emlin in his cell, and the Kraken-worshipper next to him.

Suddenly the strange prison makes sense. The cells are arranged as a compass. They've arranged saints in their cells by direction from Guerdon. No saints due north, because the goddess of Grena is dead and Haith has no saints. Only a few to the north-east, because of the Haithi god-suppression in Varinth. A few to the east; not many people have fled Lyrix for Guerdon yet, and so there are few saints from that land. The southern part of the arc, though, is crowded. Saints from Ishmere, from Severast, from Mattaur. All blessed by the same fratricidal, bloodthirsty pantheon.

When the gods draw near, their saints grow in power.

It's not just a prison. It's a weatherglass.

A machine for detecting the movements of the divine.

The old part of the prison around the central courtyard was once a fort, and that's where they bring the spy. Thick stone walls. Narrow windows, like arrow-slits. A sigil above the door has been chiselled away; he wonders what god's symbol or king's mark once lay there. Inside, it's chilly and half derelict. They pass storerooms of supplies, boxes of machine parts, spare rubber tubes coiled like entrails, canisters of whatever soul-sapping gas pervades the whole prison. Only the rooms on the inner side of the corridor are in use; those across the hall, facing the sea, are too damp. Greenish-black colonies of mould sprout around the frames of broken doors.

The guards usher him downstairs, into an older sort of prison. No open cells, no mirrored tower. A dungeon for prisoners, a row of cages. They've installed aetheric lamps in the niches where torches once burned, but for the most part these cells haven't changed in centuries. The hiss of soporific gas from a tube running along the ceiling of the corridor, out of reach of the prisoners in their cells. Little brass mouths breathe jets of gas into each cell.

"You'll need to wait here until we refer your case to the main-land," says one of the masked guards. He sounds apologetic. "The rest of the island's not safe. I'll bring down some blankets and some-thing to eat." He nods towards the other occupied cells. Two other prisoners, one unconscious, and one awake. "Don't talk to them. Pay them no heed."

They lock the spy in a cell. It's cramped and cold, but not as bad as some he's been in.

When the guards depart, he surveys his new domain. A small cot. A pot to piss in. A tiny window, high up on the inner wall. If he stands on the cot and reaches up, he can almost see out of it, get a look at the courtyard. The bars of the cell are old but sturdy; some have been replaced or remortared recently, so he doubts there's any way to escape. The lock, similarly, looks solid and hard to open without a key.

He presses his head to the bars and tries to see the other cells along the corridor. The one at the end of the corridor is occupied. The prisoner there is a young woman, unconscious, lying on the bed. Her face is bandaged and smeared with healing unguents.

From this angle, the spy can't see much of the other prisoner. Just a pair of long-fingered hands, resting on the bars. Filthy and very pale – this man hasn't seen the sun in a long time.

"Hey, you there?" says the spy. "Who are you?"

The other prisoner's voice is very soft. "I knew she'd come back to me, before the end."

"Who? Her? You know her?"

"She's Carillon." The prisoner's hands suddenly clench, viciously, like he's wringing someone's neck, then relax. He presses his face to the bars, too, so the spy can see a little of his features. A young-ish man, terribly thin, stringy hair falling over a knife-like face, a bushy beard.

"Call me Alic. What's your name?"

"Do you know what time it is? Will the bells ring soon?" asks the other prisoner.

The spy's always had a talent for keeping track of time. It's nearly six. Across the harbour, the city's church bells will be ringing. "Six o'clock, or thereabouts."

The other prisoner withdraws. The spy can hear him taking shallow breaths, faster and faster, like a bull about to—

He flings himself full force against the bars, throwing his whole body against them. Gasping as the impact knocks the air from his lungs. His pale skin scraped and bloodied by the impact. The prisoner falls heavily to the ground, lies there a moment, then stands back up and resumes lounging against the bars as though nothing has happened, as though he didn't just try to smash through his cell by sheer brute strength.

A thin smile, a wave of greeting. "I'm Miren."

INTERLUDE II

Even at this early hour the heat from the summer sun is enough to crack the stones. Rasce swears as he hurries across the courtyard of the villa, cursing the weight of the leather armour and protective gear he has to wear. It'll get worse once he puts on the breathing mask and helmet, so he leaves those off as long as he can. Without the mask, he can smell his Great-Uncle, who's sunning himself by a statue of Rasce's great-great-and-a-few-more-greats-grandmother. Great-Uncle stretches his neck lazily, spreads his wings so wide that the whole villa is plunged briefly into blessed shadow.

"It seems such a waste of a nice day, no?" says Great-Uncle. This close, Rasce can hear the dragon's voice through his feet, his spine.

"Punishment for your sins, Great-Uncle," says Rasce. A little impolite, but they're about to fly into battle together. Informality can be indulged, today.

His Great-Uncle chuckles. "Is that what this is? About time, I suppose." He coughs, scorching the already blackened stones. "A nice day for ending the world."

Rasce clambers up into the battle howdah, straps himself in. The howdah's more cramped than usual. The space normally reserved for treasures liberated from passing merchant ships is now crammed with alchemical weapons. He checks that the rip-lines for the sacks of acid seeds are clear of any tangles, then secures them where he can reach them in a hurry.

"Ready?"

The dragon chuckles again, then canters across the yard, heading for the cliff's edge. Servants scurry out of the way, hurrying for the shelter of the villa. Rasce glimpses, for an instant, the faces of two of his cousins, watching jealously from a balcony. Artolo's children. Great-Uncle picked Rasce for this flight, not them, so to hell with them. Their newly fingerless father's been sent off to count coins in some backroom. Rasce makes the sign of the fig as Great-Uncle spreads his wings and they plunge, then soar on the thermals rising from the hot beach.

The dragon banks over the little island, then turns his head south. Rasce glances back at the other isles of the Ghierdana along the coast of Lyrix. There are other dragons aloft this morning, circling on thermals over their villas. It's a clear morning – he can see the coastal villages, bristling with razor-edged church spires. He can feel the loathing of the gods of Lyrix. The Godswar may have forced a truce between those deities and their wayward creations, but they still hate the dragons and their adopted families.

Great-Uncle also senses it, and laughs. Either Lyrix survives the war, and the dragon families of the Ghierdana return to being pirates, or Lyrix falls, and the Ghierdana get to watch their former masters being destroyed by the mad gods of Ishmere. No matter what, the Ghierdana will get the last laugh.

They race south. Rasce consults the compass, tries to hold onto the chart in the rushing wind. "Down!" he shouts, thumping Great-Uncle's scaly neck for emphasis. The dragon descends. The sea below is stained a virulent green, and steam rises from it. A line of floating acid seeds, each one slowly dissolving in the water, turning the sea to poison. A wall of acidic death.

In places, the wall's been breached.

He checks his breathing mask, checks the seal on his goggles. Those fumes could blind him if he's careless.

As Great-Uncle flies over the acidic scar, Rasce releases seeds to fill the gaps. The cabbage-sized weapons tumble down to splash in the sea below. They don't have enough to plug all the breaches.

"Done!"

Great-Uncle flaps his wings, struggling to rise. The undersides of his membranous wings are now raw, burned by the fumes. They were too low. Rasce can feel tremors run through the dragon's body each time with each painful wingbeat. When they're back in the villa, his sisters will rub soothing ointments into Great-Uncle's wings.

Then the dragon banks hard, turns back south. Crosses the line of acid again.

"What is it?" Rasce ties the rip-lines back in place, unholsters his rifle.

Great-Uncle doesn't answer. He just keeps flying south, over empty ocean. Rasce checks the clouds ahead through his scope, looking for Ishmeric saints. Scans the waters. Looks for ships on the surface, or monsters moving in the deeps.

Going further south than they've dared fly in weeks.

Empty ocean. Empty as far as his scope can see.

Nothing.

No invasion force. No ravening fleet of mad gods and warrior-saints.

No end of the world today.

At least, not here.

CHAPTER 36

Eladora spends the rest of the night in a shelter in the New City, a common room in a cellar run by an old man named Cafstan. It's too dangerous to go home, she tells herself, with parts of the New City ablaze. Too dangerous for whom, though? She can still sense the terrible attention of the Kept Gods lingering upon her. She feels like she's been soaked in phlogiston, that a single spark might turn her into a pillar of fire.

Cafstan mumbles at her, tells her she'll be safe here, and that he doesn't ask questions of those who stay under his roof. She lies on a narrow cot, restless, listening to the city outside the window. Distant bells, shouting, the aftermath of the fires. The other beds are taken by those fleeing the fire. The room smells of soot and tears. She gives up her bed, finds a place on the floor instead.

Some of them are wounded. She wants to help, but fears that if she tries to treat those wounds she'll open some door within her that she cannot close. The sweet warmth of a healing miracle and the all-consuming fire of a blazing sword come from the same divine source.

She sleeps fitfully, in dream-filled bursts. Some of the dreams are familiar ones – the tomb under the hill, her grandfather's worm-fingers brushing against her skin. Then Jervas becomes Miren, young and handsome, but his hands are knives that slice into her and spill her blood. Impaled on him, she can't escape as he steps backwards over a cliff and they both plunge into darkness.

Other dreams are strange, and she doesn't think they're meant for her. Some are, she guesses, her mother's dreams. Full of brightness, like the sun seen through a cracked crystal. Full of pain, so she wakes up in agony, red welts on her breast where her mother was shot.

She dreams, distantly, of the Kept Gods. Of giants walking across the city, moving away from her.

During the night she wakes to see Cafstan sitting on a stool across the room. His scarred hands glow with a miraculous light, as though he's holding an invisible lantern. The old man cries and laughs quietly, and speaks to the light like it's a lost child.

The Holy Beggar bears a lantern. The holy light of revealed truth.

Cafstan's an unwitting saint, she guesses. One of many created by the proximity of the Kept Gods this night. She contemplates rising from her little nest of blankets and offering the man what counsel she could. How to channel and control this miraculous talent, or, better yet, how to reject it. The connection between man and god is new-made and fragile. It could still be severed, if he acted in ways displeasing to the god. She tries to bring to mind the Beggar's ancient forbiddances – scorning the dead, thievery, malice – but the thought of speaking to Cafstan while he's in the grip of sainthood scares her. There's the old man across the room, chuckling as he conjures light from his fingers, and there's the god, trying to find a foothold in the mortal world.

What would Cafstan do if he knew she'd struck down a saint of the Kept Gods earlier that night? Her own mother!

And more to the point, what would the Holy Beggar do?

The crown of flowers that Sinter gave her is still in her satchel. When Cafstan's not looking, she takes it out and dismembers it, scattering the petals and shoving the remains under a bed. The touch of the Kept Gods may feel warm and loving, but it's no different from the worm-fingers of her dead grandfather ripping a hole in her soul. *I am Eladora Duttin*, she shouts to herself, *I am not to be used*.

The next morning, she leaves Cafstan snoring, his head resting on a table. She empties her purse, keeping only enough coin to get home. Then reconsiders – is giving the man *alms* part of the Beggar's bargain? Will that ritual act deepen his connection to the god?

And who is she to decide, anyway? She scoops up the coins, stacks them neatly, and leaves a note, making it clear that it's payment for a night's accommodation, not a gift.

She doesn't even know if the gods can read.

She's home for maybe a minute before she hears a scratching at the door. Silkpurse. Sighing, Eladora undoes the locks and wards, lets the ghoul scramble inside. Silkpurse looks wilder than Eladora's seen her before. The ghoul sniffs the air; yellow eyes narrow.

"You, too? I can smell the odour of sanctity."

"My mother——" Eladora begins to explain, but Silkpurse shakes her head, waves her claws to cut her off. "Miss Duttin, it's all going wrong! You've got to talk to Kelkin! He's sent us out to find saints. All the ghouls! And young Emlin is sainted, and they've sent him to Hark, and Alic, he made me send him, too!"

In fragments, Eladora pieces together the account of last night and early this morning. Ghoul raids across the city, leading the watch to suspected saints of other gods. Most are taken to the prison on Hark Island – *like Carillon*, she thinks, suddenly remembering what Sinter ordered.

Silkpurse is right – she has to talk to Kelkin. Wearily, Eladora strips off her bloodied dress and puts on clean clothes.

From her bedroom window, she can see the shining Victory Cathedrals atop Holyhill, with the Palace of the Patros hidden behind them, and when she looks up towards those temples of the Kept Gods she feels a sudden burst of unwanted strength. Columns of thick smoke still rise from the courtyards, and she guesses those plazas in front of the cathedrals are filled with newly fervent worshippers.

Eladora checks the Vulcan coffee shop as she passes, but it's clear that Kelkin's not there. There's a clerk stationed at Kelkin's table at the back of the shop – the table is technically free for any patron to use, but it's been Kelkin's for so many years that no one else would dare use it without his permission. Not even the clerk who sits there tonight would dream of touching any of the mess of papers and empty cups that litter the desk. Kelkin knows where every scrap of paper and crumpet crumb is on that table, and woe betide anyone who interferes with his system.

She marches up Mercy Street, climbing the steep hill towards parliament. A newspaper cryer shouts something about invasion by Haith – the newspapers have been muttering about Haithi threats for years, and there's a panic every few months. She grabs a copy anyway.

Parliament's crowded. Military officers, so many it gives the impression of an armed camp. So much, she thinks, for the post-Festival election push.

She's ushered into a waiting room outside Kelkin's office. There aren't any seats left. Some she recognises; other election agents, a few sitting members of parliament. A delegation from the alchemists' guild. Priests from various churches, none of them Keepers.

The man next to her – an alchemist – spots the newspaper under Eladora's arm. "Do you mind if I borrow that?"

Eladora unfolds it, glances at the front page. The Haithi are demanding the return of "one of their embassy staff", who's rumoured to have "sought sanctuary in Guerdon". There's no stated connection to the murder of the ambassador, but the implication is clear. Nothing Eladora doesn't already know, so she hands the paper over.

"Thank you," says the alchemist.

And then, his voice low but anguished, "YOU SAW CARILLON?"

Eladora looks over. The alchemist's face is frozen in terror, his body paralysed. His eyes full of sudden panic, with a yellowish light deep in the pupils.

Eladora keeps her voice equally low. "Lord Rat, if you want to talk to me, show yourself."

"BUSY." A pause. "DOES SHE LIVE?"

"Yes." Eladora hesitates for a moment. "Sinter captured her. I think they intend to bring her to Hark."

"THE FIRES – SHE WAS HURT. BY SINTER?"

"By my m-mother."

"URRHHHR." A horrible approximation of a laugh, and then the alchemist inhales, his whole body contorting. Several people in the waiting room look over at him in surprise. Rat makes him cough as if trying to cover up his odd behaviour, but it's a horribly stilted act. "YOU STINK OF SAINTHOOD. OPEN WOUNDS OFTEN BECOME INFECTED." For a brief instant, the alchemist is freed from Rat's control, falling forward like he's just been dropped, as Rat's attention shifts elsewhere across the city. Then he's back.

"THE KEPT GODS. FEH." She can hear the ghoul's disgust and suspicion, even at this distance. The light fades from the alchemist's eyes.

"Wait!" The light glimmers again. "I don't owe them any a-a-allegiance. I'm no Safidist. And you'd have died, too, in my grandfather's tomb, if it wasn't for Saint Aleena."

The alchemist snorts like a horse, spewing gobbets of snot across his perfect suit. "I HAVE NEED OF CARILLON. THERE IS FOLLY AFOOT. MEN OF HAITH, MEDDLING IN THE DEEPS. I NEED HER TO HOLD SHUT THE TOMBS. MAKE THE UNDERCITY SAFE FOR ME AND MINE. THE LYING PRIEST HAS HIDDEN HER ON HARK. TELL NO ONE ELSE, BUT FETCH HER FOR ME, AND WE SHALL BE SUCH GOOD FRIENDS."

And he falls again, released. An instant later, a door across the waiting room opens and one of Kelkin's secretaries enters.

"ELADORA DUTTIN?" she calls. Her eyes stare ahead, unseeing. Her body's held rigid, and her voice is weirdly guttural. Rat hasn't gone far.

Eladora brushes past the possessed secretary and enters the sanctum.

There's a miserable looking aethergraph operator from the city watch sitting by the edge of Kelkin's desk, his fingers poised over the brass keys of his instrument. Around him, the office is crowded with senior IndLib figures and navy commanders. A map of the seas around Guerdon, marked with sightings of enemy ships and readings from arcane gauges.

She instantly senses the tension, the barely controlled terror in the room. This is not a drill, not an abstract discussion of possible future threats.

This is the moment before the storm breaks on the shore.

Before the Godswar comes to Guerdon.

Eladora fights back the stab of existential terror that comes with that thought, the feeling of falling into an unthinkable abyss, when invisible powers and crazed fanatics carve up reality with butcher miracles. There's also a brief, unexpected and unworthy sense of relief – she's lived with that feeling of terror for almost a year, ever since the Crisis, ever since meeting her grandfather in the tomb. Now the rest of the city will catch up with her, have their souls blighted, too, by the same nightmare. She won't have to bear the burden alone.

As Eladora enters the room, slipping in through the door quietly, Admiral Vermeil thunders at Kelkin. "Parliament is absolutely not secure! The building's a thousand years old. We can't secure it. We need to relocate to Queen's Point immediately."

Kelkin's deputy Ogilvy objects. "Minister Droupe monitored the Crisis from here just last year, and *that* was a far more immediate threat to the city than this one."

"Droupe wasn't in charge of picking his own nose," snaps Kelkin. "I'm not Droupe, understand? I'm in charge, and I'm not leaving here. You've brought up this jabbering thing," gesturing at the aethergraph, "and you're all here, so let's get on with it."

Vermeil sighs. "The monitors at Hark are still calibrating the new intake. But we have signs of hostile divine intervention here in Guerdon already. We arrested a hostile saint, on a tip-off from a Keeper priest."

"Which god?" asks Kelkin.

"The Ishmeric deity of secrets. Fate Spider. We'd expect the Spider to move ahead of the main invasion force, gathering intelligence and relaying information from spies in place in the city."

"So the god's already here, you think? Just not manifest?" Kelkin spots Eladora at the back of the room, beckons her forward. She approaches nervously, feeling exposed.

"Its influence is wide-ranging," argues Vermeil. "At the very least, it's connected to the shrine in the Ishmere embassy — they use the god's webs to send secure messages."

"But this Fate Spider isn't a war-god, or am I mistaken? Rame — ah, blast it. She's not here." Kelkin frowns, points at another woman in the room, a watch officer Eladora doesn't recognise. "You. It's not a war-god, is it?"

"The whole pantheon is belligerent, but we have no reports of Fate Spider taking the lead in any assault," answers the officer. "That's more likely to be Kraken or Lion Queen."

Vermeil shakes his head. "We've already had reports of krakens in the water. They're coming."

The Godswar. The terror threatens to overwhelm her again. She looks at the faces assembled in the room, the soldiers and generals and sorcerers bent over their instruments, tells herself they're ready for any catastrophe. *This is why the alchemists make monsters*, she thinks. Of all the cities in the world, Guerdon is supposed to be the safest.

And if the war comes here, what can she do?

The aethergraph suddenly chatters, making Eladora jump. The jar of greenish-yellow fluid at its core crackles, and lights flare in the murky depths. The keys start moving of their own accord. The operator presses his hands to the machine's controls, silently mouths words as he tries to assemble the message. The room falls silent as everyone waits for him to decode the update.

Eladora uses the momentary lull to cross to Kelkin's side.

"You shouldn't be in here," says Kelkin mildly.

"What's happening?" She gestures at the aethergraph.

"Nothing. For now. For the next few hours, maybe. What do you want, Duttin?"

"I-I—" she swallows, "they've arrested at least one of our election candidates, along with lots of innocent people — victims of the war, not saints or worshippers. And——" She was about to say *and Carillon*, but she remembers Rat's warning. She doesn't know why Rat wants her to conceal Cari's presence in the Hark internment camp, but she's not going to cross the ghoul unless she has to. "And my m-mother was attacked. By Sinter."

"Are you hurt?"

She shakes her head.

"Is your mother?"

"Yes. I-I'm not sure how badly. They took her to Holyhill, after."

"Sinter's consolidating power, all right," mutters Kelkin, his voice low. "I want to talk to you about this, soon as I'm done here."

"I need to go to Hark," says Eladora, "and get our people out of the camp."

"No. Gods below, no. Give me a list of names, and I'll see what can be done, but I have much bigger matters to deal with now, Duttin. Go home. Wait, no. Stay here in parliament. In case . . . well, the shelters here are deeper."

Ogilvy hurries over, holding a note scribbled by the aethergraph operator. "This just came in from the Patros. They've got the one who killed the ambassador."

"The fucking Keepers have him?" marvels Kelkin. "What, did the idiot go and look for sanctuary or something?"

"He was with me when my m-mother attacked us. When Sinter ambushed her," interrupts Eladora.

Kelkin actually gives her his full attention for the first time since she entered. "You and I are going to have a long fucking talk after all this is done." He shakes his head in disbelief, then looks to Ogilvy. "Are they willing to hand him over to Haith?"

"He didn't kill his brother!"

"Gods below." Kelkin grabs Eladora by the arm, drags her over to a corner. "There's a fucking Ishmeric invasion fleet out there somewhere! They didn't attack Lyrix! They've changed course, and we have one damn shot if they come at us. We've got the Keepers trying to bolster their gods. Feeding them worship, putting a king in place to make 'em think it's five hundred years ago! Goading the beasts instead of keeping them! They'll drag us into the Godswar!" He's turned purple, splutters in her face with anger. "Oh, did I mention I have Haithi troops sitting outside the city like a knife to my throat? And all this on an election platform of fucking peace and unity! If handing Erevesic over gets rid of one of my problems, then good riddance to him."

"Even if he's innocent?"

"He's a subject of the Haithi crown. The ambassador died in the Haithi embassy. It is absolutely, unquestionably, not our concern." Kelkin sighs. "Gods below. When I took you in, I hoped you'd be like Jermas was in the old days. He had fucking steel in his spine. Not you." He turns his back on her. "Where were we?"

She squashes down her anger. Holds it all in, all the shame and pride. Steps back with an awkward nod. Her mother taught her to be polite, to never makes a scene.

"The Patros says he's at the mercy of the king," reads Ogilvy, "and wants to know if the emergency committee of parliament will support the king's decision, whatever that decision is."

The aethergraph's chattering again with omens of war. Admiral Vermeil's gesturing for Kelkin to come over. Kelkin groans. The Keepers have chosen their moment perfectly – Kelkin can resolve the threat from Haith instantly, if he acknowledges the king's claim to Guerdon's long-vacant throne. A choice between his principles and the prosperity of the city.

It's never a contest. "All right. Parliament will endorse the king's decision, as long as it's the fucking right one."

He glances back at Eladora. "Go on, go and be useful somewhere." "But . . ."

"No. Stay away from Hark. Listen to me: no one there is worth the risk."

He crosses back to his generals, veterans of the Godswar, subdued and worried. Their hands shaking slightly.

The generals fall silent.

Vermeil, blustering, furiously waves another aethergraph note. "Readings from the Kraken-saint at Hark! Miracles south and east, close at hand! Ishmere is coming, sir. It's unquestionable to my mind. We have to be ready."

Kelkin glances back at Eladora for an instant, as if looking for her counsel, or her approval. Then, almost impulsively, he signs an order and hands it to Vermeil. "You are authorised to strike first. Bloody them, so they think twice about invading."

Eladora looks around the room. "Where's Dr Ramegos?"

Kelkin glares at her, as if he blames her for all this chaos. "My fucking special adviser on matters theological and arcane? She quit yesterday."

His voice quavers at the end there. She can tell he's scared.

Eladora walks briskly down the steep stairs of Castle Hill, eyes fixed straight ahead. The crowds part for her, pushed aside by a bow wave of furious purpose. A few canvassers and hawkers try to stop her, to press leaflets into her hand or lure her into one shop or another, but she ignores them resolutely.

One of them, a smiling young man, perfumed and coiffed, stumbles into her path, breaking her stride. He looks up at her, and there's a now-familiar light in his eyes.

"THIS IS NOT THE WAY TO THE ISLAND."

She wonders where Rat actually is. Previously, she's only seen the elder ghoul speak through others at a close range. Is he nearby, following her through the tunnels that riddle the city, or scuttling along the rooftops? Perched on a church spire? Or is he far away, and is only now revealing the extent of his power?

"I have to make a brief detour."

"BE QUICK." The young man laughs Rat's hideous graveyard chuckle, which turns into a choking fit as the ghoul releases him. She leaves him in the care of other passers-by and hurries down, past the House of Justice, into Venture Square.

Back into the familiar warmth and press of the Vulcan coffee shop. The clerk at Kelkin's table knows her, he's seen her in here dozens of times. She's one of Kelkin's own, everyone knows that.

"Mr Kelkin sent me down to draft some letters for his signature," she says. "I'll need the table."

The clerk bows, cedes the chair to her. He hovers near the entrance to the backroom, watching her, but not too closely.

"Fetch me a carriage, would you? I'll be done in a moment."

Kelkin keeps a signet ring and wax in this drawer. His signature is spiky and illegible. The letter itself is brief, just like he'd write it. It's even a passable imitation of his handwriting.

"Where's the carriage to?"

She folds the letter up, slips it into an envelope.

"Queen's Point."

CHAPTER 37

There's movement outside, across the prison yard. Alic watches through the little barred window as more prisoners get marched across the yard and put into their appointed slots in the divine prognosticator. They've been appraised, found to have some connection to a god that can be measured. Their sainthood's a weight on some alchemist's scale, a stain on a slide. Pinned like specimens.

Alic watches figures hurrying back and forth, between the cell where they put Emlin and the mirrored tower. At one point, he hears Emlin shouting, crying his name in terror. He calls back, but there's nothing he can do. They're watching him from that tower, too.

What can he do? Shout? Rant and rave? Throw himself against the bars? The spy in him counsels patience, as always. Lulling him, winding webs of conjecture and contingency. *If you act, you'll ruin everything. Wait. Observe. Patience.*

He watches the stars come out across a cloudless sky. Listens to the waves break on the rocky shores of Hark. Break, not shatter. No lion-headed goddess descends on a stair of fire from heaven to make war upon the city.

He considers the possibility that, in his desperate prayer, Emlin sent a warning to Ishmere. Told them that he'd been captured. Surely that wouldn't stop the invasion, though? The mad gods of Ishmere are heedless of the suffering of their worshippers. He knows that, better than anyone. They wouldn't relent just because one young saint is suffering.

Neither can the spy.

But Alic would.

The spy sits down, closes his eyes. Tries to sleep, but Alic hears screams and sobbing, and each time he wakes with a start, wondering if it's Emlin. *There's nothing you can do yet*, the spy tells Alic, *maybe nothing that can be done.* Either the machinery is in motion, or it is broken. Either the gods of Ishmere are coming, or he's failed his mission. Either way, there's nothing he can do to affect it from this jail cell, so the best use of his time is sleep.

He wonders why the other two are in this prison for saints. The boy, Miren, seems mad enough. As far as Alic can tell, he hasn't slept. He just stands there, eyes fixed on the sleeping form of the girl. She has scarcely stirred in the night, but she looks stronger this morning.

The smell of the soporific gas gets into everything. The scent isn't strong, but particles in the gas irritate the spy's throat and eyes. He feels slightly dizzy, too, detached from his body. He grabs the blankets from the bed and tries stuffing them between the bars of his cell, to block the constant trickle of gas from the ceiling tube in the corridor.

"It won't work." Miren smirks at Alic's efforts. "They check. They want us cut off from the gods."

"I'm not a saint," replies Alic, truthfully.

"I am," says Miren. "She stole my gods away. But Father says we'll bring them back together."

"Who's your father?"

Miren's expression doesn't change. "He's dead. He's buried with all the broken things."

The door at the end of the corridor rattles, and masked guards enter. Alic tears down the blanket before the guards see it, flips it back onto the bed. A model prisoner. One of the guards pauses outside his cell and hands him a plate of food. Fried sausages, bread, mushrooms, a sort of sweet paste the alchemists make. The guard removes his mask before speaking.

"A peaceful night, I hope?"

"I've had worse." They still don't know how to handle him, it seems. He's not a saint, not a criminal. They can't figure out why he was on that boat.

"We'll be with you in a moment. Get that food down you." The mask goes back down.

The spy eats while the guards check the unconscious woman. She stirs but does not wake. The guards look at one another, speak in low, worried tones.

They leave food for Miren, too, but do it cautiously, like they're feeding a wild beast. One guard takes out a heavy club, while the other gingerly slides the plate of food across the floor, careful to keep his arm out of Miren's reach. The boy reaches down and takes the plate, languid and unhurried. He glances over at the spy. "Did they give you a knife?"

Alic shakes his head. He's eating with his hands.

"I'll have a knife again," says Miren to himself, nodding.

One of the guards slams the club into the bars of Miren's cell. The boy flinches and flees back into the shadows, spilling his breakfast across the floor. "Quiet, freak," snarls the guard.

Then, to Alic. "Come on. They're ready for you."

Terevant steps out of the door of the half-house and the world explodes in his face. A light so bright he thinks first it's the dawn, the sun blazing right in his face at midnight. Then – aha – it's a dragon bomb, exploding right on top of him. That explains the pain – he and everyone else in the world is being annihilated.

No. It's just him. He's been shot.

He's on the ground. Faces and voices, hands pulling at him. Can't they see he's busy? He's holding his intestines in. They're very slippery and it's rather complicated.

Then he's walking in crisp sunlight, the frosted grass crunching under his feet. He's back in the gardens of the Erevesic estate. Children, bundled up in woollen scarves and coats, run laughing past him. He isn't sure who they are, but it strikes him that the laughter of children is the only laughter one ever hears in Haith. He makes this observation to Olthic, who snorts.

"Empire is a serious matter," says his brother. "A weighty matter, full of terrible decisions and heavy burdens. Daerinth told me that. Father told me that."

But I heard you laugh, Olthic. On the battlefield.

Olthic shrugs. Thunder rolls from the cloudless winter sky.

Then, reluctantly, Olthic says, "It was a mistake." And then he walks away through the frost-rimed, leafless trees, a forest of bone.

Terevant hurries after his brother, through the bones. He must have gone to the mansion. To the room where Father's dying.

Wait, this is a dream. He's not in Haith. He's in Guerdon. And he's been shot. He's dying in a different room, a half-room. One half perfectly made, the other half unfinished. It's oddly fitting.

Outside, the noise of fighting. Explosions, slashing, screaming. He should do his duty. Join the fray. All he needs to do is die, and resurrect. Become Vigilant. He recites the prayers to death, mentally traces the scrimshawed runes on the periapts of his wrists, his ribs, his skull. Come on! He tries to recall his training for this, lessons given by an old Vigilant in a cold hall by the shore at Shipbreak Strand.

If he dies, the Erevesic line dies, too. Olthic was supposed to be the proper heir, to carry on the family. Have another generation, then watch over them from within the sword. Now only Terevant is left, and if he's dead, the line ends. Only a living bearer can wield the full power of the sword. If he's dead, then the Erevesic sword will remain forever silent.

Is he supposed to live or die? What does the Empire want from him now?

No doubt there's some Bureau protocol for a phylactery without a bearer.

"It's happened before," says Lys. He's back in the gardens, hurrying up towards the mansion. "It'd become property of the Crown." She pulls Olthic's heavy coat around her against the cold. "I'm sorry, Ter."

Why.

"You never understood the game, and the odds were against you."

The odds were against him at Eskalind, too, and for a moment it seems like he'll fall out of that frosted garden, slip back to the horrors on that bloodied shore, when he contended against mad gods. When Yoras and so many others died. But, no – he's still dreaming of home.

"Have you found Vanth yet?" she asks as they climb the steps into the mansion.

From outside, voices. The smell of burned flesh. Like Edoric Vanth's body, soul destroyed by holy fire. Who killed Vanth, he wants to ask, but it comes out Who killed Olthic.

Lys has always been smarter than him. She grins and asks "Who ordained his death?"

Look for higher powers. The actions of the gods don't always make sense from a mortal perspective. He's lying on the floor, but he feels like he's soaring over Guerdon, seeing everything from atop the spires and towers.

He extends a hand to Lys. Wipes it on his shirt, because it must be bloody from keeping pressure on that wound. Offers it again.

Come with me.

She shakes her head. "It's not for me."

Somehow, they're now in the corridor outside Father's room. He can feel the heat of that fire. The attending necromancer's walking with them, cloaked, head bowed. Terevant feels like he's floating, being carried away from Lys. The smell of incense, the distant sounds of prayer.

He wants to warn her about touching the sword. She knows better than to touch the sword, right?

She opens the door, but it's not a sword, it's a crown. Divinity.

And then the sound of the gunshot, again. And the sun bursts.

At some point, the sound of the gunshots in his dream became the tolling of church bells, and then he could actually hear the bells ringing nearby as he woke.

Cool hands touching his. Fingers probing his wrist, checking for his periapt. Terevant struggles to open his eyes, but his eyelids feel matted together with sleep. He tries to reach up to brush them clean, but moving his arm is agony upon agony, his chest exploding in pain.

"Don't move, Ter. You're barely holding together. Let me."

Sounds. Water splashing in a bowl. Then a damp cloth wiping his eyes, his forehead. He tries to speak, but his throat is full of mucus, and coughing will bring even more agony. He groans, and Lys places a glass against his lips. "Drink," she orders. It's not water — it tastes sugary, and numbs his throat, and smells metallic. Some alchemical cure-all.

"Where?" he manages. How long has he been unconscious?

"You are in the Palace of the Patros of Guerdon. Sinter's men brought you here yesterday evening."

He manages to open one eye. Lys, sitting on the bed, dressed in black. The room richly appointed, an ancient painting of some Keeper saint on the wall. Opposite that, a window. He can see blue skies, pierced by the white spire of one of the Victory Cathedrals and a black column of smoke. They're up on Holyhill, high on the eastern side of the city. Through the window he can hear singing, the murmur of a crowd.

"Olthic," he says, and it's all he can manage.

"I know," she says. She slips him a little sad smile. "I wish you'd been here with us when things were good, Ter. It was like old times, back home."

"I didn't—" He can't finish. He rolls his head to the side, lets blood spill from his mouth, staining the white pillow.

"I never thought you did," she says, wiping the blood away. "When we were first married, when he was off in the war, I would get advance copies of the casualty lists through the Bureau. They came early in the morning. I wouldn't sleep at all the night before, not until I'd checked and made sure he wasn't dead. I thought, in Guerdon . . ." she trails off.

She looks out of the window.

"There's a purge going on outside," Lys whispers. "Not the Patros, but below him. Sinter and the city Keepers are pushing back against the Safidists. They're seizing control of all the new saints and bringing them here. They've got a dozen so far, but they won't let us have another healer for you. Sinter wants to keep me distracted." The last said with a hint of amusement or sadness, he can't tell. "We should be safe – it's an internal feud. They both need Haith."

"The embassy?" he manages.

"Shush. Rest." She walks to the window, spreads the bloodstained cloth against the windowsill, draping it like a flag. Her wedding ring glints in the sun. "Daerinth claims you killed Olthic. The Crown of Haith has demanded that Guerdon hand you over."

"I didn't do it," he insists again.

"I know."

He swallows. He has to ask. "Lys, did you kill him?"

She turns back to him, hands folded behind her back. "How could you think that?" She doesn't sound insulted – she's curious, detached. Like she's trying to see things from his perspective. Giving nothing away.

"Answer me, please. Honestly. I know the train from Haith was a setup. You stole the sword once, to make sure Olthic's deal with parliament fell apart. Is that it?" He manages to half sit up in bed, to turn and watch her. The pain in his chest feels like his heart might just fall out if he moves too quickly.

"The train was Lemuel's suggestion. He's very eager to please, and I had other things on my mind. I'm sorry for tricking you." She lowers her voice. "I told you that's it's bad back home, Ter. The Bureau, the Enshrined Houses, the Crown – they're all terrified. We're losing the Godswar. The Empire is lost, Ter, everyone knows that. It's all about saving Old Haith now, and for that the Crown needs weapons and allies." She crosses back to the bed. "The Bureau has held the royal line of Guerdon for generations, waiting for the right moment. Then Olthic came in, trampling everything.

"Maybe it was the nomination to the Fifty, and he felt he had to beat me. He tried to push a grand bargain, but we don't have the strength to fully defend Guerdon and Haith. I had to undermine him. I did it as gently as I could. But I didn't kill him. I don't know who did. If I'd been at the embassy, they'd have killed me, too. I'm protected here — that's why I didn't come when he died." Her mask slips a little, there's fear in her voice, Or is she *letting* the mask slip? How much of her is Lys, and how much is the artifice of Bureau training?

"And what about Edoric Vanth?"

"I learned what happened before I visited you at the mansion. A mad Keeper saint killed Vanth — one of the Safidist lunatics, running wild. We couldn't let one crazy saint disrupt the Bureau's plan to install Berrick as king — if Olthic found out that one of the embassy staff had been murdered by our new allies, he'd have blown everything up. He'd have gone to parliament, gone to the Houses . . . you know how loud he could be. We had to hide the Keepers' involvement in Vanth's death. And Olthic wouldn't believe me or Lem. It had to be someone he trusted. It had to be you."

"You used me?" Even though he'd suspected it, he still feels sick to his stomach to have it confirmed. Subtle variations of shame run through him — shame at being used by Lys, at unwittingly betraying Olthic, at his own foolishness . . . and at how quickly part of him wants to forgive her.

"I have to compartmentalise," she replies. "The mission comes first." She shakes her head. "The Office of Foreign Divinity warned us that returning the king would strengthen the Kept Gods, but Sinter said he could keep them in check. Their gods are idiots, Ter, and their saints are mad. It's something else we've got to navigate." She pauses. "Can I tell you something?"

"Go on."

"You made it into the Bureau. It was a close-run thing, but you passed the exams."

Even after all these years, it's a punch to the stomach. He's outside that black door again, wondering how he could have failed. Slipping and stumbling into the gutter.

"Why?"

"Olthic wrote to me, and asked me to ensure the Bureau turn you away. He wanted you by his side."

A great fit of laughter mixed with tears rises up in his chest, but he's too badly hurt to do either. He just lies back and stares at the ceiling, while the world spins around him. The past decade unspools, years flowing backwards, a train without brakes. Hurtling downhill.

"Now, listen to me, Ter. Your old life is gone. They're blaming you for Olthic's death, so—" Lys tenses, then folds away the cloth and sits up on the windowsill as if relaxing there. Terevant struggles to rise. He's got so much to ask her, so much to say – but she raises a finger to quieten him, and a moment later there's a knock at the door.

Two of the Keeper's ceremonial guards enter, plumed helmets brushing against the lintel. Behind them, a third guard stands with a wheeled wicker bathchair. "His Majesty desires to speak to the Erevesic."

Lys stands. "Of course. Give us but a moment, and—"

"The Erevesic alone, my lady."

"As he wishes." Lys helps Terevant out of bed, and as she does, she whispers in his ear. "Trust the Bureau."

The Palace of the Patros looks humble from the outside, over-shadowed by the three massive Victory Cathedrals that flank it. No marble or gilt, no ornamentation apart from on the wall that overlooks the cathedral's shared plaza, where the Patros addresses the faithful from a balcony.

As the guards push the squeaking bathchair down long marble corridors lined with statues of silver and gold, Terevant realises that the bulk of the palace is hidden. Interwoven with the city, or delved deep into the stone of Holyhill. The halls are quiet, the only sound the distant murmur of the crowd in the plaza outside. Black-robed priests and clerics vanish like ghosts as the guards pass by. It reminds Terevant of his time in Haith's holdings overseas. The palace has the air of an occupied city, the locals vanishing when the Vigilant pass by, only to reappear behind them, jeering or plotting against them. Making signs of banished gods.

Once, they pass a door that's half ajar, and Terevant catches a brief glimpse of a trio of old women, ritually stripping bloodied robes from the corpse of a Keeper priest. Sinter's consolidating power. They come to a massive set of double doors, marked with the seals of the Patros and the emblems of Saint Storm. More guards stand outside, still as Vigilants. The doors are unlocked, the wards disarmed, and they press on into this inner sanctum. Ahead, another set of doors, equally huge, but instead of going through them they bring him to a small room off the corridor. A little study, with threadbare chairs and walls lined with bookcases crammed with yellowed books. A single narrow window, looking out over the University District.

Waiting behind the desk is a man in a jewelled robe, a crown of gold upon his brow. Berrick's slight frame seems almost swallowed by his finery; instead of being made grander by his new appearance, he's diminished, occluded by the mantle and the title.

"Your Majesty, the Erevesic of Haith."

One of the guards helps Terevant out of the bathchair, although he discovers he doesn't actually need the aid. His chest still aches, but the pain's diminishing. Another healing miracle, and he might be nearly recovered.

The guards withdraw outside the door.

"My condolences on your new title," says Berrick after an awkward moment.

"My congratulations on yours," replies Terevant, cautiously.

Berrick grins, touches the crown. "Oh, that's yet to be determined. At least the gods have conspired to restock my wine cellar. Please, join me." He reaches under the desk, produces two huge silver goblets and a bottle of wine. "Drinking is a large part of my kingly duties."

He fills the cups and passes one to Terevant. "To duty!" toasts Berrick.

"I can't." Terevant puts the goblet back down without drinking.

"As you wish." Berrick sighs. "I suppose I can speak a little more freely now than I could when we met at the fair. Not much more freely, though." He waves the goblet at the bookcases. "Gods watch over this city, my friend, and they have many willing ears."

Terevant wonders how many in the Keeper's church know that

Berrick was planted by Haith? Is it common knowledge? A closely guarded secret, kept only by the highest in the clergy? Terevant has no idea. He's lost in a foggy marsh – he knows enough to realise that the footing is treacherous, but has no clue where he should be going or how to escape with his life.

Lys said everything had been taken care of. He has to trust her.

"You said that things were going to happen, whether you wanted them to or not."

"I did, didn't I? And they did. And they continue to happen, I'm afraid." Berrick sips from the goblet, turns to the window. "You know, I still haven't seen any of the city. They tell me it's my city, but you've seen more of it than I. You fled the embassy. Lived on the streets. Tell me, Terevant, how did it feel to be free?"

For some reason, he flashes back to the last night of the festival, to the mercenary woman Naola. To that moment when he turned around to walk back towards her. Just before Lemuel clubbed him, and everything fell apart. "It felt good," he admits, "but fleeting."

"Oh." King Berrick Ultgard sounds disappointed. "I suppose that's the way of things. Leap from the moving train, and you get an instant of freedom before you hit the ground. I hope it was worth it." He takes a mouthful of wine, rolls around, swallows, sighs. "I am told that it's necessary to maintain good relations with the Empire of Haith. That Guerdon's parliament and the Church of the Keepers are agreed that you are to be given over into the custody of Haith, to, ah, Daerinth?"

"Prince Daerinth."

"My royal cousin!" Berrick laughs mirthlessly. "What will he do to you, my friend?"

"I don't know. He thinks I killed my brother. He ordered the guards to kill me, in the embassy. I suppose there'll be a trial." Another court martial, and this time, no Olthic to intervene. Terevant tries to recall the protocol. It'll come before the Crown, he guesses. And with no other Erevesic heirs, the Crown will take command of the Erevesic estates and armies.

"I am also told that I can't show you mercy or set you free."

Told? "Things happen, whether you want them to happen or not."

"It's not much of a kingdom, I suppose." He wanders over to the window and opens it, listens to the distant crowd chanting his name. "I don't know what I expected. I thought nothing would come of it, when they sent me to Guerdon."

The Bureau, guesses Terevant, but he doesn't dare speak. The king's already giving away far too much to any eavesdroppers.

Berrick takes the crown from his head, and dangles it out of the window as he ruffles his hair. "It's something of a family tradition. They did the same with my grandfather, about forty years ago. Some other political strife when it might have been useful to bring back a king. But I thought it would end like that – bundled back home in the dead of night. Guests of the Crown, that's what they call my family."

"We each have our part to play." Terevant remembers the train journey with Berrick. They were both pieces being shoved around a board, but at least Berrick knew then what he was, while Terevant had been unaware of his status. Now, he too knows.

Is it better to resign oneself to being a pawn, or try to play the game and lose? Is there honour in going unflinchingly to one's fate? When he tried to join the Bureau, he tried to move against the rules, to jump to a square he wasn't permitted to move to, and he failed – or so he'd thought. At Eskalind, he tried to play like Olthic and failed. And in between, he'd knocked himself off the board in a fit of self-pity.

"Are you sure you don't want this last drink?" asks Berrick.

"I must decline."

"We both have things we must do, I suppose." Berrick raises his voice. "Guards! Take him away. Give him to Haith."

Queen's Point is in uproar when Eladora arrives. Battalions of city watch hurry past her, raptequine-drawn wagons race through the streets. They're preparing for an attack on the city.

Crowds have gathered on the quayside, to watch the ships go out. Guerdon's main naval strength is stationed down the coast at Maredon, but there are still half a dozen ships at Queen's Point and they're all going out. The crowds cheer as the newest warship in the fleet, the *Grand Retort*, is dragged out into the harbour by tugboats. She gleams in the afternoon sun like a new-polished sword. Alchemy-powered, birthed in the foundries and laboratories of Guerdon. Her hull's marked with protective spell-wards and arcane dampeners; she bristles with guns to spit alchemical shells into the face of any god or monster who dares threaten the city. She cost a fortune to build; the yards that wrought her were once owned by Eladora's family, before they were sold off to cover her grandfather's mounting debts. *Grand Retort* is another monster made possible by Jermas Thay, like Carillon or Miren. Only *Grand Retort* wears its monstrous nature openly instead of cloaking it in flesh.

There, on her forward deck, ready to be launched, is the dark shape of a god bomb. Eladora feels ill at the sight of it. It's horrible to look at, and even when she closes her eyes and looks away it's still there, like a spiked stone pressing on her head. No one else in the crowd has the same reaction. None of them know the terrible power of that weapon.

Grand Retort turns her prow south, the steel ram cutting the oily waters of the harbour.

Eladora hurries into the fortress, and shows the letter – marked with Kelkin's seal – to the officer at the desk in the main hall. Authorisation to requisition a launch to go to Hark Island. The clerk mutters to himself, fetches an officer who's struggling into a heavy greatcoat, gas mask and sorcery-ward dangling from leather straps. She holds her breath for a moment, worried that her ruse has been discovered already, wondering if she's forgotten some point of military protocol that gave her away. Then the officer bows, a grin breaking across his bearded face.

"Commander Aldras," he says, waving a gloved hand. "Can you be ready in twenty minutes or so? And is it just yourself? We're heavily loaded."

"It's just me," says Eladora, "but I'll be coming back with others."

"I wouldn't count on making the return today. It's going to be rough."

There's hardly a cloud in the sky, and the air's still, but she doesn't have time to question Aldras. She just asks where the boat is.

"Dock Four," he says, "do you know the way down?"

It's a stone's throw from Ramegos' laboratory in the bowels of Queen's Point. She's been there a dozen times. Once more, she thinks, to say goodbye.

CHAPTER 38

The waiting room down the corridor from Ramegos' office is empty; the desks in the outer office are abandoned and bare, boxes of papers stacked waiting to be brought to some archive. Eladora walks uncertainly down to the inner door. This corridor always reminded Eladora of walking down a dragon's throat. The uneven stones of the arched ceiling, hot, foul-smelling exhausts from subterranean engines. At the end of the corridor was Ramegos' office, where the sorceress served her mint tea, taught her magic, and gossiped about history. A little hedge-school, hidden in the depths of Guerdon's fortress.

But Eladora never forgot that Ramegos was as dangerous as any dragon. Humans, Ramegos taught her, are ill suited to sorcery. Casting a spell means taking hold of the unseen aether and warping it by force of will, to command the raw stuff of gods and souls directly. Casting a spell is an act of hubris. It's trespassing in the domain of the gods. There are precautions that can be employed — using a thauma-turgical fetch to take the brunt of the backlash, carefully constructing the spell so the excess energies cancel each other out, or casting along the grain of existing miracles, mimicking previous acts of gods.

Ramegos cautioned her against that last technique. Said that the weakness of Guerdon's kept gods meant that their miracles were weak, so the aetheric field around the city was chaotic and mostly unformed, so there were no local currents or channels to exploit, no grain in the world to follow. Now, Eladora wonders if Ramegos was cautioning her against getting too close to the Kept Gods.

How much did Ramegos know? Was the older woman her friend, or her keeper? Has Eladora been punished, yet again, for putting her trust in someone older and wiser?

She pauses outside the door.

Ramegos warned her not to open it without permission – the sorceress uses potent spells to guard her sanctum. One of the first sorcerous incantations that Ramegos taught Eladora was the creation of wards to seal a door. Eladora's wards might briefly stun a burglar; she's quite sure Ramegos' wards are strong enough to kill. There are other spells, too, far beyond Eladora's ability. She's spent what felt like hours studying in that office, only to find that mere minutes have passed outside.

She knocks. "Dr Ramegos?"

No answer.

"Doctor?" she calls again. Again, silence.

Is Ramegos gone already? Kelkin said she had suddenly resigned her post as the IndLibs' occult adviser – has she also left Queen's Point? She'd spoken about returning to Khebesh when her work in Guerdon was done, but it seems odd for her to depart so suddenly. Odd and cruel.

Impulsively, Eladora grabs the handle and turns. The door opens, revealing an empty room, somehow much smaller than she remembers it. A typewriter and a chair on an otherwise bare desk. Everything's gone – Ramegos' books and curios, her thaumaturgical fetches, her records. The divine icons, strung on a cord, proclaiming that all faiths were one and nothing at the same time, just eddies in some aetheric current.

As if she was never here.

Eladora sighs. Tears burn her eyes, but she wipes them away. She doesn't weep. She doesn't have time. She needs to get down to the docks, get a boat to Hark Island.

She turns and hurries back through the maze of tunnels under Queen's Point, conscious that the boat will depart soon. She files Ramegos away in the same part of her mind where she keeps Ongent and Miren, another foolish indulgence on her part. She wonders if she'll have to put Kelkin under the same heading. She's done her part – delivered him the New City, if the polling's correct. Convinced him to stay out of any doomed alliance with the Keepers. But despite all that, they still don't trust each other. Does he look at her and see her grandfather, or her mother? He didn't listen when she told him that she believed Terevant Erevesic was innocent. Letting the Church hand him over to Haith was tantamount to murder.

There's no air in these tunnels, and it's hotter here than it was on the Festival field. The aetheric lights flicker, reacting to some magical discharge elsewhere in the fortress.

She's taken a wrong turn, she realises. There should be stairs here, leading down to the docks. She should be able to smell the sea from here, smell rotting seaweed and engine oil and the stink of the city, but all she can smell is an antiseptic tang, some chemical cleaner. This part of the base is deserted, so there's no one she can ask for directions. Her heart pounds; if the boat leaves without her, Cari and Alic will be stuck on Hark Island. They need her, and she's lost in the cellars of Queen's Point.

Backtrack. Take that turning instead. For an instant, as she comes around the corner, she glimpses a hunched shape hurrying ahead. A beggar in rags, carrying a lamp – and then it's gone. The fumes are getting to her. She's seeing things . . . The chemical smell is stronger down here, emanating from a door down the corridor, and she hears a familiar voice cursing in Khebeshi.

"Dr Ramegos?" She pushes open the door. It's a morgue. A stack of empty coffins against one wall, the sealed kind they use for victims of alchemical attacks. Lying on a gurney is an oddly shaped corpse under a grey, moth-eaten sheet. Ramegos is on her hands and knees nearby, scrubbing the floor with a chemical-soaked rag like a washerwoman.

She looks up, scowling, then breaks into a smile when she sees Eladora.

"My dear! I didn't think I'd see you before I left."

"What are you doing?"

"Just a little spillage as I was packing." Ramegos stands,

carefully putting the rag down on a counter, wiping her hands with another cloth.

"You didn't tell me you were leaving."

"I've finished my work here, and I'm needed back home in Khebesh."

"K-Kelkin still needs your advice."

"I'm done here," snaps Ramegos, defensively. Eladora can tell she's had this argument with others recently. "I did everything I could, Eladora. But it's not *a* Crisis. You all need to stop thinking that what happened was an isolated event, like the city could go back to what it was before. Like it was a storm that passed, and now it's clear seas forever. This is the world now. All the gods are mad." She sighs. "I can't steer the city through the storm. All I could do was give Kelkin a fighting chance."

"And that's it? You vanish like a thief?"

Ramegos looks heartbroken. "It's coming, Eladora. I've lingered here as long as I can, but I'm not getting caught up in the Godswar." She pauses, then extends a hand to Eladora. "Neither should you. Come with me. Come to Khebesh. You'll like it — the schools there put your university to shame."

"I can't."

"El — they're coming. Look." Ramegos walks over to another table, where she's got a shapeless bag. She produces her chain of god-tokens and holds it up, divinities clinking and clattering as it unrolls. Some of the tokens seem to move and change expression as they swing from the chain. Fate Spider's legs twitch. Lion Queen roars. Saint Storm brandishes a sword. Holy Beggar lifts the lamp of truth. And the Mother of Flowers clasps her hands, cradles them as if they're painful. "You can feel it directly, can't you? The gods moving on the city. Eladora, there's a *reason* your cousin fled Guerdon — she should have stayed away. There's nothing more monstrous than the kindness of the gods. Come to Khebesh."

Eladora fretfully toys with one of the holes in the sheet. "I need to go to Hark," she says. "Carillon was arrested and brought there. And Alic—"

"Who's that?" asks Ramegos, packing the chain of gods away again.

"He's . . . " The scorched holes remind her of the little burn marks on Carillon's face, the scars from when the Black Iron Gods first reached for her. Like tiny sparks scorched holes in the sheet.

"Don't touch that," snaps Ramegos. "The body – it's tainted. Withering dust."

There's something else under the sheet. Not just a body.

"But he died in fire," says Eladora, and she doesn't know where the words come from.

Her hand twitches, and the sheet falls to the floor. The ruined body of Edoric Vanth stares back at her. The remains are more mangled than the last time she looked at the corpse. She remembers how the face and head were horribly burned. The gaping wound in the throat. Puckered wounds in the chest, stabbed and shot and burned. Those wounds she remembers from her glimpse of the corpse at Sevenshell Street. But now the rotting skin's pocked and bleached by withering dust, exposing the crumbling bones. Scars and sutures where the necromancer cut deep to reach the periapts. Fresh cuts on his arms, glittering with shards of glass. A cracked rib protruding from his broken side.

His forearms have taken the brunt of the withering dust; all the flesh has sloughed off them, and one has broken off entirely, the dust leaving the bones of his arm weak as chalk. His other hand has been scorched by some arcane discharge, the flesh discoloured and iridescent. It's as though the man's body has suffered all the wounds the city could inflict on it.

Atop him, clasped in that spell-scorched hand, is the Erevesic sword. She recognises the sigil on the crossguard. Terevant has the same sign on his uniform, Olthic on his door.

"You took it." Eladora stares at her mentor in horror. Another betrayal. She's been taken for a fool again. Like Ongent. Like Miren. Like the gods. A memory that isn't hers spills across her mind – her hands holding a burning sword, Vanth's face vanishing in a burst of holy fire. Her mother killed him. "YOU TOOK IT," she says again, and her voice is a thunderous choir. For a moment, the mortuary's bathed in heavenly light that radiates from Eladora's face.

Ramegos raises her hands, conjuring a defensive ward.

"I hoped it would be your mother who came for me, not you," sighs Ramegos. "Or did you go to them?"

"I would never choose that," Eladora says firmly, as much to herself as to Ramegos. "Sinter – he drew them on me. He used me to counter my mother's sainthood." She takes a deep breath, clears her mind. Recites a sorcerous incantation in her head. The pressure of the Kept Gods withdraws. A last echo of her mother, she hopes.

"You've been vulnerable ever since your grandfather's ritual," says Ramegos, concern in her voice warring with caution. She still has her spell to hand. "There are other things I can try—"

Eladora makes a dismissive gesture. "It doesn't matter now. Why is the Erevesic sword here? Where are you taking it?"

Ramegos relaxes a little, dropping her gesture of warding. "Back home, like I said. To Khebesh. As to why . . . that's a more complicated question." She picks up her heavy ledger, flips to one page – or, rather, the absence of a page. A whole page of records, torn out. Those records describe acts of sorcery, miracles, divine interventions, fluctuations in the aether.

"The god bomb."

"Very good," says Ramegos. "I was in Lyrix when it went off, on business for the masters of Khebesh. By the time I made it to Guerdon, the Crisis was already over. Spar had destroyed half the alchemists' guild, including their laboratories. The guildmistress, Rosha, was dead. Most of the records relating to the creation of the weapons were lost, too – and Carillon had drained the power of the Black Iron Gods from the intact bells.

"Kelkin asked me to look into the remaining weapons. We salvaged one in the first week, but the other two bells are lost to us, buried deep under the New City. We worked out where, but we couldn't get to them – not without pissing off the ghouls and causing more chaos in Guerdon.

"One bomb wasn't enough. Rosha knew that – with only a few

Black Iron bells to turn into bombs, she was looking for ways to make them count. All lost with her."

"You sound regretful," says Eladora, suspiciously.

"She was a monster," says Ramegos, "by any standard. But also a genius." She points to the Erevesic sword, careful not to touch it. "The masters wanted me to recover a god bomb. I couldn't do that – but then, I thought about the Haithi phylacteries. They're like the Black Iron Gods. Both repositories for souls, both physical structures. But you need the blessing of the Haithi death-god to make a phylactery."

"You cut a deal with Haith," says Eladora, "to get the Erevesic sword." The sword quivers. Something stirs beneath the steel of the blade.

"Any phylactery would work. But the phylacteries and the Haithi Great Houses are one and the same, and the Houses control the army – if they knew that the Crown was selling their aristocracy to convert them into weapons, there'd be a civil war. Daerinth arranged it." Ramegos brushes her hands. "I'm not proud of what's happened, child. This is bloody work, and I'll be damned for it. But it's that or war without end."

"And what did Daerinth get in return for the sword?"

"A copy of Rosha's notes, and the work I've done on them. A full report on the Crisis. The location of the unforged bombs, under the New City."

"Those are state secrets," says Eladora. The theft of such secrets is punishable by death.

"Kelkin knows."

"What?"

"He approved the bargain. Payment for my work here."

Kelkin, too. Everyone's so short-sighted, and so callous. Scrambling over one another, wrestling in the mud for momentary advantage. A litany of betrayals, and for what? Another Godswar, pitting mortals against the divine? She imagines Ramegos' grimoire as a history of this period. Confusion, contradiction, pages torn out and burned.

"Terevant Erevesic's going to die because of what you've done. It's wrong. You have to return the sword." The sword quivers again.

"Don't cross me, child." Ramegos raises her hands again, reluctantly. "I don't want this."

Anger like wildfire rushing through her mind. It's hers, but not only hers. Like she's opened a door and can't close it.

Ramegos senses the danger. "Don't—"

Saint Storm offers Eladora a sword. It's not the Erevesic sword, nor Aleena's sword, but suddenly it's in her hands.

"No!" shouts Ramegos, as Eladora flings the gurney at the older woman. There's a flash of defensive sorcery, shattering the gurney in a blaze of arcane light. The Erevesic sword spins across the room, unscathed, trailing streamers of magical fire from the broken spell.

Eladora swings her own miraculous blade wildly. Ramegos stumbles back and falls against the table, knocking her belongings to the ground. She gestures and a bolt of lightning leaps from her hands. The hasty spell splinters on Eladora's divine armour. She tries again, and Eladora slashes with the blade, the holy fires disrupting the spell before it's even cast. Ramegos sprawls at her feet, helpless.

Eladora raises the sword. Flames ripple down the blade. *Fire shall destroy them*, proclaims Eladora's mother's voice, but Eladora can't tell if it's a memory or some spiritual message from the gods.

At this moment, it's within her power to kill Ramegos. The Khebeshi sorcerer is protected by potent life-wards and defensive spells, but she can burn through them.

It's within her power to compel truth from Ramegos. The Holy Beggar holds the lantern of truth, and she can take it as easily as she took Saint Storm's sword.

The Kept Gods will exalt her. Carry her up on wings of fire. Burn her away until she's a thing of sunlight and translucent crystal, an empty vessel for their perfect purity, blazing as the sun.

She fights back. The Mother is mercy.

She can put down a sword instead.

"TELL ME MY NAME," says Eladora, and her voice is the shout of a heavenly host.

Ramegos looks up, momentarily confused. Then she understands. "Eladora Duttin."

The power shifts, flickers, but doesn't withdraw. Duttin was Eladora's father's family name. He was a simple man, honest and kind. He worked the farm until he died, never lifting his head to look at the horizon. Never looking beyond the wheel of the seasons. Eladora loved him, but his family name holds no power over her.

"IT'S NOT WORKING!" She has to hold back the blade, fight against it – the Kept Gods *want* her to strike down this sorceress, who consorts with demons and meddles with things of Black Iron.

"Eladora Thay," says Ramegos, tentatively. Then again, authoritatively. "Eladora Thay."

The name binds her and defines her. The Kept Gods recoil, no longer able to find purchase on her soul. This tether to the mortal world snaps. Eladora drops the sword, and it vanishes with her armour. She sinks to her knees, next to the older woman. Embraces her, cradling her. Ramegos is shivering, too, shaken by the presence of the gods.

"It's wrong," says Eladora again quietly.

Flakes of ash fall around them both. The remains of Edoric Vanth float down, his dust-ravaged frame disintegrated in the fray.

"All right," says Ramegos as she pulls herself up, her old bones creaking. "Where's the Erevesic?"

"The Palace of the Patros." Eladora wipes her eyes. "You'll do it?"

"Well," says Ramegos quickly, "I don't have much of a choice, do I? Without Vanth, it'd be hell to get the sword out of the city. Especially as you'll have riled it up, taking about the Erevesics and all. I can't touch the damn thing, and it unravels my spells. I can't move it. Vanth could have carried it, but now ... " She brushes Vanth's ashes off her book.

Eladora snaps her fingers. "Yoras. One of the undead guards at the embassy. Terevant trusts him. Send for Yoras."

"I'll do what I can, child – but the signs are clear. The Godswar is nearly upon Guerdon. Please, come away with me. Maybe the city escapes invasion, but I don't like the odds."

The walls of this chamber in Queen's Point are fresh concrete on three sides, but the wall at the far end is made of old stone. There's a sigil on one stone, almost invisible beneath thick layers of white-wash, but still discernible as the royal crest of Guerdon. The old royal fort, buried beneath hundreds of years of fortification. The city has been conquered before, burned before, been rebuilt before. Guerdon endures. And interwoven with all that history, her family. There were Thays in the royal court. Thays on the first ships that discovered the city, and they walked the deserted streets wondering where the first folk of the city had gone, not knowing they had gone below as ghouls.

The city changes. The city endures.

"I do," says Eladora quietly. She kisses Ramegos on the brow. "Thank you for teaching me sorcery. Go and fetch Yoras. I'll see you when all this is over."

Commander Aldras waits by the dockside for her. He's too busy shouting orders at his crew to notice her flushed face, or the fragments of Edoric Vanth that dust her skirts. Maybe he notices some lingering godsent presence in her, though, because he doesn't question her late arrival.

"Just sit there," he tells her, pointing to a bench that's out of the way of the crew as they hastily load their cargo. Coils of wire and boxes stamped with the symbol of the alchemists' guild take up some of the space on board, but the main cargo is a large box that just arrived on the back of a cart. A quartet of raptequines drew it here through the streets; they glare at Eladora, flanks gleaming with bloody sweat, jaws drooling. Sailors and dockworkers hastily secure the large crate, lifting it onto the boat using a small crane. It comes down inches away from Eladora's knees.

Immediately, they cast off from the dock, the boat juddering as the engine comes to life. Eladora's close enough to hear the bubbling and churning of the reaction chamber. Sailors clamber around, securing the crate. The boat moves smoothly along the narrow channel of Queen's Point, heading for open seas. The mountainous bulk of *Kestrel* is ahead of them, surrounded by a flotilla of tugs and escorts.

As they come around the shoulder of Queen's Point and into the open harbour, Eladora can see the whole seaward portion of the city laid out in front of her. Cheering crowds line the streets near Queen's Point, and down into the Wash.

Across the harbour, smoke drifts from the smouldering wound in the middle of the New City.

The white wharves of the New City aren't as crowded – Eladora can make out a handful of people standing on the promenade where she met Alic a few days before the festival, black dots against white stone.

One of the sailors laughs at something behind her. Turning, she spots a figure in a wide-skirted dress jumping and waving frantically on the dockside near Queen's Point, as close as a member of the public can get to the cove without being stopped or shot. The person's waving a hat of some kind, desperately trying to attract their attention. The crowds jeer. Some projectile splatters on the ground nearby. Then, desperately, the figure jumps into the water with a tremendous splash. The crowds laugh, seeing it as a comic sideshow to the display of military might. A tattered dress, empty and torn, bobs to the surface.

"Wait," orders Eladora. She rises, but the boat rolls beneath her, and she half falls against one of the crates. The sailor curses at her. Aldras looks over, and Eladora points across the water. There, head breaking the surface like a seal, swims a sleek shape. Hoof-footed ghouls don't make good swimmers, but Silkpurse's powerful arms carry her through the water towards the boat. Aldras throttles back the engine, and the boat slows, allowing the ghoul to catch up and haul herself on board. Shaking water from her hair like a wet dog.

"She's with me," says Eladora to the sailors.

Silkpurse crouches down next to Eladora. "Lord Rat sent me," she says between gasps. "Said I was t'go with you."

Eladora stands again, more careful this time, and crosses to Aldras at the helm. "Might you have a coat or something my companion can borrow?"

"The ghoul?" Ghouls usually wear rags stolen from corpses, or nothing at all. Silkpurse is exceptional among her kind. "There's an oilskin in the locker, there."

Eladora fetches the coat and gives it to Silkpurse. "Thank'ee," says the ghoul. Despite the warmth, she draws the coat close around her shoulders. "I wish we were going anywhere but Hark."

Eager to make up time, Aldras orders the boat to full speed. She labours under the weight of her cargo, but still she races already, overtaking *Grand Retort* and her escorts. Their boat darts alongside the *Retort*, running parallel to the seagoing iron mountain of her hull, bouncing along in her wake. Then out, out into the open harbour.

Guerdon dwindles behind them. The city looks so small and fragile she could hold it in one hand. A precious heirloom.

They pass the Bell Rock. Ahead, the long, low shape of Hark.

The guards take Alic to a room two levels up, still in the old part of the prison. Three chairs, a desk. And there, against one wall, a metal locker. The tools of the interrogator's trade, he guesses, or at least he's meant to think the cabinet is full of knives and thumbscrews.

Two interrogators wait for him. One's a round-faced man with a large moustache and kindly eyes that might twinkle in other circumstances. A loving grandfather, reluctantly forced to chastise, eager to forgive. The other interrogator's face is hidden behind a mask of lenses and breathing tubes; he's got a pistol at his belt. The lenses rotate and click as the spy crosses the room to sit down. Protective runes of warding glow softly; the only light in the room comes from the brazier-cage in the ceiling.

"I'm Edder," says the old man. "Alic, isn't it? I've seen you in the New City."

Edder doesn't mention the masked figure at his right hand, doesn't even acknowledge his presence. He produces a bundle of papers, reads them by the light of a handheld lamp. He peruses them in silence for a few minutes.

Cautiously, the spy rouses. Probes Alic's resolve, offering a way out. Acknowledging that the spy's false identity has, on some level, a claim on existence. *Listen to me*, the spy whispers, *follow my lead, and Alic can live.*

"I want to see Emlin. He's a child – he doesn't deserve to be here."

"No," agrees Edder, "he doesn't." The shuffle of papers, again.

Lenses click. Smoke from the brazier in the ceiling drifts down. When the light from the lamp catches the wisps of smoke, they look like torn strands of cobweb, tumbling through the air.

Deny everything, deny Emlin, and the spy can walk out of here. The spy weaves an argument in his mind: *such a tragedy, to be god-touched – he's not my son, really, he's adopted, the child of distant relatives, I brought him with me out of obligation. This is the best place for him. Jaleh couldn't gentle him, why don't you keep him? Why, it's a good thing that you were tipped off. I wonder who did it? Ah well, the kindness of strangers.*

"Would you like anything to eat or drink, before we begin?" asks Edder. "I'm going to get a cup of tea for myself, so it's no trouble."

"No. They gave me breakfast." It's sitting heavily in his stomach, though, weighing him down more than it should. Makes it even harder to concentrate. Drugs in the food, too, maybe.

"All right. Let's just get started, then." Edder takes a small rubber breathing mask from under the desk, connected to a brass bottle of some gas. He takes a deep breath. Clean air, the spy guesses, something that counteracts the soporific poison in the braziers. You'd want a clear head for an interrogation.

"You come from Mattaur?" asks Edder.

"Severast. By way of Mattaur."

"And you fled Severast after the invasion by Ishmere."

"Yes."

"After," asks Edder, "or during?"

"After."

"Were you present," asks the masked interrogator, "for the sundering?"

"That was before the invasion. They came afterwards."

"Describe it."

Alic wasn't there. The spy was.

The earth shook. The altars of the temples cracked. Blinded, maddened priests crawling across the ground. Saints killing one another. Krakens in the harbour sinking into the mud, tentacles wrapped around one another in a deathly embrace. Lion Queen throwing down her sword and taking up a shield of gold. The priests in the shadows of Fate Spider's temple, knives in their hands, finding those whose souls were closer to the gods of Ishmere than to the gods of Severast and culling them. So much blood on the temple floor, and all those sacrifices brought him here. It's up to the spy to make them count.

The spy makes Alic shrug. "A theological argument among priests. No one paid it much heed until Ishmere called us a city of heretics and attacked."

"Is Alic your real name?"

"Yes," Alic answers. The spy hastily corrects. "It is now. But back there, I was Sanhada Baradhin."

Lenses whir. Edder makes a note.

"And you arrived in Guerdon under that name?" asks Edder.

"We, I — Emlin and I didn't come through regular channels. Things were chaotic — we barely made it out of Mattaur before it fell to Ishmere, too."

"I see," mutters Edder. "These things happen, of course. Oversights. It's a little unusual, though. Tell me, did you have friends here in the city when you arrived? Former colleagues perhaps? Or people you were told about, back in Mattaur?"

"I was a merchant. I had lots of business contacts. Guerdon's a trading city."

Another note. "Was it Annah Vierz you knew, or was it Tander Vierz?"

How much do they know? Has Emlin talked? Or Dredger? No — the arms dealer's in too deep, between the illegal money for the election and the supply of weapons. Someone else. Jaleh? Silkpurse? Or someone the spy's never spoken to — the bartender at the King's Nose tavern?

He forces himself to laugh. "They come as a pair, don't they?"

"Not any more," says the masked interrogator. The mask distorts the wearer's voice.

"What was the nature of your contact with the Vierzes?"

Tander's dead. Put it on him. "I knew Tander slightly from his mercenary days. I supplied him when he was campaigning in Severast. He told me to look him up if I was ever in Guerdon."

"Did Tander ever talk to you about Guerdon's defences?"

"He might have. I don't recall."

"Let's talk about Emlin. Is he your son?"

The spy tries to recite his planned spiel, but Alic's mouth won't cooperate. He just says, "Yes". The spy hides his own alarm, his own anger at his stupidity. It's the soporific smoke, it has to be, dulling his mind and disrupting his thoughts.

Edder takes another hit of clean air from his little breather mask. Smiles at the spy, as if he can detect Alic's confusion.

"He was chosen by the Fate Spider?"

"It was an honour. The Fate Spider was worshipped in a different way there, compared to Ishmere. He wove the proper fate for all who lived in the city, and his chosen priests could walk the webs, divine the future."

"But Severast has fallen, and the Sacred Realm of Ishmere has conquered it," says the masked interrogator, a metallic note of triumph in his voice. "Did he continue to worship the Fate Spider afterwards?"

"Sometimes."

"Did he visit the Paper Tombs?" The Ishmeric temple of the Spider.

"Maybe once or twice."

"Did he manifest any supernatural gifts?" asks Edder. His pen scratching on his pad as he makes notes. The masked interrogator unmoving except for the click of lenses rotating, his hand twitching near the gun at his belt.

"No."

"Did he," asks Edder gently, "ever visit any of the shrines consecrated to the Fate Spider? Any holy places?"

The spy takes his chance. He speaks quickly, lying with dexterity, before Alic can interfere. His words are an incantation, sealing the boy's fate, and the fate of the city.

"I don't know. We met with Annah. Not Tander, I don't know where he is. But Annah took him away, in the dead of night. Up to the Street of Shrines."

"When?" The masked interrogator.

"A week ago, maybe."

"Why?"

"I think, maybe . . . I think maybe he sent a message. Annah did, through Emlin. To Ishmere. Calling them."

Edder makes another note. His hand shakes as he writes. He looks at his masked companion. "Please, give us a moment."

The two inquisitors leave the room for a few minutes, then Edder returns alone.

"What's going to happen to me?" asks the spy.

"You'll be returned to the mainland. Hark's only for divines. The city watch will have more questions for you, but it won't be our section. Wait here until you're called for."

"What about Emlin?" asks the spy.

"I'm afraid he'll have to remain here," says Edder.

"Can I see him?"

Edder looks at the spy, then shakes his head. "No."

A siren blows distantly across the waters, an industrial air horn blaring a warning.

"But if you have any messages for him," continues Edder, "I'll see that he gets 'em."

He's lying, thinks the spy. "No. No messages."

The men who take Emlin from his cell treat him gently. They're dressed in protective robes of some silvery thread, with hoods and goggles. He's seen alchemists wear robes like that. They lead him, gingerly, like he's something toxic, out of the circle of cells, away from that mirrored tower. It's hard for him to concentrate – his head feels like it's stuffed with cotton wool – but he knows what he has to do. *Live your cover*, Alic told him. He's Alic's son, and this is all a horrible misunderstanding. Alic's nearby – he'll sort it all out. Explain it away. Bring him back home to Guerdon.

And beneath that shell, that mask, there's the nameless boy who was trained in the Paper Tombs. The saint of Fate Spider. He knows he sinned when he abjured his god, but he was forgiven! The stigmata on his face are proof of Fate Spider's love! There's still a place for him in the Sacred Realm, and Ishmere is coming. Guerdon will be conquered like Severast, like Mattaur, like all the other lands, and when the war is done, he will be exalted.

The boy feels no fear as they bring him out through the main gate of the prison. Emlin's heart leaps at the sight of the sea – maybe his father's waiting there, with a boat! But the dock's empty, and the robed alchemists lead him along the stony shore, beneath the shadow of the old fort's walls. They're bringing him towards that little spit of rock on the seaward side of Hark.

There are other robed figures there, hard at work. They've built some sort of machine there, something that's like a throne with a cage around it. It's ugly, all spikes and wires, the chair made of steel and orichalcum. There are other components, too – bubbling tanks with dark shapes swimming in them, crackling aetheric vanes, heavy duty wards. Emlin's attendants help him step over thick aetheric cables and pipes that run between the machine and the fort behind him.

"What is that?" he asks, but they don't reply.

The air out here is fresh, and it clears his head. He can feel the thick spidery hairs that have grown on the back of his neck stand up. He can feel other senses awakening. The shadows aren't dark to him any more. The robes the alchemists wear are magical, woven to block his miracles, but if he pushed, then maybe he could get through. His mouth floods with saliva, and there's a little taste of the Poison Undeniable. He's getting stronger.

As they get closer, he sees there's a woman in the chair. He recognises her – she had those icons of the Kraken on Dredger's ship. She's not a Kraken-saint, but she has a little connection to the god.

Had.

The alchemists lift her contorted corpse out of the chair. Her head lolls, and bloody seawater gushes from her mouth, her water-filled lungs, to splash on the rocks and the wiring at her feet. Two robed alchemists carry her past Emlin.

She's been warped by divinity. Her fingers, now limp tentacles, trail behind her. Her skin bursts where the alchemists lift her, and water drips from the wounds.

He squares his shoulders. Alic will come for him. Or, if he dies here, Fate Spider will catch his soul. He'll live or he'll die here, and, either way, his faith will be rewarded.

"Sit down, please," orders one of the alchemists.

"What if I don't?"

They grab him, four or five of them, the fabric of their gloves rough against his skin, and force him into the chair. They lock metal chains across his chest and pull them tight. The chair was made for an adult's body, so they have to stuff a spare robe under him to boost him up. They tie leather restraints around his wrists and ankles.

He won't cry. He won't scream. He'll be brave.

One of the alchemists presses a switch, and suddenly there's a feeling of *power* all around Emlin. It *lifts* him, like his soul's been carried out of his body and into the realm of the gods. He stares at the alchemist in front of him, who's looking at a bank of instruments connected to the machine. Beneath the man's robes is his face, beneath his face his skull, beneath his skull his brain, and there is a fine web of thought—

Tell the tower we're ready here, signal the mainland. Bring the icon. A flash of the statue from the Shrine, eight legs in holy shadow, eight all-seeing eyes—

And then the alchemist flips the switch, and the power goes, and the miracle ends.

The alchemists retreat down the spit of rock, away from the machine. Some lift their skirts and jog along the shore back to the fort; others look out to sea as if waiting for a ship. None of them get too close to the water.

But Emlin's seen enough. Either Alic will come for him, or Fate Spider will come for him, and he'll be saved.

He doesn't need to be afraid. Even here, alone on this spit of rock, bound hand and foot to some awful machine, he's not scared. He knows he's loved. He trusts he'll be saved.

The dead man walks through the streets of the city. He's moving against the flow of the crowds, so he has to push through to get to Queen's Point. Passers-by mutter apologies, or curses, or say nothing as they jostle him; Guerdon is notoriously impolite, compared to the hidebound etiquette of Haith. He doesn't dare offer apologies of his own, though. The few who notice the mask flinch and give him plenty of room.

In his hand, he clutches the message that came to the embassy. By rights, he shouldn't be here – it's forbidden for the Vigilant to leave the embassy without permission. But the ambassador is dead, and Lady Erevesic and Terevant are missing, and the First Secretary is gone, too, taking most of the Vigilant garrison with him. Leaving only Yoras and Peralt to endlessly patrol the marble corridors, to watch over empty offices and reception halls, to stand sentry at the gates.

To remain Vigilant.

Yoras died in the service of the Crown, as part of the Ninth Rifles. As a Vigilant of the Crown, Yoras serves the state directly. His loyalty is supposed to be to the Crown alone, not to any one House or Bureau. That's no trouble for Yoras – in life, he never saw any House as being worth dying for, and nor the Bureau. When he was alive, the affairs of House and Bureau were like storm clouds clashing far above his head. Now, he's ascended to some exalted, chilly region of the sky, far beyond the clouds, and their intrigues cannot touch him. His death is for the Crown alone.

But in life, he knew Terevant, and he's only a year dead. The memory of friendship not yet bleached from his bones.

The message was hastily written, but quite specific. He is to arrive at a particular side door to the fortress of Castle Point, just before sundown. He is not to speak to anyone, nor is he to ask any questions. It's unsigned.

The dead are not known for their curiosity, and Yoras is no

exception. He betrays no surprise when the door opens and a small dark-eyed woman with greying hair beckons him inside. This must the infamous Dr Ramegos. "You're not here, all right? This is about Terevant Erevesic, and if you don't do as I say, he'll be the one who pays the price. Understand?"

Yes. He doesn't, but what the Vigilant lack in curiosity, they make up in dogged loyalty.

Dr Ramegos mutters a spell. The Vigilant are more resistant to sorcery than the living; Yoras has seen sorcerers collapse in fits or bleed from their eyes trying to force a spell to catch on his animated bones. Ramegos manages to ensorcel him, but she's breathing heavily as they walk down the corridor. Her spell is one of conceal-ment – the few people they meet in these tunnels beneath Guerdon's chief fortress pay no attention to the sight of a Haithi soldier here.

In the distance, alarms begin to blare. Ramegos sighs.

"It hasn't started yet," she says. "I wish I had a chance to see if the machine works. Ah well."

Then, "this way", and she opens a door into a morgue. The room's dusty, and presumably dark to human eyes – he's been dead a year, and already he's forgotten much about how the living navigate the world. A shroud lies on the ground, as if it accidentally slipped from the table. She lifts the cloth, and beneath it is—

Oh.

"The damn thing's awake. I can't touch it, and it unravels my spells. You'll have to take it to where it belongs."

To the Erevesic.

"I suppose so." She kneels down by the sword, runs her fingers almost along the weapon, but never touching it. She looks at the blade regretfully, like it's a jewel of great price. "Ah, a chance may come around again. There's power in patience, and life is long."

I beg to differ. He scoops up the blade. An unfamiliar thrill, like blood pumping through phantom veins, runs through his arm, but the Enshrined souls within the phylactery blade recognise him as Haithi. The blade doesn't strike at him – but without a living soul to channel its magic, it can't exalt him either.

Ramegos stands, brushes herself off. Takes a heavy bag from a side table and slings it on her back with a grunt. "Let's be off."

The palace guards bring Terevant back to his room, overlooking the private gardens of the Patros. Terevant expected them to hand him over to Haith immediately, but instead, they make him wait.

The gardens tumbling down the hill's eastern flank must be beautiful in the morning, but the sun's setting on the other side of Holyhill, and they're full of twisted shadows in the dusk. Servants hurry through the winding paths, lighting lamps. Beyond the gardens, parts of the city are lighting up, too. Flickering gas lamps, the harsh flare of aetheric lights, night-candles. The city's fortunes traced in light. Further out, more aetheric lights, industrial ones, mark the site of the alchemists' new half-built factories, replacing the ones buried under the New City. And there, outside the limits of Guerdon, must be where the Haithi forces are camped. A small army, sent to extract justice for Olthic's death.

The thought of Olthic dead is still an absurd one. Olthic mastered the basic rites of Vigilance at a preposterously young age, and was the heir presumptive to the Erevesic sword. More than that, he was too large for death, too strong and too loud. His death feels more like an aberration than a loss. Less grief than disorientation, as if the world is a train that's jumped its tracks and now careens into some unknown region.

The clatter of hooves outside the window. A carriage draws up in the yard below, next to the garden wall. Drawn not by raptequines, but by a quartet of black horses. A pair of Vigilants riding on it. An honour guard, here to collect the wayward Erevesic.

A key scrapes in the lock of his door. The same guards who escorted him to the Patros, here to bring him downstairs.

"This way, my lord," says one.

Seeing his injuries, the other asks, "Shall I fetch the chair again, my lord?"

"No," says Terevant. "I can walk."

CHAPTER 39

As the gunboat approaches Hark Island, Aldras comes over to Eladora and Silkpurse. He slaps the side of the big crate. "This is going to the far side of the island. I'll deliver you to to the fort first, then go on and drop this cargo off. I'll be back for you within the hour. Don't be late."

The boat came alongside the concrete jetty in the shadow of the fort. Off to their left – *port*, she corrects herself – two other boats cluster around a narrow tooth of stone offshore. There's some sort of construction underway there. A sudden wave catches the boat, rocking it. The heavy crate lurches towards Eladora. Silkpurse pulls her out of the way as the crate breaks its restraints and slams into the railing. The wood of the crate splinters, and Eladora catches a glimpse of something spindly and grey inside. *A monster* is her initial thought, but the thing isn't moving. Some sort of statue, she guesses, although it's hard to shake the impression that it's something once-living that was preserved, pickled in some alchemical compound.

It's oddly familiar, too.

There's uproar on the ship as the crew rush over to wrestle the crate back into place, and Silkpurse adds her ghoulish strength to the task. Aldras helps Eladora climb onto the deserted jetty, more to keep her out of the way than out of any sense of chivalry. After a few heaves, the box is recentred in the boat, and Silkpurse joins Eladora on the shore.

The ghoul seems subdued, and growls softly at the boat as it departs. She sniffs the air, then crouches down and sniffs the ground. She looks over towards the construction on the far shore. It's some sort of machine – she can see what looks like a metal chair surrounded by aetheric engines. Aldras' boat is already on its way there, tracing a large arc to avoid any unseen rocks near the shore.

"T'isn't safe here," mutters Silkpurse. "Not at all."

The gates of the fort open, and a pair of guards, armed and masked, emerge. Eladora has Kelkin's letter of authorisation to hand. "I need to speak to your commanding officer, in the name of the emergency committee."

"The captain's occupied, milady. You'll have to wait."

"It's urgent." Eladora draws herself up, puts on her most commanding voice. "Minister Kelkin sent me. The matter cannot wait."

She sounds, she realises, a little like her grandfather. A part of her recoils at the thought, but she remembers how terrified she was of him, how that terror made her obey Jermas Thay's commands. Very well – she can use that.

The guards exchange glances through their masks, then nod. They escort her through the fort, weaving through the courtyard of chemical misters and monitoring devices. The eyes of two dozen or more saints watch her lethargically. *There but for the lack of grace of the gods*, she thinks. How many of them chose to walk the path of sainthood, and how many were trapped by it, seized by mad gods? She scans the cells, looking for Carillon, looking for Emlin, seeing neither. Sinter said to put Cari in the deep cells, wherever those are, but surely Emlin should be part of this strange assembly of saints.

Now that she's inside the structure, the diagrams and notes that Terevant showed her start to make sense. That arc of cells, each one with a saint of a different god. Monitoring devices and observers to watch them all, to calibrate their connections to divinity and to spot any changes. Mechanised mysticism – if the gods of Ulbishe or Lyrix or Ishmere extend their supernatural influence towards Guerdon, the corresponding saints in the machine will register that influence. The changes might be subtle or gross, but the proximity of the gods always has some effect on those close to them.

She imagines, as they cross the courtyard, another half-circle of cells on the far side of that mirrored watchtower. If the city watched for the Kept Gods, would they would lock Eladora away in a cell there? Dials and gauges twitching at the Festival of Flowers, jumping into the red when Silva fought Cari in the New City.

Silkpurse retches quietly. "Can't breathe this stuff," she says.

"Do you have another mask?" asks Eladora. She wonders if she should remove her own mask and breathe deeply, quash any lingering connection to the Kept Gods, but she needs to stay sharp.

The guard shakes his head. "None that'll fit its muzzle."

"I'll wait where it's fresher," says Silkpurse. "Call for me if you need me, and I'll come running."

"Stay by the jetty," cautions the guard. "You will be shot if you leave that shore."

Silkpurse runs on all fours back to the gate, casting a glance back towards Eladora, and Eladora isn't sure who's looking out of the ghoul's eyes in that moment. Rat's words echo in her mind.

She feels very alone as she crosses the yard. The guards flanking her are anonymous behind their masks. They lead her into the mirrored tower and up a narrow spiral staircase that runs through the heart of the structure. As they climb, Eladora glimpses alchemists and sorcerers bent over their instruments, peering through telescopes at the saints, measuring magical currents and shifts in the aether. Some of the devices she recognises from Professor Ongent's crowded office of curiosities and gizmos, or Ramegos' sanctum, but others are incomprehensible to her. There's more to this machine than mere divination – there's the hum of huge engines buried deep underground.

Climbing, again. The tower's taller than the walls of the fort around it, a glittering pillar. They can see the low roofs of the fort around the prison, see the dock and spit south of the island. Three small boats out at the spit, by the machinery. Another quarter-turn of the staircase and she glimpses *Grand Retort*, cruising past Hark on the western shore, following the same route Aldras took.

They come to the topmost level of the tower. It's an observation deck, looking out over the island and the city. An aethergraph chitters, relaying messages from Queen's Point and parliament, the twitching nerves of state. Soldiers and sorcerers crowd around the windows, watching the southern approach.

"Miss Duttin?"

The commander stands by the aethergraph in the centre of the room, the axle around which everything revolves. He looks like some emanation of the fort; the sheen of sweat on his bald head glistens like the mirrored windows of the tower, and he's solid enough to withstand an artillery barrage. He takes Kelkin's letter from Eladora.

"What are the names of the prisoners you want?"

"Alic Nemon."

"He's waiting for you. Edder will show you down." One of the other guards stirs, salutes.

"His son, Emlin. I know he's g-god-touched, but—"

The commander interrupts her. "Are you mad? Is this a joke? A test?"

"No, I—" Eladora swallows. "I'd like to see him, if he can't be released."

"That's not possible," says the commander curtly.

"Also – I'm not sure what name she was admitted under, but – Carillon Thay. A woman, about my age, dark-haired, her face marked." When the man doesn't react, she adds, "The deep cells?"

The commander shakes his head. "Access to special prisoners is forbidden. It's time for you to leave. Edder, show Mr Kelkin's representative down to Bloc One, and bring the prisoner to her."

Edder shuffles over to Eladora's side. "Yes, sir. Come along, miss. Best you be out of here before it all kicks off."

But before she can move, it begins. A flare rises over the southern side of the fort, launched from Aldras' boat. Edder makes a half-hearted attempt to usher Eladora back down the stairs, but he doesn't press her very hard. He wants to linger here as much as she does.

A matching flare goes up from the *Grand Retort*, rising like a bloody comet. A secular portent.

Is this an exercise? Are they getting ready to fire? But there's nothing in sight. No enemy ships in the water, no godspawned monsters. Just the island.

"Invocation station reports ready, sir," says a sorcerer.

"Begin," orders the commander. He strides over to the southern window, picks up a telescope, focuses it on that little outcrop of stone.

A thrill of sorcery runs through the tower. Huge aetheric engines groan into life. Electro-mechanical sorcery, their wires and valves mimicking the sorcerer's will. Alchemical soul-stuff, raw power, boils through them, churning in reaction chambers. Buried cables spark and hum. The whole fortress blazes with it. Static electricity crawls along drainpipes, leaps between the bars in the cells. Along the shore, where the cables run from the walls of the fort to the rocky tooth, magical discharges flash and transmute patches of sand to glass. Under the fortress, the shadows move.

The prisoners in the cells feel it. Some scream. Some cower. Some welcome the rush of magic, even though it's not meant for them. They beat on the bars and try to snatch some fraction of the energy of that massive invocation.

Thunder rolls across the city. There's a storm somewhere off to the north-east, rolling in on the far side of Holyhill.

All eyes watch the southern approach. Even those whose attention should be fixed on their instruments can't help making furtive glances south.

All except Eladora. She's seized by a sudden, intense terror, but it's not coming from the south. It's external to her, but it's centred around the *Grand Retort*. The warship's coming around the western shore of Hark, turning in the shallow waters. Crewmen wrestle the launcher into position. The god bomb's ready to fire. In Eladora's eyes, it's loathsome, a poisonous horror so vile she can't bear to look at it. As repulsive as the sun is bright.

The tower seems to spin around her. From here all things are visible.

"Manifestation," says one of the sorcerers – and in the same moment, from far away, her mother's voice: "We are betrayed! He means to strike us!"

Where is a god? Where is a thing without physical form? Where is a living thought, a prayer once it has left the lips, a spell before it is cast?

There, in that machine that has become a shrine. Entangled, hissing in fury and frustration, a thing of shadow unfolds, forced to manifest in the mortal world. *There*, right there, bound in chains of sorcery, is a god.

And there, on Holyhill. Above and around the Palace of the Patros. In the Victory Cathedrals. In the minds of the faithful who gather to praise their newfound king. In the House of Saints. In their gilded cages. The Kept Gods.

Kept. Trapped. But not bound.

Eladora raises her hand, to shield her eyes against the lightning flash.

CHAPTER 40

The guards hustle Terevant down a back staircase. The jostling makes him gasp in pain. They move abruptly from richly decorated halls to bare rooms with peeling paint; servants' quarters and storerooms. A few servants look curiously at Terevant, but they avert their eyes when the guards glare at them.

One servant, a stoop-shouldered, bearded man carrying a bundle of gardening tools, spades and forks and a mechanical spray-pump, passes by. The man's face is familiar to Terevant, but it takes him a moment to place it – the last time he saw that bearded man, it was on the train from Haith, all those weeks ago. He was the chaperone of those girls, the man sleeping under the newspaper.

Lemuel.

As the guards pass under an archway, they're ambushed. The bearded man smashes one over the back of the head with a shovel. When the other guard turns, the spray-pump goes off, shooting a small cloud of dust into his face – and then the guard's face shrivels, collapsing and shrinking like a rotten apple as the withering dust eats it away. Terevant steps back, retching, shielding his nose and mouth.

The man pulls the false beard from his face, revealing Lemuel's customary sneer. "Stay quiet and come on."

Lemuel hustles Terevant through a warren of storerooms. "Courtesy of the Bureau," he hisses. "We'll stash you somewhere, keep you safe."

"What about Lys?"

"She's where she needs to be — she's got the ear of the king and the Patros, and they've all played their parts. The alliance between Haith and the Church holds. The Crown can't blame the Church for you getting kidnapped. And she'll deny everything, say you're the bastard who killed her husband." There's a note of admiration in Lemuel's voice. "I bloody told you to get out of the city. You should've listened."

"You attacked me! At the Festival. You knocked me out."

Lemuel rolls his eyes. "That was Daerinth's clerks, not me. His little club."

Lemuel maintains a fast pace, enough to make Terevant's injuries painfully inconvenient, and he clearly knows it. He looks sidelong at Terevant, curiosity on his face. "Did you kill him? The ambassador?"

"No."

"I would've, if she'd ever asked me to." He shrugs. "Out through the gardens."

There's a heavy door, securely locked, but Lemuel has a key.

"Quick," mutters Lemuel, leading Terevant through the maze of the gardens. He chooses a route that avoids the lamps and candles, bringing them down paths shielded by tall plants and hedges. The air's thick with unfamiliar scents, the honey-sweetness of the flowers mingling strangely with the stench of burning fat from the corpse shafts. Their escape is so swift, so sudden it's almost dreamlike, as though Terevant left some part of his soul back in the palace, and now his wounded, hollow body is stumbling after Lemuel.

The stone walls of the garden can be glimpsed through the trees, half lost beneath the ivy. Moss grows over half-ruined walls and fallen stones as the garden tumbles down the tree-greened slope. "There are ghoul tunnels round this way," says Lemuel, "We'll go below."

They plunge into a deeper, darker part of the garden, where willow trees hang over sheltered flowerbeds. Lemuel slows down, relieved that they're almost out of view. Terevant leans against a tree for a moment, to catch his breath. He looks back at the dark bulk of the palace, its uppermost levels still outlined against the fiery sunset. He looks for the window of the room where he spoke to Lys, but he can't tell which one it was, or even if it's visible from here. The last rays of the sun glancing off the polished roof conjure phantoms in the air. He blinks, seeing shapes in the sky for moment. Suddenly, there's a new energy in the air. It feels like it did at Eskalind, as he climbed towards the temples. The Kept Gods are close at hand. So close that even Terevant can sense them.

"Move," hisses Lemuel, "bloody idiot. The tunnel entrance is just down here."

Lemuel yanks his arm, pulling him down another shady avenue lined with flowers.

"Wait," says Terevant. He can tell something's wrong, something's dangerous, but it takes him a moment to spot it.

It's dusk, but all the flowers are open. He looks at one, and it looks back at him.

A human eye has sprouted in the middle of each blossom. The same eye, in all the thousands of flowers.

"Saint," he says. Tries to say. Then Lemuel's nearly swallowed by a flowerbed. Hands – the same hand, over and over – emerge from the flowers, dragging him down. Terevant grabs the other man by the belt, throws himself backwards onto the gravel bank, yanking Lemuel out of the murderous flora.

"Back," shouts Lemuel, "to the carriage!" The Haithi carriage is on the other side of the garden wall. His gun barks, blossoms exploding in showers of bloody petals. They fall back towards the carriage, the rescue abandoned, the distinctions between Bureau and House falling away in the face of divine wrath.

The Vigilants hear their shouts and come rushing to their aid, swords drawn, battle-cries of Haith like leaden weights in the air. The two skeletal warriors scramble onto the garden wall with the uncanny agility of the dead. For an instant, Terevant sees the two Vigilants standing atop the wall, like sentries on the battlements of Old Haith, scanning the undergrowth.

Lightning flashes – from the sky or from the rooftop of the palace, Terevant can't tell – and one of the Vigilants is incinerated in a flash. Shards of bone rain down amid the flowers. The other's hurled off the wall by the blast, lands heavily amid the shrubberies. She tries to run, but the hammer of the Holy Smith catches her. Invisible hammer blows knock the Vigilant to the ground, smash her skull. She tries to rise, and the unseen hammer hits her again, driving her down into the gravel of the path. Then again and again and again.

Terevant tries to run towards the ghoul tunnel Lemuel indicated, but more assassins emerge from the shadows of the garden. Two of them corner Terevant; they have pistols drawn, but they don't fire. They know he'd be more dangerous dead than alive. Instead, one of them punches him sharply in the chest, right into his bandaged wound, knocking the air from his lungs. He stumbles, and the two of them seize him.

A third grabs Lemuel, overpowering him with ease. He draws a sword, and harsh white flames leap from the edges of the blade, driving away all shadow. All the fight goes out of Lemuel – they can't hope to stand against one Keeper saint, let alone two.

Or three.

Sinter comes down the path, pushing a wheeled chair. Silva Duttin sits in it, wrapped in blankets, her head lolling to one side. A line of drool runs from one corner of her mouth; on her lap, tied to the chair, is a sword.

"Ah, hell, don't tell me the bloody skeletons got involved," curses Sinter. He spits in the direction of the smoking crater.

Silva groans, but doesn't speak. Sinter wipes the drool from her mouth, and flicks the spittle into a little crystal vial that he pockets. "She pisses holy now, our Silva does. You want this, Lem? Heals all wounds, I'll bet." He swaggers over to Lemuel. "Though not this one, you godless Haithi prick."

The sword-wielding saint drives his blade into Lemuel's chest. It goes in with horrible ease, driven with such force that it cuts through bone as smoothly as skin or muscle. The holy fire burns very briefly. Even his last scream is cut short.

Sinter turns to face Terevant. "Lemuel was a local boy with *ambitions*. You could buy the little shit for two coppers. Daerinth, Lyssada, Vanth . . . fucker even tried to sell himself to me, once."

Sinter waves his three-fingered hand, warding off the stench of the burning body. "I cannot fucking abide faithless people. They deserve everything they get."

Silva makes a noise that might be a laugh.

The fact that Sinter hasn't killed Terevant too suggests that the spymaster intends to keep him alive. To hand him over to Haith as planned, sealing the alliance between the Keepers and Haith.

"And what are you loyal to, Sinter?"

"The blessed Church," says Sinter. "The gods in their place, and me in mine, and let none fuck that up. Oh, don't worry – we won't touch Lyssada Erevesic, though I've no doubt she's behind this little escapade. She'll have her alliance – on our terms, not with a fucking Haithi puppet king. And we'll have parliament. The city made whole and holy. Put an end to all this nonsense. And Kelkin, too." He kicks Lemuel's burning remains, as if anticipating having a different defeated enemy dead at his feet.

The entrance to the ghoul tunnels is just a short distance away. A short distance, and unimaginably far. The saints can move much faster than he can, and their bullets go faster still. They can heal him, too, or kill him and wait for him to come back Vigilant. Run, or don't run, live or die, all paths lead to the same place. To disgrace back in Haith. He'll be branded a murderer, a brother-killer. The last of the line of the Erevesics, a fool to the end.

"We're done here," says Sinter. "Put the Erevesic back in his room. Send word to Prince Daerinth that we'll bring the prisoner ourselves, tomorrow morning."

The two men grab his arms. Their hands are like manacles.

The flower-saint appears at Sinter's side. Her hands are stained, red with blood and green with crushed plant juice.

"He – the Patros – wants you. Up in the palace," she says, words tumbling out in haste. "There's something happening. He said, he said *Grand Retort*'s left port."

"Who's been sighted? What gods?" demands Sinter, grabbing the girl by the shoulders. She flinches at his touch. "Is it Ishmere? Ulbishe? Lyrix?" The girl shakes her head in confusion.

Holyhill is thick with divinity. The clouds above the garden ripple and flow, becoming huge figures that seem to lean down as if listening.

Sinter spins around, grabs a decorative lantern from an ivy-wreathed arch, thrusts it into the hands of one of the saints. "Ask the Holy Beggar for fucking guidance, quick – who's out there? Who the fuck is Kelkin aiming at?"

The saint holds the lantern awkwardly. No miraculous light of revelation shines forth. Whatever miracle impends isn't the one that Sinter desires. Terevant strains against the iron grip of his captors, but they're too strong for him to break free. The presence of their gods gifts them inhuman might, and here, tonight, they're as strong as they've ever been.

As strong as they've ever been. Here, at their temples.

What did Eladora see, in those notes from the Gethis Row safehouse? He remembers how ugly they were, how functional. As if stripping the majesty and mystery from the act was a necessary part of it ...

"'To ensure complete annihilation of the aetheric weave, it is necessary to achieve a local maxima of divine presence,'" shouts Terevant.

Sinter stares at him. "What?"

"One of Vanth's documents. It's about the god bombs. Some military project. Their ideal target – a big temple, lots of saints. The gods close at hand."

Sinter freezes. "Kelkin wouldn't. He fucking wouldn't."

The grip of the saints slackens enough for Terevant to shrug. "The Bureau thinks he might."

"We are betrayed!" hisses Silva from her chair. "He means to strike us!"

Suddenly uncertain, the saints look to Sinter for guidance. The air in the garden is unnaturally still, as the heavens hold their breath. Would Kelkin betray them? Would their city turn its most terrible weapon upon them?

Sinter stands there, like a man who's knows he's been shot, but hasn't yet felt the pain.

For a moment, Terevant's back on the shore at Grena. In his memory, the seagulls wheel above that empty, godless valley. There are other figures there, too — an armoured knight with a sword of fire, a woman crowned in flowers. Two thin figures grub for scrap metal in the surf, one holding a lamp. The Kept Gods are so close that even Terevant can touch them. The silent figures move through the hollows of his memory, probing the sand of the shore.

Then.

"Scatter! Scatter, you fucking shits!" Sinter runs amid his collection of fresh-minted saints, shoving them, blaspheming at them. He names them frantically. He pulls the symbol of the Keepers from his breast and hurls it into the mud, stamps on it. If he could, he'd burn down the temples, deny the king, drive the crowds away. Anything to break up the locus of divine power above the hill. Anything to make the Kept Gods less of a target for an incoming god bomb.

Silva topples backwards, spilling out of her wheelchair, but she's caught by unseen hands. Levitating, her head still lolling, her neck limp, but her right arm strong as a tower, she lifts her sword to the heavens.

And the heavens answer.

A bolt of lightning blasts from the sky above Holyhill, blazing across the city.

CHAPTER 41

The spy waits in the empty interrogation room. The rest of the prison vibrates around him, guards hurrying this way and that, alchemists and sorcerers fussing over their machinery.

Even through the thick stone walls of the old fort, the spy can sense forces moving. As though there are great invisible cogs and wheels under the skin of the world, moving and spinning, the teeth of the gears interlocking. Alic imagines Emlin crushed by these gears.

The spy quenches that thought. The sacrifice is necessary.

At the door, a snuffling noise. A ghoul, sniffing for scents.

"Alic?" It's Silkpurse.

"I'm in here."

The door cracks. The lock snaps. Silkpurse tumbles into the room.

"We came to get to you," she says. "You and Emlin and—" Her voice changes, growing deeper. "CARILLON. HAVE YOU SEEN CARILLON?"

The girl in the prison cell. "Downstairs."

Silkpurse wrings her hands. "I've got to get her – but oh, Emlin! I smelled his scent out there, on the rocks. They took him out to this—"

She's interrupted by a massive boom of thunder, breaking right above the prison. The whole island shakes.

That wasn't the god bomb. It was something else.

"What was that?" All the spy can think is that they're under attack, that the invasion has begun.

"Up," says Silkpurse. They rush out of the door, and up a narrow staircase to the roof of the fort.

There, just off the shore, is the *Grand Retort*. Smoke pours from the hole that's been punched in her. Her screws churn desperately, but she's sinking quickly into the shallow waters off Hark. Tiny figures crawl around her burning deck. The god bomb's there, in its cradle. Dying sailors stagger towards that dark shape, trying to fire it at . . .

At.

Eight legs arch from horizon to horizon, arching higher than the sky. Eight eyes like moons blaze with madness and hatred. Mandibles quiver as they taste the secret thoughts of every living soul in the city, and fangs drop godly venom that splashes on the southern wall of the fort, melting the stones. The sun does not set — it flees the master of shadows, the lord of whispers.

Silkpurse throws herself to the floor as the gaze of the god crosses over them. Mortals cannot bear the direct attention of a god for long. In the yard below, guards and prisoners alike fling themselves to the ground; sorcerers huddle behind triple-warded blast shields, and quail at the horror they've brought forth.

The spy stays standing, watching the fate he's made. *Fire, damn you*, he thinks, urging the gunners on the *Grand Retort* to overcome the churning waves, the smoke, the chaos, and loose their weapon. *Step over the dying, you can do nothing for them. They will be remembered as martyrs. Just launch the accursed thing!*

Silver cords of destiny weave so thickly around the manifest god that they, too, become visible, a billion destinies anchored to this single point in time. Fate Spider shrieks in frustration as it tries one strand of the web, then another and another, but cannot tear itself free from the alchemists' machine. Cannot escape, not as long as its tethered to Emlin. Congruency goes both ways — the machine turns Emlin's sainthood into a snare that drags the god out of heaven, forces it to manifest. If the god bomb were ready, the trap would close.

One sailor struggles across the heaving deck of the *Retort*, gets a gloved hand to the firing mechanism. Fumbles with the trigger, his clumsy fingers struggling to repair the damage caused by the blast. So very close.

The snare is a potent one, well made, but Fate Spider is older than the world. There is no trap it cannot outwit, in the end. Spinnerets of destiny throw out a new web, new strands of possibility. One strand finds purchase in the physical world. A new destiny. A way out.

There's an instant's hesitation, though, before the miracle. Some fragment of Emlin, maybe, caught up in the terrible embrace of the god.

It gives the spy a moment to duck for cover as fate lashes out like a whip.

The fires reach the *Grand Retort*'s phlogiston reserve, and the ship erupts in a second explosion. This one rips it in half. The unlucky sailor is killed instantly, his body pulverised by the blast.

The bow sinks, taking the god bomb with it – the spy can feel the horrible shape of the weapon even as it plunges down through forty feet of water. Explosions ripple along the stern, showering the area in shards of burning metal. One large chunk – big enough to impale a man – lands inches away from where the spy was standing a moment ago.

Other pieces of shrapnel rain down across the courtyard, starting fires. Debris cracks the surface of the mirror tower, sending bright fragments of glass tumbling to earth. The roof of the processing shed is alight. Flames lick the tanks of soporific gas.

There's a third explosion, this time on the island, a lurid burst of green flame as the gas tanks ignite. Flames rush down the rubber tubes that connect the tanks to all those cells. All the saint-prisons in the arc of cells are connected to those gas tanks. So are half the rooms in the fort complex itself. The mirror tower blazes with fiery light, as it reflects a dozen or more fires starting simultaneously.

With a whine, the aetheric lights go out. A shower of sparks hisses in the sea south of the island, as the divine summoning machinery dies. The manifestation of Fate Spider vanishes, the spectral spider-god dissolving back into the unseen realms.

Silkpurse grabs the spy, drags him back down the steps. She's yelping, an animalistic noise of terror and confusion. They pass the blazing inferno that was the interrogation room. Gobbets of molten rubber drip from the ceiling as the gas-jet catches fire.

"Got to get out. Got to get out," moans Silkpurse. She stumbles to one of the windows, tries to squeeze through, but it's too narrow. She claws at the stone in terror.

"Come on!" He's leading her now, pulling her towards the stairs. The stairwell's full of smoke, but no flames yet. They rush downstairs to ground level. Outside, it's chaos. The whole fort is ablaze – maybe the whole island. Greenish-blue smoke chokes the dusk.

The sound of roaring is met by gunfire. The saints are loose. The gas has stopped, and some of them have had their prayers answered.

"We have to get off the island!" he says.

"I must get Miss Duttin. And Cari." Silkpurse clenches her clawed fists, then dashes off into the madness and fire of the courtyard.

The spy walks forward. The gate of the prison is open and unguarded.

There, ahead of him, is the jetty. He can see the lights of boats approaching it, beams cutting through the smoke that rolls over the water, coming to rescue any survivors of the conflagration. All he has to do is wait by the shore. Everyone else in the prison might burn, but the spy will survive.

For a little while, anyway. The manifestation of Fate Spider has vanished, but Ishmere is coming. Kraken swims through the seas. Cloud Mother births the horizon. Blessed Bol whispers in the clink of every coin in Guerdon's markets. Striding ahead of them all, Lion Queen. And the instrument of his revenge lies under forty feet of water on the far side of the island.

There's a strange, wordless keening noise, somewhere between a whimper and a scream. He can't tell where it's coming from, then realises he's making it.

The spy might survive, but his plan has failed.

*

Eladora watches in horror as the *Grand Retort* explodes. The prow sinks beneath the waves, carrying the linchpin of Guerdon's defences with it. Sparks and shrapnel from the blazing stern fall across the fort, lighting fires. The whole tower lurches when the gas tanks go up.

For a moment, she glimpses two figures on the roof of the old fort. Silkpurse and Alic.

"Please, I must go," she begins, but the tower commander grabs her, points to the space under a table.

"Stay there," he orders, "keep that breathing mask on."

The aethergraph clatters, a dozen messages coming through at once. The commander barks orders. Some guards are sent down to keep order in the cells. Others are sent to the walls, to signal the boats offshore to come in and take the survivors. To destroy parts of the machine, before it can be misused by escaped saints. From downstairs, Eladora hears shouts, screams, gunfire. She crouches under the table as ordered, trying to stay out of the way of the military as they mount a desperate defence of the prison. Outside, the courtyard has become the Godswar in microcosm, as mad saints from a dozen pantheons recall old grudges at the same time as they recall divine powers.

Smoke clouds fill the air outside the tower. It's like they're in a glass boat sailing on a sea of fire, disconnected from the world outside. The only tether to sanity is that chattering aethergraph. The operator reads off messages in a clipped tone, staying true to his training despite the carnage, reporting the sinking of the *Grand Retort*, responding to panicked inquiries from Queen's Point, from parliament, from a dozen other stations.

The aetherglyph chatters again.

"Sir, Queen's Point has our range. They'll fire in twenty minutes. Full howler battery."

"Sound the evacuation order," snaps the commander.

Queen's Point bristles with cannons, and her long guns can reach all the way out into the harbour. They're going to rain down howler-shells and philogiston bursts, wipe the island clean.

"We'll form up on the ground floor," says the commander, fastening his mask and checking his handgun. "Make straight for the gates. Edder, Valomar, provide covering fire from the tower." He turns to Eladora. "Miss Duttin, you're with us. Just keep your head down."

"I came here on Minister Kelkin's authority to retrieve three detainees. I can't leave without them."

"Unless they're already at the boat, Miss Duttin, there's nothing I can do."

"Effro Kelkin himself—"

He points to the aethergraph. "Send him a message if you want. Bring him here in person if you want. It won't matter. There's no time."

The spy walks down onto the stony beach, heedless of the blazing fortress behind him, ignoring the sounds of carnage. He wades into the cold waters and washes the soot from his face.

Washes away any trace of the gas.

Washes away X84, the failed agent of Ishmere.

Washes away Sanhada Baradhin, lets the man's face and name float off into the bay.

Washes away a hundred other names he's worn.

The plan has failed. Does he have the strength to start again, somewhere else? He was only a fractional being when he first came to Guerdon, and he's lost even more of himself since then.

Better, maybe, to let it go.

He begins to dissolve, to wash away the last name left to the spy, when Alic hears Emlin weeping in the distance.

The spotlight of one of the boats catches Emlin, revealing him in the darkness. He's chained to an iron chair on the tooth of rock, surrounded by occult machinery. Mechanical summoning circles, spinning like prayer wheels. Aetheric engines. Tanks of jellyfish, grown with human souls, bred to blindly adore and worship whatever deity they're shown. And behind him, the statue of the Fate Spider from the Street of Shrines.

The boat turns, the crew hurrying to bring the deck gun to bear.

Alic turns back, wades onto the shore. Then runs, leaping from rock to rock, following the spit of land out towards that rocky outcrop. He's racing the gunboat, racing the fragmentation shell from the deck gun. Shouts from the boat when the crew spot him, ordering him to turn back.

Then, when he doesn't stop, small arms fire cracks on the rocks around him. Alic doesn't care — he's a wisp, a fragment, a lie of a man. He barely exists.

But Emlin's real. Whatever else, the boy's real. Flesh and blood, so very mortal, so very fragile. An innocent child walked into the Paper Tombs in Ishmere, was offered up to the gods. He's belonged to Fate Spider ever since.

Alic runs towards his child. His heart pounds in his chest, his lungs fill with acrid smoke. He feels alive for the first time.

Emlin's head lolls to the side. He's drooling, his eyes unfocused. Blood smeared across his face, running from his ears and nose. The boy channelled the full power of a god — it'll be a miracle if he's still sane. Alic scrambles over the rocks and broken machines to his side. The metal of the summoning circle burns hot to the touch. Cracked aetheric engines leak wild magic into the world.

"Emlin?"

The boy sees Alic, and it's like he's waking from a nightmare. Gods above and below, gods of every nation, he's still alive! His eyes light up, he coughs, spits out blood, calls out to Alic.

"I want to go home."

Emlin is bound to the iron chair by heavy manacles, scored with runes of binding. Alic tears at the clasps, trying to find how to undo the mechanism, but it's too tightly sealed. He tugs at the manacles, hammers at them with a rock. Tears at them until his fingers bleed.

"What's happening?" asks Emlin, weakly. "I saw . . . is it the fleet? Are they here?"

The gunboat blares its horn, a last warning. The deck gun's armed and loaded. They're not going to relent.

There's no time to escape.

No time to say farewell.

Many and strange are the blessings of the Fate Spider.

Only time for a father's benediction, before the thundercrack of the guns, and the outcrop's annihilated by a hail of shells.

CHAPTER 42

Terevant runs through the gardens of the Patros, as best he can. Stumbling in the darkness, crashing through hedges and slipping on slick grass. Adrenaline overcoming the pain in his chest. He can feel the heat of his periapts, triggered by his injuries, as they stand ready to resurrect him if he falls, and he honestly isn't sure he's alive or dead by the time he makes it to the entrance to the tunnel. Without hesitation, he dives into the darkness.

Shouts echo down the tunnel behind him. Sinter's men are giving chase. Terevant runs, blind in the utter darkness of this underworld. He guesses that the passageway has to link up with the cellars of the palace somehow, so he hurries in that direction. Stumbling over the uneven floor, feeling his way along the moisture-slick walls. The tunnel floor gives way to rough-cut stairs, and he makes it down without breaking his neck.

The shouts still echo, but from somewhere far away. He keeps walking, stumbling, until there's nothing but the dripping silence of the underworld. It's so dark that only the dead could see down here. His shirt's wet with blood again — one of his wounds has opened. Maybe more than one.

The tunnel ends in what seems to be a pile of fallen rocks. He probes with his hands for a way through, and finds a narrow passageway off to the side. Squeezing through, he discovers it leads down. He stops, wondering if it's better to try retracing his steps in the utter darkness and search for the turning that must lead back to the cellars, or keep going. He tries to bring the maps from Gethis

Row to mind, but the tunnels below the city are more intricate and intertwined than the veins and arteries beneath the flesh of a flayed corpse.

Once, he has the impression that there's someone else here with him. The sound of someone else, breathing heavily. Smells of ash and salt. But when he reaches out, there's no one there. Just a trick of the darkness.

He finds he's on the floor. Unable to tell if the wetness on the stone is moisture trickling down from above, or his own sticky blood. Unable to tell if he's blacked out for a instant, or an hour, or many hours. Or if he's died casteless, lost forever in the darkness. Imagining himself rising as a Vigilant, only to wander the endless labyrinths beneath the city forever, never finding his way back. Maybe he'll meet Edoric Vanth some day, centuries hence, another dead man blundering through this maze. Lost in the lies.

He's back in the woods outside the Erevesic mansion, and it's very cold. There are wolves in these woods, Olthic cautions him, stay close.

You're dead, he tells Olthic, and father's dead. And I'm the Erevesic. You tried to prepare me for that, but I didn't listen.

I lost sight of it, too, says Olthic, but it's simple. Take up your sword.

Terevant tries to tell his brother that he lost the Erevesic sword, that the family blade is gone, but he falls into darkness again. His fingers are too numb to hold a blade, even if he had one.

From down the tunnel, the sound of snuffling.

An unearthly screech, and something lands against the outside of the tower with a heavy thump. For an instant, Eladora glimpses a face through the glass, the impression of an arachnid form, but it's gone before she can blink. The soldiers swivel in place, levelling their weapons at the windows, but whatever's out there scuttles away before they can fire. There's nothing visible now through the soot-stained glass.

One guard dares to open the door. "It's clear, sir."

"Form up!" orders the commander. His men rush downstairs. He looks to Eladora. "I'll leave you behind if I have to, miss."

She has to find Carillon, and Alic. And she thinks she recognised that face at the window, despite the changes. "I'll see you at the boat."

"Fifteen minutes. You shall have no more." The commander's expression is unreadable behind his mask as he turns and marches down the stairs. They charge out, guns barking, their bullets clearing a path through warped divinity.

One minute ticks by. Two. Eladora hides under the desk again, watches the room. Everything in the tower is very still. Everything outside the tower is hell.

The face appears at the window again. Spider-legs probe the glass for weaknesses, then a human fist smashes against a cracked pane. Eladora suppresses a squeak of horror at the sight of the monstrous amalgam. The creature's god-touched, his formerly human frame warped and blended with the essence of the divine Spider. Horribly long, spindly legs carry the saint across the room, his human torso hunched against the ceiling. He moves towards the commander's desk with quiet intent.

Then those eight eyes spot Eladora's hiding place. The spider-saint turns on her, yellowish venom dripping from human teeth.

It worked for Sinter, thinks Eladora, *but he's much further gone than I was.* "Emlin!" she calls, naming the mortal in front of her, and not the god entwined with him. "Emlin," she cries again. She hopes it's his real name.

Emlin pauses. His stance shifts, his expression softens. Tears well up; he swallows his venom. "Fate Spider chose me. Showed me what is coming. He gave me strength."

"Emlin! Listen," Eladora begs. "They tried to make me a saint, too. I'm still me. You don't have to obey."

"Can't stay. This place will burn. I've seen it." Emlin scuttles back, then picks up the heavy aethergraph machine from the desk, cables trailing from it like entrails. Eladora cowers, terrified that Emlin is about to hurl the machine at her, but then the saint lowers his head and bites into the machine, sinking his teeth into the metal as if he's eating a succulent fruit. Venom rushes from his fangs, discolouring the metal, mixing with the bubbling alchemical fluids at the heart of the device.

He lifts his head for a moment. "Run! It's coming." And then he bites the aethergraph again.

Eladora watches in horror and confusion as Emlin dissolves, or shrinks, somehow flowing *into* the machine.

The aetherglyph crashes to the ground when Emlin vanishes. The cables vibrate as something moves through them.

Those cables connect to the mainland, to a web of aethergraph stations. To machines throughout Guerdon, all in places of great importance. Parliament, Queen's Point, the alchemists' guildhall, city watch stations . . . all the city's organs, linked by nerves of spun orichalcum.

Eladora checks the aethergraph, wondering if she can send a warning to the mainland, but the machine's dead.

Five minutes gone.

Six, and she's at the door of the tower, the keys to the prison block clutched in her hand.

Seven, and she's in the courtyard. One of the skeletal metal towers has crashed down across the yard, blocking the mirror-tower off from the worst of the chaos. Through the smoke and flames, she can see the last of the guards holding the gate of the fort. The earth is soaked with the blood of saints.

Eight, and she's stumbling across the courtyard. The breathing mask is all that keeps her from succumbing to the foul smoke. The heat blisters her skin. There's the door to the cells.

Nine, and she's in the old fort building on the perimeter of the isle. The upper storeys are ablaze; burning sparks fall from the ceiling, and the gaps between beams in the ceiling glow a burning red. The building creaks alarmingly.

Ten, and she's downstairs. The steel door at the bottom of the stairs is locked. Silkpurse is there, scrabbling at the door, tearing at the mortar around the doorframe as she tries to force it open through sheer strength. Her muzzle's choked with blood and soot, making her breathing horribly laboured.

"Cari's in there!"

Eladora pushes past her. "Get out!" she shouts. "Go to the boat! Make them wait for us!"

The steel door is hot to the touch as she searches for the right key. Silkpurse has done so much damage to the hinges that Eladora can only partially open the door, but the gap is wide enough to squeeze through. Inside, there's no light. She takes a breath, the air in the mask stinking of sweat and ash, and – *eleven minutes* – murmurs a sorcerous incantation. The spell rises through her, tugging at bones and muscles, as she gathers the energy and spits it out as a little ball of light. It's almost funny how difficult the incantation is, compared to the power she was able to briefly wield as a saint.

The spell illuminates the corridor of cells. There's Carillon, lying on a bed in the furthermost cell. Unconscious, but stirring. Eladora hurries forward, looking for the matching key for that cell.

"Let me out."

Miren's hand shoots out of the gap between the bars, grabbing her right elbow. His fingers close on her arm, digging in, trapping her. He's so very thin, so very pale, but it's him. There was a time – a year and a lifetime ago – when she'd devoutly wished for him to touch her in any way. When she'd seen his quiet blankness as concealing hidden, tender depths.

She never saw with her own eyes the things that Miren is accused of doing. She never witnessed any of the murders, never knew he was bred by his father to be a replacement for Carillon, another saint of the Black Iron Gods. She read the reports that Kelkin and Ramegos shared with her, about how Miren eliminated his father's enemies, how he teleported around the city in secret, locked-room murders and thefts. About how he killed Spar at the height of the Crisis.

Some foolish part of her always wanted to disbelieve. She could never completely reconcile the monster in those reports with the boy she'd known.

Now she can.

Miren pulls her over to the cell, his limbs frighteningly twisted, like a python. One arm wrapping itself around her neck, pressing on her windpipe. The other hand grabbing for her left arm, trying to reach the bunch of keys.

She drops the keys, kicks them away out of reach down the corridor. He hisses in anger, and increases the pressure on her throat. She tears at his arm with her nails, but he doesn't react. She tries for a spell, and he lifts her off the ground, slamming her head against a crossbar. The pain breaks her grasp on the sorcery.

"I thought you'd come for me," he whispers in her ear. His hand moves across her, probing. He finds the letter she forged, unfolds it. "What's this? You leave me rotting here for months, but as soon as my Cari's put in jail, you come running?"

"Didn't know. You. Here." *Twelve,* says another part of her mind, remorseless and cold.

"If I let you go, will you open the lock?" he whispers in her ear.

"Yes," she gasps.

A long moment passes as he considers her words. "No. I don't think I believe you." He keeps squeezing, and squeezing. The cells are very far away now. She tries praying to the Kept Gods – a fraction of her mother's strength would be enough to rip Miren's arm off, or bend the bars of Cari's cell – but they're far away, too, and far above. She feels like she's falling into some dark abyss, populated only by echoes and the pounding noise of her own heart.

"Father always thought more of you than I." His voice sounds like it's coming from inside her, a thought running through her brain that isn't hers. Broken shapes of darkness move in the deeps. There's an awful silence there, how she imagines death must sound. An absence that smothers everything.

Miren's arm around her throat is smooth and dry, but she remembers her grandfather's wormy hands choking her, too.

She hears Carillon's voice, somehow overlapping. It's right there with her in this dark place, and echoing down from far above.

"Murderer!"

The pressure lifts, and Eladora falls to the floor. Purple lights explode in her vision as she gasps for air. Cari's there, unsteady on her feet, but free, out of the cell. She's holding the bunch of keys in her hand, and blood's dripping from one jagged key. Miren cradles a wound on his forearm. He raises his arm to his mouth and sucks the blood.

"We have the same dreams," he says to Cari. "You killed most of them, but there are still two left. Broken, like us."

"El, do you have a fucking gun? Or a knife? I'm going to kill this bastard." Cari has to lean against the wall to stay standing, but there's no hesitation in her voice.

"We have. To go." Eladora wheezes. "They're going to. To b-bomb the whole island."

"That'll do," says Cari. "Hear that, fucker?" She imitates the whistle-blast of an incoming shell. "They'll drop this whole building on top of you. Just like daddy."

Miren licks away the last of the blood. Stretches like a cat, sniffs the air. It's full of smoke, but there's no remaining smell of the gas. "Follow me, Carillon," he says, reaching out through the bars. Polite this time, offering his hand like a gentleman helping her out of a carriage. "I know a way."

Cari doesn't move. Miren withdraws. "As you wish."

He clenches his fists, and vanishes.

It's ghastly. The one time Eladora saw him teleport before, in the crypt on Gravehill, he'd simply disappeared. One heartbeat he was there, the next gone, a flickering shadow. This is different. He doesn't move, but she can tell he's laboriously *pulling* himself through whatever dimension he travels through. A dozen heartbeats, and with every one, new agonies cross his face. He fades, beat by beat, with the sound of joints cracking, of sinews snapping and reforming. Worst of all, he leaves some of himself behind – a ghostly after-image, made of leftover flesh. A moon shadow of bone, thinner than the finest china. A wisp of flesh, like onion-skin parchment. A ghost of tissue. A mist of moisture from his eyes, a few droplets of blood, a few small fragments of thread from his rags. All falling to the floor or blowing away on the hot draughts when he's gone.

"Gods below," says Cari, sinking back against the wall.

"No time," says Eladora, grabbing her. She's lost track of how long before the artillery bombardment begins, but they can't have more than a few minutes. They run through the burning fort, climbing back up to ground level, looking for a door that leads out into the courtyard near the gate. They sprint through endless abandoned rooms, the flames crackling over their heads, burning timber falling around them.

They find a window that's large enough to climb out of. On the other side is a steep drop down to rocks atop the island's eastern flank. They half clamber, half fall down, landing heavily on the hard rocks. Carillon gulps fresh air as the sea breeze cuts through the smoke. There's a goat-path from there down to the jetty. The light from the burning buildings above them is brighter than the sun.

"I'm getting woozy," says Cari, slipping on the rocks.

"It's just a little further," Eladora says, but she's interrupted by the distant crack-boom of artillery fire. She looks towards the city on the horizon. At this distance, Guerdon is a little semicircle of light, with only a few features discernible. The white bulk of the New City, the spires of Holyhill.

Smoke over Queen's Point. Tiny pinpricks of light, like fast-moving stars.

CHAPTER 43

"Swim!" Eladora pulls Cari towards the water as the first shells descend. Fortunately, the gunners' initial target is the summoning machinery on the south shore, not the fort itself. Still, they're only a few hundred yards away from the blast zone, and half the world explodes. The first barrage is howler-shells, designed to shatter hard targets. Warships, fortifications, gods. The second wave will be the same, she guesses, to destroy the remainder of the fort, rip away any shelter where a rogue saint might hide.

The next barrage will be phlogiston, to sear the island clear.

Hand in hand, they plunge into the chilly water, struggling to stay afloat. Detritus from the sunken *Retort* bobs past them. Carillon's a stronger swimmer, but she's still weak from her imprisonment. Eladora grabs a piece of floating debris large enough for her cousin to rest on as they continue to paddle towards the receding lights. Her breathing mask fills with salty water; she pulls it off and loops the strap around her wrist.

"El," says Cari weakly. "Thanks."

"Yes, well," sniffs Eladora, "it seemed like the right thing to do. I could hardly leave you there."

"Not that. Well, that, but also, y'know, kicking the shit out of your mother. I know how scary it is, letting a god in. How hard it is to stay yourself, afterwards." She coughs, shivers. "Even with Spar — he's not a god, I guess, but it's still hard to remember sometimes where he stops and I start. Sometimes, I'd get on a train and just fuck off out of the city for a few days."

"They thought you'd leave the city." Eladora rests on the floating debris, too, her body trailing in the water. She kicks off her boots to swim better, her toes freezing in the cold water. She's exhausted, and it's getting harder to kick. The currents here will sweep them back towards Hark if they stop, though, bringing them back into the line of fire.

"Sail away. Yeah. I thought about it, but . . . I don't know. I felt like I fucked everything up, so it was on me to fix it. I never used to feel like that, before . . . "

"Cari, stay awake."

"If I don't, just . . . take care of it, all right?" Cari loses her grip on their little raft, begins to slip backwards.

Eladora catches her cousin's wrist. "Carillon Thay, stay awake!"

"Trying." Cari bites her lip, squares her shoulders, and pulls herself up onto the raft.

Behind them, more shells fall on Hark. More howlers. The sky momentarily bright, then darkness closes in again. After the screeches fall to silence and the echoes die away, Eladora adds. "It was Rat who sent me to get you. He needs your help, I think."

Carillon smiles. "Fucker's still in there." She closes her eyes, as if in prayer.

Eladora holds onto Carillon's hand, feeling the pulse in her wrist, like a bell. The smoke and flickering lights from the ruin on the island behind them makes the night sky untrustworthy. Dark shapes that might be clouds, mottled with unearthly colours. She feels something move beneath her, deep in the waters. Gods circle the city like wolves, like sharks, unseen as they draw closer. And the city's only weapon is down there, too.

What does the election matter now? Will the invading gods care if it's Kelkin or Sinter or someone else at the minister's pulpit in parliament when the city falls? All the decisions and sacrifices of the last ten months – do they even warrant a footnote? She's achieved nothing lasting.

She recalls Professor Ongent lecturing her on Guerdon's history. The city has been conquered before, but those were mortal wars. The victors installed new kings and satraps, demanded tribute, dwelt in the city and became part of its fabric. Wars of territory, wars of gold. There could be compromise. Treaties and ransoms, truces and alliances. They could show mercy.

The Godswar is different. It's all-consuming. Severast showed that – the sundered gods even slaughtered their worshippers, tolerating no dissent. The city will be destroyed.

Thinking of Ongent makes her think of Miren, stepping into the darkness. It's her nightmare come to life. All those carefully buried memories, those thoughts she's locked away over the last year, come spilling out, but she's too tired and cold to feel much. They float there in the darkness of her mind, like the debris that surrounds them. She can consider them dispassionately, watch them drift and spin, forming new patterns.

Half-drowned rats scramble over the debris. Bedraggled, terrified, desperate, the creatures claw at each other as their little refuges sink beneath their combined weight.

A horrible idea presents itself. A horrible way out.

"There has to be another way," she says to herself.

"El," calls Cari. "Look."

And in the distance, a boat's coming towards them. Silkpurse perched on the prow like a figurehead, waving.

Commander Aldras drapes them both in blankets, has them sit near the hot housing of the engine. Silkpurse perches next to them, like she's a gargoyle on a tombstone in Gravehill, then remembers herself. She sits down as well, crossing her legs and borrowing one of the blankets.

"I found Alic," she says, her voice breaking. "He went to get Emlin, but they didn't make it."

"Emlin is alive." Eladora shivers at the memory of the thing she saw in the tower. The thing with the boy's voice, his eyes. "But he was transformed into a giant . . . spidery thing." She stares across the water to the city, a light's flashing in the darkness, from some tower atop Queen's Point. On and off, on and off, pulsing out a message.

"Fate Spider," says Cari. "Diviners and rumour-mongers down in Severast. Pay 'em a copper and they'll read your fate in the cobwebs, that sort of stuff. Harmless, I thought."

"The Ishmere branch of the church is different." Eladora recalls the few reports she was privy to.

"We're turning," says Cari suddenly. The blazing island behind them provides an easy reference point, so it's clear she's correct. The boat's changed course — instead of returning to Guerdon, it's now circling back, orbiting a point off the north-west shore of Hark.

Commander Aldras comes down from the wheelhouse. He glances suspiciously at Carillon, then addresses Eladora.

"New orders from Queen's Point. We're to stay here until dawn, guard the wreck of the *Grand Retort*. As soon as I can, I'll have you back on the mainland." He pauses. "There was no mention of your mission. I can signal back if you wish, but under the circumstances, you should just count your blessings."

"Fuck him," mutters Cari, once he's out of earshot. "I need to get back to Spar."

"Can you, ah, contact him from here?" asks Eladora. The New City's almost invisible in the darkness.

Silkpurse looks confused. "But — Spar's dead, dear." Then she hunches, her voice changes. "URRH. YOU HAVE HER?"

"Rat?"

"HELLO, CARILLON," says the elder ghoul. Foam wells up from Silkpurse's mouth, and Eladora wipes it away with a corner of the blanket. Silkpurse's limbs twitch, but stay locked in place, as Rat takes control of her voice from miles away.

"You tried to kill me, you fuck," says Cari.

"HAD TO. THE BLACK IRON GODS COULD HAVE RETURNED THROUGH YOU. NOT A DANGER NOW. BUT THERE ARE OTHERS DIGGING UNDER THE NEW CITY. YOU KNOW WHAT THEY SEEK. WHERE ARE YOU?"

"On a fucking boat," says Cari.

"We're at the wreck of the *Grand Retort*," whispers Eladora. "They said we wouldn't be back in the city until the morning."

"TOO LONG. URRRH." Silkpurse's body suddenly goes limp, and she collapses to the deck. Commander Aldras stands up at the same moment, but it's too far for Rat to hold onto the officer's mind. Aldras looks around in confusion, then takes a swig from a canteen and returns to his labours, his crew dropping off another marker buoy.

Silkpurse convulses again. "Rat, you'll hurt her. I'll come as quick as I can," says Cari.

"Urrgh." The light begins to fade from Silkpurse's eyes.

"Wait," Eladora says hastily. "Warn Kelkin — there's an Ishmeric saint in the aethergraphs. And Miren's loose." She has no idea what the elder ghoul will be able to do about either threat, but if she tells him, at least there's a chance that the city will be warned.

As Rat departs, a hideous smile spreads across Silkpurse's lips. Rat has wanted to kill Miren from the moment he met him.

"We've got to get back to Guerdon," says Cari. She scrambles to the railing, stares at the New City, one hand holding onto the amulet she wears around her neck, a talisman of the Black Iron Gods. Eladora shivers, remembering how Jermas placed it around her own neck when he tried to summon the gods through her. "I can't reach Spar. It's too far."

"You can't do what Miren does, can you?" asks Eladora.

"Teleport? Not really. I tried, a few times, but it's something the Black Iron Gods gave him." She slumps down. "I saw sorcerers do something similar, years ago. Down in Severast. You throw spells, these days — can you get us back to shore like that?"

"I'm not an adept," says Eladora, thinking of Ramegos. Teleportation is likely beyond her, too, although ... She takes that thought, lets it float with the rest of the debris.

"Figured. Right." Cari nods over at Commander Aldras. "Do you want to talk to him, or should I?" Cari reaches under her blanket and produces a knife.

Eladora stifles a shriek. "You just got out of prison! And then we were in the ocean! How did you get that?"

"Sailors have knives." Cari shrugs.

"Put that away." Eladora hurries over to Aldras' side. He looks up at her, half his face illuminated by the raging phlogiston flames on Hark, the rest in shadow.

"Commander, it's imperative that we return to Guerdon immediately. There are other boats here to guard the wreck – surely they can spare your vessel for a swift return trip?"

"I have my orders, miss. I may not understand them fully, but I'm not about to question them."

Eladora crosses to the railing, looks down into the dark waters. The reflections of flames dance in the waves and ripples, turning the sea to fire. Beyond that undulating ribbon of light, she can see sense a point of revulsion. The military don't need to mark the wreck of the *Retort* – anyone touched by the gods can sense the precise spot where the awful thing lies.

"Commander, down there lies a weapon that's key to the city's defence. There are two other weapons like it, and they're about to be taken by our enemies. We need to stop them."

Aldras slaps the side of the boat's searchlight. "I can signal the mainland, but we're not leaving."

The boat lurches, pushing Eladora against the railing. Aldras catches her, his other hand going to the wheel.

She looks over the side, and the reflection of the fires is distorted. The ribbon of fire's breaking into many smaller streamers, flowing away out to sea. The boat's still turning, the engine labouring to hold her in position. The topmost parts of the wreck are suddenly visible through the water.

Cari joins them in the wheelhouse. "What's happening?"

"We're being dragged," shouts Aldras.

"The water's going away," says Eladora, confused.

"Kraken." Cari pulls her away from the railing. "It's a fucking kraken, stealing the sea!"

"KRAKEN!" roars Aldras. The boat's crew stir themselves, putting on protective gear, readying weapons.

There were four other boats out there, circling the wreck. Four shapes, outlined in flame. Four lights on the dark water.

Now, there are three.

Aldras doesn't hesitate. He's Mattaur-born, and although he left that land before it fell to Ishmere, he's seen Kraken-saints before. He knows their miraculous powers. Long ago, the gods of Ishmere stole the seas; he has seen the way Kraken's miracle can turn water to a substance like liquid glass that no ship can sail through, nor any man swim in. If his boat's caught by this miracle, they'll be trapped, unable to do anything except sit and wait for the unseen monster's tentacles to rise.

He turns the boat towards Guerdon, opens the throttle. The engines roar as the gunboat struggles to break free of the current, and then they're moving quickly, plunging forward towards the distant city lights. Eladora falls to the floor, unbalanced by the rolling motion of the deck. Cari maintains her balance, knife in hand, watching for danger. Of the three, she's the only one who's travelled beyond Guerdon; she spent half her life on ships

There's three lights behind them, and they're not moving. The sea around Hark has turned to glass.

Two lights, and they're racing for the safety of the city, its inner harbour. Spray from the bow splashes over them. The engine screams.

They pass the Bell Rock. Pass Shrike Island.

One light left astern, and they're halfway there.

Then none behind them, except for the burning line of Hark on the horizon. Guerdon swells ahead of them – they can see the harbour clearly now, the New City on one side and Queen's Point on the other. Aldras frantically flashes the signal light, beating out a warning to anyone who's watching. Sensing its prey escaping, the kraken pursues, spitting miracles ahead of them. Glassy stains like oil-slicks appear in their path, and Aldras must weave a path between them.

"Hold fast," shouts Aldras. Silkpurse scrambles forward to Eladora's side. The alchemical engines belch smoke and scream as they're pressed past the point of endurance. Noxious gas hisses from some overpressured valve.

A tentacle swipes out of the water, brushing almost gently over the boat. It drips with water turned razor-sharp. Eladora winces as one droplet lands on her thigh, slicing through her dress and her skin like a knife. Silkpurse shelters her, letting her back be flayed by the passage of the tentacle.

Aldras roars in pain, falling back. His mask protected him from the worst of the saint's assault, but he's still hurt. His arms and back are covered in welts. He's holding one hand to a wound on his neck, and blood wells from between his fingers.

Cari jumps forward, grabs the wheel, while Eladora wriggles from under Silkpurse and helps treat Aldras' injuries, wishing in that moment that she could call up the healing gifts of the Kept Gods again. She can't bring herself to pray, and the gods aren't so close to her that she can draw on their power without intervention on their part.

The kraken's right behind them now – more tentacles rip at the boat's stern, trying to disable their engine. For a moment, Eladora sees a huge eye, bloodshot and watery-green, peering at her from the churning waters.

Some naval gun emplacement on the shore has seen their signal, their plight. Shots fall into the water nearby, sending spouts of water leaping high into the air or cracking patches of glass. The kraken writhes, then dives, burrowing into the murk of the sea-bed for safety. From its hiding place, it spits a final, desperate miracle.

A ripple of magic runs through the sea, and all the waters along the shore turn to glass. A scum of razors, a foam of frozen blades. From the cape of the New City to Queen's Point, the city's edge is abruptly rimed with glass. Liquid glass breaks like a wave, sends a lethal spray over the city's jetties and docks. They're cut off from landing. Thirty feet from shore, an impassable barrier of knives.

Carillon prays, and the New City quakes. One of the unlikely spires that towers over the city lurches, half toppling so it overhangs the harbour. Chunks of miracle-conjured stone fall, and where they land, the glass turns back to water.

Carillon aims the boat for the narrow gap opened in the glass and brings them home.

CHAPTER 44

They land at a jetty. The New City rises above them, a sheer cliff of unlikely architecture. This was the edge of the Gutter Miracle, the last moments of Spar's brief divinity, when he spent the accumulated power of the Black Iron Gods profligately. Fractal shapes frozen in stone, great plazas that end in abrupt cliffs, towers like fingers on the hand of a petrified giant, all growing from the same root structure. A few faces look down at them from balconies and walkways on higher levels, but the streets are unusually empty. Many of the inhabitants of the New City came to Guerdon from lands conquered by Ishmere, from Mattaur and Severest. They've seen the gods of Ishmere march to war before. They know what's coming, so they've taken shelter. Only fools and saints would stand openly against the gods in their wrath.

It's a struggle to climb out of the boat; the water level in the harbour is unnaturally low and they have to climb up a weed-tangled ladder at the side of the jetty. The falling seas have exposed discoloured walls swarming with shellfish and alchemical runoff. Seabirds flock to this sudden bounty, cawing and shrieking. Eladora catches fragments of a prayer to Cloud Mother in the calls of the gulls.

The gods are coming. None of them are safe here.

"Come on." Cari leads Eladora and Silkpurse across the quayside towards the seawall. Even after months of study, Eladora's grasp of New City geography is hazy, so it takes her a moment to realise they've landed near Sevenshell Street. Cari's old house is several levels up, but only one street over.

"Wait," shouts Aldras, scrambing out of the boat and hurrying after them. "You have to come with us to Queen's Point. You're still in custody."

"Sure," says Cari. "Come and arrest me."

She touches the stone of the seawall, and it tears like wet paper, rolling back and ripping until it's a doorway. Silkpurse and Eladora follow her through. Eladora gives an apologetic wave as the portal closes behind them.

The tunnel Cari opened leads to a stairwell. Cari looks at the narrow spiral staircase ascending into the darkness. "Fuck that," she says. "Let's talk here." She sits down on the bottom step, resting her head against the stone wall.

"Hey," she says to the stone. "I'm back."

She seems stronger already, drawing vitality from the New City.

From all around them, Eladora can hear a sound like surging water. She doesn't know if it's the sound of the city streets far above her, or the sea draining from deep tunnels, or some tremendous stone heart beating in a distant chamber.

"Water level's dropping. The whole harbour's draining." Cari sounds distracted, like she's only half listening. "Fuck. Fuck. Fuck," she mutters to herself.

"What's happening out there?" Eladora's own fears conjure a litany of horrors.

"Oh, *fuck.*"

The streets of the Wash seem deserted this night. Still, whoever's watching from spy holes or from the upper levels of the tenements that slump over the street must think them a strange couple indeed. The dead man and the sorceress hurry along the path, both carrying heavy burdens. The Erevesic sword strapped to Yoras' back seems to squirm and writhe, digging into his spine, his ribcage.

Ramegos huffs and puffs as she carries her bag and her heavy ledger of sorceries. Yoras offered to carry one or the other, but she refused. "We'll be parting ways soon enough," she said, "soon as we get to the Dowager Gate, I'll be going west and you north." North, to the Haithi camp. West to ... west, *away* from the Ishmere invasion fleet out there, in the conquered sea. Away from the wrathful gods.

A siren wails mournfully somewhere up on Castle Hill, signalling curfew.

The trains aren't running. There isn't a carriage to be had in the city. The streets are deserted, in anticipation of the storm.

The easiest route to the Dowager Gate would be to keep going through the Wash until they cross over Mercy Street, then follow that boulevard north under the viaducts, but Mercy Street and Venture Square have become armed camps in anticipation of attack, and neither Ramegos nor Yoras can afford to be stopped and questioned. Therefore, they circle around the foot of Castle Hill. The rocky cliffside has, over the centuries, been turned into a vertical city, a district of stairs and ledges under the shadow of the parliament building. It's easy to move unseen there.

Ramegos – the only living thing, it seems, in all the Wash – mutters instructions to Yoras between breaths, telling him what to say when he gets to the camp. It's clear to him that there's some intricate web of intrigues and bargains involved, but making sense of it is beyond him. He just listens while he helps the older woman up the steep steps that rise from the Wash to the rocky heights of Castle Hill.

"When you get there, don't stop. Don't let anyone take that sword off you, until you find the heir and put it right in his hand. The phylactery will know its own. Watch for ... " Ramegos clicks her tongue, then shakes her head, deciding not to put that thought into words. "I never meant any of them ill. There was never supposed to be any bloodshed on my account." She makes a curious sign with her hand, and Yoras suspects that there's some sorcerous taboo involved. Her worry about bloodshed is more that simple guilt.

He doubts whoever she conspired with feels the same. The dead do not feel as the living do. In Haith, life is a brief, wild fling with unreason and passion. The Empire is founded on cold obedience to tradition and iron-boned discipline.

There are a great many steps, and they're only halfway up Castle

Hill when Ramegos calls a halt. She reaches inside her coat, pulls out her chain of gods, examines it.

"Well, then." She turns and faces south.

Gunfire rings out over the city. It's directed away from them, out to sea. Flashes from Castle Hill, from directly above them. Then answering fire from Queen's Point, from the docks. A massive, earth-shaking fusillade – and the earth keeps shaking even after the guns of Guerdon fall silent.

There's a rushing, rumbling noise, bigger than the sky. So wide it cannot be distinguished from its echoes. The whole horizon's screaming.

Yoras can see in the dark. The living cannot. All they know is that terrible noise.

He can see the waters draining from the harbour. The white line of the surf retreating. The masts of the docked ships toppling out of sight behind the row of warehouses like felled trees. Huge freighters settling into the mud as the sea withdraws. All across the bay, the water's going away.

A dark wall, terrible and vast, rises up in the bay. A tidal wave, taller than the towers.

Long ago, Ishmere conquered the seas.

Now, the sea goes to war for the Sacred Realm.

As the wave rolls over Shrike Island, it does not break. Instead, it splits, and splits again and again. Not one wave but a dozen, a dozen arms of of water, immense, Kraken-shaped. Riding atop each of the twelve arms is a huge, grotesque warship. Misshapen things laden with shrines and relics, vessels that could never sail in mortal seas. Bourne by krakens across the endless ocean from Ishmere.

The first tentacle breaks over the harbour, sending a cascade of razor-water flooding over the quayside. Another two, three, maybe more, wrap around Queen's Point. When the tentacles collapse, they leave behind the warships they carried. There's a ship left stranded high atop the fortress, toppled over on some upper courtyard.

Another wave-tentacle stretches out of the invading ocean. It reaches over the docks, over the Wash, arching directly above Yoras' skull. He glimpses the keel of the Ishmere warship as it rides the wave, hears the battle-cries of the saints and monsters on board. The tentacle can stretch just far enough to reach the edge of the plateau of Castle Hill, and the warship grinds to rest perched atop the precipice.

Muddy water crashes down onto them. Yoras flings Ramegos into an alcove. The razor-edged water tears through his uniform and scores his bones with deep scratches, but he can endure the assault infinitely better than her mortal flesh. The stairs become a waterfall.

Ramegos is shouting something – a spell – but even though her face is only inches away from his skull, he can't hear her. The world is shattered by six more cataclysms, six more waves crashing to earth. And where each wave lands, it leaves behind a warship crewed by god-touched monsters and fanatic priests.

"We have to get below," shouts Ramegos. "The tunnels! The tunnels!"

A shrieking storm blows in with impossible speed, the clouds boiling out of the night. There are war-saints in the sky.

The feeble gods of Guerdon could only muster a single thunderbolt. The gods of Ishmere have the blessing of High Umur, and he commands the lightning-sheaf. The night sky explodes into a hundred false dawns as the gods smite gun emplacements and fortifications across the city. One bolt strikes the stairs, and the impact sends him tumbling over the edge.

He splashes into the floodwaters, and the current catches him. The streets of the Wash have become fast-flowing rivers, rushing blindly down towards the sea. He's not the only corpse carried by these waters. The dead are all around him, dancing with him as he's carried off into the maelstrom that was Guerdon.

Carillon presses her hand to the stone wall – more for support than for any magical connection to Spar, guesses Eladora. Her cousin's voice shakes as she relays what the visions tell her.

"A dozen Ishmeric ships. This . . . tidal wave tentacle thing carried them inland, way past the shore. They've landed all over the Wash.

Castle Hill, too. Saints and . . . fuck. The watch is fucked. Lots of them near Queen's Point, more down the docks. The camp down in Venture Square got washed away. It looks like there's fighting near the Keeper Churches, and in Glimmerside."

"They're going after temples," says Eladora, recalling briefings from Admiral Vermeil. In other lands conquered in the Godswar, the temples and sanctums and saints of the enemy are the first targets for any attacker. Anything that denies the gods' ability to coalesce.

She wonders if the Admiral's alive or dead. The guns up by parliament have gone silent. She remembers the spider-monster made from Emlin invading the aethergraph network, and there was an aethergraph in the war office in parliament, too. The spider could have bypassed parliament's outdated wards, jumped from Hark to the heart of government in a flash. For all Eladora knows, Kelkin and Vermeil and the rest of the emergency committee are all dead, and the city's leaderless.

Cari wrenches her attention away from the visions. "You've got to run, El. I can't leave, but you can. Get out of the city."

Everyone keeps telling her to run. Ramegos, Rat and now Cari. Telling her to escape, to look away from the danger. She's rejected her own proffered sainthood, and she's not a master sorcerer. She's not a soldier or a general or a saint or a spy. What role is left to her to play in this?

She shakes her head, unsure of what the answer might be.

"Do we hide? Go deep?" Silkpurse asks, burying her face in her hands at the thought. "That's what Rat's planning, I think. There are places under the city where even the gods of Ishmere won't find us."

"Fuck that," says Cari. "We need to stop the invasion. It's going to be a fucking slaughter. Again. We need weapons. There's the one on *Kestrel*, but that's sunk. There are two more buried down with the alchemical shit, and now Rat's complaining about Haithi soldiers in his shitty ghoul tunnels."

Eladora nearly adds *Ramegos found the bombs and sold their location to the Haithi*, but she holds her tongue. Carillon doesn't need to know that, and might react by stabbing someone.

Cari snaps her fingers. "That's fucking it. Haith's after the bombs. They're trying to break open the vault, but they've got to be careful 'cos of all the alchemical stuff down there. I can just shape the stone. We get in quick, steal 'em first, use them. Boom."

"No," says Eladora quietly.

"No what?" snaps Cari. She hops up. "What's the alternative? If you want to stay, you fight, right? Or are you going to run back to bloody Effro Kelkin? Write reports while the navy tries to fight 'em off? Because I fucking know what he'll say, El – they'll write off the New City, and the Wash, and half the low city. Like they did before. They'll defend the rich folk and tell the rest to go hang. I fucking know, El, all right? I've been protecting the New City single-handed for months!"

"Cari, calm d-down." Eladora says. "I need to think."

"We don't have time. We have to get those bombs."

"Those weapons are unfinished. They're just broken bells."

"The alchemists turned the Tower of Law bell into a weapon in a week!" spits Cari. She prowls up and down the landing, the knife she stole in her hand. Unable to sit still, consumed by the need to act.

To do something stupid.

"Do you have an alchemical foundry to hand? One designed according to the most closely guarded secrets of the alchemists? The ones who got killed when you conjured the New City on top of them?"

Cari glares, but doesn't have an answer.

"And even then, what would that achieve?"

"Kill the Ishmeric gods!"

"Ramegos designed the whole machine on Hark Island to achieve the conditions necessary to kill *one* god. The weapons aren't a solution. E-everyone's extrapolating from the Grena Valley, but that was chosen as a test site because it offered optimal conditions."

"Godsfuck. So what do we do?"

"Running off wildly won't help."

"No, let's sit here and read a book about how much smarter you are than everyone else. That'll fucking help."

Silkpurse shifts uncomfortably. "The Keepers are stronger than they used be. They have saints now. Guerdon ain't so godless. Not saying I want to live under the Kept Gods again, but better them than Ishmere. An' there's a king now, maybe it won't be so bad."

"Holyhill's fucked," declares Cari. "If they're going for the churches and temples the Keepers will go first." A savage grin on her face. "Welcome to sainthood, Silva. I bet they'll make a really nice relic from your fucking skull."

A coalition. An alliance, thinks Eladora. The Church's saints, marching to war alongside the city watch and the navy. Alchemical weapons to bolster them. And Terevant owes her a favour — maybe they can call on the Haithi troops to aid them. They can fight back, can't they?

She slumps down against the wall, pressing her hands over her ears to blot out the sounds of bombardment. All she can hear is the booming of her own blood.

What portion of the invasion fleet has landed already? Twelve ships is only a fraction of Ishmere's strength. And when Mattaur fell, there were avatars there, the gods manifested as fully as they could in the physical world. For all the carnage and destruction outside, this is still just a probing attack. Is Ishmere holding back, or is this all the force they could muster now? All the intelligence reports claimed that they were going to attack Lyrix. They've changed course for some reason. A spy, she guesses, reporting that Guerdon was more vulnerable than it appeared.

If that's true, then this is only the first wave. There'll be more ships. More saints.

It feels like she's reading all this in a history book. Detached and distant, with lists of troop numbers and estimated miracles. *The Fall of Guerdon: a critical reassessment, with special emphasis on political discord and the role of the Thay family.*

She has no idea who'd win in a conflict between this Ishmeric force and whatever coalition of city watch and Keeper saints and Haithi troops they could cobble together, but she knows that it wouldn't be a decisive victory. Ishmere has vast fleets; Haith has undying hosts. The winner would not be allowed to hold Guerdon, not while the city contained prizes like the alchemical works, the hidden god bombs. There'd be a counter-invasion, and another, and another.

Repelling the invasion won't end the war.

Think. Think.

Think as saints hurl lightning across the sky. Think as the noise of artillery fire is joined by the crack of rifles down by the docks. Think as the city groans and creaks beneath the weight of floodwater.

Silkpurse kneels down next to her.

"Miss, we're going to Lord Rat. The ghouls are gathering down below. He's called for Carillon. Are you coming?"

Eladora shakes her head again. She can't remember how to speak.

Cari pauses. "El. I know a bunch of smugglers. Spar says they're leaving tonight – they've got a boat hidden up the coast. If you want, it's your best chance to get to safety."

There'll be more waves. More gods.

She stands. She has no handkerchief, so she wipes her nose on her sleeve. "I'm going to Kelkin," she says quietly.

Cari looks disappointed. "For fuck's sake, El."

"I . . . I have an . . . an inkling of an idea. A thesis."

The ghoul beams. "Mr Kelkin will know what to do."

"Mr Kelkin," mutters Eladora, "will not like my idea."

CHAPTER 45

T he unseen creatures paw and sniff at Terevant. Long rough tongues lick his hands, slipping under the wrists of his shirt to probe his periapt-scars. Ghouls, he thinks, feral ones. The corpse-eaters were eradicated in Haith centuries ago, but he recalls old stories. Young ghouls can almost pass for human, talk like humans, and elder ghouls are monsters out of legend, necrophagic demigods of the underworld. Between those two stages is the feral period, when the monsters become savage predators and scavengers. He's in the midst of a pack of two-legged wolves.

Stay calm. No threatening gestures. But don't play dead — they eat corpses. *Death, they're probably hungry. The Church of the Keepers is supposed to feed them, but they've closed the corpse shafts.*

"I don't have any food," he says. The ghouls leer and whoop. One of them tugs at his shirt, claws pushing at the painful scar. Another shoves him, pushing him over. He can't keep his footing in the darkness.

More ghouls join the pack, dragging something behind them. He can't see them, but the tunnel's more crowded, and he can hear wet cracking noises, smell the blood. They've grabbed a corpse, and they're dismembering it. Ripping it limb from limb, picking it apart. His stomach lurches and he retches, making his chest burn with pain again. Grotesquely, one of the ghouls passes a lump of flesh back to him, offering it to him as if they expect him to share in their grisly feast. He takes the flesh and throws it aside.

One of the bigger monsters yowls, and he can't tell if it's an instruction or a question or an animalistic roar.

And then they lift him, the whole pack carrying him, dragging him at speed through the tunnels. He shouts, but they're moving so fast through the endless darkness that he can't even hear the echo of his screams. He kicks, but they're monstrously strong. Clawed hands grab his ankles, his arms, trap him in place. Clawed hands close over his mouth, muffling him. Plunging through the city's depths, a headlong rush like a runaway train. He's convinced at every turn that they'll smash his head against some unseen obstacle, or that half the ghouls will go one way and the rest another and he'll be torn apart.

Down go the ghouls. At times, their wild race through the city's underworld brings them to great open chasms – sewers, maybe, or train tunnels, or unseen caverns – and the ghouls leap across them, the chill wind rushing across Terevant's face, the synchronised grunt of the pack as they fling themselves across the abyss.

Abruptly, the pack pauses. He hears some of them move away, muttering and growling to one another in low tones. They're suddenly cautious. They lay Terevant down on the floor – it's rough, metallic, broken, like he's lying in a scrapyard. A broken pipe presses against his ribs; his cheek lies against shattered glass. He can smell a foul chemical reek, and something slimy – not a ghoul, much smaller, the size of a housecat maybe, but squishy and cold – scuttles over his calf. Where have they brought him?

The ground trembles as something elephantine walks towards him. Hot, foul breath. The yelping of the ghouls becomes subdued, even awed. Massive claws lift him from the ground – and then, worst of all, the creature takes control of his *voice*. Rotten-fruit words swell up in his stomach and pour through his throat like lumpy vomit.

"URH. A COIN LOST IN THE GUTTER. A KITTEN IN A BAG. MAN OF HAITH. WHAT GOOD ARE YOU? YOUR SOUL IS BOUND TO YOUR BONES. MUST WE CRACK OPEN THE MARROW TO FIND YOU?"

The creature drops him, sending him sprawling back on the broken ground, but his mouth keeps moving. His voice echoing in his ears. "YOUR TWO-FACED SERVING-MAN, HIM

WE COULD EAT. HE OFFERED UP ALL HIS SECRETS. YOU ARE THE LORD OF THESE SOLDIERS. THEY WILL LISTEN TO YOU."

Terevant tries to speak, tries to tell the ghouls that he's a wanted criminal, that he has no authority over the House Erevesic troops any more, but the monster still seizes his throat.

"TELL THEM THAT THEY WILL FIND NO TREASURE HERE."

The monster releases him. Terevant gasps for air. "Why are you doing this?"

"WE WERE HERE FIRST." The elder ghoul squats down next to him. Instead of speaking through him, it takes control of a chorus of its lesser kin, its voice a guttural choir of barks and grunts that somehow form jigsaw words. "ALWAYS, WHEN THE DARK TIMES COME, WE GO TO THE DEEP PLACES TO SHELTER. KELKIN'S PLANS HAVE FAILED. THERE WILL BE MUCH DEATH. WE SHALL HIDE DOWN HERE UNTIL THE STORM PASSES, AND THEN THE STREETS WILL HAVE SUCH A BOUNTY OF DEAD FLESH FOR US TO EAT. THIS IS THE WAY OF THE GHOUL." The monster leans in, so close that Terevant can hear the rasping of its tongue. "TELL THEM TO LEAVE."

"They won't listen to me."

"YOUR STRENGTH IS COMING, MAN OF HAITH. I SMELL IT. AND WHEN YOU HAVE IT, YOU WILL MAKE THEM LEAVE. MARCH AWAY TO YOUR DUSTY LAND, AND TROUBLE MY CITY NO MORE." The ghoul chuckles. "YOU CAN LEAVE US DAERINTH. THERE IS NOT MUCH *SOUL* LEFT IN HIM TO EAT, BUT I SHALL PICK MY TEETH WITH HIS BONES."

A strange light approaches. Its radiance illuminates the chamber around them. It's vast, an underground cyst hundreds of feet across. An endless junkyard, piled in drifts and mounts, shattered and twisted like some giant child had played with it before discarding his broken toys. The ceiling, by contrast, is a magnificent vault that wouldn't be out of place in the grandest cathedral in all the world, all made from a pearly white stone that—

"We're under the New City."

"Indeed." The conjurer of the light emerges from another tunnel. It's Dr Ramegos. Her robes are wet and tattered, and she's bleeding from many small cuts. Behind her are more ghouls, pushing her along like the others carried Terevant. "This used to be the old Alchemists' Quarter, up until the Crisis. The god bombs were made here. But you put an end to that, didn't you, Lord Rat?"

Now that he can see the elder ghoul, Terevant wishes it was still dark. The creature's right next to him, so close he can feel its fetid breath on his neck. It's at least twice his height, with a horned head that resembles the skinned skull of a dog. Eyes that make him think of a furnace's light, like the thing's burning souls in its emaciated belly.

The elder ghoul speaks through Terevant again. The words pushing irresistibly out of his throat. "CARILLON KILLED THE BLACK IRON GODS. SPAR BURIED WHAT WAS LEFT. IT IS WISE TO LISTEN WHEN GHOULS SPEAK OF GRAVES."

Ramegos sits down next to Terevant, facing the ghoul. "If this *creature* had let us excavate the vault, we could have recovered the remnants of the last two bells ourselves. But he wouldn't let us in—"

"YOU DO NOT KNOW WHAT YOU ASK," growls Rat, through one of the other ghouls. Terevant and Ramegos are surrounded now by a host of the scavengers, swarming like moths around the light. Ramegos doesn't flinch. She ignores the ghoul's interruption.

"He wouldn't let us in, and Effro Kelkin wasn't willing to risk the alliance with the ghouls. So, we struck a secret deal with your Crown. A phylactery in exchange for the location of the vault."

"The Erevesic sword." *She killed Olthic*, thinks Terevant. *The Crown killed Olthic.*

"SHE HAS WRONGED BOTH OF US," says Rat, "SHALL WE KILL HER?" The ghouls laugh. "SHALL I BREAK YOU, OLD WITCH, AND EAT OF YOUR SOUL?"

"You've been threatening that since I arrived," Ramegos sneers. Sorcery crackles between her hands. "He's too much of a coward to try it," she says to Terevant. "And if I've wronged you, he's done worse. Ask him who told the Keepers about Edoric Vanth. Go on, Rat, admit it."

The elder ghoul laughs again, a horrible gurgling. "COURAGE IS BORN OF FEAR. FEAR IS FOR SURFACE FOLK." A different ghoul speaks this time, but they're still Rat's words. "YOUR BARGAIN WITH HAITH WOULD HAVE BROUGHT TROUBLE DOWN ON US. HAS BROUGHT TROUBLE."

"Where's the sword?" demands Terevant. He feels like he's walked in the middle of a long-running argument.

"Young Eladora Duttin came to me, and . . . convinced me to return it to you. I tried, I really did. I gave it to your man Yoras."

"Where is he?"

Ramegos shakes her head. "I'm sorry. He's gone. We got caught in the open when Ishmere attacked. The sword's in the middle of the Wash. It's hell up there." As if to underline her words, the cavern shakes slightly, rocked by a distant explosion or divine thunderbolt far above.

"YOUR PLANS HAVE FAILED," says Rat. "THE ARMADA OF ISHMERE IS HERE. THERE WILL BE GODSWAR ON THE STREETS, AND MUCH SUFFERING."

"I thought we'd have more time," says Ramegos. "That they'd bypass Guerdon, and go and conquer Lyrix or Haith first. No offence." She sighs. "We tried. We really did. We nearly changed the world, here. If we'd had a little longer . . . "

Rat nuzzles her, his massive snout pushing against her. "LIE DOWN AND DIE, THEN, AND WE SHALL EAT OF YOUR FLESH."

"I'm not dead yet," snaps Ramegos. "I'm leaving, by the quickest road I can find."

"WITHOUT THE SWORD," growls Rat, "HE IS USELESS TO ME. YOU ARE BOTH *MEAT*." The ghoul looms over them, claws gleaming in the werelight.

Terevant scrambles to his feet. "I'm still the Erevesic! Even without the sword – those troops are mine. Bring them to me. Let me talk to them!"

"AS YOU WISH." The ghoul shrugs. "THE GODSWAR IS UPON US. IT MATTERS LITTLE HOW YOU SPEND YOUR LAST BREATHS."

The ghouls lead Terevant and Ramegos across the strange landscape of the cavern, through the wreckage. They must take a circuitous route; the ghouls may be mostly immune to the toxin pools and piles of shattered alchemical weapons, but Terevant is still mortal. He imagines he can feel the poisons seeping into his flesh. His lungs burn, his eyes water, but he can't look away. Behind him, Ramegos coughs into her sleeve. She mutters something about the place being too unstable for protective spells.

They move through the remains of the old Alchemists' Quarter. The god bombs were forged in these machines; a kingdom's ransom in weapons lies scattered across the tortured stone. They pass the corpses of monsters that Terevant doesn't recognise – misshapen things, like a dozen animals stitched together. Crawling horrors of wax. Slime pools that sprout eyes and stare at him.

There are other creatures in the darkness. Drawn by the light, they slither and lumber and pounce. Things that might once have been human, shambling wretches in the tattered remains of protective suits. Half-wax creatures, partially melted. Feral raptequines, thin as skeletal horses, pale manes matted with blood.

Ahead, the walls curve inwards. The white stone's smeared with patches of crushed metal, debris piled atop more debris and crushed by some unimaginable force. A containment vessel. He imagines a stone giant, frantically ramming handfuls of molten metal against cracks in the wall, desperate to seal away whatever lies on the far side. Something more toxic, more abhorrent than all the horrors of this outer cavern.

At the foot of the massive wall is a patch of light. Dozens of Vigilant troops in House Erevesic livery stand watch alongside a smaller continent of embassy troops. Behind them are a handful of living souls. Some wear the black robes of necromancers, others the uniform of royal engineers. Haunted faces, pale from the dust, smeared with blood and slime. They're quarrying through the wall. Terevant wonders for an instant why they don't simply blast through the wall, then remembers the piles of alchemical waste and broken weapons littering the wreckage. No wonder they aren't using explosives.

When they spot the ghouls, the Vigilants react as one, aiming their rifles into the darkness. The ghouls take cover amid the debris, leaving Terevant exposed. He advances all alone, stepping over bodies. Recently killed ghouls, a few broken Vigilants, damaged beyond repair, and beneath them a gory carpet of slaughtered abominations.

It is the Erevesic, shouts one of the undead in amazement.

The Erevesic! echo the other troops of his House. They've fought for his family for centuries. They lived and died and rose to fight again alongside his ancestors, alongside the bearer of the Erevesic sword.

Familiar skulls that he last saw back in Old Haith emerge out of the darkness. Commander Rabendath, Iorial, Brythal. Bony hands supporting him, leading him into the light.

"The city's under attack," says Terevant. "We should be up there. Brythal, your daughter's up there in the Patros' palace, it'll be their first target—"

We have our orders, lord, says Rabendath, **and you are not in command here.**

Daerinth hurries towards him accompanied by four Vigilants from the embassy staff. "Arrest him!" he croaks. "Arrest the ambassador's murderer!"

The Erevesic is in custody, says Rabendath. The House Erevesic dead close ranks around Terevant. He and Daerinth are left staring at each other through fences of bone.

"Take him to the camp! Put him on a train to Haith, so that he may stand before the Crown's justice," insists Daerinth. "He should not be here."

"Let him through," orders Terevant.

The old man pushes through the lines, clutches at Terevant's arm. He whispers, "I gave you a chance to run, you fool. I tried to avoid this."

"You murdered my brother."

"I tried to avoid the necessity. If not for your intransigence, he would be alive and crowned, but . . . it had to be done. It is for Haith I do all this."

"What have you done?"

"I never wavered. The Crown will see I never wavered." The Crown, not the Houses or the Bureau. Olthic tried to secure Guerdon by diplomacy, Lys by guile, and all the while there was a third plan, born of desperation and cold calculation.

Daerinth weakly pushes Terevant away, raises his voice.

"A kinslayer cannot hold the family sword. The souls of the Enshrined dead would reject him. The line of the Erevesics ended with Olthic. You owe this traitor no loyalty."

"I didn't kill him. I don't know how you did it, but—"

Daerinth scoffs. "More lies. You stabbed him."

"You all fought at my brother's side," says Terevant, raising his voice. "You knew his prowess as a swordsman. He was peerless with an ordinary blade – you think I alone could have beaten him when he held the Erevesic sword?"

One of the embassy troops swivels his skull to look at Daerinth. **Perhaps we should all return to the camp, your grace.**

"There is no time for that. We are too close. On the other side of this wall are the remains of the last two god-bane weapons. The Crown has commanded me to obtain them. The Crown commands me."

"He knows the weapons are there," shouts Terevant, "because he sold the Erevesic sword to find this place!"

"That is a lie. The Crown would never—"

"Dr Ramegos, come forward!"

"Ah, hell." The werelight flares into existence. Ramegos advances cautiously, emerging from the ghouls' hiding place and picking her

way across the wreckage. Daerinth stares in horror as she approaches;
Ramegos gives him an awkward nod of greeting. "It's true. There
was a deal. A phylactery for the location of the bombs, the knowledge to use them. I can't speak to what happened in the embassy,
but I had the sword."

She stands in the middle of the no man's land between the ghouls
and the dead, the pale conjured light falling around her, making her
look like some accusing spectre.

"What does it matter!?" Daerinth shrieks. "Haith is in peril!
After Guerdon falls, we are next! The Crown needs those weapons!
Bring down the wall!"

The Crown troops push against the unyielding line of House
Erevesic, and are forced back. Daerinth tries to reach to the Royal
Engineers stationed by the wall, pushing through the host of the
dead, but Rabendath steps forward and gently restrains the prince.
We shall return to the camp, your grace—

And then everything goes to hell.

Rat sees it first – or senses it first. The big ghoul starts moving,
an instant before it all begins. Scrambling up a scree of broken
metal, his hot breath steaming in the chill of the cavern, wading
through the wreckage. Claws outstretched, maw drooling. But he's
too far away.

Ramegos glances back, alarmed by the charging ghoul. The
bristle of rifles from the Haithi ranks.

For an instant, there's a shard of steel in the air next to Terevant.
A spike of bright metal, sliding out of nowhere, materialising impossibly. Then there's a man holding it, dressed in rags, young and
pale, dark tangled hair and beard, his dirt-streaked hand clasping
the handle of the knife. Moving like a dancer, always in motion,
stepping from one place to another without passing through the
intervening space.

From beyond the curtain wall, Terevant hears a distant grinding
noise, some great mass of metal shifting against stone.

The knife blade disappears like a conjuring trick, reappears in

Ramegos' chest, plunging deep into her ribcage. A spell dies unspoken on her lips, and she begins to fall.

The assassin lets go of the knife handle with smooth grace, whirling on past Ramegos. He falls apart as he moves, dissolving into a spinning cloud of rags and tatters and bloody shreds. Rat reaches the assassin an instant after he vanishes, the ghoul's massive claws closing on empty air. The name "MIREN" bursts from Terevant's throat, leaving a bitter aftertaste of frustration and hatred.

Terevant catches Ramegos before she hits the ground. Her blood-flecked lips mutter the same word, the elder ghoul's anger spilling out through every living mouth within range. The sorceress is bird-light, hollow-boned. He's shocked by the heat of her life as it floods over his hand in a wet rush. He tries to staunch the bleeding, but he's not sure how. If a soldier under his command was this badly hurt, he'd let the warrior die, start their eternal vigil. Abandon the flesh.

Rat's roaring in anger. Erevesic soldiers rush forwards, swords in hand, forming a defensive line in front of Terevant. Swords ready, threatening Rat. The elder ghoul snorts and snarls; more ghouls push forward.

Ramegos clutches at him, trying to tell him something. He catches the words "Black Iron" and what might be "saint" or "sacrifice", but nothing intelligible.

She's dying. Think. She's a sorceress. The periapts under his skin are necromantic talismans, blessed by Death to pin the soul in place, anchor it to the mortal world. He has no idea if it'll work, but he grabs her right hand, her sharp-nailed fingers, and presses them to his wrist. Pushing against his skin so she can feel the iron lump of the periapt. Blood gurgles in her throat; her lung's been pierced, but she manages to dig her nails into his wrist, and arcane energy floods through her into him, like millions of tiny bubbles rushing through his veins. The periapt grows blisteringly hot underneath his skin – she's doing something with it. Using him like a drowning woman would cling to flotsam.

Ramegos grabs his face with one hand, pushes at him. Turning his head so he looks across the cavern towards that curtain wall.

There, beyond the Vigilant, beyond Daerinth – the engineers. The military sappers brought down from Haith. There's a brief flicker of a deeper shadow there, the same pale boy who stabbed Ramegos. He's crossed the cavern in a heartbeat, teleported from the middle of the vast room to its edge.

A match flares in his hand. The sappers brought a blasting charge.

Stabbing Ramegos was a distraction, to draw attention away from that curtain wall for a moment so he could—

The wall explodes. The white soul-stone of the New City cracks and collapses, pearly shards falling like an iceberg calving. A billowing cloud of sparking dust rushes outwards, shot through with flying debris that rains down throughout the cave. He can hear shouts, screams of pain from the living engineers near the blast. Others are dead. Daerinth lies broken and bleeding.

For an instant, he can can see into another cavern beyond. It's more crowded than this wasteland of broken metal, the machinery in there more intact. A sarcophagus for all the evils of Guerdon.

He sees, in that instant, twin massive containment vessels. Hatred seethes in them, a divine emotion so intense he cannot help but share in the feeling when he looks at them. The things held in those vessels are the shattered remains of the Black Iron Gods. For three centuries, the Keepers kept them trapped in bells as mindless, truncated deities; now, they're unfinished god bombs. No longer mindless, but incapable of any thought but destruction. He glimpses other shapes in that moment, too. Wax-encrusted vats where still-living things crawl. A massive, blocky machine, adorned with a woman's face in steel. Aetheric engines, still crackling with weird sorcery. Things he cannot name, things that slither and scream.

The shockwave from the explosion washes over him, and he can hear the unholy roaring of the things kept behind that wall. The blast has brought down the wall and unleashed monstrosities. Malformed, misshapen, tortured horrors, somehow made all the worse by their own suffering.

He looks into an alchemical hell. All the worst things in the world, distilled and transmuted into metal and glass.

But he sees it only for an instant.

Impossibly, the debris flying through the air halts. Reverses. The fallen shards of wall rise up. New stone, pristine as alabaster, gleaming with its own divine light, flows to fill the cracks. The sarcophagus is resealed once more. All those alchemical monsters and broken gods are locked away again.

Across the cavern, Miren howls a wordless cry of frustration and vanishes.

Across the cavern, Carillon Thay, shaken by the effort of her miracle, replies: "Fuck you."

CHAPTER 46

Eladora's guided through the New City streets more by sound than anything else. As long as she's heading towards the Duchess Viaduct, she's going in roughly the right direction, and there are artillery pieces on the Viaduct. So, keep walking towards the gunfire. She learns to distinguish the barking cry of one cannon from another, to tell the distant roar of the big guns on Queen's Points from the staccato thunder of smaller howitzers along the docks.

The alchemical hailstorm of the guns is answered with divine wrath. Smoke Painter draws purple sigils of glowing fog in the night sky – look at one and go mad. High Umur hurls lightning. Krakens in the shallows hoot and squirt jets of razor-water far inland, directing the silvery stream with gesturing tentacles. The waterspouts are liquid spears, impaling and slicing.

Streams of people stumble out of the Wash and Glimmerside and the market district, taking shelter in the labyrinthine cellars and ghoul tunnels of the New City. It's a good plan – the New City is a blessing in stone. Its bones are divine and unyielding, and there's some lingering sanctity about it that guards against hostile miracles. It's not safe. Nowhere in Guerdon is safe, now the mad gods are here. But it's safer than the Wash.

She can see parliament atop Castle Hill, across the Wash. A brisk twenty-minute stroll, yesterday. An impossibly perilous journey tonight. She shivers, still soaked and barefoot.

A masked city watch guard gestures at her to join the throng seeking shelter.

She shakes her head, asks him where the nearest watch station is. He can't hear her over the din at first. He has to remove his mask and let her shout directly into his ear to understand her– he's terribly young, terribly scared beneath it.

"Where's the nearest watch station?" she asks, holding up her semi-sodden letter from Kelkin.

"Venture Square, but – all dead!"

"I need an aethergraph!"

The next closest station, she learns, is on the western slopes of Holyhill, but the fighting is too thick there for her risk it. She follows the arc of the New City around, darting from alleyway to alleyway, shelter to shelter. She passes a few more crowds taking shelter, but soon the streets empty out and she's all alone.

Nearby, gunfire, running feet. The scream of a flash-ghost detonation. The lumbering tread of war-saints, advancing up the slopes. The carnage is all around her, but somehow she seems to miss it every time. She darts across a boulevard in eerie stillness, and then as soon as she's clear it becomes a killing ground as the riflemen open fire. She finds aftermaths: golden statues, blood-hot to the touch, caught in the moment of screaming. A dozen soldiers, all impaled on a spear hurled by Cruel Urid, who nests in the ruins of a tailor's shop and cracks skulls on the pavement like a thrush breaking snails.

Eladora doesn't know if she's lucky, or blessed, but she crosses the New City unharmed. She suspects blessed, and mutters a thank you to the stone as she passes.

Onto half-familiar streets. Glimmerside, where she spent her student days, now filigreed and interwoven with the New City. Steep steps bring her up to the northern flank of Holyhill, to the edge of the University District.

They're setting up an artillery emplacement on the grassy quad. A spotter perched on the roof of the library shouts at her to get under cover, and the sight of her beloved college turned into a for-tress is somehow more alarming than all the rest. Terrible things can happen in the Wash, or Five Knives, or the New City; they can talk of war in parliament and Queen's Point, but the university is supposed to be inviolate and unchanging. It's home.

She remembers the city watch station by the campus as a place where her classmates stole watchmen's helmets as pranks, where drunken students who made the mistake of crossing the invisible line from Glimmerside to Holyhill were brought to dry out. Now, the station's a fortified bunker, and a rough-looking band of mercenaries stand around outside, waiting to be issued with protective breathing masks.

In the back of her mind, a little voice tells her that this implies the use of heavy gas. Another little voice is screaming.

One of the watch officers stops her, and she holds up her tattered writ. "I need to use your aethergraph."

He takes the paper off her, studies it. "This says something about taking a launch to Hark Island for the getting of prisoners. Ain't nothing here about use of an aethergraph."

Eladora stares coldly at him. "I am a representative of Mr Kelkin and the city is under attack. I need to use your machine."

He relents. "If you want to risk it, though, go ahead. The blasted thing went mad last night, and we haven't got a readable message since. Had to use runners instead."

He shows her into a small room at the back of the station, where the aethergraph sits on a rather grand writing desk borrowed from some university study. The room's been recently refurbished – she realises with a jolt that she's living in what will one day be another historical period. *Sacred and Secular Architecture in the Ashen Period* will be shelved next to – what? *Invocations and Innovations in the Post-Crisis Era*? Or *A Hasty and Expensive Folly: The Emergency Council of Guerdon*?

She prays that there will still be someone sane enough to write histories when all this is done.

This aethergraph has rarely been used. The keys are stiff when she touches them, but the contraption crackles into life when she ignites the aetheric spark. A list pasted to the wall nearby gives her the sequence for the machine in parliament.

Laboriously, she keys in her message, but that's only half of it. The machine needs a living operator at either end of the line. The alchemists, in their ingenuity, managed to reify a sorcerous incantation, replacing mental constructs with brass and copper, replacing chanted arcana with glyph-stamped keys, swapping a jar of alchemical slime for a soul, but it still needs intent. She's read that experienced aethergraph operators share each other's dreams, and that there are concerns about psychic leakage.

Kelkin offered to have one of the machines installed in her apartment – for parliamentary business only – but she'd refused without knowing why. Now, she understands why the machines disturbed her – her soul is an open wound, as Rat put it. Her grandfather tore her spirit open in his ritual, trying to make her into a hasty substitute for Carillon, and the damage will not heal. More of her could be torn away by this machine.

Foolish girl, she berates herself. The city's under divine assault, there are soldiers marching off to fight gods and saints, and she's worried about a little psychic scarring?

Anyway, if you're going to worry about anything, worry about the spider-monster that might be hiding in there, she tells herself, and presses the activation key.

HAVE RETURNED FROM HARK. NEED TO DISCUSS OPTIONS. ELADORA DUTTIN.

It's nowhere near as bad as she feared – a rush of nausea, but no more taxing than one of Ramegos' sorcerous exercises. There's an aftertaste of panic, though, a psychic backwash from whoever received the message.

The first reply clatters out of the machine almost instantly, the keys moving her under her fingers, spelling out words. A-T-H-E-R-G-R- . . .

AETHERGRAPH   LINES   COMPROMISED.   CODE-BOOK ONLY.

She has no idea what this codebook might be; some military protocol she's not privy to.

NO CODEBOOK, she replies.

The second reply comes a few moments later. It might be her imagination, but she can feel Kelkin's bristly chin pressed close to her face, smell his pipe. Hear his waspish irritation.

DO YOU HAVE THAY?

It takes her a moment to work out who he means. Carillon – her father was Aridon Thay. She's the only one in the city who might still lay legitimate claim to that storied, terrible name.

YES.

The reply comes hastily, a torrent, keyed in so quickly the machine splutters under the load.

NAVAL RELIEF EN ROUTE FROM MAREDON. REQUIRE THAY AID IN SALVAGING RETORT.

Guerdon's navy is well equipped, but too few in number to lift the siege. Even if Cari somehow brought the *Grand Retort* back up to the surface using Spar's miracles, they'd have one bomb against a raging pantheon, and no way to *constrain* the target god. Not without the machinery on Hark.

Thoughts of the the machine lead to thoughts of Alic. Silkpurse described to her how he died trying to free Emlin from that machinery. There's no time for tears now, not for the man nor what he represents.

In Alic, and the other candidates she'd recruited, the work she did, she'd hoped to shape the city. To repair it, fixing the damage done in the Crisis, assuring the next chapter of its history would unfold in safety and prosperity. To lift the crushing worry from her soul, the burden of guilt and shame and responsibility that comes with what her grandfather did.

There will be no inspiring rally in the election, no full-throated cry for freedom. No atonement by that path. Just the bitter calculus of survival, of seeing which side can throw more bodies and souls into the maw of the Godswar.

Another clatter of keys. Another message from Kelkin.

YOU ARE AUTHORISED TO NEGOTIATE WITH HAITH WIDOW, SECURE LANDWARD REINFORCEMENTS.

The Widow – it takes a moment for Eladora to realise he means

Lyssada Erevesic. Kelkin scorned Haith's offer of alliance once, but that was before the invasion. Kelkin is a man who sets a high price on his principles, but is still willing to bargain them away if he must.

Before she can respond, the keys start moving again of their own accord.

PARLIAMENT UNDER ATTACK. STAND BY FOR—

The message ends abruptly.

A moment later, the psychic wave washes over her. Eight eyes gleaming in the darkness, the sensation of a thousand thousand legs crawling over her skin. *There* he is, moving invisibly through the aether. Skittering through the web of wires and sorcery that runs through the city.

Outside, a guard hammers at the door, telling her that she's got to leave. The advancing monsters of Ishmere are prowling the university grounds. They have to fall back.

Through the machine comes a torrent of half-heard whispers, the impression of a gathering storm. Ishmere's full strength has yet to strike the city. The carnage outside is just the leading edge of the wave.

PESH LION QUEEN GODDESS OF WAR WAR IS HOLY WAR IS DIVINE PESH IS COMING IN HER FULL MIGHT AND MAJESTY

She doesn't know if it's a threat or warning. It tells her what she needed but didn't want to know.

A memory: Professor Ongent talking about naming traditions in Guerdon. How the aristocratic families adopted family names like Thay or Voller, the names of ancient houses, in imitation of Haith. But some folk of the Wash kept to the old Varinthian ways, naming sons after fathers. Taphson, Idgeson . . .

She types.

EMLIN ALICSON. I'M SORRY.

Naming the boy. Binding him.

Then she tears the orichalcum cable from the aethergraph, disconnecting it.

*

Ghouls are carrion-eaters. Connoisseurs of dead meat. Terevant assumes, therefore, that it's a good sign that the big ghoul sniffs at Ramegos, then ignores her in favour of the newcomer. Rat stalks across the cavern towards Carillon Thay.

Terevant turns to walk over to the Haithi troops as they pick through the aftermath of the explosion, but the ghoul glances back at Terevant, and he finds himself hurrying to catch up. It seems the Elder Ghoul wants to use him as a mouthpiece.

"CARI." The name rises unbidden from his throat, tinged with more warmth than Terevant expected. More than Cari expected, too, it seems, judging from her face.

"Rat, you fucker," she says, "are we pax?"

"YOU ARE NO LONGER THE HERALD OF THE BLACK IRON GODS," says Rat through Terevant. "YOU ARE NO LONGER A THREAT TO THE GHOULS." He squats down next to her, inclines his massive head forward. "I SENT ELADORA TO FETCH YOU FROM HARK. WHAT FURTHER PROOF DO YOU NEED?"

"A fucking apology would be nice."

Rat laughs his hideous gurgling chuckle. "NO."

"Bloody ghouls," says Carillon. "Right. Fuck it. What do we do about Miren?"

"SOMETHING CRUEL AND PROLONGED," says the ghoul, "BUT HE IS GONE, AND I CANNOT TRACK HIM. THIS CAVE STINKS OF HIM." Terevant wrenches control of his own voice back. "Excuse me, but I need to WHAT DO YOU WANT, MAN OF HAITH?"

The ghoul's eyes glimmer with amusement.

"I need to," begins Terevant again, and he's interrupted again by his own tongue. "LEAD YOUR DEAD ARMY BACK TO YOUR DEAD LAND? No, I need YOUR PRINCE IS DEAD, O MAN OF HAITH, stop AND YOU MAY TAKE HIM damn you stop TELL ME CARILLON, HAVE YOU SEEN ANY OF THE CAFSTAN BOYS? OR ANY OF THE OLD BROTHERHOOD CREW?"

Terevant gasps for air.

Cari snorts, then thumps Rat's leg. "All right, leave him. He's quality, you know."

"RICH OR POOR, THEY ALL END UP MEAT IN THE END."

Terevant pulls himself upright with all the dignity he can muster. "Not in Haith. The Empire is undying. Now, if you will pray excuse MAN OF HAITH I AM NOT DONE WITH YOU."

"Wait a moment," says Cari. "We need a plan. What do we do about Ishmere?"

"THE GODSWAR IS HERE. THE CITY IS LOST. WE HIDE DOWN HERE."

"'The city' includes Spar. I'm not letting him go. Not again."

"I must—" begins Terevant, but it's Rat who answers. "GUERDON IS BELOW. THE TUNNELS RUN DEEP. WHAT REMAINS OF HIM WILL ENDURE."

"He'd want us to save people, too. Even if we can't stop the gods, then we can bring people down into the tunnels. Fight a delaying action. Rat, you haven't lived with him in your head for a year. It's like having a really itchy conscience all the time."

"I must BRING THEM DOWN SAFE WHILE THEY LIVE. A LARDER FOR THE GHOULS IF THEY – OW!"

Terevant punches the ghoul squarely in the snout. Rat yelps. "*As I was saying*, I must recover my family's sword." He nods at Cari. "You're a seer – help me find the blade, and I'll order my troops out of these vaults."

Cari sticks out a grubby hand. "Deal."

Some of the Haithi engineers caught in the blast had periapts; two might be able to attain the Vigil. Terevant orders them brought back to the camp outside the city, where the House necromancers can help pull them through.

Prince Daerinth, though, is casteless dead. Terevant stares down at the man who killed his brother, who tried to blame him for the crime. Who traded the Erevesic sword for the shattered scraps of a bomb.

"Take his remains," he orders, "and treat them with the honour due to a prince of Haith. Bring them back to the Crown."

As they wrap the body, Terevant wonders what secrets died with the prince. Did the Crown command him to betray House Erevesic, or was Daerinth scheming on his own, trying to get back into favour?

Lys might know, but Terevant realises that he'll never get a straight answer from her. Everything will be distorted or shifted by the crooked glass of the Bureau. If he's learned anything in the past few days it's that they're never going to get back to that bright lawn he remembers.

"Captain Brythal." Lys's dead father snaps to attention. "Escort the casualties to the main camp. Then make for the Palace of the Patros. The Lady Erevesic is there; guard her and give her whatever aid she requires."

What of the living troops at the camp?

"Guerdon's no place for the living. Tell them to hold the camp and the railhead, to keep open our lines of retreat." Terevant picks up a sword that belonged to one of the fallen soldiers. It's an ordinary sword, without marks or sigils. It's not the Sword Erevesic, but it will serve. "Colonel Rabendath, ours is a rescue mission. The Erevesic sword is on the battlefield. Carillon can help us find it. Once we have it, we'll fall back and retreat in good order."

Rabendath's has been the right hand of the Erevesic for four centuries; Terevant remembers his father and grandfather in grave conversation with the Vigilant. The ancient warrior listens to Terevant's orders, and – is there a moment of hesitation before he salutes and says, **It shall be as you command, my lord.**

What about the sorceress? asks Brythal.

"Leave me here," groans Ramegos from the ground. "The ghouls never let me get this close to the foundries before. Got work to do."

"I'll stay with her," says one of the ghouls wearing a ragged oil-skin. The creature has salvaged a medical kit from somewhere and treated Ramegos' stab wound as best she can. She's unable to keep from licking her lips.

"What if that . . . assassin-saint returns?"

"Oh," says the ghoul, showing her teeth, "I'll have words with Master Miren, you'll see."

CHAPTER 47

E ladora is not the only person to seek shelter in the church. The grand courtyard in front of the Victory Cathedrals heaves with crowds. Most came to catch a glimpse of the new king; others fled the carnage in the city below. Now they're trapped here. A thin line of Keeper guards defends the entrance to the courtyard, pikes set against the darkness and any monsters that might come charging up the hill.

Where are their saints? wonders Eladora. Where is her mother? If the city's to be troubled by a resurgence of Keeper saints, then surely now is the time to send them out! There's some protection here, just like there is in the New City. The Victory Cathedrals were wrought by human hands, not conjured by divine intervention, but they're still sanctified. The lightning bolts and curses that the invading gods hurl at the Wash, or at parliament, or at Queen's Point haven't yet touched Holyhill.

Yet, she thinks.

She pushes through the crowd as best she can, past children clinging to weeping mothers. Old women mumbling prayers to the Mother of Mercies. Young men roaming the square, arguing what to do, doing nothing. The doors of the three cathedrals are all closed and barred; so, too, are the doors of the Palace of the Patros. There are more guards there, pikes ready to drive the crowd back. The cries of the people echo off shuttered windows.

Eladora approaches one of the guards, and he stabs his pike at her, shouting something incomprehensible as he forces her back. The crowd shouts, heaves, throws stones, but aren't willing to charge the pikes.

Yet, she thinks.

She's pushed through the crowd, this way and that. Someone tears at her oilskin jacket; someone else screams at her, gesturing towards the purple sigils in the sky. She trips over the leg of a little girl, who sits shivering on the rain-slick cobblestones. Eladora leaves her jacket with the child and finds her way to the edge of the square, where the crowd thins out. Administrative buildings, servants' quarters. Here she finds gilded saints with bronze swords and shields looking out over the square.

In the shadow of the colonnade – Sinter. The priest's walking back and forth in front of a small side door, shoulders hunched. His bald pate beaded with sweat or raindrops. He sees her and snarls. Darts forward and pulls her into the shadows.

"What's going on? Did Kelkin send you? Is there a plan?"

"I-I haven't seen Kelkin since yesterday. Since before . . ."

"Is there a plan? What's he doing?" Sinter grabs her arm like he'd prefer to be grabbing her throat. His own voice is strangled as he tries to keep from screaming at her.

"Kelkin had a plan." Eladora shoves at Sinter's arm, but he doesn't let go. "Your gods ruined it."

"They've turned on me," says Sinter. "I can't go back in. I can't go." Thunder rolls above the square, and he scurries back into the shelter of the doorway. He's staying in the cover of the pillars, she realises, keeping out of the line of sight of those gilded statues.

Everyone else in the square is here to shelter from the gods of Ishmere, but Sinter now lives in terror of the wrath of his own gods.

"I need to talk to the Patros." With parliament overrun, with Queen's Point under siege, the Patros is perhaps the highest authority in the city. Or the head of the alchemists' guild, the head of the watch. The king. The gods. Carillon.

Anyone but me. Anyone but this.

"Yes," says Sinter, "yes! You – Silva's daughter, they'll let you in. Listen, listen. Give him this." He produces a crumpled sheet of paper, ripped from a prayer book. On the back, in the margins, he's scribbled a note. A plan.

"Straight to the hand of the Patros, understand? Don't let anyone take it from you." He fumbles in his robes for a key. "I told you, didn't I? Told you that all this was spinning out of control. Now it's fucked, everything's fucked. Give him that. Tell him it's the only way. Tell him we've got to act now."

He unlocks the little side door. Just inside, there's a statue of the Mother, garlanded in fresh flowers. Sinter ducks to the side so the statue's sightless marble gaze doesn't fall on him. He closes the door behind Eladora. "Tell him," he shouts from the other side.

The flowers, she notes dispassionately, are growing from the stone. A minor miracle.

She unfolds the note. Reads it. *Mass sacrifice ... the mob in the square ... a great offering, a jubilee of souls, as Safid wrote ...* A proposal to buy his way back into the favour of the gods with the souls of everyone in the courtyard outside. *The fires of Safid shall carry the souls ... air-burst phlogiston shells ... heavy gas ...*

A monstrously cruel plan. Mistaking brutality for decisiveness, cruelty for courage.

Eladora tears up the note. "By the by," she says to the closed door, knowing he's still listening. "My cousin is still alive. Terevant Erevesic shall have his sword back. To hell with you and your schemes — I've a better plan."

Once she's inside the palace, she's ignored by the courtiers and priests who mill around. They're trapped here, unwilling to brave the city outside. The palace has become an ark, adrift on a stormy sea. Small knots of clerics conspire in twos and threes; servants either busy themselves with pointless tasks or eye the exits. Eladora's reminded of Terevant's description of the Grena river valley, after the god bomb. The Kept Gods are still here — she can distantly sense them in some corner of her soul, but the pressure of incipient sainthood is gone — but there's some absence at the heart of the church. Sinter's hiding, and no one else has taken charge yet.

She enters the golden court of the Patros. They've tried to make this into a throne room for the new king of Guerdon, too, but there seems to have been some dispute over which ruler takes precedence here. The Patros' seat has pride of place, right in front of the high altar, but the king gets a bigger and more elevated chair over at the side of the chamber. Neither the Patros nor the king are present in the room, but with the palace sealed the newly minted courtiers have nowhere else to go. As Eladora arrives, some ancient bishop tries to make himself heard over the noise of the crowd and storm outside. "The strength of the church has always been in the fields and farms. In the humble villages. In the little churches. It is to them – it is in them – we must seek renewal," he shouts.

Mhari Voller detaches herself from a group of courtiers behind the king's throne and totters over to Eladora. Voller's wearing a jacket emblazoned with the crest of the king. The Festival where the Kept Gods "discovered" the king was a week ago – Eladora wonders if Voller had the jacket embroidered in secret before the Festival, or if her family kept it in some attic for three centuries until it become politically expedient again.

"Eladora! What are you *wearing*? Were you caught without an umbrella?" Voller's breath smells of alcohol. "This is all just ghastly. Sinter has caused such a muddle – I don't quite know what happened, but Silva is quite unwell. And this trouble, now – we're discussing where to decamp to. I suggested Maredon, but the consensus seems to be some awful backwater like Wheldacre – oh, I'm sure it's delightfully rustic of course, but it's hardly—"

"This trouble?" Eladora says, incredulous.

"Whatever's going on in the harbour – we heard gunfire, earlier. Pirate raiders from Lyrix, someone said."

"It's the Godswar. It's Ishmere."

"The Godswar," says Voller, with misplaced confidence, "is very far away. Is Effro with you? He acknowledged King Berrick's claim earlier, when he endorsed the decision about Ambassador Olthic's murderer – that's the first step in him seeing sense, you know. I told you he'd come around."

Eladora stares at her for a moment, then says, "I need to see the Patros. Or the king. Both. Whoever's in command."

"Well, that's a matter of some debate. Interesting times, but—"

"Where is my mother?"

Silva's in an antechamber off the court. She sits in a bathchair, staring at the shuttered window. Bandages on her burned hands, a naked sword on her lap.

She doesn't react when Eladora enters. Doesn't react when Eladora kneels down beside her. How much of her soul is left? How much has been torn away by fickle gods when they withdrew from her? She opened herself to greater forces, and paid the price.

Eladora tries anyway. "Silva, it's Eladora. Can you hear me?"

Nothing.

There's a garland of flowers on the table. A talisman of the Mother. And the sword on Silva's knee. Tokens all, but Eladora doesn't dare touch any of them. She needs to remain spiritually intact. Re-establishing her connection to the Kept Gods, here and now, would ruin her plan. It might ruin her, leave her a hollow shell like the woman in front of her.

She tries again.

"Mother. The Godswar is here. I need ... I mean, the city needs—" She stops, assailed by doubt. "M-maybe you should ... "

When Saint Aleena spoke aloud, her voice was like a fanfare of trumpets, a triumphal thunder, the dawn breaking through the walls of night. Her words were touched with light and power; they fired the soul of anyone who harkened to them.

The voice that slithers from her mother's slack lips is the wheeze of a broken bellows, the spit and crackle of embers in a dying fire. The slow fall of ash.

"Why did you never *embrace* the gods, child? I brought you to the chapel in the hills. I taught you all the litanies. Why did you hold back?"

"I-I ... I don't know."

"Deceitful child," says Silva, and Eladora can somehow tell that the anger in those words comes from her mother, not whatever force is speaking through her – or with her. But she can't tell how much of the entity in front of her is Silva, and how much is the Kept Gods. "Three times you called the gods. Three times you were answered. Three times, you rejected them."

Three times — at Gravehill, when Jermas tried to use me as Cari's proxy in the ritual to call the Black Iron Gods. In the New City, when I fought you. And in Queen's Point, against Ramegos.

"I didn't call. I mean — it was Grandfather who . . . he damaged my soul, Mother. That's what Dr Ramegos said. A spiritual wound. And then Sinter used me to counter you. He dressed me up as a saint to fool the gods, to make them believe I was you. There was nothing to reject, it wasn't me who chose it."

Out of nowhere, that same sensation of terrible *pressure* that she felt on the Festival ground, the awful proximity of the divine. Her skull is a door, and they're pressing against it, trying to get in. Cleaving it with swords of fire.

Silva's head lifts to look at Eladora. Her eyes are sightless, unfocused, but she's not the one looking through them. "Who are you to question the will of the gods? This world is broken — the path to heaven must be made from cracked and jagged stones. It is still you who chose not to walk it."

"Cracked and jagged — you're saying that the Kept Gods *wanted* Jermas Thay to torture me? That Sinter was doing *their* bidding when he used me to hurt *you*? That's nonsense." Eladora rises. "So-called gods are self-perpetuating magical constructs that draw power from the ritual actions and *residuum* of their worshippers. They're . . . aetheric vortices, parasitic spells. No more than — spiritual tapeworms!" It's an argument that Eladora imagined having with her mother a thousand times, ever since she first went to university and studied under Professor Ongent. Now, she spits the words at her. "I won't give myself over to such things. I won't prostrate myself before them, or indulge their . . .. their ritual delusions!"

"Such arrogance. You think you can stand aloof? You think the gods are not in your blood and bone? In the earth you walk upon, and in the air? You want to be mistress of your own fate — but you shall be betrayed, time and time again." Silva rises from the bathchair, held aloft by unseen hands – and then something snaps, and she falls back. She paws at Eladora, reaching for her hand.

Eladora snatches her arm away, steps back. "I won't be your focus. I won't serve you. Not like that." She can sense, dimly, forces whirling around the palace, around Holyhill. The Kept Gods are scattered, disorganised. They need a rallying point, something to assert their shape and purpose.

It won't be her. It can't be her.

The creak of a door, the rustle of skirts. Another woman enters the little room. Slim and elegant, dressed in the black of mourning. She closes the door behind her and removes her veil, shaking out her hair. "Eladora Duttin. I've heard a great deal about you." Silva slumps back down. Eladora gently tucks her mother's arms back inside the bathchair, moves her head so it rests on a pillow, then turns to greet the newcomer.

"Lady Erevesic."

Lys moves to the shuttered window, opens it a crack. "It's very stuffy in here," she says. "What did you hope to do with the church's saints?"

Eladora swallows. "Fight the invasion."

"You can't beat the Sacred Realm, not without the god bomb. Guerdon's lost." Lys gives a little sympathetic smile.

"Is that the view of the king of Guerdon, or the Crown of Haith?"

Lys grins. "The Patros and his court want to run. My instructions from Haith are to go to the embassy and await rescue."

"And the king?"

"I'm sure the king doesn't want to lose his realm before he's even crowned. And if he must lose his realm, then he's determined to make Ishmere pay as high a price as possible." Tendrils of cloud brush down from the sky over Five Knives, smashing rooftops. Cloud Mother's saints, striking deeper into the city. Lys closes the window, turns back to Eladora. "Did Kelkin send you to fetch the Keeper saints?"

"Minister Kelkin didn't send me," admits Eladora. "I came looking for you, too."

CHAPTER 48

Terevant doesn't know how long they've marched for. He just stumbles along behind Carillon as she leads the motley host of ghouls and dead men through an endless maze of stairs and steep-sloping tunnels. Terevant's the only one in the company who's wholly human – even Carillon seems to possess unnatural vitality. She grows stronger as they climb towards the New City, while he falls behind. His chest aches where he was shot.

Rabendath steps to the side and lets the column march past him, before falling in with Terevant at the rear. **My lord, the front lines of the Godswar are no place for the living.**

"I fought on the front line," gasps Terevant, "at Eskalind."

You lost at Eskalind. Rabendath unslings a rifle and a breathing mask. **It will be street fighting, messy work. The Guerdon saint – you've seen her powers at work, I believe.**

Terevant nods, remembering the living stone of the New City miraculously changing at her command.

That may give us an edge, but we will need covering fire. He hands Terevant the rifle. **I understand that the Ninth Rifles are good marksmen.**

An hour later, he's crouched on a rooftop on the edge of the New City, overlooking the maze of twisted streets that tumble down to the docks. One of the Ishmeric landing craft came to rest on the shore there; the waters of the harbour ripple as Kraken-saints slip beneath the moonlit waves. There's an orange-red glow in the clouds over the city, but it's not a presentiment of dawn – he's facing west, towards Queen's Point. The fortress must be on fire.

Carillon slips over to him. "Over there," she says, pointing to the mouth of an alleyway. "Wait for the fifth one."

He rests the sniper rifle on a ledge and squints through the sights. The first thing to scuttle out of the alleyway is one of the sacred animals of High Umur, an *umurshix*, a creature with the body of a scorpion and the head of a bull. He holds his fire as it passes. Three Ishmeric soldiers follow, their bodies wreathed in steel-smoke armour that flows around them. They carry lightning in their hands. Fifth – fifth, for an instant, is a priest of Smoke Painter. Spindly-limbed, clad in purple, twice as tall as a man, elongated fingers smearing reality with a touch.

He squeezes the trigger. The hot flash of phlogiston igniting, and the priest topples. No blood, just hissing purplish smoke, deflating instead of bleeding. The steel-smoke armour protecting the Ishmerians dissipates – and the trap closes. Vigilants charge from the cover of nearby buildings, striking down the suddenly vulnerable warriors. The *umurshix*, trapped in the suddenly narrow street, cannot turn around to bring its claws and teeth to bear, and its venomous sting holds no terror for the already dead. The Vigilants stab at the monster's hindquarters, their swords seeking the gaps between its armour plates. Wounded, the beast bellows and scurries down the alleyway. Terevant reloads, the action as familiar to him as breathing. Six months since Eskalind, and he hasn't lost the knack.

Carillon grabs Terevant. "Get off the roof," she shouts. She doesn't wait for him – she leaps down to a neighbouring roof, landing unerringly, vanishing into a doorway.

A bank of cloud descends towards him from the seething skies. He can dimly make out a figure at its heart, and snaps off a shot from the rifle. A wild miss. The cloud extends tendrils of mist, unfolding like some exotic aerial anemone. They look as fragile as gossamer, but Terevant has seen them rip people asunder, or carry them away into the sky. He follows Carillon on her headlong flight, landing awkwardly on the far rooftop and ducking into the doorway after her. He turns to slam the door behind him and finds that it's already vanished, and there's just blank stone there now.

"This is fun," mutters Carillon. He's not sure if she's talking to him or to the city around her.

"Any sign of my sword?" He reloads in the darkness, finding the rune-scratched glass and smooth wood of the cartridge by touch.

"It's down there, in the Wash. I can't see it clearly, but it's there." She swallows. "They know it, too."

The forces of Ishmere may not be able to *touch* the sword, but they know its value. They're using it as bait, trying to lure the Haithi army into making a doomed sortie down the hill. It's an obvious trap, but every second that goes by makes it more tempting. The sword's more than a symbol – it could give Terevant the strength he needs to lead his House to victory.

Something scrapes against the exterior wall of the building. The bull-scorpion? The cloud tentacles? Another conjuration of the belligerent gods of Ishmere? The rifle will be no use in these close quarters if something breaks in. He draws his sword.

Another scratch, from below. A frustrated roar.

"The bastards are looking for us," says Carillon. Her eyes tightly closed, her hand pressed to the glimmering stone wall. "Stay still. There are more of your dead lads coming down Holyhill way."

Bryal and the troops from the camp. With their added strength, there's a chance they can push past Ishmerinans, grab the Erevesic sword, and fall back intact. At Eskalind, he lost because he over-extended himself, because he pushed the Ninth Rifles too far into enemy territory. Is he making the same mistake here? What would Olthic have done?

"Are you all right?" asks Carillon. "You look like you're about to puke."

His heart's pounding, all right. He shakes his head.

"I'm fine." Then, to distract himself: "You're not in the Bureau files. Vanth wrote a lot about the Thays, and your cousin Eladora, but not you."

Cari shrugs. "I came back to Guerdon just before the Crisis. I was sick and starving on the streets, not hanging about with spies or diplomats." She pauses, then replies to an unheard comment. "Yes, you're fucking diplomatic, fine," she says to the wall.

To Spar. Terevant brushes the wall with his fingers. It feels like stone. He can't sense anything in there. "It's like a phylactery, I suppose."

"I don't know. Maybe. Ask Eladora or someone."

"Where were you before you came back here?"

"At sea, mostly. Serevast. Ulbishe. Paravos."

"I lived in Paravos for a few months."

"Part of the Haithi garrison?"

"No. Down in the Flowing Gardens." A warren of poets and thieves, addicts and mystics.

"I loved it there. Up by the holy springs by day, and then down to the waterfront and the Dancer's temple." Cari's face breaks into a grin.

A skittering noise from the far side of the wall. The *umurshix* is still out there, inches away from them, trying to find a way in. There's a series of horrible, measured *tap-tap-tap*s as it probes the stone with its forehooves, searching for a weakness.

"Can't you, I don't know, imprison it or cast it into a sewer?" asks Terevant.

Carillon scowls. "We wait. Once your soldiers get here, I'll open another door and we can lead that bastard right to them, and they can shoot it. It can't get—"

The bull-scorpion throws its full weight against the sealed door, but the stone holds. It roars again. Terevant can hear words in the monster's bellowing; a prayer litany, or a summoning. Drawing the attention of the gods to their hiding place.

"—in. Maybe. Shit." They scramble downstairs, through rooms recently abandoned. If the inhabitants were lucky, they found shelter deeper in the New City. Carillon's also sealed the exit to ground level. She concentrates, and the stone begins to weep, beads of pale reddish liquid appearing on its surface and flowing down to pool on the floor.

"Harder to make this work down here," she mutters. "Foundations are more solid. Give me a moment."

"Why did you stay?" asks Terevant suddenly.

"When?"

"After you came back to Guerdon. It sounded awful."

"I had a friend who was better than I am," says Cari. She touches the wall, and the stone under her fingers slowly melts, folding back on itself like it's alive. Sluggishly, painfully, it opens into a hole. "Come on!" she shouts as she slithers through.

Terevant's bigger than she is, slower, and he's got to wrestle the bulky rifle through after him. He's only a few seconds slower, but it feels like minutes. She's halfway up the twisted street by the time he's through, and the bull-scorpion is right there, right on top of him, so close he can smell the digestive juices dripping from its fangs, read the sacred scriptures patterned in the creature's shell. The *umurshix*'s eyes are human — was it once a saint or worshipper of High Umur?

He scrambles up the steep street after Carillon, the monster at his heels. Above, the sky's writhing with low-hanging tentacles of solid mist.

The bull-scorpion knocks him down with a swipe of its massive hoof, sending him sprawling. It runs past him, over him, ignoring him — Carillon's a saint, the emissary of a rival god. In the sightless eye of Ishmere, Terevant's just another mortal. The saint is the threat. The *umurshix*'s stinger lashes out at him — trying to kill him as an afterthought — but he rolls to the side before it strikes. The bull-scorpion races after Carillon.

Terevant unslings his rifle, and fires. He can't tell if he hit the monster, but the *umurshix* rears up in surprise, and turns to face him again, roaring and rattling. He's got nowhere to run. Nowhere to retreat. To his left, there's a high wall of pearly stone; to his right, smouldering rubble that used to be a tower. He reaches for another cartridge, but it slips from his fingers, shatters on the ground. The monster's bullet-proof anyway.

And then the wall cracks, and a huge slab of it comes crashing down, right on top of the *umurshix*. The impact shatters the monster's shell, and there's a tremendous wet splat as the weight of the stone crushes the thing's organs.

Cari emerges from the dust and helps Terevant up. She kicks a fragment of stone, sending it splashing into the pool of ichor that oozes from the titanic corpse. "You'll kill yourself!" she mutters, bitterly. Then, to Terevant: "Come on. Stay low."

They clamber over the rubble, sneak through winding back alleys. The low-hanging clouds deny them the rooftops. The New City is a maze, but Carillon leads him unerringly through the streets until they make contact with the Haithi reinforcements.

Bony hands clap Terevant on the back, salute him as he pushes through the formation. There are living soldiers here, too; their faces wear an expression that he remembers from Eskalind – the Godswar bursting around them, the shock of sudden divine wrath and rampaging monsters, but beyond and beneath that, the overwhelming horror of knowing that the gods have gone mad. The creeping, undeniable realisation that heaven is a storm at sea, and the timbers of the world are breaking.

Still, there's less than a quarter of the soldiers he expected. Even with some left behind to guard the camp near the alchemists' factories at the rail yard, there should be more Haithi troops here. He remembers Eskalind, looking back from the threshold of the temple and seeing only a handful of the Rifles still standing. Terevant leads Carillon through the ranks, up towards the company's banner where Bryal waits. He's talking to some woman in a city watch jacket, her face hidden in a breathing mask. For a moment, Terevant's heart leaps at the thought that it might be Lys, but it's not her. Some other woman.

Bryal reassures him. **We've secured the Palace of the Patros. The king ordered us to open the doors of the Cathedrals, so the faithful in the courtyard could take refuge there. I left two companies there to guard our allies.**

"The king ordered it – or the Lady Erevesic?"

"I ordered it." Eladora pulls off her breathing mask, sniffs the air, puts it back on.

"Duttin!" gasps Terevant. "What happened? How did you ... I mean, those are my troops, so—" The last time he'd seen her, she was as broken as he was, shattered by the revelation that Sinter had used her, just like Lys had used him. They'd both been manipulated and used by others. Lost in a fog of lies.

Clearly, Eladora has been through many ordeals since then, but something has changed in her. She seems out of the fog now. Terevant envies her, envies that wellspring of certainty she's found.

"There is little time, and much to do," says Eladora.

"Thank you for ..." Terevant begins, then trails off. *Healing me when I got shot? Finding out who stole my sword?*

"We can settle all accounts if we survive, Lord Erevesic." Eladora glances back east up the hill, towards Holyhill. The sun rising behind the Cathedrals outlines their spires in rosy fire. "King Berrick and the Patros are conducting a ceremony, praying for victory over the city's enemies. I have sent ... allies ... to the House of Saints, to fetch all the holy relics they can muster. It will, I p-p ... I *think*, refocus the Kept Gods, bolster the strength of the saints. The Kept Gods will take to the defence of the city." The way she speaks reminds Terevant of when he first met her, weeks ago, in the waiting room outside Ramegos' office. Then, she sounded most confident when reciting from a history book.

Now, she sounds like she's anticipating what they'll write about her. Meeting the judgement of history without flinching, impatient for events around her to catch up.

"Full-on Godswar, El?" says Carillon quietly.

"The Kept Gods are still weak. Their newfound power is brittle – the presence of the king has given them a focus, and the faith he inspires gives them a flush of power ... like an apprentice sorcerer who's just mastered a spell for the first time. But it won't last. They're still no match for the pantheon of Ishmere." She takes a deep breath. "But they'll help you hold the line."

"What do you mean?" asks Terevant. Cari says nothing, but her dark eyes watch her cousin intently.

Eladora takes a breath, pauses for a moment at the brink.

Then.

"I need three days."

CHAPTER 49

E ladora walks in the darkness, holding Carillon's hand. She's got an alchemical lamp in her pocket, but she doesn't light it. She knows Cari can sense every footfall, every imperfection, through the stone of the tunnels around them. Eladora follows her cousin in silence, trusting in Cari to guide her down to the vault of horrors beneath the New City.

The sounds of the war fade as they descend. Soon, it's just Eladora's breath rattling in her mask, Cari's knife tapping nervously on the walls.

"Is it much further?" asks Eladora. Part of her wants these stairs to elongate, to put this off as long as possible.

"Spar buried them deep," replies Carillon, "but we're nearly there. Here, feel this." She guides Eladora's hand so she can feel the jagged metal of a broken alchemical tank that's embedded in the tunnel wall. There's some waxy residue in the tank that squirms beneath her fingers. She lingers there a moment, seeing how flexible the stuff is, how much it can be pressed before it breaks.

They emerge into the outer cavern. The fresh scar-stone of the curtain wall is dimly luminescent, but the main source of light is Ramegos' fading werelight. The sorceress lies with her head on a folded jacket, salvaged from remains of the Haithi excavation. Silkpurse sits next to her, chewing on a hunk of meat that Eladora suspects was also salvaged from Haith remains.

"Miss Duttin!" squeaks Silkpurse, running over to greet her. "Lord Rat said to tell you that they've evacuated parliament through the tunnels. The army's digging in at Gravehill, to keep 'em penned in the lower city." Castle Hill, Queen's Point and Holyhill form three points of a rough triangle around the harbour and the Wash, with the New City off to the side. "Same thing they did in the Crisis," mutters Cari. "Keep the fighting where the poor live. Can't have the quality up in Bryn Avane suffer."

"It's a matter of geography," says Eladora defensively. "The heights can be defended, and the only gaps between them are fortified. There are guns on the Duchess Viaduct."

"Good thing," says Ramegos weakly from the ground, "that gods can't fly. Or throw thunderbolts from heaven. Or—" She's stopped by a coughing fit. Silkpurse rushes to her side, lifts her so that she can breathe. "It was over when the interceptor sank."

I hoped you'd be like Jermas was in the old days, Kelkin said. *He had fucking steel in his spine.*

"I have a proposal," says Eladora.

She stoops and picks up a piece of shimmering New City stone from the ground. "Carillon, you can invoke Spar. The city is alive. You can reshape its stone – you even did it out in the harbour. You can reach out to Hark, raise the *Kestrel*."

"What? Fuck, no. It's too far for him, El – his soul's already stretched over the whole fucking New City. You can't use him for that. It'd break him. Kill him."

Eladora raises her voice, addresses the stone walls around them. "Spar Idgeson, please – can you do it?"

Cari reaches inside her shirt, finds her amulet, holds it for a moment of silent communion. The amulet was made by Jermas Thay. A relic of the Black Iron Gods for their chosen saint. The Crisis was supposed to have left it magically impotent, but it still seems to help Cari concentrate.

"Fuck you," says Cari a minute later. She stares at the floor, unwilling to meet Eladora's gaze.

"Thank you." Eladora turns to Ramegos. "The god bomb – does it require any special preparations to fire?"

"No. But . . ." Ramegos pushes herself upright. She winces at the pain from the wound in her side. "Think clearly. The Ishmeric gods aren't *constrained* – the bomb might wound them, but it won't kill them. You *might* get lucky and take out one of them, but not a whole pantheon."

"Pantheon-yield," echoes Cari, hollowly. "That's what Rosha said to me, once."

"The target," says Eladora curtly, "will be obvious, I think. I've spoke to enough refugees from Severast and Mattaur to know what to expect. The Lion Queen is their Goddess of War – I am assured she will arrive to preside over their victory."

"Even if we – *damage* – Pesh," says Ramegos, "they won't stop. It's not like the Grena Valley."

"I think it will be." Eladora looks down at Ramegos. "I've . . . I know the Kept Gods. I've shared their thoughts. I could taste how they feared the bomb. It's more than destruction – it's annihilation. You wrote that yourself. But killing a god isn't enough. It's what comes after."

Steel in the spine, she tells herself.

"I need to go through there," says Eladora, pointing towards the curtain wall.

She can feel the Black Iron Gods now, hear them. It's not like the storm-front celestial pressure of the Kept Gods, blindly pushing at her to open her soul, accept them in. It's different, more insidious. A constant, gnawing demand, a hunger for oblivion. The Black Iron Gods want to unravel her, to devour her piece by piece, cell by cell, until nothing remains but them, those archons of the hungry void.

"I don't fucking understand," says Cari angrily. "You want Spar and me to get the god bomb and save the day? Fine. We can try. But why do you——"

"You can save the day," interrupts Eladora. "But what about the next day? Or the day after that?" She looks up at the conjured heaven above their heads, the arches of unlikely creation born of Spar and stolen magic. "That's what concerns me. The future. The city's future." She thinks for a moment. "Can I borrow a knife?"

Cari snorts. "Sure."

"And . . . and the amulet."

"Should it be me going through?" asks Cari. Suddenly subdued as she thinks about what awaits Eladora on the other side of this prison wall.

"No. You have Spar. It has to be me." Eladora takes the amulet, settles it around her neck. The memory of her grandfather's wormy fingers brushing against her skin. "I'm ready."

"Wait!" groans Ramegos. With Silkpurse's help, she staggers over to the two younger women. "I'll go with you."

"I'm not coming back this way," says Eladora.

"Aye, I guessed when you asked for the amulet. You're my apprentice," says Ramegos. "Can't finish your lessons without seeing some *proper* sorcery."

She slips her arm from Silkpurse, grabs onto Eladora instead. One hand grips Eladora's wrist painfully; the other traces arcane symbols in the air that blaze with power. "Let's get to work."

Carillon prays, and the wall splits open.

The inner cavern is furnace-hot, as though the broken tallow-vats and alchemical crucibles are still running. The machinery in here is more intact than outside. Ramegos' werelight darts around them, illuminating the half-melted remains of Tallowmen. The ruins of the old alchemists' chapel, a fortune in gemstones and gold smeared across the ground. An industrial graveyard, where the barrels of titanic artillery pieces rise like unlikely pillars to support the jagged ceiling.

The wall closes behind them, the stone knitting back together. It's slower than last time. Carillon warned them that Spar was over-exerting himself. He, too, must endure.

Ramegos grunts, then says, "Over to the left, if you please."

Eladora supports Ramegos as they slowly cross the ruins, following the werelight to the wreckage of a huge machine. A press of some sort, thinks Eladora — there's a mould there in the middle, tanks and pipes like organs and entrails, but also shattered mirrors, aetheric engines – and above it all, surmounting the armoured frame, is the steel effigy of a woman's face, ten feet tall. Was it the sculptor or the alchemist who captured Rosha's sneer, or the determination in her gaze? The woman who made the god bombs stares blindly at her prison wall.

"Phylactery," says Ramegos, "though how she made it without the blessing of Haith's death-god, I don't know. Her soul was in there – mould was for making her new wax bodies whenever she wanted." Ramegos mutters a spell, and sigils glimmer along the frame. "Something's still in there."

She lingers a moment, then nods. "Let's move on."

There are other things living, or at least moving in the cavern. Whatever's out there flinches from the werelight, heaving its monstrous bulk into the shadows before Eladora can get a good look at it. Oily feathers, mismatched claws, and a dozen eyes glitter back at her. For all its size, it's fast. The eyes look human, embedded in a monstrous prison of flesh.

Lightning crackles around Ramegos' hand. "I've got one good spell left in me."

Eladora can sense the Black Iron Gods before she sees them. The two remaining deities are in the centre of the cavern, in a cage of twisted metal that used to be the alchemists' Grand Athanor. One of them used to be the bell of the Holy Beggar church down in the Wash; the other rang from the lighthouse out on Bell Rock. Neither of them are bells any more, but neither are they the cthonic idols they once were. They strike Eladora as something unearthly; alien ovoids of metal that fell from some nightmare sky.

They're aware of her. She senses their awareness groping towards her. Confused by her presence, confused by her existence. They've mistaken her for Carillon before.

She decides that the one on the left is the one from the Bell Rock. Cari touched the Holy Beggar bell once, and after that she said it knew her.

Maybe she can fool the one on the left.

"Ready?" she asks Ramegos.

"Set me down here," replies Ramegos, "and give me a moment." Eladora lowers her mentor to the floor of broken metal. Ramegos takes out her heavy ledger and hastily scribbles a few more glyphs.

"The first moments of sainthood," says Ramegos as she writes, without looking at Eladora, "are especially potent ones. When the soul first aligns with the god, when the channel is established. You're a special case — you've already been, ah, claimed, but that was forced on you."

"I can manage this," says Eladora. "I'll see it through."

Ramegos finishes writing. The pages are smeared with her own blood, but the glyphs are readable. She closes the book, hands it to Eladora with effort. "They sent me up from Khebesh to study those bombs. This is as close as I'll get to Rosha's formula. See that . . . well, you know what this all means. Either the Godswar ends, or the world does. See that it's put to good use."

"I will."

"I wish I could have shown you Khebesh. But that's too far. There's never enough time, is there? Never enough." Ramegos winces. "You'd better go."

One of the alchemical monstrosities, a shapeless thing spawned from the mixing of a dozen shattered vats, breaks into a loping run towards Eladora, drooling from all four of its mouths. Ramegos hurls a blasting spell at it, staggering it. Another creature emerges from the shadows, and another and another, and the darkness of the cavern is lit by blazing sorcery.

Eladora walks towards the god, chanting a spell that becomes a prayer that becomes a plea.

Let me walk between the cracks. Let me step across the sky. Don't you recognise me? I'm the Herald.

Let me in.

She vanishes.

Falling between darkness.

Hearing the silence between the tolling of the bell.

In the moment after the knife goes in.

How are you here? asks a thing that wears Miren's face.

Eladora recalls that when Carillon teleported with Miren, the two experienced an overwhelming sexual attraction, a yearning to recover that moment of spiritual union. She remembers the stab of jealousy.

There's nothing there any more except revulsion, and distant pity.

I'm not here, she insists, giving nothing away. *I'm there. I'm across the sea. Where there are dragons in the skies, and other gods in the forests.*

Somehow, even though they're both bodiless, timeless, little sparks of soul held aloft on the hurricane of Black Iron, he scowls.

They're mine. This is my place. Father made me for this.

She draws herself up. *No, it's mine. I am a daughter of the Thay family. My grandfather woke the Black Iron Gods. He wrote the spells to call them. He made their Herald. You — you're a thief. A squatter. You're nothing to me.*

She looks beyond Miren's face, to the Black Iron Gods beyond. *I am Eladora Thay. I require passage to Lyrix. Name your price.*

The bells' toll echoes out across the cavern, three times, and then she's gone.

CHAPTER 50

The spy crawls out of the water, onto a beach of hot ash. In places, the sand has been fused into glass that glitters in the morning light. The stench burns his lungs. He stumbles into the ruins of the Hark prison. Flames and phlogiston-patches smoulder amid the debris. The cages are ruined; the divine prisoners from a dozen pantheons all united in ecumenical incineration. The mirrored tower has toppled, and its sides are blackened and dull.

Remote gunfire echoes across the harbour. The sky above the distant city cracks with miracles.

There was gunfire at Severast, too, and many miracles, and that city still fell.

The spy hurries across Hark Island, crossing to its northern shore. He can see the churning waters where the *Grand Retort* went down. Kraken-tentacles seethe beneath the surface, a predator guarding the carcass of its kill against scavengers. *Poor Dredger*, thinks the spy, *the greatest alchemical weapons salvage in all the world is right on your doorstep, and you can't get to it.* He finds a hiding place high up amid the rocks, in case the kraken's dinner-plate eyes spot him. He wonders if the creature in the water is Ory, or some other war-saint, an outrider swimming ahead of the main invasion fleet.

He takes out a spyglass and trains it on the horizon. There's fighting in the city. The streets of the Wash gleam in the summer sun, making the slums as beautiful and magical as the New City. They've been flooded, he realises, by the Kraken-wave. The main fleet isn't here yet – not that it makes much of a difference to the spy. The means of his revenge are just there, beneath the waves, but it may as well be on the moon.

Without that purpose, that *focus*, he finds himself slipping away. The summer sun is warm, and his perch in the rocks quite comfortable. Little fragments of his being scuttle away, to find crannies in the rocks, dark places to hide from the light. He could sleep. Drift away.

Become a ghost. Haunt this empty isle. He closes his eyes, lets darkness overtake him. Like a wave rising up, blotting out the light.

He's not sure how long he rests there. The sun and moon wheel above him. The sky is wracked with storms. Cloud bands march like battalions towards the shore.

Distantly, he can hear the fighting in the city. The defenders have held the line for now – Ishmere's invasion has stalled in the lower city. Queen's Point is burning, and parliament is burning, and the Wash is a marshland of floating corpses, but they haven't managed to push back the defenders on the slopes. From the island, Guerdon is a smudge on the horizon, made larger by the pall of smoke and cloud above it, and the success of the defenders is about as meaningful. In Severast, they held back the Sacred Realm for ten days, and the city still fell.

He remembers that the temple dancers birthed monsters, their bellies swelling right in front of the terrified priests. Children conceived in the dance are holy, they belong to the Goddess. She claimed them as her weapons. Other dancers danced for fire, and fire answered. He remembers the priests of Pesh sacrificing the sacred lions and scattering the blood from censers along the shore, and from each drop of blood a lion-spirit sprang. He remembers castles of smoke and cloud in the sky.

Guerdon can muster only scanty miracles. The Crisis broke the alchemists; the Kept Gods might have recovered a little of their former strength, but have no stamina. A handful of Haithi soldiers will not tip the balance. Guerdon gambled on its god bomb, just like he did.

The spy weakly raises a hand and salutes the city. *We both lost*, he thinks.

*

They tell Terevant that it's been three days since the attack began. He takes the dead at their word. Even the summer sun can't penetrate the smoke, the flood-spawned mist, the carnivorous clouds that hang over Guerdon, and he can't remember when he last slept.

They tell him that the line has held. Of that, he's much less sure. Back in the military academy, they drew neat lines on maps, depicted formations as square blocks of ranked soldiers, the neat contour lines of hillsides. None of it bears any resemblance to the street fighting of the last three days. Fighting Ishmeric godspawn and war-crazed saints. Peshite berserkers, growing stronger with every kill. Monstrous spiders, lurking in wait. He needs to wear a breathing mask even when he's up on Holyhill now, to filter out the smell of burning from the sacrificial fires. Guerdon's dead get burned according to the old rites, to carry their souls up to the Kept Gods, and that soul-energy comes right back down again to the saints. There've been miracles, too, direct intervention. Damaged cannons remade by unseen hands, a blessing of the Smith. Lights bobbing in the smoke clouds, guiding lost soldiers to safety if they have faith in the Holy Beggar. Gods on their side.

But the Ishmerians have gods on their side, too, and theirs are much stronger.

The Duchess Viaduct fell during the night. He's not sure what hit it. A miracle of Smoke Painter, maybe – the bridge is still *visible*, but it's not *there* any more. It's a ghost structure, and the soldiers on it are ghosts too, now. Transparent, eerily silent, unable to touch anything or leave the viaduct. Pressing themselves against the invisible barrier, pleading silently for rescue. Mercifully, the Viaduct is fading from sight now, but Colonel Rabendath has already wiped the neat line of the bridge off his neat maps.

The Viaduct was a linchpin of the defence. Four train lines crossed it, and they'd parked armoured trains with long guns on all of them. All gone now. And the valley below is full of kraken, which meant the bridge was the only safe way to cross to Castle Hill without going below. Now they're effectively cut off from the western portion of the city. Holyhill and the New City – the miracle district, the mercenaries call it – are alone, unlikely allies, marooned in a growing sea of foes.

They've set up a headquarters on the edge of the university, in the old seminary. Terevant follows Rabendath through the corridors, wondering if he should take the lead.

Crystal chandeliers hang from the ceiling of the university dining hall, but the impact of distant explosions has shattered some of them. Some of the faces at the table are familiar, some aren't, but they're all haggard, soot-stained, red-eyed. Well, almost all – the massive yellow-eyed shape of Lord Rat squats in a corner. Carillon Thay paces next to him, muttering to herself. Glass from the broken chandeliers crunches underfoot as she walks. Only the dead manage to sit still and maintain decorum.

More unlikely allies arrive. Mercenary commanders, militia from the New City – turncoat saints, some of them – and then a group of Keepers. And in the middle of them is Lys.

Also: the priest, Sinter. Apparently, he and Carillon have some history, as she draws a knife and shouts at him as soon as she spots him. Rat restrains her, and Terevant takes advantage of the distraction to slip around the table and sit next to Lys. She squeezes his hand.

"Still alive?" she asks.

"I think so."

"You should have left by now," he tells her. "Get to safety."

"If I go," Lys whispers, "then Berrick goes. If Berrick goes, the Patros goes. Patros goes, the Keepers go." She shrugs. "As long as there's a chance, I've got to stay. I've not lost Guerdon yet."

It's Rat who calls the meeting to order, the same ghastly call for QUIET issuing from half a dozen mouths at one. Colonel Rabendath nods in appreciation, and rolls out a map atop the table.

The loss of the Viaduct means there is a gap in the defences. The enemy is gathering forces here, in the upper Wash, with the intent of breaking through into the inland portion of the city. *You* must defend the gap.

"Aye, that's plain to see," mutters one of the mercenaries. "but it'll take everything we have to hold them there."

"It's too far from the New City for me," says Carillon. "And I've got stuff to do."

"The Kept Gods shall keep the city safe," intones Sinter, and Terevant has to suppress a hysterical giggle at that. He opens his mouth to speak, but before he can find the words, a city watch officer stands.

"Before the aethergraphs stopped," she says, "we got word from the naval base at Maredon. They're sending reinforcements. If we contain Ishmere in the Wash, then . . . "

"Then you can bombard the Wash and kill everyone." Carillon hasn't put her knife away. "Fuck that."

"We don't know how many are still alive down there."

"I do," says Carillon. "I can still *see* down there."

Terevant raises a hand to speak, but Rabendath doesn't notice.

That brings up another matter. We have received intelligence—

"I told you," interjects Cari, sourly.

Rabendath continues. **Regarding the location of the Sword Erevesic. It is in the lower Wash.** He indicates tenements around Sumpwater Square.

"It's a trap." Sinter sounds incredulous that they'd even consider the possibility. "Ishmere knows that you want to recover the sword. They want to divide our forces. No doubt they've got some horror waiting for you to take the bait."

It is not *bait*. It is the Sword Erevesic. And this is not our city. My orders are to recover the sword and all Haithi personnel, then retreat.

"No fucking way we hold the Viaduct without the dead," says the mercenary. "No way we're doing that. We're out."

"Eladora said to give her three days," shouts Cari, "you don't need to hold it for long."

"And where the fuck is Eladora Duttin?" demands Sinter.

"I don't know!"

"You and she," says Sinter, "are ruinous. Had I but one wish, it would be that you died with the rest of your accursed family."

Time is running out. If you do not fortify the Viaduct line soon, the enemy will break through. My troops shall coordinate our advance with your deployment, draw away some of the enemy forces. Rabendath acknowledges Terevant's presence for the first time. **The Erevesic must have his sword.**

Lys squeezes Ter's hand again. He takes his hand away and stands.

"Thank you, Colonel, but ... the Erevesic can wait. Have our troops join Guerdon's in the defence of the Viaduct gap."

Rabendath's skull swivels to face him. **My lord, if we do not recover the sword now, it will likely be lost forever. The souls of your ancestors are in it. It is the Sword Erevesic.**

Hold the line, hold the city. Give Eladora her full three days. Maybe save the rest of the city. Maybe seal an alliance between Haith and Guerdon.

Or lead his troops in battle against Ishmere. Maybe win the sword. A poet's war, going for the dramatic gesture, the quest for glory. All his failures washed away as he saves Sword and House Erevesic at once. One grand moment where the world changes.

The easiest person to deceive is yourself.

"The enemy knows how valuable the sword is to us. They know what it means to me. Sinter's right – it's a trap, a scheme to divide our forces." Terevant keeps his face impassive, his voice steady. "Hold the line, Colonel," he orders.

For four hundred years I have fought under your family's banner. In all that time, I have never known defeat when the Erevesic led us.

But it's not Olthic, or anyone else. It's me.

"You have your orders, Colonel."

CHAPTER 51

The spy's slow death is interrupted by a naval engagement, close at hand. Guerdon's little fleet of ironclads have arrived from Maredon. The krakens are waiting for them – tentacles explode from the water, trying to pluck soldiers from the deck or drag the ships into the abyss. Cannons bark in response, searing the monsters with bitter clouds of withering dust or dragons-breath bursts of phlogiston. It's a standoff – the guns are enough to keep the kraken at bay, but without miracles to counter the theft of the seas the warships dare not press on into the harbour.

They hold position beyond Hark, harassing the besiegers, launching rockets and shells over the island. The spy can't tell if they're holding position, waiting for some signal, or if they're preparing to engage the main fleet when it arrives.

That would be a valiant effort.

Mortals are so good at valiant efforts.

Until a god reaches down and brushes them away.

Columns of troops march down from Holyhill towards the Viaduct gap. They go through the University District, down the Street of Philosophers, past Desiderata Street. The Vigilants in perfect formation, then ragged city watch, knots of mercenaries and irregular volunteers. Here and there a flaming sword, a divine gift.

Lys hurries to walk alongside Terevant. One of her bodyguards urges her to turn back, to return to the comparative security of Holyhill, but she brushes them away. She pulls Terevant to the side.

"You did the right thing, Ter. Without the sword, the Erevesic armies and lands will be taken into charge by the Crown. But if we save Guerdon, get control of the remaining god bombs, *I'll* be the Crown." Her eyes are bright, and her nails dig into his arm. "Olthic would understand. Hold the city, and we gain everything."

She steps back, lets the guards whisk her away.

She doesn't understand. She's seeing conspiracies and stratagems, the same dance of ambition and intrigue that Olthic tried to join.

That's not why he did it, not why at all.

One of the Erevesic troops – Iorial, he thinks, but it's hard to tell in the smoke and steam rising from the flooded city – finds Terevant in the column. He hands Terevant a satchel of rifle ammunition. **The Colonel advises that you find a position in the heights, well clear of the Viaduct gap. For your own safety.**

"I'm the Erevesic. Shouldn't I be at the head of our troops?"

As the Colonel said, the front lines are no place for the living. It's usually hard to read subtext in the sepulchral voices of the dead, but Iorial's tombstone-heavy tone is perfect for conveying the message here. Most of those who'll fight at the Viaduct gap are alive, not Vigilant, but Guerdon's mercenaries and city watch are better equipped for close-quarters battle in the Godswar than regular Haithi troops. It's not worth the argument.

Perversely, Terevant takes a left turn, following a narrow street that runs down towards the Wash, towards occupied territory. There are warehouses along Hook Row that have a commanding view over the approaches from the Wash; he can station himself there. He loads his rifle, checks his breathing mask.

There was fighting on these streets earlier. Bullet holes in the walls, stains on the cobblestones. Relatively few bodies, though. Keepers and ghouls take the human dead, and alchemist scavengers take the god-touched monsters. All boiled down for their essences. Somewhere down there, behind enemy lines, is his brother's essence. The essence of his House. But he can't gamble the city. He doesn't have the courage to stake the fate of so many others on his own skill.

He's gone too far, in the mist. Gone past the warehouses. The street ahead is half flooded, water lapping against ground-floor windows, great shoals of debris bobbing along the Kraken-swollen river.

A bizarre shape emerges from the murk. A creature of spikes and claws, lumpy and irregular, propelled by a little thrashing tail . . . and then he sees it more clearly. Mercenaries crouched on a ramshackle raft, armed with rifles and swords, watching the shore. Some swimming creature at the rear, pushing the raft through the floodwater.

He raises his rifle, in case they're Ishmeric, but the woman at the front of the raft waves to him in greeting.

"Hey," she shouts, "it's the boy from the Festival." The soldier removes her breathing mask. It's Naola, the mercenary.

Terevant stumbles down to the edge of the water, removes his own mask. "You were going to Lyrix."

"The war came here," replies Naola. "And Guerdon paid us more." Naola springs ashore to stand in front of him. "Where'd you run off to, Festival night?"

He can't help but laugh. "You wouldn't believe me."

"Maybe I would. We've seen the strangest of things. We've been fighting down in the Wash, last two days." From the look of the cargo on the raft, though, they've been doing as much looting as fighting.

"How?" The Wash is occupied territory. Ishmeric gods and monsters everywhere.

"We fell in with a bunch of refugees in the New City. Some of 'em were close to the gods back in Severast, came here gentled. Now that the gods are here, they've got power again." Naola gestures back towards the shape that pushed the raft. "We've got our own *kraken*," she says gleefully.

He stops and grabs Naola by the shoulders. "I am Terevant of House Erevesic. I'm absurdly wealthy. I'll pay you a fortune if you can sneak me into the Wash."

*

A hot wind blows across Hark, waking the spy. He stares up into a red sky, and cannot tell if it is night or day, or if all natural order is another casualty of the war. A wound opens in the crimson firmament, a slash of gold, and from it descends a whirling stairway of fire.

The stair spins and dances across the ruins of the prison, a blazing whirlwind. A tongue of flame touches the spy, and the stairs anchors itself to the ground where he lies. He is too empty to react; too tired even to blink.

Figures descend the stairs from heaven. Ishmeric soldiers. Priests of Pesh, their hands blood-slick, some carrying trumpets, others sacrificial knives. They walk ahead of Captain Isigi, who strides down the stairs carrying a bowl of freshly plucked hearts. The captain's once-beautiful face is misshapen, her skull remade too many times. She glances down at the spy. *Do you know who I am?* he thinks, but she ignores him, stepping over him to gaze at the smoke-shrouded city beyond.

Her eyes are quite, quite mad.

After Isigi follows a woman in the silken robes of a priestess of the Fate Spider, a woman who kneels down by the spy and dribbles water into his mouth from a flask, then sits back and lights a cigarette.

"X84," says Annah, "how the fuck are you still alive?"

"Just lucky," he mutters.

"Lucky," she echoes, looking at the wreck of the *Grand Retort*. "We all got lucky. You lied to us about the bomb. Do you have any idea what they'll do to you?"

"Nothing that has not been done already." His throat is so dry he can only manage a whisper, a breeze stirring cold ashes.

Annah shakes her head slowly. "Idiot. When the war is over, the gods will amuse themselves devising new ways to punish apostates and traitors. But we won't wait that long for you."

"When the war is over?" says Isigi. "The war is holy. The war is eternal." She looks at Guerdon and laughs. "But here I will dance in the ruin."

Isigi strides off across the rocks, down to the shore. She wades into the sea, careful to avoid the froth of the acid seeds. She wades until the water is up to her chest, and keeps striding forward, her skull cracking and reshaping as she dons the war-form of Pesh. Her frame swells, the waves breaking against the muscles of her back as she grows. The foam of her wake is pink-tinged with blood.

Taller than the towers, now, a goddess wading through the murky depths of the harbour. She brushes aside sandbars, breaks the Bell Rock island. Her strides send smaller waves rushing across the bay, drowning Shrike. On the Isle of Statues, terrified Stone Men fling themselves to the ground and press their faces into the dirt rather than look at her terrible countenance. Some will never rise again.

She exhales, and lion-spirits of steam and hate run ahead of Pesh, heralding the arrival of the goddess.

As she draws close to the city, a few of the remaining guns open fire upon her. Cannons on the heights of Holyhill, weapons brought over from the alchemists' warehouses and hastily put into the field. But Pesh is the war incarnate, and their fury is her fury. They cannot harm her.

She roars a lion's roar of triumph, and the world shakes. She unsheathes her claws with a trumpet blast from the priests on the shore. With one tremendous swipe of her divine paw, she crushes the seaward bastion of Queen's Point.

Godswar has come to the city.

Annah watches the goddess in her wrath. "Well, then. Not fucking smooth at all, but that's that." She counts out a handful of golden coins, leaves them on the rock next to the spy. "All accounts settled at the end."

She finishes her cigarette. "In other circumstances, we'd take you to the Paper Tombs, and my god would unmake you. Like Tammur. But Fate Spider has fled this place, because of your actions, so we have to resort to secular means."

From beneath her robe, she produces a small gun, an expensive repeater. Points it at the spy's face. "We vetted you, Baradhin. You were no one – a petty smuggler. No faith. No surviving family. No loyalties. We were *thorough*."

It's true, thinks the spy. Sanhada Baradhin was an ideal recruit for the Ishmerian Intelligence Corps. That's why he was chosen.

"You didn't sell us out to Guerdon. Was it to Haith? To Lyrix? Who bought you, Baradhin? Give me something, and maybe I'll be merciful. Mortals can be merciful. Gods cannot."

She's right. He mutters something under his breath.

"What's that?" Annah leans down, the gun aimed now at his belly. The priests of Pesh glance over, knives in hand, ready to act.

"Annah," whispers the spy. And he speaks another word, a secret word, known only to those who have worshipped at the temples, who have descended into the Paper Tombs.

She straightens up. "My god," says Annah quietly.

The gun fires one, twice, three times, four. The four priests topple. A secular sacrifice.

Annah places the gun in her own mouth and pulls the trigger. Five.

Pale spiders emerge from cracks in the rocks.

The spy walks down to the beach while the spiders cocoon the remains.

CHAPTER 52

Three days, Eladora said.

Patience has never been one of Carillon's gifts.

Over the last three days, she's taught the Ishmerians to fear the Saint of Knives. Every window is her eye. The New City streets are a maze of traps and ambushes; her soldiers a mob of thieves and sainted footpads, who mug any god who trespasses in her sacred alleyways. She prowls on rooftops and gutters, watching the monsters get closer.

At night, the ghouls came out. Rat's legion from the tunnels, to claw and strangle any invader caught out after dark. The Ishmerians turned what used to be Mercy Street into a seething river of unwater, a barrier between the occupied zone and Carillon's domain. Some of the folk of the Wash made it out before the waters rose, and now the tunnels and vaults under the New City are crowded. She protected them as best she could.

Spar protected them better, shielding them from miracles, sealing off tunnels before the monsters could reach them.

Now, the fighting's gone to other parts of Guerdon, up Mercy Street to Glimmerside, Holyhill, the Viaduct. It's a sort of victory, Carillon guesses, but it leaves her feeling frustrated.

At dawn, she visits the burned-out ruin of her house on Sevenshell Street. From there, she can see across the glittering harbour. Out beyond the horizon is Hark Island and the wreck of the *Grand Retort*.

"If they want us to fucking raise her," she mutters, "why wait?"

Eladora asked you to, comes the answer. Spar's answers in her head have started to sound less like him, more like her own voice.

"She's probably dead, you know? If she hasn't got distracted by a 'particularly fine example of pre-Crisis cloacal architecture', or started blubbering." Cari drums her fingernails on the stone. "If we're going to go, we should go."

We should wait for the right time.

"The city's under attack!"

Yes, I did notice. She can sense Spar gathering himself, his consciousness trickling through unseen channels in the stone. *I feel it all, Cari. I share in every death. I'm struck by every gunshot. But this war has been coming for longer than either of us have been alive. Waiting three days is insignificant, when you consider how long the Godswar has lasted already.*

"Easy for you to say when you're not the one getting shot. Tell everyone who dies today that we're sorry, but now's not the right time, and it serves them right for being murdered according to schedule."

That's not what I'm saying.

"It's a pretty detached perspective, is all."

I know. What more would you have me do?

It's not him that should do more. Spar's given his life already. She wants to do more. Do something. To act, not wait.

Cari listens to the distant sound of gunfire out at sea. It echoes off the seawall behind her, like the whole sky's falling.

Rat's here. The ghoul clambers down the side of a building, stalks over to where Cari sits. He folds his massive frame, bowing his horned head down until it's nearly at Carillon's level.

"TELL SPAR—" Rat tries to speak through her, but she fights him off. "Fuck that. You can speak for yourself. I'm already carrying two-thirds of the conversation. I'm not going to sit here and let you two argue through me."

Rat reaches up and waggles his wolf-like jaw. He tries to speak around his fangs. "Isn't *comfortable* to speak like this." His words sound like they've been exhumed, deep and doleful, and his breath is a graveyard stink.

"Oh, poor you." She pauses for a moment. "You heard the Keepers killed Cruel Urid?"

"A demigod," scoffs Rat, "and he'll come back. Diminished, yes, but not destroyed. Not without the god bomb." Irritated, he adds, "And they burned the body."

"How're your ghouls doing in all this?"

"We have seen the city fall before. We have known war and invasion before, plague and much death. Such times are feasts for our kind. This is different – all gods are carrion gods, these days, so desperate for souls that they'll claim the meanest corpse. There may be poor pickings for my kind in days to come – but we will survive. Dig deep. Guerdon is older than gods."

"The pair of you," says Carillon, "are shit at being comforting."

Sorry.

"You worked with Eladora in Kelkin's government, right? What's she like there?"

Rat considers the question. "I dismissed her as one of Kelkin's acolytes, but she is . . . deep-rooted. When she dies, I think her soul will be one of those that clings to the earth and the bricks, and is . . . indigestible to ghouls." He chuckles slowly. "Sometimes, actually, she reminds me of you, Spar. Other times . . . " He snorts.

The Haithi troops are forming up at the Viaduct gap, signals Spar. The thought is accompanied by the sensation of vibration, of thousands of bony feet marching in unison.

"They're going to lose, aren't they?"

Probably.

Rat's yellow eyes gaze out across the sea. He points. "Carillon."

Cari turns. Striding through the harbour, hundreds of feet tall, her face more radiant than the sun. A wake of blood behind her. "Goddess," says Carillon, and the word tastes of ash and iron.

I think this is the moment.

Naola's kraken is a sorry thing. Unlike the massive tentacled monsters out in the bay, she's still got traces of her humanity. Her legs have fused together into a mermaid's tail, her arms have grown long and branched, pale tentacles ending in vestigial human hands. Her torso, though, is still mostly human, and there are fresh bullet wounds in her back. Her face is still human, too, but her voice is lost.

She pushes a raft through the flooded streets. Around her, she invokes the Kraken-miracle, transmuting the floods back to water so their raft can sail through, then stealing the water again as they pass, replacing it with molten glass. Kraken stole the seas, but Naola's saint can borrow them back again. Her tentacle-hands run with silvery water as she works her miracle.

They sail through canyons that were streets. Reefs of debris washed out of houses and taverns and factories. All abandoned – the streets are empty of corpses. At first, Terevant wonders if the evacuation was unusually effective, but he soon realises that the bodies have all been taken by one god or another. Kidnapped to be given funeral rites, so the gods can claim the dregs of the soul left in the remains.

They pass the ruins of the Church of the Holy Beggar, one of the oldest churches in the city. The stained-glass windows have been shattered, the belltower toppled. The altar of the Kept Gods has been cast down, and now a creature of Smoke Painter sits in the nave, surrounded by incense burners and dancing shapes made of broken glass. The presence of the gods has warped this old portion of the city. The temple-ships have taken root. A tenement tower become smoke as it rises, the solid lower floors giving way to a smear of brown-grey mist in the shape of a building. Blessed Bol has claimed the old Seamarket, and now fish of solid gold wriggle through the unwater.

The enemy is all around them. *Umurshixes* perched on rooftops. They pass under a thick bank of low-hanging cloud, and the flash of an explosion illuminates the embryonic shapes wriggling inside Cloud Mother's belly. Weird things birthed from the madness of the gods wait in the alleyways. Ishmeric marines, dug in amid the chaos, held in reserve until the gods need another saint, another soul to be sanctified and consumed in equal measure. The floodwaters ripple and the buildings shake as godspawn monsters shamble through the occupied city. All waiting in anticipation of a Haithi counter-attack, ready for a legion of dead soldiers to come marching down from Holyhill to find the sword.

They're looking for the dead, not the living. Terevant and the mercenaries are on a raft, propelled by a kraken. In the fog and smoke of the tortured city, it's easy to overlook them. No one challenges them as they press onwards, into the heart of the Wash.

Naola's mercenaries are veterans of the Godswar. They hunch together, weapons ready. Their armour is studded with grounding charms and wards. They mutter prayers in an interference pattern. Watch one another for signs of religious ecstasy or divine revelation. Naola sits with Terevant in the middle of the raft. "You're the money," she whispers, like it's an oath.

They pass the ruins of a hall that Naola whispers was once the headquarters of the Brotherhood, the city's old thieves' guild. Huge black spiders scuttle in and out of broken windows, weaving a grey cocoon around the building. The broken windows remind Terevant of multifaceted insect eyes, watching the city.

The kraken-woman has no voice, but her exhaustion is evident. She strains to push the raft. They're approaching Sumpwater Square.

The sword might be nearby.

Terevant closes his eyes. Stretches out his hand. He could sense the family sword without touching it when it was in his kitbag, back on the train. He could feel the presence of his ancestors. There must be a connection.

Breath. Concentrate.

He imagines himself back at the Erevesic estate, playing in the woods with Olthic and Lys. Olthic would always climb higher than he could. In his mind's eye, he looks in the treetops, imagining his brother caught in the crook of some forked branch.

His mental image of the forest shakes. A hurricane breath blows through it, bending the trees. He hears a roar. Closer now.

He's praying. Everyone on the raft is praying in a language he doesn't know. His tongue, his lips, his throat are no longer under his control.

He opens his eyes, and sees the goddess.

Pesh, Lion Queen, Goddess of War, steps over the raft. She strides towards the Duchess Viaduct and the fall of the city. Prowling through the streets after her come lion-spirits. Walking on the waters, made of her wrath, they scent the presence of Terevant and the mercenaries.

They've come too far. They're trapped.

The last part of the New City to be conjured in Spar's apotheosis was a sheltered cove and a small jetty, made of the same miraculous stone as the rest. It was an invitation to leave. Spar's last thought in life was that Carillon should escape Guerdon, escape the shadow of her family name and the Black Iron Gods. She rejected it.

Now, she remakes it.

The stone wall of the jetty convulses and shimmers – then explodes outwards in a new miracle. Cari takes that raw creation and shapes it in her mind, drawing on the memories of half a lifetime at sea. A ship of stone, hull eggshell-thin, masts like columns. It shines as it finds its balance in the heaving waters. Sails of frozen moonlight unfurl. It's a divine impossibility, a ship of dreams. When Carillon sneaked out of Silva's house in Wheldacre and ran away to sea, this is the ship she prayed would be waiting for her.

The crew of grinning ghouls weren't part of her childhood imaginings, but she's glad to have them there.

She climbs on board, touches the stone railing. She can feel Spar's life running through the ship, but it's too small to contain more than a fragment of his mind. It can only carry a blessing, not a farewell.

"All right!" she shouts, "to Hark!"

Rat grins and yowls a command in the tongue of ghouls, and they cast off.

No earthly winds propel the ship – but she sails on no earthly seas. The waters of the harbour were stolen by Kraken; Spar wrestles for control of the sea, turning it to a milky liquid. The hull creaks as the first miracles strike it: Kraken-curses of bad fortune and shipwreck. The real attacks will come later, guesses Cari – the attention of the Ishmeric deities is turned towards the city.

They still have saints to contend with. Tentacles reach from the unwater, probing for crew to snatch and drown – but ghouls are stronger than humans, and have teeth and claws. When one tentacle tries to grab Rat, he sinks his nails into the pulpy flesh and hauls the Kraken-saint out of the ocean, beats it against the deck until it's dead. The ghouls feast.

They skip across the waves, faster than any mortal vessel. Cari laughs at the unlikely grace of their creation. Their ship is a thief's ship, a smuggler's dream. Her exhilaration lets her ignore the soul-sapping effort of the miracle. Spar is not a god; he has no worshippers, and claims no *residuum* through secret rites. He can't replenish his power – and they're spending it profligately on this heist.

They approach the island. The seas around Hark have reverted to mundane water – Kraken has withdrawn his cruel blessing – but there's a circle of steam around the wreck of the *Grand Retort*.

"Acid seeds," whispers a ghoul. The weapons slowly dissolve in seawater, releasing an alchemical compound that eats away the hulls of ships that try to cross the blockade.

"Cover your eyes," shouts Cari. She pulls a breathing mask over her own face, and spends the last few seconds wishing she'd prepared better before her ship plunges into the steam cloud.

It's a brief hell. She curls into a ball as the mists roll over her, trying to guard her exposed skin. The mist is insidious, mixing her with sweat to make rivulets of agony. Her skin blisters. The mask's filters can't cope; she can't breathe.

She holds her breath, closes her eyes tightly, and looks through the ship's eyes instead. They're lost in a caustic fog. The ghouls are tougher than Cari is, but it still burns them. They cower on the deck, meeping and grunting in pain. Only Rat is able to endure the cloud without flinching. He strides to the rear, puts one massive claw on the tiller. The other he places over Cari's head, protecting the back of her neck.

There's a horrible series of creaks and cracks from the hull. Patches of the stone peel away, rotted by the acid. Their once-shimmering vessel now resembles a victim of the Stone Plague, pockmarked with oozing patches and scales. But they're through, they're clear, into the eye.

"COME ON," roars Rat. "BRING IT UP!"

Cari concentrates. Spar's too far away — it's all on her to shape the stone. Their vessel quivers as she sends out spikes of stone, reaching down to the wreck. *It's the same as the New City*, she tells herself. On the edges, Spar interwove old and new, mortal and divine. *It's Gethis Row*, where heaven brushed against the grimy alleys of the Wash. The stone spikes divide, becoming harpoons, becoming claws, ripping at the wreckage, pulling it up towards the surface.

She can sense the god bomb now. It's very close. It's screaming at her.

The ship lurches. Water runs over Cari's feet. She's distantly aware that they're taking on water, that she's had to use too much of the substance of their vessel to conjure this unlikely claw. The *Retort* is ten times bigger than they are, and she doesn't have a fucking idea what she's doing. She thought it would be like picking a lock, but it's more like trying to rescue a drowning man.

She's being pulled down with the *Retort*. They all are.

Close the gap in the hull, she thinks, but the hull's turned solid. The divinity in the stone has calcified, eroded.

Sinking like a stone.

Terevant clings to the little raft as Naola snaps off a shot from her pistol at the nearest lion-spirit. The bullet passes right through the creature.

"Figured," she mutters. "This is going to be rough. They're only solid when they kill." The other mercenaries ready their weapons, watching the circling lionesses. When one of the Circle of Eight dies, the rest can strike. There's no question that some of them are going to die.

"Stay on the raft," mutters Naola as she reloads. Terevant's own rifle is equally useless against the spirits. He's baggage. The money.

Two hundred Haithi soldiers landed on that beach at Eskalind. Only seventy-two sailed away. Only a dozen or so of those were still alive, but they were all – living and dead alike – haunted by the war. The Godswar followed him home to Haith, clinging to him, not like a stench or a stain, but like a perverse thought he could never drive from his mind. His mind is occupied terrain. The whole world's caught in the Godswar. The whole world's a battlefield, even in places like Guerdon where the fighting has only just turned physical. It was a spiritual war for a long time before that.

A wild impulse takes hold. He strips off the signet ring from his finger, tucks it into Naola's pocket – *if they make it out, they deserve payment* – and jumps from the raft, landing in the knee-deep water. Naola shouts at him, but he's already running, wading through the muck. The lionesses roar and chase after him. Maybe the mercenaries can get away.

He runs through the flooded streets. The ground shakes with the footfalls of the goddess, and the roaring of the spirits as they chase him is a hymn to war. He runs uphill, towards the base of the stairs. He'll die with his back against the wall of Castle Hill, he decides.

The lionesses keep pace with him. Toying with him. Herding him. He dodges through a ruined building that was once a temple of the Last Days Cult. The room stinks of spilled wine and vomit – the apocalyptic cultists celebrated the invasion, danced and drank themselves to death as the Kraken-waves crashed down on them.

The war is all around him. Gunfire and the clash of swords on Castle Hill. Bodies tumble down from fighting on the cliffs above him. Naval cannon fire out in the harbour. Gods wrestling in the sky above Holyhill. Rabendath told him there were more troops coming down the railway from Haith, that three more House legions had crossed the border.

A lion-spirit appears next to him, swipes at him with a claw. He dodges into a doorway. The ground floor is abandoned, fragments of furniture and other debris floating in the water. Fearful faces on the stairs. Children, huddled together, watching him from an upstairs landing. He splashes through the water, climbs up onto the broken stairs. They don't speak.

"Hide!" he tells them, pushing them back into the nearest

doorway. Through there he sees a few piles of bedclothes, some shapes on the ground, and against the far wall is a small home-made shrine, decorated with candles. A crudely carved lion, and the sigils of Pesh carved into the wall. A bowl of what must have been some red fruit.

He rushes up the stairs. The lion-spirits keep pace, leaping from floor to floor, passing through the walls. There were bodies in that crude shrine, he realises, those were the shapes on the floor. Sacrifices to Pesh? The proximity of the goddess inspiring those who had never even heard Her name? He can't think as he climbs. The horrors churn in his brain. He passes more rooms stacked high with the dead.

The war claimed Olthic, too. And Vanth. Their murders like the small waves, breaking on the shore in advance of the rising storm. The gods invaded Guerdon with their mortal agents first, before the war of miracles began, but it's all the same war.

He emerges onto the roof through a trapdoor. He can see the remnants of the Duchess Viaduct in the distance. The Haithi forces arrayed in the gap below, between Castle Hill and Holyhill, polished armour and polished bone. Towards them, hundreds of feet tall, invincible and glorious, strides Pesh.

Terevant falls to his knees.

Haithi snipers fire at the approaching goddess. Their bullets become prayers.

Haithi swordsmen charge towards her, stabbing at her feet, slashing at her massive paws. Pesh laughs as they draw blood. She swipes with one claw, cutting deep into the rock of Castle Hill. An avalanche buries half the Haithi troops, choking the river, smashing through the breweries and warehouses along the riverbank.

One of the lions materialises on the roof nearby, slates cracking as the spirit takes physical form. It pads towards him, eyes blazing. Terevant lifts his rifle – and throws it away over the edge of the roof. It spins in the air, splashes into the water below.

"No."

"Blasphemy," says the goddess. She speaks through the lion in front of him, but it's Pesh. All things of war are Pesh. "War is holy."

"No," says Terevant again. He closes his eyes, imagines he's back in the forests outside the mansion. Waits for the lion's jaws to close.

But the goddess is there, too, in the woods. "Before you took up a sword, I knew you. How could I not, son of Haith, heir to conquerors? Great is my love for you. For a thousand generations, you have made offerings to me with sword and fire."

"I've never worshipped you!"

Pesh's claw caresses his cheek, his jaw. "All wars are mine. All war is holy. My rivals shall be dismembered, and I will eat their hearts, and raise my banner in the ruins of their temples. You still walk in my presence at Eskalind, mine forever. Did I not pull you back from my brother's webs, when you blasphemed, led astray by lies? Do you not seek revenge?"

The forest dissolves. He's back on the rooftop, but instead of Guerdon he's looking out at Old Haith. The city's on fire. Half the fortresses of the Houses all fly the Erevesic banner. The Crown's palace is under siege, the pyramid of the Bureau broken open, all their files burning. He sees Daerinth's head on a traitor's pike, sees the Houses rally to his side when he accuses the Crown of betraying the ancient compact.

"No," he says a third time.

Excuse me, sir. Yoras crawls from the attic door behind Terevant. Through the tatters of his uniform, Terevant can see that the Vigilant soldier is horribly broken. His body ends at his ribcage. His left arm is gone. His skull, cracked. He pushes the Sword Erevesic with his remaining hand.

"It's a miracle," says Terevant, his voice cracking with hysteria. There are no coincidences in the Godswar, only warring destinies decreed by mad gods.

This is yours.

Terevant takes the sword.

And Pesh laughs again.

CHAPTER 53

Carillon wrestles to keep the ship of stone afloat.

For an instant, a breath of wind forces a gap in the steam, revealing the nearby shore of Hark. A man stands on the shore, watching them. She recognises him as that IndLib politician who came up into the New City with Eladora and Silkpurse – but it can't be him. He died, shot by Sinter's men.

The spy raises one hand in a gesture of blessing.

Cari feels a rush of strength. The feeling is sickeningly familiar – back during the Crisis, when the servants of the Black Iron Gods sacrificed their victims to her – it's the same quicksilver rush in her veins, the same thrill. Rat smells it, too.

Right now, she's not going to question this gift. She takes the power, channels into the stone. There's a wrenching shift as part of the *Grand Retort* breaks free.

Working quickly now, her hands moving like a weaver, shuttling threads of Spar's miracle-transmuted flesh back and forth. The foredeck of the *Retort* is like one of the buildings of the Wash that got caught in the Gutter Miracle, oily metal intermingled with shimmering stone. The launcher mechanism holding the last god bomb rises from the sea, water cascading from its housing, and settles onto the prow of the stone ship.

The last gaps in the hull reseal. An unseen wind fills the sails again, and the ship makes a tight turn. They pass back through the seething acid. Rat cradles her exhausted body, sheltering her from the burning spray.

The stone ship looks as tattered and broken as she feels. They race north again with the rushing tide, passing the Bell Rock, passing Shrike, chasing the bloody wake of Pesh. The city flows out of the horizon, the encircling headlands embracing them on either side as they cross the harbour.

Rat carries her towards the launcher. A pair of ghouls work on fixing the machinery. They have a bag of spare parts, looted from some alchemist's foundry. The launch mechanism is comparatively simple, and they don't need to aim the weapon accurately anyway. It's just a dilute phlogiston charge, big enough to spit the ugly warhead into the air.

There, on the rail, is the god bomb. Its surface is scarred and pitted, criss-crossed with hideous welts where the alchemists welded the fragments of the bomb back together. This weapon was made from the wreckage of the House of Law bell.

This bell. This was the one that found her, that recognised and initiated her. That broke and remade her.

When she presses her palm against the wet, rough metal, she can hear the god screaming. A wordless shriek, a never-ending loop of universal loathing and hatred. The insatiable soul-hunger of the carrion god as it consumes itself. The god in the bomb eats itself whole over and over again, oscillating a billion times every second. But gods cannot die.

Suffer, thinks Cari. The fucker deserves it.

She almost regrets that they're going to end the god's torment.

The Erevesic.

Terevant claims the sword. On the rooftop in the Wash, his hand closes around the hilt.

On the Erevesic estates, he walks until he comes to the mansion. The house of his ancestors is crowded with the honoured dead. His grandmother stands at the threshold, beckons him onwards. Olthic's waiting there.

On the rooftop, Terevant springs up. The power of the sword flashes through him. Strength and grace beyond anything he's ever known.

A thousand Erevesics consider the battlefield through his eyes, judge the moment to strike. A thousand Erevesics lend him their skill with the blade, fortify his soul with theirs. He leaps, jumping across the city like a flea, the sword in his hand a blazing brand.

"I have to know," says Terevant to his brother, "what happened?" As he asks, Olthic's memories become his. The taste of whisky in his throat. He's standing in the study in the Haithi embassy, putting on his old fighting gear, drunkenly proud that it still fits. Celebrating his defeat. The cheers of the army when Olthic captured the Ishmeric flagship at Eskalind blending into the cheers of the Festival crowd. He puts the sword down on the desk to pull on his hauberk.

And then they ambush him. Anonymous embassy clerks, little grey-faced men he'd paid no attention to before. Daerinth's men, knives in hands. And in from the courtyard, skull gleaming in the moonlight, comes Edoric Vanth. Faithful beyond death, here to collect Haith's half of Daerinth's secret bargain.

Olthic fights them off. Overpowers half a dozen men, dodges faster than the dead. If he can get to the sword on the desk, he'll have the full powers of the Erevesic, be able to defeat them all with ease. He throws himself across the room, his fingers straining for the hilt.

Almost touching it.

But not quite. He never sees who kills him, never knows which of the dozen attackers got lucky and can claim the glory.

"I lost," says Olthic, unable to keep the note of wonder from his voice. "I never lost before. Everything I set my mind to accomplish, I did. Every battle I fought, I won. Until I came to Guerdon."

The vision shifts. The attackers vanish, and it's just Terevant and Olthic in the study. Olthic sits in a chair by the fire. "You know, I studied the history of Guerdon when I came here. The military history, the only sort I had patience for. It's curious — Guerdon's been conquered before, many times, but the conquerors never prosper here. An ill-fortuned prize, this city."

He shrugs, then reaches forward and clasps Terevant's hands. "Shall I take it from here, brother?"

*

The Erevesic whirls across the sky. His leap would carry him onto the span of the Viaduct, if it still stood. Instead, he lands on the roof of a city watch tower. Pesh's war-saint looms above him, a hundred feet tall. She's marching towards the host of defenders who block her path. Keeper saints, alchemy-armed riflemen, a motley gang of rogues – and a thin line of bone. House Erevesic's troops do not flinch as Pesh roars at them. Do not break when she swipes at them with her claws, rending the hillside and slaying dozens with every blow.

Terevant throws himself at her back, stabbing with the sword. She senses him, whirls around, moving with feline speed and grace despite her gargantuan size. A massive paw swipes at him, and he catches it just like Olthic would have, his left hand seizing a hank of her blood-matted fur, swings himself around so he lands on her forearm, and he drives the sword deep into the wrist of the goddess.

Divine ichor sprays across the rooftops of Guerdon. Her divine gaze, the heat from every sacked and burning city, blasts him, but he parries it with the sword. Leaps again, landing on her bare breast, hacking at her collarbone, her throat. Pesh stumbles back, her feet tangled in rubble. She nearly topples backwards, but rights herself, landing cat-like on all fours.

The remaining Haithi forces charge. Their captain is in the fray, and the dead answer. The Vigilant move as one, perfectly disciplined, immune to fear or doubt. Riflemen fire through the ranks; their comrades do not flinch, for they have fought side by side for decades, and they know each other's every thought. The dead men attack the goddess, hewing at her wounded forelimb, her snarling face.

From Holyhill come the Keepers. Flowers bloom in the rubble, and as each blossom opens, a hand emerges from each one, and in every hand is a grenade. Saints hurl lances of sunlight and spears of lightning. Pesh roars in pain as her tawny flanks are raked with holy fire.

From the New City come a motley band of saints, monsters, mercenaries and brigands. Stone Men wade through the floodwaters to hurl chunks of rubble. Sellswords, veterans of the Godswar in other lands, sneak through the ruined city, ambushing the divine monsters. Refugee saints, escaped from Hark, draw on the power of distant pantheons one last time to defend their adopted home.

Battle is joined, and Pesh welcomes it. This is war, and war is holy.

The goddess draws closer to her saint. More of her power flows into this mortal focus, this living weapon.

Terevant jumps up and attacks her again, driving Pesh back. A hail of blows from the Erevesic sword, pushing her back down Mercy Street.

Her wounds heal. She is magnified.

War, she roars, and the Keeper saints remember that Haith has long been the enemy of Guerdon. War, she roars, and the city watch turn on the criminals and illegal saints. They turn on one another, all against all.

War, she roars, and her gaze is an artillery barrage.

War, she roars, and the sun becomes a bloody heart. She reaches up and tears it from the sky, plunging the city into darkness, lit only by muzzle-flashes and the leaping flames.

War, she roars, eternal and holy.

Carillon aims the stone ship. Rat yowls and lights the fuse.

The shock of the launch cracks the keel of the stone ship, and their unlikely vessel buckles, breaks. Dissolves. They fall into the water, but Carillon's a strong swimmer. As she surfaces, surrounded by wet, dog-paddling ghouls, she realises that the constant psychic pressure of her connection to the Black Iron Gods is gone. That call, that unspeakable presence that's haunted her all her life, that forced her to leave her aunt's house at Wheldacre and run away across the seas — it's gone. There may still be two Black Iron Gods, but they're locked in their prison under her New City, far away beyond stone walls and Spar's protective presence, and they cannot reach her.

She's free.

The god-bomb rocket arcs across the city. Its trajectory brings it over the dome of the Seamarket, over Venture Square, into the heart of Guerdon. Carillon sighted along Mercy Street, and the rocket flies true.

There is no explosion. No blast. No flare of light or thunderous report.

Just nothing.

Annihilation.

CHAPTER 54

The historians would, in time, reconstruct the events of that day. Survivors speak of a sickening, unnatural peace – they had no desire to lay down their guns or cease fighting, but the alternative was, literally, unthinkable. War was an unknown thing in Guerdon that day. Those who tried to continue the battle found themselves stymied, palsied, like old, old men who had forgotten all the steps of some intricate performance. Even if they could remember the music, they could not dance.

When the fertility goddess of the valley of Grena was destroyed, the valley lost all its vitality, all its spirit. Slowly, animals and plants from outside the valley – creatures sacred to no god – crept in, colonising the margins.

War in Guerdon is like that. Those at the epicentre of the blast cannot even conceive of conflict. The wounded pass away peacefully, unwilling to fight for life. Lifelong soldiers become gentle as newborn lambs. Further out, the effects are attenuated. There is still half-hearted skirmishing between the Guerdon navy and the remaining krakens, and while the thieves of the New City might hesitate for a moment, they still cut a throat given a chance. Still, many lose their minds – the absence is like a phantom limb, a wound in their souls.

Outside invaders carry their notion of war with them, filling the conceptual void. The reinforcements from Haith bring with them Haith's war, bone discipline and tradition. In Maredon, the watch still remembers how to guard Guerdon's borders and her reclaimed seas.

In the approaching Ishmeric fleet, the priests of Pesh frantically offer sacrifices to their shattered goddess, trying to coax her back into existence. Maybe, given time, they could remake her – or maybe some other Ishmeric deity of conflict will be born. Perhaps High Umur will couple with Cloud Mother, and they will spawn a god of heavenly wrath.

Unable to kill one another in this bizarre ceasefire, the survivors jockey for position. Columns of Haithi soldiers march into Guerdon's northern suburbs, advance towards the heights on Holyhill. More Kraken-waves lap against the shore, carrying reinforcements from the fleet into the Wash.

But before the fighting can begin again, before the combatants remember how to fight a war, the sky fills with dragons.

"Land there," says Eladora, pointing to the courtyard outside parliament. She has to shout to be understood over the rushing wind, but the Ghierdana pirate sees her gesture, and transmits the instruction to the dragon. They circle down over the ruin of the Wash, while other dragons perch on the spires of Holyhill, or fly low over the docks. They position themselves between the lines, between Haith and Ishmere.

Flames rumble in their throats, but they hold their breath back. Eladora dismounts unsteadily, her legs stiff and aching from the long flight across the ocean from Lyrix. She tries to speak, but her throat is raw from shouting. "Tell them," she says weakly.

The dragon smiles like a crocodile, and advances into parliament to tell the city the price of salvation.

It is something of a civic miracle that the election for parliament is held as scheduled, under the circumstances. While the fighting was, for the most part, restricted to the parts of the city nearest the harbour, it still speaks of Guerdon's bloody-minded resilience that the citizens emerge from their shelters and queue amid the rubble to cast their votes. The occupying forces watch with bemusement at the exercise of the franchise. The Haithi dead are impassive;

the Ishmerians pronounce it ungodly; the Lyrixians gamble on the outcome.

The gamblers are disappointed. It's a hung parliament; none of the parties win a majority. The vote is split almost perfectly in three between Kelkin, the alchemists and the church.

Still, something must be done. The first votes in this new parliament are among the most important in the city's long history. They must vote on the recognition of the king, on relief for those who lost everything in the war, and — most pressing of all — they must vote on the Armistice of Hark.

In coffee shops and taverns, in smoky backrooms and in salons in Bryn Avane, in Kelkin's drawing room and the Palace of the Patros and the guildhalls, the politicking begins again. Slow at first, then feverishly quick, factions racing to take advantage of the new order. The city transformed yet again, but it's still Guerdon.

Still eager to sell you your dreams while picking your pocket.

Eladora is not part of the horse-trading. She is not welcome at the tally-houses when the votes are counted; she does not go to the party at the Vulcan after the results are announced. She is rarely seen on the streets; no one is sure where she stays. She gives no interviews to the newspapers, she makes no statements.

She is seen most often in the University District, helping repair the damage to the library, but she vanishes for days at a time. Rumours fly in some circles that she is in secret negotiations with Lyrix, or with Haith, or that she has reconciled with her mother and has been engaged to King Berrick, or that she has been arrested for sabotaging the machine at Hark and will soon be executed for treason.

On a rainy evening three weeks after the election, Eladora's reading is interrupted by a knock at the door of her hotel room. She closes *The Bone Shield* — she's nearly done, only a few short chapters left — and walks barefoot across the spartan room. The hotel's in Glimmerside, in a neutral area between the Haithi-occupied territory on Holyhill and the Ishmeric region down in what used to be the Wash, but folk are now calling the Temple Quarter. Neutral territory this close to the occupied zones isn't always safe.

She slips a handgun into the pocket of her dressing gown before going to the door. She looks through the spy hole.

A skeleton grins back at her.

It's, ah, Terevant Erevesic, says the dead man.

Chapter 55

I wanted to see you before I left, he explains.

"You're returning to Haith, I take it?" Eladora examines the skeleton who sits awkwardly in the armchair opposite, crossing his bony legs as he fiddles with a teacup. He'd poured himself a cup without thinking, and now he clearly has no idea what to do with it.

No, actually. I – I joined a mercenary company. The Company of Eight. I'm shipping out this evening.

"After what you saw, you're going *back* to the Godswar?" she marvels.

I killed a goddess, you know. Sort of. I hope my reputation proceeds me. Gives me an edge when fighting other deities. Terevant laughs. **No – it would be awkward to go back to Haith. There are, ah, political concerns.**

"So I understand." In truth, she's only read hints in the news-papers, as she's cut off from Kelkin and the flow of intelligence. There are reports, though, that the current bearer of the Crown has taken hemlock, and that a new bearer will soon be chosen. Several of the Empire's remaining colonies are in revolt, too, as the Houses recall their troops to secure Old Haith. The new bearer of the Crown will rule over a much diminished realm, but – potentially – one that can better endure the Godswar.

Lyssada's name has been mentioned in newspaper reports from Old Haith.

It is said in Haith that the dead do not love in the way the living do. I'm not sure if I agree. I don't think the living love

the same way twice, either. I'll go back one day, maybe – with fresh eyes. He touches his empty eye socket. So to speak.

"If it's not too personal a question—"

Not at all.

"You had the Erevesic sword. You could have died Enshrined, could you not?"

Faithful to the last, mutters Terevant to himself. Yes, I had the sword, thanks to you. I was the Erevesic, and it was ... glorious. But I saw the rocket coming in, and ... I didn't know how the god bomb would affect the phylactery. So, I quelled the blade. I closed the connection to the mortal world, as best I could, to protect the souls within.

He lifts his kitbag, and she sees the hilt of the ancient weapon protruding from it.

"It's ... magically inert?" She shivers, suddenly cold. She hasn't seen Carillon since she returned.

No. My ancestors' souls are still in there, but they need a living host to contact them. It was the only way to shield them from the blast.

"You're the last Erevesic."

Maybe.

He puts the teacup on a desk, pokes it with a bony finger, watches the ripples.

My mother and my younger sisters – they were lost when their ship was attacked by a kraken. They're most likely dead, but – well, one virtue of this Armistice is that one can actually *talk* to the Ishmerians. And bribe them. They took prisoners from that ship, apparently. Maybe ...

"I wish you luck."

Thank you. I wanted to thank you again. And give you this. He reaches into the kitbag, hands her an ornately written piece of paper. A bank draft. Not exactly a king's ransom, but enough to keep you for a while. I'm told you're no longer employed by the Industrial Liberal party. What have you been doing with yourself, since?

Eladora glances at the pile of papers and notes on the writing desk. She closes *The Bone Shield* and hands it back to the skeleton. "Reading and thinking." She stands. "I've been cooped up in here for days. I'll walk you down to your ship and see you off."

The second visitor comes scratching at her door one evening, like a stray dog. A defrocked priest, out of favour with the Patros, out of allies, out of tricks. He tries to threaten her, extort money from her; Eladora counters with an offer of employment.

She can use him, soiled as he is.

Another visitor, this time in the dead of night. Carillon. She doesn't knock – Eladora wakes from a nightmare to see a figure sitting on the end of her bed.

"Don't be scared," says Cari, "it's me."

Eladora isn't scared. She no longer fears Miren's knives, no longer fears the vengeance of the Black Iron Gods, at least for now. She pushes the memory of the bargain she made with them away, locks it away in an otherwise empty iron safe that she buries in the darkest recesses of her mind.

"I expect," says Eladora, "you're here to complain that I invited the Ghierdana syndicates back into the city." She picks up a pile of newspapers from the nightstand, waves them at Carillon. "Actually getting stabbed would be a nice change from the daggers of the press, so go ahead."

"It's not that. Well, it is that, but . . . fuck. El, it's Spar."

"What about him?"

"He pushed himself too hard. Ever since we raised the god bomb, he's been really . . . quiet. Weak. More than before. I can't shape the stone any more, can't pass on blows. El, I can't *hear* him most of the time – or, worse, he's not *talking* as much."

Eladora gets out of bed, conjures a werelight. Cari flinches at the light. Eladora notes that her cousin is bruised and scratched. A wound dressing on her neck, stained brown.

"What do you think I can do?" Eladora leads Cari into another room in the suite, digs out her medical kit, starts to peel away the dressing.

"I dunno. It's . . . magic stuff. God stuff. Ongent stuff."

Eladora blanches at the infected wound. "Gods below, what happened to you?"

"Remember how I kicked the fucking Ghierdana out of the city, and you teleported to Lyrix and asked them nicely to come back? That."

Eladora smears ointment on the wound, applies a fresh dressing. "There are some scholars here in the city. The university department of archaeotheology, the alchemists' guild. No true *experts* left, though." It's not entirely a lie. "But there are other cities."

Eladora crosses the room to a wardrobe, disarms the spell guarding it. "The sages of Khebesh are reputed to be the greatest authorities on 'magic stuff' in all the world. And from the sounds of things, it would be best for you, too, if you left Guerdon for a while."

That's not entirely a lie, either. There's work to be done here in the city that will go easier without Cari's presence.

"I've heard stories about Khebesh," grumbles Cari. "They never let outsiders in."

Eladora opens the wardrobe and takes out a heavy leather-bound codex. Dr Ramegos' diary of sorcery, including her notes on the construction of the god bombs and the machine on Hark. Eladora hands the book to Carillon.

"Bring them this. Trade it for what you need. I don't know if they can help Mr Idgeson, but I hope it's possible."

Carillon takes the book, holds it like it's diseased. "Could they make more god bombs with this?"

"Rosha's great insight was that the Black Iron Gods, in their imprisoned form, were immensely powerful but *static*. That could be used to interrupt the ever-recurring pattern of another god. But that only worked because their hungers had brought them extremely close to the mortal world. Such . . . proximity is rare. Dr Ramegos believed that the Haithi phylacteries might be a low-grade substitute, but even after a hundred or more generations of accumulated souls, few of the phylacteries would have sufficient spiritual force to disrupt a true deity." Eladora sniffs. "So no. Not without raw materials."

"All right. Thanks."

"Let me get you a satchel." Eladora busies herself in the wardrobe again. Fetches a bag, puts some money in it, some more medicinal ointment. Removes Cari's amulet from around her own neck, slips it in there, too.

The further the amulet is from Guerdon, the safer for both women.

"Hey," asks Cari, peering over Eladora's shoulder. "What's that aethergraph for? I thought they shut them all down." The aethergraph machine sits on the floor of the wardrobe, the silvery cables wound around it in an endless loop.

"It's disconnected," says Eladora. "It's a research project." She reaches out and strokes the metal casing, gives it a reassuring pat. *I will work to save you*, she thinks, *but not yet. Not until I'm sure.* She shuts the door, reactivates the wards.

"El," says Carillon. "Before I go . . . what did you do, down in the vault? With the Black Iron Gods? Those fuckers got in my head when I was their Herald, made me see stuff, feel stuff. Don't let them use you."

"Last year, when I visited you at Sevenshell Street, just after the Crisis – I said that you should not blame yourself for what happened." Eladora reflects for a moment, then hands Carillon the satchel. "I stand by that assessment. Don't listen to your own fears, or the jealousies of little men and little gods.

"History is the only judgement that counts."

A few days later, Eladora walks up Mercy Street, picking her way through the rubble. They've cleared a gap in the middle of the road, but it's choked with carriages on their way up to the opening of parliament. Mercy Street runs along the perimeter of the Ishmeric Zone; a permanent haze hangs over the borderlands, and those who cross without the right blessing are snatched away by Cloud Mother.

The crowd is careful not to stray over the line, making their progress even slower.

She realises, as she pushes through the mob, that she's being followed. Absalom Spyke falls in beside her, matching his long strides to her shorter ones.

"The boss wants to see you before it all kicks off," he whispers in her ear.

"I know," she replies. "Rat told me." Told her by speaking through her, disturbing her in her studies.

"Boss also wants to make sure you get there *alive*," hisses Spyke. "Lots of folks wouldn't mind seeing you dead, I hear. Kill the bitch who forced us to surrender." There's a rumble in his throat that suggests he'd be one of them, off the clock, but right now he's in Kelkin's employ.

"They are entitled to hold such opinions," says Eladora, "it's one of the benefits of being alive."

Spyke grunts. The Armistice put an end to the fighting, but at the cost of ongoing occupation. It cedes portions of the city to Ishmere, to Haith, and to Lyrix. If any of the three powers breaks the truce, the other two, plus Guerdon's forces, will ally against them. Guerdon's neutrality in the Godswar is maintained – only now, instead of being on the sidelines of the conflict, the front lines are on the city streets.

As they approach parliament, Spyke relaxes. "Your new friends'll take care of you from here."

He slips away. She catches sight of him a few minutes later, his arm around a young woman. She'd be very pretty under other circumstances, but she's terrified, trapped by Spyke's long arm. She shoots a pleading look at Eladora before Spyke drags her away into a side entrance that leads to the viewer's gallery.

She spots Mhari Voller, too. Voller's wearing a Ghierdanian-style dress, and has an elaborate piece of jewellery – a golden dragon – twining around her left arm. She catches Eladora's eye too, and waves. Mouths something about drinks. In a Lyrixian restaurant, no doubt. If the god bomb hadn't worked, then Voller would be cutting out hearts and burning them in a brazier as an offering to Pesh.

Despite all its faults, this arrangement, this Armistice, is a better fate. For Voller and the city.

Eladora crosses the courtyard outside parliament. It's crowded, but there's an open space near the dragon. The massive creature lies across the rubble of a broken wall, sunning itself like a snoozing cat. A young Ghierdanian man sits on a rock near the dragon's head. He recognises Eladora, and rises to greet her.

"Miss Eladora," says Rasce in a thick Lyrixian accent. "We've scarcely seen you since we arrived. You are healed, yes? You looked like death when you arrived!"

Arrived, she thinks. *When I bargained with the Black Iron Gods? When they tore a hole in the world, and in me, so I could cross the ocean in an instant?* She masks her scowl with a smile. "Much better, thank you."

"My great-uncle would speak with you, please. This way."

He brings her over to the dragon's head. The monster opens its eyes. "Run along, Rasce. See if your cousin has found me some goat in this barren city.

"This is a new thing you have made," says the dragon to Eladora. "You are always making new things in Guerdon. First the keeping of gods, like my nephew keeps goats. Then the killing of them. Now this. What is this, do you think?"

"Peace, I hope."

"Three men holding swords to each other's throats, and this is peace?"

"For now."

"You make your buildings small, over here," says the dragon, "and I cannot fit into your parliament. But I have keen ears, and I hear many who dislike this thing you have made. Tell me, will they take your bargain?"

"They will," she says without hesitation. She can't afford to doubt.

"No war today," says the dragon, craning its head to look out over the city.

"Not today, no."

A bell rings inside parliament. "I must go." *You can't bear the weight of a sword forever. Sooner or later, you have to put it down.*

Kelkin waits for her in a small office. In the room outside, Ogilvy and a few other IndLibs argue about the relief act. Eladora's surprised that Kelkin's not out there. Usually, he's in the thick of such discussions, eager to ensure not a penny of city money is wasted, nor an iota of credit given to anyone else.

She finds him dressed in the ermine robes of state. Worn, she inadvertently recalls, by the king's minister, in the days of the monarchy. Those days have come again, now. Kelkin's a small man, and he seems barely able to carry the heavy furs.

"Duttin. You finally came yourself. I don't have the eyesight for reading endless correspondence." He waves one of her letters at her, one she sent the day after the ceasefire. She had Silkpurse deliver it.

"I needed to withdraw," she says. "And rest. The crossing to Lyrix took a great deal of my strength."

"And who asked you to do that, eh? I fucking told you to bargain with Haith, get their reinforcements! With their dead bastards, and the bomb, we could have fought off the Ishmerians—"

"Maybe the first wave. But not the full strength of the Sacred Empire. Not the gods, Effro." Eladora glances back into the outer office, seeing who's with Ogilvy. Marking faces, names. "And say you won by some mir-mir– mischance – you'd be under Haithi occupation instead of Ishmere, and Ishmere would have attacked again. At best, we'd be a . . . satrapy, under their king."

"Oh, we could've done away with that," snaps Kelkin. *He's blustering*, thinks Eladora, *trying to convince himself.* "Spyke found some girl who was bedding a Haithi spy *and* met good King Berrick on the train from Haith. A little encouragement, and she'd testify that Berrick was a spy, too. We could bring him down – and the Keepers too, if they stuck with him. But you ruined all that, didn't you?" Kelkin's raging, but he's just a little mortal man. Eladora's faced down the Black Iron Gods. "Spyke's parading the girl up in the gallery. I've let the Keepers know that we've got something on their fucking king, that we've got leverage – but because of you, I have to spend that on getting them to back your bloody Armistice! And I'll have to kneel before that milksop of a wine merchant, and call him Majesty." He spits and it turns into a hacking cough.

"Peace, Effro. It's worth the bargain."

"Peace," he echoes mockingly. "Ramegos promised me that her bloody machine would hold back the Godswar, and now it's at my throat! What's your guarantee worth? Damn all. Damn all." He groans. "When are you coming back to work?" he mutters. "I need you."

Commotion in the outer office. Ogilvy bursts in.

"We don't have the votes."

"Parliament hasn't fucking opened yet," shouts Kelkin.

"I just got word. Twenty-five of ours, and half the Keepers are going to vote against Armistice. The turncoats are all her lot," says Ogilvy, glaring at Eladora. "They're saying that they can't make a bargain with evil gods. That they came here to escape Ishmere, and that we're selling them out."

"Who? Give me names," asks Eladora.

Ogilvy rattles off a few. They're all from the New City, all off the list Spar gave her. There's one name missing.

"Leave this with me," says Eladora.

CHAPTER 56

The ghoul leads the spy through the tunnels under parliament. Castle Rock's riddled with passageways, like the rest of Guerdon, and the city's new arrivals haven't yet come to grips with the labyrinth beneath their feet. This route is the quickest way across the Temple District, down to Queen's Point.

The spy needs to be quick. Under Alic's name, he was sworn in as a member of parliament less than an hour ago, and in a short time they'll vote on the Armistice. It's his duty to be back for that crucial vote.

Of course, if the vote fails and the truce collapses, then maybe getting as far away from the heart of the city as possible is a good idea.

"Is it much further?" he asks the ghoul. He wishes they'd sent Silkpurse to fetch him, not this younger creature, with its sardonic grin and too-sharp teeth.

"Do you tire, little father? Lie down and sleep if you will. There's meat on your bones, and precious little good eating in the Wash these days, now the Ishmeric gods are harvesting the dead, too."

"I'm in a hurry, that's all."

"Haste and haste. Not far."

The green stone of the ghoul tunnel gives way to a concrete drain that slopes steeply upwards. At the end is a heavy iron gate, open enough for him to squeeze through. He's expected.

"Down there, third door," says the ghoul, and it vanishes back into the darkness.

The spy walks cautiously down the corridor, trying to work out where he'd ended up. The corridor is whitewashed concrete, lit by aetheric lights. The ground's covered in soot and grimy footprints, dirt tracked down from the surface. There's a strange pressure in the air, and the sound of distant engines.

He laughs. Queen's Point. He's under the ruins.

Annah, Tander, you should see me now, thinks the spy. Then he's Alic again — a second draft of Alic. A more pliant, tractable Alic. A better mask.

He knocks on the third door. It's a small, bare-walled office.

"Come in," says Eladora.

"Where are we?" asks Alic.

"The office of a friend of mine. No one's down here any more. It's as . . . discreet as anywhere in the city," says Eladora. "I'm sorry for dragging you away from parliament, but this can't wait."

"That sounds ominous."

"I . . . it's about the Armistice vote. Some of our new members are voting against it. They're all people you helped elect. They all listen to you. Absalom Spyke even tells me there's been talk of a leadership challenge, when Kelkin goes." Eladora takes a sharp breath. "Did you tell them to vote against the Armistice?"

"I came out of Mattaur. I've seen the Godswar," he begins, but she interrupts him.

"Oh, don't give me that," snaps Eladora. "We've *all* seen the Godswar now. Yes, it's unbearably awful. Why undermine my peace?"

"They fled the Sacred Realm. They fear that your Armistice will give Ishmere time to regather its strength," explains Alic. His eyes flicker to the only ornament in the office, a ticking clock.

"That's why *they're* voting against it, not you."

"You can't be sure Pesh was wholly destroyed, you know. To be certain, burn her temples, kill her priests, cast down her shrines, and maybe . . ."

"Restarting the war might kill Pesh. It would definitely kill all of us." Eladora bites her lip. For the first time in weeks, she wishes she had Aleena's sword hilt with her. She remembers Aleena riding into her grandfather's crypt, driving away evil with a blazing lance of sunlight. "Terevant Erevesic is a mercenary now."

The spy shrugs. "He died a hero. Godslayer, the papers call him. I hear they're writing poems about him."

"I accompanied him down to his ship. I wasn't the only person there to see the mercenaries depart. There was another woman there. The poor thing was god-touched, warped into sort of half-kraken. She had no mouth left, so we couldn't converse, but you know me. I always have pen and paper. Her name is Oona."

Eladora draws the pistol from her pocket. Aims it at the spy.

"She described how you recruited her for espionage against Guerdon. How you broke into this very fortress. You were looking for the god bomb."

Tander's dead. Annah's dead. Emlin's dead. No one knows the real story. And the best lies have a little truth. The spy lets Alic's shoulders sink. "I suppose it doesn't matter now. I . . . I was a spy for Ishmere. They paid well, Eladora. And they let me out of Severast, when the whole place was a prison camp. I didn't have a choice. But all we did was poke around Queen's Point. I know I should have told you, but . . . when Emlin died, I was broken . . . and then the election, and everything." He lets himself sob. "It was my old life. It's not the man I am now. Please believe me."

"I do," says Eladora.

"Ishmere attacked anyway. The gods are mad, you know that. All of them. It was the Kept Gods who sank the *Grand Retort*. Everything that happened was the fault of the gods."

"The Safidists believe that it's the place of mortals to serve the gods. To align oneself complete with the will of the gods. To annihilate yourself, to make a better vessel. To be their agent." Eladora's fingernails dig into her thigh, but the hand holding the gun doesn't waver. "But . . . but I could never suborn myself like that. I wanted to be free to shape my destiny, instead of letting someone or something else do it for me. I don't know how possible that is — none of us are alone. Everything's connected. The root cause of an action is hard to determine, or there are many causes. History's never as simple as the stories tell it. You have to look hard for connections.

"Who told the city watch that there was a saint of Fate Spider in Jaleh's house?"

"I don't know!" The spy lets Alic show a little anger. The boy was Alic's son.

"You did," says Eladora. "You lured Ishmere to attack the city. You *wanted* the gods to attack, so they'd be destroyed along with Guerdon."

"They're monsters."

"History also teaches us to look for inconsistencies. Impossibilities. Cari saw you die in the New City. Silkpurse saw you die in the artillery barrage. One unlikely escape is possible. Two is . . . miraculous."

She raises the pistol. "Tell me your real name."

The spy looks at the little weapon. "That can't kill me, Eladora."

She shoots him dead.

His body slumps over in the chair.

"No," Eladora admits. "It can't."

The noise of the machine becomes deafening. Then she stands, brushes down her skirts, and crosses the hall to a room nearby.

The spy is momentarily bodiless, detached from the mortal world. A new body must be woven, and this threat dealt with. He'll come back nearby. That sewer route is the only way in or out — Eladora must be working with the ghouls. He'll reform there, before she leaves. Kill her — the thought bring him no small amount of discomfort, but it must be done. The ghouls are a larger problem, especially Rat. They guard the two remaining god bombs.

He feels along the strands of fate. There's one possibility — Alic rises through parliament, becomes minister for security. Pressures the city watch. Guerdon needs a replacement god bomb, so we must eliminate the ghouls and take the components needed before Haith or Lyrix snatch them away. Rebuild the machine on Hark. A slow process, but there are ways to accelerate it, and he won't be starting from scratch. This path is a route back to—

Alic hears Emlin's voice calling for him. He tries to dismiss it as a memory from Hark Island, nothing more, but no – the boy's alive! He's nearby! He's calling for Alic, begging for help.

– A force seizes Alic, drags him back to the mortal world. Aetheric engines, tanks of writhing alchemical creatures. Summoning circles. He's seen it all before, somewhere. He has to wrestle with his memory, fight to keep his thoughts together. On Hark. He saw it on Hark.

At the centre of the summoning circle, there's an aethergraph machine. A loop of orichalcum cable runs from to the circle – the aethergraph set is live, but talking only to him. Emlin, inside the aethergraph, calling him. The spy fights to disentangle himself from Alic, but he's caught in the web of the man's thoughts.

And then he's caught in the flesh. He materialises in the circle.

A priest stands nearby, a gun in his hand. He watches the spy hungrily. It's Sinter.

Alic takes a step towards the aethergraph, but the priest clucks his tongue and gestures with the gun. The spy stops moving. The aethergraph clatters and crackles, but before it can speak, Sinter reaches over and shuts the machine down.

Eladora appears at the entrance to the room. Her eyes are wide and fearful.

"It's you. You're ...a god," she says. "I thought ... gods can't think. You're living spells. Self-perpetuating whirlpools of psychic energy in the aetheric field. You're not ... like this."

The spy spreads his hands. "Behold the sacrifice of my priests at Severast. They walked *ahead*, into the future, and left behind a thread of being for me to cling to. They went very far ahead – and as long as that strand of fate holds, I cannot die." He peers at the crackling, roaring machinery that surrounds him. "What is this prison?" he asks.

"Dr R-r-Ramegos' prototype. A scale model of the machine at Hark. I was trying to disrupt whatever was ... reincarnating you.

But it's *you*." She glances a row of gauges on the wall. "It's not strong enough to bind a deity like the Fate Spider, but it can hold ... whatever you are."

"I am Fate Spider," says the spy. "I am worshipped in Ishmere and Severast. But when Ishmere attacked Severast, I was sundered. When my counterpart, my shadow-self is destroyed, I shall be Fate Spider entire again." He shrugs. "Failing that, I shall have revenge. I shall make *secret* Godswar upon them. I shall cast down their shrines and burn their temples, even if I must do it from behind this mask of flesh." He spreads his arms wide. "You know me now. Worship me, and be the first of my new saints, my new priests."

Eladora shakes her head. "Is that what you told Emlin?"

Sinter shoots him dead. The machine roars again.

Coming back this time, he feels weak, newborn. Like some moulting sea creature, scurrying from shell to shell, vulnerable in its softness.

"You can't kill me without a god bomb."

"As long as this machine's running, you're bound here," snarls Sinter.

He smiles. The summoning circle's already running down. The aetheric engines will run out of power; the living brains in the tanks cannot recite the secret prayers to bind him for much longer. The aethergraph is fragile. He'll murder Alic, remove this troubling connection to Emlin, escape that way. He has many options, if only he has time.

"You cannot hold me."

Sinter shoots him dead again. He reforms, and he forgets how many legs humans are supposed to have. He topples to the ground, his fingers moving like spiders across the floor, trying to drag the dead weight of his body behind him.

Eladora sighs. She gestures, and Sinter fires again.

"I know what happens to gods that are destroyed too many times."

And again.

"It wears you down, doesn't it? Every time, you're ... diminished."

And again. "And you were only a little god to begin with."

Sinter shoots him again.

When he reforms that time – slowly, painful, pulling the substance of himself out of the aether like cobwebs, his thoughts slow and rotten – Sinter presses the gun against his forehead. The barrel is hot against his mortal skin.

"You work for her, now," growls the priest, pointing at Eladora. "Understand?"

The spy doesn't know if he can die again. He yields.

"I take no pleasure in this," says Eladora. "I'm just trying to do the best for my city. I have bargained with worse gods than you."

EPILOGUE

The Armistice holds.

Three belligerents of the Godswar agree that Guerdon is shared, neutral territory. Across the seas, gods and dragons and legions of the dead may fight, but not in the city. There are breaches of the truce, betrayals, questionable incidents, but the peace holds. The city authorities are miraculously well informed about potential threats; plots to restart hostilities are thwarted with a minimum of bloodshed.

Guerdon adapts to this new regime. It's the nature of the city to remake itself, to build over the rubble. By autumn, the docks are open again, busier than ever now that warships from three nations jostle for space at the neutral quaysides. Parliament temporarily relocates to the Palace of the Patros while the fortress on Castle Hill is rebuilt; the city watch occupies old tombs and catacombs in Gravehill. There are miracles, too, now that the city is no longer godless. Money-changer priests of Blessed Bol throng the markets and the cafés, blessing the city's trade. Smoke Painter's eyeless mystics sell fantasies in Glimmerside. A temporary bridge replaces the Duchess Viaduct, hanging from skyhooks anchored in the clouds. The New City is no longer out of place; there are miracles everywhere now.

On midwinter's day, Eladora Duttin is informed that her mother is dead.

The carriage sticks in half-frozen mud in the country lane. Silkpurse hops down and puts her ghoulish strength to use, shoving the rear wheel free. She clambers back on board, her breath steaming in the cold air. Eladora hands her a cloth so Silkpurse can wipe her claws and not get mud on the ghoul's new velvet mourning dress.

"Thank'ee, miss," says the ghoul. She settles back into her seat. "What are those things in the field?"

Eladora glances. "Horses."

"Oh. They're like the carvings on Keeper churches! They're prettier than raptequines. Wonder what they taste like." A city ghoul, through and through. "I'm sorry that Carillon couldn't be here."

"It's for the best," says Eladora. "She was never happy here." *Was I?*

She looks out at the endless snow-covered fields and forests, the little cottages and barns. Grey sky over a grey land.

She sees movement in the clouds, and a dragon breaks through the pall and circles over the land, scanning for prey. Eladora makes a mental note to have a word with the Lyrixian ambassador. The dragons are straying too far from their assigned hunting grounds near the city; it's a minor breach of the Armistice agreement, but nothing involving divine monsters can be dismissed as trivial. She'll consult with Alic, see what they have on the ambassador to encourage him to take care of the matter quietly, rather than risk insulting the Ghierdanian clan by confronting the dragon directly.

The dragon, unimpressed with the barren landscape, vanishes back into the clouds.

In the distance, a farmer in black trudges across a frozen field, head down, never noticing the beast in the sky.

The funeral is better attended than Eladora expected. A cynical part of her mind wonders if they've come just to get warm. As a Safidist, Silva asked to be cremated on a pyre of sacred wood, instead of having her body sent down the corpse shafts. They've erected the pyre in the little village square in the middle of Wheldacre.

Most of the mourners are people from the village, mostly relatives from the Duttin side of the family. A few minor dignitaries from Guerdon; a Keeper bishop or two. Mhari Voller is absent, although a gaudy spray of miracle-conjured blossoms is from her, according to

a note someone hands Eladora. They push her to a place at the head
of the church, the pew nearest the altar, nearest Silva's body. They
trudge past, offering ritual condolences.

Silkpurse sits in the row behind Eladora, rests a comforting claw
on her shoulder. *It's all such a bother*, thinks Eladora. *A hollow ritual.*
These prayers are emptier than the gentling-chants of Jaleh's house;
no distant god could be ever be stirred to action by these pleas
for mercy.

She remembers a Crown of Flowers festival here. Remembers
being made to stand for hours, in the sweltering heat, holding her
hands over burning candles. Praying the candle flame would become
a burning sword, praying for the gift of sainthood.

Burn, thinks Eladora. Coming here was a mistake. Stabbing Silva
with a magic sword should have been closure enough. But formal-
ities must be observed. She sits through the long service until the
hard seats make her buttocks ache, until her carefully arranged mask
of sorrow becomes an honest scowl of irritation.

The village priest says a last prayer for the dead, and they carry
Silva out to the waiting pyre. The body is light, as if it's already
mostly burned away on the inside, and they're just finishing the
job. Eladora follows, just in case. She's seen enough people come
back from the dead in the last year that she wants to make completely sure.

A few latecomers come to pay their respects to her as the body is
laid out on the pyre. One of them, a small man with a big nose, lingers for a moment to speak to the village priest before approaching
Eladora. She's seen him before, but for a moment can't quite recall
where. Then she remembers, and forces herself not to react.

"I just wanted to say how sorry I am," says King Berrick. "I knew
your mother in the last few months, while we were both guests of
the Patros in the palace. We talked, sometimes, when she was able.
She often spoke of you. Sometimes, even fondly." He looks around
the square. "She taught me to love Guerdon, even from afar."

The Thay in her.

"Thank you, your grace. And thank you for coming."

"I have an errand to discharge. Speak to the priest before you leave."

The king takes advantage of the distraction provided by the sudden leap of flame to depart unseen.

Eladora stands in the cold and watches her mother's body burn until there's only ash.

The rambling farmhouse at Wheldacre is Eladora's now. It's too late in the evening to return to Guerdon before dark, so she and Silkpurse will stay here for the night.

She turns the key and opens the back door. The farmhouse has changed little since Eladora went away to the university. Musty books, shrines to the Kept Gods. Candle wax spilling over the sideboards.

She places the box on the table.

"What's that?" asks Silkpurse. "I saw the priest give it to you after the funeral."

"My m-mother entrusted it to him," answers Eladora, "a long time ago. It . . . it was sent to her by my grandfather, at the same time he sent Carillon to live with us."

The box is made of some dark wood, with iron hinges. The clasp is sealed with wax and marked with the sigil of the Thay family. Touching it, she feels a thrill of sorcery. It's warded.

"What's inside?" Silkpurse sniffs the box.

"My grandfather's diaries, the priest said. My mother . . . wanted me to have this now."

"Why?"

A warning. An inheritance. A trap. She doesn't know.

Her mother was a monster. Her mother was a saint. She transformed the Keepers, restored the king. The king owes everything to her.

Her grandfather was a monster. Her grandfather built the modern city. Kelkin owes everything to him.

Eladora cuts her thumb and opens the seal.

AFTERWORD

Writing a book is like jumping off a cliff. You step off that edge, it's quiet for a bit and suddenly things are happening very quickly all around you and there's a lot of screaming.

Writing a second book is like trying to take a second step while in mid-air. It is definitely an experience.

Many thanks go to my UK editor Emily Byron, who transformed my original manuscript into something far better, to Bradley and Joanna, to Nazia, and everyone else at Orbit (especially the long-suffering proofreaders who put up with notes like "there's Kraken, and there's kraken, and there's Kraken-stuff that might be krakens"). Thanks also to my agent John Jarrold.

Once again I am blessed with a Richard Anderson cover.

The poem on p. 318 is adapted from Hugh MacDiarmid's poem "Midnight", and appears courtesy of Carcanet Press. The original poem is (a) lovely and (b) full of shade towards the rest of Scotland.

Many thanks to those in any of the following sets: people who bought *The Gutter Prayer*, people who read *The Gutter Prayer*, people who reviewed *The Gutter Prayer*. If you are in the intersection of any of those sets, you are due far more than double or triple thanks – I remain hugely indebted to those reviews and readers who gave the first book in the Black Iron Legacy such an initial boost.

I remain indebted also to my friends, notably Neil for continuing to be a stalwart alpha reader, long-time co-conspirator Cat and the rest of Pelgrane, and all those who ensured I developed not one whit of an ego.

Thanking Edel is like thanking oxygen.

Finally, I must acknowledge the contributions of Tristan, Elyan and Nimuë. Contributions included "being born a few days before final edits are due", but also helping out with signings and being endlessly – well, somewhat – patient when told "Daddy's working".

extras

about the author

Gareth Hanrahan's three-month break from computer programming to concentrate on writing has now lasted fifteen years and counting. He's written more gaming books than he can readily recall, by virtue of the alchemical transmutation of tea and guilt into words. He lives in Ireland with his wife and children. Follow him on Twitter @mytholder.

Find out more about Gareth Hanrahan and other Orbit authors by registering for the free monthly newsletter at www.orbitbooks.net.

if you enjoyed
THE SHADOW SAINT

look out for

THE BONE SHIPS

Book One of the Tide Child

by

RJ Barker

Enter the Hundred Isles, where ships made from the bones of extinct dragons battle for supremacy on the high seas.

Our hero Meas Giryn must unite a crew of condemned criminals for a suicide mission when the first live dragon in centuries is spotted in far off waters . . .

I

THE CASTAWAY

"Give me your hat."

They are not the sort of words that you expect to start a legend, but they were the first words he ever heard her say.

She said them to him, of course.

It was early. The scent of fish filled his nose and worked its way into his stomach, awakening the burgeoning nausea. His head ached and his hands trembled in a way that would only be stilled by the first cup of shipwine. Then the pain in his mind would fade as the thick liquid slithered down his gullet, warming his throat and guts. After the first cup would come the second, and with that would come the numbness that told him he was on the way to deadening his mind the way his body was dead, or waiting to be. Then there would be a third cup and then a fourth and then a fifth, and the day would be over and he would slip into darkness.

But the black ship in the quiet harbour would still sit at its rope. Its bones would creak as they pulled against the tide. The crew would moan and creak as they drank on its decks, and he would fall into unconsciousness in this old flenser's hut. Here he was, shipwife in name only. Commander in word only. Failure.

Voices from outside, because even here, in the long-abandoned and ghost-haunted flensing yards there was no real escape from others. Not even the memory of Keyshan's Rot, the disease of the boneyards, could keep people from cutting through.

"The *Shattered Stone* came in this morran, said they saw an archeyex over Sleightholme. Said their windtalker fell mad and it nearly wrecked 'em. Had to kill the creature to stop it bringing a wind to throw 'em across a lee shore."

"Aren't been an archeyex seen for nigh on my lifetime. It brings nothing good — paint that on a rock for the Sea Hag." And the voices faded, lost in the hiss of the waves on the beach, eaten up by the sea as everything was destined to be, while he thought on what they said — "brings nothing good". May as well as say that Skearith's Eye will rise on the morran, for this is the Hundred Isles — when did good things ever happen here?

The next voice he heard was the challenge. Delivered while he kept his eyes closed against the tides of nausea ebbing and flowing in hot, acidic waves from his stomach.

"Give me your hat." A voice thick with the sea, a bird-shriek croak of command. The sort of voice you ran to obey, had you scurrying up the rigging to spread the wings of your ship. Maybe, just maybe, on any other day or after a single cup of shipwine, maybe he would have done what she said and handed over his two-tailed shipwife's hat, which, along with the bright dye in his hair, marked him out as a commander — though an undeserving one.

But in the restless night his sleep had been troubled by thoughts of his father and thoughts of another life, not a better one, not an easier one, but a sober one, one without shame. One in which he did not feel the pull of the Sea Hag's slimy hands trying to drag him down to his end. One of long days at the wing of a flukeboat, singing of the sea and pulling on the ropes as his father glowed with pride at how well his little fisher boy worked the winds. Of long days before his father's strong and powerful body was broken as easily as a thin varisk vine, ground to meat between the side of his boat and the pitiless hull of a boneship. His hand reaching up from black water, a bearded face, mouth open as if to call to his boy in his final agonising second. Such strength, and it had meant nothing.

So maybe he had, for once, woken with the idea of how wonderful it would be to have a little pride. And if there had been a day for him to give up the two-tailed hat of shipwife, then it was not this day.

"No," he said. He had to scrape the words out of his mind, and that was exactly how it felt, like he drew the curve of a curnow blade down the inside of his skull; words falling from his mouth slack as midtide. "I am shipwife of the *Tide Child* and this is my symbol of command." He touched the rim of the black two-tailed cap. "I am shipwife, and you will have to take this hat from me."

How strange it felt to say those words, those fleet words that he knew more from his father's stories of service than from any real experience. They were good words though, strong words with a history, and they felt right in his mouth. If he were to die then they were not bad final words for his father to hear from his place, deep below the sea, standing warm and welcome at the Hag's eternal bonefire.

He squinted at the figure before him. Thoughts fought in his aching head: which one of them had come for him? Since he'd become shipwife he knew a challenge must come. He commanded angry women and men, bad women and men, cruel women and men – and it had only ever been a matter of time before one of his crew wanted the hat and the colours. Was it Barlay who stood in the door hole of the bothy? She was a hard one, violent. But no, too small for her and the silhouette of this figure wore its hair long, not cut to the skull. Kanvey then? He was a man jealous of everything and everyone, and quick with his knife. But no, the silhouette appeared female, undoubtably so. No straight lines to her under the tight fishskin and feather. Cwell then? She would make a move, and she could swim so would have been able to get off the ship.

He levered himself up, feeling the still unfamiliar tug of the curnow at his hip.

"We fight then," said the figure and she turned, walking out into the sun. Her hair worn long, grey and streaked in the colours of command: bright reds and blues. The sun scattered off the fishskin of her clothing, tightly wound about her muscled body and held in place with straps. Hanging from the straps were knives, small crossbows and a twisting shining jingling assortment of good-luck trinkets that spoke of a lifetime of service and violence. Around her shoulders hung a precious feathered cloak, and where the fishskin scattered the sunlight the feather cloak hoarded it, twinkling and sparkling, passing motes of light from plume to plume so each and every colour shone and shouted out its hue.

I am going to die, he thought.

She idled away from the slanted bothy he had slept in, away from the small and stinking abandoned dock, and he followed. No one was around. He had chosen this place for its relative solitude, amazed at how easily that could be found; even on an isle as busy as Shipshulme people tended to flock together, to find each other, and of course they shunned such Hag-haunted places as this, where the keyshan's curse still slept.

Along the shingle beach they walked: her striding, looking for a place, and him following like a lost kuwai, one of the flightless birds they bred for meat, looking for a flock to join. Though of course there was no flock for a man like him, only the surety of the death he walked towards.

She stood with her back to him as though he were not worth her attention. She tested the beach beneath her feet, pushing at the shingle with the toes of her high boots, as if searching for something under the stones that may rear up and bite her. He was reminded of himself as a child, checking the sand for jullwyrms before playing alone with a group of imaginary friends. Ever the outsider. Ach, he should have known it would come to this.

When she turned, he recognised her, knew her. Not socially, not through any action he had fought as he had fought none. But he knew her face – the pointed nose, the sharp cheekbones, the weathered skin, the black patterns drawn around her eyes and the scintillating golds and greens on her cheeks that marked her as someone of note. He recognised her, had seen her walking before prisoners. Seen her walking before children won from raids on the Gaunt Islands, children to be made ready for the Thirteenbern's priest's thirsty blades, children to be sent to the Hag or to ride the bones of a ship as corpselights – merry colours that told of the ship's health. Seen her standing on the prow of her ship, *Arakeesian Dread*, named for the sea dragons that provided the bones for the ships and had once been cut apart on the warm beach below them. Named for the sea dragons that no longer came. Named for the sea dragons that were sinking into myth the way a body would eventually sink to the sea floor.

But oh that ship!

He'd seen that too.

Last of the great five-ribbers he was, *Arakeesian Dread*. Eighteen bright corpselights dancing above him, a huge long-beaked arakeesian skull as long as a two-ribber crowned his prow, blank eyeholes staring out, his beak covered in metal to use as a ram. Twenty huge gallowbows on each side of the maindeck and many more standard bows below in the underdeck. A crew of over four hundred that polished and shone every bone that made his frame, so he was blinding white against the sea.

He'd seen her training her crew, and he'd seen her fight. At a dock, over a matter of honour when someone mentioned the circumstances of her birth. It was not a long fight, and when asked for mercy, well, she showed none, and he did not think it was in her for she was Hundred Isles and fleet to the core. Cruel and hard. What light there was in the sky darkened as if Skearith the godbird closed its eye to his fate, the fierce heat of the air fleeing as did that small amount of hope that had been in his breast – that single fluttering possibility that he could survive. He was about to fight Meas Gilbryn, "Lucky" Meas, the most decorated, the bravest, the fiercest shipwife the Hundred Isles had ever seen.

He was going to die.

But why would Lucky Meas want his hat? Even as he prepared himself for death he could not stop his mind working. She could have any command she wanted. The only reason she would want his would be if . . .

And that was unthinkable.

Impossible.

Meas Gilbryn condemned to the black ships? Condemned to die? Sooner see an island get up and walk than that happen.

Had she been sent to kill him?

Maybe. There were those to whom his continued living was an insult. Maybe they had become bored with waiting?

"What is your name?" She croaked the words, like something hungry for carrion.

He tried to speak, found his mouth dry and not merely from last night's drink. Fear. Though he had walked with it as a companion for six months it made it no less palatable.

He swallowed, licked his lips. "My name is Joron. Joron Twiner."

"Don't know it," she said, dismissive, uninterested. "Not seen it written in the rolls of honour, not heard it in any reports of action."

"I never served before I was sent to the black ships," he said. She drew her straightsword. "I was a fisher once." Did he see a flash in her eyes, and if he did what could it mean? Annoyance, boredom?

"And?" she said, taking a practice swing with her heavy blade, contemptuous of him, barely even watching him. "How does a fisher get condemned to a ship of the dead? Never mind become a ship-wife." Another practice slash at the innocent air before her.

"I killed a man."

She stared at him.

"In combat," he added, and he had to swallow again, forcing a hard ball of cold-stone fear down his neck.

"So you can fight." Her blade came up to ready. Light flashed down its length. Something was inscribed on it, no cheap slag-iron curnow like his own.

"He was drunk and I was lucky," he said.

"Well, Joron Twiner, I am neither, despite my name," she said, eyes grey and cold. "Let's get this over with, ey?"

He drew his curnow and went straight into a lunge. No warning, no niceties. He was not a fool and he was not soft. You did not live long in the Hundred Isles if you were soft. His only chance of beating Lucky Meas lay in surprising her. His blade leaped out, a single straight thrust for the gut. A simple, concise move he had practised so many times in his life – for every woman and man of the Hundred Isles dreams of being in the fleet and using his sword to protect the islands' children. It was a perfect move he made, untouched by his exhaustion and unsullied by a body palsied with lack of drink.

She knocked his blade aside with a a small movement of her wrist, and the weighted end of the curving curnow blade dragged his sword outward, past her side. He stumbled forward, suddenly off balance. Her free hand came round, and he caught the shine of a stone ring on her knuckles, knew she wore a rockfist in the moment before it made contact with his temple.

He was on the ground. Looking up into the canopy of the wide and bright blue sky wondering where the clouds had gone. Waiting for the thrust that would finish him.

Her sword tip appeared in his line of sight.

Touched the skin of his forehead.

Raked a painful line up to his hair and pushed the hat from his head and she used the tip of her sword to flick his hat into the air and caught it, putting it on. She did not smile, showed no sense of triumph, only stared at him while the blood ran down his face and he waited for the end.

"Never lunge with a curnow, Joron Twiner," she said quietly. "Did they teach you nothing? You slash with it. It is all it is fit for."

"What poor final words for me," he said. "To die with another's advice in my ear." Did something cross her face at that, some deeply buried remembrance of what it was to laugh? Or did she simply pity him?

"Why did they make you shipwife?" she said. "You plain did not win rank in a fight."

"I——" he began.

"There are two types of ship of the dead." She leaned forward, the tip of her sword dancing before his face. "There is the type the crew run, with a weak shipwife who lets them drink themselves to death at the staystone. And there is the type a strong shipwife runs that raises his wings for trouble and lets his women and men die well."

He could not take his eyes from the tip of the blade, Lucky Meas a blur behind the weapon. "It seems to me the *Tide Child* has been the first, but now you will lead me to him and he will try what it is to be the second."

Joron opened his mouth to tell her she was wrong about him and his ship, but he did not, because she was not.

"Get up, Joron Twiner," she said. "You'll not die today on this hot and long-blooded shingle. You'll live to spend your blood in service to the Hundred Isles along with every other on that ship. Now come, we have work to do." She turned, sheathing her sword, as sure he would do as she asked as she was Skearith's Eye would rise in the morning and set at night.

The shingle moved beneath him as he rose, and something stirred within him. Anger at this woman who had taken his command from him. Who had called him weak and treated him with such contempt. She was just like every other who was lucky enough to be born whole of body and of the strong.

Sure of their place, blessed by the Sea Hag, the Maiden and the Mother and ready to trample any other before them to get what they wanted. The criminal crew of *Tide Child*, he understood them at least. They were rough, fierce and had lived with no choice but to watch out for themselves. But her and her kind? They trampled others for joy.

She had taken his hat of command from him, and though he had never wanted it before, it had suddenly come to mean something. Her theft had awoken something in him.

He intended to get it back.

Enter the monthly
Orbit sweepstakes at
www.orbitloot.com

With a different prize every month,
from advance copies of books by
your favourite authors to exclusive
merchandise packs,
**we think you'll find something
you love.**